SPECIAL EDITION, LIMITED TO 100,000 COPIES

St. ELMO

BY

AUGUSTA J. EVANS

Author of "Beulah,"
"Macaria," "At the Mercy of Tiberius,"
"Infelice," Etc., Etc.

❧

"Ah! the true rule is—a true wife in her husband's house is his servant; it is in his heart that she is queen. Whatever of the best he can conceive, it is her part to be; whatever of the highest he can hope, it is hers to promise; all that is dark in him she must purge into purity; all that is failing in him she must strengthen into truth; from her, through all the world's clamor, he must win his praise; in her, through all the world's warfare, he must find his peace."—JOHN RUSKIN.

GROSSET & DUNLAP PUBLISHERS
Eleven East Sixteenth Street New York

St. Elmo.

TO

J. C. DERBY,

IN GRATEFUL MEMORY OF MANY YEARS OF KIND AND FAITHFUL FRIENDSHIP,

THESE PAGES ARE

AFFECTIONATELY DEDICATED.

[3]

" Ah ! the true rule is—a true wife in her husband's house is his servant; it is in his heart that she is queen. Whatever of the best he can conceive, it is her part to be ; whatever of the highest he can hope, it is hers to promise; all that is dark in him she must purge into purity; all that is failing in him she must strengthen into truth; from her, through all the world's clamor, he must win his praise; in her, through all the world's warfare, he must find his peace."—JOHN RUSKIN.

[5]

ST. ELMO.

CHAPTER I.

"He stood and measured the earth; and the everlasting mountains were scattered, the perpetual hills did bow."

These words of the prophet upon Shigionoth were sung by a sweet, happy, childish voice, and to a strange, wild, anomalous tune—solemn as the Hebrew chant of Deborah, and fully as triumphant.

A slender girl of twelve years' growth steadied a pail of water on her head, with both dimpled arms thrown up, in ancient classic Caryatides attitude; and, pausing a moment beside the spring, stood fronting the great golden dawn—watching for the first level ray of the coming sun, and chanting the prayer of Habakkuk. Behind her in silent grandeur towered the huge outline of Lookout Mountain, shrouded at summit in gray mist; while centre and base showed dense masses of foliage, dim and purplish in the distance—a stern cowled monk of the Cumberland brotherhood. Low hills clustered on either side, but immediately in front stretched a wooded plain, and across this the child looked at the flushed sky, rapidly brightening into fiery and blinding radiance. Until her wild song waked echoes among the far-off rocks, the holy hush of early morning had rested like a benediction upon the scene,

as though nature laid her broad finger over her great
lips, and waited in reverent silence the advent of the
sun.   Morning among the mountains possessed witchery and glories which filled the heart of the girl with
adoration, and called from her lips rude but exultant
anthems of praise.   The young face, lifted toward the
cloudless east, might have served as a model for a pictured Syriac priestess—one of Baalbec's vestals, ministering in the olden time in that wondrous and grand
temple at Heliopolis.

The large black eyes held a singular fascination in
their mild, sparkling depths, now full of tender, loving
light and childish gladness ; and the flexible red lips
curled in lines of orthodox Greek perfection, showing
remarkable versatility of expression ; while the broad,
full, polished forehead with its prominent, swelling
brows, could not fail to recall, to even casual observers,
the calm, powerful face of Lorenzo de' Medicis, which,
if once looked on, fastens itself upon heart and brain,
to be forgotten no more.   Her hair, black, straight,
waveless as an Indian's, hung around her shoulders,
and glistened as the water from the dripping bucket
trickled through the wreath of purple morning-glories
and scarlet cypress, which she had twined about her
head, ere lifting the cedar pail to its resting-place.   She
wore a short-sleeved dress of yellow striped homespun,
which fell nearly to her ankles, and her little bare feet
gleamed pearly white on the green grass and rank
dewy creepers that clustered along the margin of the
bubbling spring.   Her complexion was unusually
transparent, and early exercise and mountain air had
rouged her cheeks till they matched the brilliant hue
of her scarlet crown.   A few steps in advance of her
stood a large, fierce yellow dog, with black, scowling face, and ears cut close to his head ; a savage,
repulsive creature, who looked as if he rejoiced
in an opportunity of making good his name, " Grip."
In the solemn beauty of that summer morning
the girl seemed to have forgotten the mission upon
which she came ; but as she loitered, the sun flashed

up, kindling diamond fringes on every dew-beaded chestnut leaf and oak-bough, and silvering the misty mantle which enveloped Lookout. A moment longer that pure-hearted Tennessee child stood watching the gorgeous spectacle, drinking draughts of joy, which mingled no drop of sin or selfishness in its crystal waves; for she had grown up alone with nature—utterly ignorant of the roar and strife, the burning hate and cunning intrigue of the great world of men and women, where, "like an Egyptian pitcher of tamed vipers, each struggles to get its head above the other." To her, earth seemed very lovely; life stretched before her like the sun's path in that clear sky, and, as free from care or foreboding as the fair June day, she walked on, preceded by her dog—and the chant burst once more from her lips:

"He stood and measured the earth: and the ever-lasting mountains were scattered, the perpetual hills ——"

The sudden, almost simultaneous report of two pistol-shots rang out sharply on the cool, calm air, and startled the child so violently that she sprang forward and dropped the bucket. The sound of voices reached her from the thick wood bordering the path, and, without reflection, she followed the dog, who bounded off toward the point whence it issued. Upon the verge of the forest she paused, and, looking down a dewy green glade where the rising sun darted the earliest arrowy rays, beheld a spectacle which burned itself indelibly upon her memory. A group of five gentlemen stood beneath the dripping chestnut and sweet-gum arches; one leaned against the trunk of a tree, two were conversing eagerly in undertones, and two faced each other fifteen paces apart, with pistols in their hands. Ere she could comprehend the scene, the brief conference ended, the seconds resumed their places to witness another fire, and like the peal of a trumpet echoed the words:

"Fire! One!—two!—three!"

The flash and ringing report mingled with the com-

mand and one of the principals threw up his arm and
fell.   When with horror in her wide-strained eyes and
pallor on her lips, the child staggered to the spot, and
looked on the prostrate form, he was dead.   The hazel
eyes stared blankly at the sky, and the hue of life and
exuberant health still glowed on the full cheek ; but
the ball had entered the heart, and the warm blood,
bubbling from his breast, dripped on the glistening
grass.   The surgeon who knelt beside him took the
pistol from his clenched fingers, and gently pressed the
lids over his glazing eyes.   Not a word was uttered,
but while the seconds sadly regarded the stiffening
form, the surviving principal coolly drew out a cigar,
lighted and placed it between his lips.   The child's
eyes had wandered to the latter from the pool of blood,
and now in a shuddering cry she broke the silence :

" Murderer !"

The party looked around instantly, and for the first
time perceived her standing there in their midst, with
loathing and horror in the gaze she fixed on the per-
petrator of the awful deed.   In great surprise he drew
back a step or two, and asked gruffly :

" Who are you ?   What business have you here ?"

" Oh ! how dared you murder him ?   Do you think
God will forgive you on the gallows ?"

He was a man probably twenty-seven years of age—
singularly fair, handsome, and hardened in iniquity,
but he cowered before the blanched and accusing face
of the appalled child ; and ere a reply could be framed,
his friend came close to him.

" Clinton, you had better be off ; you have barely
time to catch the Knoxville train, which leaves Chattanooga in half an hour.   I would advise you to make
a long stay in New York, for there will be trouble when
Dent's brother hears of this morning's work."

" Aye !   Take my word for that, and put the Atlantic between you and Dick Dent," added the surgeon,
smiling grimly, as if the anticipation of retributive
justice afforded him pleasure.

" I will simply put this between us," replied the

homicide, fitting his pistol to the palm of his hand; and as he did so, a heavy antique diamond ring flashed on his little finger.

" Come, Clinton, delay may cause you more trouble than we bargained for," urged his second.

Without even glancing toward the body of his antagonist, Clinton scowled at the child, and, turning away, was soon out of sight.

" Oh, sir! will you let him get away? will you let him go unpunished?"

" He cannot be punished," answered the surgeon, looking at her with mingled curiosity and admiration.

" I thought men were hung for murder."

" Yes—but this is not murder."

" Not murder? He shot him dead! What is it?"

" He killed him in a duel, which is considered quite right and altogether proper."

" A duel?"

She had never heard the word before, and pondered an instant.

" To take a man's life is murder. Is there no law to punish 'a duel'?"

" None strong enough to prohibit the practice. It is regarded as the only method of honorable satisfaction open to gentlemen."

" Honorable satisfaction?" she repeated—weighing the new phraseology as cautiously and fearfully as she would have handled the bloody garments of the victim.

" What is your name?" asked the surgeon.

" Edna Earl."

" Do you live near this place?"

" Yes, sir, very near."

" Is your father at home?"

" I have no father, but grandpa has not gone to the hop yet."

" Will you show me the way to the house?"

" Do you wish to carry him there?" she asked, glancing at the corpse, and shuddering violently.

"Yes, I want some assistance from your grandfather."

"I will show you the way, sir."

The surgeon spoke hurriedly to the two remaining gentlemen, and followed his guide. Slowly she retraced her steps, refilled her bucket at the spring, and walked on before the stranger. But the glory of the morning had passed away; a bloody mantle hung between the splendor of summer sunshine and the chilled heart of the awe-struck girl. The forehead of the radiant, holy June day had been suddenly red-branded like Cain, to be henceforth an occasion of hideous reminiscences; and with a blanched face and trembling limbs the child followed a narrow, beaten path, which soon terminated at the gate of a rude, unwhitewashed paling. A low, comfortless looking three-roomed house stood within, and on the steps sat an elderly man, smoking a pipe, and busily engaged in mending a bridle. The creaking of the gate attracted his attention, and he looked up wonderingly at the advancing stranger.

"Oh, grandpa! there is a murdered man lying in the grass, under the chestnut trees, down by the spring."

"Why! how do you know he was murdered?"

"Good morning, sir. Your granddaughter happened to witness a very unfortunate and distressing affair. A duel was fought at sunrise, in the edge of the woods yonder, and the challenged party, Mr. Dent, of Georgia, was killed. I came to ask permission to bring the body here, until arrangements can be made for its interment; and also to beg your assistance in obtaining a coffin."

Edna passed on to the kitchen, and as she deposited the bucket on the table, a tall, muscular, red-haired woman, who was stooping over the fire, raised her flushed face, and exclaimed angrily:

"What upon earth have you been doing? I have been half-way to the spring to call you, and hadn't a drop of water in the kitchen to make coffee! A pretty

time of day Aaron Hunt will get his breakfast! What
do you mean by such idleness?"

She advanced with threatening mien and gesture,
but stopped suddenly.

"Edna, what ails you? Have you got an ague?
You are as white as that pan of flour. Are you scared
or sick?"

"There was a man killed this morning, and the body
will be brought here directly. If you want to hear
about it, you had better go out on the porch. One of
the gentlemen is talking to grandpa."

Stunned by what she had seen, and indisposed to
narrate the horrid details, the girl went to her own
room, and seating herself in the window, tried to collect her thoughts. She was tempted to believe the
whole affair a hideous dream, which would pass away
with vigorous rubbing of her eyes; but the crushed
purple and scarlet flowers she took from her forehead,
her dripping hair and damp feet assured her of the
vivid reality of the vision. Every fibre of her frame
had received a terrible shock, and when noisy, bustling
Mrs. Hunt ran from room to room, ejaculating her
astonishment, and calling on the child to assist in putting the house in order, the latter obeyed silently, mechanically, as if in a state of somnambulism.

Mr. Dent's body was brought up on a rude litter of
boards, and temporarily placed on Edna's bed, and
toward evening when a coffin arrived from Chattanooga,
the remains were removed, and the coffin rested on
two chairs in the middle of the same room. The surgeon insisted upon an immediate interment near the
scene of combat; but the gentleman who had officiated
as second for the deceased expressed his determination to carry the unfortunate man's body back to his
home and family, and the earliest train on the following day was appointed as the time for their departure.
Late in the afternoon Edna cautiously opened the
door of the room which she had hitherto avoided, and
with her apron full of lilies, white poppies and sprigs of
rosemary, approached the coffin, and looked at the rigid

sleeper. Judging from his appearance, not more than
thirty years had gone over his handsome head; his
placid features were unusually regular, and a soft,
silky brown beard fell upon his pulseless breast. Fearful lest she should touch the icy form, the girl timidly
strewed her flowers in the coffin, and tears gathered
and dropped with the blossoms, as she noticed a plain
gold ring on the little finger, and wondered if he were
married—if his death would leave wailing orphans in
his home, and a broken-hearted widow at the desolate
hearthstone. Absorbed in her melancholy task, she
heard neither the sound of strange voices in the passage, nor the faint creak of the door as it swung back
on its rusty hinges; but a shrill scream, a wild, despairing shriek terrified her, and her heart seemed to stand
still as she bounded away from the side of the coffin.
The light of the setting sun streamed through the window, and over the white, convulsed face of a feeble
but beautiful woman, who was supported on the threshold by a venerable, gray-haired man, down whose furrowed cheeks tears coursed rapidly. Struggling to
free herself from his restraining grasp, the stranger
tottered into the middle of the room.

"O Harry! My husband! my husband!" She threw
up her wasted arms, and fell forward senseless on the
corpse.

They bore her into the adjoining apartment, where
the surgeon administered the usual restoratives, and
though finally the pulses stirred and throbbed feebly,
no symptom of returning consciousness greeted the
anxious friends who bent over her. Hour after hour
passed, during which she lay as motionless as her husband's body, and at length the physician sighed, and
pressing his fingers to his eyes, said sorrowfully to the
grief-stricken old man beside him: "It is paralysis,
Mr. Dent, and there is no hope. She may linger
twelve or twenty-four hours, but her sorrows are ended;
she and Harry will soon be reunited. Knowing her
constitution, I feared as much. You should not have
suffered her to come; you might have known that the

shock would kill her. For this reason I wished his body buried here."

"I could not restrain her. Some meddling gossip told her that my poor boy had gone to fight a duel, and she rose from her bed and started to the railroad depot. I pleaded, I reasoned with her that she could not bear the journey, but I might as well have talked to the winds. I never knew her obstinate before, but she seemed to have a presentiment of the truth. God pity her two sweet babes!"

The old man bowed his head upon her pillow, and sobbed aloud.

Throughout the night Edna crouched beside the bed, watching the wan but lovely face of the young widow, and tenderly chafing the numb, fair hands which lay so motionless on the coverlet. Children are always sanguine, because of their ignorance of the stern, inexorable realities of the untried future, and Edna could not believe that death would snatch from the world one so beautiful and so necessary to her prattling, fatherless infants. But morning showed no encouraging symptoms, the stupor was unbroken, and at noon the wife's spirit passed gently to the everlasting reunion.

Before sunrise on the ensuing day, a sad group clustered once more under the dripping chestnuts, and where a pool of blood had dyed the sod, a wide grave yawned. The coffins were lowered, the bodies of Henry and Helen Dent rested side by side, and, as the mound rose slowly above them, the solemn silence was broken by the faltering voice of the surgeon, who read the burial service.

"Man, that is born of a woman, hath but a short time to live, and is full of misery. He cometh up, and is cut down, like a flower; he fleeth as it were a shadow, and never continueth in one stay. Yet, O Lord God most holy, O Lord most mighty, O holy and most merciful Saviour, deliver us not into the pains of eternal death!"

The melancholy rite ended, the party dispersed, the

strangers took their departure for their distant homes, and quiet reigned once more in the small, dark cottage. But days and weeks brought to Edna no oblivion of the tragic events which constituted the first great epoch of her monotonous life. A nervous restlessness took possession of her, she refused to occupy her old room, and insisted upon sleeping on a pallet at the foot of her grandfather's bed. She forsook her whilom haunts about the spring and forest, and started up in terror at every sudden sound; while from each opening between the chestnut trees the hazel eyes of the dead man, and the wan, thin face of the golden-haired wife, looked out beseechingly at her. Frequently, in the warm light of day, ere shadows stalked to and fro in the thick woods, she would steal, with an apronful of wild flowers, to the solitary grave, scatter her treasures in the rank grass that waved above it, and hurry away with hushed breath and quivering limbs. Summer waned, autumn passed, and winter came, but the girl recovered in no degree from the shock which had cut short her chant of praise on that bloody June day. In her morning visit to the spring, she had stumbled upon a monster which custom had adopted and petted —which the passions and sinfulness of men had adroitly draped and fondled, and called Honorable Satisfaction; but her pure, unperverted, Ithuriel nature pierced the conventional mask, recognized the loathsome lineaments of crime, and recoiled in horror and amazement, wondering at the wickedness of her race and the forbearance of outraged Jehovah. Innocent childhood had for the first time stood face to face with Sin and Death, and could not forget the vision.

Edna Earl had lost both her parents before she was old enough to remember either. Her mother was the only daughter of Aaron Hunt, the village blacksmith, and her father, who was an intelligent, promising young carpenter, accidentally fell from the roof of the house which he was shingling, and died from the injuries sustained. Thus Mr. Hunt, who had been a widower for nearly ten years, found himself burdened with the care of an infant only six months old. His daughter had never left him, and after her death the loneliness of the house oppressed him painfully, and for the sake of his grandchild he resolved to marry again. The middle-aged widow whom he selected was a kind-hearted and generous woman, but indolent, ignorant, and exceedingly high-tempered ; and while she really loved the little orphan committed to her care, she contrived to alienate her affection, and to tighten the bonds of union between her husband and the child. Possessing a remarkably amiable and equable disposition, Edna rarely vexed Mrs. Hunt, who gradually left her more and more to the indulgence of her own views and caprices, and contented herself with exacting a certain amount of daily work, after the accomplishment of which she allowed her to amuse herself as childish whims dictated. There chanced to be no children of her own age in the neighborhood, consequently she grew up without companionship, save that furnished by her grandfather, who was dotingly fond of her, and would have utterly spoiled her, had not her temperament fortunately been one not easily injured by unrestrained liberty of action. Before she was able to walk, he would take her to the forge, and keep her for hours on a sheepskin in one corner, whence she watched, with infantile delight, the blast of the furnace, and the shower of sparks that fell from the anvil, and where she often slept, lulled by the monotonous chorus of trip and sledge. As she grew older, the mystery of bellows and slack-tub engaged her attention, and at one end of the shop, on a pile of shavings, she collected a mass of curiously shaped bits of iron and steel, and blocks of wood, from which a miniature shop threatened to rise in rivalry ; and finally, when strong enough to grasp the handles of the bellows, her greatest pleasure consisted in rendering the feeble assistance which her grandfather was always so proud to accept at her hands. Although ignorant and uncultivated, Mr. Hunt was a man of warm, tender feelings, and rare nobility of soul. He regretted the ab-

sence of early advantages which poverty had denied
him; and in teaching Edna to read and to write, and
to cipher, he never failed to impress upon her the vast
superiority which a thorough education confers.
Whether his exhortations first kindled her ambition,
or whether her aspiration for knowledge was sponta-
neous and irrepressible, he knew not; but she manifested very early a fondness for study and thirst for
learning which he gratified to the fullest extent of his
limited ability. The blacksmith's library consisted of
the family Bible, Pilgrim's Progress, a copy of Irving's
Sermons on Parables, Guy Mannering, a few tracts,
and two books which had belonged to an itinerant
minister who preached occasionally in the neighborhood, and who, having died rather suddenly at Mr.
Hunt's house, left the volumes in his saddle-bags,
which were never claimed by his family, residing in a
distant State. Those books were Plutarch's Lives and
a worn school copy of Anthon's Classical Dictionary;
and to Edna they proved a literary Ophir of inestimable
value and exhaustless interest. Plutarch especially
was a Pisgah of letters, whence the vast domain of
learning, the Canaan of human wisdom, stretched allur-
ingly before her; and as often as she climbed this
height, and viewed the wondrous scene beyond, it
seemed, indeed,

> . . . . . . "an arch where through
> Gleams that untraveled world, whose margin fades
> Forever and forever when we move."

In after years she sometimes questioned if this
mount of observation was also that of temptation, to
which ambition had led her spirit, and there bargained
for and bought her future. Love of nature, love of
books, an earnest piety and deep religious enthusiasm
were the characteristics of a noble young soul, left to
stray through the devious, checkered paths of life
without other guidance than that which she received
from communion with Greek sages and Hebrew

prophets.   An utter stranger to fashionable conven-
tionality and latitudinarian ethics, it was no marvel
that the child stared and shivered when she saw the
laws of God vetoed, and was blandly introduced to
murder as Honorable Satisfaction.

CHAPTER II.

NEARLY a mile from the small, straggling village of
Chattanooga stood Aaron Hunt's shop, shaded by a
grove of oak and chestnut trees, which grew upon the
knoll, where two roads intersected. Like the majority
of blacksmith's shops at country cross-roads, it was a
low, narrow shed, filled with dust and rubbish, with old
wheels and new single-trees, broken plows and dilapi-
dated wagons awaiting repairs, and at the rear of the
shop stood a smaller shed, where an old gray horse
quietly ate his corn and fodder, waiting to carry the
master to his home, two miles distant, as soon as the
sun had set beyond the neighboring mountain. Early
in winter, having an unusual amount of work on hand,
Mr. Hunt hurried away from home one morning,
neglecting to take the bucket which contained his
dinner, and Edna was sent to repair the oversight.
Accustomed to ramble about the woods without companionship, she walked leisurely along the rocky road,
swinging the tin bucket in one hand, and pausing now
and then to watch the shy red-birds that flitted like
flame-jets in and out of the trees as she passed. The
unbroken repose of earth and sky, the cold, still atmosphere and peaceful sunshine, touched her heart with a
sense of quiet but pure happiness, and half unconsciously she began a hymn which her grandfather often
sang over his anvil :

" Lord, in the morning Thou shalt hear
    My voice ascending high ;
  To Thee will I direct my prayer,
    To Thee lift up mine eye."

Ere the first verse was ended, the clatter of horse's hoofs hushed her song, and she glanced up as a harsh voice asked impatiently :

"Are you stone deaf? I say, is there a black-smith's shop near?"

The rider reined in his horse, a spirited, beautiful animal, and waited for an answer.

"Yes, sir. There is a shop about half a mile ahead, on the right hand side, where the road forks."

He just touched his hat with the end of his gloved fingers and galloped on. When Edna reached the shop she saw her grandfather examining the horse's shoes, while the stranger walked up and down the road before the forge. He was a very tall, strong man, with a gray shawl thrown over one shoulder, and a black fur hat drawn so far over his face that only the lower portion was visible; and this, swarthy and harsh, left a most disagreeable impression on the child's mind as she passed him and went up to the spot where Mr. Hunt was at work. Putting the bucket behind her, she stooped, kissed him on his furrrowed fore-head, and said :

"Grandpa, guess what brought me to see you to-day?"

"I forgot my dinner, and you have trudged over here to bring it. Ain't I right, Pearl? Stand back, honey, or this Satan of a horse may kick your brains out. I can hardly manage him."

Here the stranger uttered an oath, and called out, "How much longer do you intend to keep me wait-ing?"

"No longer, sir, than I can help, as I like the com-pany of polite people."

"Oh, grandpa!" whispered, Edna deprecatingly, as she saw the traveller come rapidly forward and throw his shawl down on the grass. Mr. Hunt pushed back his old battered woolen hat, and looked steadily at the master of the horse—saying gravely and resolutely :

"I'll finish the job as soon as I can, and that is as much as any reasonable man would ask. Now, sir, if

that doesn't suit you, you can take your horse and put
out, and swear at somebody else, for I won't stand it."

"It is a cursed nuisance to be detained here for such
a trifle as one shoe, and you might hurry yourself."

"Your horse is very restless and vicious, and I could
shoe two gentle ones while I am trying to quiet him."

The man muttered something indistinctly, and laying his hand heavily on the horse's mane, said very
sternly a few words, which were utterly unintelligible
to his human listeners, though they certainly exerted
a magical influence over the fiery creature, who, savage
as the pampered pets of Diomedes, soon stood tranquil and contented, rubbing his head against his
master's shoulder. Repelled by the rude harshness of
this man, Edna walked into the shop, and watched the
silent group outside, until the work was finished and
Mr. Hunt threw down his tools and wiped his face.

"What do I owe you?" said the impatient rider,
springing to his saddle, and putting his hand into his
vest pocket.

"I charge nothing for 'such trifles' as that."

"But I am in the habit of paying for my work."

"It is not worth talking about. Good day, sir."

Mr. Hunt turned and walked into his shop.

"There is a dollar, it is the only small change I
have." He rode up to the door of the shed, threw the
small gold coin toward the blacksmith, and was riding
rapidly away, when Edna darted after him, exclaiming, "Stop, sir! you have left your shawl!"

He turned in the saddle, and even under the screen
of her calico bonnet she felt the fiery gleam of his eyes,
as he stooped to take the shawl from her hand. Once
more his fingers touched his hat, he bowed and said
hastily:

"I thank you, child." Then spurring his horse, he
was out of sight in a moment.

"He is a rude, blasphemous, wicked man," said Mr.
Hunt as Edna reëntered the shop, and picked up the
coin, which lay glistening amid the cinders around the
anvil."

" Why do you think him wicked ?"

" No good man swears as he did, before you came ; and didn't you notice the vicious, wicked expression of his eyes ?"

" No, sir, I did not see much of his face, he never looked at me but once. I should not like to meet him again ; I am afraid of him."

" Never fear, Pearl, he is a stranger here, and there's little chance of your ever setting your eyes on his ugly, savage face again. Keep the money, dear; I won't have it after all the airs he put on. If, instead of shoeing his wild brute, I had knocked the fellow down for his insolence in cursing me, it would have served him right. Politeness is a cheap thing ; and a poor man, if he behaves himself, and does his work well, is as much entitled to it as the President."

" I will give the dollar to grandma, to buy a new coffee-pot ; for she said to-day the old one was burnt out, and she could not use it any longer. But what is that yonder on the grass ?   That man left something after all."

She picked up from the spot where he had thrown his shawl a handsome morocco-bound pocket copy of Dante, and opening it to discover the name of the owner, she saw written on the fly-leaf in a bold and beautiful hand, " *S. E. M., Boboli Gardens, Florence. Lasciate ogni speranza voi ch' entrate.*"

" What does this mean, grandpa ?"

She held up the book and pointed out the words of the dread inscription.

" Indeed, Pearl, how should I know ? It is Greek, or Latin, or Dutch, like the other outlandish gibberish he talked to that devilish horse. He must have spent his life among the heathens, to judge from his talk ; for he has neither manner nor religion. Honey, better put the book there in the furnace; it is not fit for your eyes."

" He may come back for it if he misses it pretty soon."

" Not he. One might almost believe that he was

running from the law.   He would not turn back for it
if it was bound in gold instead of leather.   It is no
account, I'll warrant, or he would not have been reading it, the ill-mannered heathen !"

Weeks passed, and as the owner was not heard of
again, Edna felt that she might justly claim as her own
this most marvellous of books, which, though beyond
her comprehension, furnished a source of endless
wonder and delight.   The copy was Cary's translation,
with illustrations designed by Flaxman ; and many of
the grand, gloomy passages were underlined by pencil
and annotated in the unknown tongue, which so completely baffled her curiosity.   Night and day she pored
over this new treasure; sometimes dreaming of the
hideous faces that scowled at her from the solemn,
mournful pages; and anon, when startled from sleep
by these awful visions, she would soothe herself to rest
by murmuring the metrical version of the Lord's
Prayer contained in the " Purgatory."   Most emphati-
cally did Mrs. Hunt disapprove of the studious and
contemplative habits of the ambitious child, who she
averred was indulging dreams and aspirations far above
her station in life, and well calculated to dissatisfy her
with her humble, unpretending home and uninviting
future.   Education, she contended, was useless to poor
people, who could not feed and clothe themselves with
" book learning ;" and experience had taught her that
those who lounged about with books in their hands
generally came to want, and invariably to harm.   It
was in vain that she endeavored to convince her husband of the impropriety of permitting the girl to spend
so much time over her books; he finally put the matter at rest by declaring that, in his opinion, Edna was
a remarkable child ; and if well educated, might even
rise to the position of teacher for the neighborhood,
which would confer most honorable distinction upon
the family.   Laying his brawny hand fondly on her
head, he said, tenderly :

" Let her alone, wife ! let her alone !   You will make
us proud of you, won't you, little Pearl, when you are

smart enough to teach a school? I shall be too old
to work by that time, and you will take care of me,
won't you, my little mocking-bird?"

"Oh, Grandy! that I will. But do you really think
I ever shall have sense enough to be a teacher? You
know I ought to learn everything, and I have so few
books."

"To be sure you will. Remember there is always a
way where there's a will. When I pay off the debt I
owe Peter Wood, I will see what we can do about some
new books. Put on your shawl now, Pearl, and hunt
up old Brindle, it is milking time, and she is not in
sight."

"Grandpa, are you sure you feel better this evening?" She plunged her fingers in his thick white
hair, and rubbed her round, rosy cheek softly against
his.

"Oh! yes, I am better. Hurry back, Pearl, I want
you to read to me."

It was a bright day in January, and the old man sat
in a large rocking-chair on the porch, smoking his pipe,
and sunning himself in the last rays of the sinking sun.
He had complained all day of not feeling well, and
failed to go to his work as usual; and now, as his
grandchild tied her pink calico bonnet under her chin,
and wrapped herself in her faded plaid shawl, he
watched her with a tender, loving light in his keen gray
eyes. She kissed him, buttoned his shirt collar, which
had become unfastened, drew his homespun coat closer
to his throat, and springing down the steps bounded
away in search of the cow, who often strayed so far off
that she was dispatched to drive her home. In the
grand, peaceful, solemn woods, through which the wintry wind now sighed in a soothing monotone, the
child's spirit reached an exaltation which, had she
lived two thousand years earlier, and roamed amid the
vales and fastnesses of classic Arcadia, would have
vented itself in dithyrambics to the great "Lord of
the Hyle," the Greek "All," the horned and hoofed
god, Pan. In every age, and among all people—from

the Parsee devotees and the Gosains of India to the
Pantheism of Bruno, Spinoza, and New England's
"*Illuminati*"—nature has been apotheosized ; and the
heart of the blacksmith's untutored darling stirred with
the same emotions of awe and adoration which thrilled
the worshipers of Hertha, when the veiled chariot
stood in Helgeland, and which made the groves and
grottoes of Phrygia sacred to Dindymene. Edna
loved trees and flowers, stars and clouds, with a warm,
clinging affection, as she loved those of her own race ;
and that solace and amusement which most children
find in the society of children and the sports of childhood this girl derived from the solitude and serenity
of nature. To her woods and fields were indeed vocal,
and every flitting bird and gurgling brook, every passing cloud and whispering breeze, brought messages of
God's eternal love and wisdom, and drew her tender,
yearning heart more closely to Jehovah, the Lord God
Omnipotent. To-day, in the boundless reverence and
religious euthusiasm of her character, she directed her
steps to a large spreading oak, now leafless, where in
summer she often came to read and pray ; and here
falling on her knees, she thanked God for the blessings
showered upon her. Entirely free from discontent and
querulousness, she was thoroughly happy in her poor
humble home, and over all, like a consecration, shone
the devoted love for her grandfather, which more than
compensated for any want of which she might otherwise have been conscious. Accustomed always to ask
special favor for him, his name now passed her lips in
earnest supplication, and she fervently thanked the
Father that his threatened illness had been arrested
without serious consequences. The sun had gone
down when she rose and hurried on in search of the
cow. The shadows of a winter evening gathered in
the forest and climbed like trooping spirits up the
rocky mountain side, and as she plunged deeper and
deeper into the woods, the child began a wild cattle
call that she was wont to use on such occasions. The
echoes rang out a weird Brocken chorus, and at last.

when she was growing impatient of the fruitless search, she paused to listen, and heard the welcome sound of the familiar lowing, by which the old cow recognized her summons. Following the sound, Edna soon saw the missing favorite coming slowly toward her, and ere many moments both were running homeward. As she approached the house, driving Brindle before her, and merrily singing her rude *Ranz des vaches*, the moon rose full and round, and threw a flood of light over the porch where the blacksmith still sat. Edna took off her bonnet and waved it at him, but he did not seem to notice the signal, and driving the cow into the yard, she called out as she latched the gate:

"Grandy, dear, why don't you go in to the fire? Are you waiting for me, out here in the cold? I think Brindle certainly must have been cropping grass around the old walls of Jericho, as that is the farthest off of any place I know. If she is half as tired and hungry as I am, she ought to be glad to get home." He did not answer, and running up the steps she thought he had fallen asleep. The old woolen hat shaded his face, but when she crept on tiptoe to the chair, stooped, put her arms around him, and kissed his wrinkled cheek, she started back in terror. The eyes stared at the moon, the stiff fingers clutched the pipe from which the ashes had not been shaken, and the face was cold and rigid. Aaron Hunt had indeed fallen asleep, to wake no more amid the storms and woes and tears of time.

Edna fell on her knees and grasped the icy hands. "Grandpa! wake up! Oh, grandpa! speak to me, your little pearl! Wake up, dear Grandy! I have come back! My grandpa! Oh!——"

A wild, despairing cry rent the still evening air, and shrieked dismally back from the distant hills and the gray, ghostly mountain—and the child fell on her face at the dead man's feet.

Throughout that dreary night of agony, Edna lay on the bed where her grandfather's body had been placed, holding one of the stiffened hands folded in both hers, and pressed against her lips. She neither wept nor

moaned, the shock was too terrible to admit of noisy
grief; but completely stunned, she lay mute and desolate.

For the first time in her life she could not pray; she
wanted to turn away from the thought of God and
heaven, for it seemed that she had nothing left to pray
for.   That silver-haired, wrinkled old man was the only
father she had ever known; he had cradled her in his
sinewy arms, and slept clasping her to his heart; had
taught her to walk, and surrounded her with his warm,
pitying love, making a home of peace and blessedness
for her young life.   Giving him, in return, the whole
wealth of her affection, he had become the centre of
all her hopes, joys and aspirations; now what remained?   Bitter, rebellious feelings hardened her heart
when she remembered that even while she was kneeling, thanking God for his preservation from illness, he
had already passed away; nay, his sanctified spirit
probably poised its wings close to the Eternal Throne,
and listened to the prayer which she sent up to God
for his welfare and happiness and protection while on
earth.   The souls of our dead need not the aid of San-
dalphon to interpret the whispers that rise tremulously
from the world of sin and wrestling, that float up
among the stars, through the gates of pearl, down the
golden streets of the New Jerusalem.   So we all trust,
and prate of our faith, and deceive ourselves with the
fond hope that we are resigned to the Heavenly Will;
and we go on with a show of Christian reliance, while
the morning sun smiles in gladness and plenty, and the
hymn of happy days and the dear voices of our loved
ones make music in our ears; and lo! God puts us in
the crucible.   The light of life—the hope of all future
years is blotted out; clouds of despair and the grim
night of an unbroken and unlifting desolation fall like
a pall on heart and brain; we dare not look heavenward, dreading another blow; our anchor drags, we
drift out into a hideous Dead Sea, where our idol has
gone down forever—and boasted faith and trust and
patience are swept like straws from our grasp in the

tempest of woe; while our human love cries wolfishly
for its lost darling.   Ah! we build grand and gloomy
mausoleums for our precious dead hopes, but, like
Artemisia, we refuse to sepulchre—we devour the bitter ashes of the lost, and grimly and audaciously challenge Jehovah to take the worthless, mutilated life that
his wisdom reserves for other aims and future toils.
Job's wife is immortal and ubiquitous, haunting the
sorrow-shrouded chamber of every stricken human
soul, and fiendishly prompting the bleeding, crushed
spirit to " curse God and die."   Edna had never contemplated the possibility of her grandfather's death—
it was a horror she had never forced herself to front;
and now that he was cut down in an instant, without
even the mournful consolation of parting words and
farewell kisses, she asked herself again and again:
" What have I done, that God should punish me so?
I thought I was grateful, I thought I was doing my
duty; but oh! what dreadful sin have I committed, to
deserve this awful affliction?"   During the long,
ghostly watches of that winter night, she recalled her
past life, gilded by the old man's love, and could remember no happiness with which he was not intimately
connected, and no sorrow that his hand had not soothed
and lightened.   The future was now a blank, crossed
by no projected paths, lit with no ray of hope; and at
daylight, when the cold, pale morning showed the
stony face of the corpse at her side, her unnatural
composure broke up in a storm of passionate woe, and
she sprang to her feet, almost frantic with the sense of
her loss:

    " All alone! nobody to love me! nothing to look
forward to! Oh, grandpa! did you hear me praying
for you yesterday?   Dear Grandy—my own dear
Grandy! I did pray for you while you were dying—
here alone! Oh, my God! what have I done, that you
should take him away from me?   Was not I on my
knees when he died?   Oh! what will become of me
now?   Nobody to care for Edna now! Oh, grandpa!
grandpa! beg Jesus to ask God to take me too!"

And throwing up her clasped hands, she sank back insensible on the shrouded form of the dead.

> " When some beloved voice that was to you
> Both sound and sweetness, faileth suddenly,
> And silence against which you dare not cry,
> Aches round you like a strong disease and new—
> What hope ? what help ? what music will undo
> That silence to your senses ? Not friendship's sigh,
> Not reason's subtle count.   Nay, none of these !
> Speak Thou, availing Christ ! and fill this pause."

CHAPTER III.

OF all that occurred during many ensuing weeks
Edna knew little. She retained, in after years, only a
vague, confused remembrance of keen anguish and
utter prostration, and an abiding sense of irreparable
loss. In delirious visions she saw her grandfather now
struggling in the grasp of Phlegyas, and now writhing
in the fiery tomb of Uberti, with jets of flame leaping
through his white hair, and his shrunken hands
stretched appealingly toward her, as she had seen
those of the doomed Ghibelline leader, in the hideous
Dante picture. All the appalling images evoked by
the sombre and embittered imagination of the gloomy
Tuscan had seized upon her fancy, even in happy
hours, and were now reproduced by her disordered
brain in multitudinous and aggravated forms. Her
wails of agony, her passionate prayers to God to release the beloved spirit from the tortures which her
delirium painted, were painful beyond expression to
those who watched her ravings; and it was with a
feeling of relief that they finally saw her sink into
apathy—into a quiet mental stupor—from which nothing seemed to rouse her. She did not remark Mrs.
Hunt's absence, or the presence of the neighbors at
her bedside. And one morning, when she was wrapped
up and placed by the fire, Mrs. Wood told her as
gently as possible that her grandmother had died
from a disease which was ravaging the country and
supposed to be cholera. The intelligence produced

no emotion; she merely looked up an instant, glanced mournfully around the dreary room, and, shivering slightly, drooped her head again on her hand. Week after week went slowly by, and she was removed to Mrs. Wood's house, but no improvement was discernible, and the belief became general that the child's mind had sunk into hopeless imbecility. The kindhearted miller and his wife endeavored to coax her out of her chair by the chimney-corner, but she crouched there, a wan, mute figure of woe, pitiable to contemplate; asking no questions, causing no trouble, receiving no consolation. One bright March morning she sat, as usual, with her face bowed on her thin hand, and her vacant gaze fixed on the blazing fire, when, through the open window, came the impatient lowing of a cow. Mrs. Wood saw a change pass swiftly over the girl's face, and a quiver cross the lips so long frozen. She lifted her head, rose, and followed the sound, and soon stood at the side of Brindle, who now furnished milk for the miller's family. As the gentle cow recognized and looked at her, with an expression almost human in the mild, liquid eyes, all the events of that last serene evening swept back to Edna's deadened memory, and, leaning her head on Brindle's horns, she shed the first tears that had flowed for her great loss, while sobs, thick and suffocating, shook her feeble, emaciated frame.

"Bless the poor little outcast, she will get well now. That is just exactly what she needs. I tell you, Peter, one good cry like that is worth a wagon-load of physic. Don't go near her; let her have her cry out. Poor thing! It ain't often you see a child love her granddaddy as she loves Aaron Hunt. Poor lamb!"

Mrs. Wood wiped her own eyes, and went back to her weaving; and Edna turned away from the mill and walked to her deserted home, while the tears poured ceaselessly over her white cheeks. As she approached the old house she saw that it was shut up and neglected; but when she opened the gate, Grip, the fierce yellow terror of the whole neighborhood,

sprang from the door-step, where he kept guard as
tirelessly as Maïda, and, with a dismal whine of welcome, leaped up and put his paws on her shoulders.
This had been the blacksmith's pet, fed by his hand,
chained when he went to the shop, and released at his
return ; and grim and repulsively ugly though he was,
the only playmate Edna had ever known ; had gam-
boled around her cradle, slept with her on the sheepskin, and frolicked with her through the woods, in
many a long search for Brindle. He alone remained
of all the happy past ; and as precious memories
crowded mournfully up, she sat upon the steps of the
dreary homestead, with her arms around his neck, and
wept bitterly. After an hour she left the house, and,
followed by the dog, crossed the woods in the direction of the neighborhood graveyard. In order to
reach it she was forced to pass by the spring and the
green hillock where Mr. and Mrs. Dent slept side by
side, but no nervous terror seized her now as formerly ;
the great present horror swallowed up all others, and,
though she trembled from physical debility, she
dragged herself on till the rude, rough paling of the
burying-ground stood before her. Oh, dreary desolation ! thy name is country graveyard ! Here no polished sculptured stela pointed to the Eternal Rest beyond ; no classic marbles told, in gilded characters, the
virtues of the dead ; no flowery-fringed gravel-walks
wound from murmuring waterfalls and rippling foun-
tains to crystal lakes, where trailing willows threw
their flickering shadows over silver-dusted lilies ; no
spicy perfume of purple heliotrope and starry jasmine
burdened the silent air ; none of the solemn beauties
and soothing charms of Greenwood or Mount Auburn
wooed the mourner from her weight of woe. Decaying head-boards, green with the lichen-fingered touch
of time, leaned over neglected mounds, where last
year's weeds shivered in the sighing breeze, and autumn
winds and winter rains had drifted a brown shroud of
shriveled leaves ; while here and there meek-eyed
sheep lay sunning themselves upon the trampled graves,

and the slow-measured sound of a bell dirged now and
then as cattle browsed on the scanty herbage in this
most neglected of God's Acres. Could Charles Lamb
have turned from the pompous epitaphs and high-
flown ‧ panegyrics of that English cemetery, to the
rudely-lettered boards which here briefly told the names
and ages of the sleepers in these narrow beds, he had
never asked the question which now stands as a melancholy epigram on family favoritism and human frailty.
Gold gilds even the lineaments and haunts of Death,
making *Père la Chaise* a favored spot for *fêtes cham-
petres;* while poverty hangs neither veil nor mask over
the grinning ghoul, and flees, superstition-spurred,
from the hideous precincts.

In one corner of the inclosure, where Edna's parents
slept, she found the new mounds that covered the
remains of those who had nurtured and guarded her
young life ; and on an unpainted board was written in
large letters :

"To the memory of Aaron Hunt : an honest blacksmith, and true Christian ; aged sixty-eight years and
six months."

Here, with her head on her grandfather's grave, and
the faithful dog crouched at her feet, lay the orphan,
wrestling with grief and loneliness, striving to face a
future that loomed before her spectre-thronged ; and
here Mr. Wood found her when anxiety at her long
absence induced his wife to search for the missing
invalid. The storm of sobs and tears had spent itself,
fortitude took the measure of the burden imposed,
shouldered the galling weight, and henceforth, with un-
dimmed vision, walked steadily to the appointed goal.
The miller was surprised to find her so calm, and as
they went homeward she asked the particulars of all
that had occurred, and thanked him gravely but cordially for the kind care bestowed upon her, and for the
last friendly offices performed for her grandfather.

Conscious of her complete helplessness and physical
prostration, she ventured no allusion to the future, but
waited patiently until renewed strength permitted the

execution of designs now fully mapped out. Notwithstanding her feebleness, she rendered herself invaluable to Mrs. Wood, who praised her dexterity and neatness as a seamstress, and predicted that she would make a model housekeeper.

Late one Sunday evening in May, as the miller and his wife sat upon the steps of their humble and comfortless looking home, they saw Edna slowly approaching, and surmised where she had spent the afternoon. Instead of going into the house she seated herself beside them, and, removing her bonnet, traces of tears were visible on her sad but patient face.

"You ought not to go over yonder so often, child. It is not good for you," said the miller, knocking the ashes from his pipe.

She shaded her countenance with her hand, and after a moment said, in a low but steady tone:

"I shall never go there again. I have said good-by to everything, and have nothing now to keep me here. You and Mrs. Wood have been very kind to me, and I thank you heartily; but you have a family of children, and have your hands full to support them without taking care of me. I know that our house must go to you to pay that old debt, and even the horse and cow; and there will be nothing left when you are paid. You are very good, indeed, to offer me a home here, and I never can forget your kindness; but I should not be willing to live on anybody's charity; and besides, all the world is alike to me now, and I want to get out of sight of—of—what shows my sorrow to me every day. I don't love this place now; it won't let me forget, even for a minute, and—and ——"

Here the voice faltered and she paused.

"But where could you go, and how could you make your bread, you poor little ailing thing?"

"I hear that in the town of Columbus, Georgia, even little children get wages to work in the factory, and I know I can earn enough to pay my board among the factory people."

"But you are too young to be straying about in a

strange place. If you will stay here, and help my wife
about the house and the weaving, I will take good
care of you, and clothe you till you are grown and married."

"I would rather go away, because I want to be
educated, and I can't be if I stay here."

"Fiddlestick! you will know as much as the balance
of us, and that's all you will ever have any use for. I
notice you have a hankering after books, but the
quicker you get that foolishness out of your head the
better; for books won't put bread in your mouth and
clothes on your back; and folks that want to be better
than their neighbors generally turn out worse. The
less book-learning you women have the better."

"I don't see that it is any of your business, Peter
Wood, how much learning we women choose to get,
provided your bread is baked and your socks darned
when you want 'em. A woman has as good a right as
a man to get book-learning, if she wants it; and as for
sense, I'll thank you, mine is as good as yours any day;
and folks have said it was a blessed thing for the
neighborhood when the rheumatiz laid Peter Wood up,
and his wife, Dorothy Elmira Wood, run the mill.
Now, it's of no earthly use to cut at us women over
that child's shoulders; if she wants an education she
has as much right to it as anybody, if she can pay for
it. My doctrine is, everybody has a right to whatever they can pay for, whether it is schooling or a
satin frock!"

Mrs Wood seized her snuff-bottle and plunged a
stick vigorously into the contents, and, as the miller
showed no disposition to skirmish, she continued:

"I take an interest in you, Edna Earl, because I
loved your mother, who was the only sweet-tempered
beauty that ever I knew. I think I never set my eyes
on a prettier face, with big brown eyes as meek as a
partridge's; and then her hands and feet were as small
as a queen's. Now as long as you are satisfied to stay
here I shall be glad to have you, and I will do as well
for you as for my own Tabitha; but, if you are bent

on factory work and schooling, I have got no more to say; for I have no right to say where you shall go or where you shall stay. But one thing I do want to tell you, it is a serious thing for a poor, motherless girl to be all alone among strangers."

There was a brief silence, and Edna answered slowly:

"Yes, Mrs. Wood, I know it is; but God can protect me there as well as here, and I have none now but Him. I have made up my mind to go, because I think it is the best for me, and I hope Mr. Wood will carry me to the Chattanooga depot to-morrow morning, as the train leaves early. I have a little money—seven dollars—that—that grandpa gave me at different times, and both Brindle's calves belong to me—he gave them to me—and I thought may be you would pay me a few dollars for them."

"But you are not ready to start to-morrow."

"Yes, sir, I washed and ironed my clothes yesterday, and what few I have are all packed in my box. Everything is ready now, and, as I have to go, I might as well start to-morrow."

"Don't you think you will get dreadfully homesick in about a month, and write to me to come and fetch you back?"

"I have no home and nobody to love me, how then can I ever be homesick? Grandpa's grave is all the home I have, and—and—God would not take me there when I was so sick, and—and ——" The quiver of her face showed that she was losing her self-control, and turning away, she took the cedar piggin, and went out to milk Brindle for the last time.

Feeling that they had no right to dictate her future course, neither the miller nor his wife offered any further opposition, and very early the next morning, after Mrs. Wood had given the girl what she called "some good motherly advice," and provided her with a basket containing food for the journey, she kissed her heartily several times, and saw her stowed away in the miller's covered cart, which was to convey her to

the railway station. The road ran by the old blacksmith's shop, and Mr. Wood's eyes filled as he noticed
the wistful, lingering, loving gaze which the girl fixed
upon it, until a grove of trees shut out the view ; then
the head bowed itself, and a stifled moan reached his
ears.

The engine whistled as they approached the station,
and Edna was hurried aboard the train, while her companion busied himself in transferring her box of cloth-
ing to the baggage car. She had insisted on taking her
grandfather's dog with her, and, notwithstanding the
horrified looks of the passengers and the scowl of
the conductor, he followed her into the car and threw
himself under the seat, glaring at all who passed, and
looking as hideously savage as the Norse Managarmar.

" You can't have a whole seat to yourself, and nobody wants to sit near that ugly brute," said the surly
conductor.

Edna glanced down the aisle, and saw two young
gentlemen stretched at full length on separate seats,
eyeing her curiously.

Observing that the small seat next to the door was
partially filled with the luggage of the parties who sat
in front of it, she rose and called to the dog, saying to
the conductor as she did so :

" I will take that half of a seat yonder, where I shall
be in nobody's way."

Here Mr. Wood came forward, thrust her ticket
into her fingers, and shook her hand warmly, saying
hurriedly :

" Hold on to your ticket, and don't put your head
out of the window. I told the conductor he must look
after you and your box when you left the cars ; said
he would. Good-by, Edna ; take care of yourself, and
may God bless you, child."

The locomotive whistled, the train moved slowly on,
and the miller hastened back to his cart.

As the engine got fully under way, and dashed
around a curve, the small, straggling village disappeared, trees and hills seemed to the orphan to fly

past the window ; and when she leaneu out and looked back, only the mist-mantled rocks of Lookout, and the dim, purplish outline of the Sequatchie heights were familiar.

In the shadow of that solitary sentinel peak her life had been passed ; she had gathered chestnuts and chincapins among its wooded clefts, and clambered over its gray boulders as fearlessly as the young llamas of the Parimé ; and now, as it rapidly receded and finally vanished, she felt as if the last link that bound her to the past had suddenly snapped ; the last friendly face which had daily looked down on her for twelve years was shut out forever, and she and Grip were indeed alone, in a great, struggling world of self-ishness and sin. The sun shone dazzlingly over wide fields of grain, whose green billows swelled and surged under the freshening breeze; golden butterflies flut-tered over the pink and blue morning-glories that fes-tooned the rail-fences; a brakeman whistled merrily on the platform, and children inside the car prattled and played, while at one end a slender little girlish figure, in homespun dress and pink calico bonnet, crouched in a corner of the seat, staring back in the direction of hooded Lookout, feeling that each instant bore her farther from the dear graves of her dead ; and oppressed with an intolerable sense of desolation and utter isolation in the midst of hundreds of her own race, who were too entirely absorbed in their individual speculations, fears and aims, to spare even a glance at that solitary young mariner, who saw the last headland fade from view, and found herself, with no pilot but ambition, drifting rapidly out on the great, unknown, treacherous Sea of Life, strewn with mournful human wrecks, whom the charts and buoys of six thousand years of navigation could not guide to a haven of use-fulness and peace. Interminable seemed the dreary day, which finally drew to a close, and Edna, who was weary of her cramped position, laid her aching head on the window-sill, and watched the red light of day die in the west, where a young moon hung her silvery

crescent among the dusky tree-tops, and the stars
flashed out thick and fast. Far away among strangers,
uncared for and unnoticed, come what might, she felt
that God's changeless stars smiled down as lovingly
upon her face as on her grandfather's grave; and
that the cosmopolitan language of nature knew neither
the modifications of time and space, the distinctions of
social caste, nor the limitations of national dialects.

As the night wore on, she opened the cherished copy
of Dante and tried to read, but the print was too fine
for the dim lamp which hung at some distance from
her corner. Her head ached violently, and, as sleep
was impossible, she put the book back in her pocket,
and watched the flitting trees and fences, rocky banks,
and occasional houses, which seemed weird in the
darkness. As silence deepened in the car, her sense of
loneliness became more and more painful, and finally
she turned and pressed her cheek against the fair,
chubby hand of a baby, who slept with its curly head
on its mother's shoulder, and its little dimpled arm and
hand hanging over the back of the seat. There was
comfort and a soothing sensation of human companionship in the touch of that baby's hand; it seemed a
link in the electric chain of sympathy, and, after a
time, the orphan's eyes closed—fatigue conquered
memory and sorrow, and she fell asleep with her lips
pressed to those mesmeric baby fingers, and Grip's
head resting against her knee.

Diamond-powdered "lilies of the field" folded their
perfumed petals under the Syrian dew, wherewith God
nightly baptized them in token of his ceaseless guardianship, and the sinless world of birds, the "fowls of
the air," those secure and blithe, yet improvident,
little gleaners in God's granary, nestled serenely under
the shadow of the Almighty wing; but was the all-
seeing, all-directing Eye likewise upon that desolate
and destitute young mourner who sank to rest with
"Our Father which art in heaven" upon her trembling
lips? Was it a decree in the will and wisdom of our
God, or a fiat from the blind fumbling of Atheistri

Chance, or was it in accordance with the rigid edict of Pantheistic Necessity, that at that instant the cherubim of death swooped down on the sleeping passengers, and silver cords and golden bowls were rudely snapped and crushed, amid the crash of timbers, the screams of women and children, and the groans of tortured men, that made night hideous? Over the holy hills of Judea, out of crumbling Jerusalem, the message of Messiah has floated on the wings of eighteen centuries: "What I do thou knowest not now, but thou shalt know hereafter."

Edna was awakened by a succession of shrill sounds, which indicated that the engineer was either frightened or frantic; the conductor rushed bare-headed through the car; people sprang to their feet; there was a scramble on the platform; then a shock and crash as if the day of doom had dawned—and all was chaos.

CHAPTER IV.

VIEWED by the aid of lanterns and the lurid, flickering light of torches, the scene of disaster presented a
ghastly *debris* of dead and dying, of crushed cars and
wounded men and women, who writhed and groaned
among the shattered timbers from which they found it
impossible to extricate themselves. The cries of those
who recognized relatives in the mutilated corpses that
were dragged out from the wreck increased the horrors
of the occasion ; and when Edna opened her eyes amid
the flaring of torches and the piercing wails of the be-
reaved passengers, her first impression was, that she
had died and gone to Dante's " Hell ;" but the pangs
that seized her when she attempted to move soon dispelled this frightful illusion, and by degrees the truth
presented itself to her blunted faculties. She was
held fast between timbers, one of which seemed to have
fallen across her feet and crushed them, as she was
unable to move them, and was conscious of a horrible
sensation of numbness ; one arm, too, was pinioned at
her side, and something heavy and cold lay upon her
throat and chest. Lifting this weight with her un-
injured hand, she uttered an exclamation of horror as
the white face of the little baby whose fingers she had
clasped now met her astonished gaze ; and she saw
that the sweet coral lips were pinched and purple, the
waxen lids lay rigid over the blue eyes, and the dimpled
hand was stiff and icy. The confusion increased as
day dawned and a large crowd collected to offer assistance, and Edna watched her approaching deliverers as
they cut their way through the wreck and lifted out

the wretched sufferers. Finally two men, with axes in their hands, bent down and looked into her face.

" Here is a live child and a dead baby wedged in between these beams. Are you much hurt, little one?"

" Yes, I believe I am. Please take this log off my feet."

It was a difficult matter, but at length strong arms raised her, carried her some distance from the ruins, and placed her on the grass, where several other persons were writhing and groaning. The collision which precipitated the train from trestle-work over a deep ravine, had occurred near a village station, and two physicians were busily engaged in examining the wounded. The sun had risen, and shone full on Edna's pale, suffering face, when one of the surgeons, with a countenance that indexed earnest sympathy and compassion, came to investigate the extent of her injuries, and sat down on the grass beside her. Very tenderly he handled her, and after a few moments said gently :

"I am obliged to hurt you a little, my child, for your shoulder is dislocated, and some of the bones are broken in your feet ; but I will be as tender as possible. Here, Lennox! help me."

The pain was so intense that she fainted, and after a short time, when she recovered her consciousness, her feet and ankles were tightly bandaged, and the doctor was chafing her hands and bathing her face with some powerful extract. Smoothing back her hair, he said :

" Were your parents on the cars? Do you know whether they are hurt?"

" They both died when I was a baby."

" Who was with you?"

" Nobody but Grip—my dog."

" Had you no relatives or friends on the train ?"

" I have none. I am all alone in the world."

" Where did you come from?"

" Chattanooga."

" Where were you going?"

" My grandpa died, and as I had nobody to take care

of me, I was going to Columbus to work in the cotton factory."

"Humph! Much work you will do for many a long day."

He stroked his grayish beard, and mused a moment, and Edna said timidly:

"If you please, sir, I would like to know if my dog is hurt?"

The physician smiled, and looked round inquiringly.

"Has any one seen a dog that was on the train?"

One of the brakemen, a stout Irishman, took his pipe from his mouth, and answered:

"Aye, aye, sir! and as vicious a brute as ever I set eyes on. Both his hind legs were smashed—dragged so—and I tapped him on the head with an ax to put him out of his misery. Yonder he now lies on the track."

Edna put her hand over her eyes, and turned her face down on the grass to hide tears that would not be driven back. Here the surgeon was called away, and for a half hour the child lay there, wondering what would become of her, in her present crippled and help-less condition, and questioning in her heart why God did not take her instead of that dimpled darling, whose parents were now weeping so bitterly for the untimely death that mowed their blossom ere its petals were ex-panded. The chilling belief was fast gaining ground that God had cursed and forsaken her; that misfor-tune and bereavement would dog her steps through life; and a hard, bitter expression settled about her mouth, and looked out gloomily from the sad eyes. Her painful reverie was interrupted by the cheery voice of Dr. Rodney, who came back, accompanied by an elegantly-dressed middle-aged lady.

"Ah, my brave little soldier! Tell us your name."

"Edna Earl."

"Have you no relatives?" asked the lady, stooping to scrutinze her face.

"No, ma'am."

"She is a very pretty child, Mrs. Murray, and if you

can take care of her, even for a few weeks, until she is
able to walk about, it will be a real charity. I never
saw so much fortitude displayed by one so young; but
her fever is increasing, and she needs immediate attention. Will it be convenient for you to carry her to
your house at once?"

"Certainly, doctor; order the carriage driven up as
close as possible. I brought a small mattress, and
think the ride will not be very painful. What splendid eyes she has! Poor little thing! Of course you
will come and prescribe for her, and I will see that she
is carefully nursed until she is quite well again. Here,
Henry, you and Richard must lift this child, and put
her on the mattress in the carriage. Mind you do not
stumble and hurt her."

During the drive neither spoke, and Edna was in so
much pain that she lay with her eyes closed. As they
entered a long avenue, the rattle of the wheels on the
gravel aroused the child's attention, and when the
carriage stopped, and she was carried up a flight of
broad marble steps, she saw that the house was very
large and handsome.

"Bring her into the room next to mine," said Mrs.
Murray, leading the way.

Edna was soon undressed and placed within the
snowy sheets of a heavily-carved bedstead, whose
crimson canopy shed a ruby light down on the laced
and ruffled pillows. Mrs. Murray administered a dose
of medicine given to her by Dr. Rodney, and after
closing the blinds to exclude the light, she felt the
girl's pulse, found that she had fallen into a heavy
sleep, and then, with a sigh, went down to take her
breakfast. It was several hours before Edna awoke,
and when she opened her eyes, and looked around the
elegantly furnished and beautiful room, she felt bewildered. Mrs. Murray sat in a cushioned chair, near
one of the windows, with a book in her hand, and
Edna had an opportunity of studying her face. It was
fair, proud, and handsome, but wore an expression of
habitual anxiety; and gray hairs showed themselves

under the costly lace that bordered her morning head-
dress, while lines of care marked her brow and mouth.
Children instinctively decipher the hieroglyphics which
time carves on human faces, and, in reading the countenance of her hostess, Edna felt that she was a haughty,
ambitious woman, with a kind but not very warm
heart, who would be scrupulously attentive to the
wants of a sick child, but would probably never dream
of caressing or fondling such a charge. Chancing to
glance towards the bed as she turned a leaf, Mrs. Murray met the curious gaze fastened upon her, and, rising,
approached the sufferer.

"How do you feel, Edna? I believe that is your
name."

"Thank you, my head is better, but I am very
thirsty."

The lady of the house gave her some iced water in a
silver goblet, and ordered a servant to bring up the
refreshments she had directed prepared. As she felt
the girl's pulse, Edna noticed how white and soft her
hands were, and how dazzlingly the jewels flashed on
her fingers, and she longed for the touch of those aristocratic hands on her hot brow, where the hair clustered so heavily.

"How old are you, Edna?"

"Almost thirteen."

"Had you any luggage on the train?"

"I had a small box of clothes."

"I will send a servant for it." She rang the bell as
she spoke.

"When do you think I shall be able to walk
about?"

"Probably not for many weeks. If you need or
wish anything you must not hesitate to ask for it. A
servant will sit here, and you have only to tell her
what you want."

"You are very kind, ma'am, and I thank you very
much ——" She paused, and her eyes filled with tears.

Mrs. Murray looked at her and said gravely:

"What is the matter, child?"

"I am only sorry I was so ungrateful and wicked this morning."

"How so?"

"Oh! everything that I love dies; and when I lay there on the grass, unable to move, among strangers who knew and cared nothing about me, I was wicked, and would not try to pray, and thought God wanted to make me suffer all my life, and I wished that I had been killed instead of that dear little baby, who had a father and mother to kiss and love it. It was all wrong to feel so, but I was so wretched. And then God raised up friends even among strangers, and shows me I am not forsaken if I am desolate. I begin to think He took everybody away from me, that I might see how He could take care of me without them. I know 'He doeth all things well,' but I feel it now; and I am so sorry I could not trust Him without seeing it."

Edna wiped away her tears, and Mrs. Murray's voice faltered slightly as she said:

"You are a good little girl, I have no doubt. Who taught you to be so religious?"

"Grandpa."

"How long since you lost him?"

"Four months."

"Can you read?"

"Oh! yes, ma'am."

"Well, I shall send you a Bible, and you must make yourself as contented as possible. I shall take good care of you."

As the hostess left the room a staid-looking, elderly negro woman took a seat at the window and sewed silently, now and then glancing toward the bed Exhausted with pain and fatigue, Edna slept again, and it was night when she opened her eyes and found Dr. Rodney and Mrs. Murray at her pillow. The kind surgeon talked pleasantly for some time, and, after giving ample instructions, took his leave, exhorting his patient to keep up her fortitude and all would soon be well. So passed the first day of her sojourn under the hospitable roof which appeared so fortuitously to shelter her; and the child thanked God fervently for the kind hands into which she had fallen. Day after day wore wearily away, and at the end of a fortnight, though much prostrated by fever and suffering, she was propped up in bed by pillows, while Hagar, the servant, combed and plaited the long, thick, matted hair. Mrs. Murray came often to the room, but her visits were short, and though invariably kind and considerate, Edna felt an involuntary awe of her, which rendered her manner exceedingly constrained when they were together. Hagar was almost as taciturn as her mistress, and as the girl asked few questions, she remained in complete ignorance of the household affairs, and had never seen any one but Mrs. Murray, Hagar, and the doctor. She was well supplied with books, which the former brought from the library, and thus the invalid contrived to amuse herself during the long, tedious summer days. One afternoon in June, Edna persuaded Hagar to lift her to a large, cushioned chair close to the open window which looked out on the lawn; and here, with a book on her lap, she sat gazing out at the soft blue sky, the waving elm boughs, and the glittering plumage of a beautiful Himalayan pheasant, which seemed in the golden sunshine to have forgotten the rosy glow of his native snows. Leaning her elbows on the window-sill, Edna rested her face in her palms, and after a few minutes a tide of tender memories rose and swept over her heart, bringing a touching expression of patient sorrow to her sweet, wan face, and giving a far-off wistful look to the beautiful eyes where tears often gathered but very rarely fell. Hagar had dressed her in a new white muslin wrapper, with fluted ruffles at the wrists and throat; and the fair young face, with its delicate features, and glossy folds of soft hair, was a pleasant picture, which the nurse loved to contemplate. Standing with her work-basket in her hand, she watched the graceful little figure for two or three moments, and a warm, loving light shone out over her black features ; then nodding her head resolutely, she muttered :

" I will have my way this once ; she shall stay," and passed out of the room, closing the door behind her. Edna did not remark her departure, for memory was busy among the ashes of other days, exhuming a thousand precious reminiscences of mountain home, chestnut groves, showers of sparks fringing an anvil with fire, and an old man's unpainted head-board in the deserted burying-ground. She started nervously when, a half hour later, Mrs. Murray laid her hand gently on her shoulder, and said :

" Child, of what are you thinking ?"

For an instant she could not command her voice, which faltered ; but making a strong effort, she answered in a low tone :

" Of all that I have lost, and what I am to do in future."

" Would you be willing to work all your life in a factory ?"

"No, ma'am ; only long enough to educate myself, so that I could teach."

" You could not obtain a suitable education in that way, and beside, I do not think that the factory you spoke of would be an agreeable place for you. I have made some inquiries about it since you came here."

" I know it will not be pleasant, but then I am obliged to work in some way, and I don't see what else I can do. I am not able to pay for an education now, and I am determined to have one."

Mrs. Murray's eyes wandered out toward the velvety lawn, and she mused for some minutes ; then laying her hands on the orphan's head, she said :

" Child, will you trust your future and your education to me ? I do not mean that I will teach you—oh ! no—but I will have you thoroughly educated, so that when you are grown you can support yourself by teaching. I have no daughter—I lost mine when she was a babe ; but I could not have seen her enter a factory, and as you remind me of my own child, I will

not allow you to go there. I will take care of and educate you—will see that you have everything you
require, if you are willing to be directed and advised
by me. Understand me, I do not adopt you ; nor shall
I consider you exactly as one of my family ; but I shall
prove a good friend and protector till you are eighteen,
and capable of providing for yourself. You will live
in my house and look upon it as your home, at least
for the present. What do you say to this plan ? Is it
not much better and more pleasant than a wild-goose
chase after an education through the dust and din of a
factory?"

"Oh, Mrs. Murray! You are very generous and
good, but I have no claim on you—no right to impose
such expense and trouble upon you ! I am ——"

"Hush, child ! you have that claim which poverty
always has on wealth. As for the expense, that is a
mere trifle, and I do not expect you to give me any
trouble ; perhaps you may even make yourself useful
to me."

"Thank you ! oh ! thank you, ma'am ! I am very
grateful ! I can not tell you how much I thank you ;
but I shall try to prove it, if you will let me stay here
—on one condition."

"What is that ?"

"That when I am able to pay you, you will receive
the money that my education and clothes will cost
you."

Mrs. Murray laughed, and stroked the silky black
hair.

"Where did you get such proud notions ? Pay me,
indeed ! You poor little beggar ! Ha ! ha ! ha ! Well,
yes, you may do as you please, when you are able ;
that time is rather too distant to be considered now.
Meanwhile, quit grieving over the past, and think only
of improving yourself. I do not like doleful faces, and
shall expect you to be a cheerful, contented, and obedi-
ent girl. Hagar is making you an entire set of new
clothes, and I hope to see you always neat. I shall
give you a smaller room than this—the one across the

hall; you will keep your books there, and remain there during study hours. At other times you can come to my room, or amuse yourself as you like; and when there is company here, remember, I shall always expect you to sit quietly, and listen to the conversation, as it is very improving to young girls to be in really good society. You will have a music teacher, and practice on the upright piano in the library, instead of the large one in the parlor. One thing more, if you want anything, come to me, and ask for it, and I shall be very much displeased if you talk to the servants, or encourage them to talk to you. Now, everything is understood, and I hope you will be happy, and properly improve the advantages I shall give you."

Edna drew one of the white hands down to her lips and murmured:

"Thank you—thank you! You shall never have cause to regret your goodness; and your wishes shall always guide me."

"Well, well; I shall remember this promise, and trust I may never find it necessary to remind you of it. I dare say we shall get on very happily together. Don't thank me any more, and hereafter we need not speak of the matter."

Mrs. Murray stooped, and for the first time kissed the child's white forehead; and Edna longed to throw her arms about the stately form, but the polished *hauteur* awed and repelled her.

Before she could reply, and just as Mrs. Murray was moving toward the door, it was thrown open, and a gentleman strode into the room. At sight of Edna he stopped suddenly, and dropping a bag of game on the floor, exclaimed harshly:

"What the d—l does this mean?"

"My son! I am so glad you are at home again. I was getting quite uneasy at your long absence. This is one of the victims of that terrible railroad disaster; the neighborhood is full of the sufferers. Come to my room. When did you arrive?"

She linked her arm in his, picked up the game-bag, and led him to the adjoining room, the door of which she closed and locked.

A painful thrill shot along Edna's nerves, and an indescribable sensation of dread, a presentiment of coming ill, overshadowed her heart. This was the son of her friend, and the first glimpse of him filled her with instantaneous repugnance; there was an innate and powerful repulsion which she could not analyze. He was a tall, athletic man, not exactly young, yet certainly not elderly; one of anomalous appearance, prematurely old, and, though not one white thread silvered his thick, waving, brown hair, the heavy and habitual scowl on his high, full brow had plowed deep furrows such as age claims for its monogram. His features were bold but very regular; the piercing, steel-gray eyes were unusually large, and beautifully shaded with long, heavy, black lashes, but repelled by their cynical glare ; and the finely formed mouth, which might have imparted a wonderful charm to the countenance, wore a chronic, savage sneer, as if it only opened to utter jeers and curses. Evidently the face had once been singularly handsome, in the dawn of his earthly career, when his mother's good-night kiss rested like a blessing on his smooth, boyish forehead, and the prayer learned in the nursery still crept across his pure lips; but now the fair, chiseled lineaments were blotted by dissipation, and blackened and distorted by the baleful fires of a fierce, passionate nature, and a restless, powerful, and unhallowed intellect. Symmetrical and grand as that temple of Juno, in shrouded Pompeii, whose polished shafts gleamed centuries ago in the morning sunshine of a day of woe, whose untimely night has endured for nineteen hundred years, so, in the glorious flush of his youth, this man had stood facing a noble and possibly a sanctified future; but the ungovernable flames of sin had reduced him, like that darkened and desecrated fane, to a melancholy mass of ashy arches and blackened columns, where ministering priests all holy aspirations, slumbered in the dust.

His dress was costly but negligent, and the red stain on his jacket told that his hunt had not been fruitless. He wore a straw hat, belted with broad black ribbon, and his spurred boots were damp and muddy.

What was there about this surly son of her hostess which recalled to Edna's mind her grandfather's words, "He is a rude, wicked, blasphemous man." She had not distinctly seen the face of the visitor at the shop; but something in the impatient, querulous tone, in the hasty, haughty step, and the proud lifting of the regal head, reminded her painfully of him whose overbearing insolence had so unwontedly stirred the ire of Aaron Hunt's genial and generally equable nature. While she pondered this inexplicable coincidence, voices startled her from the next room, whence the sound floated through the window.

"If you were not my mother, I should say you were a candidate for a straight-jacket and a lunatic asylum; but as those amiable proclivities are considered hered, itary, I do not favor that comparison. 'Sorry for her,' indeed! I'll bet my right arm it will not be six weeks before she makes you infinitely sorrier for your deluded self; and you will treat me to a new version of '*je me regrette!*' With your knowledge of this precious world and its holy crew, I confess it seems farcical in the extreme that open-eyed you can venture another experiment on human nature. Some fine morning you will rub your eyes and find your acolyte *non est;* ditto, your silver forks, diamonds, and gold spoons."

Edna felt the indignant blood burning in her cheeks, and as she could not walk without assistance, and shrank from listening to a conversation which was not intended for her ears, she coughed several times to arrest the attention of the speakers, but apparently without effect, for the son's voice again rose above the low tones of the mother.

"Oh, carnival of shams! She is 'pious,' you say? Then, I'll swear my watch is not safe in my pocket, and I shall sleep with the key of my cameo cabinet

tied around my neck.   A Paris police would not insure
your valuables or mine.   The fates forbid that your
pen-feathered saint should decamp with some of my
costly travel-scrapings!   'Pious,' indeed!   'Edna,'
forsooth!   No doubt her origin and morals are quite
as apocryphal as her name.   Don't talk to me about
'her being providentially thrown into your hands,'
unless you desire to hear me say things which you
have frequently taken occasion to inform me 'deeply
grieved' you.   I dare say the little vagrant whines in
what she considers orthodox phraseology, that 'God
tempers the wind to the shorn lamb!' and, like some
other pious people whom I have heard canting, will
saddle some Jewish prophet or fisherman with the *dictum*, thinking that it sounds like the Bible, whereas
Sterne said it.   Shorn lamb, forsooth!   We, or rather
you, *madame, ma mère*, will be shorn—thoroughly
fleeced!   Pious!   Ha! ha! ha!"

Here followed an earnest expostulation from Mrs.
Murray, only a few words of which were audible, and
once more the deep, strong, bitter tones rejoined :

"Interfere!   Pardon me, I am only too happy to
stand aloof and watch the little wretch play out her
game.   Most certainly it is your own affair, but you
will permit me to be amused, will you not?   And with
your accustomed suavity forgive me, if I chance inadvertently to whisper above my breath, '*Le jeu n'en vaut
pas la chandelle ?*'   What the deuce do you suppose I
care about her 'faith?'   She may run through the
whole catalogue from the mustard-seed size up, as far
as I am concerned, and you may make yourself easy
on the score of my 'contaminating' the sanctified
vagrant!"

"St. Elmo! my son! promise me that you will not
scoff and sneer at her religion ; at least in her presence," pleaded the mother.

A ringing, mirthless laugh was the only reply that
reached the girl, as she put her fingers in her ears and
hid her face on the window-sill.

It was no longer possible to doubt the identity of

the stranger; the initials on the fly-leaf meant St.
Elmo Murray; and she knew that in the son of her
friend and protectress, she had found the owner of her
Dante and the man who had cursed her grandfather
for his tardiness. If she had only known this one hour
earlier, she would have declined the offer, which once
accepted, she knew not how to reject, without acquainting Mrs. Murray with the fact that she had overheard
the conversation; and yet she could not endure the
prospect of living under the same roof with a man
whom she loathed and feared. The memory of the
blacksmith's aversion to this stranger intensified her
own; and as she pondered in shame and indignation,
the scornful and opprobrious epithets which he had bestowed on herself, she muttered through her set teeth:

"Yes, Grandy! he is cruel and wicked; and I never
can bear to look at or speak to him! How dared he
curse my dear, dear, good grandpa! How can I ever
be respectful to him, when he is not even respectful to
his own mother! Oh! I wish I had never come here!
I shall always hate him!" At this juncture, Hagar
entered, and lifted her back to her couch; and, remarking the agitation of her manner, the nurse said gravely,
as she put her fingers on the girl's pulse:

"What has flushed you so? Your face is hot; you
have tired yourself sitting up too long. Did a gentleman come into this room a while ago?"

"Yes, Mrs. Murray's son."

"Did Miss Ellen—that is, my mistress—tell you
that you were to live here, and get your education?"

"Yes, she offered to take care of me for a few
years."

"Well, I am glad it is fixed, so—you can stay; for
you can be a great comfort to Miss Ellen, if you try to
please her."

She paused, and busied herself about the room, and
remembering Mrs. Murray's injunction that she should
discourage conversation on the part of the servants,
Edna turned her face to the wall and shut her eyes.
But for once Hagar's habitual silence and non-commit-

talism were laid aside ; and, stooping over the couch,
she said hurriedly :

"Listen to me, child, for I like your patient ways,
and want to give you a friendly warning ; you are a
stranger in this house, and might stumble into trouble.
Whatever else you do, be sure not to cross Mass'
Elmo's path ! Keep out of his way, and he will keep
out of yours ; for he is shy enough of strangers, and
would walk a mile to keep from meeting anybody ;
but if he finds you in his way, he will walk roughshod
right over you—trample you. Nothing ever stops him
one minute when he makes up his mind. He does not
even wait to listen to his mother, and she is about the
only person who dares to talk to him. He hates everybody and everything ; but he doesn't tread on folks'
toes unless they are where they don't belong. He is
like a rattlesnake that crawls in his own track, and
bites everything that meddles or crosses his trail.
Above everything, child, for the love of peace and
heaven, don't argue with him ! If he says black is
white, don't contradict him ; and if he swears water
runs up stream, let him swear, and don't know it runs
down. Keep out of his sight, and you will do well
enough, but once make him mad and you had better
fight Satan hand to hand with red-hot pitchforks !
Everybody is afraid of him, and gives way to him, and
you must do like the balance that have to deal with
him. I nursed him ; but I would rather put my head
in a wolf's jaws than stir him up ; and God knows I
wish he had died when he was a baby, instead of living
to grow up the sinful, swearing, raging devil he is !
Now mind what I say. I am not given to talking, but
this time it is for your good. Mind what I tell you,
child ; and if you want to have peace, keep out of his
way."

She left the room abruptly, and the orphan lay in
the gathering gloom of twilight, perplexed, distressed,
and wondering how she could avoid all the angulari-
ties of this amiable character, under whose roof fate
seemed to have deposited her.

CHAPTER V.

AT length, by the aid of crutches, Edna was able to leave the room where she had been so long confined, and explore the house in which every day discovered some new charm. The parlors and sitting-room opened on a long, arched verandah, which extended around two sides of the building, and was paved with variegated tiles ; while the stained-glass doors of the dining-room, with its lofty frescoed ceiling and deep bow-windows, led by two white marble steps out on the terrace, whence two more steps showed the beginning of a ser-pentine gravel walk winding down to an octagonal hot-house, surmounted by a richly carved pagoda-roof. Two sentinel statues—a Bacchus and Bacchante— placed on the terrace, guarded the entrance to the dining-room ; and in front of the house, where a sculp-tured Triton threw jets of water into a gleaming circu-lar basin, a pair of crouching monsters glared from the steps. When Edna first found herself before these grim doorkeepers, she started back in unfeigned terror, and could scarcely repress a cry of alarm, for the howl-ing rage and despair of the distorted hideous heads seemed fearfully real, and years elapsed before she comprehended their significance, or the sombre mood which impelled their creation. They were imitations of that monumental lion's head, raised on the battle-field of Chæroneia, to commemorate the Bœotians slain. In the rear of and adjoining the library, a nar-row, vaulted passage with high Gothic windows of stained-glass, opened into a beautifully proportioned rotunda, and beyond this circular apartment with its

ruby-tinted skylight and Moresque frescoes, extended
two other rooms, of whose shape or contents Edna
knew nothing, save the tall arched windows that looked
down on the terrace. The door of the rotunda was
generally closed, but accidentally it stood open one
morning, and she caught a glimpse of the circular form
and the springing dome. Evidently this portion of
the mansion had been recently built, while the remainder of the house had been constructed many years earlier; but all desire to explore it was extinguished when
Mrs. Murray remarked one day :

"That passage leads to my son's apartments, and he
dislikes noise or intrusion."

Thenceforth Edna avoided it as if the plagues of
Pharaoh were pent therein. To her dazzled eyes this
luxurious home was a fairy palace, an enchanted re-
gion, and, with eager curiosity and boundless admiration, she gazed upon beautiful articles whose use she
could not even conjecture. The furniture throughout
the mansion was elegant and costly ; pictures, statues,
bronzes, marble, silver, rosewood, ebony, mosaics, satin,
velvet—naught that the most fastidious and cultivated
taste or *dilettanteism* could suggest, or lavish expenditure supply, was wanting; while the elaborate and
beautiful arrangement of the extensive grounds showed
with how prodigal a hand the owner squandered a
princely fortune. The flower garden and lawn com-
prised fifteen acres, and the subdivisions were formed
entirely by hedges, save that portion of the park surrounded by a tall iron railing, where congregated a
motley menagérie of deer, bison, a Lapland reindeer,
a Peruvian llama, some Cashmere goats, a chamois,
wounded and caught on the Jungfrau, and a large
white cow from Ava. This part of the inclosure was
thickly studded with large oaks, groups of beech and
elm, and a few enormous cedars which would not have
shamed their sacred prototypes sighing in Syrian
breezes along the rocky gorges of Lebanon. The
branches were low and spreading, and even at mid-day
the sunshine barely freckled the cool, mossy knolls

where the animals sought refuge from the summer heat of the open and smoothly-shaven lawn. Here and there, on the soft, green sward, was presented that vegetable antithesis, a circlet of martinet poplars standing *vis-a-vis* to a clump of willows whose long hair threw quivering, fringy shadows when the slanting rays of dying sunlight burnished the white and purple petals nestling among the clover tufts. Rustic seats of bark, cane and metal were scattered through the grounds, and where the well-trimmed numerous hedges divided the *parterre*, china, marble and iron vases of varied mould, held rare creepers and lovely exotics ; and rich masses of roses swung their fragrant chalices of crimson and gold, rivaling the glory of Pæstum and of Bendemer. The elevation upon which the house was placed commanded an extensive view of the surrounding country. Far away to the northeast purplish gray waves along the sky showed a range of lofty hills, and in an easterly direction, scarcely two miles distant, glittering spires told where the village clung to the railroad, and to a deep rushing creek, whose sinuous course was distinctly marked by the dense growth that clothed its steep banks. Now and then luxuriant fields of corn covered the level lands with an emerald mantle, while sheep and cattle roamed through the adjacent champaign ; and in the calm, cool morning air, a black smoke-serpent crawled above the tree-tops, mapping out the track over which the long train of cars darted and thundered. Mr. Paul Murray, the first proprietor of the estate, and father of the present owner, had early in life spent much time in France, where, espousing the royalist cause, his sympathies were fully enlisted by the desperate daring of Charette, Stofflet, and Cathelineau. On his return to his native land, his admiration of the heroism of those who dwelt upon the Loire, found expression in one of their sobriquets, " Le Bocage," which he gave to his country residence ; and certainly the venerable groves that surrounded it justified the application. While his own fortune was handsome and abundant, he married the orphan of a

rich banker, who survived her father only a short time
and died leaving Mr. Murray childless. After a few
years, when the frosts of age fell upon his head, he
married a handsome and very wealthy widow ; but,
unfortunately, having lost their first child, a daughter,
he lived only long enough to hear the infantile prattle
of his son, St. Elmo, to whom he bequeathed an im-
mense fortune, which many succeeding years of reckless expenditure had failed to materially impair.
Such was "Le Bocage," naturally a beautiful situation,
improved and embellished with everything which refined taste and world-wide travel could suggest to the
fastidious owner. Notwithstanding the countless
charms of the home so benevolently offered to her, the
blacksmith's granddaughter was conscious of a great
need, scarcely to be explained, yet fully felt—the
dreary lack of that which she had yet to learn could
not be purchased by the treasures of Oude—the price-
less peace and genial glow which only the contented,
happy hearts of its inmates can diffuse over even a
palatial homestead. She also realized, without analyz-
ing the fact, that the majestic repose and boundless
spontaneity of nature yielded a sense of companionship almost of tender, dumb sympathy, which all the
polished artificialities and *recherché* arrangements of
man utterly failed to supply. While dazzled by the
glitter and splendor of "Le Bocage," she shivered in
its silent dreariness, its cold, aristocratic formalism,
and she yearned for the soft, musical babble of the
spring-branch, where, standing ankle-deep in water
under the friendly shadow of Lookout, she had spent
long, blissful July days in striving to build a wall of
rounded pebbles down which the crystal ripples would
fall, a miniature Talulah or Tuccoa. The chrism of
nature had anointed her early life and consecrated her
heart, but fate brought her to the vestibule of the
temple of Mammon, and its defiling incense floated
about her. How long would the consecration last ?
As she slowly limped about the house and grounds,
acquainting herself with the details, she was impressed

with the belief that happiness had once held her court here, had been dethroned, exiled and now waited beyond the confines of the park, anxious but unable to renew her reign and expel usurping gloom. For some weeks after her arrival she took her meals in her own room, and having learned to recognize the hasty, heavy tread of the dreaded master of the house, she invariably fled from the sound of his steps as she would have shunned an ogre; consequently her knowledge of him was limited to the brief inspection and uncomplimentary conversation which introduced him to her acquaintance on the day of his return. Her habitual avoidance and desire of continued concealment was, however, summarily thwarted when Mrs. Murray came into her room late one night, and asked:

"Did not I see you walking this afternoon without your crutches?"

"Yes, ma'am, I was trying to see if I could not do without them entirely."

"Did the experiment cause you any pain?"

"No pain exactly, but I find my ankle still weak."

"Be careful not to overstrain it; by degrees it will strengthen if you use it moderately. By the by, you are now well enough to come to the table; and from breakfast to-morrow you will take your meals with us in the dining-room."

A shiver of apprehension seized Edna, and in a frightened tone she ejaculated:

"Ma'am!"

"I say, in future you will eat at the table instead of here in this room."

"If you please, Mrs. Murray, I would rather stay here."

"Pray, what possible objection can you have to the dining-room?"

Edna averted her head, but wrung her fingers nervously.

Mrs. Murray frowned, and continued gravely:

"Don't be silly, Edna. It is proper that you should go to the table, and learn to eat with a fork instead of a knife. You need not be ashamed to meet people; there is nothing clownish about you unless you affect it. Good-night; I shall see you at breakfast; the bell rings at eight o'clock."

There was no escape, and she awoke next morning oppressed with the thought of the ordeal that awaited her. She dressed herself even more carefully than usual, despite the trembling of her hands; and when the ringing of the little silver bell summoned her to the dining-room, her heart seemed to stand still. But though exceedingly sensitive and shy, Edna was brave, and even self-possessed, and she promptly advanced to meet the trial.

Entering the room, she saw that her benefactress had not yet come in, but was approaching the house with a basket of flowers in her hand; and one swift glance around discovered Mr. Murray standing at the window. Unobserved, she scanned the tall, powerful figure clad in a suit of white linen, and saw that he wore no beard save the heavy but closely-trimmed moustache, which now, in some degree, concealed the harshness about the handsome mouth. Only his profile was turned toward her, and she noticed that, while his forehead was singularly white, his cheeks and chin were thoroughly bronzed from exposure.

As Mrs. Murray came in, she nodded to her young *protégée*, and approached the table, saying:

"Good morning! It seems I am the laggard to-day, but Nicholas had mislaid the flower shears, and detained me. Hereafter I shall turn over this work of dressing vases to you, child. My son, this is your birthday, and here is your button-hole souvenir'"

She fastened a few sprigs of white jasmine in his linen coat, and, as he thanked her briefly, and turned to the table, she said, with marked emphasis:

"St. Elmo, let me introduce you to Edna Earl."

He looked around, and fixed his keen eyes on the orphan, whose cheeks crimsoned as she looked down and said, quite distinctly·

"Good morning, Mr. Murray."

" Good morning, Miss Earl."

" No. I protest! ' Miss Earl,' indeed! Call the child Edna."

" As you please, mother, provided you do not let the coffee and chocolate get cold while you decide the momentous question."

Neither spoke again for some time, and in the embarrassing silence Edna kept her eyes on the china, wondering if all their breakfasts would be like this. At last Mr. Murray pushed away his large coffee-cup, and said abruptly:

" After all, it is only one year to-day since I came back to America, though it seems much longer. It will soon be time to prepare for my trip to the South Sea Islands. The stagnation here is intolerable."

An expression of painful surprise flitted across the mother's countenance, but she answered quickly:

" It has been an exceedingly short, happy year to me. You are such a confirmed absentee, that when you are at home, time slips by unnoticed."

" But few and far between as my visits are, they certainly never approach the angelic. 'Welcome the coming, speed the parting guest,' must frequently recur to you."

Before his mother could reply he rose, ordered his horse, and as he drew on his gloves, and left the room, looked over his shoulder, saying indifferently, " That box of pictures from Munich is at the warehouse; I directed Henry to go after it this morning. I will open it when I come home."

A moment after he passed the window on horseback, and with a heavy sigh Mrs. Murray dropped her head on her hand, compressing her lips, and toying abstractedly with the sugar-tongs.

Edna watched the grave, troubled countenance for some seconds, and then putting her hand on the flower-basket, she asked softly:

' Shall I dress the flower-pots ?"

"Yes, child, in four rooms ; this, the parlors, and the library. Always cut the flowers very early, while the dew is on them.

Her eyes went back to the sugar-tongs, and Edna joyfully escaped from a room whose restraints and associations were irksome.

Impressed by Hagar's vehement adjuration to keep out of Mr. Murray's path, she avoided those portions of the house to which he seemed most partial, and thus although they continued to meet at meals, no words passed between them, after that brief salutation on the morning of presentation. Very often she was painfully conscious that his searching eyes scrutinized her ; but though the blood mounted instantly to her cheeks at such times, she never looked up—dreading his gaze as she would that of a basilisk. One sultry afternoon she went into the park, and threw herself down on the long grass, under a clump of cedars, near which the deer and bison were quietly browsing, while the large white merinoes huddled in the shade and blinked at the sun. Opening a pictorial history of England, which she had selected from the library, she spread it on the grass, and leaning her face in her palms, rested her elbows on the ground, and began to read. Now and then she paused as she turned a leaf, to look around at the beautiful animals, each one of which might have served as a model for Landseer or Rosa Bonheur. Gradually the languor of the atmosphere stole into her busy brain ; as the sun crept down the sky, her eyelids sunk with it, and very soon she was fast asleep, with her head on the book, and her cheeks flushed almost to a vermilion hue. From that brief summer dream she was aroused by some sudden noise, and starting up, she saw the sheep bounding far away, while a large, gaunt, wolfish, grey dog snuffed at her hands and face. Once before she had seen him chained near the stables, and Hagar told her he was "very dangerous," and was never loosed except at night ; consequently, the expression of his fierce, red

eyes, as he stood over her, was well calculated to alarm her; but at that instant Mr. Murray's voice thundered :
" Keep still! don't move! or you will be torn to pieces!" Then followed some rapid interjections and vehement words in the same unintelligible dialect which had so puzzled her once before, when her grandfather could not control the horse he was attempting to shoe. The dog was sullen and unmanageable, keeping his black muzzle close to her face, and she grew pale with terror as she noticed that his shaggy breast and snarling jaws were dripping with blood.

Leaping from his horse, Mr. Murray strode up, and with a quick movement seized the heavy brass collar of the savage creature, hurled him back on his haunches, and held him thus, giving vent the while to a volley of oaths.

Pointing to a large, half-decayed elm branch, lying at a little distance, he tightened his grasp on the collar, and said to the still trembling girl :

" Bring me that stick, yonder."

Edna complied, and there ensued a scene of cursing, thrashing, and howling, that absolutely sickened her. The dog writhed, leaped, whined, and snarled ; but the iron hold was not relaxed, and the face of the master rivaled in rage that of the brute, which seemed as ferocious as the hounds of Gian Maria Visconti, fed with human flesh, by Squarcia Giramo. Distressed by the severity and duration of the punishment, and without pausing to reflect, or to remember Hagar's warning, Edna interposed :

" Oh! please don't whip him any more! It is cruel to beat him so!"

Probably he did not hear her, and the blows fell thicker than before. She drew near, and, as the merciless arm was raised to strike, she seized it with both hands, and swung on with her whole weight, repeating her words. If one of his meek, frightened sheep had sprung at his throat to throttle him, Mr. Murray would not have been more astounded. He shook her off, threw her from him, but she carried the stick in her grasp.

" D—n you ! how dare you interfere ! What is it to you if I cut his throat, which I mean to do !"

" That will be cruel and sinful, for he does not know it is wrong ; and besides, he did not bite me."

She spoke resolutely, and for the first time ventured to look straight into his flashing eyes.

" Did not bite you ! Did not he worry down and mangle one of my finest Southdowns? It would serve you right for your impertinent meddling, if I let him tear you limb from limb !"

" He knows no better," she answered, firmly.

" Then, by G—d, I will teach him ! Hand me that stick !"

" Oh ! please, Mr. Murray ! You have nearly put out one of his eyes already !"

" Give me the stick, I tell you, or I——"

He did not finish the threat, but held out his hand with a peremptory gesture.

Edna gave one swift glance around, saw that there were no other branches within reach, saw too that the dog's face was swelling and bleeding from its bruises, and, bending the stick across her knee, she snapped it into three pieces, which she threw as far as her strength would permit. There was a brief pause, broken only by the piteous howling of the suffering creature, and, as she began to realize what she had done, Edna's face reddened, and she put her hands over her eyes to shut out the vision of the enraged man, who was absolutely dumb with indignant astonishment. Presently a sneering laugh caused her to look through her fingers, and she saw " Ali," the dog, now released, fawning and whining at his master's feet.

" Aha ! The way of all natures, human as well as brute. Pet and fondle and pamper them, they turn under your caressing hand and bite you ; but bruise and trample them, and instantly they are on their knees licking the feet that kicked them. Begone ! you bloodthirsty devil ! I'll settle the account at the kennel. Buffon is a fool, and Pennant was right after all. The blood of the jackal pricks up your ears."

He spurned the crouching culprit, and as it slunk away in the direction of the house, Edna found herself alone, face to face with the object of her aversion, and she almost wished that the earth would open and swallow her. Mr. Murray came close to her, held her hands down with one of his, and placing the other under her chin, forced her to look at him.

"How dare you defy and disobey me?"

"I did not defy you, sir, but I could not help you to do what was wrong and cruel."

"I am the judge of my actions, and neither ask your help nor intend to permit your interference with what does not concern you."

"God is the judge of mine, sir, and if I had obeyed you, I should have been guilty of all you wished to do with that stick. I don't want to interfere, sir. I try to keep out of your way, aud I am very sorry I happened to come here this evening. I did not dream of meeting you; I thought you had gone to town."

He read all her aversion in her eyes, which strove to avoid his, and smiling grimly, he continued: "You evidently think that I am the very devil himself, walking the earth like a roaring lion. Mind your own affairs hereafter, and when I give you a positive order, obey it, for I am master here, and my word is law. Meddling or disobedience I neither tolerate nor forgive. Do you understand me?"

"I shall not meddle, sir."

"That means that you will not obey me unless you think proper?"

She was silent, and her beautiful soft eyes filled with tears.

"Answer me!"

"I have nothing to say that you would like to hear."

"What? Out with it!"

"You would have a right to think me impertinent if I said any more."

" No, I swear I will not devour you, say what you may."

She shook her head, and the motion brought two tears down on her cheeks.

" Oh, you are one of the stubborn sweet saints, whose lips even Torquemada's red-hot steel fingers could not open. Child, do you hate or dread me most ? Answer that question."

He took his own handkerchief and wiped away the tears.

" I am sorry for you, sir," she said in a low voice.

He threw his head back and laughed heartily.

" Sorry for me ? For me ! Me ? The owner of as many thousands as there are hairs on your head ! Keep your pity for your poverty-stricken vagrant self ! Why the deuce are you sorry for me ?"

She withdrew her hands, which he seemed to hold unconsciously, and answered :

" Because, with all your money, you never will be happy."

" And what the d—l do I care for happiness ? I am not such a fool as to expect it; and yet after all, ' Out of the mouths of babes and sucklings.' Pshaw ! I am a fool nevertheless to waste words on you. Stop ! What do you think of my park, and the animals ? I notice you often come here."

" The first time I saw it I thought of Noah and the ark, with two of every living thing ; but an hour ago it seemed to me more like the garden of Eden, where the animals all lay down together in peace, before sin came into it."

" And Ali and I entered, like Satan, and completed the vision ? Thank you, considering the fact that you are on my premises, and know something of my an- gelic, sanctified temper, I must say you indulge in bold flights of imagery."

" I did not say that, sir."

" You thought it nevertheless. Don't be hypocriti- cal ! Is not that what you thought of ?"

She made no reply, and anxious to terminate an

interview painfully embarassing to her, stepped forward to pick up the history which lay on the grass.

"What book is that?"

She handed it to him, and the leaves happened to open at a picture representing the murder of Becket. A scowl blackened his face as he glanced at it, and turned away, muttering:

"Malice prepense! or the devil!"

At a little distance, leisurely cropping the long grass, stood his favorite horse, whose arched forehead and peculiar mouse-color proclaimed his unmistakable descent from the swift hordes that scour the Kirghise steppes, and sanctioned the whim which induced his master to call him "Tamerlane." As Mr. Murray approached his horse, Edna walked away toward the house, fearing that he might overtake her; but no sound of hoofs reached her ears, and looking back as she crossed the avenue and entered the flower-garden, she saw horse and rider standing where she left them, and wondered why Mr. Murray was so still, with one arm on the neck of his Tartar pet, and his own head bent down on his hand.

In reflecting upon what had occurred, she felt her repugnance increase, and began to think that they could not live in the same house without continual conflicts, which would force her to abandon the numerous advantages now within her grasp. The only ray of hope darted through her mind when she recalled his allusion to a contemplated visit to the South Sea Islands, and the possibility of his long absence. Insensibly her dislike of the owner extended to every thing he handled, and much as she had enjoyed the perusal of Dante, she determined to lose no time in restoring the lost volume, which she felt well assured his keen eyes would recognize the first time she inadvertently left it in the library or the greenhouse. The doubt of her honesty, which he had expressed to his mother, rankled in the orphan's memory, and for some days she had been nerving herself to anticipate a dis-

74 ST. ELMO.

covery of the book by voluntarily restoring it. The *rencontre* in the park by no means diminished her dread of addressing him on this subject; but she resolved that the rendition of Cæsar's things to Cæsar should take place that evening before she slept.

CHAPTER VI.

THE narrow, vaulted passage leading to Mr. Murray's suit of rooms was dim and gloomy when Edna approached the partly opened door of the rotunda, whence issued a stream of light. Timidly she crossed the threshold and stood within on the checkered floor, whose polished tiles glistened under the glare of gas from bronze brackets representing Telamones, that stood at regular intervals around the apartment. The walls were painted in Saracenic style, and here and there hung specimens of Oriental armor—Turcoman cimeters, Damascus swords, Bedouin lances, and a crimson silk flag, with heavy gold fringe, surmounted by a crescent. The cornice of the lofty arched ceiling was elaborately arabesque, and as Edna looked up she saw through the glass roof the flickering of stars in the summer sky. In the centre of the room, immediately under the dome, stretched a billiard-table, and near it was a circular one of black marble, inlaid with red onyx and lapis lazuli, which formed a miniature zodiac similar to that at Denderah, while in the middle of this table sat a small Murano hour-glass, filled with sand from the dreary valley of El Ghor. A huge plaster Trimurti stood close to the wall, on a triangular pedestal of black rock, and the Siva-face and the writhing cobra confronted all who entered. Just opposite grinned a red granite slab with a quaint basso-relievo taken from the ruins of Elora. Near the door were two silken divans, and a richly carved urn, three feet high, which had once ornamented the facade of a tomb in the royal days of Petra, ere the curse fell on Edom.

now stood an *in memoriam* of the original Necropolis.
For what purpose this room was designed or used
Edna could not imagine, and after a hasty survey of
its singular furniture, she crossed the rotunda, and
knocked at the door that stood slightly ajar. All was
silent ; but the smell of a cigar told her that the owner
was within, and she knocked once more.

" Come in."

" I don't wish to come in ; I only want to hand you
something."

" Oh ! the deuce you don't ! But I never meet people
even half-way, so come in you must, if you have anything to say to me. I have neither blue blazes nor
pitchforks about me, and you will be safe inside. I
give you my word there are no small devils shut up
here, to fly away with whomsoever peeps in ! Either
enter, I say, or be off."

The temptation was powerful to accept the alternative ; but as he had evidently recognized her voice,
she pushed open the door and reluctantly entered. It
was a long room, and at the end were two beautiful
fluted white marble pillars, supporting a handsome
arch, where hung heavy curtains of crimson Persian
silk, that were now partly looped back, showing the
furniture of the sleeping apartment beyond the richly
carved arch. For a moment the bright light dazzled
the orphan, and she shaded her eyes ; but the next
instant Mr. Murray rose from a sofa near the window,
and advanced a step or two, taking the cigar from his
lips.

" Come to the window and take a seat."

He pointed to the sofa ; but she shook her head, and
said quickly :

" I have something which belongs to you, Mr. Murray, which I think you must value very much, and
therefore I wanted to see it safe in your own hands."

Without raising her eyes she held the book toward
him.

" What is it ?"

He took it mechanically, and with his gaze fixed on

the girl's face ; but as she made no reply, he glanced down at it, and his stern, swarthy face lighted up joyfully.

"Is it possible? my Dante! my lost Dante! The copy that has travelled round the world in my pocket, and that I lost a year ago, somewhere in the mountains of Tennessee! Girl, where did you get it?"

"I found it where you left it—on the grass near a blacksmith's shop."

"A blacksmith's shop! where?"

"Near Chattanooga. Don't you remember the sign, under the horse-shoe, over the door, 'Aaron Hunt'?"

"No; but who was Aaron Hunt?"

For nearly a minute Edna struggled for composure, and looking suddenly up, said falteringly:

"He was my grandfather—the only person in the world I had to care for, or to love me—and—sir——"

"Well, go on."

"You cursed him because your horse fretted, and he could not shoe him in five minutes."

"Humph!"

There was an awkward silence ; St. Elmo Murray bit his lip and scowled, and, recovering her self-control, the orphan added :

"You put your shawl and book on the ground, and when you started you forgot them. I called you back and gave you your shawl ; but I did not see the book for some time after you rode out of sight."

"Yes, yes, I remember now about the shawl and the shop. Strange I did not recognize you before. But how did you learn that the book was mine?"

"I did not know it was yours until I came here by accident, and heard Mrs. Murray call your name ; then I knew that the initials written in the book spelt your name. And besides, I remembered your figure and your voice."

Again there was a pause, and her mission ended, Edna turned to go.

"Stop! Why did you not give it to me when you first came?"

She made no reply, and putting his hand on her shoulder to detain her, he said, more gently than she had ever heard him speak to any one :

" Was it because you loved my book and disliked to part with it, or was it because you feared to come and speak to a man whom you hate ?   Be truthful."

Still she was silent, and raising her face with his palm, as he had done in the park, he continued in the same low, sweet voice, which she could scarcely believe belonged to him :

" I am waiting for your answer, and I intend to have it."

Her large, sad eyes were brimming with precious memories, as she lifted them steadily to meet his, and answered :

" My grandfather was noble and good, and he was all I had in this world."

" And you can not forgive a man who happened to be rude to him ?"

" If you please, Mr. Murray, I would rather go now. I have given you your book, and that is all I came for."

" Which means that you are afraid of me, and want to get out of my sight ?"

She did not deny it, but her face flushed painfully.

" Edna Earl, you are at least honest and truthful, and those are rare traits at the present day.   I thank you for preserving and returning my Dante.   Did you read any of it ?"

" Yes, sir, all of it.   Good-night, sir."

" Wait a moment.   When did Aaron Hunt die ?"

" Two months after you saw him."

" You have no relatives ? No cousins, uncles, aunts ?"

" None that I ever heard of.   I must go, sir."

" Good-night, child.   For the present, when you go out in the grounds, be sure that wolf, Ali, is chained up, or you may be sorry that I did not cut his throat. as I am still inclined to do."

She closed the door, ran lightly across the rotunda, and regaining her own room, felt inexpressibly re-

lieved that the ordeal was over—that in future there
remained no necessity for her to address one whose
very tones made her shudder, and the touch of whose
hand filled her with vague dread and loathing.

When the echo of her retreating footsteps died
away, St. Elmo threw his cigar out of the window, and
walked up and down the quaint and elegant rooms,
whose costly *bizarrerie* would more appropriately have
adorned a villa of Parthenope or Lucanian Sybaris,
than a country-house in *soi-disant* "republican" America. The floor, covered in winter with velvet carpet,
was of white and black marble, now bare and polished
as a mirror, reflecting the figure of the owner as he
crossed it. Oval ormolu tables, buhl chairs, and oaken
and marquetrie cabinets, loaded with cameos, intaglios,
Abraxoids, whose "*erudition*" would have filled Mne-
sarchus with envy, and challenged the admiration of
the Samian lapidary who engraved the ring of Poly-
crates ; these and numberless articles of *virtu* testified
to the universality of what St. Elmo called his "world-
scrapings," and to the reckless extravagance and
archaistic taste of the collector. On a *verd-antique*
table lay a satin cushion holding a vellum MS., bound
in blue velvet, whose uncial letters were written in
purple ink, powdered with gold-dust, while the margins
were stiff with gilded illuminations ; and near the
cushion, as if prepared to shed light on the curious
cryptography, stood an exquisite white glass lamp,
shaped like a vase, and richly ornamented with
Arabic inscriptions in ultra-marine blue—a precious
relic of some ruined Laura in the Nitrian desert,
by the aid of whose rays the hoary hermits,
whom St. Macarius ruled, broke the midnight gloom
chanting, "*Kyrie eleison, Christe eleison,*" fourteen
hundred years before St. Elmo's birth. Immediately
opposite, on an embossed ivory stand, and protected
from air and dust by a glass case, were two antique
goblets, one of green-veined agate, one of blood-red
onyx ; and into the coating of wax, spread along the
ivory slab, were inserted amphoræ, one dry and empty,

the other a third full of Falernian, whose topaz drops
had grown strangely mellow and golden in the ashy
cellars of Herculaneum, and had doubtless been
destined for some luxurious triclinium in the days of
Titus. A small Byzantine picture, painted on wood,
with a silver frame ornamented with cornelian stars,
and the background heavily gilded, hung over an
etagère, where lay a leaf from Nebuchadnezzar's diary,
one of those Babylonish bricks on which his royal name
was stamped. Near it stood a pair of Bohemian vases
representing the two varieties of lotus—one velvety
white with rose-colored veins, the other with delicate
blue petals. This latter whim had cost a vast amount
of time, trouble, and money, it having been found
difficult to carefully preserve, sketch, and paint them
for the manufacturer in Bohemia, who had never seen
the holy lotus, and required specimens. But the in-
domitable will of the man, to whose wishes neither
oceans nor deserts opposed successful barriers, finally
triumphed, and the coveted treasures fully repaid their
price as they glistened in the gaslight, perfect as their
prototypes slumbering on the bosom of the Nile, under
the blazing midnight stars of rainless Egypt. Several
handsome rosewood cases were filled with rare books
—two in Pali—centuries old ; and moth-eaten volumes
and valuable MSS.—some in parchment, some bound in
boards—recalled the days of astrology and alchemy,
and the sombre mysteries of Rosicrucianism. Side by
side, on an ebony stand, lay an Elzevir Terence, printed
in red letters, and a curious Birman book, whose pages
consisted of thin leaves of ivory, gilded at the edges ;
and here too were black rhyta from Chiusi, and a cylix
from Vulci, and one of those quaint Peruvian jars,
which was so constructed that, when filled with water
the air escaped in sounds that resembled that of the
song or cry of the animal represented on the vase or
jar. In the space between the tall windows that fronted
the lawn hung a weird, life-size picture that took
strange hold on the imagination of all who looked at
it. A gray-haired Cimbrian Prophetess, in white vest-

ments and brazen girdle, with canvas mantle fastened
on the shoulder by a broad brazen clasp, stood, with
bare feet, on a low, rude scaffolding, leaning upon her
sword, and eagerly watching, with divining eyes, the
stream of blood which trickled from the throat of the
slaughtered human victim down into the large brazen
kettle beneath the scaffold. The snowy locks and
white mantle seemed to flutter in the wind ; and those
who gazed on the stony, inexorable face of the
Prophetess, and into the glittering blue eyes, shuddered and almost fancied they heard the pattering of
the gory stream against the sides of the brass caldron.
But expensive and rare as were these relics of bygone
dynasties and mouldering epochs, there was one other
object for which the master would have given everything else in this museum of curiosities, and the secret
of which no eyes but his own had yet explored. On a
sculptured slab, that once formed a portion of the
architrave of the Cave Temple at Elephanta, was a
splendid marble miniature, four feet high, of that
miracle of Saracenic architecture, the Taj Mahal at
Agra. The elaborate carving resembled lace-work,
and the beauty of the airy dome and slender, glittering
minarets of this mimic tomb of Noor-Mahal could find
no parallel, save in the superb and matchless original.
The richly-carved door that closed the arch of the
tomb swung back on golden hinges, and opened only
by c curiously-shaped golden key, which never left Mr.
Murray's watch-chain ; consequently what filled the
penetralia was left for the conjectures of the imagina-
tive ; and when his mother expressed a desire to examine it, he merely frowned and said hastily :

"That is Pandora's box, *minus* imprisoned hope. I
prefer it should not be opened."

Immediately in front of the tomb he had posted a
grim sentinel—a black marble statuette of Mors,
modeled from that hideous little brass figure which
Spence saw at Florence, representing a skeleton sitting
on the ground, resting one arm on an urn.

Filled though it was with sparkling *bijouterie* that

would have graced the Barberini or Strozzi cabinets,
the glitter of the room was cold and cheerless. No
light, childish feet had ever pattered down the long
rows of shining tiles; no gushing, mirthful laughter
had ever echoed through those lofty windows; everything pointed to the past—a classic, storied past, but
dead as the mummies of Karnac, and treacherously, repulsively lustrous as the waves that break in silver
circles over the buried battlements, and rustling palms
and defiled altars of the proud cities of the plain. No
rosy memories of early, happy manhood lingered here;
no dewy gleam of the merry morning of life, when
hope painted and peopled a smiling world; no magic
trifles that prattled of the springtime of a heart, that in
wandering to and fro through the earth, had fed itself
with dust and ashes, acrid and bitter; had studiously
collected only the melancholy symbols of mouldering
ruin, desolation, and death, and which found its best
type in the Taj Mahal, that glistened so mockingly as
the gas-light flickered over it.

A stranger looking upon St. Elmo Murray for the
first time, as he paced the floor, would have found it
difficult to realize that only thirty-four years had
plowed those deep, rugged lines in his swarthy and
colorless but still handsome face; where midnight
orgies and habitual excesses had left their unmistakable plague-spot, and Mephistopheles had stamped his
signet. *Blazé*, cynical, scoffing, and hopeless, he had
stranded his life, and was recklessly striding to his
grave, trampling upon the feelings of all with whom he
associated, and at war with a world, in which his lordly
brilliant intellect would have lifted him to any eminence he desired, and which, properly directed, would
have made him the benefactor and ornament of the
society he snubbed and derided. Like all strong though
misguided natures, the power and activity of his mind
enhanced his wretchedness, and drove him farther and
farther from the path of rectitude; while the consciousness that he was originally capable of loftier,
purer aims, and nobler pursuits than those that now

engrossed his perverted thoughts, rendered him savagely morose. For nearly fifteen dreary years, nothing but jeers and oaths and sarcasms had crossed his finely sculptured lips, which had forgotten how to smile; and it was only when the mocking demon of the wine-cup looked out from his gloomy gray eyes that his ringing, sneering laugh struck like a dagger to the heart that loved him, that of his proud but anxious and miserable mother. To-night, for the first time since his desperate plunge into the abyss of vice, conscience, which he had believed effectually strangled, stirred feebly, startling him with a faint moan, as unexpected as the echo from Morella's tomb, or the resurrection of Ligeia; and down the murdered years came wailing ghostly memories, which even his iron will could no longer scourge to silence. Clamorous as the avenging Erinnys, they refused to be exorcised, and goaded him almost to frenzy.

Those sweet, low, timid tones, " I am sorry for you," had astonished and mortified him. To be hated and dreaded was not at all unusual or surprising, but to be pitied and despised was a sensation as novel as humiliating; and the fact that all his ferocity failed to intimidate the " little vagrant " was unpleasantly puzzling.

For some time after Edna's departure he pondered all that had passed between them, and at length he muttered :

" How thoroughly she abhors me ! If I touch her, the flesh absolutely writhes away from my hand, as if I were plague-stricken or a leper. Her very eyelids shudder when she looks at me—and I believe she would more willingly confront Apollyon himself. Strange ! how she detests me. I have half a mind to make her love me, even despite herself. What a steady, brave look of scorn there was in her splendid eyes when she told me to my face I was sinful and cruel !"

He set his teeth hard, and his fingers clinched as if longing to crush something; and then came a great revulsion, a fierce spasm of remorse, and his features writhed.

"Sinful? Ay! Cruel? O my lost youth! my cursed and wrecked manhood! If there be a hell blacker than my miserable soul, man has not dreamed of nor language painted it. What would I not give for a fresh, pure, and untrampled heart, such as slumbers peacefully in yonder room, with no damning recollections to scare sleep from her pillow? Innocent childhood!"

He threw himself into a chair, and hid his face in his hands; and thus an hour went by, during which he neither moved nor sighed.

Tearing the veil from the past, he reviewed it calmly, relentlessly, vindictively, and at last, rising, he threw his head back, with his wonted defiant air, and his face hardened and darkened as he approached the marble mausoleum, and laid his hand upon the golden key.

"Too late! too late! I can not afford to reflect. The devil himself would shirk the reading of such a record."

He fitted the key in the lock, but paused and laughed scornfully as he slung it back on his chain.

"Pshaw! I am a fool! After all, I shall not need to see them, the silly, childish mood has passed."

He filled a silver goblet with some strong spicy wine, drank it, and taking down Candide, brightened the gas jets, lighted a fresh cigar, and began to read as he resumed his walk:

> "Lord of himself; that heritage of woe—
> That fearful empire which the human breast
> But holds to rob the heart within of rest."

CHAPTER VII.

MRS. MURRAY had informed Edna that the gentleman whom she had engaged to instruct her resided in
the neighboring town of ——, and one Monday morning in August she carried her to see him, telling her,
as they drove along, that he was the minister of the
largest church in the county, was an old friend of her
family, and that she considered herself exceedingly
fortunate in having prevailed upon him to consent to
undertake her education. The parsonage stood on
the skirts of the village, in a square immediately opposite the church, and was separated from it by a wide
handsome street, lined on either side with elm trees.
The old-fashioned house was of brick, with a wooden
portico jutting out over the front door, and around
the slender pillars twined honeysuckle and clematis tendrils, purple with clustering bells ; while the brick walls
were draped with luxuriant ivy, that hung in festoons
from the eaves, and clambered up the chimneys and
in at the windows. The daily-swept walk leading to
the gate was bordered with white and purple lilies—
"flags," as the villagers dubbed them—and over the
little gate sprang an arch of lattice-work loaded with
Belgian and English honeysuckle, whose fragrant
wreaths drooped till they touched the heads of all who
entered. When Mrs. Murray and Edna ascended the
steps and knocked at the open door, bearing the name
"Allan Hammond," no living thing was visible, save a
thrush that looked out shyly from the clematis vines ;
and after waiting a moment, Mrs. Murray entered
unannounced. They looked into the parlor, with its

cool matting and white curtains and polished old-fashioned mahogany furniture, but the room was unoccu-
pied; then passing on to the library or study, where
tiers of books rose to the ceiling, they saw, through
the open window, the form of the pastor, who was
stooping to gather the violets blooming in the little
shaded garden at the rear of the house. A large
white cat sunned herself on the strawberry bed, and a
mocking-bird sang in the myrtle-tree that overshadowed
the study-window. Mrs. Murray called to the minister, and taking off his straw hat he bowed, and came
to meet them.

"Mr. Hammond, I hope I do not interrupt you?"

"No, Ellen, you never interrupt me. I was merely
gathering some violets to strew in a child's coffin.
Susan Archer, poor thing! lost her little Winnie last
night, and I knew she would like some flowers to
sprinkle over her baby."

He shook hands with Mrs. Murray, and turning to
her companion offered his hand saying kindly:

"This is my pupil, Edna, I presume? I expected
you several days ago, and am very glad to see you at
last. Come into the house and let us become acquainted at once."

As he led the way to the library, talking the while
to Mrs. Murray, Edna's eyes followed him with an
expression of intense veneration, for he appeared to
her a living original of the pictured prophets—the
Samuel, Isaiah, and Ezekiel, whose faces she had
studied in the large illustrated Bible that lay on a satin
cushion in the sitting-room at Le Bocage. Sixty-five
years of wrestling and conquests on the "Quarantina"
of life had set upon his noble and benignant countenance the seal of holiness, and shed over his placid
features the mild, sweet light of a pure, serene heart,
of a lofty, trusting, sanctified soul. His white hair and
beard had the silvery sheen which seems peculiar to
prematurely gray heads, and the snowy mass wonderfully softened the outline of the face; while the pleasant
smile on his lips, the warm, cheering light in his bright

blue eyes, won the perfect trust, the profound respect, the lasting love and veneration of those who entered the charmed circle of his influence. Learned without pedantry, dignified but not pompous, genial and urbane; never forgetting the sanctity of his mission, though never thrusting its credentials into notice; judging the actions of all with a leniency which he denied to his own; zealous without bigotry, charitable yet rigidly just, as free from austerity as levity, his heart throbbed with warm, tender sympathy for his race; and while none felt his or her happiness complete until his cordial congratulations sealed it, every sad mourner realized that her burden of woe was lightened when poured into his sympathizing ears. The sage counselor of the aged among his flock, he was the loved companion of younger members, in whose juvenile sports and sorrows he was never too busy to interest himself; and it was not surprising that over all classes and denominations he wielded an influence incalculable for good.

The limits of one church could not contain his great heart, which went forth in yearning love and fellowship to his Christian brethren and co-laborers throughout the world, while the refrain of his daily work was, "Bear ye one another's burdens." So in the evening of a life blessed with the bounteous fruitage of good deeds, he walked to and fro, in the wide vineyard of God, with the light of peace, of faith, and hope, and hallowed resignation shining over his worn and aged face.

Drawing Edna to a seat beside him on the sofa, Mr. Hammond said:

"Mrs. Murray has intrusted your education entirely to me; but before I decide positively what books you will require I should like to know what particular branches of study you love best. Do you feel disposed to take up Latin?"

"Yes, sir—and——"

"Well, go on, my dear. Do not hesitate to speak freely."

" If you please, sir, I should like to study Greek also."

" Oh, nonsense, Edna! women never have any use for Greek; it would only be a waste of your time," interrupted Mrs. Murray.

Mr. Hammond smiled and shook his head

" Why do you wish to study Greek? You will scarcely be called upon to teach it."

" I should not think that I was well or thoroughly educated if I did not understand Greek and Latin; and beside, I want to read what Solon and Pericles and Demosthenes wrote in their own language."

" Why, what do you know about those men?"

" Only what Plutarch says."

" What kind of books do you read with most pleasure?"

" History and travels."

" Are you fond of arithmetic?"

" No, sir."

" But as a teacher you will have much more use for mathematics than for Greek."

" I should think that, with all my life before me, I might study both; and even if I should have no use for it, it would do me no harm to understand it Knowledge is never in the way, is it?"

" Certainly not half so often as ignorance. Very well; you shall learn Greek as fast as you please. I should like to hear you read something. Here is Goldsmith's Deserted Village; suppose you try a few lines; begin here at 'Sweet was the sound.' "

She read aloud the passage designated, and as he expressed himself satisfied, and took the book from her hand, Mrs. Murray said:

" I think the child is as inveterate a bookworm as I ever knew; but for heaven's sake, Mr. Hammond, do not make her a blue-stocking."

" Ellen, did you ever see a genuine blue-stocking?"

" I am happy to be able to say that I never was so unfortunate!"

" You consider yourself lucky then, in not having

known De Staël, Hannah More, Charlotte Brontë, and Mrs. Browning?"

"To be consistent, of course, I must answer yes: but you know we women are never supposed to understand that term, much less possess the jewel itself; and beside, sir, you take undue advantage of me, for the women you mention were truly great geniuses. I was not objecting to genius in women."

"Without those auxiliaries and adjuncts which you deprecate so earnestly, would their native genius ever have distinguished them, or charmed and benefited the world? Brilliant success makes blue-stockings autocratic, and the world flatters and crowns them; but unsuccessful aspirants are strangled with an offensive *sobriquet*, than which it were better that they had millstones tied about their necks. After all, Ellen, it is rather ludicrous, and seems very unfair, that the whole class of literary ladies should be sneered at on account of the color of Stillingfleet's stockings, eighty years ago."

"If you please, sir, I should like to know the meaning of 'blue-stocking?'" said Edna.

"You are in a fair way to understand it if you study Greek," answered Mrs. Murray, laughing at the puzzled expression of the child's countenance.

Mr. Hammond smiled, and replied:

"A 'blue-stocking,' my dear, is generally supposed to be a lady, neither young, pleasant, nor pretty (and in most instances unmarried); who is unamiable, ungraceful, and untidy; ignorant of all domestic accomplishments and truly feminine acquirements, and ambitious of appearing very learned; a woman whose fingers are more frequently adorned with ink-spots than thimble; who holds housekeeping in detestation, and talks loudly about politics, science, and philosophy; who is ugly, and learned, and cross; whose hair is never smooth and whose ruffles are never fluted. Is that a correct likeness, Ellen?"

"As good as one of Brady's photographs. Take warning, Edna."

"The title of 'blue-stocking,'" continued the pastor, "originated in a jest, many, many years ago, when a circle of very brilliant, witty, and elegant ladies in London, met at the house of Mrs. Vesey, to listen to and take part in the conversation of some of the most gifted and learned men England has ever produced. One of those gentlemen, Stillingfleet, who always wore blue stockings, was so exceedingly agreeable and instructive, that when he chanced to be absent the company declared the party was a failure without 'the blue stockings,' as he was familiarly called. A Frenchman, who heard of the circumstance, gave to these conversational gatherings the name of '*bas bleu*,' which means blue stocking ; and hence, you see, that in popular acceptation, I mean in public opinion, the humorous title, which was given in compliment to a very charming gentleman, is now supposed to belong to very tiresome, pedantic, and disagreeable ladies. Do you understand the matter now ?"

"I do not quite understand why ladies have not as good a right to be learned and wise as gentlemen."

"To satisfy you on that point would involve more historical discussion than we have time for this morning ; some day we will look into the past and find a solution of the question. Meanwhile you may study as hard as you please, and remember, my dear, that where one woman is considered a blue-stocking, and tiresomely learned, twenty are more tiresome still because they know nothing. I will obtain all the books you need, and hereafter you must come to me every morning at nine o'clock. When the weather is good, you can easily walk over from Mrs. Murray's."

As they drove homeward, Edna asked :

"Has Mr. Hammond a family?"

"No ; he lost his family years ago. But why do you ask that question?"

"I saw no lady, and I wondered who kept the house in such nice order."

"He has a very faithful servant who attends to his household affairs. In your intercourse with Mr. Hammond be careful not to allude to his domestic afflictions."

Mrs. Murray looked earnestly, searchingly at the girl, as if striving to fathom her thoughts ; then throwing her head back, with the haughty air which Edna had remarked in St. Elmo, she compressed her lips, lowered her veil, and remained silent and abstracted until they reached home.

The comprehensive and very thorough curriculum of studies now eagerly commenced by Edna, and along which she was gently and skilfully guided by the kind hand of the teacher, furnished the mental aliment for which she hungered, gave constant and judicious exercise to her active intellect, and induced her to visit the quiet parsonage library as assiduously as did Horace, Valgius, and Virgil the gardens on the Esquiline where Mæcenas held his literary assize. Instead of skimming a few text-books that cram the brain with unwieldy scientific technicalities and pompous philosophic terminology, her range of thought and study gradually stretched out into a broader, grander cycle, embracing, as she grew older, the application of those great principles that underlie modern science and crop out in ever-varying phenomena and empirical classifications. Edna's tutor seemed impressed with the fallacy of the popular system of acquiring one branch of learning at a time, locking it away as in drawers of rubbish, never to be opened, where it moulders in shapeless confusion till swept out ultimately to make room for more recent scientific invoices. Thus in lieu of the educational plan of "finishing natural philosophy and chemistry this session, and geology and astronomy next term, and taking up moral science and criticism the year we graduate," Mr. Hammond allowed his pupil to finish and lay aside none of her studies ; but sought to impress upon her the great value of Blackstone's aphorism : " For sciences are of a sociable disposition, and flourish best in the neighborhood of each other ; nor is there anv branch of learning but may be helped and improved by assistance drawn from other arts."

Finding that her imagination was remarkably fertile, he required her, as she advanced in years, to compose essays, letters, dialogues, and sometimes orations, all of which were not only written and handed in for correction, but he frequently directed her to recite them from memory, and invited her to assist him, while he dissected and criticised either her diction, line of argument, choice of metaphors, or intonation of voice. In these compositions he encouraged her to seek illustrations from every department of letters, and convert her theme into a focus, upon which to pour all the concentrated light which research could reflect, assuring her that what is often denominated "far-fetchedness," in metaphors, furnished not only evidence of the laborious industry of the writer, but is an implied compliment to the cultured taste and general knowledge of those for whose entertainment or edification they are employed—provided always said metaphors and similies really illustrate, elucidate, and adorn the theme discussed—when properly understood.

His favorite plea in such instances was, "If Humboldt and Cuvier, and Linnæus, and Ehrenberg have made mankind their debtors by scouring the physical cosmos for scientific *data*, which every living *savant* devours, assimilates, and reproduces in dynamic, physiologic, or entomologic theories, is it not equally laudable in scholars, orators, and authors—nay, is it not obligatory on them, to subsidize the vast cosmos of literature, to circumnavigate the world of *belles-lettres*, in search of new hemispheres of thought, and spice islands of illustrations ; bringing their rich gleanings to the great public mart, where men barter their intellectual merchandise ? Wide as the universe, and free as its winds should be the range of human mind."

Yielding allegiance to the axiom that "the proper study of mankind is man," and recognizing the fact that history faithfully epitomizes the magnificent triumphs and stupendous failures, the grand capacities and innate frailties of the races, he fostered and stimulated his pupil's fondness for historic investigation; while in impressing upon her memory the chronologic sequence of events he not only grouped into great epochs the principal dramas, over which Clio holds august critical tribunal, but so carefully selected her miscellaneous reading, that poetry, novels, biography, and essays reflected light upon the actors of the particular epoch which she was studying; and thus through the subtle but imperishable links of association of ideas, chained them in her mind.

The extensive library at Le Bocage, and the valuable collection of books at the parsonage, challenged research, and, with a boundless ambition, equalled only by her patient, persevering application, Edna devoted herself to the acquisition of knowledge, and astonished and delighted her teacher by the rapidity of her progress and the vigor and originality of her restless intellect.

The noble catholicity of spirit that distinguished Mr. Hammond's character encouraged her to discuss freely the ethical and psychological problems that arrested her attention as she grew older, and facilitated her appreciation and acceptance of the great fact, that all bigotry springs from narrow minds and partial knowledge. He taught her that truth, scorning monopolies and deriding patents, lends some valuable element to almost every human system; that ignorance, superstition, and intolerance are the red-handed Huns that ravage society, immolating the pioneers of progress upon the shrine ef prejudice—fettering science— blindly bent on divorcing natural and revealed truth, which "God hath joined together" in holy and eternal wedlock; and while they battle à l'outrance with every innovation, lock the wheels of human advancement, turning a deaf ear to the thrilling cry:

"Yet I doubt not through the ages one increasing purpose runs,
And the thoughts of men are widened with the process of the
suns."

If Carlyle be correct in his declaration that " Truly
a thinking man is the worst enemy the prince of darkness can have, and every time such a one announces
himself there runs a shudder through the nether em-
pire, where new emissaries are trained with new tactics,
to hoodwink and handcuff him," who can doubt that
the long dynasty of Eblis will instantly terminate,
when every pulpit in Christendom, from the frozen
shores of Spitzbergen to the green dells of Owhyhee,
from the shining spires of Europe to the rocky battlements that front the Pacific, shall be filled with meek
and holy men of ripe scholarship and resistless eloquence, whose scientific erudition keeps pace with
their evangelical piety, and whose irreproachable lives
attest that their hearts are indeed hallowed temples of
that loving charity " that suffereth long and is kind ;
that vaunteth not itself, is not puffed up ; thinketh no
evil ; beareth all things, hopeth all things, endureth
all things ?"

While Christ walked to and fro among the palms
and poppies of Palestine, glorifying anew an accursed
and degraded human nature, unlettered fishermen,
who mended their nets and trimmed their sails along
the blue waves of Galilee, were fit instruments, in his
guiding hands, for the dissemination of his Gospel ;
but when the days of the Incarnation ended, and
Jesus returned to the Father, all the learning and the
mighty genius of Saul of Tarsus were required to confront and refute the scoffing sophists who, replete with
philhellenic lore, and within sight of the marvellous
triglyphs and metopes of the Parthenon, gathered on
Mars Hill to defend their marble altars to the
Unknown God.'

CHAPTER VIII.

DURING the months of September and October Mrs. Murray filled the house with company, and parties of gentlemen came from time to time to enjoy the game season and take part in the hunts to which St. Elmo devoted himself. There were elegant dinners and *petits soupers* that would not have disgraced Tusculum, or made Lucullus blush when Pompey and Cicero sought to surprise him in the "Apollo"; there were billiard-matches and horse-races, and merry gatherings at the ten-pin alley; and laughter, and music, and dancing usurped the dominions where silence and gloom had so long reigned. Naturally shy and unaccustomed to companionship, Edna felt no desire to participate in these festivities, but became more and more absorbed in her studies, and her knowledge of the company was limited to the brief intercourse of the table, where she observed the deference yielded to the opinions of the master of the house, and the dread that all manifested lest they should fall under the lash of his merciless sarcasm. An Ishmael in society, his uplifted hand smote all conventionalities and shams, spared neither age nor sex, nor sanctuaries, and acknowledged sanctity nowhere. The punctilious courtesy of his manner polished and pointed his satire, and when a personal application of his remarks was possible, he would bow gracefully to the lady indicated, and fill her glass with wine, while he filled her heart with chagrin and rankling hate. Since the restoration of the Dante, not a word had passed between him and Edna, who regarded him with increasing detestation;

but on one occasion, when the conversation was
general, and he sat silent at the foot of the table, she
looked up at him and found his eyes fixed on her face.
Inclining his head slightly to arrest her attention, he
handed a decanter of sherry to one of the servants,
with some brief direction, and a moment after her
glass was filled, and the waiter said :

"Mr. Murray's compliments to Aaron Hunt's granddaughter." Observation had taught her what was
customary on such occasions, and she knew that he
had once noticed her taking wine with the gentleman
who sat next to her; but now repugnance conquered
politeness, the mention of her grandfather's name
seemed an insult from his lips, and putting her hand
over her glass, she looked him full in the face and
shook her head. Nevertheless he lifted his wine,
bowed, and drank the last drop in the crystal goblet :
then turned to a gentleman on his right hand, and
instantly entered into a learned discussion on the
superiority of the wines of the Levant over those of
Germany, quoting triumphantly the lines of M. de
Nevers :

> "Sur la membrane de leur sens,
> Font des sillons charmans."

When the ladies withdrew to the parlor he rose, as
was his custom, and held the door open for them.
Edna was the last of the party, and as she passed him
he smiled mockingly and said :

"It was unfortunate that my mother omitted to
enumerate etiquette in the catalogue of studies prose-
cuted at the parsonage."

Instantly the answer sprang to her lips :

"She knew I had a teacher for that branch nearer
home; but her conscience smote her, she repressed
the words, and said gravely :

"My reason was, that I think only good friends
should take wine together."

"This is your declaration of war? Very well, only

remember I raise a black flag and show no quarter.
Woe to the conquered !"

She hurried away to the library, and thenceforth
"kept out of his way " more assiduously than ever;
while the fact that he scrutinized her closely, rendered
her constrained and uncomfortable, when forced to
enter his presence. Mrs. Murray well understood her
hostile feeling toward her son, but she never alluded
to it, and his name was not mentioned by either.

One by one the guests departed; autumn passed,
winter was ushered in by wailing winds and drizzling
rains ; and one morning as Edna came out of the hothouse, with a basketful of camellias, she saw St. Elmo
bidding his mother good-bye, as he started on his long
journey to Oceanica. They stood on the steps, Mrs.
Murray's head rested on his shoulder, and bitter tears
were falling on her cheeks as she talked eagerly and
rapidly to him. Edna heard him say impatiently:

"You ask what is impossible; it is worse than useless to urge me. Better pray that I may find a peaceful grave in the cinnamon groves and under the 'plumy
palms' of the far south."

He kissed his mother's cheek and sprang into the
saddle, but checked his horse at sight of the orphan,
who stood a few yards distant.

"Are you coming to say good-by? Or do you reserve such courtesies for your 'good friends'?"

Regret for her former rudeness, and sympathy for
Mrs. Murray's uncontrollable distress, softened her
heart toward him; she selected the finest white cam-
ellia in the basket, walked close to the horse, and, ten-
dering the flower, said :

"Good-by, sir. I hope you will enjoy your
travels."

"And prolong them indefinitely ? Ah! you offer a
flag of truce ? I warned you I should not respect it.
You know my motto, 'Nemo me impune lacessit!'
Thank you, for this lovely peace-offering. Since you
are willing to negotiate, run and open the gate for me.
I may never pass through it again except as a ghost."

She placed her basket on the steps and ran down the avenue, while he paused to say something to his mother. Edna knew that he expected to be absent, possibly, several years, and while she regretted the pain which his departure gave her benefactress, she could not avoid rejoicing at the relief she promised herself during his sojourn in foreign lands.

Slowly he rode along the venerable aisle of elms that had overarched his childish head in the sunny morning of a quickly clouded life, and as he reached the gate, which Edna held open, he dismounted.

"Edna, if you are as truthful in all matters as you have proved in your dislikes, I may safely intrust this key to your keeping. It belongs to that marble temple in my sitting-room, and opens a vault that contains my will and a box of papers, and—some other things that I value. There is no possibility of entering it, except with this key, and no one but myself knows the contents. I wish to leave the key with you, on two conditions; first, that you never mention it to any one—not even my mother, or allow her to suspect that you have it; secondly, that you promise me solemnly you will not open the tomb or temple unless I fail to return at the close of four years. This is the tenth of December—four years from to-day, if I am not here, *and if you have good reason to consider me dead*, take this key (which I wish you to wear about your person) to my mother, inform her of this conversation, and then open the vault. Can you resist the temptation to look into it? Think well before you answer."

He had disengaged the golden key from his watch-chain and held it in his hand.

"I should not like to take charge of it, Mr. Murray. You can certainly trust your own mother sooner than an utter stranger like myself."

He frowned and muttered an oath; then exclaimed:

"I tell you I do not choose to leave it in any hands but yours. Will you promise or will you not?"

The dreary wretchedness, the savage hopelessness

of his countenance awed and pained the girl, and after a moment's silence, and a short struggle with her heart, she extended her hand, saying with evident reluctance :

"Give me the key, I will not betray your trust."

"Do you promise me solemnly that you will never open that vault, except in accordance with my directions? Weigh the promise well before you give it."

"Yes, sir ; I promise most solemnly."

He laid the key in her palm and continued :

"My mother loves you—try to make her happy while I am away; and if you succeed, you will be the first person to whom I have ever been indebted. I have left directions concerning my books and the various articles in my rooms. Feel no hesitation in examining any that may interest you, and see that the dust does not ruin them. Good-by, child ; take care of my mother."

He held out his hand, she gave him hers for an instant only, and he mounted, lifted his cap, and rode away.

Closing the ponderous gate, Edna leaned her face against the iron bars, and watched the lessening form. Gradually trees intervened, then at a bend in the road she saw him wheel his horse as if to return. For some moments he remained stationary, looking back, but suddenly disappeared, and, with a sigh of indescribable relief, she retraced her steps to the house. As she approached the spot where Mrs. Murray still sat, with her face hidden in her handkerchief, the touch of the little key, tightly folded in her palm, brought a painful consciousness of concealment and a tinge of shame to her cheeks; for it seemed in her eyes an insult to her benefactress that the guardianship of the papers should have been withheld from her.

She would have stolen away to her own room to secrete the key; but Mrs. Murray called her, and as she sat down beside her the miserable mother threw her arms around the orphan, and resting her cheek on her head wept bitterly. Timidly, but very gently and

tenderly, the latter strove to comfort her, caressing
the white hands that were clasped in almost despairing anguish.

"Dear Mrs. Murray, do not grieve so deeply; he
may come back much earlier than you expect. He
will get tired of travelling, and come back to his own
beautiful home, and to you, who love him so devotedly."

"No, no! he will stay away as long as possible. It
is not beautiful to him. He hates his home and forgets me! My loneliness, my anxiety are nothing in
comparison to his morbid love of change. I shall
never see him again."

"But he loves you very much, and that will bring
him to you."

"Why do you think so?"

"He pointed to you, a few moments ago, and his
face was full of wretchedness when he told me, 'Make
my mother happy while I am gone, and you will be
the first person to whom I have ever been indebted.'
Do not weep so, dear Mrs. Murray; God can preserve
him as well on sea as here at home."

"Oh! but he will not pray for himself!" sobbed
the mother.

"Then you must pray all the more for him; and
go where he will, he cannot get beyond God's sight, or
out of His merciful hands. You know Christ said,
'Whatsoever you ask in my name, I will do it'; and
if the Syrophenician's daughter was saved not by her
own prayers but by her mother's faith, why should not
God save your son if you pray and believe?"

Mrs. Murray clasped Edna closer to her heart, and
kissed her warmly.

"You are my only comfort! If I had your faith I
should not be so unhappy. My dear child, promise
me one thing, that every time you pray you will remember my son, and ask God to preserve him in his
wanderings, and bring him safely back to his mother!
I know you do not like him, but for my sake will you
not do this?"

" My prayers are not worth much, but I will always remember to pray for him ; and, Mrs. Murray, while he is away, suppose you have family prayer, and let all the household join in praying for the absent master. I think it would be such a blessing and comfort to you. Grandpa always had prayer night and morning, and it made every day seem almost as holy as Sunday."

Mrs. Murray was silent a little while, and answered hesitatingly :

"But, my dear, I should not know how to offer up prayers before the family. I can pray for myself, but I should not like to pray aloud."

There was a second pause, and finally she said :

" Edna, would you be willing to conduct prayers for me ?"

"It is your house, and God expects the head of every family to set an example. Even the pagans offered sacrifices every day for the good of the household, and you know the Jews had morning and evening sacrifices ; so it seems to me family prayer is such a beautiful offering on the altar of the hearthstone. If you do not wish to pray yourself, you could read a prayer ; there is a book called Family Prayer, with selections for every day in the week. I saw a copy at the parsonage, and I can get one like it at the book store if you desire it."

"That will suit my purpose much better than trying to compose them myself. You must get the book for me. But, Edna, don't go to school to-day, stay at home with me ; I am so lonely and low-spirited. I will tell Mr. Hammond that I could not spare you. Beside, I want you to help me arrange some valuable relics belonging to my son, and now that I think of it, he told me he wished you to use any of his books or MSS. that you might like to examine. This is a great honor, child, for he has refused many grown people admission to his rooms. Come with me, I want to lock up his curiosities."

They went through the rotunda and into the rooms together ; and Mrs. Murray busied herself in carefully removing the cameos, intaglios, antique vases, goblets, etc., etc., from the tables, and placing them in the drawers of the cabinets. As she crossed the room tears fell on the costly trifles, and finally she approached the beautiful miniature temple and stooped to look at the fastening. She selected the smallest key on the bunch, that contained a dozen, and attempted to fit it in the small opening, but it was too large; then she tried her watch-key, but without success, and a look of chagrin crossed her sad, tear-stained face.

"St. Elmo has forgotten to leave the key with me."

Edna's face grew scarlet, and stooping to pick up a heavy cornelian seal that had fallen on the carpet, she said, hastily:

"What is that marble temple intended to hold?"

"I have no idea; it is one of my son's oriental fancies. I presume he uses it as a private desk for his papers."

"Does he leave the key with you when he goes from home?"

"This is the first time he has left home for more than a few weeks since he brought this gem from the East. I must write to him about the key before he sails. He has it on his watch-chain."

The same curiosity which, in ages long past, prompted the discovery of the Eleusinian or Cabiri mysteries now suddenly took possession of Edna, as she looked wonderingly at the shining façade of the exquisite Taj Mahal, and felt that only a promise stood between her and its contents.

Escaping to her own room, she proceeded to secrete the troublesome key, and to reflect upon the unexpected circumstances which not only rendered it her duty to pray for the wanderer but necessitated her keeping always about her a *souvenir* of the man whom she could not avoid detesting, and was yet forced to remember continually.

On the following day, when she went to her usual morning recitation, and gave the reason for her absence, she noticed that Mr. Hammond's hand trembled, and a look of keen sorrow settled on his face.

"Gone again! and so soon! So far, far away from all good influences!"

He put down the Latin grammar and walked to the window, where he stood for some time, and when he returned to his armchair Edna saw that the muscles of his face were unsteady.

"Did he not stop to tell you good-by?"

"No, my dear, he never comes to the parsonage now. When he was a boy, I taught him here in this room, as I now teach you. But for fifteen years he has not crossed my threshold, and yet I never sleep until I have prayed for him."

"Oh! I am so glad to hear that! Now I know he will be saved."

The minister shook his gray head, and Edna saw tears in his mild blue eyes as he answered:

"A man's repentance and faith can not be offered by proxy to God. So long as St. Elmo Murray persists in insulting his Maker, I shudder for his final end. He has the finest intellect I have ever met among living men; but it is unsanctified—worse still, it is dedicated to the work of scoffing at and blaspheming the truths of religion. In his youth he promised to prove a blessing to his race and an ornament to Christianity; now he is a curse to the world and a dreary burden to himself."

"What changed him so sadly?"

"Some melancholy circumstances that occurred early in his life. Edna, he planned and built that beautiful church where you come on Sabbath to hear me preach, and about the time it was finished he went off to college. When he returned he avoided me, and has never yet been inside of the costly church which his taste and his money constructed. Still, while I live, I shall not cease to pray for him, hoping that in God's good time he will bring him back to the pure faith of his boyhood."

"Mr. Hammond, is he not a very wicked man?"

" He had originally the noblest heart I ever knew, and was as tender in his sympathies as a woman, while he was almost reckless in his munificent charities. But in his present irreligious state I hear that he has grown bitter and sour and illiberal. Yet, however repulsive his manner may be, I can not believe that his nature is utterly perverted. He is dissipated but not unprincipled. Let him rest, my child, in the hands of his God, who alone can judge him. We can but pray and hope. Go on with your lesson."

The recitation was resumed and ended; but Edna was well aware that for the first time her teacher was inattentive, and the heavy sighs that passed his lips almost unconsciously told her how sorely he was distressed by the erratic course of his quondam pupil.

When she rose to go home she asked the name of the author of the Family Prayers which she wished to purchase for Mrs. Murray, and the pastor's face flushed with pleasure as he heard of her cherished scheme.

" My dear child, be circumspect, be prudent; above all things, be consistent. Search your own heart; try to make your life an exposition of your faith; let profession and practice go hand in hand; ask God's special guidance in the difficult position in which you are placed, and your influence for good in Mrs. Murray's family may be beyond all computation." Laying his hands on her head, he continued tremulously : " O my God! if it be thy will, make her the instrument of rescuing, ere it be indeed too late. Help me to teach her aright; and let her pure life atone for all the inconsistencies and wrongs that have well-nigh wrought eternal ruin."

Turning quickly away, he left the room, before she could even catch a glimpse of his countenance.

The strong and lasting affection that sprang up between instructor and pupil—the sense of dependence on each other's society—rarely occurs among persons in whose ages so great a disparity exists. Spring and autumn have no affinities—age has generally no sympathy for the gushing sprightliness, the eager question-

ing, the rose-hued dreams and aspirations of young
people ; and youth shrinks chilled and constrained
from the austere companionship of those who, with
snowy locks gilded by the fading rays of a setting sun,
totter down the hill of life, journeying to the dark and
silent valley of the shadow of death.

Preferring Mr. Hammond's society to that of the
comparative strangers who visited Mrs. Murray, Edna
spent half of her time at the quiet parsonage, and the
remainder with her books and music. That under
auspices so favorable her progress was almost unpre-
cedentedly rapid, furnished matter of surprise to no one
who was capable of estimating the results of native
genius and vigorous application. Mrs. Murray watched
the expansion of her mind, and the development of
her beauty, with emotions of pride and pleasure, which,
had she analyzed them, would have told her how dear
and necessary to her happiness the orphan had become.

As Edna's reasoning powers strengthened, Mr.
Hammond led her gradually to the contemplation of
some of the gravest problems that have from time immemorial perplexed and maddened humanity, plunging one half into blind, bigoted traditionalism, and
scourging the other into the dreary, sombre, starless
wastes of Pyrrhonism. Knowing full well that of
every earnest soul and honest, profound thinker these
ontologic questions would sooner or later demand
audience, he wisely placed her in the philosophic *pal-
æstra*, encouraged her wrestlings, cheered her on,
handed her from time to time the instruments and aids
she needed, and then, when satisfied that the intellectual gymnastics had properly trained and developed
her, he invited her—where he felt assured the spirit of
the age would inevitably drive her—to the great Pythian games of speculation, where the lordly intellects of
the nineteenth century gather to test their ratiocinative
skill, and bear off the crown of bay on the point of a
syllogism or the wings of an audacious hypothesis.

Thus immersed in study, weeks, months, and years

glided by, bearing her young life swiftly across the
Enna meads of girlhood, nearer and nearer to the por-
tals of that mystic temple of womanhood, on whose
fair fretted shrine was to be offered a heart either consumed by the baleful fires of Baal, or purfied and consecrated by the Shekinah, promised through Messiah

CHAPTER IX.

DURING the first year of Mr. Murray's absence his
brief letters to his mother were written at long intervals ; in the second, they were rarer and briefer still :
but toward the close of the third he wrote more frequently, and announced his intention of revisiting
Egypt before his return to the land of his birth. Although no allusion was ever made to Edna, Mrs. Murray sometimes read aloud descriptions of beautiful
scenery, written now among the scoriæ of Mauna Roa
or Mauna Kea, and now from the pinnacle of Mount
Ophir, whence, through waving forests of nutmeg and
clove, flashed the blue waters of the Indian Ocean, or
the silver ripples of Malacca ; and, on such occasions,
the orphan listened eagerly, entranced by the tropical
luxuriance and grandeur of his imagery, by his gorgeous word-painting, which to her charmed ears seemed
scarcely inferior to the wonderful pen-portraits of Ruskin. Those letters seemed flecked with the purple and
gold, the amber and rose, the opaline and beryline
tints, of which he spoke in telling the glories of Poly-
nesian and Malaysian skies, and the matchless verdure
and floral splendors of their serene spicy dells. For
many days after the receipt of each, Mrs. Murray was
graver and sadder, but the spectre that had disquieted
Edna was thoroughly exorcised, and only when the
cold touch of the golden key startled her was she conscious of a vague dread of some far-off but slowly and
surely approaching evil. In the fourth year of her
pupilage she was possessed by an unconquerable desire
to read the Talmud, and in order to penetrate the

mysteries and seize the treasures hidden in that exhaustless mine of Oriental myths, legends, and symbolisms, she prevailed upon Mr. Hammond to teach
her Hebrew and the rudiments of Chaldee. Very
reluctantly and disapprovingly he consented, and sub-
sequently informed her that, as he had another pupil
who was also commencing Hebrew, he would class
them, and hear their recitations together. This new
student was Mr. Gordon Leigh, a lawyer in the town,
and a gentleman of wealth and high social position.
Although quite young, he gave promise of eminence
in his profession, and was a great favorite of the minister, who pronounced him the most upright and exemplary young man of his acquaintance. Edna had
seen him several times at Mrs. Murray's dinners, but
while she thought him exceedingly handsome, polite,
and agreeable, she regarded him as a stranger, until
the lessons at the Parsonage brought them every two
days around the little table in the study. They began
the language simultaneously ; but Edna, knowing the
flattering estimation in which he was held, could not
resist the temptation to measure her intellect with his,
and soon threatened to outrun him in the Talmud
race. Piqued pride and a manly resolution to conquer
spurred him on, and the venerable instructor looked on
and laughed at the generous emulation thus excited.
He saw an earnest friendship daily strengthening
between the rivals, and knew that in Gordon Leigh's
magnanimous nature there was no element which could
cause an objection to the companionship to which he
had paved the way.

Four months after the commencement of the new
study, Edna rose at daylight to complete some exercises, which she had neglected to write out on the
previous evening, and as soon as she concluded the
task, went down stairs to gather the flowers. It was
the cloudless morning of her seventeenth birthday and
as she stood clipping geraniums and jasmine and
verbena, memory flew back to the tender years in which
the grisly blacksmith had watched her career with such

fond pride and loving words of encouragement, and
painted the white-haired old man smoking on the
porch that fronted Lookout, while from his lips, tremulous with a tender smile, seemed to float the last
words he had spoken to her on that calm afternoon
when, in the fiery light of a dying day, he was gathered
to his forefathers :

"You will make me proud of you, my little Pearl,
when you are smart enough to teach a school and take
care of me, for I shall be too old to work by that
time."

Now, after the lapse of years, when her educational
course was almost finished, she recalled every word
and look and gesture ; even the thrill of horror that
shook her limbs when she kissed the lips that death
had sealed an hour before. Mournfully vivid was her
recollection of her tenth birthday, for then he had
bought her a blue ribbon for her hair, and a little
china cup and saucer ; and now tears sprang to her
eyes as she murmured : " I have studied hard and the
triumph is at hand, but I have nobody to be proud of
me now ! Ah Grandpa ! if you could only come back
to me, your little Pearl ! It is so desolate to be alone
in this great world ; so hard to have to know that
nobody cares specially whether I live or die whether I
succeed or fail ignominiously. I have only myself
to live for ; only my own heart and will to sustain and
stimulate me."

Through the fringy acacias that waved their long
hair across the hothouse windows, the golden sunshine
flickered over the graceful, rounded, lithe figure of the
orphan—over the fair young face with its delicate
cameo features, warm, healthful coloring, and brave,
hopeful expression. Four years had developed the
pretty, sad-eyed child into a lovely woman, with a
pure heart filled with humble unostentatious piety, and
a clear, vigorous intellect inured to study, and ambitious of every honorable eminence within the grasp of
true womanhood.

Edna had endeavored to realize and remember what

her Bible first taught her, and what moralists of all
creeds, climes and ages, had reiterated—that human
life was at best but "vanity and vexation of spirit,"
that "man is born to trouble as the sparks fly upward"; yet as she stood on the line, narrow and thin
as Al-Sirat, that divides girlhood and womanhood, all
seemed to her fresh, pure heart as inviting and bewitching as the magnificent panorama upon which en-
raptured lotophagi gazed from the ancient acropolis
of Cyrene.

As Edna turned to leave the hothouse, the ring of
horse's hoofs on the rocky walk attracted her attention, and a moment after, Mr. Leigh gave his horse to
the gardener and came to meet her.

"Good morning, Miss Edna. As I am bearer of
dispatches from my sister to Mrs. Murray, I have invited myself to breakfast with you."

"You are an earlier riser than I had supposed, Mr.
Leigh, from your lamentations over your exercises."

"I do not deny that I love my morning nap, and
generally indulge myself; for, like Sydney Smith, 'I
can easily make up my mind to rise early; but I can
not make up my body.' In one respect I certainly
claim equality with Thorwaldsen, my 'talent for
sleeping' is inferior neither to his nor Goethe's. Do
you know that we are both to have a holiday to-day?"

"No, sir; upon what score?"

"It happens to be my birthday as well as yours, and
as my sister, Mrs. Inge, gives a party to-night in honor
of the event, I have come to insist that my classmate
shall enjoy the same reprieve that I promise myself.
Mrs. Inge commissioned me to insure your presence
at her party."

"Thank you; but I never go out to parties."

"But bad precedents must not guide you any longer
If you persist in staying at home, I shall not enjoy the
evening, for in every dance I shall fancy my *vis-a-vis*
your spectre, with an exercise in one hand and a Hebrew grammar in the other. *A propos !* Mr. Hammond
told me to say that he would not expect you to-day

but would meet you to-night at Mrs. Inge's. You need not trouble yourself to decline, for I shall arrange matters with Mrs. Murray. In honor of my birthday will you not give me a sprig of something sweet from your basket?"

They sat down on the steps of the dining-room, and Edna selected some delicate oxalis cups and nutmeg geranium leaves, which she tied up, and handed to her companion.

Fastening them in the button-hole of his coat, he drew a small box from his pocket, and said:

"I noticed last week, when Mr. Hammond was explaining the Basilidian tenets, you manifested some curiosity concerning their amulets and mythical stones. Many years ago, while an uncle of mine was missionary in Arabia, he saved the life of a son of a wealthy sheik, and received from him, in token of his gratitude, a curious ring, which tradition said once belonged to a caliph, and had been found near the ruins of Chilminar. The ring was bequeathed to me, and is probably the best authenticated antique in this country. Presto! we are in Bagdad! in the blessed reign—

'. . . in the golden prime
Of good Haroun Alraschid!'

I am versed in neither Cufic nor Neskhi lore, but the characters engraved on this ring are said to belong to the former dialect, and to mean 'Peace be with thee,' which is, and I believe has been, from time immemorial, the national salutation of the Arabs."

He unwound the cotton that enveloped the gem, and held it before Edna's eyes.

A broad band of dusky, tarnished gold was surmounted by a large crescent-shaped emerald, set with beautiful pearls, and underneath the Arabic inscription was engraved a ram's head, bearing on one horn a small crescent, on the other a star.

As Edna bent forward to examine it Mr. Leigh continued:

"I do not quite comprehend the symbolism of the ram's head and the star ; the crescent is clear enough."

"I think I can guess the meaning." Edna's eyes kindled.

"Tell me your conjecture ; my own does not satisfy me, as the Arabic love of mutton is the only solution at which I have arrived."

"Oh, Mr. Leigh ! look at it and think a moment."

"Well, I have looked at it and thought a great deal, and I tell you mutton-broth sherbet is the only idea suggested to my mind. You need not look so shocked, for, when cooled with the snows of Caucasus, I am told it makes a beverage fit for Greek gods."

"Think of the second chapter of St. Luke."

He pondered a moment, and answered, gravely :

"I am sorry to say that I do not remember that particular chapter well enough to appreciate your clew."

She hesitated, and the color deepened on her cheek as she repeated, in a low voice :

"'And there were in the same country shepherds abiding in the field, keeping watch over their flock by night. And, lo, the angel of the Lord came upon them, and the glory of the Lord shone round about them. And suddenly there was with the angel a multitude of the heavenly host praising God, and saying, Glory to God in the highest, and on earth peace, good will toward men.'

"Mr. Leigh, the star on the ram's horn may be the Star of Bethlehem that shone over the manger, and the Arabic inscription is certainly the salutation of the angel to the shepherds. ' Peace, good will toward men,' says St. Luke ; ' Peace be with thee,' said Is- lamism."

"Your solution seems plausible, but, pardon me, is totally inadmissible, from the fact that it blends crescent and cross, and ignores antagonisms that del- uged centuries with blood."

"You forget, Mr. Leigh, that Mohammedanism is nothing but a huge eclecticism, and that its founder stole its elements from surrounding systems. The symbolism of the crescent he took from the mysteries of Isis and Astarte ; the ethical code of Christ he engrafted on the monotheism of Judasism ; his typical forms are drawn from the Old Testament or the more modern Mishma : and his pretended miracles are mere repetitions of the wonders performed by our Saviour —for instance, the basket of dates, the roasted lamb, the loaf of barley bread, in the siege of Medina. Even the Moslem Jehennam is a palpable imitation of the Hebrew Gehenna. Beside, sir, you know that Sabeanism reigned in Arabia just before the advent of Mohammed, and if you refuse to believe that the Star of Bethlehem was signified by this one shining here on the ram's horn, at least you must admit that it refers to stars studied by the shepherds who watched their flocks on the Chaldean plains. In a cabinet of coins and medals, belonging to Mr. Murray, I have examined one of silver, representing Astaroth, with the head of a woman adorned with horns and a crescent, and another of brass, containing an image of Baal—a human face on the head of an ox, with the horns surrounded by stars. However, I am very ignorant of these things, and you must refer the riddle of the ring to some one more astute and learned in such matters than your humble 'yokefellow' in Hebrew. ' Peace be with you.' "

" I repeat ' Peace be with thee,' during the new year on which we are both entering, and, as you have at least attempted to read the riddle, let me beg that you will do me the honor to accept and wear the ring in memory of our friendship and our student life."

He took her hand, and would have placed the ring on her finger, but she resisted.

" Thank you, Mr. Leigh, I appreciate the honor, but indeed you must excuse me, I cannot accept the ring."

" Why not, Miss Edna ?"

" In the first place, because it is very valuable and beautiful, and I am not willing to deprive you of it : in

the second, I do not think it proper to accept presents
from—any one but relatives or dear friends."

"I thought we were dear friends? Why can we not
be such?"

At this moment Mrs. Murray came into the dining-
room, and as she looked at the two sitting there in the
early sunshine, with the basket of flowers between
them; as she marked the heightened color and embarrassed expression on one fair, sweet face, and the eager
pleading written on the other, so full of manly beauty,
so frank and bright and genial, a possible destiny for
both flashed before her; and pleased surprise warmed
her own countenance as she hurried forward.

"Good-morning, Gordon. I am very glad to see
you. How is Clara?"

"Quite well, thank you, and entirely absorbed in
preparations for her party, as you will infer from this
note, which she charged me to deliver in person, and
for which I here pray your most favorable consideration."

As Mrs. Murray glanced over the note Edna turned
to leave the room; but Mr. Leigh exclaimed:

"Do not go just yet, I wish Mrs. Murray to decide
a matter for me."

"Well, Gordon, what is it?"

"First, do you grant my sister's petition?"

"Certainly, I will bring Edna with me to-night, unless she prefers staying at home with her books. You
know I let her do pretty much as she pleases."

"Now then for my little quarrel! Here is a curious
old ring, which she will appreciate more highly than
any one one else whom I happen to know, and I want
her to accept it as a birthday memento from me, but a
few minutes ago she refused to wear it. Can you not
come to my assistance, my dear Mrs. Murray?"

She took the ring, examined it, and said, after a
pause:

"I think, Gordon, that she did exactly right; but I
also think that now, with my approval and advice, she
need not hesitate to wear it henceforth, as a token of

your friendship. Edna, hold out your hand, my dear."

The ring was slipped on the slender finger, and as she released her hand, Mrs. Murray bent down and kissed her forehead.

"Seventeen to-day! My child, I can scarcely believe it! And you—Gordon? May I ask how old you are?"

"Twenty-five—I grieve to say! You need not tell me——"

The conversation was interrupted by the ringing of the breakfast bell, and soon after, Mr. Leigh took his departure.

Edna felt puzzled and annoyed, and as she looked down at the ring she thought that instead of "Peace be with thee," the Semitic characters must surely mean, "Disquiet seize thee!" for they had shivered the beautiful calm of her girlish nature, and thrust into her mind ideas unknown until that day. Going to her own room, she opened her books, but ere she could fix her wandering thoughts Mrs. Murray entered.

"Edna, I came to speak to you about your dress for to-night."

"Please do not say that you wish me to go, my dear Mrs. Murray, for I dread the very thought."

"But I must tell you that I insist upon your conforming to the usages of good society. Mrs. Inge belongs to one of the very first families in the State; at her house you will meet the best people, and you could not possibly make your *début* under more favorable circumstances. Beside, it is very unnatural that a young girl should not enjoy parties and the society of gay young people. You are very unnecessarily making a recluse of yourself, and I shall not permit you to refuse such an invitation as Mrs. Inge has sent. It would be rude in the extreme."

"Dear Mrs. Murray, you speak of my *début*, as if, like other girls, I had nothing else to do but fit myself for society. These people care nothing for me, and I am as little interested in them. I have no desire to move for a short time in a circle from which my work in life must soon separate me."

"To what work do you allude?"

"The support which I must make by teaching. In a few months I hope to be able to earn all I need, and then——"

"Then it will be quite time enough to determine what necessity demands; in the mean while, as long as you are in my house you must allow me to judge what is proper for you. Clara Inge is my friend, and I can not allow you to be rude to her. I have sent the carriage to town for Miss O'Riley, my mantua-maker, and Hagar will make the skirt of your dress. Come into my room and let her take the measure."

"Thank you for your kind thoughtfulness, but indeed I no not want to go. Please let me stay at home! You can frame some polite excuse, and Mrs. Inge cares not whether I go or stay. I will write my regrets and——"

"Don't be childish, Edna; I care whether you go or stay, and that fact should weigh with you much more than Mrs. Inge's wishes, for you are quite right in supposing that it is a matter of indifference to her. Do not keep Hagar waiting."

Mrs. Murray's brow clouded, and her lips contracted, as was their habit, when anything displeased her; consequently, after a quick glance, Edna followed her to the room where Hagar was at work. It was the first time the orphan had been invited to a large party, and she shrank from meeting people whose standard of gentility was confined to high birth and handsome fortunes. Mrs. Inge came frequently to Le Bocage, but Edna's acquaintance with her was comparatively slight, and in addition to her repugnance to meeting strangers she dreaded seeing Mr. Leigh again so soon, for she felt that an undefinable barrier had suddenly risen between them; the frank, fearless freedom of the old friendship at the parsonage table had vanished. She began to wish that she had never studied Hebrew; that she had never heard of Basilides, and that the sheik's ring was back among the ruins of Chilminar. Mrs. Murray saw her discomposure, but chose to take no notice of it, and superintended her toilet that night with almost as much interest as if she had been her own daughter.

During the drive she talked on indifferent subjects, and as they went up to the dressing-room had the satisfaction of seeing that her *protégée* manifested no trepidation They arrived rather late, the company had assembled, and the rooms were quite full as Mrs. Murray entered ; but Mrs. Inge met them at the threshold, and Mr. Leigh, who seemed on the watch, came forward at the same instant, and offered Edna his arm.

"Ah, Mrs. Murray! I had almost abandoned the hope of seeing you. Miss Edna, the set is just forming, and we must celebrate our birthday by having the first dance together. Excuse you, indeed ! You presume upon my well-known good nature and generosity, but this evening I am privileged to be selfish."

As he drew her into the middle of the room she noticed that he wore the flowers she had given him in the morning, and this, in conjunction with the curious scrutiny to which she was subjected, brought a sudden surge of color to her cheeks. The dance commenced, and from one corner of the room Mr. Hammond looked eagerly at his two pupils, contrasting them with the gay groups that filled the brilliant apartment.

Edna's slender, graceful figure was robed in white Swiss muslin, with a bertha of rich lace ; and rose-colored ribbons formed the sash, and floated from her shoulders. Her beautiful glossy hair was simply coiled in a large roll at the back of the head, and fastened with an ivory comb. Scrutinizing the face lifted toward Mr. Leigh's, while he talked to her, the pastor thought he had never seen a countenance half so eloquent and lovely. Turning his gaze upon her partner, he was compelled to confess that though Gordon Leigh was the handsomest man in the room, no acute observer could look at the two and fail to discover that the blacksmith's

granddaughter was far superior to the petted brother
of the aristocratic Mrs. Inge. He was so much interested in watching the couple that he did not observe
Mrs. Murray's approach until she sat down beside him
and whispered :

" Are they not a handsome couple ?"

" Gordon and Edna ?"

" Yes."

" Indeed they are ! I think that child's face is the
most attractive, the most fascinating I ever looked at.
There is such a rare combination of intelligence, holiness, strength and serenity in her countenance ; such
a calm, pure light shining in her splendid eyes ; such a
tender, loving look far down in their soft depths."

" Child ! Why she is seventeen to-day."

" No matter, Ellen ; to me she will always seem a
gentle, clinging, questioning child. I look at her often
when she is intent on her studies, and wonder how long
her pure heart will reject the vanities and baubles that
engross most women ; how long mere abstract study
will continue to charm her ; and I tremble when I
think of the future to which I know she is looking so
eagerly. Now, her emotional nature sleeps, her heart
is at rest—slumbering also, she is all intellect at present
—giving her brain no relaxation. Ah ! if it could always be so. But it will not ! There will come a time,
I fear, when her fine mind and pure, warm heart will
be arrayed against each other, will battle desperately,
and one or the other must be subordinated."

" Gordon seems to admire her very much," said Mrs.
Murray.

Mr. Hammond sighed, and a shadow crept over his
placid features, as he answered :

" Do you wonder at it, Ellen ? Can any one know
the child well, and fail to admire ? 'ove her ?"

"If he could only forget her o   birth—if he
could only consent to marry her—what a splendid
match it would be for her ?"

" Ellen ! Ellen Murray ! I am surprised at you !
Let me beg of you for her sake, for yours, for all

parties concerned, not to raise your little finger in this matter; not to utter one word to Edna that might arouse her suspicions; not to hint to Gordon that you dream such an alliance possible; for there is more at stake than you imagine——"

He was unable to conclude the sentence, for the dance had ended, and as Edna caught a glimpse of the beloved countenance of her teacher, she drew her fingers from Mr. Leigh's arm, and hastened to the pastor's side, taking his hand between both hers:

"O sir! I am glad to see you. I have looked around so often; hoping to catch sight of you. Mrs. Murray, I heard Mrs. Inge asking for you."

When the lady walked away, Edna glided into the seat next the minister, and continued:

"I want to talk to you about a change in some of my studies."

"Wait till to-morrow, my dear. I came here to-night only for a few moments, to gratify Gordon, and now I must slip away."

"But, sir, I only want to say, that as you objected at the outset to my studying Hebrew, I will not waste any more time on it just now, but take it up again after a while, when I have plenty of leisure. Don't you think that would be the best plan?"

"My child, are you tired of Hebrew?"

"No, sir; on the contrary, it possesses a singular fascination for me; but I think, if you are willing, I shall discontinue it—at least, for the present. I shall take care to forget nothing that I have already learned."

"You have some special reason for this change, I presume?"

She raised her eyes to his, and said frankly:

"Yes, sir, I have."

"Very well, my dear, do as you like. Good-night."

"I wish I could go now with you."

"Why? I thought you appeared to enjoy your dance very much. Edna, look at me."

She hesitated—then obeyed him, and he saw tears glistening on her long lashes.

Very quietly the old man drew her arm through his, and led her out on the dim verandah, where only an occasional couple promenaded.

"Something troubles you, Edna. Will you confide in me?"

"I feel as if I were occupying a false position here, and yet I do not see how I can extricate myself without displeasing Mrs. Murray, whom I can not bear to offend—she is so very kind and generous."

"Explain yourself, my dear."

"You know that I have not a cent in the world except what Mrs. Murray gives me. I shall have to make my bread by my own work just as soon as you think me competent to teach; and notwithstanding, she thinks I ought to visit and associate as she does with these people, who tolerate me now, simply because they know that while I am under her roof she will exact it of them. To-night, during the dance, I heard two of her fashionable friends criticising and sneering at me; ridiculing her for 'attempting to smuggle that spoiled creature of unknown parentage and doubtless low origin into really first circles.' Other things were said which I can not repeat, that showed me plainly how I am regarded here, and I will not remain in a position which subjects me to such remarks. Mrs. Murray thought it best for me to come ; but it was a mistaken kindness. I thought so before I came —now I have irrefragable proof that I was right in my forebodings."

"Can you not tell me all that was said ?"

"I shrink, sir, from repeating it, even to you."

"Did Mr. Leigh hear it ?"

"I hope not."

"My dear child, I am very much pained to learn that you have been so cruelly wounded ; but do not let your mind dwell upon it ; those weak, heartless, giddy people are to be pitied, are beneath your notice. Try to fix your thoughts on nobler themes, and waste no reflection on the idle words of those poor gilded moths of fashion and folly, who are incapable of realizing their own degraded and deplorable condition."

"I do not care particularly what they think of me, but I am anxious to avoid hearing their comments upon me, and therefore I am determined to keep as much out of sight as possible. I shall try to do my duty in all things, and poverty is no stigma, thank God! My grandfather was very poor, but he was noble and honest, and as courteous as a nobleman; and I honor his dear, dear memory as tenderly as if he had been reared in a palace. I am not ashamed of my parentage, for my father was as honest and industrious as he was poor, and my mother was as gentle and good as she was beautiful."

There was no faltering in the sweet voice, and no bitterness poisoning it. Mr. Hammond could not see the face, but the tone indexed all, and he was satisfied.

"I am glad, my dear little Edna, that you look at the truth so bravely, and give no more importance to this gossip than your future peace of mind demands. If you have any difficulty in convincing Mrs. Murray of the correctness of your views, let me know, and I will speak to her on the subject. Good-night! May God watch over and bless you!"

When the orphan reëntered the parlor, Mrs. Inge presented her to several gentlemen who had requested an introduction; and though her heart was heavy, and her cheeks burned painfully, she exerted herself, and danced and talked constantly until Mrs. Murray announced herself ready to depart.

Joyfully Edna ran upstairs for her wrappings, bade adieu to her hostess, who complimented her on the sensation her beauty had created; and felt relieved and comparatively happy when the carriage-door closed and she found herself alone with her benefactress.

"Well, Edna, notwithstanding your repugnance to

going, you acquitted yourself admirably, and seemed to
have a delightful time."

"I thank you, ma'am, for doing all in your power to
make the evening agreeable to me. I think your kind
desire to see me enjoy the party made me happier
than everything else."

Gratefully she drew Mrs. Murray's hand to her lips,
and the latter little dreamed that at that instant tears
were rolling over the flushed face, while the words of
the conversation which she had overheard rang mockingly in her ears :

"Mrs. Murray and even Mr. Hammond are scheming to make a match between her and Gordon Leigh.
Studying Hebrew indeed! A likely story! She had
better go back to her wash-tub and spinning-wheel!
Much Hebrew she will learn! Her eyes are set on
Gordon's fortune, and Mrs. Murray is silly enough to
think he will step into the trap. She will have to bait
it with something better than Hebrew and black eyes,
or she will miss her game. Gordon will make a fool of
her, I dare say, for, like all other young men, he can be
flattered into paying her some little attention at first. I
am surprised at Mrs. Inge to countenance the girl at
all."

Such was the orphan's initiation into the charmed
circle of fashionable society ; such her welcome to *le
beau monde.*

As she laid her head on her pillow, she could not
avoid exclaiming :

"Heaven save me from such aristocrats! and commit me rather to the horny but outstretched hands,
the brawny arms, the untutored minds, the simple but
kindly-throbbing hearts of *proletaire !*"

CHAPTER X.

WHEN Mr. Hammond mentioned Edna's determination to discontinue Hebrew, Mr. Leigh expressed no surprise, asked no explanation, but the minister noticed that he bit his lip, and beat a hurried tattoo with the heel of his boot on the stony hearth ; and as he studiously avoided all allusion to her, he felt assured that the conversation which she had overheard must have reached the ears of her partner also, and supplied him with a satisfactory solution of her change of purpose. For several weeks Edna saw nothing of her quondam schoolmate; and fixing her thoughts more firmly than ever on her studies, the painful recollection of the birthday fête was slowly fading from her mind, when one morning, as she was returning from the parsonage, Mr. Leigh joined her, and asked permission to attend her home. The sound of his voice, the touch of his hand, brought back all the embarrassment and constraint, and called up the flush of confusion so often attributed to other sources than that from which it really springs.

After a few commonplace remarks, he asked:

"When is Mr. Murray coming home ?"

"I have no idea. Even his mother is ignorant of his plans."

"How long has he been absent ?"

"Four years to-day."

"Indeed ! so long ? Where is he ?"

"I believe his last letter was written at Edfu, a he said nothing about returning."

"What do you think of his singular character ?"

"I know almost nothing about him, as I was too young when I saw him to form an estimate of him."

"Do you not correspond?"

Edna looked up with unfeigned astonishment, and could not avoid smiling at the inquiry.

"Certainly not."

A short silence followed, and then Mr. Leigh said :

"Do you not frequently ride on horseback?"

"Yes, sir."

"Will you permit me to accompany you to-morrow afternoon?"

"I have promised to make a visit with Mr. Hammond."

"To-morrow morning then, before breakfast?"

She hesitated—the blush deepened, and after a brief struggle, she said hurriedly :

"Please excuse me, Mr. Leigh; I prefer to ride alone."

He bowed, and was silent for a minute, but she saw a smile lurking about the corners of his handsome mouth, threatening to run riot over his features.

"By the by, Miss Edna, I am coming to-night, to ask your assistance in a Chaldee quandary. For several days I have been engaged in a controversy with Mr. Hammond on the old battlefield of ethnology, and, in order to establish my position of diversity of origin, have been comparing the Septuagint with some passages from the Talmud. I heard you say that there was a Rabbinical Targum in the library at Le Bocage, and I must beg you to examine it for me, and ascertain whether it contains any comments on the first chapter of Genesis. Somewhere in my most desultory reading I have seen it stated that in some of those early Targums was the declaration, that ' God originally created men red, white and black.' Mr. Hammond is charitable enough to say that I must have smoked an extra cigar, and dreamed the predicate I am so anxious to authenticate. Will you oblige me by searching for the passage?"

"Certainly, Mr. Leigh, with great pleasure ; though

perhaps you would prefer to take the book and look through it yourself? My knowledge of Chaldee is very limited."

"Pardon me! my mental *vis inertiæ* vetoes the bare suggestion. I study by proxy whenever an opportunity offers, for laziness is the only hereditary taint in the Leigh blood."

"As I am very much interested in this ethnological question, I shall enter into the search with great eagerness."

"Thank you. Do you take the unity or diversity side of the discussion?"

Her merry laugh rang out through the forest that bordered the road.

"Oh, Mr. Leigh! what a ridiculous question! I do not presume to take any side, for I do not pretend to understand or appreciate all the arguments advanced; but I am anxious to acquaint myself with the bearings of the controversy. The idea of my 'taking sides' on a subject which gray-haired *savans* have spent their laborious lives in striving to elucidate seems extremely ludicrous."

"Still, you are entitled to an idea, either *pro* or *con*, even at the outset."

"I have an idea that neither you nor I know anything about the matter; and the *per saltum* plan of 'taking sides' will only add the prop of prejudice to my ignorance. If, with all his erudition, Mr. Hammond still abstains from dogmatizing on this subject, I can well afford to hold my crude opinions in abeyance. I must stop here, Mr. Leigh, at Mrs. Carter's, on an errand for Mrs. Murray. Good morning, sir; I will hunt the passage you require."

"How have I offended you, Miss Edna?"

He took her hand and detained her.

"I am not offended, Mr. Leigh," and she drew back.

"Why do you dismiss me in such a cold, unfriendly way?"

"If I sometimes appear rude, pardon my unfortunate

manner, and believe that it results from no unfriendliness."

"You will be at home this evening?"

"Yes, sir, unless something very unusual occurs."

They parted, and during the remainder of the walk Edna could think of nothing but the revelation written in Gordon Leigh's eyes; the immemorial, yet ever new and startling truth, that opened a new vista in life, that told her she was no longer an isolated child, but a woman, regnant over the generous heart of one of the pets of society.

She saw that he intended her to believe he loved her, and suspicious as gossips had made her with reference to his conduct, she could not suppose he was guilty of heartless and contemptible trifling. She trusted his honor; yet the discovery of his affection brought a sensation of regret—of vague self-reproach, and she felt that in future he would prove a source of endless disquiet. Hitherto she had enjoyed his society, henceforth she felt that she must shun it.

She endeavored to banish the recollection of that strange expression in his generally laughing eyes, and bent over the Targum, hoping to cheat her thoughts into other channels; but the face would not "down at her bidding," and as the day drew near its close she grew nervous and restless.

The chandelier had been lighted, and Mrs. Murray was standing at the window of the sitting-room, watching for the return of a servant whom she had sent to the post-office, when Edna said:

"I believe Mr. Leigh is coming here to tea; he told me so this morning."

"Where did you see him?"

"He walked with me as far as Mrs. Carter's gate, and asked me to look out a reference which he thought I might find in one of Mr. Murray's books."

Mrs. Murray smiled, and said:

"Do you intend to receive him in that calico dress?"

"Why not? I am sure it is very neat; it is perfectly new, and fits me well."

"And is very suitable to wear to the Parsonage, but not quite appropriate when Gordon Leigh takes tea here. You will oblige me by changing your dress and rearranging your hair, which is twisted too loosely."

When she re-entered the room, a half-hour later, Mrs. Murray leaned against the mantelpiece, with an open letter in her hand and dreary disappointment printed on her face.

"I hope you have no unpleasant tidings from Mr. Murray. May I ask why you seem so much depressed?"

The mother's features twitched painfully as she restored the letter to its envelope, and answered:

"My son's letter is dated Philoe, just two months ago, and he says he intended starting next day to the interior of Persia. He says, too, that he did not expect to remain away so long, but finds that he will probably be in Central Asia for another year. The only comforting thing in the letter is the assurance that he weighs more, and is in better health, than when he left home."

The ringing of the door-bell announced Mr. Leigh's arrival, and as she led the way to the parlor, Mrs. Murray hastily fastened a drooping spray of coral berries in Edna's hair.

Before tea was ended, other visitors came in, and the orphan found relief from her confusion in the general conversation.

While Dr. Rodney, the family physician, was talking to her about some discoveries of Ehrenberg, concerning which she was very curious, Mr. Leigh engrossed Mrs. Murray's attention, and for some time their conversation was exceedingly earnest; then the latter rose and approached the sofa where Edna sat, saying gravely:

"Edna, give me this seat, I want to have a little chat with the doctor; and, by the way, my dear, I believe Mr. Leigh is waiting for you to show him some book you promised to find for him. Go into the library—there is a good fire there."

The room was tempting indeed to students, and as
the two sat down before the glowing grate, and Mr.
Leigh glanced at the warm, rich curtains sweeping
from ceiling to carpet, the black-walnut book-cases
girding the walls on all sides, and the sentinel bronze
busts keeping watch over the musty tomes within, he
rubbed his fingers and exclaimed:

"Certainly this is the most delightful library in the
world, and offers a premium for recluse life and studious
habits. How incomprehensible it is that Murray should
prefer to pass his years roaming over deserts and
wandering about neglected, comfortless khans, when he
might spend them in such an elysium as this! The
man must be demented! How do you explain the
mystery?"

"*Chacun à son gout!* I consider it none of my
business, and as I suppose he is the best judge of what
contributes to his happiness, I do not meddle with the
mystery."

"Poor Murray! his wretched disposition is a great
curse. I pity him most sincerely."

"From what I remember of him, I am afraid he
would not thank you for your pity, or admit that he
needed or merited it. Here is the Targum, Mr. Leigh,
and here is the very passage you want."

She opened an ancient Chaldee MS., and spreading it
on the library table, they examined it together, spelling
out the words, and turning frequently to a dictionary
which lay near. Neither knew much about the language; now and then they differed in the interpretation, and more than once Edna referred to the rules
of her grammar, to establish the construction of the
sentences.

Engrossed in the translation, she forgot all her apprehensions of the morning, and the old ease of manner
came back. Her eyes met his fearlessly, her smile
greeted him cheerily as in the early months of their acquaintance; and while she bent over the pages she was
deciphering, his eyes dwelt on her beaming countenance
with a fond, tender look, that most girls of her age

would have found it hard to resist, and pleasant to recall in after days.

Neither suspected that an hour had passed, until Dr. Rodney peeped into the room and called them back to the parlor, to make up a game of whist.

It was quite late when Mr. Leigh rose to say good-night; and as he drew on his gloves he looked earnestly at Edna, and said :

"I am coming again in a day or two, to show you some plans for a new house which I intend to build before long. Clara differs with me about the arrangement of some columns and arches, and I shall claim you and Mrs. Murray for my allies in this architectural war."

The orphan was silent, but the lady of the house replied promptly :

"Yes, come as often as you can, Gordon, and cheer us up; for it is terribly dull here without St. Elmo."

"Suppose you repudiate that incorrigible Vandal and adopt me in his place? I would prove a model son."

"Very well. I shall acquaint him with your proposition, and threaten an immediate compliance with it if he does not come home soon."

Mrs. Murray rang the bell for the servant to lock up the house, and said *sotto voce :*

"What a noble fellow Gordon is! If I had a daughter I would select him for her husband. Where are you going, Edna?"

"I left a MS. on the library table, and as it is very rare and valuable I want to replace it in the glass box where it belongs before I go to sleep."

Lighting a candle, she lifted the heavy Targum, and slowly approached the suite of rooms, which she was now in the habit of visiting almost daily.

Earlier in the day she had bolted the door, but left the key in the lock, expecting to bring the Targum back as soon as she had shown Mr. Leigh the controverted passage. Now, as she crossed the rotundo, an unexpected sound, as of a chair sliding on the marble floor, seemed to issue from the inner room, and she paused to listen. Under the flare of the candle the vindictive face of Siva, and the hooded viper twined about his arm, looked more hideous than ever, warning her not to approach, yet all was silent, save the tinkling of a bell far down in the park, where the sheep clustered under the cedars. Opening the door, which was ajar, she entered, held the light high over her head, and peered a little nervously around the room ; but, here, too, all was quiet as the grave, and quite as dreary, and the only moving thing seemed her shadow, that flitted slightly as the candle-light flickered over the cold, gleaming white tiles. The carpets and curtains— even the rich silk hangings of the arch—were all packed away, and Edna shivered as she looked through both rooms, satisfied herself that she had mistaken the source of the sound, and opened the box where the MSS. were kept.

At sight of them her mind reverted to the theme she had been investigating, and happening to remember the importance attached by ethnologists to the early Coptic inscriptions, she took from the book-shelves a volume containing copies of many of these characters, and drawings of the triumphal processions carved on granite, and representing the captives of various nations torn from their homes to swell the pompous retinue of some barbaric Rhamses or Sesostris.

Drifting back over the gray, waveless, tideless sea of centuries, she stood, in imagination, upon the steps of the Serapeum at Memphis; and when the wild chant of the priests had died away under the huge propylæum, she listened to the sighing of the tamarinds and cassias, and the low babble of the sacred Nile, as it rocked the lotus-leaves, under the glowing purple sky, whence a full moon flooded the ancient city with light, and kindled like a beacon the vast placid face of the Sphinx—rising solemn and lonely and weird from its desert lair—and staring blankly, hopelessly across arid yellow sands at the dim colossi of old Misraim.

Following the sinuous stream of Coptic civilization

to its inexplicable source in the date-groves of Meroe, the girl's thoughts were borne away to the Golden Fountain of the Sun, where Ammon's black doves fluttered and cooed over the shining altars and amid the mystic symbols of the marvelous friezes.

As Edna bent over the drawings in the book, oblivious for a time of everything else, she suddenly became aware of the presence of some one in the room, for though perfect stillness reigned, there was a consciousness of companionship, of the proximity of some human being, and with a start she looked up, expecting to meet a pair of eyes fastened upon her. But no living thing confronted her—the tall, bent figure of the Cimbri Prophetess gleamed ghostly white upon the wall, and the bright blue augurous eyes seemed to count the dripping blood-drops; and the unbroken, solemn silence of night brooded over all things, hushing even the chime of sheep-bells, that had died away among the elm arches. Knowing that no superstitious terrors had ever seized her heretofore, the young student rose, took up the candle, and proceeded to search the two rooms, but as unsuccessfully as before.

"There certainly is somebody here, but I can not find out where."

These words were uttered aloud, and the echo of her own voice seemed sepulchral; then the chill silence again fell upon her. She smiled at her own folly, and thought her imagination had been unduly excited by the pictures she had been examining, and that the nervous shiver that crept over her was the result of the cold. Just then the candle-light flashed over the black marble statuette, grinning horribly as it kept guard over the Taj Mahal. Edna walked up to it, placed the candle on the slab that supported the tomb, and, stooping, scrutinized the lock. A spider had ensconced himself in the golden receptacle, and spun a fine web across the front of the temple, and Edna swept the airy drapery away, and tried to drive the little weaver from his den; but he shrank further and further, and finally she took the key from her pocket and put it far

enough into the opening to eject the intruder, who
slung himself down one of the silken threads, and
crawled sullenly out of sight. Withdrawing the key,
she toyed with it, and glanced curiously at the mausoleum. Taking her handkerchief, she carefully
brushed off the cobwebs that festooned the minarets,
and murmured that fragment of Persian poetry which
she once heard the absent master repeat to his mother,
and which she had found, only a few days before,
quoted by an Eastern traveller : " The spider hath
woven his web in the imperial palaces ; and the owl
hath sung her watch-song on the towers of Afrasiab."

" It is exactly four years to-night since Mr. Murray
gave me this key, but he charged me not to open the
Taj unless I had reason to believe that he was dead.
His letter states that he is alive and well ; consequently, the time has not come for me to unseal the
mystery. It is strange that he trusted me with this
secret ; strange that he, who doubts all of his race,
could trust a child of whom he really knew so little.
Certainly it must have been a singular freak which
gave this affair into my keeping, but at least I will not
betray the confidence he reposed in me. With the
contents of that vault I can have no concern, and yet
I wish the key was safely back in his hands. It annoys
me to conceal it, and I feel all the while as if I were
deceiving his mother."

These words were uttered half unconsciously as she
fingered the key, and for a few seconds she stood there,
thinking of the master of the house, wondering what
luckless influence had so early blackened and distorted
his life, and whether he would probably return to Le
Bocage before she left it to go out and carve her
fortune in the world's noisy quarry. The light danced
over her countenance and form, showing the rich folds
of her crimson merino dress, with the gossamer lace
surrounding her white throat and dimpled wrists ; and
it seemed to linger caressingly on the shining mass of
black hair, on the beautiful, polished forehead, the

firm, delicate, scarlet lips, and made the large eyes look elfish under their heavy jet lashes.

Again the girl started and glanced over her shoulder, impressed with the same tantalizing conviction of a human presence; of some powerful influence which baffled analysis. Snatching the candle, she put the gold key in her pocket, and turned to leave the room, but stopped, for this time an unmistakable sound like the shivering of a glass or the snapping of a musical string, fell on her strained ears. She could trace it to no particular spot, and conjectured that perhaps a mouse had taken up his abode somewhere in the room, and, frightened by her presence, had run against some of the numerous glass and china ornaments on the *étagère*, jostling them until they jingled. Replacing the book which she had taken from the shelves, and fastening the box that contained the MSS., she examined the cabinets, found them securely closed, and then hurried out of the room, locked the door, took the key, and went to her own apartment with nerves more unsettled than she felt disposed to confess.

For some time after she laid her head on her pillow, she racked her brain for an explanation of the singular sensation she had experienced, and at last, annoyed by her restlessness and silly superstition, she was just sinking into dreams of Ammon and Serapis, when the fierce barking of Ali caused her to start up in terror. The dog seemed almost wild, running frantically to and fro, howling and whining; but finally the sounds receded, gradually quiet was restored, and Edna fell asleep soon after the scream of the locomotive and the rumble of the cars told her that the four o'clock train had just started to Chattanooga.

Modern zoologic science explodes the popular fallacy that chameleons assume, and reflect at will, the color of the substance on which they rest or feed; but, with a profound *salaam* to *savans*, it is respectfully submitted that the mental saurian—human thought—certainly takes its changing hues, day by day, from the books through which it crawls devouringly.

Is there not ground for plausible doubt that, if the
work-bench of Mezzofanti had not stood just beneath
the teacher's window, whence the ears of the young
carpenter were regaled from morning till night with
the rudiments of Latin and Greek, he would never
have forsworn planing for parsing, mastered forty dialects, proved a walking scarlet-capped polygot, and
attained the distinction of an honorary nomination for
the office of interpreter-general at the Tower of Babel?

The hoary associations and typical significance of
the numerous relics that crowded Mr. Murray's rooms
seized upon Edna's fancy, linked her sympathies with
the huge pantheistic systems of the Orient, and filled
her mind with waifs from the dusky realm of a mythol-
ogy that seemed to antedate all the authentic chrono-
logical computations of man. To the East, the mighty
alma mater of the human races—of letters, religions,
arts, and politics, her thoughts wandered in wondering
awe ; and Belzoni, Burckhardt, Layard, and Champollion were hierophants of whose teachings she never
wearied. As day by day she yielded more and more
to this fascinating nepenthe influence, and bent over
the granite sarcophagus in one corner of Mr. Murray's
museum, where lay a shrunken mummy shrouded in
gilded byssus, the wish strengthened to understand
the symbols in which subtle Egyptian priests masked
their theogony.

While morning and afternoon hours were given to
those branches of study in which Mr. Hammond guided
her, she generally spent the evening in Mr. Murray's
sitting-room, and sometimes the clock in the rotundo
struck midnight before she locked up the MSS. and
illuminated papyri.

Two nights after the examination of the Targum,
she was seated near the book-case looking over the
plates in that rare but very valuable volume, Spence's
Polymetis, when the idea flashed across her mind that
a rigid analysis and comparison of all the mythologies
of the world would throw some light on the problem

of ethnology, and in conjunction with philology settle the vexed question.

Pushing the Polymetis aside, she sprang up and paced the long room, and gradually her eyes kindled, her cheeks burned, as ambition pointed to a possible future, of which, till this hour, she had not dared to dream ; and hope, o'erleaping all barriers, grasped a victory that would make her name imperishable.

In her miscellaneous reading she had stumbled upon singular correspondences in the customs and religions of nations separated by surging oceans and by ages ; nations whose aboriginal records appeared to prove them distinct, and certainly furnished no hint of an ethnological bridge over which traditions traveled and symbolisms crept in satin sandals. During the past week several of these coincidences had attracted her attention.

The Druidic rites and the festival of Beltein in Scotland and Ireland, she found traced to their source in the worship of Phrygian Baal. The figure of the Scandinavian Disa, at Upsal, enveloped in a net precisely like that which surrounds some statues of Isis in Egypt. The mat or rush sails used by the Peruvians on Lake Titicaca, and their mode of handling them, pronounced identical with that which is seen upon the supulchre of Ramses III. at Thebes. The head of a Mexican priestess ornamented with a veil similar to that carved on Eastern sphinxes, while the robes resembled those of a Jewish high-priest. A very quaint and puzzling pictorial chart of the chronology of the Aztecs contained an image of Coxcox in his ark, surrounded by rushes similar to those that overshadowed Moses, and also a likeness of a dove distributing tongues to those born after the deluge.

Now, the thought of carefully gathering up these vague mythologic links, and establishing a chain of unity that would girdle the world, seized and mastered her, as if veritably clothed with all the power of a *bath kol*.

To firmly grasp the Bible for a talisman, as Ulysses

did the sprig of moly, and to stand in the Pantheon of
the universe, examining every shattered idol and crumbling defiled, altar, where worshipping humanity had
bowed ; to tear the veil from oracles and sibyls, and
show the world that the true, good and beautiful of all
theogonies and cosmogonies, of every system of religion that had waxed and waned since the gray dawn of
time, could be traced to Moses and to Jesus, seemed
to her a mission grander far than the conquest of em-
pires, and infinitely more to be desired than the crown
and heritage of Solomon.

The night wore on as she planned the work of coming years, but she still walked up and down the floor,
with slow, uncertain steps, like one who, peering at
distant objects, sees nothing close at hand. Flush and
tremor passed from her countenance, leaving the features pale and fixed ; for the first gush of enthusiasm,
like the jets of violet flame flickering over the sim-
mering mass in alchemic crucibles, had vanished—
the thought was a crystalized and consecrated purpose.

At last, when the feeble light admonished her that
she would soon be in darkness, she retreated to her
own room, and the first glimmer of day struggled in at
her window as she knelt at her bedside praying :

" Be pleased, O Lord! to make me a fit instrument
for Thy work; sanctify my heart ; quicken and enlighten my mind ; grant me patience and perseverance
and unwavering faith ; guide me into paths that lead
to truth ; enable me in all things to labor with an eye
single to thy glory, caring less for the applause of the
world than for the advancement of the cause of Christ.
O my Father and my God ! bless the work on which I
am about to enter, crown it with success, accept me as
an humble tool for the benefit of my race, and when
the days of my earthly pilgrimage are ended, receive
my soul into that eternal rest which Thou hast prepared from the foundations of the world, for the sake
of Jesus Christ."

CHAPTER XI.

ONE afternoon about a week after Mr. Leigh's last visit, as Edna returned from the parsonage, where she had been detained beyond the usual time, Mrs. Murray placed in her hand a note from Mrs. Inge, inviting both to dine with her that day, and meet some distinguished friends from a distant State. Mrs. Murray had already completed an elaborate toilet, and desired Edna to lose no time in making the requisite changes in her own dress. The latter took off her hat, laid her books down on a table and said :

" Please offer my excuses to Mrs. Inge. I can not accept the invitation, and hope you will not urge me."

" Nonsense ! Let me hear no more such childish stuff, and get ready at once ; we shall be too late, I am afraid."

The orphan leaned against the mantelpiece and shook her head.

Mrs. Murray colored angrily and drew herself up haughtily.

" Edna Earl, did you hear what I said ?"

' Yes, madam, but this time I cannot obey you. Allow me to give you my reasons, and I am sure you will forgive what may now seem mere obstinacy. On the night of the party given by Mrs. Inge I determined, under no circumstances, to accept any future invitations to her house, for I overheard a conversation between Mrs. Hill and Mrs. Montgomery which I believe was intended to reach my ears, and consequently wounded and mortified me very much. I was ridiculed and denounced as a ' poor upstart and interloper,' who was being smuggled into society far above my position in life, and pronounced an avaricious schemer, intent on thrusting myself upon Mr. Leigh's notice, and ambitious of marrying him for his fortune. They sneered at the idea that we should study Hebrew with Mr. Hammond, and declared it a mere trap to catch Mr. Leigh. Now, Mrs. Murray, you know that I never had such a thought, and the bare mention of a motive so sordid, contemptible, and unwomanly surprised and disgusted me ; but I resolved to study Hebrew by myself, and to avoid meeting Mr. Leigh at the parsonage ; for if his sister's friends entertain such an opinion of me, I know not what other people, and even Mrs. Inge, may think. Those two ladies added some other things equally unpleasant and untrue, and as I see that they are also invited to dine to-day, it would be very disagreeable for me to meet them in Mr. Leigh's presence."

Mrs. Murray frowned, and her lips curled, as she clasped a diamond bracelet on her arm.

"I have long since ceased to be surprised by any manifestation of Mrs. Montgomery's insolence. She doubtless judges your motives by those of her snub-nosed and excruciatingly fashionable daughter, Maud, who rumor says, is paying most devoted attention to that same fortune of Gordon's. I shall avail myself of the first suitable occasion to suggest to her that it is rather unbecoming in persons whose fathers were convicted of forgery, and hunted out of the State, to lay such stress on the mere poverty of young aspirants for admission into society. I have always noticed that people (women especially) whose lineage is enveloped in a certain twilight haze, constitute themselves guardians of the inviolability of their pretentious cliques, and fly at the throats of those who, they imagine, desire to enter their fashionable set—their 'mutual admiration association.' As for Mrs. Hill whose parents were positively respectable, even genteel, I expected less nervousness from her on the subject of genealogy, and should have given her credit for more courtesy and less malice; but, poor thing, nature denied her any individuality, and she serves 'her circle' in the same capacity as one of those tin reflectors fastened on locomotives. All that you heard was excessively ill-bred, and in really good society ill-breeding is more iniquitous than ill-nature; but, however annoying, it is beneath your notice, and unworthy of consideration. I would not gratify them by withdrawing from a position which you can so gracefully occupy."

"It is no privation to me to stay at home; on the contrary, I prefer it, for I would not exchange the companionship of the books in this house for all the dinners that ever were given."

"There is no necessity for you to make a recluse of yourself simply because two rude, silly gossips disgrace themselves. You have time enough to read and study, and still go out with me when I consider it advisable."

"But, my dear Mrs. Murray, my position in your family, as an unknown dependent on your charity, subject me to——"

"Is a matter which does not concern Mesdames Hill and Montgomery, as I shall most unequivocally intimate to them. I insist upon the dismissal of the whole affair from your mind. How much longer do you intend to keep me waiting?"

"I am very sorry you cannot view the subject from my standpoint, but hereafter I cannot accompany you to dinners and parties. Whenever you desire me to see company in your own house, I shall be glad to comply with your wishes and commands; but my self-respect will not permit me to go out to meet people who barely tolerate me through fear of offending you. It is exceedingly painful, dear Mrs. Murray, for me to have to appear disrespectful and stubborn toward you, but in this instance I can not comply with your wishes."

They looked at each other steadily, and Mrs. Murray's brow cleared and her lip unbent.

"What do you expect me to tell Mrs. Inge?"

"That I return my thanks for her very kind remembrance, but am closely occupied in preparing myself to teach, and have no time for gayeties."

Mrs. Murray smiled significantly.

"Do you suppose that excuse will satisfy your
friend Gordon? He will fly for consolation to the
stereotyped smile and delicious flattery of simpering
Miss Maud."

"I care not where he flies, provided I am left in
peace."

"Stop, my dear child; you do not mean what you
say. You know very well that you earnestly hope
Gordon will escape the tender mercies of silly Maud
and the machinations of her most amiable mamma;
if you don't, I do. Understand that you are not to
visit Susan Montgomery's sins on Gordon's head. I
shall come home early, and make you go to bed at
nine o'clock, to punish you for your obstinacy. By
the by, Edna, Hagar tells me that you frequently sit
up till three or four o'clock, poring over those hea-
thenish documents in my son's cabinet. This is absurd,
and will ruin your health; and beside, I doubt if what
you learn is worth your trouble. You must not sit up
longer than ten o'clock. Give me my furs."

Edna ate her dinner alone, and went into the library
to practise a difficult music lesson; but the spell of
her new project was stronger than the witchery of
music, and closing the piano, she ran into the " Egyptian Museum," as Mrs. Murray termed her son's sitting-
room.

The previous night she had been reading an account of the doctrines of Zoroaster, in which there
was an attempt to trace all the chief features of the
Zendavesta to the Old Testament and the Jews, and
now she returned to the subject with unflagging interest.

Pushing a cushioned chair close to the window, she
wrapped her shawl around her, put her feet on the
round of a neighboring chair, to keep them from the

icy floor and gave herself up to the perusal of the volume.

The sun went down in a wintry sky; the solemn red light burning on the funeral pyre of day streamed through the undraped windows, flushed the fretted façade of the Taj Mahal, glowed on the marble floor, and warmed and brightened the serene, lovely face of the earnest young student. As the flame faded in the west, where two stars leaped from the pearly ashes, the fine print of Edna's book grew dim, and she turned the page to catch the mellow, silvery radiance of the full moon, which, shining low in the east, threw a ghastly lustre on the awful form and floating white hair of the Cimbrian woman on the wall. But between the orphan and the light, close beside her chair, stood a tall, dark figure, with uncovered head and outstretched hands.

She sprang to her feet, uttering a cry of mingled alarm and delight, for she knew that erect, stately form and regal head could belong to but one person.

"Oh, Mr. Murray! Can it be possible that you have indeed come home to your sad, desolate mother? Oh! for her sake I am so glad!"

She had clasped her hands tightly in the first instant of surprise, and stood looking at him, with fear and pleasure struggling for mastery in her eloquent countenance.

"Edna, have you no word of welcome, no friendly hand, to offer a man who has been wandering for four long years among strangers in distant lands?"

It was not the harsh, bitter voice whose mocking echoes had haunted her ears during his absence, but a tone so low and deep and mournful, so inexplicably sweet, and she could not recognize it as his, and, unable to utter a word, she put her hand in his outstretched palm. His fingers closed over it with a pressure that was painful, and her eyes fell beneath the steady, searching gaze he fixed on her face.

For fully a minute they stood motionless; then he took a match from his pocket, lighted a gas globe that

hung over the Taj, and locked the door leading into
the rotundo.

"My mother is dining out, Hagar informed me.
Tell me, is she well? And have you made her happy
while I was far away?"

He came back, leaned his elbow on the carved top of
the cushioned chair, and partly shading his eyes with
his hand, looked down into the girl's face.

"Your mother is very well indeed, but anxious and
unhappy on your account, and I think you will find
her thinner and paler than when you saw her last."

"Then you have not done your duty, as I requested?"

"I could not take your place, sir, and your last
letter led her to believe that you would be absent for
another year. She thinks that at this instant you are
in the heart of Persia. Last night, when the servant
came from the post-office without the letter which she
confidently expected, her eyes filled with tears, and
she said, 'He has ceased to think of his home, and
loves the excitement of travel better than his mother's
peace of mind.' Why did you deceive her? Why did
you rob her of all the joy of anticipating your speedy
return?"

As she glanced at him, she saw the old scowl settling
heavily between his eyes, and the harshness had crept
back to the voice that answered:

"I did not deceive her. It was a sudden an unexpected circumstance that determined my return.
Moreover, she should long since have accustomed herself to find happiness from other sources than my
society; for no one knows better my detestation of
settling down in any fixed habitation."

Edna felt all her childish repugnance sweeping over
her as she saw the swift hardening of his features, and
she turned toward the door.

"Where are you going?"

"To send a messenger to your mother, acquainting
her with your arrival. She would not forgive me if I
failed to give her such good tidings at the very earliest
moment."

"You will do no such thing. I forbid any message. She thinks me in the midst of Persian ruins, and can afford to wait an hour longer among her friends. How happened it that you also are not at Mrs. Inge's?"

Either the suddenness of the question, or the intent-ness of his scrutiny, or the painful consciousness of the true cause of her failure to accept the invitation, brought back the blood which surprise had driven from her cheeks.

"I preferred remaining at home."

"Home! home!" he repeated, and continued vehe-mently: "Do you really expect me to believe that a girl of your age, with the choice of a dinner-party among the *élite*, with lace, silk, and feathers, champagne, *bon-mot*, and scandal, flattering speeches and soft looks from young gentlemen, biting words and hard looks from old ladies, or the alternative of a dull, lonely evening in this cold, dreary den of mine, shut up with mummies, MSS., and musty books, could deliberately decline the former and voluntarily select the latter? Such an anomaly in sociology, such a *lusus naturæ*, might occur in Bacon's 'Bensalem,' or in some undis-covered and unimagined realm, where the men are all brave, honest, and true, and the women conscientious and constant! But here! and now? Ah! pardon me! Impossible!"

Edna felt as if Momus' suggestion to Vulcan, of a window in the human breast, whereby one's thoughts might be rendered visible, had been adopted; for, under the empaling eye bent upon her, the secret motives of her conduct seemed spread out as on a scroll, which he read as well.

"I was invited to Mrs. Inge's, yet you find me here, because I preferred a quiet evening at home to a noisy one elsewhere. How do you explain the contradiction if you disbelieve my words?"

"I am not so inexperienced as to tax my ingenuity with any such burden. With the Penelope web of female motives may fates and furies forbid rash med-dling. Unless human nature here in America has undergone a radical change, nay, a most complete transmogrification, since I abjured it some years ago; unless this year is to be chronicled as an Avatar of truth and unselfishness, I will stake all my possessions on the assertion that some very peculiar and cogent reason, something beyond the desire to prosecute archæological researches, has driven you to decline the invitation."

She made no reply, but opened the bookcase and replaced the volume which she had been reading; and he saw that she glanced uneasily toward the door, as if longing to escape.

"Are you insulted at my presumption in thus catechising you?"

"I am sorry, sir, to find that you have lost none of your cynicism in your travels."

"Do you regard travelling as a panacea for minds diseased?"

She looked up and smiled in his face—a smile so bright and arch and merry, that even a stone might have caught the glow.

"Certainly not, Mr. Murray, as you are the most incorrigible traveller I have ever known."

But there was no answering gleam on his darkening countenance as he watched her, and the brief silence that ensued was annoying to his companion, who felt less at ease every moment, and convinced that with such antagonism of character existing between them, all her peaceful, happy days at Le Bocage were drawing to a close.

"Mr. Murray, I am cold, and I should like to go to the fire if you have no more questions to ask, and will be so kind as to unlock the door."

He glanced round the room, and taking his grey travelling shawl from a chair where he had thrown it, laid it in a heap on the marble tiles, and said :

"Yes, this floor is icy. Stand on the shawl, though I am well aware you are more tired of me than of the room."

Another long pause followed, and then St. Elmo Murray came close to his companion, saying:

"For four long years I have been making an experiment—one of those experiments which men frequently attempt, believing all the time that it is worse than child's play, and half hoping that it will prove so and sanction the wisdom of their skepticism concerning the result. When I left home I placed in your charge the key of my private desk or cabinet, exacting the promise that only upon certain conditions would you venture to open it. Those contingencies have not arisen, consequently there can be no justification for your having made yourself acquainted with the contents of the vault. I told you I trusted the key in your hands; I did not. I felt assured you would betray the confidence. It was not a trust—it was a temptation, which I believed no girl or woman would successfully resist. I am here to receive an account of your stewardship, and I tell you now I doubt you. Where is the key?"

She took from her pocket a small ivory box, and opening it drew out the little key and handed it to him.

"Mr. Murray, it was a confidence which I never solicited, which has caused me much pain, because it necessitated concealment from your mother, but which—God is my witness—I have not betrayed. There is the key, but of the contents of the tomb I know nothing. It was ungenerous in you to tempt a child as you did; to offer a premium as it were for a violation of secrecy, by whetting my curiosity and then placing in my own hands the means of gratifying it. Of course I have wondered what the mystery was, and why you selected me for its custodian; and I have often wished to inspect the interior of that marble cabinet; but child though I was, I think I would have gone to the stake sooner than violate my promise."

As he took the key she observed that his hand trembled and that a sudden pallor overspread his face.

"Edna Earl, I give you one last chance to be truthful with me. If you yielded to the temptation—and what woman, what girl, would not ?—it would be no more than I really expected, and you will scarcely have disappointed me ; for, as I told you, I put no faith in you. But even if you succumbed to a natural curiosity, be honest and confess it !"

She looked up steadily into his inquisitorial eyes, and answered :

"I have nothing to confess."

He laid his hand heavily on her shoulder, and his tone was eager, vehement, pleading, tremulous :

"Can you look me in the eye—so—and say that you never put this key in yonder lock ? Edna ! more hangs on your words than you dream of. Be truthful ! as if you were indeed in the presence of the God you worship. I can forgive you for prying into my affairs, but I can not and will not pardon you for trifling with me now."

"I never unlocked the vault ; I never had the key near it but once—about a week ago—when I found the tomb covered with cobwebs, and twisted the key partly into the hole to drive out the spider. I give you my most solemn assurance that I never unlocked it, never saw the interior. Your suspicions are ungenerous and unjust—derogatory to you and insulting to me."

"The proof is at hand, and if I have indeed unjustly suspected you, atonement full and ample shall be made."

Clasping one of her hands so firmly that she could not extricate it, he drew her before the Taj Mahal, and stooping, fitted the key to the lock. There was a dull click as he turned it, but even then he paused and scrutinized her face. It was flushed, and wore a proud, defiant, grieved look ; his own was colorless as the marble that reflected it, and she felt the heavy, rapid beating of his blood, and saw the cords thickening on his brow.

" If you have faithfully kept your promise, there will be an explosion when I open the vault."

Slowly he turned the key a second time ; and as the arched door opened and swung back on its golden hinges, there was a flash and sharp report from a pistol within.

Edna started involuntarily notwithstanding the warning, and clung to his arm an instant, but he took no notice of her whatever. His fingers relaxed their iron grasp of hers, his hand dropped to his side, and leaning forward, he bowed his head on the marble dome of the little temple. How long he stood there she knew not ; but the few moments seemed to her interminable as she silently watched his motionless figure.

He was so still, that finally she conjectured he might possibly have fainted from some cause unknown to her ; and averse though she was to addressing him, she said timidly :

" Mr. Murray, are you ill ? Give me the key of the door and I will bring you some wine."

There was no answer, and in alarm she put her hand on his.

Tightly he clasped it, and drawing her suddenly close to his side, said without raising his face :

" Edna Earl, I have been ill—for years—but I shall be better henceforth. O child ! child ! your calm, pure, guileless soul can not comprehend the blackness and dreariness of mine. Better that you should lie down now in death, with all the unfolded freshness of your life gathered in your grave, than live to know the world as I have proved it. For many years I have lived without hope or trust or faith in any thing—in any body. To-night I stand here lacking sympathy with or respect for my race, and my confidence in human nature was dead ; but, child, you have galvanized the corpse."

Again the mournful music of his voice touched her heart, and she felt her tears rising as she answered in a low, hesitating tone :

"It was not death, Mr. Murray, it was merely syn-cope and this is a healthful reaction from disease."

"No, it will not last. It is but an *ignis fatuus* that will decoy to deeper gloom and darker morasses. I have swept and garnished, and the seven other devils will dwell with me forever! My child, I have tempted you, and you stood firm. Forgive my suspicions. Twenty years hence, if you are so luckless as to live that long, you will not wonder that I doubted you, but that my doubt proved unjust. This little vault contains no skeleton, no state secrets; only a picture and a few jewels, my will, and the history of a wrecked, worthless, utterly ruined life. Perhaps if you continue true, and make my mother happy, I may put all in your hands some day, when I die; and then you will not wonder at my aimless, hopeless, useless life. One thing I wish to say now, if at any time you need as-sistance of any kind—if you are troubled—come to me. I am not quite so selfish as the world paints me, and even if I seem rude and harsh, do not fear to come to me. You have conferred a favor on me, and I do not like to remain in anybody's debt. Make me repay you as soon as possible."

"I am afraid, sir, we never can be friends."

"Why not?"

"Because you have no confidence in me, and I would much sooner go for sympathy to one of your bronze monsters yonder on the doorsteps, than to you. Neither of us likes the other, and consequently a sham cordiality would be intolerably irksome. I shall not be here much longer; but while we are in the same house, I trust no bitter or unkind feelings will be en-tertained. I thank you, sir, for your polite offer of as-sistance, but hope I shall soon be able to maintain myself without burdening your mother any longer."

"How long have you burdened her?"

"Ever since that night when I was picked up lame and helpless, and placed in her kind hands."

"I should like to know whether you really love my mother?"

"Next to the memory of my grandfather, I love her and Mr. Hammond ; and I feel that my gratitude is beyond expression. There, your mother is coming! I hear the carriage. Shall I tell her you are here?"

Without raising his face, he took the key of the door from his pocket, and held it toward her. "No ; I will meet her in her own room."

Edna hastened to the library, and throwing herself into a chair, tried to collect her thoughts and reflect upon what had passed in the " Egyptian Museum."

Very soon Mrs. Murray's cry of joyful surprise rang through the house, and tears of sympathy rose to Edna's eyes as fancy pictured the happy meeting in the neighboring room. Notwithstanding the strong antipathy to Mr. Murray which she had assiduously cultivated, and despite her conviction that he held in derision the religious faith, to which she clung so tenaciously, she was now disquieted and pained to discover that his bronzed face possessed an attraction —an indescribable fascination—which she had found nowhere else. In striving to analyze the interest she was for the first time conscious of feeling, she soothed herself with the belief that it arose from curiosity concerning his past life, and sympathy for his evident misanthropy. It was in vain that she endeavored to fix her thoughts on a book ; his eyes met hers on every page, and when the bell summoned her to a late supper, she was glad to escape from her own confused reflections.

Mrs. Murray and her son were standing on the rug before the grate, and as Edna entered, the former held out her hand.

" Have you seen my son? Come and congratulate me." She kissed the girl's forehead, and continued: " St. Elmo, has she not changed astonishingly? Would you have known her had you met her away from home?"

" I should certainly have known her under all circumstances."

He did not look at her, but resumed the conversa-

tion with his mother which her entrance had interrupted, and during supper Edna could scarcely realize that the cold, distant man, who took no more notice
of her than of one of the salt cellars, was the same
whom she had left leaning over the Taj. Not the
faintest trace of emotion lingered on the dark, stony
features, over which occasionally flickered the light of
a sarcastic smile, as he briefly outlined the course of
his wanderings; and now that she could, without
being observed, study his countenance, she saw that he
looked much older, more worn and haggard and hopeless, than when last at home, and that the thick, curling hair that clung in glosssy rings to his temples was
turning grey.

When they rose from the table, Mrs. Murray took
an exquisite bouquet from the mantelpiece and said :

"Edna, I was requested to place this in your hands,
as a token of the regard and remembrance of your
friend and admirer, Gordon Leigh, who charged me to
assure you that your absence spoiled his enjoyment of
the day. As he seemed quite inconsolable because of
your non-attendance, I promised that you should ride
with him to-morrow afternoon."

As Edna glanced up to receive the flowers, she met
the merciless gaze she so much dreaded, and in her
confusion let the bouquet fall on the carpet. Mr.
Murray picked it up, inhaled the fragrance, rearranged
some of the geranium leaves that had been crushed,
and, smiling bitterly all the while, bowed, and put it
securely in her hand.

"Edna, you have no other engagement for to-
morrow?"

"Yes, madam, I have promised to spend it with Mr.
Hammond."

"Then you must excuse yourself, for I will not have
Gordon disappointed again."

Too much annoyed to answer, Edna left the room,
but paused in the hall and beckoned to Mrs. Murray,
who instantly joined her.

"Of course, you will not have prayers to-night, as Mr. Murray has returned?"

"For that very reason I want to have them, to make a public acknowledgment of my gratitude that my son has been restored to me. Oh! if he would only consent to be present!"

"It is late, and he will probably plead fatigue."

"Leave that with me, and when I ring the bell, come to the library."

The orphan went to her room and diligently copied an essay which she intended to submit to Mr. Hammond for criticism on the following day; and as the comparative merits of the Solonian and Lycurgan codes constituted her theme, she soon became absorbed by Grecian politics, and was only reminded of the events of the evening, when the muezzin bell sounded, calling the household to prayer.

She laid down her pen and hurried to the library, whither Mrs. Murray had enticed her son, who was standing before one of the bookcases, looking over the table of contents of a new scientific work. The servants came in and ranged themselves near the door, and suddenly Mrs. Murray said:

"You must take my place to-night, Edna; I can not read aloud."

The orphan looked up appealingly, but an imperative gesture silenced her, and she sat down before the table, bewildered and frightened. Mr. Murray glanced around the room, and with a look of wrath and scorn threw down the book and turned toward the door; but his mother's hand seized his—

"My son, for my sake, do not go! Out of respect for me, remain this first evening of your return. For my sake, St. Elmo!"

He frowned, shook off her hands, and strode to the door; then reconsidered the matter, came back, and stood at the fireplace, leaning his elbow on the mantel, looking gloomily at the coals.

Although painfully embarrassed as she took her seat and prepared to conduct the services in his pres-

ence, Edna felt a great calm steal over her spirit when
she opened the Bible and read her favorite chapter,
the fourteenth of St. John.

Her sweet, flexible voice, gradually losing its tremor,
rolled soothingly through the room ; and when she
knelt and repeated the prayer selected for the occasion—a prayer of thanks for the safe return of a traveller to the haven of home—her tone was full of pathos
and an earnestness that strangely stirred the proud
heart of the wanderer as he stood there, looking
through his fingers at her uplifted face, and listening to
the first prayer that had reached his ears for nearly
nineteen weary years of sin and scoffing.

When Edna rose from her knees he had left the
room, and she heard his swift steps echoing drearily
through the rotundo.

CHAPTER XII.

" I DO not wish to interrupt you. There is certainly room enough in this library for both, and my entrance need not prove the signal for your departure."

Mr. Murray closed the door as he came in, and walking up to the bookcases, stood carefully examining the titles of the numerous volumes. It was a cold, dismal morning, and sobbing wintry winds and the ceaseless pattering of rain made the outer world seem dreary in comparison with the genial atmosphere and the ruddy glow of the cosy, luxurious library, where choice exotics breathed their fragrance and early hyacinths exhaled their rich perfume. In the centre of the morocco-covered table stood a tall glass bowl, filled with white camellias, and from its scalloped edges drooped a fringe of scarlet fuchsias; while near the window was a china statuette, in whose daily adornment Edna took unwearied interest. It was a lovely Flora, whose slender fingers held aloft small tulip-shaped vases, into which fresh blossoms were inserted every morning. The head was so arranged as to contain water, and thus preserve the wreath of natural flowers which crowned the goddess. To-day golden crocuses nestled down on the streaming hair, and purple pansies filled the fairy hands, while the tiny, rosy feet sank deep in the cushion of fine, green mosses, studded with double violets.

Edna had risen to leave the room when the master of the house entered, but at his request resumed her seat and continued reading.

After searching the shelves unavailingly, he glanced over his shoulder and asked :

"Have you seen my copy of De Guérin's 'Centaur' anywhere about the house? I had it a week ago."

"I beg your pardon, sir, for causing such a fruitless search; here is the book. I picked it up on the front steps, where you were reading a few afternoons since, and it opened at a passage that attracted my attention."

She closed the volume and held it toward him, but he waved it back.

"Keep it if it interests you. I have read it once, and merely wished to refer to a particular passage. Can you guess what sentence most frequently recurs to me? If so, read it to me."

He drew a chair close to the hearth and lighted his cigar.

Hesitatingly Edna turned the leaves.

"I am afraid, sir, that my selection would displease you."

"I will risk it, as, notwithstanding your flattering opinion to the contrary, I am not altogether so unreasonable as to take offense at a compliance with my own request."

Still she shrank from the task he imposed, and her fingers toyed with the scarlet fuchsias; but after eyeing her for a while, he leaned forward and pushed the glass bowl beyond her reach.

"Edna, I am waiting."

"Well, then, Mr. Murray, I should think that these two passages would impress you with peculiar force."

Raising the book she read with much emphasis:

"Thou pursuest after wisdom, O Melampus! which is the science of the will of the gods; *and thou roamest from people to people, like a mortal driven by the destinies.* In the times when I kept my night-watches before the caverns, I have sometimes believed that I was about to surprise the thoughts of the sleeping Cybele, and that the mother of the gods, betrayed by her dreams, would let fall some of her secrets. But I have never yet made out more than sounds which faded away in the murmur of night, of words inarticulate as the bubbling of the rivers.

*   *   *   *   *   *

"Seekest thou to know the gods, O Macareus! and from what source men, animals, and the elements of the universal fire have their origin? The aged ocean, the father of all things, keeps locked within his own breast these secrets; and the nymphs who stand around sing as they weave their eternal dance before him, to cover any sound which might escape from his lips, half opened by slumber. Mortals dear to the gods for their virtue have received from their hands lyres to give delight to man, or the seeds of new plants to make him rich, but from their inexorable lips—nothing!"

"Mr. Murray, am I correct in my conjecture?"

"Quite correct," he answered, smiling grimly.

Taking the book from her hand he threw it on the table, and tossed his cigar into the grate, adding in a defiant, challenging tone:

"The mantle of Solomon did not fall at Le Cayla on the shoulders of Maurice de Guérin. After all, he was a wretched hypochondriac, and a tinge of *le cahier vert* doubtless crept into his eyes."

"Do you forget, sir, that he said, 'When one is a wanderer, one feels that one fulfills the true condition of humanity'? and that among his last words are these, 'The stream of travel is full of delight. Oh! who will set me adrift on this Nile?'"

"Pardon me if I remind you, *par parenthèse*, of the preliminary and courteous *En garde!* which should be pronounced before a thrust. De Guérin felt starved in Languedoc, and no wonder! But had he penetrated every nook and cranny of the habitable globe, and traversed the vast zaarahs which science accords the universe, he would have died at last as hungry as Ugolino. I speak advisedly, for the true Io gad-fly, *ennui*, has stung me from hemisphere to hemisphere, across tempestuous oceans, scorching deserts, and icy mountain ranges. I have faced alike the bourrans of the steppes and the Samieli of Shamo, and the result of my vandal life is best epitomized in those grand but grim words of Bossuet : '*On trouve au fond de tout le vide et le néant.*' Nineteen years ago, to satisfy my hunger, I set out to hunt the daintiest food this world could furnish, and, like other fools, have learned finally, that life is but a huge, mellow, golden Ösher, that mockingly sifts its bitter dust upon our eager lips. Ah! truly, *on trouve au fond de tout le vide et le néant !*"

" Mr. Murray, if you insist upon your bitter Ösher simile, why shut your eyes to the palpable analogy suggested? Naturalists assert that the Solanum, or apple of Sodom, contains in its normal state neither dust nor ashes, unless it is punctured by an insect (the Tenthredo), which converts the whole of the inside into dust, leaving nothing but the rind entire, without any loss of color. Human life is as fair and tempting as the fruit of ' Ain Jidy,' till stung and poisoned by the Tenthredo of sin.''

All conceivable *suaviter in modo* characterized his mocking countenance and tone, as he inclined his haughty head and asked :

" Will you favor me by lifting on the point of your dissecting-knife this stinging sin of mine to which you refer? The noxious brood swarm so teasingly about my ears that they deprive me of your cool, clear, philosophic discrimination. Which particular Tenthredo of the buzzing swarm around my spoiled apple of life would you advise me to select for my *anathema maranatha ?*"

" Of your history, sir, I am entirely ignorant; and even if I were not, I should not presume to levy a tax upon it in discussions with you ; for, however vulnerable you may possibly be, I regard an *argumentum ad hominem* as the weakest weapon in the armory of dialectics—a weapon too often dipped in the venom of personal malevolence. I merely gave expression to my belief that miserable, useless lives are sinful lives; that when God framed the world, and called the human race into it, he made most munificent provision for all healthful hunger, whether physical, intellectual, or moral; and that it is a morbid, diseased, distorted nature that wears out its allotted years on earth in bitter carping and blasphemous dissatisfaction. The Greeks recognized this immemorial truth—wrapped it in classic traditions, and the myth of Tantalus constituted its swaddling-clothes. You are a scholar, Mr. Murray; look back and analyze the derivation and significance of that fable. Tantalus, the son of Pluto, or Wealth, was, according to Pindar, 'a wanderer from happiness,' and the name represents a man abounding in wealth, but whose appetite was so insatiable, even at the ambrosial feast of the gods, that it ultimately doomed him to eternal unsatisfied thirst and hunger in Tartarus. The same truth crops out in the legend of Midas, who found himself starving while his touch converted all things to gold."

"Doubtless you have arrived at the charitable conclusion that, as I am endowed with all the amiable idiosyncrasies of ancient cynics, I shall inevitably join the snarling Dives Club in Hades, and swell the howling chorus. Probably I shall not disappoint your kind and eminently Christian expectations; nor will I deprive you of the gentle satisfaction of hissing across the gulf of perdition, which will then divide us, that *summum bonum* of feminine felicity, 'I told you so!'"

The reckless mockery of his manner made Edna shiver, and a tremor crept across her beautiful lips as she answered sadly:

"You torture my words into an interpretation of which I never dreamed, and look upon all things through the distorting lenses of your own moodiness. It is worse than useless for us to attempt an amicable discussion, for your bitterness never slumbers, your suspicions are ever on the *qui vive*."

She rose, but he quickly laid his hand on her shoulder, and pressed her back into the chair.

"You will be so good as to sit still, and hear me out. I have a right to all my charming, rose-colored views of this world. I have gone to and fro on the earth.

and life has proved a Barmecide's banquet of just thir-
ty-eight years' duration."

" But, sir, you lacked the patience and resolution of
Shacabac, or, like him, you would have finally grasped
the splendid realities. The world must be conquered,
held in bondage to God's law and man's reason, before
we can hope to levy tribute that will support our moral
and mental natures ; and it is only when humanity
finds itself in the inverted order of serfdom to the
world, that it dwarfs its capacities, and even then dies
of famine."

The scornful gleam died out of his eyes, and mournful compassion stole in.

" Ah ! how impetuously youth springs to the battlefield of life ! Hope exorcises the gaunt spectre of defeat, and fancy fingers unwon trophies and fadeless
bays ; but slow-stepping experience, pallid, blood-
stained, spent with toil, lays her icy hand on the rosy
veil that floats before bright, brave, young eyes, and
lo ! the hideous wreck, the bleaching bones, the grinning, ghastly horrors that strew the scene of combat !
No burnished eagles nor streaming banners, neither
spoils of victory nor peans of triumph, only silence and
gloom and death—slow-sailing vultures—and a voiceless desolation ! Oh, child ! if you would find a suitable type of that torn and trampled battlefield—the
human heart—when vice and virtue, love and hate, revenge and remorse, have wrestled fiercely for the mastery—go back to your Tacitus, and study there the dismal picture of that lonely Teutoburgium, where Varus
and his legions went down in the red burial of battle !
You talk of ' conquering the world—holding it in bondage !' What do you know of its perils and subtle
temptations—of the glistening quicksands whose
smooth lips already gape to engulf you ? The very
vilest fiend in hell might afford to pause and pity your
delusion ere turning to machinations destined to rouse
you rudely from your silly dreams. Ah! you remind
me of a little innocent, happy child, playing on some

shining beach, when the sky is quiet, the winds are
hushed, and all things wrapped in rest, save

> ' The water lapping on the crag,
>   And the long ripple washing in the reeds '—

a fair, fearless child, gathering polished pearly shells
with which to build fairy palaces, and suddenly, as she
catches the mournful murmur of the immemorial sea,
that echoes in the flushed and folded chambers of the
stranded shells, her face pales with awe and wonder—
the childish lips part, the childish eyes are strained to
discover the mystery ; and while the whispering monotone admonishes of howling storms and sinking argo-
sies, she smiles and listens, sees only the glowing car-
mine of the fluted cells, hears only the magic music of
the sea sirens—and the sky blackens, the winds leap to
their track of ruin, the great deep rises wrathful and
murderous, bellowing for victims, and Cyclone reigns !
Thundering waves sweep over and bear away the frail
palaces that decked the strand, and even while the
shell symphony still charms the ear, the child's rosy
feet are washed from their sandy resting-place ; she is
borne on howling billows far out to a lashed and maddened main, strewn with human drift ; and numb with
horror she sinks swiftly to a long and final rest among
purple algæ ! Even so, Edna, you stop your ears with
shells, and my warning falls like snow-flakes that melt
and vanish on the bosom of a stream.

" No, sir, I am willing to be advised. Against what
would you warn me ?"

" The hollowness of life, the fatuity of your hopes,
the treachery of that human nature of which you speak
so tenderly and reverently. So surely as you put
faith in the truth and nobility of humanity, you will
find it as soft-lipped and vicious as Paolo Orsini, who
folded his wife, Isabella de Medici, most lovingly in
his arms, and while he tenderly pressed her to his
heart, slipped a cord around her neck and strangled
her."

"I know, sir, that human nature is weak, selfish, sinful—that such treacherous monsters as Ezzolino and the Visconti have stained the annals of our race with blood-blotches, which the stream of time will never efface ; but the law of compensation operates here as well as in other departments, and brings to light a '*fidus Achates*' and Antoninus. I believe that human nature is a curious amalgam of meanness, malice and magnanimity, and that an earnest, loving Christian charity, is the only safe touchstone, and furnishes (if you will tolerate the simile) the only elective affinity in moral chemistry. Because ingots are not dug out of the earth, is it not equally unwise and ungrateful to ridicule and denounce the hopeful, patient, tireless laborers who handle the alloy and ultimately disintegrate the precious metal ? Even if the world were bankrupt in morality and religion—which, thank God, it is not—one grand shining example, like Mr. Hammond, whose unswerving consistency, noble charity, and sublime unselfishness all concede and revere, ought to leaven the mass of sneering cynics, and win them to a belief in their capacity for rising to pure, holy, almost perfect lives."

"Spare me a repetition of the rhapsodies of Madame Guyon ! I am not surprised that such a novice as you prove yourself should, in the stereotyped style of orthodoxy, swear by the hoary Tartuffe, that hypocritical wolf, Allan Hammond——"

"Stop, Mr. Murray ! You must not, shall not use such language in my presence concerning one whom I love and revere above all other human beings ! How dare you malign that noble Christian, whose lips daily lift your name to God, praying for pardon and for peace ? Oh ! how ungrateful, how unworthy you are of his affection and his prayers !"

She had interrupted him with an imperious wave of her hand, and stood regarding him with an expression of indignation and detestation.

"I neither possess nor desire his affection or his prayers."

"Sir, you know that you do not deserve, but you most certainly have both."

"How did you obtain your information?"

"Accidentally, when he was so surprised and grieved to hear that you had started on your long voyage to Oceanica."

"He availed himself of that occasion to acquaint you with all my heinous sins, my youthful crimes and follies, my——"

"No, sir! he told me nothing, except that you no longer loved him as in your boyhood; that you had become estranged from him; and then he wept, and added, ' I love him still; I shall pray for him as long as I live.' "

"Impossible! You can not deceive me! In the depths of his heart he hates and curses me. Even a brooding dove—pshaw! Allan Hammond is but a man, and it would be unnatural—utterly impossible that he could still think kindly of his old pupil. Impossible!"

Mr. Murray rose and stood before the grate with his face averted, and his companion seized the opportunity to say in a low, determined tone:

"Of the causes that induced your estrangement I am absolutely ignorant. Nothing has been told me, and it is a matter about which I have conjectured little. But, sir, I have seen Mr. Hammond every day for four years, and I know what I say when I tell you that he loves you as well as if you were his own son. Moreover, he——"

"Hush! you talk of what you do not understand. Believe in him if you will, but be careful not to chant his praises in my presence; not to parade your credulity before my eyes, if you do not desire that I shall disenchant you. Just now you are duped—so was I at your age. Your judgment slumbers, experience is in its swaddling-clothes; but I shall bide my time, and the day will come ere long when these hymns of hero-worship shall he hushed, and you stand clearer-eyed, darker-hearted, before the mouldering altar of your god of clay."

"From such an awakening may God preserve me! Even if our religion were not divine, I should clasp to my heart the system and the faith that make Mr. Hammond's life serene and sublime.   Oh! that I may be 'duped' into that perfection of character which makes his example beckon me ever onward and upward.   If you have no gratitude, no reverence left, at least remember the veneration with which I regard him, and do not in my hearing couple his name with sneers and insults."

"'Ephraim is joined to idols; let him alone!'" muttered the master of the house, with one of those graceful, mocking bows that always disconcerted the orphan.

She was nervously twisting Mr. Leigh's ring around her finger, and as it was too large, it slipped off, rung on the hearth, and rolled to Mr. Murray's feet.

Picking it up he examined the emerald, and repeating the inscription, asked:

"Do you understand these words?"

"I only know that they have been translated, 'Peace be with thee, or upon thee.'"

"How came Gordon Leigh's ring on your hand? Has Tartuffe's Hebrew scheme succeeded so soon and so thoroughly?"

"I do not understand you, Mr. Murray."

"Madame ma mère proves an admirable ally in this clerical matchmaker's deft hands, and Gordon's pathway is widened and weeded.   Happy Gordon! blessed with such able coadjutors!"

The cold, sarcastic glitter of his eyes wounded and humilated the girl, and her tone was haughty and defiant—

"You deal in innuendoes which I cannot condescend to notice.   Mr. Leigh is my friend, and gave me this ring as a birthday present.   As your mother advised me to accept it, and indeed placed it on my finger, her sanction should certainly exempt me from your censure."

"Censure! Pardon me! It is no part of my business; but I happen to know something of gem symbols, and must be allowed to suggest that this selection is scarcely *comme il faut* for a betrothal ring."

Edna's face crimsoned, and the blood tingled to her fingers' ends.

"As it was never intended as such, your carping criticism loses its point."

He stood with the jewel between his thumb and forefinger, eyeing her fixedly, and on his handsome features shone a smile, treacherous and chilling as arctic snowblink.

"Pliny's injunction to lapidaries to spare the smooth surface of emeralds seems to have been forgotten when this ring was fashioned. It was particularly unkind, nay, cruel to put it on the hand of a woman, who of course must and will follow the example of all her sex, and go out fishing most diligently in the matrimonial sea; for if you have chanced to look into gem history, you will remember what befell the fish on the coast of Cyprus, where the emerald eyes of the marble lion glared down so mercilessly through the nets, that the fishermen could catch nothing until they removed the jewels that constituted the eyes of the lion. Do you recollect the account?"

"No, sir, I never read it."

"Indeed! How deplorably your education has been neglected! I thought your adored Dominie Sampson down yonder at the parsonage was teaching you a prodigious amount?"

"Give me my ring, Mr. Murray, and I will leave you."

"Shall I not enlighten you on the subject of emeralds?"

"Thank you, sir, I believe not, as what I have already heard does not tempt me to prosecute the subject."

"You think me insufferably presumptuous?"

"That is a word which I should scarcely be justified in applying to you."

"You regard me as meddlesome and tyrannical?"

She shook her head.

"I generally prefer to receive answers to my questions. Pray, what do you consider me?"

She hesitated a moment, and said sadly and gently:

"Mr. Murray, is it generous in you to question me thus in your own house?"

"I do not claim to be generous, and the world would indignantly defend me from such an imputation! Generous? On the contrary, I declare explicitly that, unlike some 'whited supulchres' of my acquaintance, I do not intend to stand labeled with patent virtues! Neither do I parade *mezuzoth* on my doors. I humbly beg you to recollect that I am not a carefully-printed perambulating advertisement of Christianity."

Raising her face, Edna looked steadfastly at him, and pain, compassion, shuddering dread filled her soft, sad eyes.

"Well, you are reading me. What is the verdict?"

A long, heavily-drawn sigh was the only response.

"Will you be good enough to reply to my questions?"

"No, Mr. Murray. In lieu of perpetual strife and biting words, let there be silence between us. We can not be friends, and it would be painful to wage war here under your roof; consequently, I hope to disarm your hostility by assuring you that in future I shall not attempt to argue with you, shall not pick up the verbal gauntlets you seem disposed to throw down to me. Surely, sir, if not generous you are at least sufficiently courteous to abstain from attacks which you have been notified will not be resisted?"

"You wish me to understand that hereafter I, the owner and ruler of this establishment, shall on no account presume to address my remarks to Aaron Hunt's grandchild?"

"My words were very clear, Mr. Murray, and I

meant what I said, and said what I meant. But one thing I wish to add: while I remain here, if at any time I can aid or serve you, Aaron Hunt's grandchild will most gladly do so. I do not flatter myself that you will ever require or accept my assistance in anything, nevertheless I would cheerfully render it should occasion arise."

He bowed and returned the emerald, and Edna turned to leave the library.

"Before you go, examine this bauble."

He took from his vest pocket a velvet case containing a large ring, which he laid in the palm of her hand.

It was composed of an oval jacinth, with a splendid scarlet fire leaping out as the light shone on it, and the diamonds that clustered around it were very costly and brilliant. There was no inscription, but upon the surface of the jacinth was engraved a female head crowned with oak leaves, among which serpents writhed and hissed, and just beneath the face grinned a dog's head. The small but exquisitely carved human face was savage, sullen, sinister, and fiery rays seemed to dart from the relentless eyes.

"Is it a Medusa?"

"No."

"It is certainly very beautiful, but I do not recognize the face. Interpret for me."

"It is Hecate, Brimo, Empusa—all phases of the same malignant power; and it remains a mere matter of taste which of the titles you select. I call it Hecate."

"I have never seen you wear it."

"You never will."

"It is exceedingly beautiful."

Edna held it toward the grate, flashed the flame now on this side, now on that, and handed it back to the owner.

"Edna, I bought this ring in Naples, intending to ask your acceptance of it, in token of my appreciation of your care of that little gold key, provided I found

you trustworthy. After your pronunciamento uttered
a few minutes since, I presume I may save myself the
trouble of offering it to you. Beside, Gordon might
object to having his emerald overshadowed by my
matchless jacinth. Of course, your tender conscience
will veto the thought of your wearing it?"

"I thank you, Mr. Murray; the ring is, by far, the
most beautiful I have ever seen, but I certainly can
not accept it."

"*Bithus contra Bacchium!*" exclaimed Mr. Murray,
with a short, mirthless laugh that made his companion
shrink back a few steps.

Holding the ring at arm's length above his head, he
continued:

"To the 'infernal flames,' your fit type, I devote
you, my costly Queen of Samothrace!"

Leaning over the grate, he dropped the jewel in the
glowing coals.

"Oh, Mr. Murray! save it from destruction!"

She seized the tongs and sprang forward, but he put
out his arm and held her back.

"Stand aside, if you please. Cleopatra quaffed
liquid pearl in honor of Antony, Nero shivered his
precious crystal goblets, and Suger pounded up
sapphires to color the windows of old St. Denis!
Chacun à son gout! If I choose to indulge myself in
a diamond cremation in honor of my tutelary goddess
Brimo, who has the right to expostulate? True, such
costly amusements have been rare since the days of
the 'Cyranides' and the 'Seven Seals' of Hermes
Trismegistus. See what a tawny, angry glare leaps
from my royal jacinth! Old Hecate holds high carnival down there in her congenial flames."

He stood with one arm extended to bar Edna's approach, the other rested on the mantel; and a laughing, reckless demon looked out of his eyes, which
were fastened on the fire.

Before the orphan could recover from her sorrowful amazement the library door opened, and Henry
looked in.

"Mr. Leigh is in the parlor, and asked for Miss Edna."

Perplexed, irresolute, and annoyed, Edna stood still, watching the red coals; and after a brief silence, Mr. Murray smiled, and turned to look at her.

"Pray, do not let me detain you, and rest assured that I understand your decree. You have entrenched yourself in impenetrable silence, and hung out your banner, '*noli me tangere!*' Withdraw your pickets; I shall attempt neither seige nor escalade. Good morning. Leave my De Guérin on the table; it will be at your disposal after to-day."

He stooped to light a cigar, and she walked away to her own room.

As the door closed behind her, he laughed and reiterated the favorite proverb that often crossed his lips '*Bithus contra Bacchium!*'

CHAPTER XIII.

THE darling scheme of authorship had seized upon
Edna's mind with a tenacity that conquered and
expelled all other purposes, and though timidity and
a haunting dread of the failure of the experiment
prompted her to conceal the matter, even from her
beloved pastor, she pondered it in secret, and bent
every faculty to its successful accomplishment. Her
veneration for books—the great eleemosynary gran-
aries of human knowledge to which the world resorts
—extended to those who created them ; and her
imagination invested authors with peculiar sanctity, as
the real hierophants anointed with the chrism of truth.
The glittering pinnacle of consecrated and successful
authorship seemed to her longing gaze as sublime, and
well-nigh as inaccessible, as the everlasting and
untrodden Himalayan solitudes appear to some curious
child of Thibet or Nepaul ; who gamboling among
pheasants and rhododendrons, shades her dazzled eyes
with her hand, and looks up awe-stricken and wondering at the ice-domes and snow-minarets of lonely
Deodunga, earth's loftiest and purest altar, nimbused
with the dawning and the dying light of the day.
There were times when the thought of presenting herself as a candidate for admission into the band of
literary exoterics seemed to Edna unpardonably presumptuous, almost sacrilegious, and she shrank back,
humbled and abashed ; for writers were teachers, inter-
preters, expounders, discoverers, or creators—and
what could she, just stumbling through the alphabet
of science and art, hope to donate to her race that

would ennoble human motives or elevate aspirations?
Was she, an unknown and inexperienced girl, worthy
to be girded with the ephod that draped so royally the
Levites of literature? Had God's own hand set the
Urim and Thummim of Genius in her soul? Above
all, was she mitred with the plate of pure gold—" Holiness into the Lord?"

Solemnly and prayerfully she weighed the subject,
and having finally resolved to make one attempt, she
looked trustingly to heaven for aid and went vigorously to work.

To write *currente calamo* for the mere pastime of
author and readers, without aiming to inculcate some
regenerative principle, or to photograph some valuable phase of protean truth, was in her estimation
ignoble; for her high standard demanded that all
books should be to a certain extent didactic, wandering like evangels among the people, and making some
man, woman, or child happier, or wiser, or better—
more patient or more hopeful—by their utterances.
Believing that every earnest author's mind should
prove a mint, where all valuable ores are collected
from the rich veins of a universe—are cautiously
coined, and thence munificently circulated—she applied herself diligently to the task of gathering from
various sources the *data* required for her projected
work : a vindication of the unity of mythologies. The
vastness of the cosmic field she was now compelled to
traverse, the innumerable ramifications of polytheistic
and monotheistic creeds, necessitated unwearied research, as she rent asunder the superstitious veils
which various nations and successive epochs had woven
before the shining features of truth. To-day peering
into the golden Gardens of the Sun at Cuzco; to-
morrow clambering over Thibet glaciers, to find the
mystic lake of Yamuna ; now delighted to recognize
in Teoyamiqui (the wife of the Aztec God of War) the
unmistakable features of Scandinavian Valkyrias ; and
now surprised to discover the Greek Fates sitting
under the Norse tree Ygdrasil, deciding the destinies

of mortals, and calling themselves Nornas; she spent
her days in pilgrimages to mouldering shrines, and
midnight often found her groping in the classic dust
of extinct systems. Having once grappled with her
theme, she wrestled as obstinately as Jacob for the
blessing of a successful solution, and in order to popu-
larize a subject bristling with recondite archaisms and
philologic problems, she cast it in the mould of fiction.
The information and pleasure which she had derived
from the perusal of Vaughan's delightful Hours with
the Mystics, suggested the idea of adopting a similar
plan for her own book, and investing it with the
additional interest of a complicated plot and more
numerous characters. To avoid anachronisms, she
endeavored to treat the religions of the world in their
chronologic sequence, and resorted to the expedient
of introducing pagan personages. A fair young
priestess of the temple of Neith, in the sacred city of
Sais—where people of all climes collected to witness
the festival of lamps—becoming skeptical of the
miraculous attributes of the statues she had been
trained to serve and worship, and impelled by an
earnest love of truth to seek a faith that would satisfy
her reason and purify her heart, is induced to question
minutely the religious tenets of travellers who visited
the temple, and thus familiarized herself with all existing creeds and hierarchies. The lore so carefully
garnered is finally analyzed, classified, and inscribed on
papyrus. The delineation of scenes and sanctuaries
in different latitudes, from Lhasa to Copan, gave full
exercise to Edna's descriptive power, but imposed
much labor in the departments of physical geography
and architecture.

Verily! an ambitious literary programme for a girl
over whose head scarcely eighteen years had hung
their dripping drab wintry skies, and pearly summer
clouds.

One March morning, as Edna entered the breakfast-room, she saw unusual gravity printed on Mrs.
Murray's face; and observing an open letter on the

table, conjectured the cause of her changed countenance. A moment after the master came in, and as he seated himself his mother said :

" St. Elmo, your cousin Estelle's letter contains bad news. Her father is dead ; the estate is wretchedly insolvent ; and she is coming to reside with us."

" Then I am off for Hammerfest and the midnight sun ! Who the deuce invited her I should like to know ?"

" Remember she is my sister's child ; she has no other home, and I am sure it is very natural that she should come to me, her nearest relative, for sympathy and protection."

" Write to her by return mail that you will gladly allow her three thousand a year, provided she ensconces herself under some other roof than this."

" Impossible ! I could not wound her so deeply."

" You imagine that she entertains a most tender and profound regard for both of us ?"

" Certainly, my son ; we have every reason to believe that she does."

Leaning back in his chair, St. Elmo laughed.

" I should really enjoy stumbling upon something that would overtax your most marvellous and indefinitely extensible credulity ! When Estelle Harding becomes an inmate of this house I shall pack my valise, and start to Tromso ! She approaches like Discord, uninvited, armed with an apple or a dagger. I am perfectly willing to share my fortune with her, but I'll swear I would rather prowl for a month through the plague-stricken district of Constantinople than see her domesticated here ! You tried the experiment when she was a child, and we fought and scratched as indefatigably as those two amiable young Theban bullies, who are so often cited as scarecrows for quarrelsome juveniles. Of course, we shall renew the battle at sight."

" But, my dear son, there are claims urged by natural affection which it is impossible to ignore. Poor Estelle is very desolate, and has a right to our sympathy and love."

"Poor Estelle! *Hæredipetæ!* The frailties of old Rome survive her virtues and her ruins!"

Mr. Murray laughed again, beat a tattoo with his fork on the edge of his plate, and, rising, left the room.

Mrs. Murray looked puzzled, and said:

"Edna, do you know what he meant? He often amuses himself by mystifying me, and I will not gratify him by asking an explanation."

"*Hæredipetæ* were legacy-hunters in Rome, where their sycophantic devotion to people of wealth furnished a constant theme for satire."

Mrs. Murray sighed heavily, and the orphan asked:

"When do you expect your niece?"

"Day after to-morrow. I have not seen her for some years, but report says she is very fascinating, and even St. Elmo, who met her in Europe, admits that she is handsome. As you heard him say just now, they formerly quarreled most outrageously and shamefully, and he took an unaccountable aversion to her; but I trust all juvenile reminiscences will vanish when they know each other better. My dear, I have several engagements for to-day, and I must rely upon you to superintend the arrangement of Estelle's room. She will occupy the one next to yours. See that everything is in order. You know Hagar is sick, and the other servants are careless."

Sympathy for Miss Harding's recent and severe affliction prepared Edna's heart to receive her cordially, and the fact that an irreconcilable feud existed between the stranger and St. Elmo, induced the orphan to hope that she might find a congenial companion in the expected visitor.

On the afternoon of her arrival, Edna leaned eagerly forward to catch a glimpse of her countenance, and as she threw back her long mourning-vail, and received her aunt's affectionate greeting, the first impression was, "How exceedingly handsome—how commanding she is!" But a few minutes later, when Mrs. Murray

introduced them, and the stranger's keen, bright, restless eyes fell upon the orphan's face, the latter drew
back, involuntarily repelled, and a slight shiver crept
over her, for an unerring instinctive repulsion told her
they could never be friends.

Estelle Harding was no longer young ; years had
hardened the outline of her features, and imparted a
certain staidness or fixedness to her calm countenance,
where strong feeling or passionate impulse was never
permitted to slip the elegant mask of polished suavity.
She was surprisingly like Mrs. Murray, but not one
line of her face resembled her cousin's. Fixing her
eyes on Edna, with a cold, almost stern scrutiny more
searching than courteous, she said :

"I was not aware, Aunt Ellen, that you had company in the house."

"I have no company at present, my dear. Edna
resides here. Do you not remember one of my letters
in which I mentioned the child who was injured by
the railroad accident ?"

"True. I expected to see a child, certainly not a
woman."

"She seems merely a child to me. But come up to
your room ; you must be very much fatigued by your
journey."

When they left the sitting-room Edna sat down in
one corner of the sofa, disappointed and perplexed.

"She does not like me, that is patent ; and I certainly do not like her. She is handsome and very
graceful, and quite heartless. There is no inner light
from her soul shining in her eyes ; nothing tender and
loving and kind in their clear depths ; they are cold,
bright eyes, but not soft, winning, womanly eyes.
They might, and doubtless would, hold an angry dog
in check, but never draw a tired, fretful child to lean
its drooping head on her lap. If she really has any
feeling, her eyes should be indicted for slander. I
am sorry I don't like her, and I am afraid we never
shall be nearer each other than touching our finger-
tips."

Such was Edna's unsatisfactory conclusion, and dis-
missing the subject, she picked up a book, and read
until the ladies returned and seated themselves around
the fire.

To Mrs. Murray's great chagrin and mortification
her son had positively declined going to meet his
cousin, had been absent since breakfast, and proved
himself shamefully derelict in the courtesy demanded
of him.   It was almost dark when the quick gallop of
his horse announced his return, and, as he passed the
window on his way to the stables, Edna noticed a
sudden change in Estelle's countenance.   During the
next quarter of an hour her eyes never wandered from
the door, though her head was turned to listen to Mrs.
Murray's remarks.   Soon after, Mr. Murray's rapid
footsteps sounded in the hall, and as he entered she
rose and advanced to meet him.   He held out his
hand, shook hers vigorously, and said, as he dropped
it :

"Mine ancient enemy, declare a truce and quiet my
apprehensions ; for I dreamed last night that, on sight,
we flew at each other's throats, and renewed the san-
guinary scuffles of our juvenile acquaintance.   Most
appallingly vivid is my recollection of a certain scar
here on my left arm, where you set your pearly teeth
some years ago."

"My dear cousin, as I have had no provocation since
I was separated from you, I believe I have grown
harmless and amiable.   How very well you look, St.
Elmo."

"Thank you.   I should like to return the compliment, but facts forbid.   You are thinner than when
we dined together in Paris.   Are you really in love
with that excruciating Brummell of a Count who
danced such indefatigable attendance upon you ?"

"To whom do you allude ?"

"That youth with languishing brown eyes, who
parted his ' hyacinthine tresses ' in the middle of his
head ; whose moustache required Ehrenberg's strongest glasses—and who absolutely believed that Ristori

singled him out of her vast audiences as the most appreciative of her listeners ; who was eternally humming ' Ernani ' and raving about ' Traviata.' Your memory is treacherous—as your conscience ? Well, then, that man, who I once told you reminded me of what Guilleragues is reported to have said about Pelisson, ' that he abused the permission men have to be ugly.' "

" Ah ! you mean poor Victor ! He spent the winter in Seville. I had a letter last week."

" When do you propose to make him my cousin ?"

" Not until I become an inmate of a lunatic asylum."

" Poor wretch ! If he only had courage to sue you for breach of promise, I would, with pleasure, furnish sufficient testimony to convict you and secure him heavy damages ; for I will swear you played *fiancée* to perfection. Your lavish expenditure of affection seemed to me altogether uncalled for, considering the fact that the fish already floundered at your feet."

The reminiscence evidently annoyed her, though her lips smiled, and Edna saw that, while his words were pointed with a sarcasm lost upon herself, it was fully appreciated by his cousin.

" St. Elmo, I am sorry to see that you have not improved one iota; that all your wickedness clings to you like Sinbad's burden."

Standing at his side, she put her hand on his shoulder. As he looked down at her, his lips curled.

" Nevertheless, Estelle, I find a pale ghost of pity for you wandering up and down what was once my heart. After the glorious intoxication of Parisian life, how can you endure the tedium of this dullest of humdrum—this most moral and stupid of all country towns? Little gossip, few flirtations, neither *beaux esprits* nor *bons vivants*—what will become of you ? Now, whatever amusement, edification, or warning you may be able to extract from my society, I here beg permission to express the hope that you will appropriate unsparingly. I shall, with exemplary hospitality, dedicate myself to your service—shall try to make amends for *votre cher* Victor's absence, and

solemnly promise to do everything in my power to
assist you in strangling time, except parting my hair
in the middle of my head, and making love to you.
With these stipulated reservations, command me *ad
libitum.*"

Her face flushed slightly, she withdrew her hand
and sat down.

Taking his favorite position on the rug, with one
hand thrust into his pocket and the other dallying with
his watch-chain, Mr. Murray continued :

" Entire honesty on my part, and a pardonable and
amiable weakness for descanting on the charms of my
native village, compel me to assure you, that, notwithstanding the deprivation of opera and theatre, *bal
masqué* and the Bois de Bologne, I believe you will be
surprised to find that the tone of society here is quite
up to the lofty standard of the ' Society of Arcueil,'
or even the requirements of the Academy of Sciences.
Our pastors are erudite as Abelard, and rigid as Trap-
pists ; our young ladies are learned as that ancient
blue-stocking daughter of Pythagoras, and as pious as
St. Salvia, who never washed her face. For instance,
girls yet in their teens are much better acquainted
with Hebrew than Miriam was, when she sung it on the
shore of the Red Sea (where, by the by, Talmudic tradition says Pharaoh was not drowned), and they will
vehemently contend for the superiority of the Targum
of Onkelos over that on the Hagiographa, ascribed to
one-eyed Joseph of Sora ! You look incredulous, my
fair cousin. Nay, permit me to complete the inven-
tory of the acquirements of your future companions.
They quote fluently from the Megilloth, and will entertain you by fighting over again the battle of the
school of Hillel *versus* the school of Shammai ! Their
attainments in philology reflect discredit on the super-
ficiality of Max Müller ; and if an incidental allusion
is made to archæology, 10 ! they bombard you with a
broadside of authorities, and recondite terminology
that would absolutely make the hair of Lepsius and
Champollion stand on end. I assure you the *savants*

of the Old World would catch their breath with envious amazement, if they could only enjoy the advantage of the conversation of these orthodox and erudite
refugees from the nursery! The unfortunate men of
this community are kept in pitiable terror lest they
commit an anachronism, and if, after a careful recon-
noissance of the slippery ground, they tremblingly
venture an anecdote of Selwyn or Hood, or Beaumar-
chais, they are invariably driven back in confusion by
the inquiry, if they remember this or that *bon mot* uttered at the court of Aurungzebe or of one of the
early Incas! Ah! would I were Moliére to repaint
Les Precieuses Ridicules !"

Although his eyes had never once wandered from
his cousin's face, toward the corner where Edna sat
embroidering some mats, she felt the blood burning in
her cheeks, and forced herself to look up. At that
moment, as he stood in the soft glow of the firelight,
he was handsomer than she had ever seen him ; and
when he glanced swiftly over his shoulder to mark the
effect of his words, their eyes met, and she smiled involuntarily.

"For shame, St. Elmo! I will have you presented
by the grand jury of this county for wholesome defam-
ation of the inhabitants thereof," said his mother,
shaking her finger at him.

Estelle laughed and shrugged her shoulders.

"My poor cousin! how I pity you, and the remainder of the men here, surrounded by such a formidable coterie of blues."

"Believe me, even if their shadows are as blue as
those which I have seen thrown upon the snow of
Eyriks Jökull, in Iceland, where I would have sworn
that every shade cast on the mountain was a blot of
indigo. Sometimes I seriously contemplate erecting
an observatory and telescope, in order to sweep our
sky and render visible what I am convinced exist there
undiscovered—some of those deep blue nebulæ which
Sir John Herschel found in the southern hemisphere !
If the astronomical conjectures be correct, concerning

the possibility of a galaxy of blue stars, a huge cluster
hangs in this neighborhood and furnishes an explanation of the color of the women."

"Henceforth, St. Elmo, the sole study of my life
shall be to forget my alphabet. Miss Earl, do you
understand Hebrew?"

"Oh! no; I have only begun to study it."

"Estelle, it is the popular and fashionable amusement here. Young ladies and young gentlemen form
classes for mutual aid and 'mutual admiration,' while
they clasp hands over the Masora. If Lord Brougham,
and other members of the 'Society for the Diffusion
of Useful Knowledge,' could only have been induced
to investigate the intellectual *status* of the 'rising generation' of our village, there is little room to doubt
that, as they are not deemed advocates for works of
supererogation, they would long ago have appreciated
the expediency of disbanding said society. I imagine
Tennyson is a *clairvoyant*, and was looking at the
young people of this vicinage, when he wrote:

'Knowledge comes, but wisdom lingers.'

Not even egoistic infallible 'Brain Town'—that self-
complacent and pretentious 'Hub,' can show a more
ambitious covey of literary fledgelings!"

"Your random firing seems to produce no confusion
on the part of your game," answered his cousin, withdrawing her gaze from Edna's tranquil features, on
which a half smile still lingered.

He did not seem to hear her words, but his eyebrows
thickened, as he drew a couple of letters from his
pocket and looked at the superscription.

Giving one to his mother, who sat looking over a
newspaper, he crossed the room and silently laid the
other on Edna's lap.

It was post-marked in a distant city and directed in
a gentleman's large, round business handwriting.
The girl's face flushed with pleasure as she broke the

seal, glanced at the signature, and without pausing for a perusal, hastily put the letter into her pocket.

"Who can be writing to you, Edna?" asked Mrs. Murray, when she had finished reading her own letter.

"Oh! doubtless some Syrian scribe has indited a Chaldee *billet-doux*, which she can not spell out without the friendly aid of dictionary and grammar. Permit her to withdraw and decipher it. Meantime here comes Henry to announce dinner, and a plate of soup will strengthen her for her task."

Mr. Murray offered his arm to his cousin, and during dinner he talked constantly, rapidly, brilliantly of men and things abroad; now hurling a sarcasm at Estelle's head, now laughing at his mother's expostulations, and studiously avoiding any further notice of Edna, who was never so thoroughly at ease as when he seemed to forget her presence.

Estelle sat at his right hand, and suddenly refilling his glass with bubbling champagne, he leaned over and whispered a few words in her ear that brought a look of surprise and pleasure into her eyes. Edna only saw the expression of his face, and the tenderness, the pleading written there astonished and puzzled her. The next moment they rose from the table, and as Mr. Murray drew his cousin's hand under his arm, Edna hurried away to her own room.

Among the numerous magazines to which St. Elmo subscribed, was one renowned for the lofty tone of its articles and the asperity of its carping criticisms, and this periodical Edna always singled out and read with avidity.

The name of the editor swung *in terrorum* in the imagination of all humble authorlings, and had become a synonym for merciless critical excoriation.

To this literary Fouquier Tinville, the orphan had daringly written some weeks before, stating her determination to attempt a book, and asking permission to submit the first chapter to his searching inspection. She wrote that she expected him to find faults—he always did; and she preferred that her work should be roughly handled by him, rather than patted and smeared with faint praise by men of inferior critical astuteness.

The anxiously expected reply had come at last, and as she locked her door and sat down to read it, she trembled from head to foot. In the centre of a handsome sheet of tinted paper she found these lines.

"MADAM: In reply to your very extraordinary request I have the honor to inform you, that my time is so entirely consumed by necessary and important claims, that I find no leisure at my command for the examination of the embryonic chapter of a contemplated book. I am, madam,

"Very respectfully,
"DOUGLASS G. MANNING."

Tears of disappointment filled her eyes and for a moment she bit her lip with uncontrolled vexation; then refolding the letter, she put it in a drawer of her desk, and said sorrowfully:

"I certainly had no right to expect anything more polite from him. He snubs even his popular contributors, and of course he would not be particularly courteous to an unknown scribbler. Perhaps some day I may make him regret that letter; and such a triumph will more than compensate for this mortification. One might think that all literary people, editors, authors, reviewers, would sympathize with each other, and stretch out their hands to aid one another; but it seems there is less free-masonry among *literati* than other guilds. They wage an internecine war among themselves, though it certainly can not be termed ' civil strife,' judging from Mr. Douglass Manning's letter."

Chagrined and perplexed she walked up and down the room, wondering what step would be most expedient in the present state of affairs; and trying to persuade herself that she ought to consult Mr. Hammond. But she wished to surprise him, to hear his impartial opinion of a printed article which he could not suspect that she had written, and finally she resolved to say nothing to any one, to work on in silence, relying upon herself. With this determination she sat down before her desk, opened the MS. of her book, and very soon became absorbed in writing the second chapter. Before she had finished even the first sentence a hasty rap summoned her to the door.

She opened it, and found Mr. Murray standing in the hall, with a candle in his hand.

"Where is that volume of chess problems which you had last week?"

"It is here, sir."

She took it from the table, and as she approached him, Mr. Murray held the light close to her countenance, and gave her one of those keen looks which always reminded her of the descriptions of the scrutiny of the Council of Ten, in the days when "lion's mouths" grinned at the street-corners in Venice.

Something in the curious expression of his face, and the evident satisfaction which he derived from his hasty investigation, told Edna that the book was a mere pretext. She drew back and asked:

"Have I any other book that you need?"

"No; I have all I came for."

Smiling half mischievously, half maliciously, he turned and left her.

"I wonder what he saw in my face that amused him?"

She walked up to the bureau and examined her own image in the mirror; and there, on her cheeks, were the unmistakable traces of the tears of vexation and disappointment.

"At least he can have no idea of the cause, and that is some comfort, for he is too honorable to open my letters."

But just here a doubt flashed into her mind.

"How do I know that he is honorable? Can any man be worthy of trust who holds nothing sacred, and sneers at all religions? No; he has no conscience; and yet——"

She sighed and went back to her MS., and though for a while St. Elmo Murray's mocking eyes seemed to glitter on the pages, her thoughts ere long were anchored once more with the olive-crowned priestess in the temple at Sais.

CHAPTER XIV.

IF the seers of geology are correct in assuming that the age of the human race is coincident with that of the alluvial stratum, from eighty to one hundred centuries, are not domestic traditions and household customs the great arteries in which beats the social life of humanity, linking the race in homogeneity? Roman women suffered no first day of May to pass without celebrating the festival of *Bona Dea*; and two thousand years later, girls who know as little of the manners and customs of ancient Italy, as of the municipal regulations of fabulous " Manoa," lie down to sleep on the last day of April, and kissing the fond, maternal face that bends above their pillows, eagerly repeat :

" You must wake and call me early, call me early, mother dear;
To-morrow 'll be the happiest time of all the glad new-year;
Of all the glad new-year, mother, the maddest, merriest day,
For I'm to be Queen o' the May, mother, I'm to be Queen o'
the May."

For a fortnight Edna had been busily engaged in writing colloquies and speeches for the Sabbath-school children of the village, and in attending the rehearsals for the perfection of the various parts. Assisted by Mr. Hammond and the ladies of his congregation, she had prepared a varied programme, and was almost as much interested in the success of the youthful orators, as the superintendent of the school, or the parents of the children. The day was propitious—clear, balmy, all that could be asked of the blue-eyed month—and as the festival was to be celebrated in a beautiful grove of elms and chestnuts, almost in sight of Le Bocage, Edna went over very early to aid in arranging the tables, decking the platforms with flowers, and training one juvenile Demosthenes, whose elocution was as unpromising as that of his Greek model.

Despite her patient teaching this boy's awkwardness threatened to spoil everything, and as she watched the nervous wringing of his hands and desperate shuffling of his feet, she was tempted to give him up in despair. The dew hung heavily on grass and foliage, and the matin carol of the birds still swelled through the leafy aisles of the grove, when she took the trembling boy to a secluded spot, directed him to stand on a mossy log, where two lizards lay blinking, and repeat his speech.

He stammered most unsatisfactorily through it, and, intent on his improvement, Edna climbed upon a stump and delivered his speech for him, gesticulating and emphasizing just as she wished him to do. As the last words of the peroration passed her lips, and while she stood on the stump, a sudden clapping of hands startled her, and Gordon Leigh's cheerful voice exclaimed:

"Encore! Encore! Since the days of Hypatia you have not had your equal among female elocutionists. I would not have missed it for any consideration, so pray forgive me for eavesdropping." He came forward, held out his hand and added: "Allow me to assist you in dismounting from your temporary rostrum, whence you bear your 'blushing honors thick upon you.' Jamie, do you think you can do as well as Miss Edna when your time comes?"

"Oh! no, sir; but I will try not to make her ashamed of me."

He snatched his hat from the log and ran off, leaving the friends to walk back more leisurely to the spot selected for the tables. Edna had been too much disconcerted by his unexpected appearance, to utter a word until now, and her tone expressed annoyance as she said :

"I am very sorry you interrupted me, for Jamie will make an ignominious failure. Have you nothing better to do than stray about the woods like a satyr?"

"I am quite willing to be satyrized even by you on this occasion; for what man, whose blood is not curdled by cynicism, can prefer to spend Mayday among musty law books and red tape, when he has the alternative of listening to such declamation as you favored me with just now, or of participating in the sports of one hundred happy children? Beside, my good 'familiar,' or rather my *sortes Prænestinæ*, told me that I should find you here; and I wanted to see you before the company assembled; why have you so pertinaciously avoided me of late?"

They stood close to each other in the shade of the elms, and Gordon thought that never before had she looked so beautiful, as the mild perfumed breeze stirred the folds of her dress, and fluttered the blue ribbons that looped her hair and girdled her waist.

Just at that instant, ere she could reply, a rustling of the undergrowth arrested further conversation, and Mr. Murray stepped out of the adjoining thicket, with his gun in his hand, and his grim pet Ali at his heels. Whatever surprise he may have felt, his countenance certainly betrayed none, as he lifted his hat and said:

"Good morning, Leigh. I shall not intrude upon the Sanhedrim, on which I have happened to stumble, longer than is necessary to ask if you are so fortunate as to have a match with you? I find my case empty."

Mr. Leigh took a match from his pocket, and while Mr. Murray lighted his cigar, his eyes rested for an instant only on Edna's flushed face.

"Are you not coming to the children's celebration?" asked Gordon.

"No, indeed! I own that I am as lazy as a Turk; but while I am constitutionally and habitually opposed to labor, I swear I should prefer to plough or break stones till sundown, sooner than listen to all the rant

and fustian that spectators will be called on to endure
this morning. I have not sufficient courage to remain
and witness what would certainly recall ' the manner of
Bombastes Furioso making love to Distaffina !' Will
you have a cigar? Good morning."

He lifted his hat, shouldered his gun, and calling to
his dog, disappeared among the thick undergrowth.

"What an incorrigible savage!" muttered Mr.
Leigh, replacing the match-case in his pocket.

His companion made no answer and was hurrying
on, but he caught her dress and detained her.

" Do not go until you hear what I have to say to
you. More than once you have denied me an opportunity of expressing what you must long ago have
suspected. Edna, you know very well that I love you
better than every thing else—that I have loved you
from the first day of our acquaintance ; and I have
come to tell you that my happiness is in your dear
little hands; that my future will be joyless unless you
share it ; that the one darling hope of my life is to
call you my wife. Do not draw your hand from
mine ! Dear Edna, let me keep it always. Do I
mistake your feelings when I hope that you return my
affection ?"

" You entirely mistake them, Mr. Leigh, in supposing that you can ever be more to me than a very
dear and valued friend. It grieves me very much to
be forced to give you pain or cause you disappointment ; but I should wrong you even more than myself, were I to leave you in doubt concerning my
feeling toward you. I like your society, and you
have my entire confidence and highest esteem ; but
it is impossible that I can ever be your wife."

" Why, impossible ?"

" Because I never could love you as I think I ought
to love the man I marry."

" My dear Edna, answer one question candidly.
Do you love any one else better than you love me ?"

" No, Mr. Leigh."

"Does Mr. Murray stand between your heart and mine?"

"Oh! no, Mr. Leigh."

"Then I will not yield the hope of winning your love. If your heart is free, I will have it all my own one day! O Edna! why can not you love me? I would make you very happy. My darling's home should possess all that fortune and devoted affection could supply; not one wish should remain ungratified."

"I am able to earn a home; I do not intend to marry for one."

"Ah! your pride is your only fault, and it will cause us both much suffering, I fear. Edna, I know how sensative you are, and how deeply your delicacy has been wounded by the malicious meddling of ill-mannered gossips. I know why you abandoned your Hebrew recitations, and a wish to spare your feelings alone prevented me from punishing certain scandalmongers as they deserved. But, dearest, do not visit their offences upon me! Because they dared ascribe their own ignoble motives to you, do not lock your heart against me and refuse me the privilege of making your life happy."

"Mr. Leigh, you are not necessary to my happiness. While our tastes are in many respects congenial, and it is pleasant to be with you occasionally, it would not cause me any deep grief if I were never to see you again."

"O Edna! you are cruel, unlike yourself!"

"Forgive me, sir, if I seem so, and believe me when I assure you that it pains me more to say it than you to hear it. No woman should marry a man whose affection and society are not absolutely essential to her peace of mind and heart. Applying this test to you, I find that mine is in no degree dependent on you; and though you have no warmer friend, I must tell you it is utterly useless for you to hope that I shall ever love you as you wish. Mr. Leigh, I regret that I can not; and if my heart were only puppet of my will, I

would try to reciprocate your affection, because I appreciate so fully and so gratefully all that you generously offer me. To-day you stretch out your hand to
a poor girl, of unknown parentage, reared by charity
—a girl considered by your family and friends an obscure interloper in aristocratic circles, and with a noble
magnanimity, for which I shall thank you always, you
say, ' Come, take my name, share my fortune, wrap
yourself in my love, and be happy ! I will give you a
lofty position in society, whence you can look down
on those who sneer at your poverty and lineage.' O,
Mr. Leigh ! God knows I wish I loved you as you deserve ! Ambition and gratitude alike plead for you ;
but it is impossible that I could ever consent to be
your wife."

Her eyes were full of tears as she looked in his
handsome face, hitherto so bright and genial, now
clouded and saddened by a bitter disappointment ;
and suddenly catching both his hands in hers, she
stooped and pressed her lips to them.

"Although you refuse to encourage, you cannot
crush the hope that my affection will, after a while,
win yours in return. You are very young, and as yet
scarcely know your own heart, and unshaken constancy
on my part will plead for me in coming years. I will
be patient, and as long as you are Edna Earl—as long
as you remain mistress of your own heart—I shall
cling fondly to the only hope that gladdens my future.
Over my feelings you have no control ; you may refuse
me your hand—that is your right—but while I shall
abstain from demonstrations of affection, I shall certainly cherish the hope of possessing it. Meantime,
permit me to ask whether you still contemplate leaving Mrs. Murray's house ? Miss Harding told my sister
yesterday that in a few months you would obtain a
situation as governess or teacher in a school."

"Such is certainly my intention ; but I am at a loss
to conjecture how Miss Harding obtained her information, as the matter has not been alluded to since her
arrival."

"I trust you will pardon me the liberty I take, in warning you to be exceedingly circumspect in your intercourse with her, for I have reason to believe that her sentiments toward you are not so friendly as might be desired."

"Thank you, Mr. Leigh. I am aware of her antipathy, though of its cause I am ignorant; and our intercourse is limited to the salutations of the day, and the courtesies of the table."

Drawing from her finger the emerald which had occasioned so many disquieting reflections, Edna continued:

"You must allow me to return the ring, which I have hitherto worn as a token of friendship, and which I cannot consent to retain any longer. 'Peace be with you,' dear friend, is the earnest prayer of my heart. Our paths in life will soon diverge so widely that we shall probably see each other rarely; but none of your friends will rejoice more sincerely than I to hear of your happiness and prosperity, for no one else has such cause to hold you in grateful remembrance. Goodby, Mr. Leigh. Think of me hereafter only as a friend."

She gave him both hands for a minute, left the ring in his palm, and, with tears in her eyes, went back to the tables and platforms.

Very rapidly chattering groups of happy children collected in the grove; red-cheeked boys clad in white linen suits, with new straw hats belted with black, and fair-browed girls robed in spotless muslin, garlanded with flowers, and bright with rosy badges. Sparkling eyes, laughing lips, sweet, mirthful, eager voices, and shadowless hearts. Ah! that Mayday could stretch from the fairy tropic-land of childhood to the Arctic zone of age, where snows fall chilling and desolate, drifting over the dead but unburied hopes which the great stream of time bears and buffets on its broad, swift surface.

The celebration was a complete success; even awkward Jamie acquitted himself with more ease and

grace than his friends had dared to hope. Speeches
and songs were warmly applauded, proud parents
watched their merry darlings with eyes that brimmed
with tenderness ; and the heart of Semiramis never
throbbed more triumphantly than that of the delighted
young Queen of the May, who would not have exchanged her floral crown for all the jewels that glittered in the diadem of the Assyrian sovereign.

Late in the evening of that festal day Mr. Hammond sat alone on the portico of the old-fashioned
parsonage.   The full moon, rising over the arched windows of the neighboring church, shone on the marble
monuments that marked the rows of graves ; and
the golden beams stealing through the thick vines
which clustered around the wooden columns, broidered
in glittering arabesque the polished floor at the old
man's feet.

That solemn, mysterious silence which nature reverently folds like a velvet pall over the bier of the pale,
dead day, when the sky is

> " Filling more and more with crystal light,
> . As pensive evening deepens into night,"

was now hushing the hum and stir of the village ; and
only the occasional far-off bark of a dog, and the clear,
sweet vesper-song of a mocking-bird swinging in the
myrtle tree, broke the repose so soothing after the
bustle of the day.   To labor and to pray from dawn
till dusk is the sole legacy which sin-stained man
brought through the flaming gate of Eden, and, in the
gray gloaming, mother Earth stretches her vast hands
tenderly over her drooping, toil spent children, and
mercifully murmurs *nunc dimittis*.

Close to the minister's armchair stood a small table
covered with a snowy cloth, on which was placed the
evening meal, consisting of strawberries, honey, bread,
butter and milk.   At his feet lay the white cat, bathed
in moonshine, and playing with a fragrant spray of
honeysuckle which trailed within reach of her paws,

and swung to and fro, like a spicy censer, as the soft
breeze stole up from the starry south. The supper
was untasted, the old man's silvered head leaned
wearily on his shrunken hand, and through a tearful
mist his mild eyes looked toward the churchyard,
where gleamed the monumental shafts that guarded
his mouldering household idols, his white-robed, darling dead.

His past was a wide, fair, fruitful field of hallowed
labor, bounteous with promise for that prophetic harvest whereof God's angels are reapers ; and his future,
whose near horizon was already rimmed with the light
of eternity, was full of that blessed ' peace which passeth all understanding.' Yet to-night, precious reminiscences laid their soft, mesmeric fingers on his heart,
and before him, all unbidden, floated visions of other
Maydays, long, long ago, when the queen of his boyish
affections had worn her crown of flowers ; and many,
many years later, when, as the queen of his home, and
the proud mother of his children, she had stood with
her quivering hand nestled in his, listening breathlessly
to the Mayday speech of their golden-haired daughter,

> " Why does the sea of thought thus backward roll ?
> Memory's the breeze that through the cordage raves,
> And ever drives us on some homeward shoal,
> As if she loved the melancholy waves
> That, murmuring shoreward, break o'er a reef of graves."

The song of the mocking-bird still rang from the
downy cradle of myrtle blossoms, and a whip-poor-
will answered from a cedar in the churchyard, when
the slamming of the parsonage gate startled the shy
thrush that slept in the vines that overarched it, and
Mr. Leigh came slowly up the walk, which was lined
with purple and white lilies whose loveliness, undi-
minished by the wear of centuries, still rivaled the
glory of Solomon.

As he ascended the steps and removed his hat, the
pastor rose and placed a chair for him near his own.

"Good evening, Gordon. Where did you immure yourself all day ? I expected to find you taking part in the children's festival, and hunted for you in the crowd."

" I expected to attend, but this morning something occurred which unfitted me for enjoyment of any kind; consequently I thought it best to keep myself and my moodiness out of sight."

" I trust nothing serious has happened ?"

" Yes, something that threatens to blast all my hopes, and make my life one great disappointment. Has not Edna told you ?"

" She has told me nothing relative to yourself, but I noticed that she was depressed and grieved about something. She was abstracted and restless, and went home very early, pleading fatigue and headache."

" I wish I had a shadow of hope that her heart ached also ! Mr. Hammond, I am very wretched, and have come to you for sympathy and counsel. Of course you have seen for a long time that I loved her very devotedly, that I intended if possible to make her my wife. Although she was very shy and guarded, and never gave me any reason to believe she returned my affection, I thought—I hoped she would not reject me, and I admired her even more because of her reticence, for I could not value a love which I knew was mine unasked. To-day I mentioned the subject to her, told her how entirely my heart was hers, offered her my hand and fortune, and was refused most decidedly. Her manner more than her words distressed and dis- couraged me. She showed so plainly that she felt only friendship for me, and entertained only regret for the pain she gave me. She was kind and delicate, but oh ! so crushingly positive ! I saw that I had no more place in her heart than that whip-poor-will in the cedars yonder. And yet I shall not give her up ; while I live I will cling to the hope that I may finally win her. Thousands of women have rejected a man again and again and at last yielded and accepted him ; and I do not believe Edna can withstand the devotion of a lifetime."

"Do not deceive yourself, Gordon. It is true many women are flattered by a man's perseverance, their vanity is gratified. They first reproach themselves for the suffering they inflict, then gratitude for constancy comes to plead for the inconsolable suitor, and at last they persuade themselves that such devotion can not fail to make them happy. Such a woman Edna is not, and if I have correctly understood her character, never can be. I sympathize with you, Gordon, and it is because I love you so sincerely that I warn you against a hope destined to cheat you."

"But she admitted that she loved no one else, and I can see no reason why, after a while, she may not give me her heart."

"I have watched her for years. I think I know her nature better than any other human being, and I tell you, Edna Earl will never coax and persuade herself to marry any man, no matter what his position and endowments may be. She is not a dependent woman ; the circumstances of her life have forced her to dispense with companionship, she is sufficient for herself ; and while she loves her friends warmly and tenderly, she feels the need of no one. If she ever marries, it will not be from gratitude or devotion, but because she learned to love, almost against her will, some strong, vigorous thinker, some man whose will and intellect master hers, who compels her heart's homage, and without whose society she can not persuade herself to live."

"And why may I not hope that such will, one day, be my good fortune ?"

For a few minutes Mr. Hammond was silent, walking up and down the wide portico ; and when he resumed his seat, he laid his hand affectionately on the young man's shoulder, saying :

"My dear Gordon, your happiness as well as hers is very dear to me. I love you both, and you will, you must, forgive me if what I am about to say should wound or mortify you. Knowing you both as I do, and wishing to save you future disappointment, I should, even were you my own son, certainly tell you. Gordon, you will never be Edna's husband, because intellectually she is your superior. She feels this, and will not marry one to whose mind her own does not bow in reverence. To rule the man she married would make her miserable, and she could only find happiness in being ruled by an intellect to which she looked up admiringly. I know that many very gifted women have married their inferiors, but Edna is peculiar, and in some respects totally unlike any other woman whose character I have carefully studied. Gordon, you are not offended with me?"

Mr. Leigh put out his hand, grasped that of his companion, and his voice was marked by unwonted tremor as he answered :

" You pain and humiliate me beyond expression, but I could never be offended at words which I am obliged to feel are dictated by genuine affection. Mr. Hammond, might not years of thought and study remove the obstacle to which you allude? Can I not acquire all that you deem requisite? I would dedicate my life to the attainment of knowledge, to the improvement of my faculties."

" Erudition would not satisfy her. Do you suppose she could wed a mere walking encyclopædia? She is naturally more gifted than you are, and, unfortunately for you, she discovered the fact when you were studying together."

" But, sir, women listen to the promptings of heart much oftener than to the cold, stern dictates of reason."

" Very true, Gordon ; but her heart declares against you."

" Do you know any one whom you regard as fully worthy of her—any one who will probably win her?"

" I know no man whose noble, generous heart renders him so worthy of her as yourself ; and if she could only love you as you deserve, I should be rejoiced ; but that I believe to be impossible."

"Do you know how soon she expects to leave Le Bocage?"

"Probably about the close of the year."

"I cannot bear to think of her as going out among strangers—being buffeted by the world, while she toils to earn a maintenance. It is inexpressibly bitter for me to reflect, that the girl whom I love above everything upon earth, who would preside so gracefully, so elegantly over my home, and make my life so proud and happy, should prefer to shut herself up in a schoolroom, and wear out her life in teaching fretful, spoiled, trying children! Oh, Mr. Hammond! can you not prevail upon her to abandon this scheme? Think what a complete sacrifice it will be."

"If she feels that the hand of duty points out this destiny as hers, I shall not attempt to dissuade her; for peace of mind and heart is found nowhere, save in accordance with the dictates of conscience and judgment. Since Miss Harding's arrival at Le Bocage, I fear Edna will realize rapidly that she is no longer needed as a companion by Mrs. Murray, and her proud spirit will rebel against the surveillance to which I apprehend she is already subjected. She has always expressed a desire to maintain herself by teaching, but I suspect that she will do so by her pen. When she prepares to quit Mrs. Murray's house I shall offer her a home in mine; but I have little hope that she will accept it, much as she loves me, for she wants to see something of that strange mask called 'life' by the world. She wishes to go to some large city, where she can command advantages beyond her reach in this quiet little place, and where her own exertions will pay for the roof that covers her. However we may deplore this decision, certainly we can not blame her for the feeling that prompts it."

"I have racked my brain for some plan by which I could share my fortune with her without her suspecting the donor; for if she rejects my hand, I know she would not accept one cent from me. Can you suggest any feasible scheme?"

Mr. Hammond shook his head, and after some reflection answered:

"We can do nothing but wait and watch for an opportunity of aiding her. I confess, Gordon, her future fills me with serious apprehension; she is so proud, so sensitive, so scrupulous, and yet so boundlessly ambitious. Should her high hopes, her fond dreams be destined to the sharp and summary defeat which frequently overtakes ambitious men and women early in life, I shudder for her closing years and the almost unendurable bitterness of her disappointed soul."

"Why do you suppose that she aspires to authorship?"

"She has never intimated such a purpose to me; but she can not be ignorant of the fact that she possesses great talent, and she is too conscientious to bury it."

"Mr. Hammond, you may be correct in your predictions, but I trust you are wrong; and I can not believe that any woman whose heart is as warm and noble as Edna's, will continue to reject such love as I shall always offer her. Of one thing I feel assured, no man will ever love her as well, or better than I do, and to this knowledge she will awake some day. God bless her! she is the only woman I shall ever want to call my wife."

"I sympathize most keenly with your severe disappointment, my dear young friend, and shall earnestly pray that in this matter God will overrule all things for your happiness as well as hers. He who notes the death of sparrows, and numbers even the hairs of our heads, will not doom your noble, tender heart to life-long loneliness and hunger."

With a long, close clasp of hands they parted. Gordon Leigh walked sadly between the royal lily-rows, hoping that the future would redeem the past; and the old man sat alone in the serene, silent night, watching the shimmer of the moon on the marble that covered his dead.

CHAPTER XV.

"IT is impossible, Estelle! The girl is not a fool, and nothing less than idiocy can explain such conduct!"

Flushed and angry, Mrs. Murray walked up and down the floor of the sitting-room ; and playing with the jet bracelet on her rounded arm, Miss Harding replied :

"As Mrs. Inge happens to be his sister, I presume she speaks *ex cathedra,* and she certainly expressed very great delight at the failure of Gordon Leigh's suit. She told me that he was much depressed in consequence of Edna's rejection, and manifested more feeling than she had deemed possible under the circumstances. Of course she is much gratified that her family is saved from the disgrace of such a *mésalliance.*"

"You will oblige me by being more choice in the selection of your words, Estelle, as it is a poor compliment to me to remark that any man would be disgraced by marrying a girl whom I have raised and educated, and trained as carefully as if she were my own daughter. Barring her obscure birth, Edna is as worthy of Gordon as any dainty pet of fashion who lounges in Clara Inge's parlors, and I shall take occasion to tell her so if ever she hints at '*mésalliance*' in my presence."

"In that event she will doubtless retort by asking you in her bland and thoroughly well-bred style, whether you intend to give your consent to Edna's marriage with my cousin, St. Elmo?"

Mrs. Murray stopped suddenly, and confronting her niece, said sternly:

"What do you mean, Estelle Harding?"

"My dear aunt, the goodness of your heart has strangely blinded you to the character of the girl you have taken into your house, and honored with your confidence and affection.   Be patient with me while I unmask this shrewd little *intrigante*.   She is poor and unknown, and if she leaves your roof, as she pretends is her purpose, she must work for her own maintenance, which no one will do from choice, when an alternative of luxurious ease is within reach.   Mr. Leigh is very handsome, very agreeable, wealthy and intelligent, and is considered a fine match for any girl ; yet your *protegée* discards him most positively, alleging as a reason that she does not love him, and prefers hard labor as a teacher to securing an elegant home by becoming his wife.   That she can decline so brilliant an offer seems to you incredible, but I knew from the beginning that she would not accept it.   My dear Aunt Ellen, she aspires to the honor of becoming your daughter-in-law, and can well afford to refuse Mr. Leigh's hand, when she hopes to be mistress of Le Bocage.   She is pretty, and she knows it, and her cunning handling of her cards would really amuse and interest me, if I were not grieved at the deception she is practicing upon you.   It has, I confess, greatly surprised me that, with your extraordinary astuteness in other matters, you should prove so obtuse concerning the machinations which that girl carries on in your own house.   Can you not see how adroitly she flatters St. Elmo by poring over his stupid MSS., and professing devotion to his pet authors?   Your own penetration will show you how unnatural it is that any pretty young girl like Edna should sympathize so intensely with my cousin's *outré* studies and tastes.   Before I had been in this house twenty-four hours, I saw the game she plays so skillfully, and only wonder that you, my dear aunt, should be victimized by the cunning of one on whom you have lavished so much kindness.   Look at the facts.   She certainly has refused to marry Mr. Leigh, and situated as she is, how can you explain the mystery by any other solution than that which I have given, and which I assure you is patent to every one save yourself?"

Painful surprise kept Mrs. Murray silent for some moments, and at last shaking her head, she exclaimed:

"I do not believe a word of it! I know her much better than you possibly can, and so far from wishing to marry my son, she fears and dislikes him exceedingly. Her evident aversion to him has even caused me regret, and at times they scarcely treat each other with ordinary courtesy. She systematically avoids him, and occasionally, when I request her to take a message to him, I have been amused at the expression of her face, and her manœuvres to find a substitute. No! no! she is too conscientious to wear a mask. You must tax your ingenuity for some better solution."

"She is shrewd enough to see that St. Elmo is satiated with flattery and homage; she suspects that pique alone can force an entrance into the citadel of his heart, and her demonstrations of aversion are only a *ruse de guerre.* My poor aunt! I pity the disappointment and mortification to which you are destined, when you discover how complete is the imposture she practices."

"I tell you, Estelle, I am neither blind nor exactly in my dotage, and that girl has no more intention of——"

The door opened, and Mr. Murray came in. Glancing round the room, and observing the sudden silence —his mother's flushed cheeks and angry eyes, his cousin's lurking smile, he threw himself on the sofa, saying:

"*Tantæne animis cœlestibus iræ?* Pray what dire calamity has raised a feud between you two? Has the French Count grown importunate, and does my mother refuse her consent to your tardy decision to follow the dictates of your long outraged conscience, and bestow speedily upon him that pretty hand of yours, which has so often been surrendered to his tender clasp? If my intercession in behalf of said

Victor is considered worthy of acceptance, pray command me, Estelle, for I swear I never keep Runic faith with an ally."

" My son, did it ever occur to you that your eloquence might be more successfully and agreeably exercised in your own behalf ?"

Mrs. Murray looked keenly at her neice as she spoke.

" My profound and proverbial humility never permitted the ghost of such a suggestion to affright my soul! Judging from the confusion which greeted my entrance, I am forced to conclude that it was *mal apropos*. But prudent regard for the reputation of the household, urged me to venture near enough to the line of battle to inform you that the noise of the conflict proclaims it to the servants, and the unmistakable tones arrested my attention even in the yard. Family feuds become really respectable if only waged *sotto voce*."

He rose as if to leave the room, but his mother motioned him to remain.

" I am very much annoyed at a matter which surprises me beyond expression. Do you know that Gordon Leigh has made Edna an offer of marriage, and she has been insane enough to refuse him ? Was ever a girl so stupidly blind to her true interest ? She can not hope to make half so brilliant a match, for he is certainly one of the most promising young men in the State, and would give her a position in the world that otherwise she can never attain."

" Refused him! Refused affluence, fashionable social *status!* diamonds, laces, rose-curtained boudoir, and hothouses! Refused the glorious privilege of calling Mrs. Inge ' sister,' and the opportunity of snubbing *le beau monde* who persistently snub her. Impossible ! You are growing old and oblivious of the strategy you indulged in when throwing your toils around your devoted admirer, whom I, ultimately had the honor of calling my father. Your pet vagrant, Edna, is no simpleton; she can take care of her own

interests, and, accept my word for it, intends to do so.
She is only practising a little harmless coquetry—toying with her victim, as fish circle round and round the
bait which they fully intend to swallow. Were she
Aphæa herself, I should say Gordon's success is as
fixed as any other decree—

> ' In the chamber of Fate, where, through tremulous hands,
> Hum the threads from an old-fashioned distaff uncurled,
> And those three blind old women sit spinning the world !'

Be not cast down, O my mother ! Your *protegée* is a
true daughter of Eve, and she eyes Leigh's fortune as
hungrily as the aforesaid venerable mother of mankind
did the tempting apple."

"St. Elmo, it is neither respectful nor courteous to
be eternally sneering at women in the presence of your
own mother. As for Edna, I am intensely provoked
at her deplorable decision, for I know that when she
once decides on a course of conduct neither persuasion
nor argument will move her one iota. She is incapable of the contemptible coquetry you imputed to her,
and Gordon may as well look elsewhere for a bride."

"You are quite right, Aunt Ellen ; her refusal was
most positive."

"Did she inform you of the fact ?" asked Mr. Murray.

"No, but Mr. Leigh told his sister that she gave him
no hope whatever."

"Then, for the first time in my life, I have succeeded
in slandering human nature ! which, hitherto, I deemed
quite impossible. *Peccavi, peccavi !* O my race ! And
she absolutely, positively declines to sell herself ? I
am unpleasantly startled in my pet theories concerning the cunning, lynx selfishness of women, by this
feminine phenomenon ! Why, I would have bet half
my estate on Gordon's chances ; for his handsome face,
aided by such incomparable coadjutors as my mother
here and the infallible sage and oracle of the parsonage
constituted a ' triple alliance' more formidable, more

invincible, than those that threatened Louis XIV. or Alberoni! I imagined the girl was clay in the experienced hands of matrimonial potters, and that Hebrew strategy would prove triumphant! Accept, my dear mother, my most heartfelt sympathy in your ignominious defeat. You will not doubt the sincerity of my condolence when I confess that it springs from the mortifying consciousness of having found that all women are not so entirely unscrupulous as I prefer to believe them. Permit me to comfort you with the assurance that the campaign has been conducted with distinguished ability on your part. You have displayed topographical accuracy, wariness, and an insight into the character of your antagonist, which entitle you to an exalted place among modern tacticians; and you have the consolation of knowing that you have been defeated most unscientifically, and in direct opposition to every well-established maxim and rule of strategy, by this rash, incomprehensible, feminine Napoleon! Believe me——"

"Hush, St. Elmo! I don't wish to hear anything more about the miserable affair. Edna is very obstinate and exceedingly ungrateful after all the interest I have manifested in her welfare, and henceforth I shall not concern myself about her future. If she prefers to drudge through life as a teacher, I shall certainly advise her to commence as soon as possible ; for if she can so entirely dispense with my counsel, she no longer needs my protection."

"Have you reasoned with her concerning this singular obliquity of her mental vision ?"

"No. She knows my wishes, and since she defies them, I certainly shall not condescend to open my lips to her on this subject."

"Women arrogate such marvellous astuteness in reading each other's motives, that I should imagine Estelle's ingenuity would furnish an *open sesame* to the locked chamber of this girl's heart, and supply some satisfactory explanation of her incomprehensible course."

Mr. Murray took his cousin's hand and drew her to a seat beside him on the sofa.

"The solution is very easy, my dear cynic. Edna can well afford to decline Gordon Leigh's offer when she expects and manœuvres to sell herself for a much higher sum than he can command."

As Miss Harding uttered these words, Mrs. Murray turned quickly to observe their effect.

The cousins looked steadily at each other, and St. Elmo laughed bitterly, and patted Estelle's cheek, saying :

"Bravo! 'Set a thief to catch a thief!' I knew you would hit the nail on the head! But who the d—l is this fellow who is writing to her from New York? This is the second letter I have taken out of the office, and there is no telling how often they come ; for, on both occasions, when I troubled myself to ride to the post-office, I have found letters directed to her in this same handwriting."

He drew a letter from his pocket and laid it on his knee, and as Estelle looked at it, and then glanced with a puzzled expression toward her aunt's equally curious face, Mr. Murray passed his hand across his eyes, to hide their malicious twinkle.

"Give me the letter, St. Elmo ; it is my duty to examine it ; for as long as she is under my protection she has no right to carry on a clandestine correspondence with strangers."

"Pardon me if I presume to dispute your prerogative to open her letters. It is neither your business nor mine to dictate with whom she shall or shall not correspond, now that she is no longer a child. Doubtless you remember that I warned you against her from the first day I ever set my eyes upon her, and predicted that you would repent in sackcloth and ashes your charitable credulity? I swore then she would prove a thief; you vowed she was a saint! But, nevertheless, I have no intention of turning spy at this late day, and assisting you in the eminently honorable work of waylaying letters from her distant swain."

Very coolly he put the letter back in his pocket.

Mrs. Murray bit her lip, and held out her hand, saying peremptorily:

"I insist upon having the letter. Since you are so spasmodically and exceedingly scrupulous, I will carry it immediately to her and demand a perusal of the contents. St. Elmo, I am in no mood for jesting."

He only shook his head, and laughed.

"The dictates of filial respect forbid that I should subject my mother's curiosity to so severe an ordeal. Moreover, were the letter once in your hands, your conscience would persuade you that it is your imperative duty to a 'poor, inexperienced, motherless' girl, to inspect it ere her eager fingers have seized it. Beside, she is coming, and will save you the trouble of seeking her. I heard her run up the steps a moment ago."

Before Mrs. Murray could frame her indignation in suitable words, Edna entered, holding in one hand her straw hat, in the other a basket, lined with grape-leaves, and filled with remarkably large and fine strawberries. Exercise had deepened the color in her fair, sweet face, which had never looked more lovely than now, as she approached her benefactress, holding up the fragrant, tempting fruit.

"Mrs. Murray, here is a present from Mr. Hammond, who desired me to tell you that these berries are the first he has gathered from the new bed, next to the row of lilacs. It is the variety he ordered from New York last fall, and some roots of which he says he sent to you. Are they not the most perfect specimens you ever saw? We measured them at the parsonage and six filled a saucer."

She was selecting a cluster to hold up for inspection, and had not remarked the cloud on Mrs. Murray's brow.

"The strawberries are very fine. I am much obliged to Mr. Hammond."

The severity of the tone astonished Edna, who looked up quickly, saw the stern displeasure written on her face, and glanced inquiringly at the cousins. There was an awkward silence, and feeling the eyes of all fixed upon her, the orphan picked up her hat, which had fallen on the floor, and asked:

"Shall I carry the basket to the dining-room, or leave it here?"

"You need not trouble yourself to carry it anywhere."

Mrs. Murray laid her hand on the bell-cord and rang sharply. Edna placed the fruit on the centre-table, and suspecting that she must be *de trop*, moved toward the door, but Mr. Murray rose and stood before her.

"Here is a letter which arrived yesterday."

He put it in her hand, and as she recognized the peculiar superscription, a look of delight flashed over her features, and raising her beaming eyes to his, she murmured, "Thank you, sir," and retreated to her own room.

Mr. Murray turned to his mother and said carelessly:

"I neglected to tell you that I heard from Clinton to-day. He has invited himself to spend some days here, and wrote to say that he might be expected next week. At least his visit will be welcome to you, Estelle, and I congratulate you on the prospect of adding to your list of admirers the most fastidious exquisite it has ever been my misfortune to encounter."

"St. Elmo, you ought to be ashamed to mention your father's nephew in such terms. You certainly have less respect and affection for your relatives than any man I ever saw."

"Which fact is entirely attributable to my thorough knowledge of their characters. I have generally found that high appreciation and intimate acquaintance are in inverse ratios. As for Clinton Allston, were he my father's son, instead of his nephew, I imagine my flattering estimate of him would be substantially the same. Estelle, do you know him?"

"I have not that pleasure, but report prepares me

to find him extremely agreeable. I am rejoiced at the prospect of meeting him. Some time ago, just before I left Paris, I received a message from him, challenging me to a flirtation at sight so soon as an opportunity presented itself."

"For your sake, Estelle, I am glad Clinton is coming, for St. Elmo is so shamefully selfish, and oblivious of his duties as host, that I know time often hangs very heavily on your hands."

Mrs. Murray was too thoroughly out of humor to heed the dangerous sparkle in her son's eyes.

"Very true, mother, his amiable and accommodating disposition commends him strongly to your affection ; and knowing what is expected of him, he will politely declare himself her most devoted lover before he has been thirty-six hours in her society. Now, if she can accept him for a husband, and you will only consent to receive him as your son, I swear I will reserve a mere scanty annuity for my travelling expenses ; I will gladly divide the estate between them, and transport myself permanently and joyfully beyond the animadversion on my inherited sweetness of temper. If you, my dear coz, can only coax Clinton into this arrangement for your own and my mother's happiness, you will render me eternally grateful, and smooth the way for a trip to Thibet and Siberia, which I have long contemplated. Bear this proposition in mind, will you, especially when the charms of Le Bocage most favorably impress you ? Remember you will become its mistress the day that you marry Clinton, make my mother adopt him, and release me. If my terms are not sufficiently liberal, confer with Clinton as soon as maidenly propriety will permit, and acquaint me with your ultimatum ; for I am so thoroughly weary and disgusted with this place that I am anxious to get away on almost any terms. Here come the autocrats of the neighborhood, the *nouveaux enrichis !* your friends the Montgomeries and Hills, than whom I would sooner shake hands with the Asiatic plague ! I hear Madame Montgomery asking if I am not at home, as well as the ladies! Tell her I am in Spitzbergen or Mantchooria, where I certainly intend to be ere long."

As the visitors approached the sitting-room, he sprang through the window opening on the terrace and disappeared.

The contents of the unexpected letter surprised and delighted Edna much more than she would willingly have confessed. Mr. Manning wrote that upon the eve of leaving home for a tour of some weeks' travel, he chanced to stumble upon her letter, and in a second perusal some peculiarity of style induced him to reconsider the offer it contained, and he determined to permit her to send the manuscript (as far as written) for his examination. If promptly forwarded, it would reach him before he left home, and expedite an answer.

Drawing all happy auguries from this second letter, and trembling with pleasure, Edna hastened to prepare her manuscript for immediate transmission. Carefully enveloping it in a thick paper, she sealed and directed it, then fell on her knees, and, with clasped hands resting on the package, prayed earnestly, vehemently, that God's blessing would accompany it, would crown her efforts with success.

Afraid to trust it to the hand of a servant, she put on her hat and walked back to town.

The express agent gave her a receipt for the parcel, assured her that it would be forwarded by the evening train, and with a sigh of relief she turned her steps homeward.

"Ah! it was a frail paper bark, freighted with the noblest, purest aspirations that ever possessed a woman's soul, launched upon the tempestuous sea of popular favor, with ambition at the helm, ' hope for a compass, and the gaunt spectre of failure grinning in the shrouds. Would it successfully weather the gales of malice, envy and detraction? Would it battle valiantly and triumphantly with the piratical hordes of critics who prowl hungrily along the track over which

it must sail ? Would it become a melancholy wreck
on the mighty ocean of literature, or would it proudly
ride at anchor in the harbor of immortality, with her
name floating for ever at the masthead ?

It was an experiment such as had stranded the
hopes of hundreds and thousands ; and the pinched,
starved features of Chatterton, and the white, pleading
face of Keats, stabbed to death by reviewers' poisoned
pens, rose like friendly phantoms and whispered sepulchral warnings.

But to-day the world wore only rosy garments, unspotted by shadows, and the silvery voice of youthful
enthusiasm sung only of victory and spoils, as hope
gayly struck the cymbals and fingered the timbrels.

When Edna returned to her room, she sat down before her desk to reperuse the letter which had given
her so much gratification ; and, as she refolded it,
Mrs. Murray came in and closed the door after her.

Her face was stern and pale ; she walked up to the
orphan, looked at her suspiciously, and when she spoke
her voice was hard and cold.

" I wish to see that letter which you received to-day,
as it is very improper that you should, without my
knowledge, carry on a correspondence with a stranger.
I would not have believed that you could be guilty of
such conduct."

" I am very much pained, Mrs. Murray, that you
should even for a moment have supposed that I had
forfeited your confidence. The nature of the correspondence certainly sanctions my engaging in it, even
without consulting you. This letter is the second I
have received from Mr. Manning, the editor of ⸺
Magazine, and was written in answer to a request of
mine, with reference to a literary matter which concerns nobody but myself. I will show you the signature ; there it is—Douglass G. Manning. You know
his literary reputation and his high position. If you
demand it, of course I can not refuse to allow you to
read it ; but, dear Mrs. Murray, I hope you will not
insist upon it, as I prefer that no one should see the

contents, at least at present. As I have never deceived you, I think you might trust me when I assure you that the correspondence is entirely restricted to literary subjects."

" Why, then, should you object to my reading it ?"

" For a reason which I will explain at some future day, if you will only have confidence in me. Still, if you are determined to examine the letter, of course I must submit, though it would distress me exceedingly to know that you can not, or will not, trust me in so small a matter."

She laid the open letter on the desk and covered her face with her hands.

Mrs. Murray took up the sheet, glanced at the signature, and said :

" Look at me; don't hide your face, that argues something wrong."

Edna raised her head, an¹ lifted her eyes full of tears to meet the scrutiny from which there was no escape.

" Mr. Manning's signature somewhat reassures me, and beside, I never knew you to prevaricate or attempt to deceive me. Your habitual truthfulness encourages me to believe you, and I will not insist on reading this letter, though I can not imagine why you should object to it. But, Edna, I am disappointed in you, and in return for the confidence I have always reposed in you, I want you to answer candidly the question I am about to ask. Why did you refuse to marry Gordon Leigh ?"

" Because I did not love him."

" Oh, pooh ! that seems incredible, for he is handsome and very attractive, and some young ladies show very plainly that they love him, though they have never been requested to do so. There is only one way in which I can account for your refusal, and I wish you to tell me the truth. You are unwilling to marry Gordon because you love somebody else better. Child, whom do you love ?"

" No, indeed, no ! I like Mr. Leigh as well as any

gentleman I know; but I love no one except you and
Mr. Hammond."

Mrs. Murray put her hand under the girl's chin,
looked at her for some seconds, and sighed heavily.

"Child, I find it difficult to believe you."

"Why, whom do you suppose I could love? Mr.
Leigh is certainly more agreeable than anybody else I
know."

"But girls sometimes take strange whims in these
matters. Do you ever expect to receive a better offer
than Mr. Leigh's?"

"As far as fortune is concerned, I presume I never
shall have so good an opportunity again. But, Mrs.
Murray, I would rather marry a poor man, whom I
really loved, and who had to earn his daily bread, than
to be Mr. Leigh's wife and own that beautiful house
he is building. I know you wish me to accept him,
and that you think me very unwise, very short-sighted;
but it is a question which I have settled after consulting my conscience and my heart."

"And you give me your word of honor that you
love no other gentleman better than Gordon?"

"Yes, Mrs. Murray, I assure you that I do not."

As the mistress of the house looked down into the
girl's beautiful face, and passed her hand tenderly
over the thick, glossy folds of hair that crowned the
pure brow, she wondered if it were possible that her
son could ever regard the orphan with affection; and
she asked her own heart why she could not willingly
receive her as a daughter.

Mrs. Murray believed that she entertained a sincere
friendship for Mrs. Inge, and yet she had earnestly
endeavored to marry her brother to a girl whom she
could not consent to see the wife of her own son.
Verily, when human friendships are analyzed, it seems
a mere poetic fiction that—

"Love took up the harp of Life, and smote on all the chords
    with might;
Smote the chord of Self, that, trembling, passed in music out
    of sight."

CHAPTER XVI.

ONE afternoon, about ten days after the receipt of Mr. Manning's letter, when Edna returned from the parsonage, she found the family assembled on the front verandah, and saw that the expected visitor had arrived. As Mrs. Murray introduced her to Mr. Allston, the latter rose, advanced a few steps, and held out his hand. Edna was in the act of giving him hers, when the heart-shaped diamond cluster on his finger flashed, and one swift glance at his face and figure made her snatch away her hand ere it touched his, and draw back with a half-smothered exclamation.

He bit his lip, looked inquiringly around the circle, smiled, and returning to his seat beside Estelle, resumed the gay conversation in which he had been engaged.

Mrs. Murray was leaning over the iron balustrade, twining a wreath of multiflora around one of the fluted columns, and did not witness the brief pantomime ; but when she looked around she could not avoid remarking the unwonted pallor and troubled expression of the girl's face.

"What is the matter, child? You look as if you were either ill or dreadfully fatigued."

"I am tired, thank you," was the rather abstracted reply, and she walked into the house and sat down before the open window in the library.

The sun had just gone down behind a fleecy cloud-mountain and kindled a volcano, from whose silver-rimmed crater fiery rays of scarlet shot up, almost to the clear blue zenith ; while here and there, through

clefts and vapory gorges, the lurid lava light streamed
down toward the horizon.

Vacantly her eyes rested on this sky-Hecla, and its
splendor passed away unheeded, for she was looking
far beyond the western gates of day, and saw a pool of
blood—a ghastly face turned up to the sky—a coffined
corpse strewn with white poppies and rosemary—a
wan, dying woman, whose waving hair braided the pillow with gold—a wide, deep grave under the rustling
chestnuts, from whose green arches rang the despairing wail of a broken heart:

"Oh, Harry! my husband!"

Imagination travelling into the past, painted two
sunny-haired, prattling babes, suddenly smitten with
orphanage, and robed in mourning garments for parents whose fond, watchful eyes were closed forever
under wild clover and trailing brambles. Absorbed in
retrospection of that June day, when she stood by the
spring, and watched

"God make himself an awful rose of dawn,"

she sat with her head resting against the window-
facing, and was not aware of Mr. Murray's entrance
until his harsh, querulous voice startled her.

"Edna Earl! what apology have you to offer for insulting a relative and guest of mine under my roof?"

"None, sir."

"What! How dare you treat with unparalleled
rudeness a visitor, whose claim upon the courtesy and
hospitality of this household is certainly more legiti-
mate and easily recognized than that of——"

He stopped and kicked out of his way a stool upon
which Edna's feet had been resting. She had risen,
and they stood face to face.

"I am waiting to hear the remainder of your sentence, Mr. Murray."

He uttered an oath, and hurled his cigar through
the window.

"Why the d—l did you refuse to shake hands with

Allston? I intend to know the truth, and it may prove an economy of trouble for you to speak it at once."

"If you demand my reasons, you must not be offended at the plainness of my language. Your cousin is a murderer, and ought to be hung! I could not force myself to touch a hand all smeared with blood."

Mr. Murray leaned down and looked into her eyes.

"You are either delirious or utterly mistaken with reference to the identity of the man. Clinton is no more guilty of murder than you are, and I have been led to suppose that you are rather too 'pious' to attempt the rôle of Marguérite de Brinvilliers or Joanna of Hainault! Cufic lore has turned your brain; 'too much learning hath made thee mad.'"

"No, sir, it is no hallucination; there can be no mistake; it is a horrible, awful fact, which I witnessed, which is burned on my memory, and which will haunt my brain as long as I live. I saw him shoot Mr. Dent, and heard all that passed on that dreadful morning. He is doubly criminal—is as much the murderer of Mrs. Dent as of her husband, for the shock killed her. Oh! that I could forget her look and scream of agony as she fainted over her husband's coffin!"

A puzzled expression crossed Mr. Murray's face; then he muttered:

"Dent? Dent? Ah! yes; that was the name of the man whom Clinton killed in a duel. Pshaw! you have whipped up a syllabub storm in a tea-cup! Allston only took 'satisfaction' for an insult offered publicly by Dent."

His tone was sneering and his lip curled, but a strange pallor crept from chin to temples; and a savage glare in his eyes, and a thickening scowl that bent his brows till they met, told of the brewing of no slight tempest of passion.

"I know, sir, that custom, public opinion, sanctions —at least tolerates that relic of barbarous ages—that blot upon Christian civilization which, under the name of 'duelling,' I recognize as a crime, a heinous crime, which I abhor and detest above all other crimes! Sir, I call things by their proper names, stripped of the glozing drapery of conventional usage. You say 'honorable satisfaction;' I say murder! aggravated, unpardonable murder; murder without even the poor palliation of the sudden heat of anger. Cool, deliberate, willful murder, that stabs the happiness of wives and children, and for which it would seem that even the infinite mercy of Almighty God could scarcely accord forgiveness! Oh! save me from the presence of that man who can derive 'satisfaction' from the reflection that he has laid Henry and Helen Dent in one grave, under the quiet shadow of Lookout, and brought desolation and orphanage to their two innocent, tender darlings! Shake hands with Clinton Allston? I would sooner stretch out my fingers to clasp those of Gardiner, reeking with the blood of his victims, or those of Ravaillac! Ah! well might Dante shudder in painting the chilling horrors of Caïna."

The room was dusky with the shadow of coming night; but the fading flush, low in the west, showed St. Elmo's face colorless, rigid, repulsive in its wrathful defiance.

He bent forward, seized her hands, folded them together, and grasping them in both his, crushed them against his breast.

"Ha! I knew that hell and heaven were leagued to poison your mind! That your childish conscience was frightened by tales of horror, and your imagination harrowed up, your heart lacerated by the cunning devices of that arch maudlin old hypocrite! The seeds of clerical hate fell in good ground, and I see a bountiful harvest nodding for my sickle! Oh! you are more pliable than I had fancied! You have been thoroughly trained down yonder at the parsonage. But I will be——"

There was a trembling pant in his voice like that of some wild creature driven from its jungle, hopeless of escape, holding its hunters temporarily at bay, waiting for death.

The girl's hand ached in his unyielding grasp and after two ineffectual efforts to free them, a sigh of pain passed her lips and she said proudly :

" No, sir ; my detestation of that form of legalized murder, politely called ' duelling,' was not taught me at the parsonage. I learned it in my early childhood, before I ever saw Mr. Hammond ; and though I doubt not he agrees with me in my abhorrence of the custom, I have never heard him mention the subject."

"Hypocrite ! hypocrite ! Meek little wolf in lamb's wool ! Do you dream that you can deceive me ? Do you think me an idiot, to be cajoled by your low-spoken denials of a fact which I know ? A fact, to the truth of which I will swear till every star falls !"

" Mr. Murray, I never deceived you, and I know that however incensed you may be, however harsh and unjust, I know that in your heart you do not doubt my truthfulness. Why you invariably denounce Mr. Hammond when you happen to be displeased with me, I can not conjecture ; but I tell you solemnly that he has never even indirectly alluded to the question of ' duelling ' since I have known him. Mr. Murray, I know you do entirely believe me when I utter these words."

A tinge of red leaped into his cheek, something that would have been called hope in any other man's eyes looked out shyly from under his heavy black lashes, and a tremor shook off the sneering curl of his blood-less lips.

Drawing her so close to him that his hair touched her forehead, he whispered :

" If I believe in you, my—it is in defiance of judg-ment, will, and experience, and some day you will make me pay a most humiliating penalty for my momentary weakness. To-night I trust you as im-plicitly as Samson did the smooth-lipped Delilah ; to-morrow I shall realize that, like him, I richly deserve to be shorn for my silly credulity."

He threw her hands rudely from him, turned hastily and left the library.

Edna sat down and covered her face with her bruised and benumbed fingers, but she could not shut out the sight of something that astonished and frightened her—of something that made her shudder from head to foot, and crouch down in her chair cowed and humiliated. Hitherto she had fancied that she thoroughly understood and sternly governed her heart—that conscience and reason ruled it; but within the past hour it had suddenly risen in dangerous rebellion, thrown off its allegiance to all things else, and insolently proclaimed St. Elmo Murray its king. She could not analyze her new feelings, they would not obey the summons to the tribunal of her outraged self-respect ; and with bitter shame and reproach and abject contrition, she realized that she had begun to love the sinful, blasphemous man who had insulted her revered grandfather, and who barely tolerated her presence in his house.

This danger had never once occurred to her, for she had always believed that love could only exist where high esteem and unbounded reverence prepared the soil ; and she was well aware that this man's character had from the first hour of their acquaintance excited her aversion and dread. Ten days before she had positively disliked and feared him ; now, to her amazement, she found him throned in her heart, defying ejection. The sudden revulsion bewildered and mortified her, and she resolved to crush out the feeling at once, cost what it might. When Mrs. Murray had asked if she loved any one else better than Mr. Leigh, she thought, nay she knew, she answered truly in the negative. But now, when she attempted to compare the two men, such a strange, yearning tenderness pleaded for St. Elmo, and paliated his grave faults, that the girl's self-accusing severity wrung a groan from the very depths of her soul.

When the sad discovery was first made, conscience lifted its hands in horror, because of the man's reckless wickedness; but after a little while a still louder clamor was raised by womanly pride, which bled at the thought of tolerating a love unsought, unvalued; and with this fierce rush of reinforcements to aid conscience, the insurgent heart seemed destined to summary subjugation. Until this hour, although conscious of many faults, she had not supposed that there was anything especially contemptible in her character; but now the feeling of self-abasement was unutterably galling. She despised herself most cordially, and the consistent dignity of life which she had striven to attain appeared hopelessly shattered.

While the battle of reason *versus* love was at its height, Mrs. Murray put her head in the room and asked: "Edna! Where are you, Edna?"

"Here I am."

"Why are you sitting in the dark? I have searched the house for you."

She groped her way across the room, lighted the gas, and came to the window.

"What is the matter, child? Are you sick?"

"I think something must be the matter, for I do not feel at all like myself," stammered the orphan, as she hid her face on the window-sill.

"Does your head ache?"

"No, ma'am."

She might have said very truly that her heart did.

"Give me your hand, let me feel your pulse. It is very quick, but shows nervous excitement rather than fever. Child, let me see your tongue, I hear there are some typhoid cases in the neighborhood. Why, how hot your cheeks are!"

"Yes, I shall go up and bathe them, and perhaps I may feel better."

"I wish you would come into the parlor as soon as you can, for Estelle says Clinton thought you were very rude to him; and though I apologized on the score of indisposition, I prefer that you should make your appearance this evening. Stop, you have dropped your handkerchief."

Edna stooped to pick it up, saw Mr. Murray's name printed in one corner, and her first impulse was to thrust it into her pocket; but instantly she held it toward his mother.

"It is not mine, but your son's. He was here about an hour ago and must have dropped it."

"I thought he had gone out over the grounds with Clinton. What brought him here?"

"He came to scold me for not shaking hands with his cousin."

"Indeed! you must have been singularly rude if he noticed any want of courtesy. Change your dress and come down."

It was in vain that Edna bathed her hot face and pressed her cold hands to her cheeks. She felt as if all curious eyes read her troubled heart. She was ashamed to meet the family—above all things to see Mr. Murray. Heretofore she had shunned him from dislike; now she wished to avoid him because she began to feel that she loved him, and because she dreaded that his inquisitorial eyes would discover the contemptible, and, in her estimation, unwomanly weakness.

Taking the basket which contained her sewing utensils and a piece of light needlework, she went into the parlor and seated herself near the centre-table, over which hung the chandelier.

Mr. Murray and his mother were sitting on a sofa, the former engaged in cutting the leaves of a new book, and Estelle Harding was describing in glowing terms a scene in "*Phèdre*," which owed its charm to Rachel's marvelous acting. As she repeated the soliloquy beginning:

"O toi, qui vois la honte où je suis descendue,
Implacable Vénus, suis-je assez confondue!"

Edna felt as if her own great weakness were known to the world, and she bent her face close to her basket and tumbled the contents into inextricable confusion.

To-night Estelle seemed in unusually fine spirits,

and talked on rapidly, till St. Elmo suddenly appeared to become aware of the import of her words, and in a few trenchant sentences he refuted the criticism on *Phèdre*, advising his cousin to confine her comments to dramas with which she was better acquainted.

His tone and manner surprised Mr. Allston, who remarked :

" Were I Czar, I would issue a ukase, chaining you to the steepest rock on the crest of the Ural, till you learned the courtesy due to lady disputants. Upon my word, St. Elmo, you assault Miss Estelle with as much *élan* as if you were carrying a redoubt. One would suppose that you had been in good society long enough to discover that the *fortiter in re* style is not allowable in discussions with ladies."

" When women put on boxing-gloves and show their faces in the ring, they challenge rough handling, and are rarely disappointed. I am sick of sciolism, especially that phase where it crops out in shallow criticism, and every day something recalls the reprimand of Apelles to the shoemaker. If a worthy and able literary tribunal and critical code could be established, it would be well to revive an ancient Locrian custom, which required that the originators of new laws or propositions should be brought before the assembled wisdom, with halters round their necks, ready for speedy execution if the innovation proved, on examination, to be utterly unsound or puerile. Ah ! what a wholesale hanging of sciolists would gladden my eyes !"

Mr. Murray bowed to his cousin as he spoke, and rising, took his favorite position on the rug.

" Really, Aunt Ellen, I would advise you to have him re-christened, under the name of Timon," said Mr. Allston.

" No, no. I decidedly object to any such gratification of his would-be classic freaks; and, as he is evidently aping Timon, though, unfortunately, nature denied him the Attic salt requisite to flavor the character, I would suggest, as a more suitable *sobriquet*, that

bestowed on Louis X., ' *Le Hutin* '—freely translated,
' The Quarrelsome !' What say you, St. Elmo ?"

Estelle walked up to her cousin and stood at his
side.

" That it is very bad policy to borrow one's boxing-
gloves ; and I happened to overhear Edna Earl when
she made that same suggestion to Gordon Leigh,
with reference to my amiable temperament. However,
there is a maxim which will cover your retreat, and
which you can conscientiously utter with much emphasis, if your memory is only as good in repeating all
the things you may have heard : *Pereant qui ante nos
nostra dixerunt !* Shall I translate ?"

She laughed lightly, and answered :

" So much for eavesdropping ! Of all the gentlemen of my acquaintance, I should fancy you were the
very last who could afford to indulge in that amusement."

" Miss Estelle, is this your first, second or third
Punic war ? You and St. Elmo, or rather, my cousin
' The Quarrelsome,' seem to wage it in genuine Cartha-
ginian style."

" I never signed a treaty, sir, and, consequently,
keep no records."

" Clinton, there is a chronic *casus belli* between us,
the original spring of which antedates my memory.
But at present, Estelle is directing all her genius and
energy to effect, for my individual benefit, a practical
reënactment of the old *Papia Poppæa*, which Augustus
hurled at the heads of all peaceful, happy bachelor-
dom !"

For the first time during the conversation Edna
glanced up at Estelle, for, much as she disliked her,
she regretted this thrust ; but her pity was utterly
wasted, and she was surprised to find her countenance
calm and smiling.

Mr. Allston shrugged his shoulders, and Mrs. Murray exclaimed :

" I sound a truce ! For heaven's sake, St. Elmo,
lock up your learning with your mummies, and when

you *will* say barbarous things, use language that will enable us to understand that we are being snubbed. Now who do you suppose comprehends ' Papia Poppæa ?' You are insufferably pedantic !"

" My dear mother, do you remember ever to have read or heard the celebrated reply of a certain urbane lexicographer to the rashly ambitious individual who attempted to find fault with his dictionary ? Permit me, most respectfully, to offer it for your consideration. ' I am bound to furnish good definitions, but not brains to comprehend them.' "

" I think, sir, that it is a very great misfortune for those who have to associate with you now that you were not raised in Sparta, where it was everybody's privilege to whip their neighbor's vicious, spoiled children? Such a regimen would doubtless have converted you into an amiable, or at least endurable member of society."

Miss Harding tapped his hand with her fan.

" That is problematical, my fair cousin, for if my provocative playmate had accompanied me, I'll be sworn but I think the supply of Spartan birch would have utterly failed to sweeten my temper. I should have shared the fate of those unfortunate boys who were whipped to death in Lacedæmon, in honor of Diana ; said whipping-festival (I here remark parenthetically, for my mother's enjoyment) being known in classic parlance as *Diamastigosis !"*

Her mother answered laughingly :

" Estelle is quite right ; you contrived to grow up without the necessary and healthful *quota* of sound whipping which you richly deserved."

Mr. Murray did not seem to hear her words ; he was looking down intently, smilingly into his cousin's handsome face, and, passing his arm around her waist, drew her close to his side. He murmured something that made her throw her head quickly back against his shoulder and look up at him.

" If such is the end of all your quarrels, it offers a premium for unamiability," said Mr. Allston, who had been studying Edna's face, and now turned again to his cousin. Curling the end of his moustache, he continued :

"St. Elmo, you have travelled more extensively than any one I know, and under peculiarly favorable circumstances. Of all the spots you have visited, which would you pronounce the most desirable for a permanent residence ?"

"Have you an idea of expatriating yourself—of 'quitting your country for your country's good' ?"

"One never knows what contingencies may arise, and I should like to avail myself of your knowledge; for I feel assured only very charming places would have detained you long."

"Then, were I at liberty to select a home, tranquil, blessed beyond all expression, I should certainly lose no time in domesticating myself in the Peninsula of Mount Athos."

"Ah! yes; the scenery all along that coast is described as surprisingly beautiful and picturesque."

Oh, bah ! the scenery is quite as grand in fifty other places. Its peculiar attraction consists in something far more precious."

"To what do you refer ?"

"It's marvelous and bewildering charm is to be found entirely in the fact that, since the days of Constantine, no woman has set foot on its peaceful soil ; and the happy dwellers in that sole remaining earthly Eden are so vigilant, dreading the entrance of another Eve, that no female animal is permitted to intrude upon the sacred precincts. The embargo extends even to cats, cows, dogs, lest the innate female proclivity to make mischief should be found dangerous in the brute creation. Constantine lived in the latter part of the third and beginning of the fourth century. Think of the divine repose, the unapproachable beatification of residing in a land where no woman has even peeped for fifteen hundred years !"

"May all good angels help me to steer as far as possible from such a nest of cynics ! I would sooner

confront an army of Amazons headed by Penthesilea
herself, than trust myself among a people unhumanized
and uncivilized by the refining influence and companionship of women ! St. Elmo, you are the most
abominable misogamist I ever met, and you deserve to
fall into the clutches of those 'eight mighty daughters
of the plow,' to which Tennyson's Princess consigned
the Prince. Most heartily I pity you !"

"For shame, St. Elmo ! A stranger listening to
your gallant diatribe, would inevitably conclude that
your mother was as unnatural and unamiable as Lord
Byron's ; and that I, your most devoted, meek, and
loving cousin, was quite as angelic as Miss Edgeworth's
Modern Griselda !"

Affecting great indignation, Estelle attempted to
quit his side ; but, tightening his arm, Mr. Murray
bowed and resumed :

"Had your imaginary stranger ever heard of the
science of logic, or even dreamed of Whately or Mill,
the conclusion would, as you say, be inevitable. More
fortunate than Rasselas, I found a happy spot where
the names of women are never called, where the myths
of Até and Pandora are forgotten, and where the only
females that have successfully run the rigid blockade
are the tormenting fleas, that wage a ceaseless war with
the unoffending men, and justify their nervous horror
lest any other creature of the same sex should smuggle
herself into their blissful retreat. I have seen crowned
heads, statesmen, great military chieftains, and geniuses,
whose names are destined to immortality ; but standing here, reviewing my certainly extended acquaintance, I swear I envy above all others that handsome
monk whom Curzon found at Simopetra, who had
never seen a woman ! He was transplanted to the
Holy Mountain while a mere infant, and though assured he had had a mother, he accepted the statement
with the same blind faith, which was required for some
of the religious dogmas he was called on to swallow.
I have frequently wondered whether the ghost of poor
Socrates would not be allowed, in consideration of his

past sufferings and trials, to wander forever in that peaceful realm where even female ghosts are tabooed."

"There is some terrible retribution in store for your libels on our sex! How I do long to meet some woman brave and wily enough to marry and tame you, my chivalric cousin! to revenge the insults you have heaped upon her sisterhood!"

"By fully establishing the correctness of my estimate of their amiability? That were dire punishment indeed for what you deem my heresies. If I could realize the possibility of such a calamity, I should certainly bewail my fate in the mournful words of that most astute of female wits, who is reported to have exclaimed, in considering the angelic idiosyncrasies of her gentle sisterhood, 'The only thought which can reconcile me to being a woman is that I shall not have to marry one.'"

The expression with which Mr. Murray regarded Estelle reminded Edna of the account given by a traveller of the playful mood of a lion, who, having devoured one gazelle, kept his paw on another, and amid occasional growls, teased and toyed with his victim.

As the orphan sat bending over her work listening to the conversation, she asked herself scornfully:

"What hallucination has seized me? The man is a mocking devil, unworthy the respect or toleration of any Christian woman. What redeeming trait can even my partial eyes discover in his distorted, sinful nature? Not one. No, not one!"

She was rejoiced when he uttered a sarcasm or an opinion that shocked her, for she hoped that his irony would cauterize what she considered a cancerous spot in her heart.

"Edna, as you are not well, I advise you to put aside that embroidery, which must try your eyes very severely," said Mrs. Murray.

So she folded up the piece of cambric and was putting it in her basket, when Mr. Allston asked

with more effrontery than the orphan was prepared
for :

"Miss Earl, have I not seen you before to-day?"

"Yes, sir."

"May I ask where?"

"In a chestnut grove, where you shot Mr. Dent."

"Indeed! Did you witness that affair? It happened many years ago."

There was not a shadow of pain or sorrow in his
countenance or tone, and rising, Edna said with unmistakable emphasis :

"I saw all that occurred, and may God preserve
me from ever witnessing another murder so revolt-
ing!"

In the silence that ensued she turned toward
Mrs. Murray, bowed, and said as she quitted the
parlor :

"Mrs. Murray, as I am not very well, you will
please excuse my retiring early."

"Just what you deserve for bringing the subject on
tapis, I warned you not to allude to it." As St. Elmo
muttered these words he pushed Estelle from him,
and nodded to Mr. Allston, who seemed as nearly
nonplused as ·his habitual impudence rendered possible.

Thoroughly dissatisfied with herself, and too restless to sleep, the orphan passed the weary hours of
night in endeavoring to complete a chapter on Budd-
hism, which she had commenced some days before;
and the birds were chirping their *reveille*, and the sky
blanched and reddened ere she lay down her pen and
locked up her MS. Throwing open the blinds of the
eastern window she stood for some time looking out,
gathering strength from the holy calm of the dewy
morning, resolving to watch her own heart ceaselessly,
to crush promptly the feeling she had found there, and
to devote herself unreservedly to her studies. At that
moment the sound of horse's hoofs on the stony walk
attracted her attention, and she saw Mr. Murray riding
from the stables. As he passed her window he glanced

up, their eyes met, and he lifted his hat and rode on. Were those the same sinister, sneering features she had looked at the evening before? His face was paler, sterner, and sadder than she had ever seen it, and covering her own with her hands she murmured:

"God help me to resist that man's wicked magnetism! Oh, Grandpa! are you looking down on your poor little Pearl? Will you forgive me for allowing myself ever to have thought kindly and tenderly of this strange temptation which Satan has sent to draw my heart away from my God and my duty? Ah, Grandpa! I will crush it—I will conquer it! I will not yield!"

CHAPTER XVII.

AVOIDING as much as possible the society of Mrs. Murray's guests, as well as that of her son, Edna turned to her books with increased energy and steadfastness, while her manner was marked by a studied reticence hitherto unnoticed. The house was thronged with visitors, and families residing in the neighborhood were frequently invited to dinner; but the orphan generally contrived on these occasions to have an engagement at the parsonage; and as Mrs. Murray no longer required, or seemed to desire her presence, she spent much of her time alone, and rarely saw the members of the household, except at breakfast. She noticed that Mr. Allston either felt or feigned unbounded admiration of Estelle, who graciously received his devoted attentions; while Mr. Murray now and then sneered openly at both, and appeared daily more impatient to quit the home, of which he spoke with undisguised disgust. As day after day, and week after week slipped by without bringing tidings of Edna's MS., her heart became oppressed with anxious forebodings, and she found it difficult to wait patiently for the verdict upon which hung all her hopes.

One Thursday afternoon, when a number of persons had been invited to dine at Le Bocage, and Mrs. Murray was engrossed by preparations for their entertainment, Edna took her Greek books and stole away unobserved to the parsonage, where she spent a quiet evening in reading aloud from the Organon of Aristotle.

It was quite late when Mr. Hammond took her home

in his buggy, and bade her good-night at the doorstep.
As she entered the house she saw several couples
promenading on the verandah, and heard Estelle and
Clinton Allston singing a duet from "Il Trovatore."
Passing the parlor door one quick glance showed her
Mr. Murray and Mr. Leigh standing together under
the chandelier—the latter gentleman talking earnestly,
the former with his gaze fastened on the carpet, and a
chilling smile fixed on his lip. The faces of the two
presented a painful contrast—one fair, hopeful, bright
with noble aims, and youthful yet manly beauty; the
other swarthy, cold, repulsive as some bronze image of
Abaddon. For more than three weeks Edna had not
spoken to Mr. Murray, except to say "good morning,"
as she entered the dining-room or passed him in the
hall; and now with a sigh which she did not possess
the courage to analyze, she went up to her room and
sat down to read.

Among the books on her desk was Machiavelli's
Prince and History of Florence, and the copy, which
was an exceedingly handsome one, contained a portrait
of the author. Between the regular features of the
Florentine satirist and those of the master of the house,
Edna had so frequently found a startling resemblance,
that she one day mentioned the subject to Mrs. Murray, who, after a careful examination of the picture,
was forced to admit, rather ungraciously, that "they
certainly looked somewhat alike." To-night, as the
orphan lifted the volume from its resting-place, it
opened at the portrait, and she looked long at the
handsome face which, had the lips been thinner, and
the hair thicker and more curling at the temples, might
have been daguerreotyped from that one down stairs
under the chandelier.

One maxim of the Prince had certainly been adopted
by Mr. Murray, "It is safer to be feared than to be
loved"; and while the orphan detested the crafty and
unscrupulous policy of Niccolo Machiavelli, her reason
told her that the character of St. Elmo Murray was
scarcely more worthy of respect.

She heard the guests take their departure, heard Mrs. Murray ask Hagar whether " Edna had returned from the parsonage," and then doors were closed and the house grew silent.

Vain were the girl's efforts to concentrate her thoughts on her books or upon her MS.; they wandered toward the portrait; and finally remembering that she needed a book of reference, she lighted a candle, took the copy of Machiavelli, which she determined to put out of sight, and went down to the library.   The smell of a cigar aroused her suspicions as she entered, and glancing nervously around the room she saw Mr. Murray seated before the window.

His face was turned from her, and hoping to escape unnoticed, she was retracing her steps when he rose.

" Come in, Edna.   I am waiting for you, for I knew you would be here some time before day."

Taking the candle from her hand, he held it close to her face, and compressed his lips tightly for an instant.

" How long do you suppose your constitution will endure the tax you impose upon it?   Midnight toil has already robbed you of your color, and converted a rosy, robust child into a pale, weary, hollow-eyed woman.   What do you want here?"

" The Edda."

" What business have you with Norse myths, with runes and scalds and sagas?   You can't have the book. I carried it to my room yesterday, and I am in no mood to-night to play errand-boy for any one."

Edna turned to place the copy of Machiavelli on the shelves, and he continued:

" It is a marvel that the *index expurgatorius* of your saintly tutor does not taboo the infamous doctrines of the greatest statesman of Italy.   I am told that you do me the honor to discover a marked likeness between his countenance and mine.   May I flatter myself so highly as to believe the statement ?"

" Even your mother admits the resemblance."

"Think you the analogy extends further than the

mere *physique*, or do you trace it only in the corporeal development ?"

"I believe, sir, that your character is as much a counterpart of his as your features ; that your code is quite as lax as his."

She had abstained from looking at him, but now her eyes met his fearlessly, and in their beautiful depths he read an expression of helpless repulsion, such as a bird might evince for the serpent whose glittering eyes enchained it.

"Ah! at least your honesty is refreshing in these accursed days of hypocritical sycophancy ! I wonder how much more training it will require before your lips learn fashionable lying tricks? But you understand me as little as the world understood poor Machiavelli, of whom Burke justly remarked, 'He is obliged to bear the iniquities of those whose maxims and rules of government he published. His speculation is more abhorred than their practice.' We are both painted blacker than——"

"I came here, sir, to discuss neither his character nor yours. If is a topic for which I have as little leisure as inclination. Good-night, Mr. Murray."

He bowed low, and spoke through set teeth :

"I regret the necessity of detaining you a moment longer, but I believe you have been anxiously expecting a letter for some time, as I hear that you every day anticipate my inquiries at the post-office. This afternoon the express agent gave me this package."

He handed her a parcel and smiled as he watched the startled look, the expression of dismay, of keen disappointment that came into her face.

The frail bark had struck the reefs ; she felt that her hopes were going down to ruin, and her lips quivered with pain as she recognized Mr. Manning's bold chirography on the paper wrapping.

"What is the matter, child ?"

"Something that concerns only myself."

"Are you unwilling to trust me with your secret, whatever it may be ? It would sooner find betrayal from the grinning skeletons in monastic crypts than from my lips."

Smothering a sigh she shook her head impatiently.

"That means that red-hot steel could not pinch it out of you ; and that despite your boasted charity and love of humanity you really entertain as little confidence in your race as it is my pleasure to indulge. I applaud your wisdom, but certainly did not credit you with so much craftiness. My reason for not delivering the parcel more promptly, was simply the wish to screen you from the Argus scrutiny with which we are both favored by some now resident at Bocage. As your letters subjected you to suspicion, I presumed it would be more agreeable to you to receive them without witnesses."

He took a letter from his pocket and gave it to her.

"Thank you, Mr. Murray ; you are very kind."

"Pardon me ! that is indeed a novel accusation ! Kind, I never professed to be. I am simply not quite a brute, nor altogether a devil of the most malicious and vindictive variety, as you doubtless consider it your religious duty to believe. However, having hopelessly lost my character, I shall not trespass on your precious time by wasting words in pronouncing a eulogy upon it, as Antony did over the stabbed corpse of Cæsar ! I stand in much the same relation to society that King John did to Christendom, when Innocent III. excommunicated him ; only I snap my fingers in the face of my pontiff, the world, and jingle my Peterpence in my pocket ; whereas poor John's knees quaked until he found himself at the feet of Innocent, meekly receiving Langton, and paying tribute ! Child, you are in trouble ; and your truthful countenance reveals it as unmistakably as did the Phrygian reeds that babbled of the personal beauties of Midas. Of course it does not concern me—it is not my business—and you certainly have as good a right as any other child of Adam, to fret and cry and pout over your girlish griefs, to sit up all night, ruin your eyes, and grow rapidly and prematurely old and ugly. But whenever I chance to stumble over a wounded creature trying to drag itself out of sight, I generally either wring its neck, or set my heel on it to end its torment ; or else, if there is a fair prospect of the injury healing by 'first intention,' I take it gently on the tip of my boot, and help it out of my way. Something has hurt you, and I suspect I can aid you. Your anxiety about those letters proves that you doubt your idol. You and your lover have quarrelled ? Be frank with me ; tell me his name, and I swear upon the honor of a gentleman, I will rectify the trouble —will bring him in contrition to your feet."

Whether he dealt in irony, as was his habit, or really meant what he said, she was unable to determine ; and her quick glance at his countenance showed her only a dangerous sparkle in his eyes.

" Mr. Murray, you are wrong in your conjecture ; I have no lover."

"Oh ! call him what you please ! I shall not presume to dictate your terms of endearment. I merely wish to say, that if poverty stands forbiddingly between you and happiness, why, command me to the extent of half my fortune, I will give you a dowry that shall equal the expectations of any ambitious suitor in the land. Trust me, child, with your sorrow, and I will prove a faithful friend. Who has your heart ?"

The unexpected question alarmed and astonished her, and a shivering dread took possession of her that he suspected her real feelings, and was laughing at her folly. Treacherous blood began to paint confusion in her face, and vehement and rapid were her words.

" God and my conscience own my heart. I know no man to whom I would willingly give it ; and the correspondence to which you allude contains not a syllable of love. My time is rather too valuable to be frittered away in such trifling."

" Edna, would you prefer to have me a sworn ally or an avowed enemy ?"

" I should certainly prefer to consider you as neither."

"Did you ever know me to fail in any matter which I had determined to accomplish?"

"Yes, sir; your entire life is a huge, hideous, woful failure, which mocks and maddens you."

"What the d—l do you know of my life? It is not ended yet, and it remains to be seen whether a grand success is not destined to crown it. Mark you! the grapple is not quite over, and I may yet throttle the furies whose cursed fingers clutched me in my boyhood. If I am conquered finally, take my oath for it, I shall die so hard that the howling hags will be welcome to their prey. Single-handed I am fighting the world, the flesh, and the devil, and I want neither inspection, nor sympathy, nor assistance. Do you understand me?"

"Yes, sir. And as I certainly desire to thrust neither upon you, I will bid you good-night."

"One moment! What does that package contain?"

"The contents belong exclusively to me—could not possibly interest you—would only challenge your sarcasm, and furnish food for derision. Consequently, Mr. Murray, you must excuse me if I decline answering your question."

"I'll wager my title to Le Bocage that I can guess so accurately, that you will regret that you did not make a grace of necessity, and tell me."

A vague terror overshadowed her features as she examined the seals on the package, and replied:

"That, sir, is impossible, if you are the honorable gentleman I have always tried to force myself to believe."

"Silly child! Do you imagine I would condescend to soil my fingers with the wax that secures that trash? That I could stoop to an inspection of the correspondence of a village blacksmith's granddaughter? I will give you one more chance to close the breach between us by proving your trust. Edna, have you no confidence in me?"

"None, Mr. Murray."

" Will you oblige me by looking me full in the face,
and repeating your flattering words ?"

She raised her head, and though her heart throbbed
fiercely as she met his eyes, her voice was cold steady,
and resolute :

" None, Mr. Murray."

" Thank you. Some day those same red lips will
humbly, tremblingly crave my pardon for what they
utter now ; and then, Edna Earl, I shall take my revenge, and you will look back to this night and realize
the full force of my parting words—*væ victis !*"

He stooped and picked up a bow of rose-colored
ribbon which had fallen from her throat, handed it to
her, smiled, and, with one of those low, graceful,
haughty bows so indicative of his imperious nature, he
left the library. A moment after she heard his peculiar
laugh, mirthless and bitter, ring through the rotundo ;
then the door was slammed violently, and quiet
reigned once more through the mansion.

Taking the candle from the table where Mr. Murray
had placed it, Edna went back to her own room and
sat down before the window.

On her lap lay the package and letter, which she no
longer felt any desire to open, and her hands drooped
listlessly at her side. The fact that her MS. was returned rung a knell for all her sanguine hopes, for
such was her confidence in the critical acumen of Mr.
Manning that she deemed it utterly useless to appeal
to any other tribunal. A higher one she knew not ;
a lower she scorned to consult.

She felt like Alice Lisle on that day of doom, when
Jeffreys pronounced the fatal sentence ; and after a
time, when she summoned courage to open the letter,
her cheeks were wan and her lips compressed so firmly
that their curves of beauty were no longer traceable.

" MISS EARL : I return your MS., not because it is
devoid of merit, but from the conviction that were I to
accept it, the day would inevitably come when you
would regret its premature publication. While it

contains irrefragable evidence of extraordinary ability,
and abounds in descriptions of great beauty, your style
is characterized by more strength than polish, and is
marred by crudities which a dainty public would never
tolerate. The subject you have undertaken is beyond
your capacity—no woman could successfully handle it
—and the sooner you realize your over-estimate of
your powers, the sooner your aspirations find their
proper level, the sooner you will succeed in your treatment of some theme better suited to your feminine
ability. Burn the enclosed MS., the erudition and
archaisms of which would fatally nauseate the intellectual dyspeptics who read my 'Maga,' and write
sketches of home life—descriptions of places and
things that you understand better than recondite anal-
ogies of ethical creeds and mythologic systems, or
the subtle lore of Coptic priests. Remember that
women never write histories or epics ; never compose
oratorios that go sounding down the centuries ; never
paint ' Last Suppers' and ' Judgment Days'; though
now and then one gives to the world a pretty ballad
that sounds sweet and soothing when sung over a
cradle, or another paints a pleasant little *genre* sketch
which will hang appropriately in some quiet corner,
and rest and refresh eyes that are weary with gazing
at the sublime spiritualism of Fra Bartolomeo, or the
gloomy grandeur of Salvator Rosa. If you have any
short articles that you desire to see in print, you may
forward them, and I will select any for publication,
which I think you will not blush to acknowledge in
future years.

            " Very respectfully,
                " Your obedient Servant,
                        "DOUGLASS G. MANNING."

Unwrapping the MS., she laid it with its death-war-
rant in a drawer, then sat down, crossed her arms on
the top of her desk, and rested her head upon them.
The face was not concealed, and, as the light shone on
it, an experienced physiognomist would have read

there profound disappointment, a patient weariness,
but unbending resolution and no vestige of bitterness.
The large, thoughtful eyes were sad but dry, and none
who looked into them could have imagined for an instant that she would follow the advice she had so
eagerly sought. During her long reverie, she wondered whether all women were browbeaten for aspiring
to literary honors; whether the poignant pain and
mortification gnawing at her heart was the inexorable
initiation-fee for entrance upon that arena, where fame
adjudges laurel crowns, and reluctantly and sullenly
drops one now and then on female brows. To possess
herself of the golden apple of immortality, was a purpose from which she had never swerved; but how to
baffle the dragon critics who jealously guarded it was
a problem whose solution puzzled her.

To abandon her right to erudition formed no part of
the programme which she was mentally arranging as
she sat there watching a moth singe its filmy, spotted
wings in the gas-flame; for she was obstinately wedded
to the unpardonable heresy, that, in the nineteenth
century, it was a woman's privilege to be as learned as
Cuvier, or Sir William Hamilton, or Humboldt, provided the learning was accurate, and gave out no hollow, counterfeit ring under the merciless hammering
of the dragons. If women chose to blister their fair,
tender hands in turning the windlass of that fabled
well where truth is hidden, and bruised their pretty,
white feet in groping finally on the rocky bottom, was
the treasure which they ultimately discovered and
dragged to light any the less truth because stentorian,
manly voices were not the first to shout Eureka?

She could not understand why, in the vineyard of
letters, the laborer was not equally worthy of hire,
whether the work was successfully accomplished in the
toga virilis or the gay kirtle of *contadina*.

Gradually the expression of pain passed from the
girl's countenance, and, lifting her head, she took from
her desk several small MSS., that she had carefully
written from time to time, as her reading suggested the

ideas embodied in the articles. Among the number were two, upon which she had bestowed much thought, which she determined to send to Mr. Manning.

One was an elaborate description of that huge iconoclasm attributed to Alcibiades, and considered by some philosophic students of history the chief cause of the ruin of Athens. In order to reflect all possible light on this curious occurrence, she had most assiduously gleaned the pages of history, and massed the grains of truth; had studied maps of the city and descriptions of travellers, that she might thoroughly understand the topography of the scene of the great desecration. So fearful was she of committing some anachronism, or of soaring on the wings of fancy beyond the realm of well-authenticated facts, that she searched the ancient records to ascertain whether on that night in May, 415 B.C., a full or a new moon looked down on the bronze helmet of Minerva Promachus and the fretted frieze of the Parthenon.

The other MS., upon which she had expended much labor, was entitled "Keeping the Vigil of St. Martin under the Pines of Grütli"; and while her vivid imagination reveled in the weird and solemn surroundings of the lonely place of rendezvous, the sketch contained a glowing and eloquent tribute to the liberators of Helvetia, the Confederates of Schweitz, Uri, and Underwalden.

Whether Mr. Manning would consider either of these articles worthy of preservation in the pages of his magazine, she thought exceedingly doubtful; but she had resolved to make one more appeal to his fastidious judgment, and accordingly sealed and directed the roll of paper.

Weary but sleepless, she pushed back the heavy folds of hair that had fallen on her forehead, brightened the gas-light, and turned to the completion of a chapter in that MS. which the editor had recommended her to commit to the flames. So entirely was she absorbed in her work that the hours passed unheeded.

Now and then, when her thoughts failed to flow smoothly into graceful sentence moulds, she laid aside her pen, walked up and down the floor, turning the idea over and over, fitting it first to one phrase, then to another, until the verbal drapery fully suited her.

The whistle of the locomotive at the station told her that it was four o'clock before her task was accomplished; and, praying that God's blessing would rest upon it, she left it unfinished, and threw herself down to sleep.

But slumber brought no relaxation to the busy brain that toiled on in fitful, grotesque dreams; and when sunshine streamed through the open window at the foot of her bed, it showed no warm flush of healthful sleep on the beautiful face, but weariness and pallor. Incoherent words stirred the lips, troubled thought knitted the delicately-arched brows, and the white, dimpled arms were tossed restlessly above her head.

Was the tired midnight worker worthy of her hire? The world would one day pay her wages in the currency of gibes, and denunciation, and envious censoriousness; but the praise of men had not tempted her to the vineyard, and she looked in faith to Him "who seeth in secret," and whose rewards are at variance with those of the taskmasters of earth. "Wherefore," O lonely but conscientious student! "be ye steadfast, unmovable, always abounding in the work of the Lord, forasmuch as ye know that your labor is not in vain."

Literary women, whose avocation is selected simply because they fancy it easier to write than to sew for bread, or because they covet the applause and adulation heaped upon successful genius, or desire mere notoriety, generally barter their birthright of quiet, life-long happiness in the peaceful seclusion of home for a nauseous mess of poisoned pottage that will not appease their hunger; and they go down to untimely graves disappointed, embittered, hating the public for whose praises they toiled, cheated out of the price for which they bargained away fireside joys and domestic serenity.

The fondest hope of Edna's heart was to be useful in " her day and generation "—to be an instrument of some good to her race ; and while she hoped for popularity as an avenue to the accomplishment of her object, the fear of ridicule and censure had no power to deter her from the line of labor upon which she constantly invoked the guidance and blessing of God.

The noble words of Kepler rang a ceaseless silvery chime in her soul, and while they sustained and strengthened her, she sought to mould her life in harmony with their sublime teachings :

" Lo ! I have done the work of my life with that power of intellect which Thou hast given. If I, a worm before thine eyes, and born in the bonds of sin, have brought forth any thing that is unworthy of thy counsels, inspire me with thy spirit, that I may correct it. If by the wonderful beauty of thy works I have been led into boldness—if I have sought my own honor among men as I advanced in the work which was destined to thine honor, pardon me in kindness and charity, and by thy grace grant that my teaching may be to thy glory and the welfare of all men. Praise ye the Lord, ye heavenly harmonies ! and ye that understand the new harmonies, praise the Lord !"

CHAPTER XVIII.

"Mr. Hammond, are you ill? What can be the matter?"'

Edna threw down her books and put her hand on the old man's shoulder. His face was concealed in his arms, and his half-stifled groan told that some fierce trial had overtaken him.

"Oh, child! I am troubled, perplexed, and my heart is heavy with a sorrow which I thought I had crushed."

He raised his head for a moment, looked sadly into the girl's face, and dropped his furrowed cheek on his hand.

"Has anything happened since I saw you yesterday?"

"Yes, I have been surprised by the arrival of some of my relatives, whose presence in my house revives very painful associations connected with earlier years. My niece, Mrs. Powell, and her daughter Gertrude, came very unexpectedly last night to make me a visit of some length; and to you, my child, I can frankly say the surprise is a painful one. Many years have elapsed since I received any tidings of Agnes Powell, and I knew not, until she suddenly appeared before me last night, that she was a widow, and bereft of a handsome fortune. She claims a temporary home under my roof; and though she has caused me much suffering, I feel that I must endeavor to be patient and kind to her and her child. I have endured many trials, but this is one of the severest I have yet been called to pass through."

Distressed by the look of anguish on his pale face, Edna took his hand between both hers, and stroking it caressingly, said :

" My dear sir, if it is your duty, God will strengthen and sustain you. Cheer up ; I can't bear to see you looking so troubled. A cloud on your face, my dear Mr. Hammond, is to me like an eclipse of the sun. Pray do not keep me in shadow."

" If I could know that no mischief would result from Agnes's presence, I would not regret it so earnestly. I do not wish to be uncharitable or suspicious ; but I fear that her motives are not such as I could——"

" May I intrude, Uncle Allan ?"

The stranger's voice was very sweet and winning, and as she entered the room Edna could scarcely repress an exclamation of admiration ; for the world sees but rarely such perfect beauty as was the portion of Agnes Powell.

She was one of those few women who seem the pets of time, whose form and features catch some new grace and charm from every passing year ; and but for the tall, lovely girl who clung to her hand and called her " mother," a stranger would have believed her only twenty-six or eight.

Fair, rosy, with a complexion fresh as a child's, and a face faultless in contour as that of a Greek goddess, it was impossible to resist the fascination which she exerted over all who looked upon her. Her waving yellow hair flashed in the morning sunshine, and as she raised one hand to shade her large, clear, blue eyes, her open sleeve fell back, disclosing an arm dazzlingly white and exquisitely moulded. As Mr. Hammond introduced his pupil to his guests, Mrs. Powell smiled pleasantly, and pressed the offered hand ; but the eyes, blue and cold as the stalactites of Capri, scanned the orphan's countenance, and when Edna had seen fully into their depths, she could not avoid recalling Heine's poem of the Loreley.

" My daughter Gertrude promises herself much pleasure in your society, Miss Earl ; for uncle's praises prepare her to expect a most charming companion. She is about your age, but I fear you will find great disparity in her attainments, as she has not been so fortunate as to receive her education from Uncle Allan. You are, I believe, an adopted daughter of Mrs. Murray?"

" No, madam ; only a resident in her house until my education is pronounced sufficiently advanced to justify my teaching."

" I have a friend, Miss Harding, who has recently removed to Le Bocage, and intends making it her home. How is she?"

" Quite well, I believe."

Mr. Hammond left the study for a moment, and Mrs. Powell added :

"Her friends at the North tell me that she is to marry her cousin, Mr. Murray, very soon."

" I had not heard the report."

" Then you think there are no grounds for the rumor?"

" Indeed, madam, I know nothing whatever concerning the matter."

" Estelle is handsome and brilliant."

Edna made no reply; and after waiting a few seconds, Mrs. Powell asked :

" Does Mr. Murray go much into society now?"

" I believe not."

" Is he as handsome as ever?"

" I do not know when you saw him last, but the ladies here seem rather to dread than admire him. Mrs. Powell, you are dipping your sleeve in your uncle's inkstand."

She by no means relished this catechism, and resolved to end it. Picking up her books, she said to Mr. Hammond, who now stood in the door :

" I presume I need not wait, as you will be too much occupied to-day to attend to my lessons."

" Yes, I must give you holiday until Monday."

" Miss Earl, may I trouble you to hand this letter to Miss Harding? It was entrusted to my care by one of

her friends in New York. Pray be so good as to deliver it, with my kindest regards."

As Edna left the house, the pastor took his hat from
the rack in the hall, and walked silently beside her until she reached the gate.

"Mr. Hammond, your niece is the most beautiful
woman I have ever seen."

He sighed heavily, and answered hesitatingly:

"Yes, yes. She is more beautiful now than when
she first grew up."

"How long has she been a widow?"

"Not quite a year."

The troubled expression settled once more over his
placid face, and when Edna bade him good morning,
and had walked some distance, she happened to look
back, and saw him still leaning on the little gate under
the drooping honeysuckle tendrils, with his gray head
bent down on his hand.

That Mrs. Powell was in some way connected with
Mr. Murray's estrangement from the minister Edna
felt assured, and the curiosity which the inquiries of
the former had betrayed, told her that she must be
guarded in her intercourse with a woman who was an
object of distrust even to her own uncle.

Very often she had been tempted to ask Mr. Hammond why Mr. Murray so sedulously shunned him;
but the shadow which fell upon his countenance whenever St. Elmo's name was accidentally mentioned,
made her shrink from alluding to a subject which he
evidently avoided discussing.

Before she had walked beyond the outskirts of the
village, Mr. Leigh joined her, and she felt the color rise
in her cheeks as his fine eyes rested on her face, and
his hand pressed hers. "You must forgive me for telling you how bitterly I was disappointed in not seeing
you two days ago. Why did you absent yourself from
the table?"

"Because I had no desire to meet Mrs. Murray's
guests, and preferred to spend my time with Mr. Hammond."

" If he were not old enough to be your grandfather,
I believe I should be jealous of him. Edna, do not be
offended, I am so anxious about you—so pained at
the change in your appearance. Last Sunday as you
sat in church I noticed how very pale and worn you
looked, and with what weariness you leaned your head
upon your hand. Mrs. Murray says you are very well,
but I know better. You are either sick in body or
mind ; which is it ?"

" Neither, Mr. Leigh. I am quite well, I assure
you."

" You are grieved about something, which you are
unwilling to confide to me. Edna, it is a keen pain
that sometimes brings that quiver to your lips, and if
you would only tell me ! Edna, I know that I——"

" You conjure up a spectre. I have nothing to confide, and there is no trouble which you can relieve."
They walked on silently for a while, and then Gordon
said :

" I am going away day after to-morrow, to be absent
at least for several months, and I have come to ask a
favor which you are too generous to deny. I want
your ambrotype or photograph, and I hope you will
give it to me without hesitation."

" I have never had a likeness of any kind taken."

" There is a good artist here ; will you not go to-day
and have one taken for me ?"

" No, Mr. Leigh."

" Oh, Edna ! Why not ?"

" Because I do not wish you to think of or remember me. The sooner you forget me entirely, save as a
mere friend, the happier we both shall be."

" But that is impossible. If you withhold your picture it will do no good, for I have your face here in my
heart, and you cannot take that image from me."

" At least I will not encourage feelings which can
bring only pain to me and disappointment to yourself.
I consider it unprincipled and contemptible in a woman to foster or promote in any degree an affection
which she knows she can never reciprocate. If I had

fifty photographs I would not give you one. My
dear friend, let the past be forgotten ; it saddens me
whenever I think of it, and is a barrier to all pleasant
friendly intercourse. Good-by, Mr. Leigh. You have
my best wishes on your journey."

" Will you not allow me to see you home?"

" I think it is best—I prefer that you should not.
Mr. Leigh, promise me that you will struggle against
this feeling which distresses me beyond expression."

She turned and put out her hand. He shook his
head mournfully and said as he left her :

" God bless you ! It will be a dreary, dreary season
with me till I return and see your face again. God
preserve you till then !"

Walking rapidly homeward, Edna wondered why
she could not return Gordon Leigh's affection—why
his noble face never haunted her dreams instead of
another's—of which she dreaded to think.

Looking rigorously into the past few weeks, she felt
that long before she was aware of the fact, an image to
which she refused homage must have stood between
her heart and Gordon's.

When she reached home she inquired for Miss Harding, and was informed that she and Mrs. Murray had
gone visiting with Mr. Allston ; had taken lunch, and
would not return until late in the afternoon. Hagar
told her that Mr. Murray had started at daylight to one
of his plantations about twelve miles distant, and
would not be back in time for dinner ; and, rejoiced at
the prospect of a quiet day, she determined to complete the chapter which she had left unfinished two
nights previous.

Needing a reference in the book which Mr. Murray
had taken from the library, she went up to copy it ;
and as she sat down and opened the volume to find the
passage she required, a letter slipped out and fell at
her feet. She glanced at the envelope as she picked it
up, and her heart bounded painfully as she saw Mr.
Murray's name written in Mr. Manning's peculiar and
unmistakable chirography.

The postmark and date corresponded exactly with
the one that she had received the night Mr. Murray
gave her the roll of MS., and the strongest temptation
of her life here assailed her. She would almost have
given her right hand to know the contents of that letter, and Mr. Murray's confident assertion concerning
the package was now fully explained. He had recognized the handwriting on her letters, and suspected
her ambitious scheme. He was not a stranger to Mr.
Manning, and must have known the nature of their
correspondence ; consequently his taunt about a lover
was entirely ironical.

She turned the unsealed envelope over and over
longing to know what it contained.

The house was deserted—there was, she knew, no
human being nearer than the kitchen, and no eye
but God's upon her. She looked once more at the
superscription of the letter, sighed, and put it back
into the book without opening the envelope.

She copied into her note-book the reference she was
seeking, and replacing the volume on the window-sill
where she had found it, went back to her own room
and tried to banish the subject of the letter from her
mind.

After all, it was not probable that Mr. Murray had
ever mentioned her name to his correspondent ; and
as she had not alluded to Le Bocage or its inmates in
writing to Mr. Manning, St. Elmo's hints concerning
her MS. were merely based on conjecture. She felt as
if she would rather face any other disaster sooner than
have him scoffing at her daring project ; and more annoyed and puzzled than she chose to confess, she resolutely bent her thoughts upon her work.

It was almost dusk before Mrs. Murray and her
guests returned ; and when it grew so dark that Edna
could not see the lines of her paper, she smoothed her
hair, changed her dress, and went down to the parlor.

Mrs. Murray was resting in a corner of the sofa, fanning herself vigorously, and Mr. Allston smoked on

the verandah, and talked to her through the open window.

" Well, Edna, where have you been all day ?"

" With my books."

"I am tired almost to death ! This country visiting is an intolerable bore ! I am worn out with small talk and backbiting. Society nowadays is composed of cannibals—infinitely more to be dreaded than the Fijians—who only devour the body and leave the character of an individual intact. Child, let us have some music by way of variety. Play that symphony of Beethoven that I heard you practicing last week."

She laid her head on the arm of the sofa, and shut her eyes, and Edna opened the piano and played the piece designated.

The delicacy of her touch enabled her to render it with peculiar pathos and power ; and she played on and on, unmindful of Miss Harding's entrance—oblivious of everything but the sublime strains of the great master.

The light streamed over her face, and showed a gladness, an exaltation of expression there, as if her soul had broken from its earthly moorings, and was making its way joyfully into the infinite sea of eternal love and blessedness.

At last her fingers fell from the keys, and as she rose she saw Mr. Murray standing outside of the parlor door, with his fingers shading his eyes.

He came in soon after, and his mother held out her hand, saying :

" Here is a seat, my son. Have you just returned ?"

" No, I have been here some time."

" How are affairs at the plantation ?"

" I really have no idea."

" Why ? I thought you went there to-day."

" I started ; but found my horse so lame, that I went no further than town."

" Indeed ! Hagar told me you had not returned, when I came in from visiting."

" Like some other people of my acquaintance, Hagar

reckons without her host. I have been at home ever since twelve o'clock, and saw the carriage as you drove off."

"And pray how have you employed yourself, you incorrigible *ignis fatuus ?* O my cousin! you are well named. Aunt Ellen must have had an intuitive insight into your character when she had you christened St. Elmo; only she should have added the 'Fire——' How have you spent the day, sir?"

"Most serenely and charmingly, my fair cousin, in the solitude of my den. If my mother could give me satisfactory security that all my days would prove as quiet and happy as this has been, I would enter into bonds never to quit the confines of Le Bocage again. Ah! the indescribable relief of feeling that nothing was expected of me; that the galling gyves of hospitality and etiquette were snapped, and that I was entirely free from all danger of intrusion. This day shall be marked with a white stone; for I entered my rooms at twelve o'clock, and remained there in uninterrupted peace till five minutes ago; when I put on my social shackles once more, and hobbled down to entertain my fair guest."

Edna was arranging some sheets of music that were scattered on the piano; but as he mentioned the hour of his return, she remembered that the clock struck one just as she went into the sitting-room where he kept his books and cabinets; and she knew now that he was at that very time in the inner room, beyond the arch. She put her hand to her forehead, and endeavored to recollect the appearance of the apartment. The silk curtains, she was sure, were hanging over the arch; for she remembered distinctly having noticed a large and very beautiful golden butterfly which had fluttered in from the terrace, and was flitting over the glowing folds that fell from the carved intrados to the marble floor. But though screened from her view, he must have heard and seen her, as she sat before his book-case, turning his letter curiously between her fingers.

She dared not look up, and bent down to examine the music, so absorbed in her own emotions of chagrin and astonishment, that she heard not one word of what Miss Harding was saying. She felt well assured that if Mr. Murray were cognizant of her visit to the " Egyptian museum," he intended her to know it, and she knew that his countenance would solve her painful doubt.

Gathering up her courage, she raised her eyes quickly in the direction of the sofa, where he had thrown himself, and met just what she most dreaded, his keen gaze riveted on her face. Evidently he had been waiting for this eager, startling, questioning glance; for instantly he smiled, inclined his head slightly, and arched his eyebrows, as if much amused. Never before had she seen his face so bright and happy, so free from bitterness. If he had said, "Yes, I saw you; are you not thoroughly discomfited, and ashamed of your idle curiosity? What interest can you possibly have in carefully studying the outside of my letters? How do you propose to mend matters?"—he could not have more fully conveyed his meaning. Edna's face crimsoned, and she put up her hand to shield it; but Mr. Murray turned toward the window, and coolly discussed the merits of a popular race-horse, upon which Clinton Allston lavished extravagant praise.

Estelle leaned against the window, listening to the controversy, and after a time, when the subject seemed very effectually settled by an oath from the master of the house, Edna availed herself of the lull in the conversation to deliver the letter.

"Miss Harding, I was requested to hand you this."

Estelle broke the seal, glanced rapidly over the letter and exclaimed:

"Is it possible? Can she be here? Who gave you this letter?"

"Mrs. Powell, Mr. Hammond's niece."

"Agnes Powell?"

"Yes. Agnes Powell."

During the next three minutes one might have distinctly heard a pin fall, for the ticking of two watches was very audible.

Estelle glanced first at her cousin, then at her aunt, then back at her cousin. Mrs. Murray involuntarily laid her hand on her son's knee, and watched his face with an expression of breathless anxiety; and Edna saw that, though his lips blanched, not a muscle moved, not a nerve twitched; and only the deadly hate, that appeared to leap into his large shadowy eyes, told that the name stirred some bitter memory.

The silence was growing intolerable when Mr. Murray turned his gaze full on Estelle, and said in his usual sarcastic tone :

"Have you seen a ghost? Your letter must contain tidings of Victor's untimely demise; for, if there is such a thing as retribution, such a personage as Nemesis, I swear that poor devil of a Count has crept into her garments and come to haunt you. Did he cut his white womanish throat with a penknife, or smother himself with charcoal fumes, or light a poisoned candle and let his poor homœopathic soul drift out dreamily into eternity? If so, Gabriel will require a powerful microscope to find him. Notwithstanding the fact that you destined him for my cousin, the little curly creature always impressed me as being a stray specimen of an otherwise extinct type of intellectual Lacrymatoria. Is he really dead? Peace to his infusorial soul! Who had the courage to write and break the melancholy tidings to you ? Or perhaps, after all, it is only the ghost of your own conscience that has brought that scared look into your face."

She laughed and shrugged her shoulders.

"How insanely jealous you are of Victor ! He's neither dead nor dreaming of suicide, but enjoying himself vastly in Baden-Baden. Edna, did Mrs. Powell bring Gertrude with her?"

"Yes."

"Do you know how long she intends remaining at the parsonage?"

"I think her visit is of indefinite duration."

"Edna, will you oblige me by inquiring whether Henry intends to give us any supper to-night? He forgets we have had no dinner. St. Elmo, do turn down that gas—the wind makes it flare dreadfully."

Edna left the room to obey Mrs. Murray's command, and did not return immediately; but, after the party seated themselves at the table, she noticed that the master seemed in unusually high spirits; and when the meal was concluded, he challenged his cousins to a game of billiards.

They repaired to the rotundo, and Mrs. Murray beckoned to Edna to follow her. As they entered her apartment she carefully closed the door.

"Edna, when did Mrs. Powell arrive?"

"Last night."

"Did you see her?"

"Yes ma'am."

"Is she very pretty?"

"She is the most beautiful woman I ever met."

"How did Mr. Hammond receive her?"

"Her visit evidently annoys him, but he gave me no explanation of the matter, which I confess puzzles me. I should suppose her society would cheer and interest him."

"Oh, pooh! Talk of what you understand. She surely has not come here to live?"

"I think he fears she has. She is very poor."

Mrs. Murray set her teeth together, and muttered something which her companion did not understand.

"Edna, is she handsomer than Estelle?"

"Infinitely handsomer, I think. Indeed, they are so totally unlike it would be impossible to compare them. Your neice is very fine-looking, very commanding; Mrs. Powell is beautiful."

"But she is no longer young. She has a grown daughter."

"True; but in looking at her you do not realize it. Did you never see her?"

"No; and I trust I never may! I am astonished that Mr. Hammond can endure the sight of her. You say he has told you nothing about her?"

"Nothing which explains the chagrin her presence seems to cause."

"He is very wise. But, Edna, avoid her society as much as possible. She is doubtless very fascinating; but I do not like what I have heard of her, and prefer that you should have little conversation or intercourse with her. On the whole, you might as well stay at home now; it is very warm, and you can study without Mr. Hammond's assistance."

"You do not mean that my visits must cease altogether?"

"Oh! no; go occasionally—once or twice a week— but certainly not every day, as formerly. And, Edna, be careful not to mention that woman's name again; I dislike her exceedingly."

The orphan longed to ask for an explanation, but was too proud to solicit confidence so studiously withheld.

Mrs. Murray leaned back in her large rocking-chair and fell into a reverie. Edna waited patiently for some time, and finally rose.

"Mrs. Murray, have you anything more to say to me to-night? You look very much fatigued!"

"Nothing, I believe. Good-night, child. Send Hagar to me."

Edna went back to her desk and resolutely turned to her work; for it was one of the peculiar traits of her character that she could at will fasten her thoughts upon whatever subject she desired to master. All irrelevant ideas were sternly banished until such season as she chose to give them audience; and to-night she tore her mind from the events of the day, and diligently toiled among the fragments of Scandinavian lore for the missing links in her mythologic chain.

Now and then peals of laughter from the billiard-room startled her; and more than once Mr. Murray's clear, cold voice rose above the subdued chatter of Estelle and Clinton.

After a while the game ended, good-nights were exchanged, the party dispersed, doors were closed, and all grew silent.

While Edna wrote on, an unexpected sound arrested her pen. She listened, and heard the slow walk of a horse beneath her window. As it passed she rose and looked out. The moon was up, and Mr. Murray was riding down the avenue.

The girl returned to her MS., and worked on without intermission for another hour; then the last paragraph was carefully punctuated, the long and difficult chapter was finished. She laid aside her pen, and locked her desk.

Shaking down the mass of hair that had been tightly coiled at the back of her head, she extinguished the light, and drawing a chair to the window, seated herself.

Silence and peace brooded over the world; not a sound broke the solemn repose of nature.

The summer breeze had rocked itself to rest in the elm boughs, and only the waning moon seemed alive and toiling as it climbed slowly up a cloudless sky, passing starry sentinels whose mighty challenge was lost in vast vortices of blue, as they paced their ceaseless round in the mighty camp of constellations.

With her eyes fixed on the gloomy, groined archway of elms, where an occasional slip of moonshine silvered the ground, Edna watched and waited. The blood beat heavily in her temples and throbbed sullenly at her heart; but she sat mute and motionless as the summer night, reviewing all that had occurred during the day.

Presently the distant sound of hoofs on the rocky road leading to town fell upon her strained ear; the hard, quick gallop ceased at the gate, and very slowly Mr. Murray walked his horse up the dusky avenue, and on toward the stable.

From the shadow of her muslin curtain, Edna looked down on the walk beneath, and after a few moments saw him coming to the house.

He paused on the terrace, took off his hat, swept back the thick hair from his forehead, and stood look-ing out over the quiet lawn.

Then a heavy, heavy sigh, almost a moan, seemed to burst from the depths of his heart, and he turned and went into the house.

The night was far spent, and the moon had cradled herself on the tree-tops, when Edna raised her face all blistered with tears. Stretching out her arms she fell on her knees, while a passionate, sobbing prayer strug-gled brokenly across her trembling lips:

"O my God! have mercy upon him! save his wretched soul from eternal death! Help me so to live and govern myself that I bring no shame on the cause of Christ. And if it be thy will, O my God! grant that I may be instrumental in winning this precious but wandering, sinful soul back to the faith as it is in Jesus!"

Ah! verily—

> " . . . . More things are wrought by prayer
> Than this world dreams of. Wherefore let thy voice
> Rise like a fountain for him night and day.
> For what are men better than sheep or goats,
> That nourish a blind life within the brain,
> If, knowing God, they lift not hands of prayer
> Both for themselves, and those who call them friend?"

CHAPTER XIX.

"WHERE are you going, St. Elmo? I know it is one of your amiable decrees that your movements are not to be questioned, but I dare to brave your ire."

" I am going to that blessed retreat familiarly known as ' Murray's den,' where, secure from feminine intrusion, as if in the cool cloisters of Coutloumoussi, I surrender my happy soul to science and cigars, and revel in complete forgetfulness of that awful curse which Jove hurled against all mankind, because of Prometheus's robbery."

"There are asylums for lunatics and inebriates, and I wonder it has never occurred to some benevolent millionaire to found one for such abominable cynics as you, my most angelic cousin! where the snarling brutes can only snap at and worry one another."

" An admirable idea, Estelle, which I fondly imagined I had successfully carried out when I built those rooms of mine."

" You are as hateful as Momus, *minus* his wit! He was kicked out of heaven for grumbling, and you richly deserve his fate."

" I have a vague recollection that the Goddess Discord shared the fate of the celestial growler. I certainly plead guilty to an earnest sympathy with Momus's dissatisfaction with the house that Minerva built, and only wish that mine was movable, as he recommended, in order to escape bad neighborhoods and tiresome companions."

" Hospitable, upon my word! You spin some spiteful idea out of every sentence I utter and are not even

entitled to the compliment which Chesterfield paid old
Samuel Johnson, 'The utmost I can do for him is to
consider him a respectable Hottentot.' If I did not
know that instead of proving a punishment it would
gratify you beyond measure, I would take a vow not to
speak to you again for a month; but the consciousness
of the happiness I should thereby bestow upon you,
vetoes the resolution.   Do you know that even a
Comanche chief, or a Bechuana of the desert, shames
your inhospitality? I assure you I am the victim of
hopeless *ennui*, am driven to the verge of desperation;
for Mr. Allston will probably not return until to-morrow, and it is raining so hard that I can not wander
out of doors.   Here I am shut up in this dreary house,
which reminds me of the descriptions of that doleful
retreat for sinners in Normandy, where the inmates
pray eleven hours a day, dig their own graves every
evening, and if they chance to meet one another, salute
each other with ' *Memento mori !*' Ugh! if there remains one latent spark of chivalry in your soul, I
beseech you be merciful! Do not go off to your den,
but stay here and entertain me.   It is said that you
read bewitchingly, and with unrivalled effect; pray
favor me this morning.   I will promise to lay my hand
on my lips ; is it not white enough for a flag of truce?
I will be meek, amiable, docile, absolutely silent."

Estelle swept aside a mass of papers from the corner
of the sofa, and, taking Mr. Murray's hand, drew him
to a seat beside her.

"Your 'amiable silence,' my fair cousin, is but a
cunningly fashioned wooden horse.   *Timeo Danaos et
dona ferentes !*   I am to understand that you actually
offer me your hand as a flag of truce? It is wonderfully white and pretty; but excuse me, *C'est une main
de fer, gantée de velours !*   Your countenance, so
serenely radiant, reminds me of what Madame Noblet
said of M. de Vitri, 'His face looked just like a *strata-
gem !*'   Reading aloud is a practice in which I never
indulge, simply because I cordially detest it, and knowing this fact, it is a truly feminine refinement of cruelty

on your part to select this mode of penance. Nevertheless, your appeal to my chivalry, which always springs up, armed *cap-à-pie* 'to do or die'; and since read I must, I only stipulate that I may be allowed to select my book. Just now I am profoundly interested in a French work on infusoria, by Dujardin; and as you have probably not studied it, I will select those portions which treat of the animalcula that inhabit grains of sugar and salt and drops of water; so that by the time lunch is ready, your appetite will be whetted by a knowledge of the nature of your repast. According to Leeuwenhoek, Müller, Gleichen, and others, the campaigns of Zenzis-Khan, Alexander, Attila, were not half so murderous as a single fashionable dinner; and the battle of Marengo was a farce in comparison with the swallowing of a cup of tea, which contains——"

"For shame, you tormentor! when you know that I love tea as well as did your model of politeness, Dr. Johnson! Not one line of all that nauseatiug scientific stuff shall you read to me. Here is a volume of poems of the 'Female Poets'; do be agreeable for once in your life, and select me some sweet little rhythmic gem of Mrs. Browning, or Mrs. Norton, or L. E. L."

"Estelle, did you ever hear of the Peishwah of the Mahrattas?"

"I most assuredly never had even a hint of a syllable on the subject. What of him, her, or it?"

"Enough, that though you are evidently ambitious of playing his despotic *rôle* at Le Bocage, you will never succeed in reducing me to that condition of abject subjugation necessary to make me endure the perusal of 'female poetry.' I have always desired an opportunity of voting my cordial thanks to the wit who expressed so felicitously my own thorough conviction, that Pegasus had an unconquerable repugnance, hatred, to side-saddles. You vow you will not listen to science; and I swear I won't read poetry! Suppose we compromise on this new number of the —— Magazine? It is the ablest periodical published in this country. Let me see the contents of this number."

It was a dark, rainy morning in July. Mrs. Murray was winding a quantity of zephyr wool, of various bright colors, which she had requested Edna to hold on her wrists; and at the mention of the magazine the latter looked up suddenly at the master of the house.

Holding his cigar between his thumb and third finger, his eye ran over the table of contents.

"'Who smote the Marble Gods of Greece?' Humph! rather a difficult question to answer after the lapse of twenty-two centuries. But doubtless our archæologists are so much wiser than the Athenian Senate of Five Hundred, who investigated the affair the day after it happened, that a perusal will be exceedingly edifying. Now, then, for a solution of this classic mystery of the nocturnal iconoclasm; which, in my humble opinion, only the brazen lips of Minerva Promachus could satisfactorily explain."

Turning to the article he read it aloud, without pausing to comment, while Edna's heart bounded so rapidly that she could scarcely conceal her agitation. It was, indeed, a treat to listen to him; and as his musical voice filled the room, she thought of Jean Paul Richter's description of Goethe's reading: "There is nothing comparable to it. It is like deep-toned thunder blended with whispering rain-drops."

But the orphan's pleasure was of short duration, and as Mr. Murray concluded the perusal, he tossed the magazine contemptuously across the room, and exclaimed:

"Pretentious and shallow! A tissue of pedantry and error from beginning to end—written, I will wager my head, by some scribbler who never saw Athens! Moreover, the whole article is based upon a glaring blunder; for, according to Plutarch and Diodorus, on the memorable night in question there was a new moon. Pshaw! it is a tasteless, insipid plagiarism from Grote; and if I am to be bored with such insufferable twaddle, I will stop my subscription. For some time I have noticed symptoms of deterioration, but this is altogether intolerable ; and I shall write to Manning that, if he cannot do better, it would be advisable for him to suspend at once before his magazine loses its reputation. If I were not aware that his low estimate of female intellect coincides fully with my own, I should be tempted to suppose that some silly but ambitious woman wrote that stuff, which sounds learned and is simply stupid."

He did not even glance toward Edna, but the peculiar emphasis of his words left no doubt in her mind that he suspected, nay, felt assured, that she was the luckless author. Raising her head which had been drooped over the woolen skeins, she said, firmly, yet very quietly :

"If you will permit me to differ with you, Mr. Murray, I will say that it seems to me all the testimony is in favor of the full-moon theory. Beside, Grote is the latest and best authority ; he has carefully collected and sifted the evidence, and certainly sanctions the position taken by the author of the article which you condemn."

"Ah! how long since you investigated the matter ? The affair is so essentially Paganish that I should imagine that it possessed no charm for so orthodox a Christian as yourself. Estelle, what say you concerning this historic sphinx ?"

"That I am blissfully ignorant of the whole question, and have a vague impression that it is not worth the paper it is written on, much less a quarrel with you, Monsieur ' Le Hutin '; that it is the merest matter of moonshine—new moon *versus* full moon, and must have been written by a lunatic. But, my Chevalier Bayard, one thing I do intend to say most decidedly, and that is, that your lunge at female intellect, was as unnecessary and ill-timed and ill-bred as it was ill-natured. The mental equality of the sexes is now as unquestioned, as universally admitted, as any other well-established fact in science or history ; and the sooner you men gracefully concede us our rights, the

sooner we shall cease wrangling, and settle back into
our traditional amiability."

"The universality of the admission I should certainly deny, were the subject of sufficient importance
to justify a discussion. However, I have been absent
so long from America, that I confess my ignorance of
the last social advance in the striding enlightenment
of this most progressive people. According to Moleschott's celebrated *dictum*—'Without phosphorus no
thought,' and if there be any truth in physiology and
phrenology, you women have been stinted by nature
in the supply of phosphorus. Peacock's measurements
prove that in the average weight of male and female
brains, you fall below our standard by not less than
six ounces. I should conjecture that in the scales of
equality six ounces of ideas would turn the balance in
favor of our superiority."

"If you reduce it to a mere question of avoirdupois,
please be so good as to remember that even greater
difference exists among men. For instance, your
brain (which is certainly not considered over average)
weighs from three to three and a half pounds, while
Cuvier's brain weighed over four pounds, giving him
the advantage of more than eight ounces over our household oracle! Accidental difference in brain weight
proves nothing; for you will not admit your mental
inferiority to any man, simply because his head requires a larger hat than yours."

"Pardon me, I always bow before facts, no matter
how unflattering, and I consider one of Cuvier's ideas
worthy of just exactly eight degrees more of reverence
than any phosphorescent sparkle which I might choose
to hold up for public acceptance and guidance. Without doubt, the most thoroughly ludicrous scene I ever
witnessed was furnished by a 'woman's right's meeting,' which I looked in upon one night in New-York,
as I returned from Europe. The speaker was a raw-
boned, wiry, angular, short-haired, lemon-visaged
female of very certain age; with a hand like a bronze
gauntlet, and a voice as distracting as the shrill squeak

of a cracked cornet-a-piston. Over the wrongs and grievances of her down-trodden, writhing sisterhood she ranted and raved and howled, gesticulating the while with a marvelous grace, which I can compare only to the antics of those inspired goats who strayed too near the Pythian cave, and were thrown into convulsions. Though I pulled my hat over my eyes and clapped both hands to my ears, as I rushed out of the hall after a stay of five minutes, the vision of horror followed me, and for the first and only time in my life, I had such a hideous nightmare that night, that the man who slept in the next room broke open my door to ascertain who was strangling me. Of all my pet aversions my most supreme abhorrence is of what are denominated 'gifted women'; strong-minded (that is, weak-brained but loud-tongued), would-be literary females, who, puffed up with insufferable conceit, imagine they rise to the dignity and height of man's intellect, proclaim that their 'mission' is to write or lecture, and set themselves up as shining female lights, each aspiring to the rank of protomartyr of reform. Heaven grant us a Bellerophon to relieve the age of these noisy Amazons! I should really enjoy seeing them tied down to their spinning-wheels, and gagged with their own books, magazines, and lectures! When I was abroad and contrasted the land of my birth with those I visited, the only thing for which, as an American, I felt myself called on to blush, was my countrywomen. An insolent young count who had traveled through the Eastern and Northern States of America, asked me one day in Berlin, if it were really true that the male editors, lawyers, doctors and lecturers in the United States were contemplating a hegira, in consequence of the rough elbowing by the women, and if I could inform him at what age the New England girls generally commenced writing learned articles, and affixing LL.D., F.E.S., F.S.A., and M.M.S.S. to their signature?"

" 'Lay on, Macduff!' I wish you distinctly to understand that my toes are not bruised in the slightest degree; for I am entirely innocent of any attempt at erudition or authorship, and the sole literary dream of my life is to improve the present popular recipe for *biscuit glacé*. But mark you, 'Sir Oracle,' I must 'ope my lips' and bark a little under my breath at your inconsistencies. Now, if there are two living men whom, above all others, you swear by, they are John Stuart Mill and John Ruskin. Well do I recollect your eulogy of both, on that ever-memorable day in Paris, when we dined with that French encyclopædia, Count W——, and the leading lettered men of the day were discussed. I was frightened out of my wits, and dared not raise my eyes higher than the top of my wineglass, lest I should be asked my opinion of some book or subject of which I had never even heard, and in trying to appear well-educated, make as horrible a blunder as poor Madame Talleyrand committed, when she talked to Denon about his man Friday, believing that he wrote 'Robinson Crusoe.' At that time I had never read either Mill or Ruskin; but my profound reverence for the wisdom of your opinions taught me how shamefully ignorant I was, and thus, to fit myself for your companionship, I immediately bought their books. Lo, to my indescribable amazement, I found that Mill claimed for women what I never once dreamed we were worthy of—not only equality, but the right of suffrage. He, the foremost dialectician of England and the most learned of political economists, demands that, for the sake of equity and 'social improvement,' we women (minus the required six ounces of brains) should be allowed to vote. Behold the Corypheus of the 'woman's rights' school! Were I to follow his teachings, I should certainly begin to clamor for my right of suffrage—for the ladylike privilege of elbowing you away from the ballot-box at the next election.

"I am quite as far from admitting the infallibility of man as the equality of the sexes. The clearest thinkers of the world have had soft spots in their brains; for instance, the dæmon belief of Socrates and the ludicrous superstitions of Pythagoras; and you have laid your finger on the softened spot in Mill's skull, 'suffrage.' That is a jaded, spavined hobby of his, and he is too shrewd a logician to involve himself in the inconsistency of 'extended suffrage' which excludes women. When I read his 'Representative Government' I saw that his reason had dragged anchor, the prestige of his great name vanished, and I threw the book into the fire and eschewed him henceforth. *Sic transit.*"

Here Mrs. Murray looked up and said:

"John Stuart Mill—let me see—Edna, is he not the man who wrote that touching dedication of one of his books to his wife's memory? You quoted it for me a few days ago, and said that you had committed it to memory because it was such a glowing tribute to the intellectual capacity of woman. My dear, I wish you would repeat it now; I should like to hear it again."

With her fingers full of purple woolen skeins, and her eyes bent down, Edna recited, in a low, sweet voice the most eloquent panegyric which man's heart ever pronounced on woman's intellect:

"To the beloved and deplored memory of her who was the inspirer, and in part, the author, of all that is best in my writings, the friend and wife whose exalted sense of truth and right was my strongest incitement, and whose approbation was my chief reward, I dedicate this volume. Like all that I have written for many years, it belongs as much to her as to me; but the work as it stands has had, in a very insufficient degree, the inestimable advantage of her revision; some of the most important portions having been reserved for a more careful re-examination, which they are now never destined to receive. Were I but capable of interpreting to the world one half the great thoughts and noble feelings which are buried in her grave, I should be the medium of a greater benefit to it than is ever likely to arise from anything that I can write unprompted and unassisted by her all but unrivalled wisdom."

"Where did you find that dedication?" asked Mr.
Murray.

"In Mill's book on liberty."

"It is not in my library."

"I borrowed it from Mr. Hammond."

"Strange that a plant so noxious should be permitted in such a sanctified atmosphere! Do you happen to
recollect the following sentences? 'I regard utility as the
ultimate appeal on all ethical questions!' 'There is a
Greek ideal of self-development which the Platonic
and Christian ideal of self-government blends with but
does not supersede. It may be better to be a John
Knox than an Alcibiades, but it is better to be a
Pericles than either.'"

"Yes, sir. They occur in the same book; but, Mr.
Murray, I have been advised by my teacher to bear
always in mind that noble maxim, 'I can tolerate everything else but every other man's intolerance;' and it
is with his consent and by his instructions that I go
like Ruth, gleaning in the great fields of literature."

"Take care you don't find Boaz instead of barley.
After all, the universal mania for match-making schemes
and manœuvers which continually stir society from its
dregs to the painted foam-bubble dancing on its crested
wave, is peculiar to no age or condition, but is an
immemorial and hereditary female proclivity; for I
defy Paris or London to furnish a more perfectly developed specimen of a 'manœuvring mamma' than
was crafty Naomi, when she sent that pretty little
Moabitish widow out husband-hunting."

"I heartily wish she was only here to outwit you!"
laughed his cousin, nestling her head against his arm
as they sat together on the sofa.

"Who? The widow or the match-maker?"

"Oh! the match-maker, of course. There is more
than one Ruth already in the field."

The last clause was whispered so low that only St.
Elmo heard it, and any other woman but Estelle Harding would have shrunk away in utter humiliation from
the eye and the voice that answered:

"Yourself and Mrs. Powell! Eat Boaz's barley as long as you like—nay, divide Boaz's broad fields between you ; an you love your lives, keep out of Boaz's way."

"You ought both to be ashamed of yourselves. I am surprised at you, Estelle, to encourage St. Elmo's irreverence," said Mrs. Murray, severely.

"I am sure, Aunt Ellen, I am just as much shocked as you are ; but when he does not respect even your opinions, how dare I presume to hope he will show any deference to mine? St. Elmo, what think you of the last Sibylline leaves of your favorite Ruskin? In looking over his new book, I was surprised to find this strong assertion . . . Here is the volume now— listen to this, will you ?"

"'Shakespeare has no heroes ; he has only heroines. In his labored and perfect plays you find no hero, but almost always a perfect woman; steadfast in grave hope and errorless purpose. The catastrophe of every play is caused always by the folly or fault of a man; the redemption, if there be any, is by the wisdom and virtue of a woman, and failing that, there is none !'"

"For instance, Lady Macbeth, Ophelia, Regan, Goneril, and last, but not least, Petruchio's sweet and gentle Kate! *De gustibus!*" answered Mr. Murray.

"Those are the exceptions, and of course you pounce upon them. Ruskin continues : 'In all cases with Scott, as with Shakespeare, it is the woman who watches over, teaches and guides the youth ; it is never by any chance the man who watches over or educates her; and thus——'"

"Meg Merrilies, Madge Wildfire, Mause Headrigg, Effie Deans, and Rob Roy's freckle-faced, red-haired, angelic Helen!" interrupted her cousin.

"Don't be rude, St. Elmo. You fly in my face like an exasperated wasp. I resume : 'Dante's great poem is a song of praise for Beatrice's watch over his soul ; she saves him from hell, and leads him star by star up into heaven——'"

"Permit me to suggest that conjugal devotion

should have led him to apostrophize the superlative charms of his own wife, Gemma, from whom he was forced to separate ; and that his vision of hell was a faint reflex of his domestic felicity."

"Mask your battery, sir, till I finish this page, which I am resolved you shall hear : 'Greek literature proves the same thing, as witness the devoted tenderness of Andromache, the wisdom of Cassandra, the domestic excellence of Penolope, the love of Antigone, the resignation of Iphigenia, the faithfulness of——' "

"Allow me to assist him in completing the list : the world-renowned constancy of Helen to Menelaus, the devotion of Clytemnestra to her Agamemnon, the sublime filial affection of Medea, and the bewitching——"

"Hush, sir ! Aunt Ellen, do call him to order ! I will have a hearing, and I close the argument by the unanswerable assertion of Ruskin : 'That the Egyptians and Greeks (the most civilized of the ancients) both gave to their spirit of wisdom the form of a woman, and for symbols, the weaver's shuttle and the olive !"

"An inevitable consequence of the fact, that they considered wisdom as synonymous with sleepless and unscrupulous cunning ! Schiller declares that 'man depicts himself in his gods '; and even a cursory inspection of the classics proves that all the abhorred and hideous ideas of the ancients were personified by woman. Pluto was affable, and beneficent, and gentlemanly, in comparison with Brimo ; ditto might be said of Loke and Hela, and the most appalling idea that ever attacked the brain of mankind, found incarnation in the Fates and Furies, who are always women. Unfortunately the mythologies of the world crystallized before the age of chivalry, and a little research will establish the unflattering fact that human sins and woes are traced primarily to female agency ; while it is patent that all the rows and squabbles that disgraced Olympus were stirred up by scheming goddesses!

"Thank heaven! here comes Mr. Allston; I can smooth the ruffled plumes of my self-love in his sunny smiles, and forget your growls. Good morning, Mr. Allston; what happy accident brought you again so soon to Le Bocage and its disconsolate inmates?"

Edna picked up the magazine which lay in one corner, and made her escape.

The gratification arising from the acceptance and prompt publication of her essay, was marred by Mr. Murray's sneering comments; but still her heart was happier than it had been for many weeks, and as she turned to the Editor's Table and read a few lines complimenting "the article of a new contributor," and promising another from the same pen for the ensuing month, her face flushed joyfully.

While she felt it difficult to realize that her writings had found favor in Mr. Manning's critical eyes, she thanked God that she was considered worthy of communicating with her race through the medium of a magazine so influential and celebrated. She thought it probable that Mr. Manning had written her a few lines, and wondered whether at that moment a letter was not hidden in St. Elmo's pocket.

Taking the magazine, she went into Mrs. Murray's room, and found her resting on a lounge. Her face wore a troubled expression, and Edna saw traces of tears on the pillow.

"Come in, child; I was just thinking of you."

She put out her hand, drew the girl to a seat near the lounge, and sighed heavily.

"Dear Mrs. Murray, I am very, very happy, and I have come to make a confession and ask your congratulations."

She knelt down beside her, and, taking the white fingers of her benefactress, pressed her forehead against them.

"A confession, Edna! What have you done?"

Mrs. Murray started up and lifted the blushing face.

"Some time ago you questioned me concerning some letters which excited your suspicion, and which

I promised to explain at some future day. I dare say
you will think me very presumptuous when I tell you
that I have been aspiring to authorship; that I was
corresponding with Mr. Manning on the subject of a
MS. which I had sent for his examination, and now I
have come to show you what I have been doing. You
heard Mr. Murray read an essay this morning from the
—— Magazine, which he ridiculed very bitterly, but
which Mr. Manning at least thought worthy of a place
in his pages. Mrs. Murray, I wrote that article."

"Is it possible? Who assisted you—who revised it?
Mr. Hammond? I did not suppose that you, my child,
could ever write so elegantly, so gracefully."

"No one saw the MS. until Mr. Manning gave it to
the printers. I wished to surprise Mr. Hammond, and
therefore told him nothing of my ambitious scheme.
I was very apprehensive that I should fail, and for that
reason was unwilling to acquaint you with the precise
subject of the correspondence until I was sure of success. Oh, Mrs. Murray! I have no mother, and feeling that I owe everything to you—that without your
generous aid and protection I should never have been
able to accomplish this one hope of my life, I come to
you to share my triumph, for I know you will fully
sympathize with me. Here is the magazine containing Mr. Manning's praise of my work, and here are the
letters which I was once so reluctant to put into your
hands. When I asked you to trust me, you did so nobly
and freely; and thanking you more than my feeble
words can express, I want to show you that I was not
unworthy of your confidence."

She laid magazine and letters on Mrs. Murray's lap,
and in silence the proud, reserved woman wound her
arms tightly around the orphan, pressing the bright
young face against her shoulder, and resting her own
cheek on the girl's fair forehead.

The door was partly ajar, and at that instant St.
Elmo entered.

He stopped, looked at the kneeling figure locked so
closely in his mother's arms, and over his stern face

broke a light that transformed it into such beauty as Lucifer's might have worn before his sin and banishment, when God—

> " 'Lucifer'—kindly said as ' Gabriel,'
>   'Lucifer'—soft as ' Michael' ; while serene
> He, standing in the glory of the lamps,
> Answered, ' My Father,' innocent of shame
> And of the sense of thunder !"

Yearningly he extended his arms toward the two, who, absorbed in their low talk, were unconscious of his presence ; then the hands fell heavily to his side, the brief smile was swallowed up by scowling shadows, and he turned silently away and went to his own gloomy rooms.

CHAPTER XX.

" Mrs. Powell and her daughter to see Miss Estelle and Miss Edna."

"Why did you not say we were at dinner?" cried Mrs. Murray, impatiently, darting an angry glance at the servant.

"I did, ma'am, but they said they would wait."

As Estelle folded up her napkin and slipped it into the silver ring, she looked furtively at St. Elmo, who, holding up a bunch of purple grapes, said in an indifferent tone to his mother:

"The vineyards of Axarquia show nothing more per fect. This cluster might challenge comparison with those from which Red Hermitage is made, and the seeds of which are said to have been brought from Schiraz. Even on the sunny slopes of Cyprus and Naxos I found no finer grapes than these. *A propos !* I want a basketful this afternoon. Henry, tell old Simon to gather them immediately."

"Pray what use have you for them? I am sure the courteous idea of sending them as a present never could have forced an entrance into your mind, much less have carried the outworks of your heart!"

As his cousin spoke she came to the back of his chair and leaned over his shoulder.

"I shall go out on the terrace and renew the obsolete Dionysia, shouting '*Evoe! Eleleus!*' I shall crown and pelt my marble Bacchus yonder with the grapes till his dainty sculptured limbs are bathed in their purple sacrificial blood. What other use could I possibly have for them?"

He threw his head back and added something in a lower tone, at which Estelle laughed, and put up her red, full lip.

Mrs. Murray frowned, and said sternly :

"If you intend to see those persons, I advise you to do so promptly."

Her niece moved toward the door, but glanced over her shoulder.

"I presume Gertrude expects to see Edna, as she asked for her."

The orphan had been watching Mr. Murray's face, but could detect no alteration in its expression, save a brief gleam as of triumph when the visitors were announced. Rising, she approached Mrs. Murray, whose clouded brow betokened more than ordinary displeasure, and whispered :

"Gertrude is exceedingly anxious to see the house and grounds ; have I your permission to show her over the place? She is particularly anxious to see the deer."

"Of course, if she requests it ; but their effrontery in coming here caps the climax of all the impudence I ever heard of. Have as little to say as possible."

Edna went to the parlor, leaving mother and son together.

Mrs. Powell had laid aside her mourning garments and wore a dress of blue muslin which heightened her beauty, and as the orphan looked from her to Gertrude she found it difficult to decide who was the loveliest. After a few desultory remarks she rose, saying :

"As you have repeatedly expressed a desire to examine the park and hothouses, I will show you the way this afternoon."

"Take care, my love, that you do not fatigue yourself," were Mrs. Powell's low, tenderly spoken words as her daughter rose to leave the room.

Edna went first to the greenhouse, and though her companion chattered ceaselessly, she took little interest in her exclamations of delight, and was conjecturing the probable cause of Mrs. Murray's great indignation.

For some weeks she had been thrown frequently into the society of Mr. Hammond's guests, and while her distrust of Mrs. Powell, her aversion to her melting, musical voice, increased at every interview, a genuine affection for Gertrude had taken root in her heart.

They were the same age; but one was an earnest woman, the other a fragile, careless, gleeful, enthusiastic child. Although the orphan found it impossible to make a companion of this beautiful, warm-hearted girl, who hated books and turned pale at the mention of study, still Edna liked to watch the lovely, radiant face, with its cheeks tinted like sea-shells, its soft, childish blue eyes sparkling with joyousness; and she began to caress and to love her, as she would have petted a canary or one of the spotted fawns gamboling over the lawn.

As they stood hand in hand, admiring some gold-fish in a small aquarium in the centre of the greenhouse, Gertrude exclaimed:

"The place is as fascinating as its master! Do tell me something about him; I wonder very often why you never mention him. I know I ought not to say it; but really, after he has talked to me for a few minutes, I forget every thing else, and think only of what he says for days and days after."

"You certainly do not allude to Mr. Murray?" said Edna.

"I certainly do. What makes you look so astonished?"

"I was not aware that you knew him."

"Oh! I have known him since the week after our arrival here. Mamma and I met him at Mrs. Inge's. Mr. Inge had some gentlemen to dinner, and they came into the parlor while we were calling. Mrs. Murray sat down and talked to me then for some time, and I have frequently met him since; for it seems he loves to stroll about the woods almost as well as I do, and sometimes we walk together. You know he and my uncle are not friendly, and I believe mamma does not like him, so he never comes to the parsonage ; and never seems to see me if I am with her or Uncle Allan. But is he not very fascinating ? If he were not a little too old for me, I believe I should really be very much in love with him."

An expression of disgust passed swiftly over Edna's pale face; she dropped her companion's hand, and asked coldly :

" Does your mother approve of your walks with Mr. Murray ?"

" For heaven's sake, don't look so solemn ! I—she —really I don't know ! I never told her a word about it. Once I mentioned having met him, and showed her some flowers he gave me ; and she took very little notice of the matter. Several times since he has sent me bouquets, and though I kept them out of uncle's sight, she saw them in my room, and must have suspected where they came from. Of course he can not come to the parsonage to see me when he does not speak to my uncle or to mamma ; but I do not see any harm in his walking and talking with me, when I happen to meet him. Oh ! how lovely those lilies are, leaning over the edge of the aquarium ! Mr. Murray said that some day he would show me all the beautiful things at Le Bocage ; but he has forgotten his promise, I am afraid and I——"

" Ah ! Miss Gertrude, how could you doubt me ? I am here to fulfill my promise."

He pushed aside the boughs of a guava which stood between them, and, coming forward, took Gertrude's hand, drew it under his arm, and looked down eagerly, admiringly, into her blushing face.

" Oh, Mr. Murray ! I had no idea you were anywhere near me. I am sure I could——"

" Did you imagine you could escape my eyes, which are always seeking you ? Permit me to be your *cicerone* over Le Bocage, instead of Miss Edna here, who looks as if she had been scolding you. Perhaps she

will be so good as to wait for us, and I will bring you
back in a half-hour at least."

"Edna, will you wait here for me?" asked Gertrude.

"Why can not Mr. Murray bring you to the house?
There is nothing more to see here."

"Allow us to judge for ourselves, if you please.
There is a late Paris paper, which will amuse you till
we return."

St. Elmo threw a newspaper at her feet, and led
Gertrude away through one of the glass doors into the
park.

Edna sat down on the edge of the aquarium, and
the hungry little fish crowded close to her, looking up
wistfully for the crumbs she was wont to scatter there
daily; but now their mute appeal was unheeded.

Her colorless face and clasped hands grew cold as
the marble basin on which they rested, and the great,
hopeless agony that seized her heart came to her large
eyes and looked out drearily.

It was in vain that she said to herself:

"St. Elmo Murray is nothing to me; why should I
care if he loves Gertrude? She is so beautiful and
confiding and winning. Of course, if he knows her
well he must love her. It is no business of mine. We
are not even friends; we are worse than strangers;
and it can not concern me whom he loves or whom he
hates."

Her own heart laughed her words to scorn, and
answered defiantly: "He is my king! my king! I
have crowned and sceptred him, and right royally he
rules!"

In pitiable humiliation she acknowledged that she
had found it impossible to tear her thoughts from him;
that his dark face followed—haunted her, sleeping and
waking. While she shrank from his presence, and
dreaded his character, he could not witness his fond
manner to Gertrude without a pang of the keenest pain
she had ever endured.

The suddenness of the discovery shocked her into a
thorough understanding of her own feelings. The

grinning fiend of jealousy had swept aside the flimsy veil which she had never before fully lifted ; and looking sorrowfully down into the bared holy of holies, she saw standing between the hovering wings of golden cherubim an idol of clay demanding homage, daring the wrath of conscience, the high priest. She saw all now, and saw, too, at the same instant, whither her line of duty led.

The atmosphere was sultry, but she shivered ; and if a mirror could have been held before her eyes, she would have started back from the gray, stony face so unlike hers.

It seemed so strange that the heart of the accomplished misanthrope—the man of letters and science, who had ransacked the world for information and amusement—should surrender itself to the prattle of a pretty young thing, who could sympathize in no degree with his pursuits, and was as utterly incapable of understanding his nature as his Tartar horse or his pet bloodhound.

She had often heard Mrs. Murray say, " If there is one thing more uncertain even than the verdict of a jury—if there is one thing which is known neither in heaven, earth, nor hell, and which angels and demons alike waste time in guessing at—it is what style of woman any man will fancy and select for his wife. It is utterly impossible to predict what matrimonial caprice may or may not seize even the wisest, most experienced, most practical, and reasonable of men ; and I would sooner undertake to conjecture how high the thermometer stands at this instant on the crest of Mount Copernicus up yonder in the moon, than attempt to guess what freak will decide a man's choice of a bride."

Sternly Edna faced the future, and pictured Gertrude as Mr. Murray's wife ; for if he loved her, (and did not his eyes declare it ?) of course he would sweep every objection, every obstacle to the winds, and marry her speedily. She tried to think of him—the cold, harsh scoffer—as the fond husband of that laughing child; and though the vision was indescribably painful, she forced herself to dwell upon it.

The idea that he would ever love any one or anything had never until this hour occurred to her; and while she could neither tolerate his opinions or respect his character, she found herself smitten with a great, voiceless anguish at the thought of his giving his sinful bitter heart to any woman.

> Why did she love him? Curious fool, be still!
> Is human love the growth of human will?"

Pressing her hand to her eyes she murmured:

"Gertrude is right; he is fascinating, but it is the fascination of a tempting demon! Ah! if I had never come here, if I had never been cursed with the sight of his face! But I am no weak, silly child like Gertrude Powell; I know what my duty is, and I am strong enough to conquer, and if necessary to crush my foolish heart. Oh! I know you, Mr. Murray, and I can defy you. To-day, shortsighted as I have been, I look down on you You are beneath me, and the time will come when I shall look back to this hour and wonder if I were temporarily bewitched or insane. Wake up! wake up! come to your senses, Edna Earl! Put an end to this sinful folly; blush for your unwomanly weakness!"

As Gertrude's merry laugh floated up through the trees the orphan lifted her head, and the blood came back to her cheeks while she watched the two figures sauntering across the smooth lawn. Gertrude leaned on Mr. Murray's arm, and as he talked to her his head was bent down, so that he could see the flushed face shaded by her straw hat.

She drew her hand from his arm when they reached the greenhouse, and looking much embarrassed, said hurriedly:

"I am afraid I have kept you waiting an unconscionable time; but Mr. Murray had so many beautiful things to show me, that I quite forgot we had left you here alone."

"I dare say your mother thinks I have run away with you ; and as I have an engagement, I must either bid you good-bye and leave you here with Mr. Murray, or go back at once with you to the house."

The orphan's voice was firm and quiet ; and as she handed the French paper to St. Elmo, she turned her eyes full on his face.

"Have you read it already?" he asked, giving her one of his steely, probing glances.

"No, sir, I did not open it, as I take little interest in continental politics. Gertrude, will you go or stay ?"

Mr. Murray put out his hand, took Gertrude's, and said :

"Good-bye till to-morrow. Do not forget your promise."

Turning away, he went in the direction of the stables.

In silence Edna walked on to the house, and presently Gertrude's soft fingers grasped hers.

"Edna, I hope you are not mad with me. Do you really think it is wrong for me to talk to Mr. Murray, and to like him so much?"

"Gertrude, you must judge for yourself concerning the propriety of your conduct. I shall not presume to advise you ; but the fact that you are unwilling to acquaint your mother with your courre ought to make you look closely at your own heart. When a girl is afraid to trust her mother, I should think there were grounds for uneasiness."

They had reached the steps, and Mrs. Powell came out to meet them.

"Where have you two runaways been? I have waited a half hour for you. Estelle, do come and see me. It is very dreary at the parsonage, and your visits are cheering and precious. Come, Gertrude."

When Gertrude kissed her friend, she whispered :

"Don't be mad with me, dearie. I will remember what you said, and talk to mamma this very evening."

Edna saw mother and daughter descend the long

avenue and then running up to her room, she tied on her hat and walked rapidly across the park in an opposite direction.

About a mile and a half from Le Bocage, on a winding and unfrequented road leading to a sawmill, stood a small log-house containing only two rooms. The yard was neglected, full of rank weeds, and the gate was falling from its rusty hinges.

Edna walked up the decaying steps, and without pausing to knock, entered one of the comfortless-looking rooms.

On a cot in one corner lay an elderly man in the last stage of consumption, and by his side, busily engaged in knitting, sat a child about ten years old, whose pretty white face wore that touching look of patient placidity peculiar to the blind. Huldah Reed had never seen the light, but a marvellous change came over her countenance when Edna's light step and clear, sweet voice fell on her ear.

"Huldah, how is your father to-day?"

"Not as well as he was yesterday; but he is asleep now, and will be better when he wakes."

"Has the doctor been here to-day?"

"No, he has not been here since Sunday."

Edna stood for a while watching the labored breathing of the sleeper, and putting her hand on Huldah's head, she whispered:

"Do you want me to read to you this evening? It is late, but I shall have time for a short chapter."

"Oh! please do, if it is only a few lines. It will not wake him."

The child rose, spread out her hands, and groped her way across the room to a small table, whence she took an old Bible.

The two sat down together by the western window, and Edna asked:

"Is there any particular chapter you would like to hear?"

"Please read about blind Bartimeus sitting by the roadside, waiting for Jesus."

Edna turned to the verses and read in a subdued tone for some moments. In her eager interest Huldah slid down on her knees, rested her thin hands on her companion's lap and raised her sweet face, with its wide, vacant, sad, hazel eyes.

When Edna read the twenty-fourth verse of the next chapter, the small hands were laid upon the page to arrest her attention.

" Edna, do you believe that ? ' What things soever you desire, when ye pray believe that ye receive them, *and ye shall have them !*' Jesus said that : and if I pray that my eyes may be opened, do you believe I shall see ? They tell me that—that pa will not live. Oh ! do you think if I pray day and night, and if I believe, and oh ! I do believe, I will believe ! do you think Jesus will let me see him—my father—before he dies ? If I could only see his dear face once, I would be willing to be blind afterward. All my life I have felt his face, and I knew it by my fingers; but oh ! I can't feel it in the grave ! I have been praying so hard ever since the doctor said he must die ; praying that Jesus would have mercy on me, and let me see him just once. Last night I dreamed Christ came and put his hands on my eyes, and said to me too, ' Thy faith hath made thee whole '; and I waked up crying, and my own fingers were pulling my eyes open ; but it was all dark, dark. Edna, won't you help me pray ! And do you believe I shall see him ?"

Edna took the quivering face in her soft palms, and tenderly kissed the lips several times.

" My dear Huldah, you know the days of miracles are over, and Jesus is not walking in the world now to cure the suffering and the blind and the dumb."

" But he is sitting close to the throne of God, and he could send some angel down to touch my eyes, and let me see my dear, dear pa once—ah ! just once. Oh ! he is the same Jesus now as when he felt sorry for Bartimeus. And why won't he pity me too ? I pray and I believe, and that is what he said I must do."

" I think that the promise relates to spiritual things,

and means that when we pray for strength to resist
temptation and sin, Jesus sends the Holy Spirit to assist all who earnestly strive to do their duty. But,
dear Huldah, one thing is very certain, even if you are
blind in this world, there will come a day when God
will open your eyes, and you shall see those you love
face to face ; ' for there shall be no night there ' in that
city of rest—no need of sun or moon, for ' the Lamb is
the light thereof."

" Huldah—daughter !"

The child glided swiftly to the cot, and, looking
round, Edna doubted the evidence of her senses; for
by the side of the sufferer stood a figure so like Mr.
Murray that her heart began to throb painfully.

The corner of the room was dim and shadowy, but
a strong, deep voice soon dispelled all doubt.

"I hope you are better to-day, Reed. Here are
some grapes which will refresh you, and you can eat
them as freely as your appetite prompts."

Mr. Murray placed a luscious cluster in the emaciated hands, and put the basket down on the floor
near the cot. As he drew a chair from the wall and
seated himself, Edna crossed the room stealthily, and,
laying her hand on Huldah's shoulder, led her out to
the front steps.

" Huldah, has Mr. Murray ever been here before ?"

" Oh ! yes—often and often ; but he generally comes
later than this. He brings all the wine poor pa drinks,
and very often peaches and grapes. Oh! he is so
good to us. I love to hear him come up the steps ;
and many a time, when pa is asleep, I sit here at night,
listening for the gallop of Mr. Murray's horse. Somehow I feel so safe, as if nothing could go wrong, when
he is in the house."

"Why did you never tell me this before ? Why
have you not spoken of him ?"

" Because he charged me not to speak to any one
about it—said he did not choose to have it known that
he ever came here. There ! pa is calling me. Won't
you come in and speak to him ?"

"Not this evening. Good-bye. I will come again soon."

Edna stooped, kissed the child hastily, and walked away.

She had only reached the gate, where Tamerlane was fastened, when Mr. Murray came out of the house.

"Edna!"

Reluctantly she stopped and waited for him.

"Are you not afraid to walk home alone?"

"No, sir; I am out frequently even later than this."

"It is not exactly prudent for you to go home now alone; for it will be quite dark before you can possibly reach the park gate."

He passed his horse's reins over his arm, and led him along the road.

"I am not going that way, sir. There is a path through the woods that is much shorter than the road and I can get through an opening in the orchard fence. Good evening."

She turned abruptly from the beaten road, but he caught her dress and detained her.

"I told you some time ago that I never permitted espionage in my affairs; and now with reference to what occurred at the greenhouse, I advice you to keep silent. Do you understand me?"

"In the first place, sir, I could not condescend to play spy on the actions of any one; and in the second, you may rest assured I shall not trouble myself to comment upon your affairs, in which I certainly have no interest. Your estimate of me must be contemptible indeed, if you imagine that I can only employ myself in watching your career. Dismiss your apprehensions, and rest in the assurance that I consider it no business of mine where you go or what you may choose to do."

"My only desire is to shield my pretty Gertrude's head from the wrath that may be bottled up for her."

Edna looked up fixedly into the deep, glittering eyes that watched hers, and answered quietly:

"Mr. Murray, if you love her half as well as I do, you will be more careful in future not to subject her to the opening of the vials of wrath."

He laughed contemptuously, and exclaimed :

"You are doubtless experienced in such matters, and fully competent to advise me."

"No, sir, it does not concern me, and I presume neither to criticise nor to advise. Please be so good as to detain me no longer, and believe me when I repeat that I have no intention whatever of meddling with any of your affairs, or reporting your actions."

Putting his hands suddenly on her shoulders, he stooped, looked keenly at her, and she heard him mutter an oath. When he spoke again it was through set teeth :

"You will be wise if you adhere to that decision. Tell them at home not to wait supper for me."

He sprang into his saddle and rode toward the village ; and Edna hurried homeward, asking herself :

"What first took Mr. Murray to the blacksmith's hovel? Why is he so anxious that his visits should remain undiscovered? After all, is there some latent nobility in his character? Is he so much better or worse than I have thought him? Perhaps his love for Gertrude has softened his heart, perhaps that love may be his salvation. God grant it! God grant it!"

The evening breeze rose and sang solemnly through the pine trees, but to her it seemed only to chant the melancholy refrain, "My pretty Gertrude, my pretty Gertrude."

The chill light of stars fell on the orphan's pathway, and over her pale features, where dwelt the reflection of a loneliness—a silent desolation, such as she had never realized, even when her grandfather was snatched from her clinging arms. She passed through the orchard, startling a covey of partridges that nestled in the long grass, and a rabbit that had stolen out under cover of dusk ; and when she came to the fountain, she paused and looked out over the dark, quiet grounds. Hitherto duty had worn a smiling, loving counten-

ance, and walked gently by her side as she crossed
the flowery vales of girlhood; now, the guide was
transformed into an angel of wrath, pointing with
drawn sword to the gate of Eden.

As the girl's slight fingers locked themselves tightly,
her beautiful lips uttered mournfully:

> " What hast thou done, O soul of mine
>   That thou tremblest so?
> Hast thou wrought His task, and kept the line
>   He bade thee go?
> Ah! the cloud is dark, and day by day
>   I am moving thither:
> I must pass beneath it on my way—
>   God pity me! Whither?''

When Mrs. Murray went to her own room later
than usual that night, she found Edna sitting by the
table, with her Bible lying open on her lap, and her
eyes fixed on the floor.

"I thought you were fast asleep before this. I sat
up waiting for St. Elmo, as I wished to speak to him
about some engagements for to-morrow."

The lady of the house threw herself wearily upon
the lounge, and sighed as she unclasped her bracelets
and took off the diamond cross that fastened her collar.

"Edna, ring for Hagar."

"Will you not let me take her place to-night? I
want to talk to you before I go to sleep."

"Well, then, unlace my gaiters and take down my
hair. Child, what makes you look so very serious?"

" Because what I am about to say saddens me very
much. My dear Mrs. Murray, I have been in this
house five peaceful, happy, blessed years; I have
become warmly attached to every thing about the
home where I have been so kindly sheltered during my
girlhood, and the thought of leaving it is exceedingly
painful to me."

"What do you mean, Edna? Have you come to
your senses at last, and consented to make Gordon
happy?"

ST. ELMO.

"No, no. I am going to New York to try to make my bread."

"You are going to a lunatic asylum! Stuff! nonsense! What can you do in New York? It is already overstocked with poor men and women, who are on the verge of starvation. Pooh! pooh! you look like making your bread. Don't be silly."

"I know that I am competent now to take a situation as teacher in a school, or family, and I am determined to make the experiment immediately. I want to go to New York because I can command advantages there which no poor girl can obtain in any Southern city; and the magazine for which I expect to write is published there. Mr. Manning says he will pay me liberally for such articles as he accepts, and if I can only get a situation which I hear is now vacant, I can easily support myself. Mrs. Powell received a letter yesterday from a wealthy friend in New York who desires to secure a governess for her young children, one of whom is deformed. She said she was excessively particular as to the character of the woman to whose care she committed her crippled boy, and that she had advertised for one who could teach him Greek. I shall ask Mrs. Powell and Mr. Hammond to telegraph to her to-morrow and request her not to engage any one till a letter can reach her from Mr. Hammond and myself. I believe he knows the lady, who is very distantly related to Mrs. Powell. Still, before I took this step, I felt that I owed it to you to acquaint you with my intention."

"It is a step which I can not sanction. I detest that Mrs. Powell—I utterly loathe the sound of her name, and I should be altogether unwilling to see you domesticated with any of her ' friends.' I am surprised that Mr. Hammond could encourage any such foolish scheme on your part."

"As yet he is entirely ignorant of my plan, for I have mentioned it to no one except yourself; but I do not think he will oppose it. Dear Mrs. Murray, much as I love you, I can not remain here any longer, for I could not continue to owe my bread even to your kind and tender charity. You have educated me, and only God knows how inexpressibly grateful I am for all your goodness; but now, I could no longer preserve my self-respect or be happy as a dependent on your bounty."

She had taken Mrs. Murray's hand, and while tears gathered in her eyes, she kissed the fingers and pressed them against her cheek.

"If you are too proud to remain here as you have done for so many years, how do you suppose you can endure the humiliations and affronts which will certainly be your portion when you accept a hireling's position in the family of a stranger? Don't you know that of all drudgery that required of governesses is most fraught with vexation and bitterness of spirit? I have never treated you as an upper servant, but loved you and shielded you from slights and insults as if you were my niece or my daughter. Edna, you could not endure the lot you have selected; your proud, sensitive nature would be galled to desperation. Stay here and help me keep house; write and study as much as you like, and do as you please; only don't leave me."

She drew the girl to her bosom, and while she kissed her, tears fell on the pale face.

"Oh, Mrs. Murray! it is hard to leave you! For indeed I love you more than you will ever believe or realize; but I must go! I feel that it is my duty, and you would not wish me to stay here and be unhappy."

"Unhappy here! Why so? Something is wrong, and I must know just what it is. Somebody has been meddling—taunting you. Edna, I ask a plain question, and I want the whole truth. You and Estelle do not like each other; is her presence here the cause of your determination to quit my house?"

"No, Mrs. Murray; if she were not here I should still feel it my duty to go out and earn my living. You are correct in saying we do not particularly like each other; there is little sympathy between us, but no bad feeling that I am aware of, and she is not the cause of my departure."

Mrs. Murray was silent a moment, scrutinizing the face on her shoulder.

" Edna, can it be my son? Has some harsh speech of St. Elmo's piqued and wounded you ?"

" Oh ! no. His manner toward me is quite as polite, nay, rather more considerate than when I first came here. Beside, you know, we are almost strangers; sometimes weeks elapse without our exchanging a word."

" Are you sure you have not had a quarrel with him? I know you dislike him ; I know how exceedingly provoking he frequently is ; but, child, he is unfortunately constituted ; he is bitterly rude to everybody, and does not mean to wound you particularly."

" I have no complaint to make of Mr. Murray's manner to me. I do not expect or desire that it should be other than it is. Why do you doubt the sincerity of the reason I gave for quitting dear old Bocage ? I have never expected to live here longer than was necessary to qualify myself for the work I have chosen."

" I doubt it because it is so incomprehensible that a young girl, who might be Gordon Leigh's happy wife and mistress of his elegant home, surrounded by every luxury, and idolized by one of the noblest, handsomest men I ever knew, should prefer to go among strangers and toil for a scanty livelihood. Now I know something of human nature, and I know that your course is very singular, very unnatural. Edna, my child ! My dear, little girl ! I can't let you go. I want you ! I can't spare you ! I find I love you too well, my sweet comforter in all my troubles ! My only real companion !"

She clasped the orphan closer and wept.

" Oh ! you don't know how precious your love is to my heart, dear, dear Mrs. Murray ! In all this wide world whom have I to love me but you and Mr. Hammond ? Even in the great sorrow of leaving you, it will gladden me to feel that I possess so fully your confidence and affection. But I must go away; and after a little while you will not miss me; for Estelle will be with you, and you will not need me. Oh, it is hard to leave you! it is a bitter trial! But I know what my duty is; and were it even more difficult, I would not hesitate. I hope you will not think me unduly obstinate when I tell you, that I have fully determined to apply for that situation in New York."

Mrs. Murray pushed the girl from her, and, with a sob, buried her face in her arms.

Edna waited in vain for her to speak, and finally she stooped, kissed one of the hands, and said brokenly as she left the room:

"Good-night—my dearest—my best friend. If you could only look into my heart and see how it aches at the thought of separation, you would not add the pain of your displeasure to that which I already suffer."

When the orphan opened her eyes on the following morning, the found a note pinned to her pillow:

"MY DEAR EDNA: I could not sleep last night in consequence of your unfortunate resolution, and I write to beg you, for my sake if not for your own, to reconsider the matter. I will gladly pay you the same salary that you expect to receive as governess, if you will remain as my companion and assistant at Le Bocage. I cannot consent to give you up; I love you too well, my child, to see you quit my house. I shall soon be an old woman, and then what should I do without my little orphan girl? Stay with me always, and you shall never know what want and toil and hardship mean. As soon as you are awake, come and kiss me good-morning, and I shall know that you are my own dear, little Edna.

"Affectionately yours,
"ELLEN MURRAY."

Edna knelt and prayed for strength to do what she felt duty sternly dictated; but, though her will did

not falter her heart bled, as she wrote a few lines
thanking her benefactress for the affection that had
brightened and warmed her whole lonely life, and
assuring her that the reasons which induced her to
leave Le Bocage were imperative and unanswerable.

An hour later she entered the breakfast-room, and
found the members of the family already assembled.
While Mrs. Murray was cold and haughty, taking no
notice of Edna's salutation, Estelle talked gayly with
Mr. Allston concerning a horseback ride they intended
to take that morning ; and Mr. Murray, leaning back
in his chair, seemed engrossed in the columns of the
London *Times* which contained a recent speech of
Gladstone's.   Presently he threw down the paper,
looked at his watch and ordered his horse.

" St. Elmo, where are you going ? Do allow yourself to be prevailed upon to wait and ride with us."

Estelle's tone was musical and coaxing as she
approached her cousin and put one of her fingers
through the button-hole of his coat.

" Not for all the kingdoms that Satan pointed out
from the pinnacle of Mount Quarantina ! I have as
insuperable an objection to constituting one of a trio
as some superstitious people have to forming part of
a dinner-company of thirteen.   Where am I going ?
To that 'Sea of Serenity' which astronomers tell us
is located in the left eye of the face known in common
parlance as the man in the moon.   Where am I going ?
To Western Ross-shire, to pitch my tent and smoke
my cigar in peace, on the brink of that blessed Loch
Maree, whereof Pennant wrote."

He shook off Estelle's touch, walked to the mantelpiece, and taking a match from the china case, drew
it across the heel of his boot.

" Where is Loch Maree ? I do not remember ever
to have seen the name," said Mrs. Murray, pushing
aside her coffee-cup.

" Oh ! pardon me, mother, if I decline to undertake
your geographical education.   Ask that incipient
Isotta Nogarole, sitting there at your right hand.

Doubtless she will find it a pleasing task to instruct you in Scottish topography, while I have an engagement that forces me most reluctantly and respectfully to decline the honor of enlightening you. Confound these matches! they are all damp."

Involuntarily Mrs. Murray's eyes turned to Edna, who had not even glanced at St. Elmo since her entrance. Now she looked up, and though she had not read Pennant, she remembered the lines written on the old Druidic well by an American poet. Yielding to some inexplicable impulse, she slowly and gently repeated two verses:

> " 'Oh, restless heart and fevered brain !
>   Unquiet and unstable,
> That holy well of Loch Maree
>   Is more than idle fable !
> The shadows of a humble will
>   And contrite heart are o'er it :
> Go read its legend—" TRUST IN GOD "—
>   On Faith's white stones before it !' "

CHAPTER XXI.

"While your decision is very painful to me, I shall
not attempt to dissuade you from a resolution which
I know has not been lightly or hastily taken. But,
ah, my child! what shall I do without you?"

Mr. Hammond's eyes filled with tears as he looked
at his pupil, and his hand trembled when he stroked
her bowed head.

"I dread the separation from you and Mrs. Murray; but I know I ought to go; and I feel that when
duty commands me to follow a path, lonely and dreary
though it may seem, a light will be shed before my feet,
and a staff will be put into my hands. I have often
wondered what the Etrurians intended to personify in
in their *Dii Involuti*, before whose awful decrees all
other gods bowed. Now I feel assured that the chief
of the 'Shrouded Gods' is Duty, veiling her features
with a silver-lined cloud, scorning to parley, but whose
unbending finger signs our way—an unerring pillar of
cloud by day, of fire by night. Mr. Hammond, I
shall follow that stern finger till the clods on my coffin shut it from my sight."

The August sun shining through the lilac and myrtle boughs that rustled close to the study-window
glinted over the pure, pale face of the orphan, and
showed a calm mournfulness in the eyes which looked
out at the quiet parsonage garden, and far away to
the waving lines against the sky, where

A golden lustre slept upon the hills."

Just beyond the low, ivy-wreathed stone wall that

marked the boundary of the garden ran a little stream,
overhung with alders and willows, under whose tremulous shadows rested contented cattle—some knee-
deep in water, some browsing leisurely on purple-
tufted clover. From the wide, hot field, stretching
away on the opposite side, came the clear metallic ring
of the scythes, as the mowers sharpened them ; the
mellow whistle of the driver lying on top of the huge
hay mass, beneath which the oxen crawled toward the
lowered bars ; and the sweet gurgling laughter of two
romping, sunburned children, who swung on at the
back of the wagon.

Edna pointed to the peaceful picture, and said :
" If Rosa Bonheur could only put that on canvas for
me, I would hang it upon my walls in the great city
whither I am going ; and when my weary days of work
ended, I could sit down before it, and fold my tired
hands and look at it through the mist of tears till its
blessed calm stole into my heart, and I believed myself once more with you, gazing out of the study-window. Ah! blessed among all gifted women is Rosa
Bonheur! accounted worthy to wear what other
women may not aspire to—the Cross of the Legion of
Honor! Yesterday when I read the description of
the visit of the Empress to the studio, I think I was
almost as proud and happy as that patient worker at
the easel, when over her shoulders was hung the ribbon which France decrees only to the mighty souls
who increase her glory, and before whom she bows in
reverent gratitude. I am glad that a woman's hand
laid that badge of immortality on womanly shoulders
—a crowned head crowning the Queen of Artists. I
wonder if, when obscure and in disguise, she haunted
the *abattoir du Roule*, and worked on amid the lowing
and bleating of the victims—I wonder if faith prophe-
sied of that distant day of glorious recompense, when
the ribbon of the Legion fluttered from Eugenie's
white fingers and she was exalted above all thrones ?
Ah, Mr. Hammond ! we all wear our crosses, but they
do not belong to the order of the Legion of Honor."

The minister enclosed in his own the hand which she had laid on his knee, and said gently but gravely :

" My child, your ambition is your besetting sin. It is Satan pointing to the tree of knowledge, tempting you to eat and become ' as gods.' Search your heart, and I fear you will find that while you believe you are dedicating your talent entirely to the service of God, there is a spring of selfishness underlying all. You are too proud, too ambitious of distinction, too eager to climb to some lofty niche in the temple of fame, where your name, now unknown, shall shine in the annals of literature and serve as a beacon to encourage others equally as anxious for celebrity. I was not surprised to see you in print ; for long, long ago, before you realized the extent of your mental dowry, I saw the kindling of that ambitious spark whose flame generally consumes the women in whose hearts it burns. The history of literary females is not calculated to allay the apprehension that oppresses me, as I watch you just setting out on a career so fraught with trials of which you have never dreamed. As a class they are martyrs, uncrowned and uncanonized ; jeered at by the masses, sincerely pitied by a few earnest souls, and wept over by the relatives who really love them. Thousands of women have toiled over books that proved millstones and drowned them in the sea of letters. How many of the hundreds of female writers scattered through the world in this century, will be remembered six months after the coffin closes over their weary, haggard faces ? You may answer, ' They made their bread.' Ah, child ! it would have been sweeter if earned at the wash-tub, or in the dairy, or by their needles. It is the rough handling, the jars, the tension of the heartstrings that sap the foundations of a woman's life and consign her to an early grave ; and a Cherokee rose-hedge is not more thickly set with thorns than a literary career with grievous, vexatious, tormenting disappointments. If you succeed after years of labor and anxiety and harrassing fears, you will become a target for envy and malice, and, possibly, for slander. Your own sex will be jealous of your eminence, considering your superiority an insult to their mediocrity; and mine will either ridicule or barely tolerate you; for men detest female competitors in the Olympian game of literature. If you fail, you will be sneered down till you become embittered, soured, misanthropic; a curse to yourself, a burden to the friends who sympathize with your blasted hopes. Edna, you have talent, you write well, you are conscientious; but you are not De Staël, or Hannah More, or Charlotte Brontë, or Elizabeth Browning; and I shudder when I think of the disappointment that may overtake all your eager aspirations. If I could be always near you, I should indulge less apprehension for your future; for I believe that I could help you to bear patiently whatever is in store for you. But far away among strangers you must struggle alone."

"Mr. Hammond, I do not rely upon myself; my hope is in God."

"My child, the days of miraculous inspiration are ended."

"Ah! do not discourage me. When the Bishop of Noyon hesitated to consecrate St. Radegund, she said to him, 'Thou wilt have to render thy account, and the Shepherd will require of thee the souls of his sheep.' My dear sir, your approbation is the consecration that I desire upon my purpose. God will not forsake me; He will strengthen and guide me and bless my writing, even as He blesses your preaching. Because He gave you five talents and to me only one, do you think that in the great day of reckoning mine will not be required of me? I do not expect to 'enter into the joy of my Lord' as you will be worthy to do; but with the blessing of God, I trust the doom of the altogether unprofitable servant will not be pronounced against me."

She had bowed her head till it rested on his knee, and presently the old man put his hands upon the glossy hair and murmured solemnly:

"And the peace of God, which passeth all understanding, shall keep your heart and mind through Christ Jesus."

A brief silence reigned in the study, broken first by the shout of the haymakers and the rippling laugh of the children in the adjacent field, and then by the calm voice of the pastor:

"I have offered you a home with me as long as I have a roof that I can call my own; but you prefer to go to New York, and henceforth I shall never cease to pray that your resolution may prove fortunate in all respects. You no longer require my direction in your studies, but I will suggest that it might be expedient for you to give more attention to positive and less to abstract science. Remember those noble words of Sir David Brewster, to which, I believe, I have already called your attention, 'If the God of love is most appropriately worshipped in the Christian temple, the God of nature may be equally honored in the temple of science. Even from its lofty minarets the philosopher may summon the faithful to prayer, and the priest and the sage may exchange altars without the compromise of faith or of knowledge;' Infidelity has shifted the battlefield from metaphysics to physics, from idealism and rationalism to positivism or rank materialism; and in order to combat it successfully, in order to build up an imperishable system of Christian teleology, it is necessary that you should thoroughly acquaint yourself with the 'natural sciences,' with dynamics, and all the so-called 'inherent forces in nature,' or what Humboldt terms 'primordial necessity.' This apotheosis of dirt, by such men as Moleschott, Buchner, and Vogt, is the real Antæus which, though continually overthrown, springs from mother earth with renewed vigor, and after a little while some Hercules of science will lift the boaster in his inexorable arms and crush him."

Here Mrs. Powell entered the room, and Edna rose and tied on her hat.

"Mr. Hammond, will you go over to see Huldah

his afternoon? Poor little thing! she is in great distress about her father."

"I fear he can not live many days. I went to see him yesterday morning, and would go again with you now, but have promised to baptize two children this evening."

Edna was opening the gate when Gertrude called to her from a shaded corner of the yard, and turning, she saw her playing with a fawn, about whose neck she had twined a long spray of honeysuckle.

"Do come and see the beautiful present Mr. Murray sent me several days ago. It is as gentle and playful as a kitten, and seems to know me already."

Gertrude patted the head of her pretty pet and continued:

"I have often read about gazelle's eyes, and I wonder if these are not quite as lovely? Very often when I look at them they remind me of yours. There is such a soft, sad, patient expression, as if she knew perfectly well that some day the hunters would be sure to catch her and kill her, and she was meekly biding her time to be turned into venison steak. I never will eat another piece! The dear little thing! Edna, do you know that you have the most beautiful eyes in the world, except Mr. Murray's? His glitter like great stars under long, long black silk fringe. By the way, how is he? I have not seen him for some days and you can have no idea how I do want to look into his face, and hear his voice, which is so wonderfully sweet and low. I wrote him a note thanking him for this little spotted darling; but he has not answered it—has not come near me, and I was afraid he might be sick."

Gertrude stole one arm around her companion's neck and nestled her golden head against the orphan's shoulder.

"Mr. Murray is very well; at least, appears so. I saw him at breakfast."

"Does he ever talk about me?"

"No; I never heard him mention your name but once, and then it occurred incidentally."

"Oh, Edna! is it wrong for me to think about him so constantly? Don't press your lips together in that stern, hard way. Dearie, put your arms around me, and kiss me. Oh! if you could know how very much I love him! How happy I am when he is with me. Edna, how can I help it? When he touches my hand, and smiles down at me, I forget everything else! I feel as if I would follow him to the end of the earth. He is a great deal older than I am; but how can I remember that when he is looking at me with those wonderful eyes? The last time I saw him, he said —— well, something very sweet, and I was sure he loved me, and I leaned my head against his shoulder; but he would not let me touch him; he pushed me away with a terrible frown, that wrinkled and blackened his face. Oh! it seems an age since then."

Edna kissed the lovely coral lips, and smoothed the bright curls that the wind had blown about the exquisitely moulded cheeks.

"Gertrude, when he asks you to love him, you will have a right to indulge your affection; but until then you ought not to allow him to know your feelings, or permit yourself to think so entirely of him."

"But do you believe it is wrong for me to love him so much?"

"That is a question which your own heart must answer."

Edna felt that her own lips were growing cold, and she disengaged the girl's clasping arms.

"Edna, I know you love me; will you do something for me? Please give him this note. I am afraid that he did not receive the other, or that he is offended with me."

She drew a dainty three-cornered envelope from her pocket.

"No, Gertrude; I can be a party to no clandestine correspondence. I have too much respect for your uncle, to assist in smuggling letters in and out of his house. Beside, your mother would not sanction the course you are pursuing."

"Oh! I showed her the other note, and she only laughed, and patted my cheek, and said, 'Why, Mignonne! he is old enough to be your father.' This note is only to find out whether he received the other. I sent it by the servant who brought this fawn——oh dear me! just see what a hole the pretty little wretch has nibbled in my new Swiss muslin dress! Won't mamma scold! There, do go away, pet; I will feed you presently. Indeed, Edna, there is no harm in your taking the note, for I give you my word mamma does not care. Do you think I would tell you a story? Please, Edna. It will reach him so much sooner if you carry it over, than if I were to drop it into the post-office where it may stay for a week; and Uncle Allan has no extra servants to run around on errands for me."

"Gertrude, are you not deceiving me? Are you sure your mother read the other note and sanctions this?"

"Certainly; you may ask her if you doubt me. There! I must hurry in; mamma is calling me. Dear Edna, if you love me! Yes, mamma, I am coming."

Edna could not resist the pleading of the lovely face pressed close to hers, and with a sigh she took the tiny note and turned away.

More than a week had elapsed since Mr. Hammond and Mrs. Powell had written, recommending her for the situation in Mrs. Andrews's family; and with feverish impatience she awaited the result. During this interval she had not exchanged a word with Mr. Murray—had spent much of her time in writing down in her note-book such references from the library as she required in her MS.; and while Estelle seemed unusually high-spirited, Mrs. Murray watched in silence the orphan's preparations for departure.

Absorbed in very painful reflections, the girl walked on rapidly till she reached the cheerless home of the blacksmith, and knocked at the door.

ST. ELMO. 299

"Come in, Mr. Murray."
Edna pushed open the door and walked in.
"It is not Mr. Murray this time."
"Oh, Edna! I am so glad you happened to come.
He would not let me tell you; he said he did not wish
it known. But now you are here, you will stay with
me, won't you, till it is over?"

Huldah was kneeling at the side of her father's cot,
and Edna was startled by the look of eager, breathless
anxiety printed on her white, trembling face.

"What does she mean, Mr. Reed?"

"Poor little lamb, she is so excited she can hardly
speak, and I am not strong enough to talk much.
Huldah, daughter, tell Miss Edna all about it."

"Mr. Murray heard all I said to you about praying
to have my eyes opened, and he went to town that
same evening, and telegraphed to some doctor in Philadelphia, who cures blindness, to come on and see if he
could do anything for my eyes. Mr. Murray was here
this morning, and said he had heard from the doctor,
and that he would come this afternoon. He said he
could only stay till the cars left for Chattanooga, as
he must go back at once You know he——hush!
There! there! I hear the carriage now. Oh, Edna!
pray for me! Pa, pray for my poor eyes!"

The sweet, childish face was colorless, and tears
filled the filmy, hazel eyes as Huldah clasped her
hands. Her lips moved rapidly, though no sound was
audible.

Edna stepped behind the door, and peeped through
a crack in the planks.

Mr. Murray entered first and beckoned to the stranger, who paused at the threshold, with a case of instruments in his hand.

"Come in, Hugh; here is your patient, very much
frightened, too, I am afraid. Huldah, come to the
light."

He drew her to the window, lifted her to a chair,
and the doctor bent down, pushed back his spectacles,
and cautiously examined the child's eyes.

"Don't tremble so, Huldah; there is nothing to be afraid of. The doctor will not hurt you."

"Oh! it is not that I fear to be hurt! Edna, are you praying for me?"

"Edna is not here," answered Mr. Murray, glancing round the room.

"Yes, she is here. I did not tell her, but she happened to come a little while ago. Edna, won't you hold one of my hands? Oh, Edna! Edna!"

Reluctantly the orphan came forward, and, without lifting her eyes, took one of the little outstretched hands firmly in both her own. While Mr. Murray silently appropriated the other, Huldah whispered:

"Please, both of you pray for me."

The doctor raised the eyelids several times, peered long and curiously at the eyeballs, and opened his case of instruments.

"This is one of those instances of congenital cataract which might have been relieved long ago. A slight operation will remove the difficulty. St. Elmo, you asked me about the probability of an instantaneous restoration, and I had begun to tell you about that case which Wardrop mentions of a woman, blind from her birth till she was forty-six years of age. She could not distinguish objects for several days—— "

"Oh, sir! will I see? Will I see my father?" Her fingers closed spasmodically over those that clasped them, and the agonizing suspense written in her countenance was pitiable to contemplate.

"Yes, my dear, I hope so—I think so. You know, Murray, the eye has to be trained; but Haller mentions a case of a nobleman who saw distinctly at various distances, immediately after the cataract was removed from the axis of vision. Now, my little girl, hold just as still as possible. I shall not hurt you."

Skilfully he cut through the membrane and drew it down, then held his hat between her eyes and the light streaming through the window.

Some seconds elapsed and suddenly a cry broke from the child's lips.

"Oh! something shines! there is a light, I believe!"

Mr. Murray threw his handkerchief over her head, caught her in his arms and placed her on the side of the cot.

"The first face her eyes ever look upon, shall be that which she loves best—her father's."

As he withdrew the handkerchief Mr. Reed feebly raised his arms toward his child, and whispered:

"My little Huldah—my daughter, can you see me?"

She stooped, put her face close to his, swept her small fingers repeatedly over the emaciated features, to convince herself of the identity of the new sensation of sight with the old and reliable sense of touch; then she threw her head back with a wild laugh, a scream of delight.

"Oh! I see! Thank God I see my father's face! My dear pa! my own dear pa!"

For some moments she hung over the sufferer kissing him, murmuring brokenly her happy, tender words, and now and then resorting to the old sense of touch.

While Edna wiped away tears of joyful sympathy which she strove in vain to restrain, she glanced at Mr. Murray, and wondered how he could stand there watching the scene with such bright, dry eyes.

Seeming suddenly to remember that there were other countenances in the world beside that tear-stained one on the pillow, Huldah slipped down from the cot, turned toward the group, and shaded her eyes with her fingers.

"Oh, Edna! a'n't you glad for me? Where are you? I knew Jesus would hear me. 'What things soever ye desire, when ye pray believe that ye receive them, and ye shall have them.' I did believe, and I see! I see! I prayed that God would send down some angel to touch my eyes, and He sent Mr. Murray and the doctor."

After a pause, during, which the oculist prepared some bandages, Huldah added.

"Which one is Mr. Murray? Will you, please,

come to me? My ears and my fingers know you, but my eyes don't."

He stepped forward and putting out her hands she grasped his, and turned her untutored eyes upon him. Before he could suspect her design she fell at his feet, threw her arms around his knees, and exclaimed :

"How good you are! How shall I ever thank you enough? How good." She clung to him and sobbed hysterically.

Edna saw him lift her from the floor and put her back beside her father, while the doctor bandaged her eyes ; and waiting to hear no more, the orphan glided away and hurried along the road.

Ere she had proceeded far, she heard she quick trot of the horses, the roll of the carriage. Leaning out as they overtook her, Mr. Murray directed the driver to stop, and swinging open the door, he stepped out and approached her.

"The doctor dines at Le Bocage ; will you take a seat with us, or do you, as usual, prefer to walk alone?"

"Thank you, sir; I am not going home now. I shall walk on."

He bowed, and was turning away, but she drew the delicately perfumed envelope from her pocket.

"Mr. Murray, I was requested by the writer to hand you this note, as she feared its predecessor was lost by the servant to whom she entrusted it "

He took it, glanced at the small, cramped, school-girlish handwriting, smiled, and thrust it into his vest pocket, saying in a low, earnest tone :

"This is, indeed, a joyful surprise. You are certainly more reliable than Henry. Accept my cordial thanks, which I have not time to reiterate. I generally prefer to owe my happiness entirely to Gertrude ; but in this instance I can bear to receive it through the medium of your hands. As you are so prompt and trusty, I may trouble you to carry my answer."

The carriage rolled on, leaving a cloud of dust which

the evening sunshine converted into a glittering track of glory, and seating herself on a grassy bank, Edna leaned her head against the body of a tree; and all the glory passed swiftly away, and she was alone in the dust.

As the sun went down, the pillared forest aisles stretching westward, filled first with golden haze, then glowed with a light redder than Phthiotan wine poured from the burning beaker of the sun; and only the mournful cooing of doves broke the solemn silence as the pine organ whispered its low coranach for the dead day; and the cool shadow of coming night crept, purple-mantled, velvet-sandaled, down the forest glades.

"Oh! if I had gone away a week ago! before I knew there was any redeeming charity in his sinful nature! If I could only despise him utterly, it would be so much easier to forget him. Ah! God pity me! God help me!— What right have I to think of Gertrude's lover—Gertrude's husband! I ought to be glad that he is nobler than I thought, but I am not! Oh! I am not! I wish I had never known the good that he has done. Oh, Edna Earl! has it come to this? How I despise—how I hate myself!"

Rising, she shook back her thick hair, passed her hands over her hot temples, and stood listening to the distant whistle of a partridge—to the plaint of the lonely dove nestled among the pine boughs high above her; and gradually a holy calm stole over her face, fixing it as the merciful touch of death stills features that have long writhed in mortal agony. Into her struggling heart entered a strength which comes only when weary, wrestling, honest souls turn from human sympathy, seek the hallowed cloisters of Nature, and are folded tenderly in the loving arms of Mother Cybele, who "never did betray the heart that loved her."

"Whose dwelling is the light of setting suns,
  And the round ocean and the living air,
  And the blue sky * * * 'Tis her privilege,
Through all the years of this our life, to lead

> From joy to joy ; for she can so inform
> The mind that is within us, so impress
> With quietness and beauty, and so feed
> With lofty thoughts, that neither evil tongues,
> Rash judgments, nor the sneers of selfish men,
> Nor greetings where no kindness is—nor all
> The dreary intercourse of daily life,
> Shall e'er prevail against us or disturb
> Our cheerful faith, that all which we behold
> Is full of blessing."

To her dewy altars among the mountains of Gilead fled Jephthah's daughter, in the days when she sought for strength to fulfill her father's battle-vow ; and into her pitying starry eyes looked stricken Rizpah, from those dreary rocks where love held faithful vigil, guarding the bleaching bones of her darling dead, sacrificed for the sins of Saul.

CHAPTER XXII.

"Mrs. Andrews writes that I must go on with as little delay as possible, and I shall start early Monday morning, as I wish to stop one day at Chattanooga."

Edna rose and took her hat from the study table, and Mr. Hammond asked:

"Do you intend to travel alone?"

"I shall be compelled to do so, as I know of no one who is going on to New York. Of course, I dislike very much to travel alone, but in this instance I do not see how I can avoid it."

"Do not put on your hat—stay and spend the evening with me."

"Thank you, sir, I want to go to the church and practise for the last time on the organ. After to-morrow, I may never sing again in our dear choir. Perhaps I may come back after awhile and stay an hour or two with you."

During the past year she had accustomed herself to practising every Saturday afternoon the hymns selected by Mr. Hammond for the services of the ensuing day, and for this purpose had been furnished by the sexton with a key, which enabled her to enter the church whenever inclination prompted. The church-yard was peaceful and silent as the pulseless dust in its numerous sepulchres; a beautiful redbird sat on the edge of a marble vase that crowned the top of one of the monuments, and leisurely drank the water which yesterday's clouds had poured there, and a rabbit nibbled the leaves of a cluster of pinks growing near a child's grave.

Edna entered the cool church, went up into the gallery and sat down before the organ. For some time the low, solemn tones whispered among the fluted columns that supported the gallery, and gradually swelled louder and fuller and richer as she sang:

"Cast thy burden on the Lord."

Her sweet, well-trained voice faltered more than once, and tears fell thick and fast on the keys. Finally she turned and looked down at the sacred spot where she had been baptized by Mr. Hammond, and where she had so often knelt to receive the sacrament of the Lord's Supper.

The church was remarkably handsome and certainly justified the pride with which the villagers exhibited it to all strangers. The massive mahogany pew-doors were elaborately carved and surmounted by small crosses; the tall, arched windows were of superb stained glass, representing the twelve apostles; the floor and balustrade of the altar, and the grand Gothic pillared pulpit, were all of the purest white marble; and the capitals of the airy, elegant columns of the same material, that supported the organ gallery, were ornamented with rich grape-leaf mouldings; while the large window behind and above the pulpit contained a figure of Christ bearing his Cross—a noble copy of the great painting of Solario, at Berlin.

As the afternoon sun shone on the glass, a flood of ruby light fell from the garments of Jesus upon the glittering marble beneath, and the nimbus that radiated around the crown of thorns caught a glory that was dazzling.

With a feeling of adoration that no language could adequately express, Edna had watched and studied this costly painted window for five long years; had found a marvellous fascination in the pallid face stained with purplish blood-drops; in the parted lips quivering with human pain and anguish of spirit; in the unfathomable, divine eyes that pierced the veil and rested upon the Father's face. Not all the sermons of Bossuet, or Chalmers, or Jeremy Taylor, or Melville, had power to stir the great deeps of her soul like one glance at that pale, thorn-crowned Christ, who looked in voiceless woe and sublime resignation over the world he was dying to redeem.

To-day she gazed up at the picture of Emmanuel till her eyes grew dim with tears, and she leaned her head against the mahogany railing and murmured sadly:

"'And he that taketh not his cross, and followeth after me, is not worthy of me!' Strengthen me, O my Saviour! so that I neither faint nor stagger under mine!"

The echo of her words died away among the arches of the roof, and all was still in the sanctuary. The swaying of the trees outside of the windows threw now a golden shimmer, then a violet shadow over the gleaming altar pavement; and the sun sunk lower, and the nimbus faded, and the wan Christ looked ghastly and toil-spent.

"Edna! My darling! my darling!"

The pleading cry, the tremulous, tender voice so full of pathos, rang startlingly through the silent church, and the orphan sprang up and saw Mr. Murray standing at her side, with his arms extended toward her, and a glow on his face and a look in his eyes which she had never seen there before.

She drew back a few steps and gazed wonderingly at him; but he followed, threw his arm around her, and, despite her resistance, strained her to his heart.

"Did you believe that I would let you go? Did you dream that I would see my darling leave me, and go out into the world to be buffeted and sorely tried, to struggle with poverty—and to suffer alone? Oh, silly child! I would part with my own life sooner than give you up! Of what value would it be without you, my pearl, my sole hope, my only love, my own, pure Edna——"

"Such language you have no right to utter, and I

none to hear! It is dishonorable in you and insulting to me. Gertrude's lover can not, and shall not, address such words to me. Unwind your arms instantly! Let me go!"

She struggled hard to free herself, but his clasp tightened, and as he pressed her face against his bosom, he threw his head back and laughed:

"'Gertrude's lover!' Knowing my history, how could you believe that possible? Am I, think you, so meek and forgiving a spirit as to turn and kiss the hand that smote me? Gertrude's lover! Ha! ha!! Your jealousy blinds you, my——"

"I know nothing of your history; I have never asked; I have never been told one word! But I am not blind, I know that you love her, and I know, too, that she fully returns your affection. If you do not wish me to despise you utterly, leave me at once."

He laughed again, and put his lips close to her ear, saying softly, tenderly—ah! how tenderly:

"Upon my honor as a gentleman, I solemnly swear that I love but one woman; that I love her as no other woman ever was loved; with a love that passes all language; a love that is the only light and hope of a wrecked, cursed, unutterably miserable life; and that idol which I have set up in the lonely gray ruins of my heart is Edna Earl!"

"I do not believe you! You have no honor! With the touch of Gertrude's lips and arms still on yours, you come to me and dare to perjure yourself! Oh, Mr. Murray! Mr. Murray! I did not believe you capable of such despicable dissimulation! In the catalogue of your sins, I never counted deceit. I thought you too proud to play the hypocrite. If you could realize how I loathe and abhor you, you would get out of my sight! You would not waste time in words that sink you deeper and deeper in shameful duplicity. Poor Gertrude! How entirely you mistake your lover's character! How your love will change to scorn and detestation!"

In vain she endeavored to wrench away his arm, a

band of steel would have been as flexible; but St. Elmo's voice hardened, and Edna felt his heart throb fiercely against her cheek as he answered:

"When you are my wife you will repent your rash words, and blush at the remembrance of having told your husband that he was devoid of honor. You are piqued and jealous, just as I intended you should be; but, darling, I am not a patient man, and it frets me to feel you struggling so desperately in the arms that henceforth will always enfold you. Be quiet and hear me, for I have much to tell you. Don't turn your face away from mine, your lips belong to me. I never kissed Gertrude in my life, and so help me God, I never will! Hear——"

"No! I will hear nothing! Your touch is profanation. I would sooner go down into my grave, out there in the churchyard, under the granite slabs, than become the wife of a man so unprincipled. I am neither piqued nor jealous, for your affairs cannot affect my life; I am only astonished, and mortified and grieved. I would sooner feel the coil of a serpent around my waist than your arms."

Instantly they fell away. He crossed them on his chest, and his voice sank to a husky whisper, as the wind hushes itself just before the storm breaks.

"Edna, God is my witness that I am not deceiving you; that my words come from the great troubled depths of a wretched heart. You said you knew nothing of my history. I find it more difficult to believe you than you to credit my declarations. Answer one question: Has not your pastor taught you to distrust me? Can it be possible that no hint of the past has fallen from his lips?"

"Not one unkind word, not one syllable of your history has he uttered. I know no more of your past than if it were buried in mid-ocean."

Mr. Murray placed her in one of the cushioned chairs designed for the use of the choir, and leaning back against the railing of the gallery, fixed his eyes on Edna's face.

"Then it is not surprising that you distrust me, for you know not my provocation. Edna, will you be patient? Will you go back with me over the scorched and blackened track of an accursed and sinful life? It is a hideous waste I am inviting you to traverse! Will you?"

"I will hear you, Mr. Murray, but nothing that you can say will justify your duplicity to Gertrude, and——"

"D—n Gertrude! I ask you to listen, and suspend your judgment till you know the circumstances."

He covered his eyes with his hand, and in the brief silence she heard the ticking of his watch.

"Edna, I roll away the stone from the charnel house of the past, and call forth the Lazarus of my buried youth, my hopes, my faith in God, my trust in human nature, my charity, my slaughtered manhood! My Lazarus has tenanted the grave for nearly twenty years, and comes forth, at my bidding, a grinning skeleton. You may or may not know that my father, Paul Murray, died when I was an infant, leaving my mother the sole guardian of my property and person. I grew up at Le Bocage under the training of Mr. Hammond, my tutor; and my only associate, my companion from earliest recollection, was his son Murray, who was two years my senior, and named for my father. The hold which that boy took upon my affection was wonderful, inexplicable! He wound me around his finger as you wind the silken threads with which you embroider. We studied, read, played together. I was never contented out of his sight, never satisfied until I saw him liberally supplied with everything that gave me pleasure. I believe I was very precocious, and made extraordinary strides in the path of learning; at all events, at sixteen I was considered a remarkable boy. Mr. Hammond had six children; and as his salary was rather meagre I insisted on paying his son's expenses as well as my own when I went to Yale. I could not bear that my Damon, my Jonathan, should be out of my sight: I must have my idol always with me. His father was educating him for the ministry, and he had already commenced the study of theology'; but no! I must have him with me at Yale, and so to Yale we went. I had fancied myself a Christian, had joined the church, was zealous and faithful in all my religious duties. In a fit of pious enthusiasm I planned this church—ordered it built. The cost was enormous, and my mother objected, but I intended it as a shrine for the ' apple of my eye,' and where he was concerned, what mattered the expenditure of thousands? Was not my fortune quite as much at his disposal as at mine? I looked forward with fond pride to the time when I should see my idol—Murray Hammond—standing in yonder shining pulpit. Ha! at this instant it is filled with a hideous spectre! I see him there! His form and features mocking me, daring me to forget! Handsome as Apollo! treacherous as Apollyon!"

He paused, pointing to the pure marble pile where a violet flame seemed flickering, and then with a groan bowed his head upon the railing. When he spoke again, his face wore an ashy hue, and his stern mouth was unsteady.

" Hallowed days of my blessed boyhood! Ah! they rise before me now, like holy, burning stars, breaking out in a stormy, howling night, making the blackness blacker still! My short happy springtime of life! So full of noble aspirations, of glowing hopes, of philanthropic schemes, of all charitable projects! I would do so much good with my money! my heart was brimming with generous impulses, with warm sympathy and care for my fellow-creatures. Every needy sufferer should find relief at my hands as long as I possessed a dollar or a crust! As I look back now at that dead self, and remember all that I was, all the purity of my life, the nobility of my character, the tenderness of my heart—I do not wonder that people who knew me then, predicted that I would prove an honor, a blessing to my race! Mark you! that was St. Elmo Murray—as nature fashioned him · before man spoiled God's handiwork. Back! back to your

shroud and sepulchre, O Lazarus of my youth! and
when I am called to the final judgment, rise for me!
stand in my place, and confront those who slaughtered you! * * * My affection for my chum,
Murray, increased as I grew up to manhood, and
there was not a dream of my brain, a hope of my
heart which was not confided to him. I reverenced, I
trusted, I almost—nay, I quite worshipped him!
When I was only eighteen I began to love his cousin,
whose father was pastor of a church in New Haven,
and whose mother was Mr. Hammond's sister. You
have seen her. She is beautiful even now, and you can
imagine how lovely Agnes Hunt was in her girlhood.
She was the belle and pet of the students, and before
I had known her a month, I was her accepted lover.
I loved her with all the devotion of my chivalric,
ardent, boyish nature; and for me she professed the
most profound attachment. Her parents favored our
wishes for an early marriage, but my mother refused
to sanction such an idea until I had completed my
education and visited the old world. I was an obedi-
ent, affectionate son then, and yielded respectfully;
but as vacation approached, I prepared to come home,
hoping to prevail on mother to consent to my being
married just before we sailed for Europe the ensuing
year, after I left Yale. Murray was my confidant and
adviser. In his sympathizing ears I poured all my
fond hopes, and he insisted that I ought to take my
lovely bride with me; it would be cruel to leave her
so long; and, beside, he was so impatient for the
happy day when he should call me his cousin. He
declined coming home, on the plea of desiring to prosecute his theological studies with his uncle, Mr. Hunt.
Well do I recollect the parting between us. I had
left Agnes in tears—inconsolable because of my departure; and I flew to Murray for words of consolation. When I bade him good-bye my eyes were full
of tears, and as he passed his arm around my shoulders,
I whispered, 'Murray, take care of my angel Agnes
for me! watch over and comfort her while I am away.'

Ah! as I stand here to-day, I hear again ringing over the ruins of the past twenty years, his loving musical tones answering:

"'My dear boy, trust her to my care. St. Elmo, for your dear sake I will steal time from my books to cheer her while you are absent. But hurry back, for you know I find black-letter more attractive than blue. eyes. God bless you, my precious friend. Write to me constantly.'

"Since then, I always shudder involuntarily when I hear parting friends bless each other—for well, well do I know the stinging curse coiled up in those smooth liquid words! I came home and busied myself in the erection of this church; in plans for Murray's advancement in life, as well as my own. My importunity prevailed over my mother's sensible objections, and she finally consented that I should take my bride to Europe; while I had informed Mr. Hammond that I wished Murray to accompany us; that I would gladly pay his travelling expenses—I was so anxious for him to see the East, especially Palestine. Full of happy hopes, I hurried back earlier than I had intended, and reached New Haven very unexpectedly. The night was bright with moonshine, my heart was bright with hope, and too eager to see Agnes, whose letters had breathed the most tender solicitude and attachment, I rushed up the steps, and was told that she was walking in the little flower-garden. Down the path I hurried, and stopped as I heard her silvery laugh blended with Murray's; then my name was pronounced in tones that almost petrified me. Under a large apple-tree in the parsonage-garden they sat on a wooden bench, and only the tendrils and branches of an Isabella grape vine divided us. I stood there, grasping the vine—looking through the leaves at the two whom I had so idolized; and saw her golden head flashing in the moonlight as she rested it on her cousin's breast; heard and saw their kisses; heard——what wrecked, blasted, me! I heard myself ridiculed— sneered at—maligned: heard that I was to be a mere puppet—a cat's paw, that I was a doting, silly fool—easily hoodwinked; that she found it difficult, almost impossible, to endure my caresses; that she shuddered in my arms, and flew for happiness to his! I heard that from the beginning I had been duped; that they had always loved each other—always would; but poverty stubbornly barred their marriage—and she must be sacrificed to secure my fortune for the use of both! All that was uttered I can not now recapitulate; but it is carefully embalmed, and lies in the little Taj Mahal, among other cherished souvenirs of my precious friendships! While I stood there, I was transformed · the soul of St. Elmo seemed to pass away—a fiend took possession of me; love died, hope with it—and an insatiable thirst for vengeance set my blood on fire. During those ten minutes my whole nature was warped, distorted; my life blasted—mutilated—deformed. The loss of Agnes's love I could have borne, nay—fool that I was!—I think my quondam generous affection for Murray would have made me relinquish her almost resignedly, if his happiness had demanded the sacrifice on my part. If he had come to me frankly and acknowledged all, my insane idolatry would have made me place her hand in his, and remove the barrier of poverty; and the assurance that I had secured his life-long happiness would have sufficed for mine. Oh! the height and depth and marvellous strength of my love for that man passes comprehension! But their scorn, their sneers at my weak credulity, their bitter ridicule of my awkward, overgrown boyishness, stung me to desperation. I wondered if I were insane, or dreaming, or the victim of some horrible delusion. My veins ran fire as I listened to the tangling of her silvery voice with the rich melody of his, and I turned and left the garden, and walked back toward the town. The moon was full, but I staggered and groped my way, like one blind, to the college buildings. I knew where a pair of pistols was kept by one of the students, and possessing myself of them, I wandered out on the road leading to the parsonage. I was aware that Murray intended coming into the town, and at last I reeled into a shaded spot near the road, and waited for him. Oh! the mocking glory of that cloudless night! To this day I hate the cold glitter of stars, and the golden sheen of midnight moons! For the first time in my life, I cursed the world and all it held; cursed the contented cricket singing in the grass at my feet; cursed the blood in my arteries, that beat so thick and fast I could not listen for the footsteps I was waiting for. At last I heard him whistling a favorite tune, which all our lives we had whistled together, as we hunted through the woods around Le Bocage; and, as the familiar sound of 'The Braes of Balquither' drew nearer and nearer, I sprang up with a cry that must have rung on the night air like the yell of some beast of prey. Of all that passed I only know that I cursed and insulted and maddened him till he accepted the pistol, which I thrust into his hand. We moved ten paces apart—and a couple of students, who happened accidently to pass along the road and heard our altercation, stopped at our request, gave the word of command, and we fired simultaneously. The ball entered Murray's heart, and he fell dead without a word. I was severely wounded in the chest, and now I wear the ball here in my side. Ah! a precious *in memoriam* of murdered confidence!"

Until now Edna had listened breathlessly, with her eyes upon his; but here a groan escaped her, and she shuddered violently, and hid her face in her hands.

Mr. Murray came nearer, stood close to her, and hurried on.

"My last memory of my old idol is as he lay with his handsome, treacherous face turned up to the moon; and the hair which Agnes had been fingering, dabbled with dew and the blood that oozed down from his side. When I recovered my consciousness, Murray Hammond had been three weeks in his grave. As soon as I was able to travel, my mother took me to Europe, and for five years we lived in Paris, Naples, or wandered to and fro. Then she came home, and I plunged into the heart of Asia. After two years I returned to Paris, and gave myself up to every species of dissipation. I drank, gambled, and my midnight carousals would sicken your soul were I to paint all their hideousness. You have read in the Scriptures of persons possessed of devils? A savage, mocking, tearing devil held me in bondage. I sold myself to my Mephistopheles on condition that my revenge might be complete. I hated the whole world with an intolerable, murderous hate; and to mock and make my race suffer was the only real pleasure I found. The very name, the bare mention of religion maddened me. A minister's daughter, a minister's son, a minister himself, had withered my young life, and I blasphemously derided all holy things. Oh, Edna! my darling! it is impossible to paint all the awful wretchedness of that period, when I walked in the world seeking victims and finding many. Verily,

> ' There's not a crime
> But takes its proper change out still in crime,
> If once rung on the counter of this world,
> Let sinners look to it.'

Ah! upon how many lovely women have I visited Agnes's sin of hypocrisy! Into how many ears have I poured tender words, until fair hands were as good as offered to me, and I turned their love to mockery! I hated and despised all womanhood; and even in Paris I became notorious as a heartless trifler with the affections I won and trampled under my feet. Whenever a brilliant and beautiful woman crossed my path, I attached myself to her train of admirers, until I made her acknowledge my power and give public and unmistakable manifestation of her preference for me; then I left her—a target for the laughter of her circle. It was not vanity; 'oh! no, no! That springs from self-love, and I had none. It was hate of every thing human, especially of every thing feminine. One of the fairest faces that ever brightened the haunts of fashion—a queenly, elegant girl—the pet of her family and of society, now wears serge garments and a black veil, and is immured in an Italian convent, because I entirely won her heart ; and when she waited for me to declare my affection and ask her to become my wife, I quitted her side for that of another belle, and never visited her again. On the day when she bade adieu to the world, I was among the spectators; and as her mournful but lovely eyes sought mine, I laughed, and gloried in the desolation I had wrought. Sick of Europe, I came home. . . .

And to a part I come where no light shines.'

My tempting fiend pointed to one whose suffering would atone for much of my misery. Edna, I with-hold nothing ; there is much I might conceal, but I scorn to do so. During one terribly fatal winter, scarlet-fever had deprived Mr. Hammond of four chil-dren, leaving him an only daughter—Annie—the image of her brother Murray. Her health was feeble ; con-sumption was stretching its skeleton hands toward her, and her father watched her as a gardener tends his pet, choice, delicate exotic. She was about sixteen, very pretty, very attractive. After Murray's death, I never spoke to Mr. Hammond, never crossed his path; but I met his daughter without his knowledge, and finally I made her confess her love for me. I offered her my hand ; she accepted it. A day was appointed for an elopement and marriage; the hour came ; she left the parsonage, but I did not meet her here on the steps of this church as I had promised, and she received a note that announced my inability to fulfill the engagement. Two hours later her father found her insensible on the steps, and the marble was dripping with a hemorrhage of blood from her lungs. The dark stain is still there ; you must have noticed it. I never saw her again. She kept her room from that day, and died three months after. When on her deathbed she sent for me, but I refused to obey the summons. As I stand here, I see through the window the gray, granite vault overgrown

with ivy, and the marble slab where sleep in untimely
death Murray and Annie Hammond, the victims of
my insatiable revenge. Do you wonder that I doubted
you when you said that afflicted father, Allan Hammond, had never uttered one unkind word about
me ?"

Mr. Murray pointed to a quiet corner of the churchyard, but Edna did not lift her face, and he heard the
half-smothered, shuddering moan that struggled up as
she listened to him.

He put his hand on hers, but she shivered and
shrank away from him.

" Years passed. I grew more and more savage ; the
very power of loving seemed to have died out in my
nature. My mother endeavored to drag me into society, but I was surfeited, sick of the world—sick of
my own excesses ; and gradually I became a recluse, a
surly misanthrope. How often have I laughed bitterly
over those words of Mill's : ' Yet nothing is more certain than that improvement in human affairs is wholly
the work of the uncontented characters !' My indescribable, my tormenting discontent, daily belied his
aphorism. My mother is a woman of stern integrity
of character and sincerity of purpose ; but she is
worldly and ambitious, and inordinately proud, and
for her religion I had lost all respect. Again I went
abroad, solely to kill time ; was absent two years, and
came back. I had ransacked the world, and was disgusted, hopeless, prematurely old. A week after
my return I was attacked by a very malignant fever,
and my life was despaired of, but I exulted in the
thought that at last I should find oblivion. I refused
all remedies, and set at defiance all medical advice,
hoping to hasten the end ; but death cheated me. I
rose from my bed of sickness, cursing the mockery,
realizing that indeed :

> ' The good die first,
> And they whose hearts are dry as summer dust
> Burn to the socket.'

Some months after my recovery, while I was out on a camp-hunt, you were brought to Le Bocage, and the sight of you made me more vindictive than ever. I believed you selfishly designing, and I could not bear that you should remain under the same roof with me. I hated children as I hated men and women. But that day when you defied me in the park, and told me I was sinful and cruel, I began to notice you closely. I weighed your words, watched you when you little dreamed that I was present, and often concealed myself in order to listen to your conversation. I saw in your character traits that annoyed me, because they were noble and unlike what I had believed all womanhood or girlhood to be. I was aware that you dreaded and disliked me; I saw that very clearly every time I had occasion to speak to you. How it all came to pass I can not tell—I know not—and it has always been a mystery even to me ; but, Edna, after the long lapse of years of sin and reckless dissipation, my heart stirred and turned to you, child though you were, and a strange strange, invincible love for you sprang from the bitter ashes of a dead affection for Agnes Hunt. I wondered at myself ; I sneered at my idiocy; I cursed my mad folly, and tried to believe you as unprincipled as I had found others ; but the singular fascination strengthened day by day. Finally I determined to tempt you, hoping that your duplicity and deceit would wake me from the second dream into which I feared there was danger of my falling. Thinking that at your age curiosity was the strongest emotion, I carefully arranged the interior of the Taj Mahal, so that it would be impossible for you to open it without being discovered ; and putting the key in your hands, I went abroad. I wanted to satisfy myself that you were unworthy, and believed you would betray the trust. For four years I wandered, restless, impatient, scorning myself more and more because I could not forget your sweet, pure, haunting face ; because, despite my jeers, I knew that I loved you. At last I wrote to my mother from Egypt that I should go to Central

Persia, and so I intended. But one night as I sat
alone, smoking, amid the ruins of the propylon at Philæ,
a vision of Le Bocage rose before me, and your dear
face looked at me from the lotus-crowned columns of
the ancient temple. I forgot the hate I bore all mankind; I forgot every thing but you; your pure, calm,
magnificent eyes; and the longing to see you, my
darling—the yearning to look into your eyes once
more, took possession of me. I sat there till the great,
golden, dewless dawn of the desert fell upon Egypt,
and then came a struggle long and desperate. I
laughed and swore at my folly; but far down in the
abysses of my distorted nature hope had kindled a
little feeble, flickering ray. I tried to smother it, but
its flame clung to some crevice in my heart, and would
not be crushed. While I debated, a pigeon that dwelt
somewhere in the crumbling temple fluttered down at
my feet, cooed softly, looked in my face, then perched
on a mutilated red granite sphinx immediately in front
of me, and after a moment rose, circled above me in the
pure, rainless air and flew westward. I accepted it as
an omen, and started to America instead of to Persia.
On the night of the tenth of December, four years
after I bade you good-bye at the park gate, I was again
at Le Bocage. Silently and undiscovered I stole into
my own house, and secreted myself behind the curtains
in the library. I had been there one hour when you
and Gordon Leigh came in to examine the Targum.
Oh, Edna! how little you dreamed of the eager,
hungry eyes that watched you! During that hour
that you two sat there bending over the same book, I
became thoroughly convinced that while I loved you
as I never expected to love any one, Gordon also loved
you, and intended if possible to make you his wife. I
contrasted my worn, haggard face and grayish locks
with his, so full of manly hope and youthful beauty,
and I could not doubt that any girl would prefer him
to me. Edna, my retribution began then. I felt that
my devil was mocking me, as I had long mocked others,
and made me love you when it was impossible to win

you. Then and there I was tempted to spring upon
and throttle you both before he triumphantly called
you his. At last Leigh left, and I escaped to my own
rooms. I was pacing the floor when I heard you cross
the rotundo, and saw the glimmer of the light you
carried. Hoping to see you open the little Taj, I
crawled behind the sarcophagus that holds my two
mummies, crouched close to the floor, and peeped at
you across the gilded byssus that covered them. My
eyes, I have often been told, possess magnetic or
mesmeric power. At all events, you felt my eager
gaze, you were restless, and searched the room to discover whence that feeling of a human presence came.
Darling, were you superstitious, that you avoided
looking into the dark corner where the mummies lay?
Presently you stopped in front of the little tomb, and
swept away the spider-web, and took the key from
your pocket, and as you put it into the lock I almost
shouted aloud in my savage triumph! I absolutely
panted to find Leigh's future wife as unworthy of
confidence as I believed the remainder of her sex.
But you did not open it. You merely drove away the
spider and rubbed the marble clean with your handkerchief, and held the key between your fingers. Then
my heart seemed to stand still, as I watched the light
streaming over your beautiful, holy face and warm,
crimson dress; and when you put the key in your
pocket and turned away, my groan almost betrayed
me. I had taken out my watch to see the hour, and
in my suspense I clutched it so tightly that the gold
case and the crystal within all crushed in my hand.
You heard the tingling sound and wondered whence
it came; and when you had locked the door and gone,
I raised one of the windows and swung myself down
to the terrace. Do you remember that night?"

"Yes, Mr. Murray."

Her voice was tremulous and almost inaudible.

"I had business in Tennessee, no matter now, what,
or where, and I went on that night. After a week I
returned, that afternoon when I found you reading in

my sitting-room. Still I was sceptical, and not until I
opened the tomb, was I convinced that you had not
betrayed the trust which you supposed I placed in
you. Then, as you stood beside me in all your noble
purity and touching girlish beauty—as you looked up
half reproachfully, half defiantly at me—it cost me a
terrible effort to master myself—to abstain from clasping you to my heart, and telling you all that you were
to me. Oh! how I longed to take you in my arms
and feed my poor famished heart with one touch of
your lips! I dared not look at you, lest I should lose
my self-control. The belief that Gordon was a successful rival sealed my lips on that occasion; and ah!
the dreary wretchedness of the days of suspense that
followed. I was a starving beggar who stood before
what I coveted above everything else on earth, and
saw it labelled with another man's name and beyond
my reach. The daily sight of that emerald ring on
your finger maddened me; and you can form no ad-
equate idea of the bitterness of feeling with which I
noted my mother's earnest efforts and manœuvres to
secure for Gordon Leigh—to sell to him—the little
hand which her own son would have given worlds to
claim in the sight of God and man! Continually I
watched you when you least suspected me; I strewed
infidel books where I knew you must see them; I
tempted you more than you dreamed of; I teased
and tormented and wounded you whenever an opportunity offered; for I hoped to find some flaw in your
character, some defect in your temper, some inconsistency between your professions and your practice. I
knew Leigh was not your equal, and I said bitterly,
'She is poor and unknown, and will surely marry him
for his money, for his position—as Agnes would have
married me.' But you did not! and when I knew
that you had positively refused his fortune, I felt that
a great dazzling light had broken suddenly upon my
darkened life; and, for the first time since I parted
with Murray Hammond, tears of joy filled my eyes. I
ceased to struggle against my love—I gave myself up

to it, and only asked, How can I overcome her aversion to me? You were the only tie that linked me with my race, and for your sake I almost felt as if I could forget my hate. But you shrank more and more from me, and my punishment overtook me when I saw how you hated Clinton Allston's blood-smeared hands, and with what unfeigned horror you regarded his career. When you declared so vehemently that his fingers should never touch yours—oh! it was the fearful apprehension of losing you that made me catch your dear hands and press them to my aching heart. I was stretched upon a rack that taught me the full import of Isaac Taylor's grim words, 'Remorse is man's dread prerogative!' Believing that you knew all my history and that your aversion was based upon it, I was too proud to show you my affection. Douglass Manning was as much my friend as I permitted any man to be; we had travelled together through Arabia, and with his handwriting I was familiar. Suspecting your literary schemes, and dreading a rival in your ambition, I wrote to him on the subject, discovered all I wished to ascertain, and requested him, for my sake, to reconsider and examine your MS. He did so to oblige me, and I insisted that he should treat your letters and your MS. with such severity as to utterly crush your literary aspirations. Oh, child! do you see how entirely you fill my mind and heart? How I scrutinize your words and actions? Oh, my darling——"

He paused, and leaned over her, putting his hand on her head, but she shook off his touch and exclaimed:

"But Gertrude! Gertrude!"

"Be patient, and you shall know all; for as God reigns above us, there is no recess of my heart into which you shall not look. It is, perhaps, needless to tell you that Estelle came here to marry me for my fortune. It is not agreeable to say such things of one's own cousin, but to-day I deal only in truths, and facts sustain me. She professes to love me! has absolutely avowed it more than once in days gone by.

Whether she really loves anything but wealth and
luxury, I have never troubled myself to find out ; but
my mother fancies that if Estelle were my wife, I
might be less cynical. Once or twice I tried to be affectionate toward her, solely to see what effect it would
have upon you ; but I discovered that you could not
easily be deceived in that direction—the mask was too
transparent, and beside, the game disgusted me. I
have no respect for Estelle, but I have a shadowy traditional reverence for the blood in her veins which
forbids my flirting with her as she deserves. The
very devil himself brought Agnes here. She had
married a rich old banker only a few months after
Murray's death, and lived in ease and splendor until a
short time since, when her husband failed and died,
leaving her without a cent. She knew how utterly she
had blasted my life, and imagined that I had never
married because I still loved her ! With unparalleled
effrontery she came here, and trusting to her wonderfully preserved beauty, threw herself and her daughter
in my way. When I heard *she* was at the parsonage,
all the old burning hate leaped up strong as ever. I
fancied that she was the real cause of your dislike to
me, and that night, when the game of billiards ended,
I went to the parsonage for the first time since Murray's death. Oh ! the ghostly thronging memories
that met me at the gate, trooped after me up the walk,
and hovered like vultures as I stood in the shadow of
the trees, where my idol and I had chatted and
romped and shouted and whistled in the far past, in
the sinless bygone ! Unobserved I stood there, and
looked once more, after the lapse of twenty years, on
the face that had caused my crime and ruin. I listened to her clear laugh, silvery as when I heard it
chiming with Murray's under the apple-tree on the
night that branded me and drove me forth to wander
like Cain ; and I resolved, if she really loved her
daughter, to make her suffer for all that she had inflicted on me. The first time I met Gertrude I could
have sworn my boyhood's love was restored to me;

she is so entirely the image of what Agnes was. To possess themselves of my home and property is all that brought them here; and whether as my wife or as my mother-in-law I think Agnes cares little. The first she sees is impracticable, and now to make me wed Gertrude is her aim. Like mother, like daughter!"

"Oh! no, no! visit not her mother's sins on her innocent head! Gertrude is true and affectionate, and she loves you dearly."

Edna spoke with a great effort, and the strange tones of her own voice frightened her.

"Loves me? Ha, ha! just about as tenderly as her mother did before her! That they do both ' dearly love '—my purse, I grant you. Hear me out. Agnes threw the girl constantly and adroitly in my way; the demon here in my heart prompted revenge, and, above all, I resolved to find out whether you were indeed as utterly indifferent to me as you seemed. I know that jealousy will make a woman betray her affection sooner than any other cause, and I deliberately set myself to work to make you believe that I loved that pretty cheat over yonder at the parsonage—that frolicsome wax-doll, who would rather play with a kitten than talk to Cicero; who intercepts me almost daily, to favor me with manifestations of devotion, and shows me continually that I have only to put out my hand and take her to rule over my house, and trample my heart under her pretty feet! When you gave me that note of hers a week ago, and looked so calmly, so coolly in my face, I felt as if all hope were dying in my heart; for I could not believe that, if you had one atom of affection for me, you could be so generous, so unselfish toward one whom you considered your rival. That night I did not close my eyes, and had almost decided to revisit South America; but next morning my mother told me you were going to New York— that all entreaties had failed to shake your resolution Then once more a hope cheered me, and I believed that I understood why you had determined to leave those

whom I know you love tenderly—to quit the home my
mother offered you and struggle among strangers. Yesterday they told me you would leave on Monday, and I
went out to seek you ; but you were with Mr. Hammond,
as usual, and instead of you I met—that curse of my life
—Agnes! Face to face, at last, with my red-lipped
Lamia! Oh! it was a scene that made jubilee down
in Pandemonium! She plead for her child's happiness—ha, ha, ha!—implored me most pathetically to
love her Gertrude as well as Gertrude loved me, and
that my happiness would make me forget the unfortunate past! She would willingly give me her daughter,
for did she not know how deep, how lasting, how
deathless was my affection? I had Gertrude's whole
heart, and I was too generous to trifle with her tender
love! Edna, darling! I will not tell you all she said
—you would blush for your sisterhood. But my vengeance was complete when I declined the honor she
was so eager to force upon me ; when I overwhelmed
her with my scorn, and told her that there was only one
woman whom I respected or trusted ; only one woman
upon the broad earth whom I loved ; only one woman
who could ever be my wife, and her name was—Edna
Earl!"

His voice died away, and all was still as the dead in
their grassy graves.

The orphan's face was concealed, and after a moment
St. Elmo Murray opened his arms, and said in that
low winning tone which so many women had found it
impossible to resist : " Come to me now, my pure,
noble Edna. You whom I love, as only such a man as
I have shown myself to be can love."

" No, Mr. Murray : Gertrude stands between us."

"Gertrude! Do not make me swear here, in your
presence—do not madden me by repeating her name !
I tell you she is a silly child, who cares no more for me
than her mother did before her. Nothing shall stand
between us. I love you ; the God above us is my witness that I love you as I never loved any human being,
and I will not—I swear I will not live without you!

You are mine, and all the legions in hell shall not part us!"

He stooped, snatched her from the chair as if she had been an infant, and folded her in his strong arms.

"Mr. Murray, I know she loves you. My poor little trusting friend! You trifled with her warm heart, as you hope to trifle with mine; but I know you; you have shown me how utterly heartless, remorseless, unprincipled you are. You had no right to punish Gertrude for her mother's sins; and if you had one spark of honor in your nature, you would marry her, and try to atone for the injury you have already done."

"By pretending to give her a heart which belongs entirely to you? If I wished to deceive you now, think you I would have told all that hideous past, which you can not abhor one half as much as I do?"

"Your heart is not mine! It belongs to sin, or you could not have so maliciously deceived poor Gertrude. You love nothing but your ignoble revenge and the gratification of your self-love! You——"

"Take care, do not rouse me. Be reasonable, little darling. You doubt my love? Well, I ought not to wonder at your scepticism after all you have heard. But you can feel how my heart throbs against your cheek, and if you will look into my eyes, you will be convinced that I am fearfully in earnest, when I beg you to be my wife to-morrow—to-day—now! if you will only let me send for a minister or a magistrate! You are——"

"You asked Annie to be your wife, and——"

"Hush! hush! Look at me. Edna, raise your head and look at me."

She tried to break away, and finding it impossible, pressed both hands over her face and hid it against his shoulder.

He laughed, and whispered:

"My darling, I know what that means. You dare not look up because you cannot trust your own eyes! Because you dread for me to see something there

which you want to hide, which you think it your duty
to conceal."

He felt a long shudder creep over her, and she
answered resolutely:

"Do you think, sir, that I could love a murderer?
A man whose hands are red with the blood of the son
of my best friend?"

"Look at me then."

He raised her head, drew down her hands, took them
firmly in one of his, and placing the other under her
chin, lifted the burning face close to his own.

She dreaded the power of his lustrous, mesmeric
eyes, and instantly her long silky lashes swept her
flushed cheeks.

"Ah! you dare not! You can not look me steadily
in the eye and say, 'St. Elmo, I never have loved—do
not—and never can love you!' You are too truthful;
your lips can not dissemble. I know you do not want
to love me. Your reason, your conscience forbid it;
you are struggling to crush your heart. You think it
your duty to despise and hate me. But, my own,
Edna—my darling! my darling! you do love me!
You know you do love me, though you will not confess
it! My proud darling!"

He drew the face tenderly to his own, and kissed her
quivering lips repeatedly, and at last a moan of anguish
told how she was wrestling with her heart.

"Do you think you can hide your love from my
eager eyes? Oh! I know that I am unworthy of you!
I feel it more and more every day, every hour. It is
because you seem so noble—so holy—to my eyes, that
I reverence while I love you. You are so far above
all other women—so glorified in your pure, consistent
piety—that you only have the power to make my
future life—redeem the wretched and sinful past. I
tempted and tried you, and when you proved so true
and honest and womanly, you kindled a faint beam of
hope that, after all, there might be truth and saving,
purifying power in religion. Do you know that since
this church was finished I have never entered it until a

month ago, when I followed you here, and crouched downstairs—yonder, behind one of the pillars, and heard your sacred songs, your hymns so full of grandeur, so full of pathos, that I could not keep back my tears while I listened. Since then I have come every Saturday afternoon, and during the hour spent here my unholy nature was touched and softened as no sermon ever touched it. Oh! you wield a power over me—over all my future, which ought to make you tremble! The first generous impulse that has stirred my callous, bitter soul since I was a boy, I owe to you. I went first to see poor Reed, in order to discover what took you so often to that cheerless place; and my interest in little Huldah arose from the fact that you loved the child. Oh, my darling! I know I have been sinful and cruel and blasphemous; but it is not too late for me to atone! It is not too late for me to do some good in the world; and if you will only love me, and trust me, and help me——"

His voice faltered, his tears fell upon her forehead, and stooping he kissed her lips softly, reverently, as if he realized the presence of something sacred.

"My precious Edna, no oath shall ever soil my lips again; the touch of yours has purified them. I have been mad—I think, for many, many years, and I loathe my past life; but remember how sorely I was tried, and be merciful when you judge me. With your dear little hand in mine to lead me, I will make amends for the ruin and suffering I have wrought, and my Edna—my own wife, shall save me!"

Before the orphan's mental vision rose the picture of Gertrude, the trembling coral mouth, the childish wistful eyes, the lovely head nestled down so often and so lovingly on her shoulder; and she saw, too, the bent figure and white locks of her beloved pastor, as he sat in his old age, in his childless, desolate home, facing the graves of his murdered children.

"Oh, Mr. Murray! You can not atone! You can not call your victims from their tombs. You can not undo what you have done! What amends can you

make to Mr. Hammond, and to my poor little confiding Gertrude? I can not help you! I can not save
you!"

"Hush! You can, you shall! Do you think I will
ever give you up? Have mercy on my lonely life! my
wretched, darkened soul. Lean your dear head here
on my heart, and say, 'St. Elmo, what a wife can do
to save her erring, sinful husband, I will do for you.'
If I am ever to be saved, you, you only can effect my
redemption; for I trust, I reverence you. Edna, as
you value my soul, my eternal welfare, give yourself to
me! Give your pure, sinless life to purify mine."

With a sudden bound she sprang from his embrace,
and lifted her arms toward the Christ, who seemed to
shudder as the flickering light of fading day fell
through waving foliage upon it.

"Look yonder to Jesus, bleeding! Only his blood
can wash away your guilt. Mr. Murray, I can never be
your wife. I have no confidence in you. Knowing
how systematically you have deceived others, how
devoid of conscientious scruples you are, I should
never be sure that I too was not the victim of your
heartless cynicism. Beside, I——"

"Hush! hush! To your keeping I commit my con-
cience and my heart."

"No! no! I am no vicegerent of an outraged and
insulted God! I put no faith in any man whose con-
cience another keeps. From the species of fascination
which you exert, I shrink with unconquerable dread
and aversion, and would almost as soon entertain the
thought of marrying Lucifer himself. Oh! your perverted nature shocks, repels, astonishes, grieves me. I
can neither respect nor trust you. Mr. Murray, have
mercy upon yourself! Go yonder to Jesus. He only
can save and purify you."

"Edna, you do not, you can not intend to leave me?
Darling——"

He held out his arms and moved toward her, but
she sprang past him, down the steps of the gallery,
out of the church, and paused only at sight of the

dark, dull spot on the white steps, where Annie Hammond had lain insensible.

An hour later, St. Elmo Murray raised his face from the mahogany railing where it had rested since Edna left him, and looked around the noble pile which his munificence had erected. A full moon eyed him pityingly through the stained glass, and the gleam of the marble pulpit was chill and ghostly; and in that weird light the Christ was threatening, wrathful, appalling.

As St. Elmo stood there alone, confronting the picture—confronting the past—memory, like the Witch of Endor, called up visions of the departed that were more terrible than the mantled form of Israel's prophet; and the proud, hopeless man bowed his haughty head, with a cry of anguish that rose mournfully to the vaulted ceiling of the sanctuary:

"It went up single, echoless, 'My God! I am forsaken!'"

CHAPTER XXIII.

THE weather was so inclement on the following day
that no service was held in the church ; but, notwithstanding the heavy rain, Edna went to the parsonage
to bid adieu to her pastor and teacher.   When she
ascended the steps Mr. Hammond was walking up and
down the portico with his hands clasped behind him,
as was his habit when engrossed by earnest thought ;
and he greeted his pupil with a degree of mournful
tenderness very soothing to her sad heart.

Leading the way to his study, where Mrs. Powell
sat with an open book on her lap, he said gently :

" Agnes, will you be so kind as to leave us for a
while ?   This is the last interview I shall have with
Edna for a long time, perhaps forever, and there are
some things I wish to say to her alone.   You will find
a better light in the dining-room, where all is quiet."

As Mrs. Powell withdrew he locked the door, and
for some seconds paced the floor; then, taking a
seat on the chintz-covered lounge beside his pupil, he
said, eagerly :

" St. Elmo was at the church yesterday afternoon.
Are you willing to tell me what passed between you ?"

" Mr. Hammond, he told me his meloncholy history.   I know all now—know why he shrinks from
meeting you, whom he has injured so cruelly ; know
all his guilt and your desolation."

The old man bowed his white head on his bosom,
and there was a painful silence.   When he spoke, his
voice was scarcely audible.

" The punishment of Eli has fallen heavily upon

me, and there have been hours when I thought that it
was greater than I could bear—that it would utterly
crush me; but the bitterness of the curse has passed
away, and I can say truly of that ' meekest angel of
God,' the Angel of Patience :

> ' He walks with thee, that angel kind,
> And gently whispers, Be resigned ;
> Bear up, bear on ; the end shall tell,
> The dear Lord ordereth all things well !'

"I tried to train up my children in the fear and
admonition of the Lord; but I must have failed
signally in my duty, though I have never been able to
discover in what respect I was negligent. One of the
sins of my life was my inordinate pride in my only
boy—my gifted, gifted, handsome son. My love
for Murray was almost idolatrous ; and when my heart
throbbed with proudest hopes and aspirations, my
idol was broken and laid low in the dust ; and, like
David mourning for his rebellious child Absalom, I
cried out in my affliction, ' My son ! my son ! would
God I had died for thee !' Murray Hammond was
my precious diadem of earthly glory; and suddenly I
found myself uncrowned, and sackcloth and ashes were
my portion."

"Why did you never confide these sorrows to me ?
Did you doubt my earnest sympathy ?"

"No, my child ; but I thought it best that St. Elmo
should lift the veil and show you all that he wished you
to know. I felt assured that the time would come
when he considered it due to himself to acquaint you
with his sad history ; and when I saw him go into the
church yesterday I knew that the hour had arrived.
I did not wish to prejudice you against him ; for I
believed that through your agency the prayers of
twenty years would be answered, and that his wandering, embittered heart would follow you to that cross
before which he bowed in his boyhood. Edna, it was
through my son's sin and duplicity that St. Elmo's
noble career was blasted, and his most admirable char-

acter perverted ; and I have hoped and believed that
through your influence, my beloved pupil, he would
be redeemed from his reckless course. My dear little
Edna, you are very lovely and winning, and I believed
he would love you as he never loved any one else.
Oh! I have hoped every thing from your influence!
Far, far beyond all computation is the good which a
pious, consistent, Christian wife can accomplish in the
heart of a husband who truly loves her."

"Oh, Mr. Hammond! you pain and astonish me.
Surely you would not be willing to see me marry a
man who scoffs at the very name of religion ; who
willfully deceives and trifles with the feelings of all who
are sufficiently credulous to trust his hollow professions—whose hands are red with the blood of your
children! What hope of happiness or peace could
you indulge for me, in view of such a union? I should
merit all the wretchedness that would inevitably be
my life-long portion if, knowing his crimes, I could
consent to link my future with his."

"He would not deceive you, my child! If you
knew him as well as I do, if you could realize all that
he was before his tender, loving heart was stabbed by
the two whom he almost adored, you would judge him
more leniently. Edna, if I whom he has robbed of all
that made life beautiful—if I, standing here in my
lonely old age, in sight of the graves of my murdered
darlings—if I can forgive him, and pray for him, and,
as God is my witness, love him! you have no right to
visit my injuries and my sorrows upon him !"

Edna looked in amazement at his troubled earnest
countenance, and exclaimed :

"Oh! if he knew all your noble charity, your unparalleled magnanimity, surely, surely, your influence
would be his salvation! His stubborn, bitter heart
would be melted. But, sir, I should have a right to
expect Annie's sad fate if I could forget her sufferings
and her wrongs."

Mr. Hammond rose and walked to the window, and
after a time, when he resumed his seat, his eyes were

full of tears, and his wrinkled face was strangely pallid.

"My darling Annie, my sweet, fragile flower, my precious little daughter, so like her sainted mother! Ah! it is not surprising that she could not resist his fascinations. But, Edna, he never loved my pet lamb. Do you know that you have become almost as dear to me as my own dead child? She deceived me! she was willing to forsake her father in his old age; but through long years you have never once betrayed my perfect confidence."

The old man put his thin hand on the orphan's head and turned the countenance toward him.

"My dear little girl, you will not think me impertinently curious when I ask you a question, which my sincere affection for and interest in you certainly sanction? Do you love St. Elmo?"

"Mr. Hammond, it is not love; for esteem, respect, confidence, belong to love. But I can not deny that he exerts a very singular, a wicked fascination over me. I dread his evil influence, I avoid his presence, and know that he is utterly unworthy of any woman's trust; and yet—and yet—Oh, sir! I feel that I am very weak, and I fear that I am unwomanly; but I can not despise, I can not hate him as I ought to do!"

"Is not this feeling, on your part, one of the causes that hurry you away to New York?"

"That is certainly one of the reasons why I am anxious to go as early as possible. Oh, Mr. Hammond! much as I love, much as I owe you and Mrs. Murray, I sometimes wish that I had never come here! Never seen Le Bocage, and the mocking, jeering man who owns it!"

"Try to believe that somehow in the mysterious Divine economy it is all for the best. In reviewing the apparently accidental circumstances that placed you among us, I have thought that, because this was your appointed field of labor, God in his wisdom brought you where he designed you to work. Does

Mrs. Murray know that her son has offered to make you his wife?"

"No! no! I hope she never will; for it would mortify her exceedingly to know that he could be willing to give his proud name to one of whose lineage she is so ignorant. How did you know it?"

"I knew what his errand must be when he forced himself to visit a spot so fraught with painful memories as my church. Edna, I shall not urge you; but ponder well the step you are taking; for St. Elmo's future will be colored by your decision. I have an abiding and comforting faith that he will yet lift himself out of the abyss of sinful dissipation and scoffing scepticism, and your hand would aid him as none other human can."

"Mr. Hammond, it seems incredible that you can plead for him. Oh! do not tempt me! Do not make me believe that I could restore his purity of faith and life. Do not tell me that it would be right to give my hand to a blasphemous murderer? Oh! my own heart is weak enough already! I know that I am right in my estimate of his unscrupulous character, and I am neither so vain nor so blind as to imagine that my feeble efforts could accomplish for him, what all your noble magnanimity and patient endeavors have entirely failed to effect. If he can obstinately resist the influence of your life, he would laugh mine to scorn. It is hard enough for me to leave him, when I feel that duty demands it. Oh, my dear Mr. Hammond! do not attempt to take from me that only staff which can carry me firmly away—do not make my trial even more severe. I must not see his face; for I will not be his wife. Instead of weakening my resolution by holding out flattering hopes of reforming him, pray for me! oh! pray for me! that I may be strengthened to flee from a great temptation! I will marry no man who is not an earnest, humble believer in the religion of our Lord Jesus Christ. Rather than become the wife of a sacrilegious scoffer, such as I know Mr. Mur-

ray to be, I will, so help me God ! live and work alone,
and go down to my grave, Edna Earl !"

The minister sighed heavily.

"Bear one thing in mind. It has been said, that in
disavowing guardianship, we sometimes slaughter Abel.
You can not understand my interest in St. Elmo. Remember that if his wretched soul is lost at last, it will
be required at the hands of my son, in that dread day
—*Dies Iræ! Dies Illa!*—when we shall all stand at the
final judgment ! Do you wonder that I struggle in
prayer, and in all possible human endeavor to rescue
him from ruin ; so that when I am called from earth,
I can meet the spirit of my only boy with the blessed
tidings that the soul he jeoparded, and well-nigh
wrecked, has been redeemed ! is safe ! anchored once
more in the faith of Christ ? But I will say no more.
Your own heart and conscience must guide you in this
matter. It would pour a flood of glorious sunshine
upon my sad and anxious heart, as I go down to my
grave, if I could know that you, whose life and character I have in great degree moulded, were instrumental in saving one whom I have loved so long, so
well, and under such afflicting circumstances, as my
poor St. Elmo."

"To the mercy of his Maker, and the intercession of
his Saviour, I commit him.

'As for me, I go my way, onward, upward.'"

A short silence ensued, and at last Edna rose to say
good-bye.

"Do you still intend to leave at four o'clock in the
morning? I fear you will have bad weather for your
journey."

"Yes, sir, I shall certainly start to-morrow. And
now, I must leave you. Oh, my best friend ! how can
I tell you good-bye !"

The minister folded her in his trembling arms, and
his silver locks mingled with her black hair, while he solemnly blessed her. She sobbed as he pressed his lips

to her forehead, and gently put her from him; and turning, she hurried away, anxious to escape the sight of Gertrude's accusing face; for she supposed that Mrs. Powell had repeated to her daughter Mr. Murray's taunting words.

Since the previous evening she had not spoken to St. Elmo, who did not appear at breakfast; but when she passed him in the hall an hour later, he was talking to his mother, and took no notice of her bow.

Now as the carriage approached the house, she glanced in the direction of his apartments, and saw him sitting at the window, with his elbow resting on the sill, and his cheek on his hand.

She went at once to Mrs. Murray, and the interview was long and painful. The latter wept freely, and insisted that if the orphan grew weary of teaching (as she knew would happen), she should come back immediately to Le Bocage; where a home would always be hers, and to which a true friend would welcome her.

At length, when Estelle Harding came in with some letters, which she wished to submit to her aunt's inspection, Edna retreated to her own quiet room. She went to her bureau to complete the packing of her clothes, and found on the marble slab a box and note directed to her.

Mr. Murray's handwriting was remarkably graceful, and Edna broke the seal which bore his motto, *Nemo me impune lacessit.*

"EDNA: I send for your examination the contents of the little tomb, which you guarded so faithfully. Read the letters written before I was betrayed. The locket attached to a ribbon was always worn over my heart, and the miniatures which it contains are those of Agnes Hunt and Murray Hammond. Read all the record, and then judge me, as you hope to be judged. I sit alone, amid the mouldering, blackened ruins of my youth; will you not listen to the prayer of my heart, and the half-smothered pleadings of your own, and come to me in my desolation, and help me to build

up a new and noble life? Oh, my darling, you can
make me what you will. While you read and ponder,
I am praying. Aye, praying for the first time in
twenty years! praying that if God ever hears prayer,
He will influence your decision, and bring you to me.
Edna, my darling! I wait for you.

"Your own

"ST. ELMO."

Ah! how her tortured heart writhed and bled;
how piteously it pleaded for him, and for itself!

Edna opened the locket, and if Gertrude had
stepped into the golden frame, the likeness could not
have been more startling. She looked at it until her
lips blanched and were tightly compressed, and the
memory of Gertrude became paramount. Murray
Hammond's face she barely glanced at, and its extraordinary beauty stared at her like that of some avenging angel. With a shudder she put it away, and
turned to the letters that St. Elmo had written to
Agnes and to Murray, in the early, happy days of his
engagement.

Tender, beautiful, loving letters, that breathed the
most devoted attachment and the purest piety; letters
that were full of lofty aspirations, and religious fervor,
and generous schemes for the assistance and enlightenment of the poor about Le Bocage; and especially for
"my noble, matchless Murray." Among the papers
were several designs for charitable buildings: a house
of industry, an asylum for the blind, and a free school-
house. In an exquisite ivory casket, containing a
splendid set of diamonds, and the costly betrothal
ring, bearing the initials, Edna found a sheet of paper
around which the blazing necklace was twisted. Disengaging it, she saw that it was a narration of all that
had stung him to desperation on the night of the
murder.

As she read the burning taunts, the insults, the ridi
cule heaped by the two under the apple-tree upon the
fond, faithful, generous, absent friend, she felt the in-

dignant blood gush into her face; but she read on and on, and two hours elapsed ere she finished the package. Then came a trial, a long, fierce, agonizing trial, such as few women have ever been called upon to pass through; such as the world believes no woman ever triumphantly endured. Girded by prayer, the girl went down resolutely into the flames of the furnace, and the ordeal was terrible indeed. But as often as Love showed her the figure of Mr. Murray, alone in his dreary sitting-room, waiting, watching for her, she turned and asked of Duty, the portrait of Gertrude's sweet, anxious face; the picture of dying Annie; the mournful countenance of a nun, shut up by iron bars from God's beautiful world, from the home and the family who had fondly cherished her in her happy girlhood, ere St. Elmo trailed his poison across her sunny path.

After another hour, the orphan went to her desk, and while she wrote, a pale, cold rigidity settled upon her features, which told that she was calmly, deliberately shaking hands with the expelled, the departing Hagar of her heart's hope and happiness.

"To the mercy of God, and the love of Christ, and the judgment of your own conscience, I commit you. Henceforth we walk different paths, and after to-night, it is my wish that we meet no more on earth. Mr. Murray, I cannot lift up your darkened soul; and you would only drag mine down. For your final salvation I shall never cease to pray till we stand face to face before the Bar of God.

"EDNA EARL."

Ringing for a servant, she sent back the box, and even his own note, which she longed to keep, but would not trust herself to see again; and dreading reflection, and too miserable to sleep, she went to Mrs. Murray's room, and remained with her till three o'clock.

Then Mr. Murray's voice rang through the house, calling for the carriage, and as Edna put on her bonnet and shawl, he knocked at his mother's door.

" It is raining very hard, and you must not think of going to the train, as you intended."

" But, my son, the carriage is close and——"

" I can not permit you to expose yourself so unnecessarily, and, in short, I will not take you, so there is an end of it. Of course I can stand the weather, and I will go over with Edna, and put her under the care of some one on the train. As soon as possible send her down to the carriage. I shall order her trunks strapped on."

He was very pale and stern, and his voice rang coldly clear as he turned and went down stairs.

The parting was very painful, and Mrs. Murray followed the orphan to the front door.

" St. Elmo, I wish you would let me go. I do not mind the rain."

" Impossible. You know I have an unconquerable horror of scenes, and I do not at all fancy witnessing one that threatens to last until the train leaves. Go up-stairs and cry yourself to sleep in ten minutes ; that will be much more sensible. Come, Edna, are you ready ?"

The orphan was folded in a last embrace, and Mr. Murray held out his hand, drew her from his mother's arms, and taking his seat beside her in the carriage, ordered the coachman to drive on.

The night was very dark, the wind sobbed down the avenue, and the rain fell in such torrents that as Edna leaned out for a last look at the stately mansion, which she had learned to love so well, she could only discern the outline of the bronze monsters by the glimmer of the light burning in the hall. She shrank far back in one corner, and her fingers clutched each other convulsively ; but when they had passed through the gate and entered the main road Mr. Murray's hand was laid on hers—the cold fingers were unlocked gently but firmly, and raised to his lips.

She made an effort to withdraw them, but found it useless, and the trial which she had fancied was at an end seemed only beginning.

"Edna, this is the last time I shall ever speak to you of myself; the last time I shall ever allude to all that has passed. Is it entirely useless for me to ask you to reconsider? If you have no pity for me, have some mercy on yourself. You can not know how I dread the thought of your leaving me, and being roughly handled by a cold, selfish, ruthless world. Oh! it maddens me when I think of your giving your precious life, which would so glorify my home and gladden my desolate heart, to a public, who will trample upon you if possible, and, if it can not entirely crush you, will only value you as you deserve, when, with ruined health and withered hopes, you sink into the early grave malice and envy will have dug for you. Already your dear face has grown pale, and your eyes have a restless, troubled look, and shadows are gathering about your young, pure, fresh spirit. My darling, you are not strong enough to wrestle with the world; you will be trodden down by the masses in this conflict, upon which you enter so eagerly. Do you not know that *literati*' means literally the branded? The lettered slave! Oh! if not for my sake, at least for your own, reconsider before the hot irons sear your brow; and hide it here, my love; keep it white and pure and unfurrowed here, in the arms that will never weary of sheltering and clasping you close and safe from the burning brand of fame. *Literati!* A bondage worse than Roman slavery! Help me to make a proper use of my fortune, and you will do more real good to your race than by all you can ever accomplish with your pen, no matter how successful it may prove. If you were selfish and heartless as other women, adulation and celebrity and the praise of the public might satisfy you. But you are not, and I have studied your nature too thoroughly to mistake the result of your ambitious career. My darling, ambition is the mirage of the literary desert you are anxious to traverse; it is the Bahr

Sheitan, the Satan's water, which will ever recede and mock your thirsty, toil-spent soul. Dear little pilgrim, do not scorch your feet and wear out your life in the hot, blinding sands, struggling in vain for the constantly fading, vanishing oasis of happy literary celebrity. Ah! the Sahara of letters is full of bleaching bones that tell where many of your sex as well as of mine fell and perished miserably, even before the noon of life. Ambitious spirit, come, rest in peace in the cool, quiet, happy, palm-grove that I offer you. My shrinking violet, sweeter than all Pæstum boasts! You can not cope successfully with the world of selfish men and frivolous, heartless women, of whom you know absolutely nothing. To-day I found a passage which you had marked in one of my books, and it echoes ceaselessly in my heart :

> " ' *My future will not copy fair my past.*'
> I wrote that once; and thinking at my side
> My ministering life-angel justified
> The word by his appealing look upcast
> To the white throne of God, I turned at last,
> And there instead saw thee, not unallied
> To angels in thy soul! * * Then I, long tried
> By natural ills, received the comfort fast;
> While budding at thy sight, my pilgrim's staff
> Gave out green leaves with morning dews impearled.
> I seek no copy now of life's first half :
> Leave here the pages with long musing curled,
> Write me new my future's epigraph.
> New angel mine—unhoped-for in the world !' "

He had passed his arm around her and drawn her close to his side, and the pleading tenderness of his low voice was indeed hard to resist.

"No, Mr. Murray, my decision is unalterable. If you do really love me, spare me, spare me, further entreaty. Before we part there are some things I should like to say, and I have little time left. Will you hear me ?"

He did not answer, but tightened his arm, drew her head to his bosom, and leaned his face down on hers.

ST. ELMO.

"Mr. Murray, I want to leave my Bible with you, because there are many passages marked which would greatly comfort and help you. It is the most precious thing I possess, for Grandpa gave it to me when I was a little girl, and I could not bear to leave it with any one but you. I have it here in my hand; will you look into it sometimes if I give it to you?"

He merely put out his hand and took it from her.

She paused a few seconds, and as he remained silent, she continued:

"Mr. Hammond is the best friend you have on earth. Yesterday, having seen you enter the church and suspecting what passed, he spoke to me of you, and oh! he pleaded for you as only he could! He urged me not to judge you too harshly; not to leave you, and these were his words: 'Edna, if I, whom he has robbed of all that made life beautiful; if I, standing here alone in my old age, in sight of the graves of my murdered darlings, if I can forgive him, and pray for him, and, as God is my witness, love him! you have no right to visit my injuries and my sorrows upon him!' Mr. Murray, he can help you, and he will, if you will only permit him. If you could realize how deeply he is interested in your happiness, you could not fail to reverence that religion which enables him to triumph over all the natural feelings of resentment. Mr. Murray, you have declared again and again that you love me. Oh! if it be true, meet me in heaven! I know that I am weak and sinful; but I am trying to correct the faults of my character, I am striving to do what I believe to be my duty, and I hope at last to find a home with my God. For several years, ever since you went abroad, I have been praying for you; and while I live I shall not cease to do so. Oh! will you not pray for yourself? Mr. Murray, I believe I shall not be happy even in heaven if I do not see you there. On earth we are parted—your crimes divide us; but there! there! Oh! for my sake, make an effort to redeem yourself, and meet me there!"

She felt his strong frame tremble, and a heavy

shuddering sigh broke from his lips and swept across
her cheek. But when he spoke his words contained
no hint of the promise she longed to receive:

"Edna, my shadow has fallen across your heart,
and I am not afraid that you will forget me. You
will try to do so, you will give me as little thought as
possible; you will struggle to crush your aching heart,
and endeavor to be famous. But amid your ova-
tions the memory of a lonely man, who loves you
infinitely better than all the world for which you
forsook him, will come like a breath from the sepulchre, to wither your bays; and my words, my pleading words, will haunt you, rising above the pæans
of your public worshippers. When the laurel crown
you covet now shall become a chaplet of thorns
piercing your temples, or a band of iron that makes
your brow ache, you will think mournfully of the days
gone by, when I prayed for the privilege of resting
your weary head here on my heart. You can not forget me. Sinful and all unworthy as I confess myself,
I am conqueror, I triumph now, even though you
never permit me to look upon your face again; for I
believe I have a place in my darling's heart which no
other man, which not the whole world can usurp or
fill! You are too proud to acknowledge it, too truthful to deny it; but, my pure Pearl, my heart feels it
as well as yours, and it is a comfort of which all time
can not rob me. Without it, how could I face my
future, so desolate, sombre, lonely? Edna, the hour
has come when, in accordance with your own decree,
we part. For twenty years no woman's lips, except
my mother's, have touched mine until yesterday,
when they pressed yours. Perhaps we may never
meet again in this world, and, ah! do not shrink away
from me, I want to kiss you once more, my darling!
my darling! I shall wear it on my lips till death stiff-
ens them; and I am not at all afraid that any other
man will ever be allowed to touch lips that belong to
me alone; that I have made, and here seal, all my
own! Good-bye."

He strained her to him and pressed his lips twice to
hers, then the carriage stopped at the railroad station.

He handed her out, found a seat for her in the cars,
which had just arrived, arranged her wrappings comfortably, and went back to attend to her trunks.   She
sat near an open window, and though it rained heavily,
he buttoned his coat to the throat, and stood just beneath it, with his eyes bent down.   Twice she pronounced his name, but he did not seem to hear her,
and Edna put her hand lightly on his shoulder and
said :

"Do not stand here in the rain.   In a few minutes
we shall start, and I prefer that you should not wait.
Please go home at once, Mr. Murray."

He shook his head, but caught her hand and leaned
his cheek against the soft palm, passing it gently and
caressingly over his haggard face.

The engine whistled ; Mr. Murray pressed a long,
warm kiss on the hand he had taken, the cars moved
on ; and as he lifted his hat, giving her one of his imperial, graceful bows, Edna had a last glimpse of the
dark, chiselled, repulsive yet handsome face that had
thrown its baleful image deep in her young heart, and
defied all her efforts to expel it.   The wind howled
around the cars, the rain fell heavily, beating a dismal
tattoo on the glass, the night was mournfully dreary,
and the orphan sank back and lowered her veil, and
hid her face in her hands.

Henceforth she felt that in obedience to her own
decision and fiat

> "They stood aloof, the scars remaining
> Like cliffs that had been rent asunder ;
> A dreary sea now flows between ;
> But neither heat nor frost nor thunder
> Shall wholly do away, I ween,
> The marks of that which once hath been."

CHAPTER XXIV.

As DAY dawned the drab clouds blanched, broke up
in marbled masses, the rain ceased, the wind sang out
of the west, heralding the coming blue and gold, and
at noon not one pearly vapor sail dotted the sky.
During the afternoon Edna looked anxiously for the
first glimpse of "Lookout," but a trifling accident
detained the train for several hours, and it was almost
twilight when she saw it, a purple spot staining the
clear beryl horizon; spreading rapidly, shifting its
Tyrian mantle for gray robes; and at length the rising moon silvered its rocky crest, as it towered in
silent majesty over the little village nestled at its
base. The kind and gentlemanly conductor on the
cars accompanied Edna to the hotel, and gave her
a parcel containing several late papers. As she sat
in her small room, weary and yet sleepless, she tried
to divert her thoughts by reading the journals, and
found in three of them notices of the last number
of —— Magazine, and especial mention of her essay :
"Keeping the Vigil of St. Martin under the Pines
of Grütli."

The extravagant laudations of this article surprised her, and she saw that while much curiosity
was indulged concerning the authorship, one of the
editors ventured to attribute it to a celebrated and
very able writer, whose genius and erudition had
lifted him to an enviable eminence in the world of
American letters. The criticisms were excessively
flattering, and the young author, gratified at the
complete success that had crowned her efforts, cut

out the friendly notices, intending to enclose them in a letter to Mrs. Murray.

Unable to sleep, giving audience to memories of her early childhood, she passed the night at her window, watching the constellations go down behind the dark, frowning mass of rock that lifted its parapets to the midnight sky, and in the morning light saw the cold, misty cowl drawn over the venerable hoary head.

The village had changed so materially that she could scarcely recognize any of the old landmarks, and the people who kept the hotel could tell her nothing about Peter Wood, the miller. After breakfast she took a box containing some flowers packed in wet cotton, and walked out on the road leading in the direction of the blacksmith's shop. Very soon the trees became familiar, she remembered every turn of the road and bend of the fences; and at last the grove of oak and chestnut shading the knoll at the intersection of the roads met her eye. She looked for the forge and bellows, for the anvil and slack-tub; but shop and shed had fallen to decay, and only a heap of rubbish, overgrown with rank weeds and vines, marked the spot where she had spent so many happy hours. The glowing yellow chestnut leaves dropped down at her feet, and the oaks tossed their gnarled arms as if welcoming the wanderer whose head they had shaded in infancy, and, stifling a moan, the orphan hurried on.

She saw that the timber had been cut down, and fences enclosed cultivated fields where forests had stood when she went away. At a sudden bend in the narrow, irregular road when she held her breath and leaned forward to see the old house where she was born and reared, a sharp cry of pain escaped her. Not a vestige of the homestead remained, save the rocky chimney, standing *in memoriam* in the centre of a cornfield. She leaned against the low fence, and tears trickled down her cheeks as memory rebuilt the log-house, and placed the split-bottomed rocking-chair on the porch in front, and filled it with the figure of a white-haired old man, with his pipe in his hand and his blurred eyes staring at the moon.

Through the brown corn-stalks she could see the gaping mouth of the well, now partly filled with rubbish ; and the wreaths of scarlet cypress which once fringed the shed above it and hung their flaming trumpets down till they almost touched her childish head, as she sang at the well where she scoured the cedar piggin, were bereft of all support and trailed helplessly over the ground. Close to the fence, and beyond the reach of plough and hoe, a yellow four-o'clock with closed flowers marked the location of the little garden ; and one tall larkspur leaned against the fence, sole survivor of the blue pets that Edna had loved so well in the early years. She put her fingers through a crevice, broke the plumy spray, and as she pressed it to her face, she dropped her head upon the rails and gave herself up to the flood of painful yet inexpressibly precious memories.

How carefully she had worked and weeded this little plat ; how proud she once was of her rosemary and pinks, her double feathery poppies, her sweet-scented lemon-grass ; how eagerly she had transplanted wood violets and purple phlox from the forest; how often she had sat on the steps watching for her grandfather's return, and stringing those four-o'clock blossoms into golden crowns for her own young head ; and how gayly she had sometimes swung them over Brindle's horns, when she went out to milk her.

> "Ah! sad and strange, as in dark summer dawns
> The earliest pipe of half-awakened birds
> To dying ears, when unto dying eyes
> The casement slowly grows a glimmering square ;
> So sad, so strange, the days that are no more."

With a sob she turned away and walked in the direction of the burying-ground; for there, certainly, she would find all unchanged ; graves at least were permanent.

The little spring bubbled as of yore, the brush

creepers made a tangled tapestry around it, and crimson and blue convolvulus swung their velvety, dew-
beaded chalices above it, as on that June morning
long ago when she stood there filling her bucket, waiting for the sunrise.

She took off her gloves, knelt down beside the spring,
and dipping up the cold, sparkling water in her palms,
drank and wept, and drank again. She bathed her
aching eyes, and almost cheated herself into the belief
that she heard again Grip's fierce bark ringing through
the woods, and the slow, drowsy tinkle of Brindle's
bell. Turning aside from the beaten track, she entered
the thick grove of chestnuts, and looked around for
the grave of the Dents ; but the mound had disappeared, and though she recognized the particular tree
which had formerly overhung it, and searched the
ground carefully, she could discover no trace of the
hillock where she had so often scattered flowers. A
squirrel leaped and frisked in the boughs above her,
and she startled a rabbit from the thick grass and fallen
yellow leaves; but neither these, nor the twitter of
gossiping orioles, nor the harsh, hungry cry of a blue-
bird told her a syllable of all that had happened in her
absence.

She conjectured that the bodies had probably been
disinterred by friends and removed to Georgia; and
she hurried on toward the hillside, where the neighborhood graveyard was situated. The rude, unpainted
paling still enclosed it, and rows of headboards
stretched away among grass and weeds; but whose
was that shining marble shaft, standing in the centre
of a neatly arranged square, around which ran a handsome iron railing ? On that very spot, in years gone
by, had stood a piece of pine board : " Sacred to the
memory of Aaron Hunt, an honest blacksmith and
true Christian."

Who had dared to disturb his bones, to violate his
last resting-place, and to steal his grave for the interment of some wealthy stranger? A cry of horror
and astonishment broke from the orphan's trembling

lips, and she shaded her eyes with her hand, and tried to read the name inscribed on the monument of the sacrilegious interloper. But bitter, scalding tears of indignation blinded her. She dashed them away, but they gathered and fell faster ; and, unbolting the gate, she entered the enclosure and stepped close to the marble.

ERECTED

IN HONOR OF

AARON HUNT:

BY HIS DEVOTED GRANDDAUGHTER.

These gilded words were traced on the polished surface of the pure white obelisk, and on each corner of the square pedestal or base stood beautifully carved vases, from which drooped glossy tendrils of ivy.

As Edna looked in amazement at the glittering shaft, which rose twenty feet in the autumn air ; as she rubbed her eyes and re-read the golden inscription, and looked at the sanded walks, and the well-trimmed evergreens, which told that careful hands kept the lot in order, she sank down at the base of the beautiful monument, and laid her hot cheek on the cold marble.

"Oh, Grandpa, Grandpa! He is not altogether wicked and callous as we once thought him, or he could never have done this ! Forgive your poor little Pearl. if she can not help loving one who, for her sake, honors your dear name and memory ! Oh, Grandpa ! if I had never gone away from here. If I could have died before I saw him again ! before this great pain fell upon my heart !"

She knew now where St. Elmo Murray went that night, after he had watched her from behind the sarcophagus and the mummies ; knew that only his hand could have erected this noble pillar of record ; and most fully did she appreciate the delicate feeling which made him so proudly reticent on this subject. He

wished no element of gratitude in the love he had endeavored to win, and scorned to take advantage of her
devoted affection for her grandfather, by touching her
heart with a knowledge of the tribute paid to his
memory.   Until this moment she had sternly refused to
permit herself to believe all his protestations of love;
had tried to think that he merely desired to make her
acknowledge his power, and confess an affection flattering to his vanity.   But to-day she felt that all he had
avowed was true; that his proud, bitter heart was indeed entirely hers; that this assurance filled her own
heart with a measureless joy, a rapture that made her
eyes sparkle through their tears and brought a momentary glow to her cheeks.   Hour after hour passed;
she took no note of time, and sat there pondering her
past life, thinking how the dusty heart deep under the
marble would have throbbed with fond pride, if it
could only have known what the world said of her
writings.   That she should prove competent to teach
the neighbor's children had been Aaron Hunt's loftiest ambition for his darling; and now she was deemed
worthy to speak to her race through the columns of a
periodical that few women were considered able to
fill.

She wondered if he were not really cognizant of it
all; if he were not watching her struggles and her
triumph; and she asked herself why he was not allowed, in token of tender sympathy, to drop one palm-
leaf on her head, from the fadeless branch he waved in
heaven?

> "Oh! how far,
> How far and safe, God, dost thou keep thy saints
> When once gone from us!   We may call against
> The lighted windows of thy fair June heaven
> Where all the souls are happy; and not one,
> Not even my father, look from work or play,
> To ask, 'Who is it that cries after us,
> Below there, in the dark?"

The shaft threw a long slanting shadow eastward as
the orphan rose, and, taking from the box the fragrant

exotics which she had brought from Le Bocage, arranged them in the damp soil of one of the vases, and twined their bright-hued petals among the dark green ivy leaves. One shining wreath she broke and laid away tenderly in the box, a hallowed souvenir of the sacred spot where it grew; and as she stood there, looking at a garland of poppy leaves chiselled around the inscription, neither flush nor tremor told aught that passed in her mind, and her sculptured features were calm, as the afternoon sun showed how pale and fixed her face had grown. She climbed upon the broad base and pressed her lips to her grandfather's name, and there was a mournful sweetness in her voice as she said aloud :

"Pray God to pardon him, Grandpa! Pray Christ to comfort and save his precious soul! Oh, Grandpa! pray the Holy Spirit to melt and sanctify his suffering heart!"

It was painfnl to quit the place. She lingered, and started away, and came back, and at last knelt down and hid her face, and prayed long and silently.

Then turning quickly, she closed the iron gate, and without trusting herself for another look, walked away. She passed the spring and the homestead ruins, and finally found herself in sight of the miller's house, which alone seemed unchanged. As she lifted the latch of the gate and entered the yard, it seemed but yesterday that she was driven away to the depot in the miller's covered cart.

An ancient apple-tree, that she well remembered, stood near the house, and the spreading branches were bent almost to the earth with the weight of red-streaked apples, round and ripe. The shaggy, black dog, that so often frolicked with Grip in the days gone by, now lay on the step, blinking at the sun and the flies that now and then buzzed over the golden balsam, whose crimson seed glowed in the evening sunshine.

Over the rocky well rose a rude arbor, where a

scuppernong vine clambered and hung its rich, luscious brown clusters ; and here, with a pipe between her
lips, and at her feet a basket full of red pepper-pods,
which she was busily engaged in stringing, sat an
elderly woman. She was clad in blue and yellow plaid
homespun, and wore a white apron and a snowy muslin
cap, whose crimped ruffles pressed caressingly the
grizzled hair combed so smoothly over her temples.
Presently she laid her pipe down on the top of the
mossy well, where the dripping bucket sat, and lifted
the scarlet wreath of peppers, eyed it satisfactorily,
and, as she resumed her work, began to hum " Auld
Lang Syne."

> " Should auld acquaintance be forgot,
>   And never brought to mind ?
>   Should auld acquaintance be forgot,
>   And days o' lang syne ?"

The countenance was so peaceful and earnest and
honest, that, as Edna stood watching it, a warm, loving
light came into her own beautiful eyes, and she put
out both hands unconsciously, and stepped into the
little arbor.

Her shadow fell upon the matronly face, and the
woman rose and courtesied.

" Good evening, miss. Will you be seated ? There
is room enough for two on my bench."

The orphan did not speak for a moment, but looked
up in the brown, wrinkled face, and then, pushing
back her bonnet and veil, she said eagerly :

" Mrs. Wood, don't you know me ?"

The miller's wife looked curiously at her visitor,
glanced at her dress, and shook her head.

" No, miss ; if ever I set my eyes on you before, it's
more than I remember, and Dorothy Wood has a
powerful memory, they say, and seldom forgets faces."

" Do you remember Aaron Hunt, and his daughter
Hester ?"

" To be sure I do ; but you a'n't neither the one nor

the other, I take it. Stop—let me see. Aha! Tabitha, Willis, you children, run here—quick! But, no—it can't be. You can't be Edna Earl?"

She shaded her eyes from the glare of the sun and stooped forward, and looked searchingly at the stranger; then the coral wreath fell from her fingers, she stretched out her arms, and the large mouth trembled and twitched.

"Are you—can you be—little Edna? Aaron Hunt's grandchild?"

"I am the poor little Edna you took such tender care of in her great affliction——"

"Samson and the Philistines! Little Edna—so you are! What was I thinking about, that I didn't know you right away? God bless your pretty white face!"

She caught the orphan in her strong arms and kissed her, and cried and laughed alternately.

A young girl, apparently about Edna's age, and a tall, lank young man, with yellow hair full of meal-dust, came out of the house, and looked on in stupid wonder.

"Why, children! don't you know little Edna that lived at Aaron Hunt's—his granddaughter? This is my Tabitha and my son Willis, that tends the mill and takes care of us, now my poor Peter—God rest his soul! —is dead and buried these three years. Bring some seats, Willis. Sit down here by me, Edna, and take off your bonnet, child, and let me see you. Umph! umph! Who'd have thought it? What a powerful hand-some woman you have made, to be sure! to be sure! Well! well! The very saints up in glory can't begin to tell what children will turn out! Lean your face this way. Why, you a'n't no more like that little bare-footed, tangle-haired, rosy-faced Edna that used to run around these woods in striped homespun, hunting the cows, than I, Dorothy Elmira Wood, am like the Queen of Sheba when she went up visiting to Jeru-salem to call on Solomon. How wonderful pretty you are! And how soft and white your hands are! Now

I look at you good I see you are like your mother, Hester Earl; and she was the loveliest, mild little pink in the county. You are taller than your mother, and prouder-looking; but you have got her big, soft, shining, black eyes; and your mouth is sweet and sorrowful, and patient as hers always was, after your father fell off that frosty roof and broke his neck. Little Edna come back a fine, handsome woman, looking like a queen! But, honey, you don't seem healthy, like my Tabitha. See what a bright red she has in her face. You are too pale; you look as if you had just been bled. A'n't you well, child?"

Mrs. Wood felt the girl's arms and shoulders, and found them thinner than her standard of health demanded.

"I am very well, thank you, but tired from my journey, and from walking all about the old place."

"And like enough you've cried a deal. Your eyes are heavy. You know, honey, the old house burnt down one blustry night in March, and so we sold the place; for when my old man died we were hard-pressed, we were, and a man by the name of Simmons, he bought it and planted it in corn. Edna, have you been to your Grandpa's grave?"

"Yes, ma'am, I was there a long time to-day."

"Oh! a'n't it beautiful! It would be a real comfort to die, if folks knew such lovely gravestones would cover 'em. I think your Grandpa's grave is the prettiest place I ever saw, and I wonder, sometimes, what Aaron Hunt would say if he could rise out of his coffin and see what is over him. Poor thing! You haven't got over it yet, I see. I thought we should have buried you, too, when he died; for never did I see a child grieve so."

"Mrs. Wood, who keeps the walks so clean, and the evergreens so nicely cut!"

"My Willis, to be sure. The gentleman that came here and fixed everything last December, paid Willis one hundred dollars to attend to it, and keep the weeds down. He said he might come back unex-

pectedly almost any time, and that he did not want
to see so much as a blade of grass in the walks;
so you see Willis goes there every Saturday and
straightens up things. What is his name, and who
is he anyhow? He only told us he was a friend of
yours, and that his mother had adopted you."

"What sort of a looking person was he, Mrs.
Wood?"

"Oh, child! if he is so good to you, I ought not to
say; but he was a powerful, grim-looking man, with
fierce eyes and a thick mustache, and hair almost
pepper-and-salt; and bless your soul, honey! his
shoulders were as broad as a barn-door. While he
talked I didn't like his countenance, it was dark like a
pirates, or one of those prowling cattle-thieves over in
the coves. He asked a power of questions about you
and your Grandpa, and when I said you had no kin on
earth, that ever I heard of, he laughed, that is, he
showed his teeth, and said, 'So much the better! so
much the better! What is his name?"

"Mr. Murray, and he has been very kind to me."

"But, Edna, I thought you went to the factory to
work? Do tell me how you fell into the hands of
such rich people?"

Edna briefly acquainted her with what had occurred during her long absence, and informed her of
her plans for the future; and while she listened Mrs.
Wood lighted her pipe, and resting her elbow on her
knee, dropped her face on her hands, and watched her
visitor's countenance.

Finally she nodded to her daughter, saying: "Do
you hear that, Bitha? She can write for the papers
and get paid for it! And she is smart enough to
teach! Well! well! that makes me say what I do
say, and I stick to it, where there's a will there's a
way! and where there's no hearty will, all the ways in
creation won't take folks to an education! Some
children can't be kicked and kept down; spite of all
the world they will manage to scuffle up somehow;
and then again, some can't be cuffed and coaxed and

dragged up by the ears! Here's Edna, that always
had a hankering after books, and she has made something of herself; and here's my girl, that I wanted to
get book-learning, and I slaved and I saved to send
her to school, and sure enough she has got no more
use for reading, and knows as little as her poor mother,
who never had a chance to learn. It is no earthly use
to fly in the face of blood and nature! 'What is
bred in the bone, won't come out in the flesh!'
Some are cut out for one thing and some for another!
Jerusalem artichokes won't bear hops, and persim-
mons don't grow on blackjacks!"

She put her brawny brown hand on Edna's forehead,
and smoothed the bands of hair, and sighed heavily.

"Mrs. Wood, I should like to see Brindle once
more."

"Lord bless your soul, honey! she has been dead
these three years! Why, you forget cows don't hang
on as long as Methuselah, and Brindle was no yearling
when we took her. She mired down in the swamp,
back of the millpond, and before we could find her
she was dead. But her calf is as pretty a young thing
as ever you saw; speckled all over, most as thick as
a guinea, and the children call her 'Speckle.' Willis,
step out and see if the heifer is in sight. Edna, a'n't
you going to stay with me to-night?"

"Thank you, Mrs. Wood, I should like very much
to do so, but have not time, and must get back to
Chattanooga before the train leaves, for I am obliged
to go on to-night."

"Well, any how, lay off your bonnet and stay and
let me give you some supper, and then we will all go
back with you, that is, if you a'n't too proud to ride to
town in our cart? We have got a new cart, but it is
only a miller's cart, and may be it won't suit your
fine fashionable clothes."

"I shall be very glad to stay, and I only wish it was
the same old cart that took me to the depot, more
than five years ago. Please give me some water."

Mrs. Wood rolled up her sleeves, put away her

pretty peppers, and talking vigorously all the time, prepared some refreshments for her guest.

A table was set under the apple-tree, a snowy cotton cloth spread over it, and yellow butter, tempting as Goshen's, and a loaf of fresh bread, and honey amber-hued, and buttermilk, and cider, and stewed pears, and a dish of ripe red apples crowned the board.

The air was laden with the fragrance it stole in crossing a hayfield beyond the road, the bees darted in and out of their hives, and a peacock spread his iridescent feathers to catch the level yellow rays of the setting sun, and from the distant millpond came the gabble of geese, as the noisy fleet breasted the ripples.

Speckle, who had been driven to the gate for Edna's inspection, stood close to the paling, thrusting her pearly horns through the cracks, and watching the party at the table with her large, liquid, beautiful, earnest eyes; and afar off Lookout rose solemn and sombre.

"Edna, you eat nothing. What ails you, child? They say too much brainwork is not healthy, and I reckon you study too hard. Better stay here with me, honey, and run around the woods and get some red in your face, and churn and spin and drink buttermilk, and get plump, and go chestnutting with my children. Goodness knows they are strong enough and hearty enough, and too much study will never make shads of them; for they won't work their brains, even to learn the multiplication table. See here, Edna, if you will stay a while with me, I will give Speckle to you."

"Thank you, dear Mrs. Wood, I wish I could; but the lady who engaged me to teach her children, wrote that I was very much needed; and, consequently, I must hurry on. Speckle is a perfect little beauty, but I would not be so selfish as to take her away from you."

Clouds began to gather in the southwest, and as the covered cart was brought to the gate, a distant mutter of thunder told that a storm was brewing.

Mrs. Wood and her two children accompanied the orphan, and as they drove through the woods, myriads of fireflies starred the gloom. It was dark when they reached the station, and Willis brought the trunks from the hotel, and found seats for the party in the cars, which were rapidly filling with passengers. Presently the down-train from Knoxville came thundering in, and the usual rush and bustle ensued.

Mrs. Wood gave the orphan a hearty kiss and warm embrace, and bidding her "Be sure to write soon, and say how you are getting along!" the kind-hearted woman left the cars, wiping her eyes with the corner of her apron.

At last the locomotive signaled that all was ready; and as the train moved on, Edna caught a glimpse of a form standing under a lamp, leaning with folded arms against the post—a form strangely like Mr. Murray's. She leaned out and watched it till the cars swept round a curve, and lamp and figure and village vanished. How could he possibly be in Chattanooga? The conjecture was absurd; she was the victim of some optical illusion. With a long, heavily-drawn sigh, she leaned against the window-frame and looked at the dark mountain mass looming behind her; and after a time, when the storm drew nearer, she saw it only now and then, as

"A vivid, vindictive, and serpentine flash
Gored the darkness, and shore it across with a gash."

CHAPTER XXV.

IN one of those brown-stone, palatial houses on Fifth Avenue, which make the name of the street a synonym for almost royal luxury and magnificence, sat Mrs. Andrews's " new governess," a week after her arrival in New York. Her reception, though cold and formal, had been punctiliously courteous; and a few days sufficed to give the stranger an accurate insight into the characters and customs of the family with whom she was now domesticated.

Though good-natured, intelligent, and charitable, Mrs. Andrews was devoted to society, and gave to the demands of fashion much of the time which had been better expended at home in training her children, and making her hearthstone rival the attractions of the club, where Mr. Andrews generally spent his leisure hours. She was much younger than her husband, was handsome, gay, and ambitious, and the polished *hauteur* of her bearing often reminded Edna of Mrs. Murray; while Mr. Andrews seemed immersed in business during the day, and was rarely at home except at his meals.

Felix, the eldest of the two children, was a peevish, spoiled, exacting boy of twelve years of age, endowed with a remarkably active intellect, but pitiably dwarfed in body and hopelessly lame in consequence of a deformed foot. His sister Hattie was only eight years old, a bright, pretty, affectionate girl, over whom Felix tyrannized unmercifully, and who from earliest recollection had been accustomed to yield both her rights and privileges to the fretful invalid.

The room occupied by the governess was small but beautifully furnished, and as it was situated in the fourth story, the windows commanded a view of the trees in a neighboring park, and the waving outline of Long Island.

On the day of her arrival Mrs. Andrews entered into a minute analysis of the characters of the children, indicated the course which she wished pursued toward them, and, impressing upon Edna the grave responsibility of her position, the mother gave her children to the stranger's guardianship and seemed to consider her maternal duties fully discharged.

Edna soon ascertained that her predecessors had found the path intolerably thorny, and abandoned it in consequence of Felix's uncontrollable fits of sullenness and passion. Tutors and governesses had quickly alternated, and as the cripple finally declared he would not tolerate the former, his mother resolved to humor his caprice in the choice of a teacher.

Fortunately the boy was exceedingly fond of his books, and as the physicians forbade the constant use of his eyes, the governess was called on to read aloud at least one half of the day. From eight o'clock in the morning till eight at night the whole care of these children devolved on Edna; who ate, talked, drove with them, accompanied them wherever their inclination led, and had not one quiet moment from breakfast until her pupils went to sleep. Sometimes Felix was restless and wakeful, and on such occasions he insisted that his governess should come and read him to sleep.

Notwithstanding the boy's imperious nature, he possessed some redeeming traits, and Edna soon became much attached to him; while his affection for his new keeper astonished and delighted his mother.

For a week after Edna's arrival, inclement weather prevented the customary daily drive which contributed largely to the happiness of the little cripple; but one afternoon as the three sat in the schoolroom, Felix

threw his Latin grammar against the wall and exclaimed:

"I want to see the swans in Central Park, and I
mean to go, even if it does rain! Hattie, ring for Patrick to bring the *coupé* round to the door. Miss Earl,
don't you want to go?"

"Yes, for there is no longer any danger of rain, the
sun is shining beautifully; and besides, I hope you
will be more amiable when you get into the open air."

She gave him his hat and crutches, took his gray
shawl on her arm, and they went down to the neat
carriage drawn by a handsome chestnut horse, and set
apart for the use of the children.

As they entered the park, Edna noticed that the
boy's eyes brightened, and that he looked eagerly at
every passing face.

"Now, Hattie, you must watch on your side, and I
will keep a good lookout on mine. I wonder if she
will come this evening?"

"For whom are you both looking?" asked the
teacher.

"Oh! for little Lila, Bro' Felix's sweetheart!"
laughed Hattie, glancing at him with a mischievous
twinkle in her bright eyes.

"No such thing! Never had a sweetheart in my
life! Don't be silly, Hattie! mind your window, or I
guess we shan't see her."

"Well, any how, I heard Uncle Gray tell Mamma
that he kissed his sweetheart's hand at the party, and
I saw Bro' Felix kiss Lila's last week."

"I didn't, Miss Earl!" cried the cripple, reddening
as he spoke.

"Oh! he did, Miss Earl! Stop pinching me, Bro'
Felix. My arm is all black and blue, now. There
she is! Look, here on my side! Here is 'Red Rid-
inghood!'"

Edna saw a little girl clad in scarlet, and led by a
grave, middle-aged nurse, who was walking leisurely
toward one of the lakes.

Felix put his head out of the window and called to the woman.

"Hannah, are you going to feed the swans?"

"Good evening. Yes, we are going there now."

"Well, we will meet you there."

"What is the child's name?" asked Edna.

"Lila Manning, and she is deaf and dumb. We talk to her on our fingers."

They left the carriage, and approached the groups of children gathered on the edge of the water, and at sight of Felix, the little girl in scarlet sprang to meet him, moving her slender fingers rapidly as she conversed with him. She was an exceedingly lovely but fragile child, apparently about Hattie's age; and as Edna watched the changing expression of her delicate features, she turned to the nurse and asked:

"Is she an orphan?"

"Yes, miss; but she will never find it out as long as her uncle lives. He makes a great pet of her."

"What is his name, and where does he live?"

"Mr. Douglass G. Manning. He boards at No. — Twenty-third street; but he spends most of his time at the office. No matter what time of night he comes home, he never goes to his own room till he has looked at Lila, and kissed her good-night. Master Felix, please don't untie her hat, the wind will blow her hair all out of curl."

For some time the children were much amused in watching the swans, and when they expressed themselves willing to resume their drive, an arrangement was made with Hannah to meet at the same place the ensuing day. They returned to the carriage, and Felix said:

"Don't you think Lila is a little beauty?"

"Yes, I quite agree with you. Do you know her uncle?"

"No, and don't want to know him; he is too cross and sour. I have seen him walking sometimes with Lila, and mamma has him at her parties and dinners; but Hattie and I never see the company unless we peep, and, above all things, I hate peeping! It is ungenteel and vulgar; only poor people peep. Mr. Manning is an old bachelor, and very crabbed, so my uncle Grey says. He is the editor of the —— Magazine, that mamma declares she can't live without. Look! look, Hattie! There goes mamma this minute! Stop, Patrick! Uncle Grey! Uncle Grey! hold up, won't you, and let me see the new horses!"

An elegant phaeton, drawn by a pair of superb black horses, drew up close to the *coupé*, and Mrs. Andrews and her only brother, Mr. Grey Chilton, leaned forward and spoke to the children; while Mr. Chilton, who was driving, teased Hattie by touching her head and shoulders with his whip.

"Uncle Grey, I think the bays are the handsomest."

"Which proves you utterly incapable of judging horseflesh; for these are the finest horses in the city. I presume this is Miss Earl, though nobody seems polite enough to introduce us."

He raised his hat slightly, bowed, and drove on.

"Is this the first time you have met my uncle?" asked Felix.

"Yes. Does he live in the city?"

"Why! he lives with us! Haven't you seen him about the house? You must have heard him romping around with Hattie; for they make noise enough to call in the police. I think my uncle Grey is the handsomest man I ever saw, except Edwin Booth, when he plays 'Hamlet.' What do you say?"

"As I had barely a glimpse of your uncle, I formed no opinion. Felix, button your coat and draw your shawl over your shoulders; it is getting cold."

When they reached home the children begged for some music, and placing her hat on a chair, Edna sat down before the piano, and played and sang; while Felix stood leaning on his crutches, gazing earnestly into the face of his teacher.

The song was Longfellow's "Rainy Day," and when she concluded it, the cripple laid his thin hand on hers and said:

" Sing the last verse again. I feel as if I should always be a good boy, if you would only sing that for me every day. ' Into each life some rain must fall?' Yes, lameness fell into mine."

While she complied with his request, Edna watched his sallow face, and saw tears gather in the large, sad eyes, and she felt that henceforth the boy's evil spirit could be exorcised.

" Miss Earl, we never had a governess at all like you. They were old, and cross, and ugly, and didn't love to play chess, and could not sing, and I hated them! But I do like you, and I will try to be good."

He rested his head against her arm, and she turned and kissed his pale, broad forehead.

" Halloo, Felix! flirting with you governess? This is a new phase of school life. You ought to feel quite honored, Miss Earl, though upon my word I am sorry for you. The excessive amiability of my nephew has driven not less than six of your predecessors in confusion from the field, leaving him victorious. I warn you he is an incipient Turenne, and the schoolroom is the Franche Comté of his campaigns."

Mr. Chilton came up to the piano, and curiously scanned Edna's face ; but taking her hat and veil, she rose and moved toward the door, saying :

" I am disposed to believe that he has been quite as much sinned against as sinning. Come, children, it is time for your tea."

From that hour her influence over the boy strengthened so rapidly that before she had been a month in the house he yielded implicit obedience to her wishes, and could not bear for her to leave him, even for a moment. When more than usually fretful, and inclined to tyrannize over Hattie, or speak disrespectfully to his mother, a warning glance or word from Edna, or the soft touch of her hand, would suffice to restrain the threatened outbreak.

Her days were passed in teaching, reading aloud. and talking to the children ; and when released from her duties she went invariably to her desk, devoting more than half the night to the completion of her MS.

As she took her meals with her pupils, she rarely saw the other members of the household, and though Mr. Chilton now and then sauntered into the school-room and frolicked with Hattie, his visits were coldly received by the teacher; who met his attempts at conversation with very discouraging monosyllabic replies.

His manner led her to suspect that the good-looking lounger was as vain and heartless as he was frivolous, and she felt no inclination to listen to his trifling, *sans souci* chatter; consequently, when he thrust himself into her presence, she either picked up a book or left him to be entertained by the children.

One evening in November she sat in her own room preparing to write, and pondering the probable fate of a sketch which she had finished and dispatched two days before to the office of the magazine.

The principal aim of the little tale was to portray the horrors and sin of duelling, and she had written it with great care; but well aware of the vast, powerful current of popular opinion that she was bravely striving to stem, and fully conscious that it would subject her to severe animadversion from those who defended the custom, she could not divest herself of apprehension lest the article should be rejected.

The door bell rang, and soon after a servant brought her a card: "Mr. D. G. Manning. To see Miss Earl."

Flattered and frightened by a visit from one whose opinions she valued so highly, Edna smoothed her hair, and with trembling fingers changed her collar and cuffs and went down-stairs, feeling as if all the blood in her body were beating a tattoo on the drum of her ears.

As she entered the library, into which he had been shown (Mrs. Andrews having guests in the parlors),

Edna had an opportunity of looking unobserved at
this critical ogre, of whom she stood in such profound
awe.

Douglass Manning was forty years old, tall, and well
built ; wore slender, steel-rimmed spectacles which
somewhat softened the light of his keen, cold, black
eyes ; and carried his slightly bald head with the
haughty air of one who habitually hurled his gauntlet
in the teeth of public opinion.

He stood looking up at a pair of bronze griffins that
crouched on the top of the rosewood book-case, and
the gaslight falling full on his face, showed his stern,
massive features, which, in their granitic cast, reminded
Edna of those of Egyptian Androsphinx—vast, serene,
changeless.

There were no furrows on cheek or brow, no beard
veiled the lines and angles about the mouth, but as
she marked the chilling repose of the countenance,
so indicative of conscious power and well-regulated
strength, why did memory travel swiftly back among
the "Stones of Venice," repeating the description of
the hawthorn on Bourges Cathedral ? "A perfect
Niobe of May." Had this man petrified in his youth
before the steady stylus of time left on his features
that subtle tracery which passing years engrave on human faces? The motto of his magazine, *Veritas sine
clementia*, ruled his life, and, putting aside the lenses
of passion and prejudice, he coolly, quietly, relentlessly judged men and women and their works ; neither
loving nor hating, pitying nor despising his race ; looking neither to right nor left ; laboring steadily as a
thoroughly well-balanced, a marvellously perfect intellectual automaton.

"Good evening, Mr. Manning. I am very glad to
meet you ; for I fear my letters have very inadequately
expressed my gratitude for your kindness."

Her voice trembled slightly, and she put out her
hand. He turned, bowed, offered her a chair, and, as
they seated themselves, he examined her face as he

would have searched the title-page of some new book for an insight into its contents.

"When did you reach New York, Miss Earl?"

"Six weeks ago."

"I was not aware that you were in the city, until I received your note two days since. How long do you intend to remain?"

"Probably the rest of my life, if I find it possible to support myself comfortably."

"Is Mrs. Andrews an old friend?"

"No, sir; she was a stranger to me when I entered her house as governess for her children."

"Miss Earl, you are much younger than I had supposed. Your writings led me to imagine that you were at least thirty, whereas I find you almost a child. Will your duties as governess conflict with your literary labors?"

"No, sir. I shall continue to write."

"You appear to have acted upon my suggestion, to abandon the idea of a book, and confine your attention to short sketches."

"No, sir. I adhere to my original purpose, and am at work upon the manuscript which you advised me to destroy."

He fitted his glasses more firmly on his nose, and she saw the gleam of his strong white teeth, as a half smile moved his lips.

"Miss Earl, my desk is very near a window, and as I was writing late last night, I noticed several large moths beating against the glass which fortunately barred their approach to the flame of the gas inside. Perhaps inexperience whispered that it was a cruel fate that shut them out; but which heals soonest, disappointed curiosity or singed wings?"

"Mr. Manning, why do you apprehend more danger from writing a book than from the preparation of magazine articles?"

"Simply because the peril is inherent in the nature of the book you contemplate. Unless I totally misunderstand your views, you indulge in the rather extraordinary belief that all works of fiction should be eminently didactic, and inculcate not only sound morality but scientific theories. Herein, permit me to say, you entirely misapprehend the spirit of the age. People read novels merely to be amused, not educated; and they will not tolerate technicalities and abstract speculation in lieu of exciting plots and melodramatic *dénouements*. Persons who desire to learn something of astronomy, geology, chemistry, philology, etc., never think of finding what they require in the pages of a novel, but apply at once to the text-books of the respective sciences, and would as soon hunt for a lover's sentimental dialogue in Newton's ' Principia,' or spicy small-talk in Kant's ' Critique,' as expect an epitome of modern science in a work of fiction."

" But, sir, how many habitual novel readers do you suppose will educate themselves thoroughly from the text-books to which you refer ?"

"A modicum, I grant you; yet it is equally true that those who merely read to be amused will not digest the scientific dishes you set before them. On the contrary, far from appreciating your charitable efforts to elevate and broaden their range of vision, they will either sneer at the author's pedantry, or skip over every passage that necessitates thought to comprehend it, and rush on to the next page to discover whether the heroine, Miss Imogene Arethusa Penelope Brown, wore blue or pink tarlatan to her first ball, or whether on the day of her elopement the indignant papa succeeded in preventing the consummation of her felicity with Mr. Belshazzar Algernon Nebuchadnezzar Smith. I neither magnify nor dwarf, I merely state a simple fact."

" But, Mr. Manning, do you not regard the writers of each age as the custodians of its tastes as well as its morals ?"

"Certainly not; they simply reflect and do not mould public taste. Shakespeare, Hogarth, Rabelais, portrayed men and things as they found them ; not as they might, could, would, or should have been. Was

Sir Peter Lely responsible for the style of dress worn by court beauties in the reign of Charles II.? He faithfully painted what passed before him. Miss Earl, the objection I urge against the novel you are preparing does not apply to magazine essays, where an author may concentrate all the erudition he can obtain and ventilate it unchallenged ; for review writers now serve the public in much the same capacity that cup-bearers did royalty in ancient days ; and they are expected to taste strong liquors as well as sweet cordials and sour light wines. Moreover, a certain haze of sanctity envelops the precincts of ' Maga,' whence the incognito ' we ' thunders with oracular power ; for, notwithstanding the rapid annihilation of all classic faith in modern times which permits the conversion of Virgil's Avernus into a model oyster-farm, the credulous public fondly cling to the myth that editorial sanctums alone possess the sacred tripod of Delphi. Curiosity is the best stimulant for public interest, and it has become exceedingly difficult to conceal the authorship of a book, while that of magazine articles can readily be disguised. I repeat, the world of novel-readers constitute a huge hippodrome, where, if you can succeed in amusing your spectators or make them gasp in amazement at your rhetorical legerdemain, they will applaud vociferously, and pet you, as they would a graceful *danseuse,* or a dexterous acrobat, or a daring equestrian ; but if you attempt to educate or lecture them, you will either declaim to empty benches or be hissed down. They expect you to help them kill time, not improve it."

" Sir, is it not nobler to struggle against than to float ignominiously with the tide of degenerate opinion ?"

" That depends altogether on the earnestness of your desire for martyrdom by drowning. I have seen stronger swimmers than you go down, after desperate efforts to keep their heads above water."

Edna folded her hands in her lap, and looked

steadily into the calm, cold eyes of the editor, then
shook her head, and answered :

"I shall not drown. At all events I will risk it. I
would rather sink in the effort than live without attempting it."

"When you require ointment for singed wings, I
shall have no [sympathy with which to anoint them ;
for, like most of your sex, I see you mistake blind obstinacy for rational, heroic firmness. The next number of the magazine will contain the contribution you
sent me two days since ; and, while I do not accept
all your views, I think it by far the best thing I have
yet seen from your pen. It will, of course, provoke
controversy, but for that result, I presume you are
prepared. Miss Earl, you are a stranger in New York,
and if I can serve you in any way, I shall be glad to
do so."

"Thank you, Mr. Manning. I need some books
which I am not able to purchase, and can not find in
this house ; if you can spare them temporarily from
your library, you will confer a great favor on me."

"Certainly. Have you a list of those which you
require ?"

"No, sir, but——"

"Here is a pencil and piece of paper ; write down
the titles, and I will have them sent to you in the
morning."

She turned to the table to prepare the list, and all
the while Mr. Manning's keen eyes scanned her countenance, dress, and figure. A half-smile once more
stirred his grave lips when she gave him the paper,
over which he glanced indifferently.

"Miss Earl, I fear you will regret your determination to make literature a profession ; for your letters
informed me that you are poor ; and doubtless you remember the witticism concerning the 'republic of letters which contained not a sovereign.' Your friend,
Mr. Murray, appreciated the obstacles you are destined to encounter, and I am afraid you will not find

life in New York as agreeable as it was under his roof."

"When did you hear from him?"

"I received a letter this morning."

"And you called to see me because he requested you to do so?"

"I had determined to come before his letter arrived."

He noticed the incredulous smile that flitted across her face, and, after a moment's pause, he continued:

"I do not wish to discourage you, on the contrary, I sincerely desire to aid you, but Mill has analyzed the subject very ably in his 'Political Economy,' and declares that ' on any rational calculation of chances in the existing competition, no writer can hope to gain a living by books; and to do so by magazines and reviews becomes daily more difficult.' "

"Yes, sir, that passage is not encouraging; but I comfort myself with another from the same book: ' In a national or universal point of view the labor of the savant or speculative thinker is as much a part of production, in the very narrowest sense, as that of the inventor of a practical art. The electro-magnetic telegraph was the wonderful and most unexpected consequence of the experiments of Oersted, and the mathematical investigations of Ampère; and the modern art of navigation is an unforeseen emanation from the purely speculative and apparently merely curious inquiry, by the mathematicians of Alexandria, into the properties of three curves formed by the intersection of a plane surface and a cone. No limit can be set to the importance, even in a purely productive and material point of view, of mere thought.' Sir, the economic law which regulates the wages of mechanics should operate correspondingly in the realm of letters."

"Your memory is remarkably accurate."

"Not always, sir; but when I put it on its honor, and trust some special treasure to its guardianship, it rarely proves treacherous."

"I think you can command better wages for your

work in New York than anywhere else on this continent. You have begun well ; permit me to say to you
be careful, do not write too rapidly, and do not despise adverse criticism. If agreeable to you, I will call
early next week and accompany you to the public
libraries, which contain much that may interest you. I
will send you a note as soon as I ascertain when I can
command the requisite leisure ; and should you need
my services, I hope you will not hesitate to claim them.
Good-evening, Miss Earl."

He bowed himself out of the library, and Edna
went back to her own room, thinking of the brief interview, and confessing her disappointment in the conversation of this most dreaded of critics.

"He is polished as an icicle, and quite as cold. He
may be very accurate and astute and profound, but
certainly he is not half so brilliant as——"

She did not complete the parallel, but compressed
her lips, took up her pen, and began to write.

On the following morning Mrs. Andrews came into
the schoolroom, and, after kissing her children, turned
blandly to the governess.

"Miss Earl, I believe Mr. Manning called upon you
last evening. Where did you know him ?"

"I never saw him until yesterday, but we have corresponded for some time."

"Indeed ! you are quite honored. He is considered
very fastidious."

"He is certainly hypercritical, yet I have found
him kind and gentlemanly, even courteous. Our correspondence is entirely attributable to the fact that I
write for his magazine."

Mrs. Andrews dropped her ivory crotchet-needle
and sat, for a moment, the picture of wild-eyed amazement.

"Is it possible ! I had no idea you were an author.
Why did you not tell me before? What have you
written ?"

Edna mentioned the titles of her published articles,
and the lady of the house exclaimed :

" Oh ! that ' Vigil of Grütli ' is one of the most beautiful things I ever read, and I have often teased Mr.
Manning to tell me who wrote it. That apostrophe
to the Thirty Confederates is so mournfully grand that
it brings tears to my eyes. Why, Miss Earl, you will
be famous some day ! If I had your genius, I should
never think of plodding through life as a governess."

" But, my dear madam, I must make my bread, and
am compelled to teach while I write.'

" I do not see what time you have for writing. I
notice you never leave the children till they are
asleep ; and you must sleep enough to keep yourself
alive. Are you writing anything at present ?"

" I finished an article several days ago which will be
published in the next number of the magazine. Of
course, I have no leisure during the day, but I work
till late at night."

" Miss Earl, if you have no objection to acquainting
me with your history, I should like very much to know
something of your early life and education."

While Edna gave a brief account of her childhood,
Felix nestled his hand into hers, and laid his head on
her knee, listening eagerly to every word.

When she concluded, Mrs. Andrews mused a moment, and then said :

" Henceforth, Miss Earl, you will occupy a different
position in my house ; and I shall take pleasure in introducing you to such of my friends as will appreciate
your talent. I hope you will not confine yourself exclusively to my children, but come down sometimes in
the evening and sit with me ; and, moreover, I prefer
that you should dine with us, instead of with these
nursery folks, who are not quite capable of appreciating you——"

" How do you know that, mamma ? I can tell you
one thing, I appreciated her before I found out that
she was likely to be ' famous'! Before I knew that
Mr. Manning condescended to notice her. We
' nursery folk ' judge for ourselves, we don't wait to
find out what other people think, and I shan't give up

Miss Earl! She is my governess, and I wish you would just let her alone!"

There was a touch of scorn in the boy's impatient tone, and his mother bit her lip, and laughed constrainedly.

"Really, Felix! who gave you a bill of sale to Miss Earl? She should consider herself exceedingly fortunate, as she is the first of all your teachers with whom you have not quarrelled most shamefully, even fought and scratched."

"And because she is sweet, and good and pretty, and I love her, you must interfere and take her off to entertain your company. She came here to take care of Hattie and me, and not to go down-stairs to see visitors. She can't go, mamma! I want her myself. You have all the world to talk to, and I have only her. Don't meddle, mamma."

"You are very selfish and ill-tempered, my poor little boy, and I am heartily ashamed of you.'

"If I am, it is because——"

"Hush, Felix!"

Edna laid her hand on the pale, curling lips of the cripple, and luckily at this instant Mrs. Andrews was summoned from the room.

Scarcely waiting till the door closed after her, the boy exclaimed passionately :

"Felix! don't call me Felix! That means happy, lucky! and she had no right to give me such a name. I am Infelix! nobody loves me! nobody cares for me, except to pity me, and I would rather be strangled than pitied! I wish I was dead and at rest in Greenwood! I wish somebody would knock my brains out with my crutch! and save me from hobbling through life. Even my mother is ashamed of my deformity! She ought to have treated me as the Spartans did their dwarfs! She ought to have thrown me into the East River before I was a day old! I wish I was dead! Oh! I do! I do!"

"Felix, it is very wicked to——"

"I tell you I won't be called Felix. Whenever I

hear the name it makes me feel as I did one day when my crutches slipped on the ice, and I fell on the pavement before the door, and some newsboys stood and laughed at me. Infelix Andrews! I want that written on my tombstone when I am buried."

He trembled from head to foot, and angry tears dimmed his large, flashing eyes, while Hattie sat with her elbows resting on her knees, and her chin in her hands, looking sorrowfully at her brother.

Edna put her arm around the boy's shoulder, and drew his head down on her lap, saying tenderly:

"Your mother did not mean that she was ashamed of her son, but only grieved and mortified by his ungovernable temper, which made him disrespectful to her. I know that she is very proud of your fine intellect, and your ambition to become a thorough scholar, and——"

"Oh! yes, and of my handsome body! and my pretty feet!"

"My dear little boy, it is sinful for you to speak in that way, and God will punish you if you do not struggle against such feelings."

"I don't see how I can be punished any more than I have been already. To be a lame dwarf is the worst that can happen."

"Suppose you were poor and friendless—an orphan with no one to care for you? Suppose you had no dear, good, little sister like Hattie to love you? Now, Felix, I know that the very fact that you are not as strong and well-grown as most boys of your age, only makes your mother and all of us love you more tenderly; and it is very ungrateful in you to talk so bitterly when we are trying to make you happy and good and useful. Look at little Lila, shut up in silence, unable to speak one word, or to hear a bird sing or a baby laugh, and yet see how merry and good-natured she is. How much more afflicted she is than you are! Suppose she was always fretting and complaining, looking miserable and sour, and out of

humor, do you think you would love her half as well
as you do now ?"

He made no reply, but his thin hands covered his
sallow face.

Hattie came close to him, sat down on the carpet,
and put her head, thickly crowned with yellow curls,
on his knee. Her uncle Grey had given her a pretty
ring the day before, and now she silently and softly
took it from her own finger, and slipped it on her
brother's.

"Felix, you and Hattie were so delighted with that
little poem which I read to you from the Journal of
Eugénie de Guérin, that I have tried to set it to music
for you. The tune does not suit it exactly, but we
can use it until I find a better one."

She went to the piano and sang that pretty nursery
ballad, "JOUJOU, THE ANGEL OF THE PLAYTHINGS."

Hattie clapped her hands with delight, and Felix
partly forgot his woes and grievances.

"Now, I want you both to learn to sing it, and I
will teach Hattie the accompaniment. On Felix's
birthday, which is not very distant, you can surprise
your father and mother by singing it for them. In
gratitude to the author I think every little child should
sing it and call it 'Eugénie's Angel Song.' Hattie, it
is eleven o'clock, and time for you to practise your
music-lesson."

The little girl climbed upon the piano-stool and began to count aloud, and after a while Edna bent
down and put her hand on Felix's shoulder.

"You grieved your mother this morning and spoke
very disrespectfully to her. I know you regret it, and
you ought to tell her so and ask her to forgive you.
You would feel happier all day if you would only acknowledge your fault. I hear your mother in her own
room ; will you not go and kiss her ?"

He averted his head and muttered :

" I don't want to kiss her."

"But you ought to be a dutiful son, and you are
not : and your mother has cause to be displeased with

you. If you should ever be so unfortunate as to lose her, and stand as I do, motherless, in the world, you will regret the pain you gave her this morning. Oh! if I had the privilege of kissing my mother, I could bear almost any sorrow patiently. If it mortifies you to acknowledge your bad behavior, it is the more necessary that you should humble your pride. Felix, sometimes I think it requires more nobility of soul to ask pardon for our faults than to resist the temptation to commit them."

She turned away and busied herself in correcting his Latin exercise, and for some time the boy sat sullen and silent.

At length he sighed heavily, and, taking his crutches, came up to the table where she sat.

"Suppose you tell my mother I am sorry I was disrespectful."

"Felix, are you really sorry?"

"Yes."

"Well, then, go and tell her so, and she will love you a thousand times more than ever before. The confession should come from your own lips."

He stood irresolute and sighed again :

"I will go if you will go with me."

She rose and they went to Mrs. Andrews's room. The mother was superbly dressed in visiting costume, and was tying on her bonnet when they entered.

"Mrs. Andrews, your son wishes to say something which I think you will be glad to hear."

"Indeed! Well, Felix, what is it?"

"Mamma—I believe—I know I was very cross—and disrespectful to you—and oh, mamma! I hope you will forgive me!"

He dropped his crutches and stretched out his arms, and Mrs. Andrews threw down the diamond cluster, with which she was fastening her ribbons, and caught the boy to her bosom.

"My precious child! my darling! Of course I forgive you gladly. My dear son, if you only knew half

how well I love you, you would not grieve me so often
by your passionate temper. My darling!——"
    She stooped to kiss him, and when she turned to
look for the girlish form of the governess, it was no
longer visible ; mother and son were alone.

CHAPTER XXVI.

DURING the first few months after her removal to New York, Edna received frequent letters from Mrs. Murray and Mr. Hammond ; but as winter advanced they wrote more rarely and hurriedly, and finally, many weeks elapsed without bringing any tidings from Le Bocage. St. Elmo's name was never mentioned, and while the girl's heart ached, she crushed it more ruthlessly day by day, and in retaliation imposed additional and unremitting toil upon her brain.

Mr. Manning had called twice to escort her to the libraries and art galleries, and occasionally he sent her new books, and English and French periodicals ; but his chill, imperturbable calmness oppressed and embarrassed Edna, and formed a barrier to all friendly warmth in their intercourse. He so completely overawed her that in his august presence she was unable to do herself justice, and felt that she was not gaining ground in his good opinion. The brooding serenity of his grave, Egyptic face was not contagious ; and she was conscious of a vague disquiet, a painful restlessness, when in his company and under his cold, changeless eyes.

One morning in January, as she sat listening to Felix's recitations, Mrs. Andrews came into the schoolroom with an open note in one hand, and an exquisite bouquet in the other.

" Miss Earl, here is an invitation for you to accompany Mr. Manning to the opera, to-night ; and here, too, is a bouquet from the same considerate gentleman. As he does me the honor to request my company also,

I came to confer with you before sending a reply. Of course, you will go ?"

"Yes, Mrs. Andrews, if you will go with me."

Edna bent over her flowers, and recognizing many favorites that recalled the hothouse at Le Bocage, her eyes filled with tears, and she hastily put her lips to the snowy cups of an oxalis. How often she had seen just such fragile petals nestling in the buttonhole of Mr. Murray's coat.

"I shall write and invite him to come early and take tea with us. Now, Miss Earl, pardon my candor, I should like to know what you intend to wear? You know that Mr. Manning is quite lionized here, and you will have to face a terrific battery of eyes and lorgnettes; for everybody will stretch his or her neck to find out, first, who you are, and secondly, how you are dressed. Now I think I understand rather better than you do what is *comme il faut* in these matters, and I hope you will allow me to dictate on this occasion. Moreover, our distinguished escort is extremely fastidious concerning ladies' *toilettes.*"

"Here are my keys, Mrs. Andrews ; examine my wardrobe and select what you consider appropriate for to-night."

"On condition that you permit me to supply any deficiencies which I may discover ? Come to my room at six o'clock, and let Victorine dress your hair. Let me see, I expect *à la Grec* will best suit your head and face,"

Edna turned to her pupils and their books, but all day the flowers in the vase on the table prattled of days gone by ; of purple sunsets streaming through golden starred acacia boughs ; of long, languid, luxurious Southern afternoons dying slowly on beds of heliotrope and jasmine, spicy geraniums and gorgeous pelargoniums ; of dewy, delicious summer mornings, for ever and ever past, when standing beside a quivering snowbank of Lamarque roses, she had watched Tamerlane and his gloomy rider go down the shadowy avenue of elms.

The monotonous hum of the children's voices seemed thin and strange and far, far off, jarring the sweet bouquet babble ; and still as the hours passed, and the winter day waned, the flower Fugue swelled on and on, through the cold and dreary chambers of her heart; now rising stormy and passionate, like a battle-blast, from the deep orange trumpet of a bignonia ; and now whispering and sobbing and pleading, from the pearly white lips of hallowed oxalis.

When she sat that night in Mr. Manning's box at the Academy of Music, the editor raised his opera-glass, swept the crowded house, scanning the lovely, beaming faces wreathed with smiles, and then his grave, piercing glance came back and dwelt on the countenance at his side. The cherry silk lining and puffings on her opera-cloak threw a delicate stain of color over her exquisitely moulded cheeks, and in the braid of black hair which rested like a coronal on her polished brow, burned a scarlet anemone. Her long lashes drooped as she looked down at the bouquet between her fingers, and listening to the Fugue which memory played on the petals, she sighed involuntarily.

" Miss Earl, is this your first night at the opera ?"

" No, sir ; I was here once before with Mr. Andrews and his children."

" I judge from your writings that you are particularly fond of music."

" Yes, sir ; I think few persons love it better than I do."

" What style do you prefer ?"

" Sacred music—oratorios rather than operas."

The orchestra began an overture of Verdi's, and Edna's eyes went back to her flowers.

Presently Mrs. Andrews said eagerly :

"Look, Miss Earl! Yonder, in the box directly opposite, is the celebrated Sir Roger Percival, the English nobleman about whom all Gotham is running mad. If he has not more sense than most men of his age, his head will be completely turned by the flattery heaped upon him. What a commentary on Republican

Americans, that we are so dazzled by the glitter of a title! However, he really is very agreeable; I have met him several times, dined with him last week at the Coltons. He has been watching us for some minutes. Ah! there is a bow for me; and one I presume for you, Mr. Manning."

"Yes, I knew him abroad. We spent a month together at Dresden, and his brain is strong enough to bear all the adulation New Yorkers offer his title."

Edna looked into the opposite box, and saw a tall, elegantly-dressed man, with huge whiskers and a glittering opera-glass; and then as the curtain rose on the first act of "Ernani," she turned to the stage, and gave her entire attention to the music.

At the close of the second act Mrs. Andrews said:

"Pray who is that handsome man down yonder in the *parquet*, fanning himself with a libretto! I do not think his eyes have moved from this box for the last ten minutes. He is a stranger to me,"

She turned her fan in the direction of the person indicated, and Mr. Manning looked down and answered:

"He is unknown to me."

Edna's eyes involuntarily wandered over the sea of heads, and the editor saw her start and lean forward, and noticed the sudden joy that flashed into her face, as she met the earnest, upward gaze of Gordon Leigh.

"An acquaintance of yours, Miss Earl?"

"Yes, sir; an old friend from the South."

The door of the box opened, and Sir Roger Percival came in and seated himself near Mrs. Andrews, who in her cordial welcome seemed utterly to forget the presence of the governess.

Mr. Manning sat close to Edna, and taking a couple of letters from his pocket he laid them on her lap, saying:

"These letters were directed to my care by persons who are ignorant of your name and address. If you will not consider me unpardonably curious, I should like to know the nature of their contents."

She broke the seals and read the most flattering commendations of her magazine sketches, the most cordial thanks for the pleasure derived from their perusal ; but the signatures were unknown to her.

A sudden wave of crimson surged into her face as she silently put the letters into Mr. Manning's hand, and watched his grave, fixed, undemonstrative features, while he read, refolded, and returned them to her.

" Miss Earl, I have received several documents of a similar character asking for your address. Do you still desire to write incognito, or do you wish your name given to your admirers ?"

"That is a matter which I am willing to leave to your superior judgment."

" Pardon me, but I much prefer that you determine it for yourself."

" Then you may give my name to those who are sufficiently interested in me to write and make the inquiry."

Mr. Manning smiled slightly, and lowered his voice as he said :

" Sir Roger Percival came here to-night to be introduced to you. He has expressed much curiosity to see the author of the last article which you contributed to the magazine ; and I told him that you would be in my box this evening. Shall I present him now ?"

Mr. Manning was rising, but Edna put her hand on his arm, and answered hurriedly:

" No, no ! He in engaged in conversation with Mrs. Andrews, and, moreover, I believe I do not particularly desire to be presented to him."

" Here comes your friend ; I will vacate this seat in his favor."

He rose, bowed to Gordon Leigh, and gave him the chair which he had occupied.

" Edna ! how I have longed to see you once more !"

Gordon's hand seized hers, and his handsome face

was eloquent with feelings which he felt no inclination
to conceal.

"The sight of your countenance is an unexpected
pleasure in New York. Mr. Leigh, when did you
arrive ?"

"This afternoon. Mr. Hammond gave me your
address, and I called to see you, but was told that
you were here."

"How are they all at home ?"

"Do you mean at Le Bocage or the Parsonage ?"

"I mean how are all my friends ?"

"Mrs. Murray is very well, Miss Estelle, ditto. Mr.
Hammond has been sick, but was better and able to
preach before I left. I brought a letter for you from
him, but unfortunately left it in the pocket of my
travelling coat. Edna, you have changed very much
since I saw you last."

"In what respect, Mr. Leigh ?"

The crash of the orchestra filled the house, and people turned once more to the stage. Standing with his
arms folded, Mr. Manning saw the earnest look on
Gordon's face as, with his arm resting on the back of
Edna's chair, he talked in a low, eager tone ; and a
pitying smile partly curved the editor's granite mouth
as he noticed the expression of pain on the girl's face,
and heard her say coldly :

"No, Mr. Leigh ; what I told you then I repeat
now. Time has made no change."

The opera ended, the curtain fell, and an enthusiastic
audience called out the popular prima donna.

While bouquets were showered upon her, Mr. Manning stooped and put his hand on Edna's :

"Shall I throw your tribute for you ?"

She hastily caught the bouquet from his fingers, and
replied :

"Oh ! no, thank you ! I am so selfish, I can not
spare it."

"I shall call at ten o'clock to-morrow to deliver your
letter," said Gordon, as he stood hat in hand.

"I shall be glad to see you, Mr. Leigh."

He shook hands with her and with Mr. Manning, to whom she had introduced him, and left the box.

Sir Roger Percival gave his arm to Mrs. Andrews, and the editor drew Edna's cloak over her shoulders, took her hand and led her down the steps.

As her little gloved fingers rested in his, the feeling of awe and restraint melted away, and looking into his face she said :

"Mr. Manning, I do not think you will ever know half how much I thank you for all your kindness to an unknown authorling. I have enjoyed the music very much indeed. How is Lila to-night ?"

A slight tremor crossed his lips ; the petrified haw-thorn was quivering into life.

"She is quite well, thank you. Pray, what do you know about her ? I was not aware that I had ever mentioned her name in your presence."

"My pupil, Felix, is her most devoted knight, and I see her almost every afternoon when I go with the children to Central Park."

They reached the carriage where the Englishman stood talking to Mrs. Andrews, and when Mr. Manning had handed Edna in, he turned and said something to Sir Roger, who laughed lightly and walked away.

During the drive Mrs. Andrews talked volubly of the foreigner's ease and elegance and fastidious musical taste, and Mr. Manning listened courteously and bowed coldly in reply. When they reached home she invited him to dinner on the following Thursday, to meet Sir Roger Percival.

As the editor bade them good-night, he said to Edna :

"Go to sleep at once ; do not sit up to work to-night."

Did she follow his sage advice ? Ask of the stars that watched her through the long winter night, and the dappled dawn that saw her stooping wearily over her desk.

At the appointed hour on the following morning Mr. Leigh called, and after some desultory remarks he asked, rather abruptly :

"Has St. Elmo Murray written to you about his last whim?"

"I do not correspond with Mr. Murray."

"Everybody wonders what droll freak will next seize him. Reed, the blacksmith, died several months ago and, to the astonishment of our people, Mr. Murray has taken his orphan, Huldah, to Le Bocage ; has adopted her I believe; at all events, is educating her."

Edna's face grew radiant.

"Oh! I am glad to hear it! Poor little Huldah needed a friend, and she could not possibly have fallen into kinder hands than Mr. Murray's."

"There certainly exists some diversity of opinion on that subject. He is rather too grim a guardian, I fancy, for one so young as Huldah Reed."

"Is Mr. Hammond teaching Huldah?"

"Oh! no. Herein consists the wonder. Murray himself hears her lessons, so Estelle told my sister. *A propos!* rumor announces the approaching marriage of the cousins. My sister informed me that it would take place early in the spring."

"Do you allude to Mr. Murray and Miss Harding?"

"I do. They will go to Europe immediately after their marriage."

Gordon looked searchingly at his companion, but saw only a faint, incredulous smile cross her calm face.

"My sister is Estelle's confidante, so you see I speak advisedly. I know that her *trousseau* has been ordered from Paris."

Edna's fingers closed spasmodically over each other, but she laughed as she answered :

"How then dare you betray her confidence? Mr. Leigh, how long will you remain in New York?"

"I shall leave to-morrow, unless I have reason to hope that a longer visit will give you pleasure. I came here solely to see you."

He attempted to unclasp her fingers, but she shook off his hand and said quickly:

"I know what you are about to say, and I would rather not hear what would only distress us both. If you wish me to respect you, Mr. Leigh, you must never again allude to a subject which I showed you last night was exceedingly painful to me. While I value you as a friend, and am rejoiced to see you again, I should regret to learn that you had prolonged your stay even one hour on my account."

"You are ungrateful, Edna! And I begin to realize that you are utterly heartless."

"If I am, at least I have never trifled with or deceived you, Mr. Leigh."

"You have no heart, or you certainly could not so coldly reject an affection which any other woman would proudly accept. A few years hence, when your insane ambition is fully satiated, and your beauty fades, and your writings pall upon public taste, and your smooth-tongued flatterers forsake your shrine to bow before that of some new and more popular idol, then Edna, you will rue your folly."

She rose and answered quietly:

"The future may contain only disappointments for me, but however lonely, however sad my lot may prove, I think I shall never fall so low as to regret not having married a man whom I find it impossible to love. The sooner this interview ends the longer our friendship will last. My time is not now my own, and as my duties claim me in the schoolroom, I must bid you good-bye."

"Edna, if you send me away from you now, you shall never look upon my face again in this world!"

Mournfully her tearful eyes sought his, but her voice was low and steady as she put out both hands, and said solemnly:

"Farewell, dear friend. God grant that when next we see each other's faces they may be overshadowed by the shining, white plumes of our angel wings, in that city of God, 'where the wicked cease from troubling and the weary are at rest.' 'Never again in this world,' ah! such words are dreary and funereal as the

dull fall of clods on a coffin-lid ; but so be it. Thank
God! time brings us all to one inevitable tryst before
the great white throne."

He took the hands, bowed his forehead upon them
and groaned; then drew them to his lips and left
her.

With a slow, weary step she turned and went up to
her room and read Mr. Hammond's letter. It was
long and kind, full of affection and wise counsel, but
contained no allusion to Mr. Murray.

As she refolded it she saw a slip of paper which had
fallen unnoticed on the carpet, and picking it up she
read these words :

" It grieves me to have to tell you that, after all, I
fear St. Elmo will marry Estelle Harding. He does
not love her, she can not influence him to redeem himself ; his future looks hopeless indeed. Edna, my
child! what have you done! Oh! what have you
done !"

Her heart gave a sudden, wild bound, then a spasm
seemed to seize it, and presently the fluttering ceased,
her pulses stopped, and a chill darkness fell upon
her.

Her head sank heavily on her chest, and when she
recovered her memory she felt an intolerable sensation
of suffocation, and a sharp pain that seemed to stab
the heart, whose throbs were slow and feeble.

She raised the window and leaned out panting for
breath, and the freezing wind powdered her face with
fine snowflakes, and sprinkled its fairy flower-crystals
over her hair.

The outer world was chill and dreary, the leafless
limbs of the trees in the park looked ghostly and weird
against the dense dun clouds which seemed to stretch
like a smoke mantle just above the sea of roofs ; and,
dimly seen through the white mist, Brooklyn's heights
and Staten's hills were huge outlines monstrous as
Echidna.

Physical pain blanched Edna's lips, and she pressed
her hand repeatedly to her heart, wondering what

caused those keen pangs. At last, when the bodily suffering passed away, and she sat down exhausted, her mind reverted to the sentence in Mr. Hammond's letter.

She knew the words were not lightly written, and that his reproachful appeal had broken from the depths of his aching heart, and was intended to rouse her to some action.

"I can do nothing, say nothing! Must sit still and wait patiently—prayerfully. To-day, if I could put out my hand and touch Mr. Murray, and bind him to me for ever, I would not. No, no! Not a finger must I lift, even between him and Estelle! But he will not marry her! I know—I feel that he will not. Though I never look upon his face again, he belongs to me! He is mine, and no other woman can take him from me."

A strange, mysterious, shadowy smile settled on her pallid features, and faintly and dreamily she repeated:

> "And yet I know past all doubting, truly—
> A knowledge greater than grief can dim—
> I know as he loved, he will love me duly,
> Yea, better, e'en better than I love him.
> And as I walk by the vast, calm river,
> The awful river so dread to see,
> I say, 'Thy breadth and thy depth for ever
> Are bridged by his thoughts that cross to me.'"

Her lashes drooped, her head fell back against the top of the chair, and she lost all her woes until Felix's voice roused her, and she saw the frightened boy standing at her side, shaking her hand and calling piteously upon her.

"Oh! I thought you were dead! You looked so white and felt so cold. Are you very sick? Shall I go for mamma?"

For a moment she looked in his face with a perplexed, bewildered expression, then made an effort to rise.

"I suppose that I must have fainted, for I had a

terrible pain here, and——" She laid her hand over her heart.

"Felix, let us go down-stairs. I think if your mother would give me some wine, it might strengthen me."

Notwithstanding the snow, Mrs. Andrews had gone out ; but Felix had the wine brought to the school-room, and after a little while the blood showed itself shyly in the governess's white lips, and she took the boy's Latin book and heard him recite his lesson.

The day appeared wearily long, but she omitted none of the appointed tasks, and it was nearly nine o'clock before Felix fell asleep that night. Softly unclasping his thin fingers which clung to her hand, she went up to her own room, feeling the full force of those mournful words in Eugénie de Guérin's Journal :

"It goes on in the soul. No one is aware of what I feel ; no one suffers from it. I only pour out my heart before God—and here. Oh ! to-day what efforts I make to shake off this profitless sadness—this sadness without tears—arid, bruising the heart like a hammer!"

There was no recurrence of the physical agony ; and after two days the feeling of prostration passed away, and only the memory of the attack remained.

The idea of lionizing her children's governess, and introducing her to *soi-disant* "fashionable society," had taken possession of Mrs. Andrews's mind, and she was quite as much delighted with her patronizing scheme as a child would have been with a new hobby-horse. Dreams at which even Macenas might have laughed floated through her busy brain, and filled her kind heart with generous anticipations. On Thursday she informed Edna that she desired her presence at dinner, and urged her request with such pertinacious earnestness that no alternative remained but acqui-escence, and reluctantly the governess prepared to meet a formidable party of strangers.

When Mrs. Andrews presented Sir Roger Percival,

he bowed rather haughtily, and with a distant politeness, which assured Edna that he was cognizant of
her refusal to make his acquaintance at the opera.

During the early part of dinner he divided his gay
words between his hostess and a pretty Miss Morton,
who was evidently laying seige to his heart and
carefully flattering his vanity; but whenever Edna,
his *vis-à-vis*, looked toward him, she invariably found
his fine brown eyes scrutinizing her face.

Mr. Manning, who sat next to Edna, engaged her
in an animated discussion concerning the value of a
small volume containing two essays by Buckle, which
he had sent her a few days previous.

Something which she said to the editor with reference to Buckle's extravagant estimate of Mill, brought
a smile to the Englishman's lip, and bowing slightly,
he said:

" Pardon me, Miss Earl, if I interrupt you a moment
to express my surprise at hearing Mill denounced by
an American. His books on Representative Government and Liberty are so essentially democratic that
I expected only gratitude and eulogy from his readers
on this side of the Atlantic."

Despite her efforts to control it, embarrassment
unstrung her nerves, and threw a quiver into her
voice, as she answered :

" I do not presume, sir, to ' denounce ' a man
whom Buckle ranks above all other living writers and
statesmen, but, in anticipating the inevitable result
of the adoption of some of Mill's proposed social
reforms, I could not avoid recalling that wise *dictum*
of Frederick the Great concerning philosophers—a
saying which Buckle quotes so triumphantly against
Plato, Aristotle, Descartes—even Bacon, Newton,
and a long list of names illustrious in the annals of
English literature. Frederick declared : ' If I wanted
to ruin one of my provinces I would make over its
government to the philosophers.' With due deference
to Buckle's superior learning and astuteness, I confess my study of Mill's philosophy assures me that.

if society should be turned over to the government of his theory of Liberty and Suffrage, it would go to ruin more rapidly than Frederick's province. Under his teachings the women of England might soon marshal their amazonian legions, and storm not only Parnassus but the ballot-box, the bench, and the forum. That this should occur in a country where a woman nominally rules, and certainly reigns, is not so surprising, but I dread the contagion of such an example upon America."

"His influence is powerful, from the fact that he never takes up his pen without using it to break some social shackles ; and its strokes are tremendous as those of the hammer of Thor. But surely, Miss Earl, you Americans can not with either good taste, grace, or consistency, upbraid England on the score of woman's rights' movements ?"

"At least, sir, our statesmen are not yet attacked by this most loathsome of political leprosies. Only a few crazy fanatics have fallen victims to it, and if lunatic asylums were not frequently cheated of their dues, these would not be left at large, but shut up together in high-walled enclosures, where, like Sydney Smith's 'graminivorous metaphysicians,' or Reaumur's spiders, they could only injure one another and destroy their own webs. America has no Bentham, Bailey, Hare or Mill, to lend countenance or strength to the ridiculous clamor raised by a few unamiable and wretched wives, and as many embittered, disappointed, old maids of New England. The noble apology which Edmund Burke once offered for his countrymen, always recurs to my mind when I hear these ' women's conventions ' alluded to : ' Because half-a-dozen grasshoppers under a fern make the field ring with their importunate chink, while thousands of great cattle repose beneath the shade of the British oak, chew the cud, and are silent, pray do not imagine that those who make the noise are the only inhabitants of the field ; that, of course, they are many in number, or that, after all, they are other than the little, shrivelled, meagre, hopping, though loud and troublesome insects of the hour.' I think, sir, that the noble and true women of this continent earnestly believe that the day which invests them with the elective franchise would be the blackest in the annals of humanity, would ring the death-knell of modern civilization, of national prosperity, social morality, and domestic happiness! and would consign the race to a night of degradation and horror infinitely more appalling than a return to primeval barbarism."

"Even my brief sojourn in America has taught me the demoralizing tendency of the doctrine of 'equality of races and of sexes,' and you must admit, Miss Earl, that your countrywomen are growing dangerously learned," answered Sir Roger, smiling.

"I am afraid, sir, that it is rather the quality than the quantity of their learning that makes them troublesome. One of your own noble seers has most gracefully declared : 'a woman may always help her husband,' (or race,) 'by what she knows, however little; by what she half knows or misknows, she will only tease him.'"

Sir Roger bowed, and Mr. Manning said :

"Very 'true, good, and beautiful,' as a mere theory in sociology, but in an age when those hideous hermaphrodites, ycleped 'strong-minded women,' are becoming so alarmingly numerous, our eyes are rarely gladdened by a conjunction of highly cultivated intellects; noble, loving hearts ; tender, womanly sensibilities. Can you shoulder the *onus probandi ?*"

"Sir, that rests with those who assert that learning renders women disagreeable and unfeminine ; the burden of proof remains for you."

"Permit me to lift the weight for you, Manning, by asking Miss Earl what she thinks of the comparative merits of the 'Princess,' and of 'Aurora Leigh,' as correctives of the tendency she deprecates ?"

Hitherto the discussion had been confined to the trio, while the conversation was general, but now silence reigned around the table, and when the Englishman's question forced Edna to look up, she saw all eyes turned upon her; and embarrassment flushed her face, and her lashes drooped as she answered :

"It has often been asserted by those who claim proficiency in the analysis of character, that women are the most infallible judges of womanly, and men of manly natures; but I am afraid that the poems referred to would veto this decision. While I yield to no human being in admiration of, and loving gratitude to Mrs. Browning, and regard the first eight books of 'Aurora Leigh' as vigorous, grand, and marvellously beautiful, I can not deny that a painful feeling of mortification seizes me when I read the ninth and concluding book, wherein 'Aurora,' with most unwomanly vehemence, voluntarily declares and reiterates her love for 'Romney.' Tennyson's 'Princess' seems to me more feminine and refined and lovely than 'Aurora'; and it is because I love and revere Mrs. Browning, and consider her not only the pride of her own sex, but an ornament to the world, that I find it difficult to forgive the unwomanly inconsistency into which she betrays her heroine. Allow me to say that in my humble opinion nothing in the whole range of literature so fully portrays a perfect woman as that noble sketch by Wordsworth, and the inimitable description in Rogers's 'Human Life.'"

"The first is, I presume, familiar to all of us, but the last, I confess, escapes my memory. Will you be good enough to repeat it?" said the editor, knitting his brows slightly.

"Excuse me, sir; it is too long to be quoted here, and it seems that I have already monopolized the conversation much longer than I expected or desired. Moreover, to quote Rogers to an Englishman would be equivalent to 'carrying coal to Newcastle,' or peddling 'owls in Athens.'"

Sir Roger smiled as he said:

"Indeed, Miss Earl, while you spoke, I was earnestly ransacking my memory for the passage to which you allude; but I am ashamed to say, it is as fruitless an effort as 'calling spirits from the vasty deep.' Pray be so kind as to repeat it for me."

At that instant little Hattie crept softly to the back of Edna's chair, and whispered :

" Bro' Felix says, won't you please come back soon, and finish that story where you left off reading last night ?"

Very glad to possess so good an excuse, the governess rose at once ; but Mrs. Andrews said :

"Wait, Miss Earl. What do you want, Hattie ?"

" Bro' Felix wants Miss Earl, and sent me to beg her to come."

" Go back and tell him he is in a hopeless minority, and that in this country the majority rule. There are fifteen here who want to talk to Miss Earl, and he can't have her in the schoolroom just now," said Grey Chilton, slyly pelting his niece with almonds.

" But Felix is really sick to-day, and if Mrs. Andrews will excuse me, I prefer to go."

She looked imploringly at the lady of the house, who said nothing ; and Sir Roger beckoned Hattie to him, and exclaimed :

"Pray, may I inquire, Mrs. Andrews, why your children do not make their appearance ? I am sure you need not fear a repetition of the sarcastic rebuke of that wit who, when dining at a house where the children were noisy and unruly, lifted his glass, bowed to the troublesome little ones, and drank to the memory of King Herod. I am very certain 'the murder of the innocents ' would never be recalled here, unless—forgive me, Miss Earl ! but from the sparkle in your eyes, I believe you anticipate me. Do you really know what I am about to say ?"

" I think, sir, I can guess."

" Let me see whether you are a clairvoyant !"

" On one occasion when a sign for a children's school was needed, and the lady teacher applied to Lamb to suggest a design, he meekly advised that of ' The Murder of the Innocents.' Thank you, sir. However, I am not surprised that you entertain such flattering

opinions of a profession which in England boasts
'Squeers' as its national type and representative."

The young man laughed good-humoredly, and answered :

"For the honor of my worthy pedagogical countrymen, permit me to assure you that the aforesaid
'Squeers' is simply one of Dickens's inimitable cari-
catures."

"Nevertheless I have somewhere seen the statement that when 'Nicholas Nickleby' first made its
appearance, only six irate schoolmasters went immediately to London to thrash the author ; each believing
that he recognized his own features in the amiable
portrait of 'Squeers.'"

She bowed and turned from the table, but Mrs.
Andrews exclaimed :

"Before you go, repeat that passage from Rogers ;
then we will excuse you."

With one hand clasping Hattie's, and the other resting on the back of her chair, Edna fixed her eyes on
Mrs. Andrew's face, and gave the quotation.

> "His house she enters, there to be a light
> Shining within when all without is night ;
> A guardian angel o'er his life presiding,
> Doubling his pleasures and his cares dividing ;
> Winning him back, when mingling in the throng
> From a vain world we love, alas ! too long,
> To fireside happiness and hours of ease,
> Blest with that charm, the certainty to please.
> How oft her eyes read his ! her gentle mind
> To all his wishes, all his thoughts inclined ;
> Still subject—ever on the watch to borrow
> Mirth of his mirth, and sorrow of his sorrow."

CHAPTER XXVII.

FLOWERY as Sicilian meads was the parsonage garden on that quiet afternoon late in May, when Mr. Hammond closed the honeysuckle-crowned gate, crossed the street, and walked slowly into the church-yard, down the sacred streets of the silent city of the dead, and entered the enclosure where slept his white-robed household band.

The air was thick with perfume, as if some strong, daring south wind had blown wide the mystic doors of Astarte's huge laboratory, and overturned the myriad alembics, and deluged the world with her fragrant and subtle distillations.

Honey-burdened bees hummed their hymns to labor, as they swung to and fro ; and numbers of Psyche-symbols, golden butterflies, floated dreamily in and around and over the tombs, now and then poising on velvet wings, as if waiting, listening for the clarion voice of Gabriel, to rouse and reanimate the slumbering bodies beneath the gleaming slabs. Canary-colored orioles flitted in and out of the trailing willows, a red-bird perched on the brow of a sculptured angel guarding a child's grave, and poured his sad, sweet, monotonous notes on the spicy air ; two purple pigeons, with rain-bow necklaces, cooed and fluttered up and down from the church belfry, and close under the projecting roof of the granite vault, a pair of meek brown wrens were building their nest and twittering softly one to another.

The pastor cut down the rank grass and fringy ferns, the flaunting weeds and coreopsis that threatened to

choke his more delicate flowers, and, stooping, tied up
the crimson pinks, and wound the tendrils of the blue-
veined clematis around its slender trellis, and straightened the white petunias and the orange-tinted crocaes,
which the last heavy shower had beaten to the ground.

The small, gray vault was overrun with ivy, whose
dark, polished leaves threatened to encroach on a
plain slab of pure marble that stood very near it ; and
as the minister pruned away the wreaths, his eyes rested
on the black letters in the centre of the slab : " Murray
Hammond. Aged 21."

Elsewhere the sunshine streamed warm and bright
over the graves, but here the rays were intercepted by
the church, and its cool shadow rested over vault and
slab and flowers.

The old man was weary from stooping so long, and
now he took off his hat and passed his hand over his
forehead, and sighed as he leaned against the door
of the vault, where fine, fairy-fingered mosses were
weaving their green arabesque *immortelles*.

In a mournfully measured, yet tranquil tone, he
said aloud :

" Ah ! truly, throughout all the years of my life I
have never heard the promise of perfect love, without
seeing aloft amongst the stars, fingers as of a man's
hand, writing the secret legend : ' *Ashes to ashes ! dust
to dust !* ' "

Age was bending his body toward the earth with
which it was soon to mingle ; the ripe and perfect
wheat nodded lower and lower day by day, as the
Angel of the Sickle delayed ; but his noble face wore
that blessed and marvellous calm, that unearthly peace
which generally comes some hours after death, when
all traces of temporal passions and woes are lost in
eternity's repose.

A low, wailing symphony throbbed through the
church, where the organist was practising ; and then
out of the windows, and far away on the evening air,
rolled the solemn waves of that matchlessly mournful
Requiem which, under prophetic shadows, Mozart

began on earth and finished, perhaps in heaven, on one of those golden harps whose apocalyptic ringing smote St. John's eager ears among the lonely rocks of Ægean-girdled Patmos. The sun had paused as if to listen on the wooded crest of a distant hill, but as the requiem ended and the organ sobbed itself to rest, he gathered up his burning rays and disappeared; and the spotted butterflies, like "winged tulips," flitted silently away, and the evening breeze bowed the large yellow primroses, and fluttered the phlox; the red nasturtiums that climbed up at the foot of the slab shuddered and shook their blood-colored banners over the polished marble. A holy hush fell upon all things save a towering poplar that leaned against the church, and rustled its leaves ceaselessly, and shivered and turned white, as tradition avers it has done since that day, when Christ staggered along the *Via Dolorosa* bearing his cross, carved out of poplar wood.

Leaning with his hands folded on the handle of the weeding hoe, his gray beard sweeping over his bosom, his bare, silvered head bowed, and his mild, peaceful blue eyes resting on his son's tomb, Mr. Hammond stood listening to the music; and when the strains ceased, his thoughts travelled onward and upward till they crossed the sea of crystal before the Throne, and in imagination he heard the song of the four and twenty elders.

From this brief reverie some slight sound aroused him, and lifting his eyes, he saw a man clad in white linen garments, wearing oxalis clusters in his coat, standing on the opposite side of the monumental slab.

"St. Elmo! my poor, suffering wanderer! Oh, St. Elmo! come to me once more before I die!"

The old man's voice was husky, and his arms trembled as he stretched them across the grave that intervened.

Mr. Murray looked into the tender, tearful, pleading countenance, and the sorrow that seized his own, making his features writhe, beggars language. He in-

stinctively put out his arms, then drew them back, and
hid his face in his hands; saying in low, broken, almost
inaudible tones :

"I am too unworthy. Dripping with the blood of
your children, I dare not touch you."

The pastor tottered around the tomb, and stood at
Mr. Murray's side, and the next moment the old man's
arms were clasped around the tall form, and his white
hair fell on his pupil's shoulder.

"God be praised! After twenty years' separation
I hold you once more to the heart that, even in its
hours of deepest sorrow, has never ceased to love you !
St. Elmo!——"

He wept aloud, and strained the prodigal convulsively to his breast.

After a moment Mr. Murray's lips moved, twitched;
and with a groan that shook his powerful frame from
head to foot, he asked :

"Will you ever, ever forgive me ?"

"God is my witness that I freely and fully forgave
you many, many years ago ! The dearest hope of my
lonely life has been that I might tell you so, and make
you realize how ceaselessly my prayers and my love
have followed you in all your dreary wanderings. Oh !
I thank God that, at last ! at last you have come to
me, my dear, dear boy ! My poor, proud prodigal !"

A magnificent *jubilate* swelled triumphantly though
church and churchyard, as if the organist up in the
gallery knew what was happening at Murray Hammond's grave ; and when the thrilling music died away
St. Elmo broke from the encircling arms, and knelt
with his face shrouded in his hands and pressed
against the marble that covered his victim.

After a little while the pastor sat down on the edge
of the slab, and laid his shrunken fingers softly and
caressingly upon the bowed head.

"Do not dwell upon a past that is fraught only with
bitterness to you, and from which you can draw no
balm. Throw your painful memories behind you, and
turn resolutely to a future which may be rendered

noble and useful and holy. There is truth, precious truth in George Herbert's words :

> ' For all may have,
> If they dare choose, a glorious life or grave !'

and the years to come may, by the grace of God, more than cancel those that have gone by."

"What have I to hope for—in time or eternity? Oh! none but Almighty God can ever know the dreary blackness and wretchedness of my despairing soul! the keen, sleepless pain of my remorse ! my utter loathing of my accursed, distorted nature !"

"And His pitying eyes see all, and Christ stretches out his hands to lift you up to himself, and his own words of loving sympathy and pardon are spoken again to you : ' Come unto me, all ye weary and heavy laden, and I will give you rest.' Throw all your galling load of memories down at the foot of the cross, and 'the peace that passeth all understanding' shall enter your sorrowing soul, and abide there for ever. St. Elmo, only prayer could have sustained and soothed me since we parted that bright summer morning twenty long, long years ago. Prayer took away the sting and sanctified my sorrows for the good of my soul ; and, my dear, dear boy, it will extract the poison and the bitterness from yours. That God answers prayer and comforts the afflicted among men, I am a living attestation. It is by His grace only that ' I am what I am '; erring and unworthy I humbly own, but patient at least, and fully resigned to His will. The only remaining cause of disquiet passed away just now, when I saw that you had come back to me. St. Elmo, do you ever pray for yourself ?"

"For some weeks I have been trying to pray, but my words seem a mockery ; they do not rise, they fall back hissing upon my heart. I have injured and insulted you ; I have cursed you and yours, have robbed you of your peace of mind, have murdered your children——"

" Hush ! hush ! we will not disinter the dead. My
peace of mind you have to-day given back to me ; and
the hope of your salvation is dearer to me than the
remembered faces of my darlings, sleeping here beside
us.   Oh, St. Elmo, I have prayed for you as I never
prayed even for my own Murray; and I know, I feel
that all my wrestling before the Throne of Grace has
not been in vain.   Sometimes my faith grew faint, and
as the years dragged on and I saw no melting of your
haughty, bitter spirit, I almost lost hope; but I did
not, thank God, I did not !   I held on to the precious
promise, and prayed more fervently, and, blessed be
His holy name ! at last, just before I go hence, the
answer comes.   As I see you kneeling here at my
Murray's grave, I know now that your soul is snatched
'as a brand from the burning !'   Oh ! I bless my merciful God, that in that day when we stand for final
judgment, and your precious soul is required at my
son's hands, the joyful cry of the recording angel shall
be, 'Saved ! saved ! for ever and ever, through the
blood of the Lamb !' "

Overwhelmed with emotion, the pastor dropped his
white head on his bosom ; and once more silence fell
over the darkening cemetery.

One by one the birds hushed their twitter and went
to rest, and only the soft cooing of the pigeons floated
down now and then from the lofty belfry.

On the eastern horizon a thin, fleecy scarf of clouds
was silvered by the rising moon, the west was a huge
shrine of beryl whereon burned ruby flakes of vapor,
watched by a solitary vestal star ; and the sapphire
arch overhead was beautiful and mellow as any that
ever vaulted above the sculptured marbles of Pisan
Campo Santo.

Mr. Murray rose and stood with his head uncovered
and his eyes fixed on the nodding nasturtiums that
glowed like blood-spots.

"Mr. Hammond, your magnanimity unmans me ;
and if your words be true, I feel in your presence like
a leper and should lay my lips in the dust, crying, 'Un-

clean! unclean!" For all that I have inflicted on you,
I have neither apology nor defence to offer; and I
could much better have borne curses from you than
words of sympathy and affection. You amaze me, for
I hate and scorn myself so thoroughly, that I marvel
at the interest you still indulge for me; I can not
understand how you can endure the sight of my
features, the sound of my voice. Oh! if I could atone!
If I could give Annie back to your arms, there is no
suffering, no torture that I would not gladly embrace!
No penance of body or soul from which I would
shrink!"

"My dear boy, (for such you still seem to me, notwithstanding the lapse of time,) let my little darling
rest with her God. She went down early to her long
home, and though I missed her sweet laugh, and her
soft, tender hands about my face, and have felt a chill
silence in my house, where music once was, she has
been spared much suffering and many trials; and I
would not recall her if I could, for after a few more
days I shall gather her back to my bosom in that
eternal land where the blighting dew of death never
falls ; where

'Adieus and farewells are a sound unknown.'

Atone? Ah, St. Elmo! you can atone. Save your
soul, redeem your life, and I shall die blessing your
name. Look at me in my loneliness and infirmity. I
am childless; you took my idols from me, long, long
ago ; you left my heart desolate; and now I have a
right to turn to you, to stretch out my feeble, empty
arms, and say, Come, be my child, fill my son's place,
let me lean upon you in my old age, as I once fondly
dreamed I should lean on my own Murray! St. Elmo,
will you come? Will you give me your heart, my son!
my son!"

He put out his trembling hands, and a yearning
tenderness shone in his eyes as he raised them to the
tall, stern man before him.

Mr. Murray bent eagerly forward, and looked wonderingly at him.

"Do you, can you mean it? It appears so impossible, and I have been so long sceptical of all nobility
in my race. Will you indeed shelter Murray's murderer in your generous, loving heart?"

"I call my God to witness, that it has been my
dearest hope for dreary years that I might win your
heart back before I die."

"It is but a wreck, a hideous ruin, black with sins;
but such as I am, my future, my all, I lay at your feet!
If there is any efficacy in bitter repentance and remorse; if there is any mercy left in my Maker's hands;
if there be saving power in human will, I will atone! I
will atone!"

The strong man trembled like a wave-lashed reed,
as he sank on one knee at the minister's feet, and
buried his face in his arms; and speading his palms
over the drooped head, Mr. Hammond gently and
solemnly blessed him.

For some time both were silent, and then Mr.
Murray stretched out one arm over the slab, and said
brokenly:

"Kneeling here at Murray's tomb, a strange, incomprehensible feeling creeps into my heart. The fierce,
burning hate I have borne him seems to have passed
away; and something, ah! something, mournfully like
the old yearning toward him, comes back, as I look at his
name. Oh, idol of my youth! hurled down and crushed
by my own savage hands! For the first time since I
destroyed him, since I saw his handsome face whitening in death, I think of him kindly. For the first time
since that night, I feel that—that—I can forgive him.
Murray! Murray! you wronged me! you wrecked me!
but oh! if I could give you back the life I took in my
madness! how joyfully would I forgive you all, my
injuries! His blood dyes my hands, my heart, my
soul!"

"The blood of Jesus will wash out those stains. The
law was fully satisfied when He hung on Calvary;

there, ample atonement was made for just such sins as yours, and you have only to claim and plead his sufferings to secure your salvation. St. Elmo, bury your past here, in Murray's grave, and give all your thoughts to the future. Half of your life has ebbed out, and yet your life-work remains undone, untouched. You have no time to spend in looking over your unimproved years."

"'Bury my past!' Impossible, even for one hour. I tell you I am chained to it, as the Aloides were chained to the pillars of Tartarus! and the croaking fiend that will not let me sleep in memory! Memory of sins that—that avenge your wrongs, old man! that goad me sometimes to the very verge of suicide! Do you know, ha! how could you possibly know? Shall I tell you that only one thought has often stood between me and self-destruction? It was not the fear of death, no, no, no! It was not even the dread of facing an outraged God! but it was the horrible fear of meeting Murray! Not all eternity was wide enough to hold us both! The hate I bore him made me shrink from a deed which I felt would instantly set us face to face once more in the land of souls. Ah! a change has come over me ; now, if I could see his face, I might learn to forget that look it wore when last I gazed upon it. Time bears healing for some natures ; to mine it has brought only poison. It is useless to bid me forget. Memory is earth's retribution for man's sins. I have bought at a terrible price my conviction of the melancholy truth, that he who touches the weapons of Nemesis effectually slaughters his own peace of mind, and challenges her maledictions, from which there is no escape. In my insanity I said, 'Vengeance is mine! I will repay!' and in the hour when I daringly grasped the prerogative of God, His curse smote me! Mr. Hammond, friend of my happy youth, guide of my innocent boyhood! if you could know all the depths of my abasement, you would pity me indeed! My miserable heart is like the crater of some extinct volcano ; the flames of sin have burned

out, and left it rugged, rent, blackened. I do not think
that——"

"St. Elmo, do not upbraid yourself so bitterly——"

"Sir, your words are kind and noble and full of
Christian charity; they are well meant, and I thank
you; but they cannot comfort me. My desolation,
my utter wretchedness isolate me from the sympathy
of my race, whom I have despised and trampled so relentlessly. Yesterday I read a passage which depicts
so accurately my dreary isolation, that I have been
unable to expel it; I find it creeping even now to my
lips:

> "'O misery and mourning! I have felt—
> Yes, I have felt like some deserted world
> That God had done with, and had cast aside
> To rock and stagger through the gulfs of space,
> He never looking on it any more;
> Untilled, no use, no pleasure, not desired,
> Nor lighted on by angels in their flight
> From heaven to happier planets; and the race
> That once hath dwelt on it withdrawn or dead.
> *Could such a world have hope that some blest day
> God would remember her, and fashion her
> Anew?'*"

"Yes, my dear St. Elmo, so surely as God reigns
above us, he will refashion it, and make the light of his
pardoning love and the refreshing dew of his grace fall
upon it! And the waste places shall bloom as Sharon,
and the purpling vineyards shame Engedi, and the lilies
of peace shall lift up their stately heads, and the 'voice
of the turtle shall be heard in the land!' Have faith,
grapple yourself by prayer to the feet of God, and he
will gird, and lift up, and guide you."

Mr. Murray shook his head mournfully, and the
moonlight shining on his face showed it colorless, haggard, hopeless.

The pastor rose, put on his hat, and took St. Elmo's
arm.

"Come home with me. This spot is fraught with
painful associations that open afresh all your wounds."

They walked on together until they reached the parsonage gate, and as the minister raised the latch, his
companion gently disengaged the arm clasped to the
old man's side.

"Not to-night. After a few days I will try to
come."

"St. Elmo, to-morrow is Sunday, and——"

He paused, and did not speak the request that
looked out from his eyes.

It cost Mr. Murray a severe struggle, and he did not
answer immediately. When he spoke his voice was
unsteady.

"Yes, I know what you wish. Once I swore I would
tear the church down, scatter its dust to the winds,
leave not a stone to mark the site! But I will come
and hear you preach for the first time since that sunny
Sabbath, twenty years dead, when your text was, '*Cast
thy bread upon the waters; for thou shalt find it after
many days.*' Sodden, and bitter, and worthless
from long tossing in the great deep of sin, it drifts
back at last to your feet; and instead of stooping tenderly to gather up the useless fragments, I wonder that
you do not spurn the stranded ruin from you. Yes, I
will come."

"Thank God! Oh! what a weight you have lifted
from my heart! St. Elmo, my son!"

There was a long, lingering clasp of hands, and the
pastor went into his home with tears of joy on his furrowed face, while his smiling lips whispered to his
grateful soul:

"In the morning sow thy seed, and in the evening
withhold not thy hand; for thou knowest not whether
shall prosper, either this or that, or whether they both
shall be alike good."

Mr. Murray watched the stooping form until it disappeared, and then went slowly back to the silent bury-
ing ground, and sat down on the steps of the church.

Hour after hour passed and still he sat there, almost
as motionless as one of the monuments, while his eyes
dwelt as if spellbound, on the dark, dull stain where

Annie Hammond had rested, in days long, long past; and Remorse, more powerful than Erictho, evoked from the charnel house the sweet girlish features and fairy figure of the early dead.

His pale face was propped on his hand, and there in the silent watches of the moon-lighted midnight, he held communion with God and his own darkened spirit.

> "What hast thou wrought for Right and Truth,
> For God and man,
> From the golden hours of bright-eyed youth,
> To life's mid-span?'

His almost Satanic pride was laid low as the dead in their mouldering shrouds, and all the giant strength of his perverted nature was gathered up and hurled in a new direction. The Dead Sea Past moaned and swelled, and bitter waves surged and broke over his heart, but he silently buffeted them; and the moon rode in mid-heaven when he rose, went around the church, and knelt and prayed, with his forehead pressed to the marble that covered Murray Hammond's last resting-place,

> "Oh! that the mist which veileth my To Come
> Would so dissolve and yield unto mine eyes
> A worthy path! I'd count not wearisome
> Long toil nor enterprise,
> But strain to reach it; ay, with wrestlings stout
> Is there such path already made to fit
> The measure of my foot? It shall atone
> For much, if I at length may light on it
> And know it for mine own."

CHAPTER XXVIII.

"OH! how grand and beautiful it is! Whenever I look at it, I feel exactly as I did on Easter-Sunday, when I went to the cathedral to hear the music. It is a solemn feeling, as if I were in a holy place. Miss Earl, what makes me feel so?"

Felix stood in an art-gallery, and leaning on his crutches looked up at Church's "Heart of the Andes."

"You are impressed by the solemnity and the holy repose of nature; for here you look upon a pictured cathedral, built not by mortal hands, but by the architect of the universe. Felix, does it not recall to your mind something of which we often speak?"

The boy was silent for a few seconds, and then his thin, sallow face brightened.

"Yes, indeed! You mean that splendid description which you read to me from 'Modern Painters?' How fond you are of that passage, and how very often you think of it! Let me see whether I can remember it:

Slowly yet accurately he repeated the eloquent tribute to "Mountain Glory," from the fourth volume of "Modern Painters."

"Felix, you know that a celebrated English poet, Keats, has said, 'A thing of beauty is a joy for ever'; and as I can never hope to express my ideas in half such beautiful language as Mr. Ruskin uses, it is an economy of trouble to quote his words. Some of his expressions are like certain songs which, the more frequently we sing them, the more valuable and eloquent they become; and as we rarely learn a fine piece of music to be played once or twice and then thrown aside, why should we not be allowed the same privilege with verbal melodies? Last week you asked me to explain to you what is meant by 'aerial perspective,' and if you will study the atmosphere in this great picture, Mr. Church will explain it much more clearly to you than I was able to do."

"Yes, Miss Earl, I see it now. The eye could travel up and up, and on and on, and never get out of that sky; and it seems to me those birds yonder would fly entirely away, out of sight, through that air in the picture. But, Miss Earl, do you really believe that the Chimborazo in South America is as grand as Mr. Church's? I do not, because I have noticed that pictures are much handsomer than the real things they stand for. Mamma carried me last spring to see some paintings of scenes on the Hudson river, and when we went travelling in the summer I saw the very spot where the artist stood when he sketched the hills and the bend of the river, and it was not half so pretty as the picture. And yet I know God is the greatest painter. Is it the far-off look that everything wears when painted?"

"Yes, the 'far-off look,' as you call it, is one cause of the effect you wish to understand; and it has been rather more elegantly expressed by Campbell, in the line:

'Tis distance lends enchantment to the view.'

I have seen this fact exemplified in a very singular manner, at a house in Georgia, where I was once visiting. From the front door I had a very fine prospect or view of lofty hills, and a dense forest, and a pretty little town where the steeples of the churches glittered in the sunshine, and I stood for some time admiring the landscape; but presently, when I turned to speak to the lady of the house, I saw, in the glass sidelights of the door, a miniature reflection of the very same scene that was much more beautiful. I was puzzled, and could not comprehend how the mere fact of diminishing the size of the various objects, by increasing the distance, could enhance their loveliness; and I asked myself whether all far-off things were handsomer than those close at hand? In my perplexity I went as usual to Mr. Ruskin, wondering whether he had ever noticed the same thing; and of course he had, and has a noble passage about it in one of his books on architecture. I will see if my memory appreciates it as it deserves: 'Are not all natural things, it may be asked, as lovely near as far away? Nay, not so. Look at the clouds, and watch the delicate sculpture of their alabaster sides and the rounded lustre of their magnificent rolling. They are meant to be beheld far away; they were shaped for their place, high above your head; approach them, and they fuse into vague mists, or whirl away in fierce fragments of thunderous vapor.' (And here, Felix, your question about Chimborazo is answered.) 'Look at the crest of the Alps, from the far-away plains over which its light is cast, whence human souls have communion with it by their myriads. The child looks up to it in the dawn, and the husbandman in the burden and heat of the day, and the old man in the going down of the sun, and it is to them all as the celestial city on the world's horizon; dyed with the depths of heaven and clothed with the calm of eternity. There was it set for holy dominion by Him who marked for the sun his journey, and bade the moon know her going down. It was built for its place in the far-off sky; approach it, and the glory of its aspect fades into blanched fearfulness; its purple walls are rent into grisly rocks, its silver fretwork saddened into wasting snow; the stormbrands of ages are on its breast, the ashes of its own ruin lie solemnly on its white raiment!' Felix, in rambling about the fields, you will frequently be reminded of this. I have noticed that the meadow in the distance is always greener and more velvety, and seems more thickly studded with flowers, than the one I am crossing, or the hillside far away has a golden gleam on its rocky slopes, and the shadow spots are softer and cooler and more purple than those I am climbing and panting over; and I have hurried on, and after a little, turning to look back, lo! all the glory I saw beckoning me on has flown, and settled over the meadow and the hillside that I have passed, and the halo is behind! Perfect beauty in scenery is like the mirage that you read about yesterday; it fades and flits out of your grasp, as you travel toward it. When we go home I will read you something which Emerson has said concerning this same lovely *ignis fatuus;* for I can remember only a few words: 'What splendid distance, what recesses of ineffable pomp and loveliness in the sunset! But who can go where they are, or lay his hand, or plant his foot thereon? Off they fall from the round world for ever.' Felix, I suppose it is because we see all the imperfections and inequalities of objects close at hand, but the fairy film of air like a silvery mist hides these when at a distance; and we are charmed with the heightened beauties, which alone are visible."

Edna's eyes went back to the painting, and rested there; and little Hattie, who had been gazing up at her governess in curious perplexity, pulled her brother's sleeve and said:

" Bro' Felix, do you understand all that? I guess I don't; for I know when I am hungry (and seems to me I always am); why, when I am hungry the closer I get to my dinner the nicer it looks! And then there was that hateful, spiteful old Miss Abby Tompkins, that mamma would have to teach you! Ugh! I have watched her many a time coming up the street, (you know she never would ride in stages for fear of pick-pockets,) and she always looked just as ugly as far off as I could see her as when she came close to me——"

A hearty laugh cut short Hattie's observation; and, coming forward, Sir Roger Percival put his hand on her head, saying:

" How often children tumble down 'the step from the sublime to the ridiculous,' and drag staid, dignified folks after them? Miss Earl, I have been watching your little party for some time, listening to your incipient art-lecture. You Americans are queer people; and when I go home I shall tell Mr. Ruskin that I heard a little boy criticizing 'The Heart of the Andes,' and quoting from 'Modern Painters.' Felix, as I wish to be accurate, will you tell me your age?"

The poor sensitive cripple imagined that he was being ridiculed, and he only reddened and frowned and bit his thin lips.

Edna laid her hand on his shoulder, and answered for him.

"Just thirteen years old; and though Mr. Ruskin is a distinguished exception to the rule that 'prophets are not without honor, save in their own country,' I think he has no reader who loves and admires his writings more than Felix Andrews.

Here the boy raised his eyes and asked:

"Why is it that prophets have no honor among their own people? Is it because they too have to be seen from a great distance in order to seem grand? I heard mamma say the other day that if some book written in America had only come from England everybody would be raving about it."

"Some other time, Felix, we will talk of that problem. Hattie, you look sleepy."

"I think it will be lunch time before we get home," replied the yawning child.

Sir Roger took her by her shoulders, and shook her gently, saying:

"Come, wake up, little sweetheart! How can you get sleepy or hungry with all these handsome pictures staring at you from the walls?"

The good-natured child laughed; but her brother, who had an unconquerable aversion to Sir Roger's huge whiskers, curled his lips, and exclaimed scornfully:

"Hattie, you ought to be ashamed of yourself! Hungry, indeed! You are almost as bad as that English Lady——, who, when her husband was admiring some beautiful lambs, and called her attention to them, answered. 'Yes, lambs are beautiful—*boiled!*'"

Desirous of conciliating him, Sir Roger replied:

"When you and Hattie come to see me in England, I will show you the most beautiful lambs in the United Kingdom; and your sister shall have boiled lamb three times a day, if she wishes it. Miss Earl, you are so fond of paintings that you would enjoy a European tour more than any lady whom I have met in this country. I have seen miles of canvas in Boston, New York, and Philadelphia, but very few good pictures."

"And yet, sir, when on exhibition in Europe this great work here before us received most extravagant praise from transatlantic critics, who are very loath to accord merit to American artists. If I am ever so fortunate as to be able to visit Europe, and cultivate and improve my taste, I think I shall still be very proud of the names of Allston, West, Church, Bierstadt, Kensett and Gifford."

She turned to quit the gallery, and Sir Roger said:

"I leave to-morrow for Canada, and may possibly sail for England without returning to New York. Will you allow me the pleasure of driving you to the Park this afternoon? Two months ago you refused a similar request, but since then I flatter myself we have become better friends."

"Thank you, Sir Roger. I presume the children can spare me, and I will go with pleasure."

"I will call at five o'clock."

He handed her and Hattie into the *coupé*, tenderly assisted Felix, and saw them driven away.

Presently Felix laughed, and exclaimed:

"Oh! I hope Miss Morton will be in the Park this evening. It would be glorious fun to see her meet you and Sir Roger."

"Why, Felix?"

"Oh! because she meddles. I heard Uncle Grey tell mamma that she was making desperate efforts to catch the Englishman; and that she turned up her nose tremendously at the idea of his visiting you. When Uncle Grey told her how often he came to our house, she bit her lips almost till the blood spouted. Sir Roger drives very fine horses, uncle says, and Miss Morton hints outrageously for him to ask her to ride, but she can't manage to get the invitation. So she will be furious when she sees you this afternoon. Yonder is Goupil's; let us stop and have a look at those new engravings mamma told us about yesterday. Hattie, you can curl up in your corner, and go to sleep and dream of boiled lamb till we come back."

Later in the day Mrs. Andrews went up to Edna's room, and found her correcting an exercise.

"At work as usual. You are incorrigible. Any other woman would be so charmed with her conquest that her head would be quite turned by a certain pair of brown eyes that are considered irresistible. Come, get ready for your drive; it is almost five o'clock, and you know foreigners are too polite, too thoroughly well-bred not to be punctual. No, no, Miss Earl; not that hat, on the peril of your life! Where is that new one that I ordered sent up to you two days ago? It will match this delicate white shawl of mine, which I brought up for you to wear; and come, no scruples if you please! Stand up and let me see whether its folds hang properly. You should have heard Madame De G—— when she put it around my shoulders for the first time, '*Juste ciel!* Madame Andrews, you are a Greek statue!' Miss Earl, put your hair back a little from the left temple. There, now the veins show! Where are your gloves? You look charmingly, my dear; only too pale, too pale! If you don't contrive to get up some color, people will swear that Sir Roger was airing the ghost of a pretty girl. There is the bell! Just as I told you, he is punctual. Five o'clock to a minute."

She stepped to the window, and looked down at the equipage before the door.

"What superb horses! You will be the envy of the city."

There was something in the appearance and manner of Sir Roger which often reminded Edna of Gordon

Leigh; and during the spring he visited her so constantly, sent her so frequently baskets of elegant
flowers, that he succeeded in overcoming her reticence, and established himself on an exceedingly
friendly footing in Mrs. Andrews's house.

Now, as they drove along the avenue and entered
the Park, their spirits rose; and Sir Roger turned
very often to look at the fair face of his companion,
which he found more and more attractive each day.
He saw, too, that under his earnest gaze the faint color
deepened, until her cheeks glowed like sea-shells; and
when he spoke he bent his face much nearer to hers
than was necessary to make her hear his words. They
talked of books, flowers, music, mountain scenery, and
the green lanes of "Merry England." Edna was
perfectly at ease, and in a mood to enjoy everything.

They dashed on, and the sunlight disappeared, and
the gas glittered all over the city before Sir Roger
turned his horses' heads homeward. When they
reached Mrs. Andrews's door he dismissed his carriage
and spent the evening. At eleven o'clock he rose to
say good-bye.

"Miss Earl, I hope I shall have the pleasure of
renewing our acquaintance at an early day; if not in
America in Europe. The brightest reminiscences I
shall carry across the ocean are those that cluster
about the hours I have spent with you. If I should
not return to New York, will you allow me the privilege of hearing from you occasionally?"

His clasp of the girl's hand was close, but she
withdrew it, and her face flushed painfully as she answered:

"Will you excuse me, Sir Roger, when I tell you
that I am so constantly occupied I have not time to
write, even to my old and dearest friends."

Passing the door of Felix's room, on her way to her
own apartment, the boy called to her: "Miss Earl,
are you very tired?"

"Oh, no. Do you want anything?"

"My head aches and I can't go to sleep. Please read to me a little while."

He raised himself on his elbow, and looked up fondly at her.

"Ah! how very pretty you are to-night! Kiss me, won't you?"

She stooped and kissed the poor parched lips, and as she opened a volume of the Waverly Novels, he said:

"Did you see Miss Morton?"

"Yes; she was on horseback, and we passed her twice."

"Glad of it! She does not like you. I guess she finds it as hard to get to sleep to-night as I do."

Edna commenced reading, and it was nearly an hour before Felix's eyes closed, and his fingers relaxed their grasp on hers. Softly she put the book back on the shelf, extinguished the light, and stole upstairs to her desk. That night, as Sir Roger tossed restlessly on his pillow, thinking of her, recalling all that she had said during the drive, he would not have been either comforted or flattered by a knowledge of the fact that she was so entirely engrossed by her MS. that she had no thought of him or his impending departure.

When the clock struck three she laid down her pen; and the mournful expression that crept into her eyes told that memory was busy with the past years. When she fell asleep she dreamed not of Sir Roger but of Le Bocage and its master, of whom she would not permit herself to think in her waking hours.

The influence which Mr. Manning exerted over Edna increased as their acquaintance ripened; and the admiring reverence with which she regarded the editor was exceedingly flattering to him. With curious interest he watched the expansion of her mind, and now and then warned her of some error into which she seemed inclined to plunge, or wisely advised some new branch of research.

So firm was her confidence in his mature and dispassionate judgment, that she yielded to his opinions a deferential homage, such as she had scarcely paid even to Mr. Hammond.

Gradually and unconsciously she learned to lean upon his strong, clear mind, and to find in his society a quiet but very precious happiness. The antagonism of their characters was doubtless one cause of the attraction which each found in the other, and furnished the balance-wheel which both required.

Edna's intense and dreamy idealism demanded a check, which the positivitism of the editor supplied; and his extensive and rigidly accurate information, on almost all scientific topics, constituted a valuable treasury of knowledge to which he never denied her access.

His faith in Christianity was like his conviction of the truth of mathematics, more an intellectual process and the careful deduction of logic than the result of some emotional impulse ; his religion like his dialectics was cold, consistent, irreproachable, unanswerable. Never seeking a controversy on any subject, he never shunned one, and, during its continuance, his demeanor was invariably courteous, but unyielding, and even when severe he was rarely bitter.

Very early in life his intellectual seemed to have swallowed up his emotional nature, as Aaron's rod did those of the magicians of Pharaoh, and only the absence of dogmatism, and the habitual suavity of his manner, atoned for his unbending obstinacy on all points.

Edna's fervid and beautiful enthusiasm surged and chafed and broke over this man's stern, flinty realism, like the warm, blue waters of the Gulf Stream that throw their silvery spray and foam against the glittering walls of sapphire icebergs sailing slowly southward. Her glowing imagery fell upon the bristling points of his close phalanx of arguments, as gorgeous tropical garlands caught and empaled by bayonets until they faded.

Merciless as an anatomical lecturer, he would smilingly take up one of her metaphors and dissect it, and over the pages of her MSS. for "Maga" his gravely spoken criticisms fell withering as hoar frost.

They differed in all respects, yet daily they felt the need of each other's society. The frozen man of forty sunned himself in the genial presence of a lovely girl of nineteen, and in the dawn of her literary career she felt a sense of security from his proffered guidance, even as a wayward and ambitious child, just learning to walk, totters along with less apprehension when the strong, steady hand it refuses to hold is yet near enough to catch and save from a serious fall.

While fearlessly attacking all heresy, whether political, scientific, or ethical, all latitudinarianism in manners and sciolism in letters, he commanded the confidence and esteem of all, and became in great degree the centre around which the *savants* and *literati* of the city revolved.

Through his influence Edna made the acquaintance of some of the most eminent scholars and artists who formed this *clique*, and she found that his friendship and recommendation was an "open sesame" to the charmed circle.

One Saturday she sat with her bonnet on, waiting for Mr. Manning, who had promised to accompany her on her first visit to Greenwood, and, as she put on her gloves, Felix handed her a letter which his father had just brought up.

Recognizing Mrs. Murray's writing, the governess read it immediately, and, while her eyes ran over the sheet, an expression, first of painful, then of joyful, surprise, came into her countenance.

" MY DEAR CHILD : Doubtless you will be amazed to hear that your *quondam* lover has utterly driven your image from his fickle heart ; and that he ignores your existence as completely as if you were buried twenty feet in the ruins of Herculaneum. Last night Gordon Leigh was married to Gertrude Powell, and the happy pair, attended by that despicable mother, Agnes Powell, will set out for Europe early next week. My

dear, it is growing fashionable to 'marry for spite.' I
have seen two instances recently, *and know of a third
which will take place ere long*. Poor Gordon will rue
his rashness, and, before the year expires, he will
arrive at the conclusion that he is an unmitigated fool,
and has simply performed, with great success, an
operation familiarly know as cutting off one's nose to
spite one's face! Your rejection of his renewed offer
piqued him beyond expression, and when he returned
from New York he was in exactly the most accommodating frame of mind which Mrs. Powell could desire.
She immediately laid siege to him. Gertrude's undisguised preference for his society was extremely soothing to his vanity, which you had so severely wounded,
and in fine, the indefatigable manœuvres of the wily
mamma, and the continual flattery of the girl, who is
really very pretty, accomplished the result. I once
credited Gordon with more sense than he has manifested, but each year convinces me more firmly of the
truth of my belief, that no man is proof against the
subtle and persistent flattery of a beautiful woman.
When he announced his engagement to me, we were
sitting in the library, and I looked him full in the face,
and answered: 'Indeed! Engaged to Miss Powell?
I thought you swore that so long as Edna Earl remained unmarried you would never relinquish your
suit?" He pointed to that lovely satuette of Pallas
that stands on the mantelpiece, and said bitterly,
'Edna Earl has no more heart than that marble
Athena.' Whereupon I replied, 'Take care, Gordon.
I notice that of late you seem inclined to deal rather
too freely in hyperbole. Edna's heart may resemble
the rich veins of gold, which in some mines run not
near the surface but deep in the masses of quartz.
Because you can not obtain it, you have no right to
declare that it does not exist. You will probably live
to hear some more fortunate suitor shout *Eureka!*
over the treasure.' He turned pale as the Pallas and
put his hand over his face. Then I said, 'Gordon, my
young friend, I have always been deeply interested in

your happiness ; tell me frankly, do you love this girl Gertrude ?' He seemed much embarrassed, but finally made his confession: ' Mrs. Murray, I believe I shall be fond of her after a while. She is very lovely, and deeply, deeply attached to me, (vanity you see, Edna,) and I am grateful for her affection. She will brighten my lonely home, and at least I can be proud of her rare beauty. But I never expect to love any woman as I loved Edna Earl. I can pet Gertrude ; I should have worshipped my first love, my proud, gifted, peerless Edna ! Oh ! she will never realize all she threw away when she coldly dismissed me.' Poor Gordon ! Well, he is married ; but his bride might have found cause of disquiet in his restless, abstracted manner on the evening of his wedding. What do you suppose was St. Elmo's criticism on this matrimonial mismatch ? ' Poor devil ! Before a year rolls over his head he will feel like plunging into the Atlantic, with Plymouth Rock for a necklace ! Leigh deserves a better fate, and I would rather see him tied to wild horses and dragged across the Andes.' These pique marriages are terrible mistakes ; so, my dear, I trust you will duly repent of your cruelty to poor Gordon."

As Edna put the letter in her pocket, she wondered whether Gertrude really loved her husband, or whether chagrin at Mr. Murray's heartless desertion had not goaded the girl to accept Mr. Leigh.

"Perhaps after all, Mr. Murray was correct in his estimate of her character, when he said that she was a mere child, and was capable of no very earnest affection. I hope so—I hope so."

Edna sighed as she tried to assure herself of the probability that the newly-married pair would become more attached as time passed ; and her thoughts returned to that paragraph in Mrs. Murray's letter which seemed intentionally mysterious : " I know of a third instance which will take place ere long."

Did she allude to her son and her niece ? Edna could not believe this possible, and shook her head at the suggestion ; but her lips grew cold, and her fingers locked each other as in a clasp of steel.

When Mr. Manning called, and assisted her into the carriage, he observed an unusual preoccupancy of mind ; but after a few desultory remarks she rallied, gave him her undivided attention, and seemed engrossed by his conversation.

It was a fine, sunny day, bright but cool, with a fresh and stiffening west wind rippling the waters of the harbor.

The week had been one of unusual trial, for Felix was sick, and even more than ordinarily fretful and exacting ; and weary of writing and of teaching so constantly, the governness enjoyed the brief season of emancipation.

Mr. Manning's long residence in the city had familiarized him with the beauties of Greenwood, and the history of many who slept dreamlessly in the costly mausoleums which they paused to examine and admire ; and when at last he directed the driver to return, Edna sank back in one corner of the carriage and said : "Some morning I will come with the children and spend the entire day."

She closed her eyes, and her thoughts travelled swiftly to that pure white obelisk standing in the shadow of Lookout ; and melancholy memories brought a sigh to her lips and a slight cloud to the face that for two hours past had been singularly bright and animated. The silence had lasted some minutes, when Mr. Manning who was gazing abstractedly out of the window, turned to his companion and said :

"You look pale and badly to-day."

"I have not felt as strong as usual, and it is a great treat to get away from the schoolroom and out into the open air, which is bracing and delightful. I believe I have enjoyed this outing more than any I have taken since I came North ; and you must allow me to tell you how earnestly I thank you for your considerate remembrance of me."

"Miss Earl, what I am about to say will perhaps

seem premature, and will doubtless surprise you ; but I beg you to believe that it is the result of mature deliberation———"

He paused and looked earnestly at her.

"You certainly have not decided to give up the editorship of 'Maga,' as you spoke of doing last winter? It would not survive your desertion six months."

"My allusion was to yourself, not to the magazine, which I presume I shall edit as long as I live. Miss Earl, this state of affairs cannot continue. You have no regard for your health, which is suffering materially, and you are destroying yourself. You must let me take care of you, and save you from the ceaseless toil in which you are rapidly wearing out your life. To teach, as you do, all day, and then sit up nearly all night to write, would exhaust a constitution of steel or brass. You are probably not aware of the great change which has taken place in your appearance during the last three months. Hitherto circumstances may have left you no alternative, but one is now offered you. My property is sufficient to render you comfortable. I have already purchased a pleasant home, to which I shall remove next week, and I want you to share it with me—to share my future—all that I have. You have known me scarcely a year, but you are not a stranger to my character or position, and I think that you repose implicit confidence in me. Notwithstanding the unfortunate disparity in our years, I believe we are becoming mutually dependent on each other, and in your society I find a charm such as no other human being possesses; though I have no right to expect that a girl of your age can derive equal pleasure from the companionship of a man old enough to be her father. I am not demonstrative, but my feelings are warm and deep ; and however incredulous you may be, I assure you that you are the first, the only woman I have ever asked to be my wife. I have known many who were handsome and intellectual, whose society I have really enjoyed, but not one until I met you whom I would have married. To you alone am I willing to entrust the education of my little Lila. She was but six months old when we were wrecked off Barnegat, and, in attempting to save his wife, my brother was lost. With the child in my arms I clung to a spar, and finally swam ashore; and since then, regarding her as a sacred treasure committed to my guardianship, I have faithfully endeavored to supply her father's place. There is a singular magnetism about you, Edna Earl, which makes me wish to see your face always at my hearthstone; and for the first time in my life I want to say to the world, 'This woman wears my name, and belongs to me for ever!' You are inordinately ambitious; I can lift you to a position that will fully satisfy you, and place you above the necessity of daily labor—a position of happiness and ease, where your genius can properly develop itself. Can you consent to be Douglass Manning's wife?"

There was no more tremor in his voice than in the measured beat of a base drum; and in his granite face not a feature moved, not a muscle twitched, not a nerve quivered.

So entirely unexpected was this proposal that Edna could not utter a word. The idea that he could ever wish to marry anybody seemed incredible, and that he should need her society appeared utterly absurd. For an instant she wondered if she had fallen asleep in the soft, luxurious corner of the carriage, and dreamed it all.

Completely bewildered, she sat looking wonderingly at him.

"Miss Earl, you do not seem to comprehend me, and yet my words are certainly very explicit. Once more I ask you, can you put your hand in mine and be my wife?"

He laid one hand on hers, and with the other pushed back his glasses.

Withdrawing her hands, she covered her face with them, and answered almost inaudibly:

"Let me think—for you astonish me."

" Take a day, or a week, if necessary, for consideration, and then give me your answer."

Mr. Manning leaned back in the carriage, folded his
hands, and looked quietly out of the window ; and for
a half hour silence reigned.

Brief but sharp was the struggle in Edna's heart.
Probably no woman's literary vanity and ambition has
ever been more fully gratified than was hers, by this
most unexpected offer of marriage from one whom she
had been taught to regard as the noblest ornament of
the profession she had selected. Thinking of the hour
when she sat alone, shedding tears of mortification and
bitter disappointment over his curt letter rejecting her
MS., she glanced at the stately form beside her, the
mysteriously calm, commanding face, the large white,
finely moulded hands, waiting to clasp hers for all time,
and her triumph seemed complete.

To rule the destiny of that strong man, whose intellect was so influential in the world of letters, was a conquest of which, until this hour, she had never dreamed ;
and the blacksmith's darling was, after all, a mere
woman, and the honor dazzled her.

To one of her peculiar temperament wealth offered
no temptation ; but Douglass Manning had climbed to
a grand eminence, and, looking up at it, she knew that
any woman might well be proud to share it.

He filled her ideal, he came fully up to her loftly
moral and mental standard. She knew that his superior
she could never hope to meet, and her confidence in his
integrity of character was boundless.

She felt that his society had become necessary to
her peace of mind ; for only in his presence was it
possible to forget her past. Either she must marry
him, or live single, and work and die—alone.

To a girl of nineteen the latter alternative seems
more appalling than to a woman of thirty, whose eyes
have grown strong in the gray, cold, sunless light of
confirmed old-maidenhood ; even as the vision of those
who live in dim caverns requires not the lamps needed
by new-comers fresh from the dazzling outer world.

Edna was weary of battling with precious memories of that reckless, fascinating cynic whom, without trusting, she had learned to love ; and she thought that, perhaps, if she were the wife of Mr. Manning, whom without loving she fully trusted, it would help her to forget St. Elmo.

She did not deceive herself ; she knew that, despite her struggles and stern interdicts, she loved him as she could never hope to love any one else. Impatiently she said to herself :

" Mr. Murray is as old as Mr. Manning, and in the estimation of the public is his inferior. Oh! why can not my weak, wayward heart follow my strong, clear-eyed judgment ? I would give ten years of my life to love Mr. Manning as I love——"

She compared a swarthy, electrical face, scowling and often repulsively harsh, with one cloudless and noble, over which brooded a solemn and perpetual peace ; and she almost groaned aloud in her chagrin and self-contempt, as she thought, " Surely, if ever a woman was infatuated—possessed by an evil spirit—I certainly am."

In attempting to institute a parallel between the two men, one seemed serene, majestic, and pure as the vast snow-dome of Oraefa, glittering in the chill light of midsummer-midnight suns ; the other fiery, thunderous, destructive as Izalco—one moment crowned with flames and lava-lashed—the next wrapped in gloom and dust and ashes.

While she sat there wrestling as she had never done before, even on that day of trial in the church, memory, as if leagued with Satan, brought up the image of Mr. Murray as he stood pleading for himself, for his future. She heard once more his thrilling, passionate cry, "Oh, my darling! my darling! come to me!" And pressing her face to the lining of the carriage to stifle a groan, she seemed to feel again the close clasp of his arms, the throbbing of his heart against her cheek, the warm, tender, lingering pressure of his lips on hers.

When they had crossed the ferry and were rattling

over the streets of New York, Edna took her hands from her eyes; and there was a rigid paleness in her face and a mournful hollowness in her voice, as she said almost sorrowfully:

"No, Mr. Manning! We do not love each other, and I can never be your wife. It is useless for me to assure you that I am flattered by your preference; that I am inexpressibly proud of the distinction you have generously offered to confer upon me. Sir, you can not doubt that I do most fully and gratefully appreciate this honor, which I had neither the right to expect nor the presumption to dream of. My reverence and admiration are, I confess, almost boundless, but I find not one atom of love; and an examination of my feelings satisfies me that I could never yield you that homage of heart, that devoted affection which God demands that every wife should pay her husband. You have quite as little love for me. We enjoy each other's society because our pursuits are similar, our tastes congenial, our aspirations identical. In pleasant and profitable companionship we can certainly indulge as heretofore, and it would greatly pain me to be deprived of it in future; but this can be ours without the sinful mockery of a marriage—for such I hold a loveless union. I feel that I must have your esteem and your society, but your love I neither desire nor ever expect to possess; for the sentiments you cherish for me are precisely similar to those which I entertain toward you. Mr. Manning, we shall always be firm friends, but nothing more."

An expression of surprise and disappointment drifted across, but did not settle on the editor's quiet countenance.

Turning to her, he answered with grave gentleness:

"Judge your own heart, Edna; and accept my verdict with reference to mine. Do you suppose that after living single all these years I would ultimately marry a woman for whom I had no affection? You spoke last week of the mirror of John Galeazzo Visconte, which showed his beloved Correggia her own image; and though I am a proud and reticent man, I beg you to believe that could you look into my heart you would find it such a mirror. Permit me to ask whether you intend to accept the love which I have reason to believe Mr. Murray has offered you?"

"Mr. Manning, I never expect to marry any one, for I know I shall never meet your superior, and yet I can not accept your most flattering offer. You fill all my requirements of noble, Christian manhood; but after to-day this subject must not be alluded to."

"Are you not too hasty? Will you not take more time for reflection? Is your decision mature and final?"

"Yes, Mr. Manning—final, unchangeable. But do not throw me from you! I am very, very lonely, and you surely will not forsake me?"

There were tears in her eyes as she looked up pleadingly in his face, and the editor sighed and paused a moment before he replied:

"Edna, if under any circumstances you feel that I can aid or advise you, I shall be exceedingly glad to render all the assistance in my power. Rest assured I shall not forsake you as long as we both shall live. Call upon me without hesitation, and I will respond as readily and promptly as to the claims of my little Lila. In my heart you are associated with her. You must not tax yourself so unremittingly, or you will soon ruin your constitution. There is a weariness in your face and a languor in your manner mournfully prophetic of failing health. Either give up your situation as governess or abandon your writing. I certainly recommend the former, as I can not spare you from 'Maga.'"

Here the carriage stopped at Mrs. Andrews's door, and as he handed her out Mr. Manning said:

"Edna, my friend, promise me that you will not write to-night."

"Thank you, Mr. Manning; I promise."

She did not go to her desk; but Felix was restless, feverish, querulous, and it was after midnight when she laid her head on her pillow. The milkmen in their noisy carts were clattering along the streets next morning, before her heavy eyelids closed, and she fell into a brief, troubled slumber ; over which flitted a Fata Morgana of dreams, where the central figure was always that tall one whom she had seen last standing at the railroad station with the rain dripping over him.

CHAPTER XXIX.

" LET thy abundant blessing rest upon it, O Almighty God ! else indeed my labor will be in vain. ' Paul planted, Apollos watered, but thou only can give the increase. It is finished ; look down in mercy, and sanctify it, and accept it."

The night was almost spent when Edna laid down her pen, and raised her clasped hands over the MS., which she had just completed.

For many weary months she had toiled to render it worthy of its noble theme, had spared neither time nor severe trains of thought ; by day and by night she had searched and pondered ; she had prayed fervently and ceaselessly, and worked arduously, unflaggingly to accomplish this darling hope of her heart, to embody successfully this ambitious dream, and at last the book was finished.

The manuscript was a mental tapestry, into which she had woven exquisite shades of thought, and curious and quaint devices and rich, glowing imagery that flecked the groundwork with purple and amber and gold.

But would the design be duly understood and appreciated by the great, busy, bustling world, for whose amusement and improvement she had labored so assiduously at the spinning-wheels of fancy—the loom of thought ?   Would her fellow-creatures accept it in the earnest, loving spirit in which it had been manufactured ? Would they hang this Gobelin of her brain along the walls of memory, and turn to it tenderly, reading reverently its ciphers and its illuminations ; or would it be rent and ridiculed, and trampled under foot? This book was a shrine to which her purest thoughts, her holiest aspirations traveled like pilgrims, offering the best of which her nature was capable. Would those for whom she had patiently chiselled and built it guard and prize and keep it; or smite and overturn and defile it?

Looking down at the mass of MS. now ready for the printer, a sad, tender, yearning expression filled the author's eyes; and her little white hands passed caressingly over its closely-written pages, as a mother's soft fingers might lovingly stroke the face of a child about to be thrust out into a hurrying crowd of cold, indifferent strangers, who perhaps would rudely jeer at and browbeat her darling.

For several days past Edna had worked hard to complete the book, and now at last she could fold her tired hands, and rest her weary brain.

But outraged nature suddenly swore vengeance, and her overworked nerves rose in fierce rebellion, refusing to be calm. She had so long anticipated this hour that its arrival was greeted by emotions beyond her control. As she contemplated the possible future of that pile of MS., her heart bounded madly, and then once more a fearful agony seized her, and darkness and a sense of suffocation came upon her. Rising, she strained her eyes and groped her way toward the window, but ere she reached it fell, and lost all consciousness.

The sound of the fall, the crash of a china vase which her hand had swept from the table, echoed startlingly through the silent house, and aroused some of its inmates. Mrs. Andrews ran upstairs and into Felix's room, saw that he was sleeping soundly, and then she hastened up another flight of steps, to the apartment occupied by the governess. The gas burned dazzlingly over the table where rested the roll of MS. and on the floor near the window lay Edna.

Ringing the bell furiously to summon her husband, and the servants, Mrs. Andrews knelt, raised the girl's head, and rubbing her cold hands, tried to rouse her.

The heart beat faintly, and seemed to stop now and then, and the white, rigid face was as ghastly as if the dread kiss of Samaël had indeed been pressed upon her still lips.

Finding all her restoratives ineffectual, Mrs. Andrews sent her husband for the family physician, and with the assistance of the servants, laid the girl on her bed.

When the doctor arrived and questioned her, she could furnish no clew to the cause of the attack, save by pointing to the table, where pen and paper showed that the sufferer had been at work.

Edna opened her eyes at last, and looked around at the group of anxious faces, but in a moment the spasm of pain returned. Twice she muttered something, and putting his ear close to her mouth, the doctor heard her whispering to herself :

"Never mind; it is done at last! Now I can rest."

An hour elapsed before the paroxysms entirely subsided, and then, with her ivory-like hands clasped and thrown up over her head, the governess slept heavily, dreamlessly.

For two days she remained in her own apartment, and on the morning of the third came down to the schoolroom, with a slow, weary step and a bloodless face, and a feeling of hopeless helplessness.

She dispatched her MS. to the publisher to whom she had resolved to offer it, and, leaning far back in her chair, took up Felix's Greek grammar.

Since the days of Dionysius Thrax, it had probably never appeared so tedious, so intolerably tiresome, as she found it now, and she felt relieved, almost grateful when Mrs. Andrews sent for her to come to the library, where Dr. Howell was waiting to see her.

Seating himself beside her, the physician examined her countenance and pulse, and put his ear close to her heart.

"Miss Earl, have you had many such attacks as the one whose effects have not yet passed away ?"

" This is the second time I have suffered so severely ; though very frequently I find a disagreeable fluttering about my heart, which is not very painful."

" What mode of treatment have you been following ?"

" None, sir. I have never consulted a physician."

" Humph ! Is it possible ?"

He looked at her with the keen, incisive eye of his profession, and pressed his ear once more to her heart, listening to the irregular and rapid pulsations.

" Miss Earl, are you an orphan ?"

" Yes, sir."

" Have you any living relatives ?"

" None that I ever heard of."

" Did any of your family die suddenly ?"

" Yes, I have been told that my mother died while apparently as well as usual, and engaged in spinning ; and my grandfather I found dead, sitting in his rocking-chair, smoking his pipe."

Dr. Howell cleared his throat, sighed, and was silent.

He saw a strange, startled expression leap into the large shadowy eyes, and the mouth quivered, the wan face grew whiter, and the thin fingers grasped each other ; but she said nothing, and they sat looking at one another.

The physician had come like Daniel to the banquet of life, and solved for the Belshazzar of youth the hideous riddle scrawled on the walls.

" Dr. Howell, can you do nothing for me ?"

Her voice had sunk to a whisper, and she leaned eagerly forward to catch his answer.

" Miss Earl, do you know what is meant by hypertrophy of the heart ?"

" Yes, yes, I know."

She shivered slightly.

" Whether you inherited your disease, I am not prepared to say, but certainly in your case there are some grounds for the belief."

Presently she said abstractedly :

" But grandpa lived to be an old man."

The doctor's eyes fell upon the mosaic floor of the library; and then she knew that he could give her no hope.

When at last he looked up again, he saw that she had dropped her face in her palms, and he was awed by the deathlike repose of her figure, the calm fortitude she evinced.

" Miss Earl, I never deceive my patients. It is useless to dose you with medicine, and drug you into semi-insensibility. You must have rest and quiet; rest for mind as well as body; there must be no more teaching or writing. You are overworked, and incessant mental labor has hastened the approach of a disease which, under other circumstances, might have encroached very slowly and imperceptibly. If latent (which is barely possible) it has contributed to a fearfully rapid development. Refrain from study, avoid all excitement, exercise moderately but regularly in the open air; and, above all things, do not tax your brain. If you carefully observe these directions, you may live to be as old as your grandfather. Heart diseases baffle prophecy, and I make no predictions."

He rose and took his hat from the table.

" Miss Earl, I have read your writings with great pleasure, and watched your brightening career with more interest than I ever felt in any other female author; and God knows it is exceedingly painful for me to tear away the veil from your eyes. From the first time you were pointed out to me in church, I saw that in your countenance which distressed and alarmed me; for its marble pallor whispered that your days were numbered. Frequently I have been tempted to come and expostulate with you, but I knew it would be useless. You have no reader who would more earnestly deplore the loss of your writings, but, for your own sake, I beg you to throw away your pen and rest."

She raised her head and a faint smile crept feebly across her face.

"Rest! rest! If my time is so short I can not afford to rest. There is so much to do, so much that I have planned and hoped to accomplish. I am only beginning to learn how to handle my tools, my life-work is as yet barely begun. When my long rest overtakes me, I must not be found idle sitting with folded hands. Since I was thirteen years old I have never once rested; and now I am afraid I never shall. I would rather die working than live a drone."

"But, my dear Miss Earl, those who love you have claims upon you."

"I am alone in this world. I have no family to love me, and my work is to me what I suppose dear relatives must be to other women. For six years I have been studying to fit myself for usefulness, have lived with and for books; and though I have a few noble and kind friends, do you suppose I ever forget that I am kinless? It is a mournful thing to know that you are utterly isolated among millions of human beings; that not a drop of your blood flows in any other veins. My God only has a claim upon me. Dr. Howell, I thank you for your candor. It is best that I should know the truth; and I am glad that, instead of treating me like a child, you have frankly told me all. More than once I have had a singular feeling, a shadowy presentiment that I should not live to be an old woman, but I thought it the relic of childish superstition, and I did not imagine that—that I might be called away at any instant. I did not suspect that just as I had arranged my workshop, and sharpened all my tools, and measured off my work, that my morning sun would set suddenly in the glowing east, and the long, cold night fall upon me, 'wherein no man can work'——"

Her voice faltered, and the physician turned away, and looked out of the window.

"I am not afraid of death, nor am I so wrapped up in the mere happiness which this world gives; no, no; but I love my work! Ah! I want to live long enough to finish something grand and noble, something that will live when the hands that fashioned it have crum-

bled back to dust; something that will follow me
across and beyond the dark, silent valley; something
that can not be hushed and straightened and bandaged and screwed down under my coffin-lid—oh! something that will echo in eternity! that grandpa and I
can hear 'sounding down the ages,' making music for
the people, when I go to my final rest! And, please
God! I shall! I will! Oh, doctor! I have a feeling
here which assures me I shall be spared till I finish my
darling scheme. You know Glanville said, and Poe
quoted, 'Man doth not yield himself to the angels, nor
unto death utterly, save only through the weakness of
his feeble will.' Mine is strong, invincible; it will sustain me for a longer period than you seem to believe.
The end is not yet. Doctor, do not tell people what
you have told me. I do not want to be watched and
pitied, like a doomed victim who walks about the scaffold with a rope already around his neck. Let the
secret rest between you and me."

He looked wonderingly at the electric white face,
and something in its chill radiance reminded him of
the borealis light, that waves its ghostly banners over
a cold midnight sky.

"God grant that I may be in error concerning your
disease; and that threescore years and ten may be
allotted you, to embody the airy dreams you love so
well. I repeat, if you wish to prolong your days, give
yourself more rest. I can do you little good; still, if
at any time you fancy that I can aid or relieve you, do
not hesitate to send for me. I shall come to see you
as a friend, who reads and loves all that has yet fallen
from your pen. God help and bless you, child!"

As he left the room she locked the door, and walked
slowly back to the low mantelpiece. Resting her
arms on the black marble, she laid her head down upon them, and ambition and death stared face to face,
and held grim parley over the coveted prey.

Taking the probable measure of her remaining days,
Edna fearlessly fronted the future, and pondered the

possibility of crowding into two years the work which she had designed for twenty.

To tell the girl to "rest," was a mockery; the tides of thought ebbed and flowed as ceaselessly as those of ocean, and work had become a necessity of her existence. She was far, far beyond the cool, quiet palms of rest, far out on the burning sands; and the Bahr-Sheitan rippled and glittered and beckoned, and she panted and pressed on.

One book was finished, but before she had completed it the form and features of another struggled in her busy brain, and she longed to put them on paper.

The design of the second book appeared to her partial eyes almost perfect, and the first seemed insignificant in comparison. Trains of thought that had charmed her, making her heart throb and her temples flush; and metaphors that glowed as she wrote them down, ah! how tame and trite all looked now, in the brighter light of a newer revelation! The attained, the achieved tarnished in her grasp. All behind was dun; all beyond clothed with a dazzling glory that lured her on.

Once the fondest hopes of her heart had been to finish the book now in the publisher's hands; but ere it could be printed, other characters, other aims, other scenes usurped her attention. If she could only live long enough to incarnate the new ideal!

Moreover, she knew that memory would spring up and renew its almost intolerable torture the moment that she gave herself to aimless reveries; and she felt that her sole hope of peace of mind, her only rest, was in earnest and unceasing labor. Subtle associations, merciless as the chains of Bonnivard, bound her to a past which she was earnestly striving to forget; and she continually paced as far off as her shackles would permit, sternly refusing to sit down meekly at the foot of the stake. She worked late at night until her body was exhausted, because she dreaded to lie awake, tossing helplessly on her pillow; haunted by precious recollections of days gone by forever.

Her name was known in the world of letters, her reputation was already enviable; extravagant expectations were entertained concerning her future; and to maintain her hold on public esteem, to climb higher, had become necessary for her happiness.

Through Mr. Manning's influence and friendship she was daily making the acquaintance of leading men in literature, and their letters and conversation stimulated her to renewed exertion.

Yet she had never stooped to conciliate popular prejudices, had never written a line which her conscience did not dictate and her religious convictions sanction; had bravely attacked some of the pet vices and shameless follies of society, and had never penned a page without a prayer for guidance from on High.

Now in her path rose God's Reaper, swinging his shining sickle, threatening to cut off and lay low her budding laurel wreath.

While she stood silent and motionless in the quiet library, the woman's soul was wrestling with God for permission to toil a little while longer on earth, to do some good for her race, and to assist in saving a darkened soul almost as dear to her as her own.

She never knew how long that struggle for life lasted; but when the prayer ended, and she lifted her face, the shadows and the sorrowful dread had passed away, and the old calm, the old sweet, patient smile reigned over pale, worn features.

Early in July, Felix's feeble health forced his mother to abandon her projected tour to the White Mountains; and in accordance with Dr. Howell's advice, Mr. Andrews removed his family to a seaside summer-place, which he had owned for some years, but rarely occupied, as his wife preferred Newport, Saratoga, and Nahant.

The house at the "Willows" was large and airy, the ceilings were high, windows wide, and a broad piazza, stretching across the front, was shaded by two aged and enormous willows, that stood on either side of the steps, and gave a name to the place.

The fresh matting on the floors, the light cane sofa
and chairs, the white muslin curtains and newly-
painted green blinds imparted an appearance of delicious coolness and repose to the rooms; and while
not one bright-hued painting was visible, the walls
were hung with soft, gray, misty engravings of Landseer's pictures, framed in carved ebony and rosewood
and oak.

The gilded splendor of the Fifth Avenue house was
left behind; here simplicity and quiet comfort held
sway. Even the china wore no glitter, but was enam-
elled with green wreaths of vine-leaves; and the vases
held only plumy ferns, fresh and dewy.

Low salt meadow-lands extended east and west,
waving fields of corn stretched northward, and the
slight knoll on which the building stood sloped
smoothly down to the ever-moaning, foam-fretted
bosom of the blue Atlantic.

To the governess and her pupils the change from
New York heat and bustle to seaside rest, was welcome and delightful; and during the long July days,
when the strong ocean breeze tossed aside the willow
boughs, and swept through the rustling blinds, and
lifted the hair on Edna's hot temples, she felt as if she
had indeed taken a new lease on life.

For several weeks her book had been announced as
in press, and her publishers printed most flattering cir-
culars, which heightened expectation, and paved the
way for its favorable reception. Save the first chapter, rejected by Mr. Manning long before, no one had
seen the MS.; and while the reading public was on the
qui vive, the author was rapidly maturing the plot of a
second work.

Finally, the book was bound; editors' copies winged
their way throughout the country; the curious eagerly
supplied themselves with the latest publication; and
Edna's destiny as an author hung in the balance.

It was with strange emotions that she handled the
copy sent to her, for it seemed indeed a part of herself. She knew that her own heart was throbbing in

its pages, and wondered whether the great world-pulses would beat in unison.

Instead of a preface she had quoted on the title-page those pithy lines in "Aurora Leigh":

> "My critic Belfair wants a book
> Entirely different, which will sell and live ;
> A striking book, yet not a startling book—
> The public blames originalities.
> You must not pump spring-water unawares
> Upon a gracious public full of nerves—
> Good things, not subtle—new, yet orthodox ;
> As easy reading as the dog-eared page
> That's fingered by said public fifty years,
> Since first taught spelling by its grandmother,
> And yet a revelation in some sort :
> That's hard, my critic Belfair!"

Now, as Edna nestled her fingers among the pages of her book, a tear fell and moistened them, and the unvoiced language of her soul was, "Grandpa ! do you keep close enough to me to read my book? Oh ! do you like it ? are you satisfied ? Are you proud of your poor little Pearl ?"

The days were tediously long while she waited in suspense for the result of the weighing in editors' sanctums, for the awful verdict of the critical Sanhedrim. A week dragged itself away ; and the severity of the decree might have entitled it to one of those slips of blue paper upon which Frederick the Great required his courts to inscribe their sentences of death. Enda learned the full import of the words :

> "He that writes,
> Or makes a feast, more certainly invites
> His judges than his friends ; there's not a guest
> But will find something wanting or ill-drest."

Newspapers pronounced her book a failure. Some sneered in a gentlemanly manner, employing polite phraseology ; others coarsely caricatured it. Many were insulted by its incomprehensible erudition ; a few growled at its shallowness. To-day there was a hint at plagiarism; to-morrow an outright, wholesale theft was asserted. Now she was a pedant; and then a sciolist. Reviews poured in upon her thick and fast; all found grievous faults, but no two reviewers settled on the same error. What one seemed disposed to consider almost laudable the other denounced violently. One eminently shrewd, lynx-eyed editor discovered that two of her characters were stolen from a book which Edna had never seen; and another, equally ingenious and penetrating, found her entire plot in a work of which she had never heard; while a third, shocked at her pedantry, indignantly assured her readers that they had been imposed upon, that the learning was all " picked up from encyclopædias"; whereat the young author could not help laughing heartily, and wondered why, if her learning had been so easily gleaned, her irate and insulted critics did not follow her example.

The book was for many days snubbed, buffeted, brow-beaten; and the carefully-woven tapestry was torn into shreds and trampled upon; and it seemed that the patiently scupltured shrine was overturned and despised and desecrated.

Edna was astonished. She knew that her work was not perfect, but she was equally sure that it was not contemptible. She was surprised rather than mortified, and was convinced, from the universal howling, that she had wounded more people than she dreamed were vulnerable.

She felt that the impetuosity and savageness of the attacks must necessitate a recoil; and though it was difficult to be patient under such circumstances, she waited quietly, undismayed by the clamor.

Meantime the book sold rapidly, the publishers could scarcely supply the demand; and at last Mr. Manning's Magazine appeared, and the yelping pack of Dandie Dinmont's pets—Auld Mustard and little Mustard, Auld Pepper and Little Pepper, young Mustard and Young Pepper, stood silent and listened to the roar of the lion.

The review of Edna's work was headed by that calm
retort of Job to his self-complacent censors, " No
doubt but ye are the people, and wisdom shall die with
you "; and it contained a withering rebuke to those
who had so flippantly essayed to crush the young
writer.

Mr. Manning handled the book with the stern
impartiality which gave such value to his criticisms—
treating it as if it had been written by an utter stranger.

He analyzed it thoroughly ; and while pointing out
some serious errors which had escaped all eyes but his,
he bestowed upon a few passages praise which no
other American writer had ever received from him,
and predicted that they would live when those who
attempted to ridicule them were utterly forgotten in
their graves.

The young author was told that she had not
succeeded in her grand aim, because the subject was
too vast for the limits of a novel, and her acquaintance
with the mythologies of the world was not sufficiently
extensive or intimate. But she was encouraged to
select other themes more in accordance with the spirit
of the age in which she lived ; and the assurance was
given to her, that her writings were destined to exert
a powerful influence on her race. Some faults of style
were gravely reprimanded, some beauties most cordially eulogized and held up for the admiration of the
world.

Edna had as little literary conceit as personal vanity;
she saw and acknowledged the errors pointed out by
Mr. Manning, and resolved to avoid them in future.
She felt that some objections urged against her book
were valid, but knew that she was honest and earnest
in her work, and could not justly be accused of trifling.

Gratefully and joyfully she accepted Mr. Manning's
verdict, and turned her undivided attention upon her
new manuscript.

While the critics snarled, the mass of readers warmly
approved ; and many who did not fully appreciate all
her arguments and illustrations, were at least clear-eyed

enough to perceive that it was their misfortune, not her fault.

Gradually the book took firm hold on the affections of the people; and a few editors came boldly to the rescue, and ably championed it.

During these days of trial, Edna could not avoid observing one humiliating fact, that saddened without embittering her nature. She found that instead of sympathizing with her, she received no mercy from authors, who, as a class, out-Heroded Herod in their denunciations, and left her little room to doubt that—

> "Envy's a sharper spur than pay,
> And unprovoked 'twill court the fray;
> No author ever spared a brother;
> Wits are gamecocks to one another."

CHAPTER XXX.

"Miss Earl, you promised that as soon as I finished the 'Antiquary' you would read me a description of the spot which Sir Walter Scott selected for the scene of his story. We have read the last chapter; now please remember your promise."

"Felix, in your hunger for books you remind me of the accounts given of cormorants. The 'Antiquary' ought to satisfy you for the present, and furnish food for thought that would last at least till to-morrow; still, if you exact an immediate fulfillment of my promise, I am quite ready to comply."

Edna took from her workbasket a new and handsomely illustrated volume, and read Bertram's graphic description of Auchmithie and the coast of Forfarshire.

Finding that her pupils were deeply interested in the "Fisher Folk," she read on and on; and when she began the pathetic story of the widow at Prestonpans, Hattie's eyes widened with wonder, and Felix's were dim with tears:

"We kent then that we micht look across the sea; but ower the waters would never blink the een that made sunshine around our hearths; ower the waters would never come the voices that were mair delightfu' than the music o' the simmer winds, when the leaves gang dancing till they sang. My story, sir, is dune. I hae nae mair tae tell. Sufficient and suffice it till say, that there was great grief at the Pans—Rachel weeping for her weans, and wouldna be comforted. The windows were darkened, and the air was heavy wi' sighin' and sabbin'."

The governess closed the book, laid it back in her basket, and raising the lid of the piano, she sang that sad, wailing lyric of Kingsley's, "The Three Fishers."

It was one of those rare and royal afternoons late in August, when summer, conscious that her reign is well-nigh ended, gathers all her gorgeous drapery, and proudly robes the world in regal pomp and short-lived splendor. Pearly cloud islets, with silver strands, clustered in the calm blue of the upper air ; soft, salmon-hued cumulus masses sailed solemnly along the eastern horizon—atmospheric ships freighted in the tropics with crystal showers for thirsty fields and parched meadows—with snow crowns for Icelandic mountain brows, and shrouds of sleet for mouldering masts, tossed high and helpless on desolate Arctic cliffs. Restless gulls flashed their spotless wings, as they circled and dipped in the shining waves ; and in the magic light of evening, the swelling canvas of a distant sloop glittered like plate-glass smitten with sunshine. A strong, steady, southern breeze curled and crested the beautiful, bounding billows, over which a fishing-smack danced like a gilded bubble ; and as the aged willows bowed their heads, it whispered messages from citron, palm, and orange groves, gleaming far, far away under the white fire of the Southern Crown.

Strange tidings these " winged winds " waft over sea and land ; and to-day, listening to low tones that traveled to her from Le Bocage, Edna looked out over the ever-changing, wrinkled face of the ocean, and fell into a reverie.

Silence reigned in the sitting-room ; Hattie fitted a new tarlatan dress on her doll, and Felix was dreaming of Prestonpans.

The breeze swept over the cluster of Tuscan jasmine and the tall, snowy phlox nodding in the green vase on the table, and shook the muslin curtains till light and shadow chased each other like waves over the noble Longhi engraving of Raphael's " Vision of Ezekiel," which hung just above the piano. After a while Felix took his chin from the window-sill, and his

eyes from the sparkling, tossing water, and his gaze
sought the beloved countenance of his governess.

> " The mouth with steady sweetness set,
>   And eyes conveying unaware
>   The distant hint of some regret
>   That harbored there."

Her dress was of white mull, with lace gathered
around the neck and wristbands ; a delicate fringy
fern leaf was caught by the cameo that pinned the
lace collar, and around the heavy coil of hair at the
back of her head, Hattie had twined a spray of scarlet
tecoma.

Save the faint red on her thin, flexible lips, her face
was as stainless as that of the Hebrew Mary, in a
carved ivory " Descent from the Cross," which hung
over the mantelpiece.

As the boy watched her he thought the beautiful
eyes were larger and deeper, and burned more brilliantly than ever before ; and the violet shadows
beneath them seemed to widen day by day, telling of
hard study and continued vigils. Pale and peaceful,
patiently sad, without a trace of bitterness or harshness,
her countenance might have served as a model for
some which Ary Scheffer dimly saw in his rapt mus-
ings over " Wilhelm Meister."

" Oh ! yonder comes mamma and—Uncle Grey !
No ; that is not my uncle Grey. Who can it be ? It
is—Sir Roger !"

Hattie ran out to meet her mother, who had been to
New York ; and Felix frowned, took up his crutches,
and put on his hat.

Edna turned and went to her own room, and in a
few moments Hattie brought her a package of letters,
and a message from Mrs. Andrews, desiring her to
come back to the sitting-room.

Glancing over the directions the governess saw that
all the letters were from strangers, except one from
Mrs. Murray, which she eagerly opened. The contents
were melancholy and unexpected. Mr. Hammond

had been very ill for weeks, was not now in immediate danger, but was confined to his room ; and the physicians thought that he would never be well again. He had requested Mrs. Murray to write, and beg Edna to come to him, and remain in his house. Mrs. Powell was in Europe with Gertrude and Gordon, and the old man was alone in his home, Mrs. Murray and her son having taken care of him thus far. At the bottom of the page Mr. Hammond had scrawled almost illegibly : "My dear child, I need you. Come to me at once."

Mrs. Murray had added a postscript to tell her that if she would telegraph them upon what day she could arrange to start, Mr. Murray would come to New York for her.

Edna put the letter out of sight, and girded herself for a desperate battle with her famishing heart, which bounded wildly at the tempting joys spread almost within reach. The yearning to go back to the dear old parsonage, to the revered teacher, to cheer and brighten his declining days, and, above all, to see Mr. Murray's face, to hear his voice once more, oh! the temptation was strong indeed, and the cost of resistance bitter beyond precedent. Having heard incidentally of the reconciliation that had taken place, she knew why Mr. Hammond so earnestly desired her presence in a house where Mr. Murray now spent much of his time; she knew all the arguments, all the pleadings to which she must listen, and she dared not trust her heart.

"Enter not into temptation!" was the warning which she uttered again and again to her own soul ; and though she feared the pastor would be pained, she felt that he would not consider her ungrateful—knew that his warm, tender heart would understand hers.

Though she had always studiously endeavored to expel Mr. Murray from her thoughts, there came hours when his image conquered ; when the longing, the intense wish to see him was overmastering ; when she felt that she would give ten years of her life for one long look into his face, or for a picture of him.

Now, when she had only to say, "Come!" and he would be with her, she sternly denied her starving heart, and instead of bread gave it stones and serpents.

She took her pen to answer the letter, but a pang which she had learned to understand told her that she was not now strong enough; and, swallowing some medicine which Dr. Howell had prescribed, she snatched up a crimson scarf and went down to the beach.

The serenity of her countenance had broken up in a fearful tempest, and her face writhed as she hurried along to overtake Felix. Just now she dreaded to be alone, and yet the only companionship she could endure was that of the feeble cripple, whom she had learned to love, as woman can love only when all her early idols are in the dust.

"Wait for me, Felix!"

The boy stopped, turned, and limped back to meet her, for there was a strange, pleading intonation in her mournfully sweet voice.

"What is the matter, Miss Earl? You look troubled."

"I only want to walk with you, for I feel lonely this evening."

"Miss Earl, have you seen Sir Roger Percival?"

"No, no; why should I see him? Felix, my darling, my little brother! do not call me Miss Earl any longer. Call me Edna. Ah, child! I am utterly alone; I must have somebody to love me. My heart turns to you."

She passed her arm around the boy's shoulders and leaned against him, while he rested on his crutches and looked up at her with fond pride.

"Edna! I have wanted to call you so since the day I first saw you. You know very well that I love you better than every thing else in the world. If there is any good in me, I shall have to thank you for it; if ever I am useful, it will be your work. I am wicked still; but I never look at you without trying to be a better boy. You do not need me—you who are so great and gifted; whose writings everybody reads and admires; whose name is already famous. Oh! you can not need any one, and, least of all, a poor little helpless cripple! who can only worship you, and love the sound of your voice better than all the music that ever was played! If I thought that you, Miss Earl—whose book all the world is talking about—if I thought you really cared for me—Oh, Edna! Edna! I believe my heart would be too big for my poor little body!"

"Felix, we need each other. Do you suppose I would have followed you out here, if I did not prefer your society to that of others?"

"Something has happened since you sang the 'Three Fishers' and sat looking out of the window an hour ago. Your face has changed. What is it, Edna? Can't you trust me?"

"Yes. I received a letter which troubles me. It announces the feeble health of a dear and noble friend, who writes begging me to come to him, and nurse and remain with him as long as he lives. You need not start and shiver so—I am not going. I shall not leave you; but it distresses me to know that he has asked an impossible thing. Now you can understand why I did not wish to be alone."

She leaned her cheek down on the boy's head, and both stood silent, looking over the wide heaving waste of immemorial waters.

A glowing orange sky overarched an orange ocean, which slowly became in turn ruby, and rose, and violet, and pearly gray, powdered with a few dim stars. As the rising waves broke along the beach, the stiffening breeze bent the spray till it streamed like silvery plumes; and the low musical murmur swelled to a monotonous moan, that seemed to come over the darkening waters like wails of the lost from some far, far "isles of the sea."

Awed by the mysterious solemnity which ever broods over the ocean, Felix slowly repeated that dirge of Tennyson's, "Break, break, break!" and

when he commenced the last verse, Edna's voice, low
and quivering, joined his.

Out of the eastern sea, up through gauzy cloud-
bars, rose the moon, round, radiant, almost full, shaking off the mists, burnishing the waves with a ghostly
lustre.

The wind rose and fluttered Edna's scarlet scarf
like a pirate's pennon, and the low moan became a
deep, sullen, ominous mutter.

"There will be a gale before daylight ; it is brewing
down yonder at the southwest.   The wind has veered
since we came out.   There! did you notice what a
savage snort there was in that last gust ?"

Felix pointed to the distant water-line, where now
and then a bluish flash of lightning showed the teeth
of the storm raging far away under southern constellations, extinguishing for a time the golden flame of
Canopus.

"Yes, you must go in, Felix.   I ought not to have
kept you out so long."

Reluctantly she turned from the beach, and they
had proceeded but a few yards in the direction of the
house when they met Mrs. Andrews and her guest.

"Felix, my son !   Too late, too late for you ! Come
in with me.   Miss Earl, as you are so fond of the
beach, I hope you will show Sir Roger all its beauties.
I commit him to your care."

She went toward the house with her boy, and as Sir
Roger took Edna's hand and bent forward, looking
eagerly into her face, she saw a pained and startled
expression cross his own.

"Miss Earl, did you ;receive a letter from me written immediately after the perusal of your book ?"

"Yes, Sir Roger, and your cordial congratulations
and flattering opinion were, I assure you, exceedingly
gratifying, especially as you were among the first who
found anything in it to praise."

"You have no idea with what intense interest I
have watched its reception at the hands of the press,
and I think the shallow, flippant criticisms were

almost as nauseous to me as they must have been to you. Your book has had a fierce struggle with these self-consecrated, red-handed, high-priests of the literary Yama ; but its success is now established, and I bring you news of its advent in England, where it has been republished. You can well afford to exclaim with Drayton :

> 'We that calumnious critic may aschew,
>   That blasteth all things with his poisoned breath.
> Detracting what laboriously we do
>   Only with that which he but idly saith.'

The numerous assaults made upon you reminded me constantly of the remarks of Blackwood a year or two since : ' Formerly critics were as scarce and formidable, and consequently as well known as mastiffs in a country parish ; but now no luckless traveller can show his face in a village without finding a whole pack yelping at his heels.' Fortunately, Miss Earl, though they show their teeth, and are evidently anxious to mangle, they are not strong enough to do much harm. Have you answered any of these attacks ?"

"No, sir. Had I ever commenced filling the sieve of the Danaides, I should have time for nothing else. If you will not regard me as exceedingly presumptious, and utterly ridiculous by the comparison, I will add that, with reference to unfavorable criticism, I have followed the illustrious example of Buffon, who said, when critics opened their batteries, ' *Je n'ai jamais répondu à aucune critique, et je garderai le même silence sur celle-ci.*' "

"But, my dear Miss Earl, I see that you have been accused of plagiarizing. Have you not refuted this statement ?"

"Again I find Buffon's words rising to answer for me, as they did for himself under similar circumstances, ' *Il vaut mieux laisser ces mauvaises gens dans l'incertitude !*' Moreover, sir, I have no right to complain, for if it is necessary in well-regulated municipalities to have inspectors of all other commodities, why not of

books also! I do not object to the rigid balancing—I
wish to pass for no more than I weigh; but I do feel
inclined to protest sometimes, when I see myself denounced simply because the scales are too small to hold
what is ambitiously piled upon them, and my book is
either thrown out pettishly, or whittled and scraped
down to fit the scales. The storm, Sir Roger, was very
severe at first—nay, it is not yet ended; but I hope, I
believe I shall weather it safely. If my literary bark
had proved unworthy, and sprung a leak and foundered,
it would only have shown that it did not deserve to
live; that it was better it should go down alone
and early, than when attempting to pilot others on the
rough unknown sea of letters. I can not agree with
you in thinking that critics are more abundant now
than formerly. More books are written, and consequently more are tabooed; but the history of literature proves that, from the days of Congreve,

'Critics to plays for the same end resort
That surgeons wait on trials in a court;
For innocence condemned they've no respect
Provided they've a body to dissect.'

After all, it cannot be denied that some of the best
portions of Byron's and Pope's writings were scourged
out of them by the scorpion thongs of adverse criticism; and the virulence of the *Xenien Sturm* waged by
Schiller and Goethe against the army of critics who assaulted them, attests the fact that even appreciative
Germany sometimes nods in her critical councils. Certainly I have had my share of scourging; for my
critics have most religiously observed the warning of
' Spare the rod and spoil the child '; and henceforth if
my writings are not model, well-behaved, puritanical
literary children, my censors must be exonerated from
all blame, and I will give testimony in favor of the
zeal and punctuality of these self-elected officials of
the public whipping-post. The canons have not varied
one iota for ages; if authors merely reflect the ordinary normal aspect of society, without melodramatic

exaggeration or ludicrous caricature, they are voted trite, humdrum, commonplace, and live no longer than their contemporaries. If they venture a step in advance, and attempt to lead, to lift up the masses, or to elevate the standard of thought and extend its range, they are scoffed at as pedants, and die unhonored prophets; and just as the tomb is sealed above them, people peer more closely into their books, and whisper, 'There is something here after all; great men have been among us.' The next generation chants pæans, and casts chaplets on the graves, and so the world rings with the names of ghosts, and fame pours generous libations to appease the manes of genius slaughtered on the altar of criticism. Once Schiller said, 'Against public stupidity the gods themselves are powerless.' Since then, that same public lifted him to the pedestal of a demi-god ; now all Germany proudly claims him; and who shall tell us where sleep his long-forgotten critics ? Such has been the history of the race since Homer groped through vine-clad Chios, and poor Dante was hunted from city to city. If the great hierarchs of literature are sometimes stabbed while ministering at the shrine, what can we humble acolytes expect but to be scourged entirely out of the temple ? We all get our dues at last; for yonder, among the stars, Astræa laughs at man's valuations, and shakes her infallible balance and re-weighs us."

She had crossed her arms on the low stone wall that enclosed the lawn, and bending forward, the moon shone full on her face, and her eyes and her thoughts went out to sea, Her companion stood watching her countenance, and some strange expression there recalled to his mind that vivid description :

"And then she raised her head, and upward cast
Wild looks from *homeless eyes*, whose liquid light
Gleamed out between deep folds of blue-black hair,
As gleam twin lakes between the purple peaks
Of deep Parnassus, at the mournful moon."

After a short silence, Sir Roger said :

"Miss Earl, I can find no triumph written on your features, and I doubt whether you realize how very proud your friends are of your success."

"As yet, sir, it is not assured. My next book will determine my *status* in literature; and I have too much to accomplish—I have achieved too little, to pause and look back, and pat my own shoulder, and cry, *Io triumphe!* I am not so indifferent as you seem to imagine. Praise gratifies, and censure pains me; but I value both as mere gauges of my work, indexing the amount of good I may or may not hope to effect. I wish to be popular—that is natural, and, surely, pardonable; but I desire it not as an end, but as a means to an end—usefulness to my fellow-creatures;

'And whether crowned or crownless, when I fall,
It matters not, so as God's work is done.'

I love my race, I honor my race; I believe that human nature, sublimated by Christianity, is capable of attaining nobler heights than pagan philosophers and infidel seers ever dreamed of. And because my heart yearns toward my fellow-creatures, I want to clasp one hand in the warm throbbing palm of sinful humanity, and with the other hold up the lamp that God gave me to carry through this world, and so struggle onward, heavenward, with this generation of men and women. I claim no clear Uriel vision, now and then I stumble and grope; but at least I try to keep my little lamp trimmed, and I am not so blind as some, who reel and stagger in the Maremme of crime and fashionable vice. As a pilgrim toiling through a world of sinful temptation, and the night of time where the stars are often shrouded, I cry to those beyond and above me, 'Hold high your lights, that I may see my way!' and to those behind and below me, 'Brothers! sisters! come on, come up!' Ah! these steeps of human life are hard enough to climb when each shares his light and divides his neighbor's grievous burden. God help us all to help one another! Mecca pilgrims stop in the Valley of Muna to stone the Devil; sometimes I fear that in the Muna of life we only stone each other and martyr Stephen. Last week I read a lecture on architecture, and since then I find myself repeating one of the passages: 'And therefore, lastly and chiefly, you must love the creatures to whom you minister, your fellowmen; for if you do not love them, not only will you be little interested in the passing events of life, but in all your gazing at humanity, you will be apt to be struck only by outside form, and not by expression. It is only kindness and tenderness which will ever enable you to see what beauty there is in the dark eyes that are sunk with weeping, and in the paleness of those fixed faces which the earth's adversity has compassed about, till they shine in their patience like dying watch-fires through twilight.' In some sort I think we are all mechanics—moral architects, designing as apprentices on the sands of time that, which, as master builders, we shall surely erect on the jasper pavements of eternity. So let us all heed the noble words."

She seemed talking rather to herself, or to the surging sea where her eyes rested, than to Sir Roger : and as he noticed the passionless pallor of her face, he sighed, and put his hands on hers.

"Come, walk with me on the beach, and let me tell you why I came back to New York, instead of sailing from Canada, as I once intended."

A half hour elapsed, and Mrs. Andrews, who was sitting alone on the piazza, saw the governess coming slowly up the walk. As she ascended the steps, the lady of the house exclaimed :

"Where is Sir Roger ?"

"He has gone."

"Well, my dear! Pardon me for anticipating you, but as I happen to know all about the affair, accept my congratulations. You are the luckiest woman in America."

Mrs. Andrews put her arm around Edna's waist, but something in the countenance astonished and disappointed her.

" Mrs. Andrews, Sir Roger sails to-morrow for England. He desired me to beg that you would excuse
him for not coming in to bid you good-bye."

" Sails to-morrow ! When does he return to
America ?"

" Probably never."

" Edna Earl, you are an idiot ! You may have any
amount of genius, but certainly not one grain of common sense ! I have no patience with you ! I had set
my heart on seeing you his wife."

" But, unfortunately for me, I could not set my
heart on him. I am very sorry. I wish we had never
met, for indeed I like Sir Roger. But it is useless to
discuss what is past and irremediable. Where are the
children ?"

" Asleep, I suppose. After all, show me ' a gifted
woman, a genius,' and I will show you a fool."

Mrs. Andrews bit her lip, and walked off; and Edna
went up-stairs to Felix's room.

The boy was sitting by the open window, watching
gray clouds trailing across the moon, checkering the
face of the mighty deep, now with shadow, now with
sheen. So absorbed was he in his communing with
the mysterious spirit of the sea, that he did not notice
the entrance of the governess until he felt her hand
on his shoulder.

" Ah ! have you come at last ? Edna, I was wishing
for you a little while ago, for as I sat looking over the
waves, a pretty thought came into my mind, and I
want to tell you about it. Last week, if you remember, we were reading about Antony and Cleopatra :
and just now, while I was watching a large star yonder
making a shining track across the sea, a ragged, hungry-
looking cloud crept up, and nibbled at the edge of the
star, and swallowed it ! And I called the cloud Cleopatra swallowing her pearl !"

Edna looked wonderingly into the boy's bright eyes,
and drew his head to her shoulder.

" My dear Felix, are you sure you never heard that
same thought read or quoted ? It is beautiful, but this

is not the first time I have heard it. Think, my dear little boy; try to remember where you saw it written."

"Indeed, Edna, I never saw it anywhere. I am sure I never heard it either; for it seemed quite new when it bounced into my mind just now. Who else ever thought of it?"

"Mr. Stanyan Bigg, an English poet, whose writings are comparatively unknown in this country. His works I have never seen, but I read a review of them in an English book, which contained many extracts; and that pretty metaphor which you used just now, was among them."

"Is that review in our library?"

"No, I am sure it is not; but you may have seen the lines quoted somewhere else."

"Edna, I am very certain I never heard it before. Do you recollect how it is written in the Englishman's poem? If you can repeat it, I shall know instantly, because my memory is very good."

"I think I can give you one stanza, for I read it when I was in great sorrow, and it made an impression upon me:

'The clouds, like grim black faces, come and go;
    One tall tree stretches up against the sky;
It lets the rain through, like a trembling hand
    Pressing thin fingers on a watery eye.
The moon came, but shrank back, like a young girl
    Who has burst in upon funereal sadness;
One star came—Cleopatra-like, the Night
    Swallowed this one pearl in a fit of madness!'

"Well, Felix, you are a truthful boy, and I can trust you!"

"I never heard the poetry before, and I tell you, Edna, the idea is just as much mine as it is Mr. Bigg's!"

"I believe you. Such coincidences are rare, and people are very loth to admit the possibility; but that they do occasionally occur, I have no doubt. Perhaps some day when you write a noble poem, and become a

shining light in literature, you may tell this circumstance to the world ; and bid it beware how it idly
throws the charge of plagiarism against the set teeth
of earnest, honest workers."

"Edna, I look at my twisted feet sometimes, and
I feel thankful that it is my body, not my mind, that
is deformed. If I am ever able to tell the world anything, it will be how much I owe you ; for I trace all
holy thoughts and pretty ideas to you and your music
and your writings."

They sat there awhile in silence, watching heavy
masses of cloud darken sea and sky ; and then Felix
lifted his face from Edna's shoulder, and asked timidly :

"Did you send Sir Roger away ?"

"He goes to Europe, to-morrow, I believe."

"Poor Sir Roger! I am sorry for him. I told
mamma you never thought of him ; that you loved
nothing but books and flowers and music."

"How do you know that ?"

"I have watched you, and when he was with you I
never saw that great shining light in your eyes, or that
strange moving of your lower lip, that always shows
me when you are really glad ; as you were that Sunday when the music was so grand ; or that rainy morning when we saw the pictures of the 'Two Marys at
the Sepulchre.' I almost hated poor Sir Roger, because I was afraid he might take you to England, and
then, what would have become of me ? Oh! the world
seems so different, so beautiful, so peaceful, as long as
I have you with me. Everybody praises you, and is
proud of you, but nobody loves you, as I do."

He took her hand, passed it over his cheek and forehead, and kissed it tenderly.

"Felix, do you feel at all sleepy ?"

"Not at all. Tell me something more about the
animalcula that cause that phosphorescence yonder—
making the top of each wave look like a fringe of fire.
Is it true that they are little round things that look
like jelly—so small that it takes one hundred and

seventy, all in a row, to make an inch ; and that a wineglass can hold millions of them ?"

" I do not feel well enough to-night to talk about animalcula. I am afraid I shall have one of those terrible attacks I had last winter. Felix, please don't go to bed for a while at least ; and if you hear me call, come to me quickly. I must write a letter before I sleep. Sit here, will you, till I come back ?"

For the first time in her life she shrank from the thought of suffering alone, and felt the need of a human presence.

" Edna, let me call mamma. I saw this afternoon that you were not well."

" No, it may pass off ; and I want nobody about me but you."

Only a narrow passage divided her room from his ; and leaving the door open, she sat down before her desk to answer Mr. Hammond's appeal.

As the night wore on, the wind became a gale; the fitful, bluish glare of the lightning showed fearful ranks of ravenous waves scowling over each others' shoulders; a roar as of universal thunder shook the shore, and in the coral-columned cathedral of the great deep, wrathful ocean played a wild and weird fugue.

Felix waited patiently, listening amid the dead diapason of wind and wave, for the voice of his governess. But no sound came from the opposite room ; and at last, alarmed by the ominous silence, he took up his crutches and crossed the passage.

The muslin curtains, blown from their ribbon fastenings, streamed like signals of distress on the breath of the tempest, and the lamplight flickered and leaped to the top of its glass chimney.

On the desk lay two letters addressed respectively to Mr. Hammond and Mrs. Murray, and beside them were scattered half a dozen notes from unknown correspondents, asking for the autograph and photograph of the young author.

Edna knelt on the floor, hiding her face in the arms which were crossed on the lid of the desk.

The cripple came close to her and hesitated a moment, then touched her lightly :

"Edna, are you ill, or are you only praying?"

She lifted her head instantly, and the blanched, weary face reminded the boy of a picture of Gethsemane, which, having once seen, he could never recall without a shudder.

"Forgive me, Felix ! I forgot that you were waiting—forgot that I asked you to sit up."

She rose, took the thin little form in her arms, and whispered :

"I am sorry I kept you up so long. The pain has passed away. I think the danger is over now. Go back to your room, and go to sleep as soon as possible. Good-night, my darling."

They kissed each other and separated ; but the fury of the tempest forbade all idea of sleep, and thinking of the " Fisher Folk " exposed to its wrath, governess and pupil committed them to Him who calmed the Galilean gale.

> "The sea was all a boiling, seething froth,
> And God Almighty's guns were going off,
> And the land trembled."

CHAPTER XXXI.

THE Greek myth concerning Demophoön embodies a valuable truth, which the literary career of Edna Earl was destined to exemplify. Harsh critics, like disguised Ceres, plunged the young author into the flames; and fortunately for her, as no short-sighted, loving Metanira snatched her from the fiery ordeal, she ultimately obtained the boon of immortality. Her regular contributions to the magazine enhanced her reputation, and broadened the sphere of her influence.

Profoundly impressed by the conviction that she held her talent in trust, she worked steadily, looking neither to the right nor left, but keeping her eyes fixed upon that day when she should be called to render an account to Him who would demand his own with interest. Instead of becoming flushed with success, she grew daily more cautious, more timid, lest inadvertence or haste should betray her into errors. Consequently as the months rolled away, each magazine article seemed an improvement on the last, and lifted her higher in public favor. The blacksmith's grandchild had become a power in society.

Feeling that a recluse life would give her only partial glimpses of that humanity which she wished to study, she moved in the circle of cultivated friends who now eagerly stretched out their arms to receive her; and "keeping herself unspotted from the world," she earnestly scutinized social leprosy, and calmly watched the tendency of American thought and feeling.

Among philosophic minds she saw an inclination to

ignore the principles of such systems as Sir William Hamilton's, and to embrace the modified and subtle materialism of Buckle and Mill, or the gross atheism of Buchner and Moleschott. Positivism in philosophy and pre-Raphælitism in art, confronted her in the ranks of the literary,—lofty idealism seemed trodden down—pawed over by Carlyle's "Monster Utilitaria."

When she turned to the next social stratum she found altars of mammon—groves of Bael, shining Schoe Dagon—set up by business men and women of fashion. Society appeared intent only upon reviving the offering to propitiate evil spirits; and sometimes it seemed thickly sprinkled with very thinly disguised refugee Yezidees, who, in the East, openly worship the Devil.

Statesmen were almost extinct in America—a mere corporal's guard remained, battling desperately to save the stabbed constitution from howling demagogues and fanatics, who raved and ranted where Washington, Webster, and Calhoun had once swayed a free and happy people. The old venerated barriers and well-guarded outposts, which decorum and true womanly modesty had erected on the frontiers of propriety, were swept away in the crevasse of *sans souci* manners that threatened to inundate the entire land; and latitudinarianism in dress and conversation was rapidly reducing the sexes to an equality, dangerous to morals and subversive of all chivalric respect for woman.

A double-faced idol, fashion and flirtation, engrossed the homage of the majority of females, while a few misguided ones, weary of the inanity of the mass of womanhood and desiring to effect a reform, mistook the sources of the evil and, rushing to the opposite extreme, demanded *power*, which as a *privilege* they already possessed, but as a *right* could not extort.

A casual glance at the surface of society seemed to justify Burke's conclusion, that "this earth is the bedlam of our system"; but Edna looked deeper, and

found much that encouraged her, much that warmed
and bound her sympathies to her fellow-creatures.
Instead of following the beaten track she struck out a
new path, and tried the plan of denouncing the of-
fence, not the offender; of attacking the sin while she
pitied the sinner.

Ruthlessly she assaulted the darling follies, the pet,
velvet-masked vices that society had adopted, and
called the reading world to a friendly parley; demanding that men and women should pause and reflect in
their mad career. Because she was earnest and not
bitter, because the white banner of Christian charity
floated over the conference ground, because she showed
so clearly that she loved the race whose recklessness
grieved her, because her rebukes were free from scorn,
and written rather in tears than gall, people turned
their heads and stopped to listen.

So it came to pass that finally, after toiling over
many obstacles, she reached the vine-clad valley of
Eshcol.

Each day brought her noble fruitage, as letters
came from all regions of the country, asking for advice
and assistance in little trials of which the world knew
nothing. Over the young of her own sex she held a
singular sway; and orphan girls of all ranks and ages
wrote of their respective sorrows and difficulties, and
requested her kind counsel. To these her womanly
heart turned yearningly; and she accepted their affectionate confidence as an indication of her proper circle
of useful labor.

Believing that the intelligent, refined, modest Christian women of the United States were the real custodians of national purity, and the sole agents who
could successfully arrest the tide of demoralization
breaking over the land, she addressed herself to the
wives, mothers, and daughters of America; calling
upon them to smite their false gods, and purify the
shrines at which they worshipped. Jealously she contended for every woman's right which God and nature
had decreed the sex. The right to be learned, wise,

noble, useful, in woman's divinely limited sphere; the right to influence and exalt the circle in which she moved; the right to mount the sanctified bema of her own quiet hearthstone; the right to modify and direct her husband's opinions, if he considered her worthy and competent to guide him; the right to make her children ornaments to their nation, and a crown of glory to their race; the right to advise, to plead, to pray; the right to make her desk a Delphi, if God so permitted; the right to be all that the phrase "noble, Christian woman" means. But not the right to vote; to harangue from the hustings; to trail her heaven-born purity through the dust and mire of political strife; to ascend the rostra of statesmen, whither she may send a worthy husband, son, or brother, but whither she can never go, without disgracing all woman-hood.

Edna was conscious of the influence she exerted, and ceaselessly she prayed that she might wield it aright. While aware of the prejudice that exists against liter-ary women, she endeavored to avoid the *outré* idiosyn-crasies that justly render so many of that class unpop-ular and ridiculous.

She felt that she was a target at which observers aimed random shafts; and while devoting herself to study, she endeavored to give due attention to the rules of etiquette, and the harmonious laws of the toilette.

The friendship between Mr. Manning and herself strengthened, as each learned more fully the character of the other; and an affectionate, confiding frankness marked their intercourse. As her popularity increased she turned to him more frequently for advice, for suc-cess only rendered her cautious; and day by day she weighed more carefully all that fell from her pen, dread-ing lest some error should creep into her writings and lead others astray.

In her publisher—an honorable, kind-hearted, and generous gentleman—she found a valued friend; and as her book sold extensively, the hope of a competency was realized, and she was soon relieved from the necessity of teaching. She was a pet with the reading public ; it became fashionable to lionize her ; her pictures and autographs were eagerly sought after ; and the little, barefooted Tennessee child had grown up to celebrity.

Sometimes, when a basket of flowers, or a handsome book, or a letter of thanks and cordial praise was received from an unknown reader, the young author was so overwhelmed with grateful appreciation of these little tokens of kindness and affection, that she wept over them, or prayed tremulously that she might make herself more worthy of the good opinion entertained of her by strangers.

Mr. Manning, whose cold, searching eye was ever upon her, could detect no exultation in her manner. She was earnestly grateful for every kind word uttered by her friends and admirers, for every favorable sentence penned about her writings ; but she seemed only gravely glad, and was as little changed by praise as she had been by severe animadversion. The sweet, patient expression still rested on her face, and her beautiful eyes beamed with the steady light of resignation rather than the starry sparkle of extravagant joy.

Sometimes when the editor missed her at the literary reunions, where her presence always contributed largely to the enjoyment of the evening, and sought her in the schoolroom, he was often surprised to find her seated beside Felix, reading to him or listening to his conversation with a degree of interest which she did not always offer to the celebrities who visited her.

Her power over the cripple was boundless. His character was as clay in her hands, and she was faithfully striving to model a noble, hallowed life ; for she believed that he was destined to achieve distinction, and fondly hoped to stamp upon his mind principles and aims that would fructify abundantly when she was silent in the grave.

Mrs. Andrews often told her that she was the only person who had ever controlled or influenced the boy

—that she could make him just what she pleased ; and she devoted herself to him, resolved to spare no toil in her efforts to correct the evil tendencies of his strong, obstinate, stormy nature.

His fondness for history, and for all that involved theories of government, led his governess to hope that at some future day he might recruit the depleted ranks of statesmen—that he might reflect lustre upon his country ; and with this trust spurring her ever on, she became more and more absorbed in her schemes for developing his intellect and sanctifying his heart. People wondered how the lovely woman, whom society flattered and fêted, could voluntarily shut herself up in a schoolroom, and few understood the sympathy which bound her so firmly to the broad-browed, sallow little cripple.

One December day, several months after their return from the seaside, Edna and Felix sat in the library. The boy had just completed Prescott's " Philip II.," and the governess had promised to read to him Schiller's " Don Carlos " and Goethe's " Egmont," in order to impress upon his memory the great actors of the Netherland revolution. She took up the copy of " Don Carlos," and crossing his arms on the top of his crutches, as was his habit, the pupil fixed his eyes on her face.

The reading had continued probably a half-hour, when Felix heard a whisper at the door, and, looking over his shoulder, saw a stranger standing on the threshold. He rose ; the movement attracted the attention of the governess, and, as she looked up, a cry of joy rang through the room. She dropped the book and sprang forward with open arms.

" Oh, Mrs. Murray ! dear friend !"

For some moments they stood locked in a warm embrace, and as Felix limped out of the room he heard his governess sobbing.

Mrs. Murray held the girl at arm's length, and as she looked at the wan, thin face, she exclaimed :

" My poor Edna ! my dear little girl ! why did not

you tell me you were ill? You are a mere ghost of
your former self. My child, why did you not come
home long ago? I should have been here a month
earlier, but was detained by Estelle's marriage."

Edna looked vacantly at her benefactress, and her
lips whitened as she asked:

"Did you say Estelle—was married?"

"Yes, my dear. She is now in New York with her
husband. They are going to Paris——"

"She married your——" The head fell forward on
Mrs. Murray's bosom, and as in a dream she heard the
answer:

"Estelle married that young Frenchman, Victor
De Sanssure, whom she met in Europe. Edna, what
is the matter? My child!"

She found that she could not rouse her, and in
great alarm called for assistance.

Mrs. Andrews promptly resorted to the remedies
advised by Dr. Howell; but it was long before Edna
fully recovered, and then she lay with her eyes closed,
and her hands clasped across her forehead.

Mrs. Murray sat beside the sofa weeping silently,
while Mrs. Andrews briefly acquainted her with the
circumstances attending former attacks. When the
latter was summoned from the room and all was quiet,
Edna looked up at Mrs. Murray, and tears rolled over
her cheeks as she said:

"I was so glad to see you, the great joy and the
surprise overcame me. I am not as strong as I used
to be in the old happy days at Le Bocage, but after a
little I shall be myself. It is only occasionally that I
have these attacks of faintness. Put your hand on my
forehead, as you did years ago, and let me think that I
am a little child again. Oh, the unspeakable happiness
of being with you once more!"

"Hush! do not talk now, you are not strong
enough!"

Mrs. Murray kissed her, and tenderly smoothed the
hair back from her blue-veined temples, where the blood
still fluttered irregularly.

For some minutes the girl's eyes wandered eagerly over her companion's countenance, tracing there the outlines of another and far dearer face, and finding a resemblance between mother and son which she had never noticed before. Then she closed her eyes again, and a half smile curved her trembling mouth, for the voice and the touch of the hand seemed indeed Mr. Murray's.

"Edna, I shall never forgive you for not writing to me, telling me frankly of your failing health."

"Oh! scold me as much as you please. It is a luxury to hear your voice even in reproof."

"I knew mischief would come of this separation from me. You belong to me, and I mean to have my own, and take proper care of you in future. The idea of your working yourself to a skeleton for the amusement of those who care nothing about you is simply preposterous, and I intend to put an end to such nonsense."

"Mrs. Murray, why have you not mentioned Mr. Hammond? I almost dread to ask about him."

"Because you do not deserve to hear from him. A grateful and affectionate pupil you have proved, to be sure. Oh, Edna! what has come over you, child? Are you so intoxicated with your triumphs that you utterly forget your old friends, who loved you when you were unknown to the world? At first I thought so. I believed that you were heartless, like all of your class, and completely wrapped up in ambitious schemes. But, my little darling, I see I wronged you. Your poor white face reproaches me for my injustice, and I feel that success has not spoiled you; that you are still my little Edna—my sweet child—my daughter. Be quiet now, and listen to me, and try to keep that flutter out of your lips. Mr. Hammond is no worse than he has been for many months, but he is very feeble, and can not live much longer. You know very well that he loves you tenderly, and he says he can not die in peace without seeing you once more. Every day, when I go over to the parsonage, his first question

is, ' Ellen, is she coming?—have you heard from her?'
I wish you could have seen him when St. Elmo was
reading your book to him. It was the copy you sent;
and when we read aloud the joint dedication to him
and to myself, the old man wept, and asked for his
glasses, and tried to read it, but could not. He—— "

Edna put out her hand with a mute gesture, which
her friend well understood, and she paused and was
silent; while the governess turned her face to the wall,
and wept softly, trying to compose herself.

Ten minutes passed, and she said: " Please go on
now, Mrs. Murray, and tell me all he said. You can
have no idea how I have longed to know what you all
at home thought of my little book. Oh! I have been
so hungry for home praise! I sent the very earliest
copies to you and to Mr. Hammond, and I thought it
so hard that you never mentioned them at all."

My dear, it was my fault, and I confess it freely.
Mr. Hammond, of course, could not write, but he
trusted to me to thank you in his name for the book
and the dedication. I was really angry with you for
not coming home when I wrote for you ; and I was
jealous of your book, and would not praise it, because
I knew you expected it. But because I was silent, do
you suppose I was not proud of my little girl? If you
could have seen the tears I shed over some of the
eulogies pronounced upon you, and heard all the ugly
words I could not avoid uttering against some of your
critics, you could not doubt my thorough appreciation
of your success. My dear, it is impossible to describe
Mr. Hammond's delight, as we read your novel to him.
Often he would say : 'St. Elmo, read that passage
again. I knew she was a gifted child, but I did not
expect that she would ever write such a book as this.'
When we read the last chapter he was completely
overcome, and said, repeatedly, ' God bless my little
Edna! It is a noble book, it will do good—much
good!' To me it seems almost incredible that the
popular author is the same little lame, crushed orphan,

whom I lifted from the grass at the railroad track, seven years ago."

Edna had risen, and was sitting on the edge of the sofa, with one hand supporting her cheek, and a tender, glad smile shining over her features, as she listened to the commendation of those dearer than all the world beside. Mrs. Murray watched her anxiously, and sighed, as she continued :

" If ever a woman had a worshipper, you certainly possess one in Huldah Reed. It would be amusing, if it were not touching, to see her bending in ecstasy over everything you write ; over every notice of you that meets her eye. She regards you as her model in all respects. You would be surprised at the rapidity with which she acquires knowledge. She is a pet of St. Elmo's, and repays his care and kindness with a devotion that makes people stare ; for you know my son is regarded as an ogre, and the child's affection for him seems incomprehensible to those who only see the rough surface of his character. She never saw a frown on his face or heard a harsh word from him, for he is strangely tender in his treatment of the little thing. Sometimes it makes me start when I hear her merry laugh ringing through the house, for the sound carries me far back into the past, when my own children romped and shouted at Le Bocage. You were always a quiet, demure, and rather solemn child ; but this Huldah is a gay little sprite. St. Elmo is so astonishingly patient with her, that Estelle accuses him of being in his dotage. Oh, Edna ! it would make you glad to see my son and that orphan child sitting together reading the Bible. Last week I found them in the library ; she was fast asleep with her head on his knee, and he sat with his open Bible in his hand. He is so changed in his manner that you would scarcely know him, and oh ! I am so happy and so grateful, I can never thank God sufficiently for the blessing !"

Mrs. Murray sobbed, and Edna bent her own head lower in her palms.

For some seconds both were silent. Mrs. Murray

seated herself close to the governess, and clasped her arms around her.

"Edna, why did you not tell me all? Why did you leave me to find out by accident that which should have been confided to me?"

The girl trembled, and a fiery spot burned on her cheeks as she pressed her forehead against Mrs. Murray's bosom, and said hastily:

"To what do you allude?"

"Why did you not tell me that my son loved you, and wished to make you his wife? I never knew what passed between you until about a month ago, and then I learned it from Mr. Hammond. Although I wondered why St. Elmo went as far as Chattanooga with you on your way North, I did not suspect any special interest, for his manner betrayed none when, after his return, he merely said that he found no one on the train to whose care he could commit you. Now I know all—know why you left 'Le Bocage'; and I know, too, that in God's hands you have been the instrument of bringing St. Elmo back to his duty—to his old noble self! Oh! Edna, my child! if you could know how I love and thank you! How I long to fold you in my arms—so! and call you my daughter! Edna Murray—St. Elmo's wife! Ah! how proud I shall be of my own daughter! When I took a little bruised, moaning, homespun-clad girl into my house, how little I dreamed that I was sheltering unawares the angel who was to bring back happiness to my son's heart, and peace to my own!"

She lifted the burning face, and kissed the quivering lips repeatedly.

"Edna, my brave darling! how could you resist St. Elmo's pleading? How could you tear yourself away from him? Was it because you feared that I would not willingly receive you as a daughter? Do not shiver so—answer me."

"Oh! do not ask me! Mrs. Murray spare me! This is a subject which I can not discuss with you."

" Why not, my child ? Can you not trust the mother of the man you love ?"

Edna unwound the arms that clasped her, and rising, walked away to the mantelpiece. Leaning heavily against it, she stood for some time with her face averted, and beneath the veil of long, floating hair Mrs. Murray saw the slight figure sway to and fro, like a reed shaken by the breeze.

" Edna, I must talk to you about a matter which alone brought me to New York. My son's happiness is dearer to me than my life, and I have come to plead with you, for his sake, if not for your own, at least to——"

" It is useless ! Do not mention his name again ! Oh, Mrs. Murray ! I am feeble to-day ; spare me ! Have mercy on my weakness !"

She put out her hand appealingly, but in vain.

" One thing you must tell me. Why did you reject him ?"

" Because I could not respect his character. Oh ! forgive me ! You force me to say it—because I knew that he was unworthy of any woman's confidence and affection."

The mother's face flushed angrily, and she rose and threw her head back with the haughty defiance peculiar to her family.

" Edna Earl, how dare you speak to me in such terms of my own son ? There is not a woman on the face of the broad earth who ought not to feel honored by his preference—who might not be proud of his hand. What right have you to pronounce him unworthy of trust ? Answer me !"

" The right to judge him from his own account of his past life. The history which he gave me condemns him. His crimes make me shrink from him."

" Crimes ? take care, Edna ! You must be beside yourself ! My son is no criminal ! He was unfortunate and rash, but his impetuosity was certainly pardonable under the circumstances."

" All things are susceptible of palliation in a mother's partial eyes," answered the governess.

" St. Elmo fought a duel, and afterward carried on several flirtations with women who were weak enough to allow themselves to be trifled with; moreover, I shall not deny that at one period of his life he was lamentably dissipated ; but all that happened long ago, before you knew him. How many young gentlemen indulge in the same things, and are never even reprimanded by society, much less denounced as criminals? The world sanctions duelling and flirting, and you have no right to set your extremely rigid notions of propriety above the verdict of modern society. Custom justifies many things which you seem to hold in utter abhorrence. Take care that you do not find yourself playing the Pharisee on the street corners."

Mrs. Murray walked up and down the room twice, then came to the hearth.

" Well, Edna, I am waiting to hear you."

" There is nothing that I can say which would not wound or displease you ; therefore, dear Mrs. Murray, I must be silent."

" Retract the hasty words you uttered just now ; they express more than you intended."

" I cannot ! I meant all I said. Offences against God's law, which you consider pardonable—and which the world winks at and permits, and even defends—I regard as grievous sins. I believe that every man who kills another in a duel deserves the curse of Cain, and should be shunned as a murderer. My conscience assures me that a man who can deliberately seek to gain a woman's heart merely to gratify his vanity, or to wreak his hate by holding her up to scorn, or trifling with the love which he has won, is unprincipled, and should be ostracized by every true woman. Were you the mother of Murray and Annie Hammond, do you think you could so easily forgive their murderer ?"

" Their father forgives and trusts my son, and you have no right to sit in judgment upon him. Do you suppose that you are holier than that white-haired saint

whose crown of glory is waiting for him in heaven?
Are you so much purer than Allan Hammond that you
fear contamination from one to whom he clings?"

"No—no—no! You wrong me. If you could know
how humble is my estimate of myself, you would not
taunt me so cruelly; you would only—pity me!"

The despairing agony in the orphan's voice touched
Mrs. Murray's proud heart, and tears softened the indignant expression of her eyes, as she looked at the
feeble form before her.

"Edna, my poor child, you must trust me. One
thing I must know—I have a right to ask—do you not
love my son? You need not blush to acknowledge it
to me."

She waited awhile, but there was no reply, and softly
her arm stole around the girl's waist.

"My daughter, you need not be ashamed of your
affection for St. Elmo."

Edna lifted her face from the mantel, and clasping
her hands across her head, exclaimed:

"Do I love him? Oh! none but God can ever
know how entirely my heart is his! I have struggled
against his fascination—oh! indeed I have wrestled
and prayed against it! But to-day—I do not deceive
myself—I feel that I love him as I can never love any
other human being. You are his mother, and you will
pity me when I tell you that I fall asleep praying for
him—that in my dreams I am with him once more—
that the first thought on waking is still of him. What
do you suppose it cost me to give him up? Oh! is it
hard, think you, to live in the same world and yet
never look on his face, never hear his voice? God
only knows how hard! If he were dead, I could bear
it better. But, ah! to live with this great sea of silence
between us—a dreary, cold, mocking sea, crossed by
no word, no whisper, filled only with slowly, sadly-
sailing ghosts of precious memories! Yes, yes! despite all his unworthiness—despite the verdict of my
judgment, and the upbraiding of my conscience—I love

him! I love him! You can sympathize with me. Do not reproach me; pity me, oh! pity me in my feebleness!"

She put out her arms like a weary child and dropped her face on Mrs. Murray's shoulder.

" My child, if you had seen him the night before I left home, you could not have resisted any longer the promptings of your own heart. He told me all that had ever passed between you; how he had watched and tempted you ; how devotedly he loved you ; how he reverenced your purity of character ; how your influence, your example, had first called him back to his early faith ; and then he covered his face and said, ' Mother! mother! if God would only give her to me, I could, I would be a better man !' Edna, I feel as if my son's soul rested in your hands ! If you throw him off utterly, he may grow desperate, and go back to his old habits of reckless dissipation and blasphemy ; and if he should! oh ! if he is lost at last, I will hold you accountable, and charge you before God with his destruction ! Edna, beware! You have a strange power over him ; you can make him almost what you will. If you will not listen to your own suffering heart, or to his love, hear me ! Hear a mother pleading for her son's eternal safety!"

The haughty woman fell on her knees before the orphan and wept, and Edna instantly knelt beside her and clung to her.

" I pray for him continually. My latest breath shall be a prayer for his salvation. His eternal welfare is almost as precious to me as my own; for if I get to heaven at last, do you suppose I could be happy even there without him? But, Mrs. Murray, I can not be his wife. If he is indeed conscientiously striving to atone for his past life, he will be saved without my influence ; and if his remorseful convictions of duty do not reform him, his affection for me would not accomplish it. Oh! of all mournful lots in life, I think mine is the saddest ! To find it impossible to tear my heart from a man whom I distrust, whom I can not

honor, whose fascination I dread. I know my duty in
this matter—my conscience leaves me no room to
doubt—and from the resolution which I made in sight
of Annie's grave, I must not swerve. I have confessed to you how completely my love belongs to him,
how fruitless are my efforts to forget him. I have
told you what bitter suffering our separation costs me,
that you may know how useless it is for you to urge
me. Ah! if I can withstand the wailing of my own
lonely, aching heart, there is nothing else that can
draw me from the path of duty; no, no! not even
your entreaties, dear Mrs. Murray, much as I love and
owe you. God, who alone sees all, will help me to bear
my loneliness. He only can comfort and sustain me;
and in His own good time He will save Mr. Murray,
and send peace into his troubled soul. Until then, let
us pray patiently."

Flush and tremor had passed away, the features
were locked in rigid whiteness; and the unhappy
mother saw that further entreaty would indeed be
fruitless.

She rose and paced the floor for some moments.
At last Edna said:

"How long will you remain in New York?"

"Two days. Edna, I came here against my son's
advice, in opposition to his wishes, to intercede in his
behalf and to prevail on you to go home with me. He
knew you better it seems than I did; for he predicted
the result, and desired to save me from mortification;
but I obstinately clung to the belief that you cherish
some feeling of affectionate gratitude toward me. You
have undeceived me. Mr. Hammond is eagerly expecting you, and it will be a keen disappointment to
the old man if I return without you. Is it useless to
tell you that you ought to go and see him? You need
not hesitate on St. Elmo's account; for unless you
wish to meet him, you will certainly not see him. My
son is too proud to thrust himself into the presence of
any one, much less into yours, Edna Earl."

" I will go with you, Mrs. Murray, and remain at the parsonage—at least for a few weeks."

" I scarcely think Mr. Hammond will live until spring ; and it will make him very happy to have you in his home."

Mrs. Murray wrapped her shawl around her and put on her gloves.

" I shall be engaged with Estelle while I am here, and shall not call again ; but of course you will come to the hotel to see her, and we will start homeward day after to-morrow evening."

She turned toward the door, but Edna caught her dress.

" Mrs. Murray, kiss me before you go, and tell me you forgive the sorrow I am obliged to cause you to-day. My burden is heavy enough without the weight of your displeasure."

But the proud face did not relax ; the mother shook her head, disengaged her dress, and left the room.

An hour after Felix came in, and approaching the sofa where his governess rested, said vehemently :

" Is it true, Edna? Are you going South with Mrs. Murray?"

" Yes ; I am going to see a dear friend who is probably dying."

" Oh, Edna ! what will become of me?"

" I shall be absent only a few weeks——"

" I have a horrible dread that if you go you will never come back ! Don't leave me ! Nobody needs you half as much as I do. Edna, you said once you would never forsake me. Remember your promise !"

" My dear little boy, I am not forsaking you ; I shall only be separated from you for a month or two ; and it is my duty to go to my sick friend. Do not look so wretched ! for just so surely as I live, I shall come back to you."

" You think so now ; but your old friends will persuade you to stay, and you will forget me, and——and——"

He turned around and hid his face on the back of his chair.

It was in vain that she endeavored, by promises and caresses, to reconcile him to her temporary absence. He would not be comforted; and his tear-stained, woe-begone, sallow face, as she saw it on the evening of her departure, pursued her on her journey South.

CHAPTER XXXII.

THE mocking-bird sang as of old in the myrtle-boughs that shaded the study-window, and within the parsonage reigned the peaceful repose which seemed ever to rest like a benediction upon it. A ray of sunshine stealing through the myrtle-leaves made golden ripples on the wall; a bright wood-fire blazed in the wide, deep, old-fashioned chimney; the white cat slept on the rug, with her pink paws turned toward the crackling flames; and blue and white hyacinths hung their fragrant bells over the gilded edge of the vases on the mantelpiece. Huldah sat on one side of the hearth peeling a red apple ; and, snugly wrapped in his palm-leaf cashmere dressing-gown, Mr. Hammond rested in his cushioned easy-chair, with his head thrown far back, and his fingers clasping a large bunch of his favorite violets. His snowy hair drifted away from a face thin and pale, but serene and happy, and in his bright blue eyes there was a humorous twinkle, and on his lips a half-smothered smile, as he listened to the witticisms of his Scotch countrymen in " Noctes Ambrosianæ."

Close to his chair sat Edna, reading aloud from the quaint and inimitable book he loved so well, and pausing now and then to explain some word which Huldah did not understand, or to watch for symptoms of weariness in the countenance of the invalid.

The three faces contrasted vividly in the ruddy glow of the fire. That of the little girl, round, rosy, red-lipped, dimpled, merry-eyed ; the aged pastor's wrinkled cheeks and furrowed brow and streaming

silver beard; and the carved-ivory features of the
governess, borrowing no color from the soft folds of
her rich crimson merino dress. As daylight ebbed, the
ripple danced up to the ceiling and vanished, like the
pricked bubble of a human hope; the mocking-bird
hushed his vesper hymn; and Edna closed the book
and replaced it on the shelf.

Huldah tied on her scarlet-lined hood, kissed her
friends good-bye, and went back to Le Bocage; and
the old man and the orphan sat looking at the grotesque flicker of the flames on the burnished andirons.

" Edna, are you tired, or can you sing some for me ?"

" Reading aloud rarely fatigues me. What shall I
sing ?"

" That solemn, weird thing in the ' Prophet,' which
suits your voice so well."

She sang " *Ah, mon fils !*" and then, without waiting
for the request which she knew would follow, gave him
some of his favorite Scotch songs.

As the last sweet strains of " Mary of Argyle "
echoed through the study, the pastor shut his eyes,
and memory flew back to the early years when his
own wife Mary had sung those words in that room,
and his dead darlings clustered eagerly around the
piano to listen to their mother's music. Five fair-
browed, innocent young faces circling about the idolized wife, and baby Annie nestling in her cradle beside
the hearth, playing with her waxen fingers and crow-
ing softly. Death had stolen his household jewels;
but recollection robbed the grave, and music's magic
touch unsealed " memory's golden urn."

" Oh ! death in life, the days that are no more !"

Edna thought he had fallen asleep, he was so still,
his face was so placid; and she came softly back to
her chair and looked at the ruby temples and towers,
the glittering domes and ash-gray ruined arcades
built by the oak coals.

A month had elapsed since her arrival at the par-

sonage, and during that short period Mr. Hammond
had rallied and recovered his strength so unexpectedly
that hopes were entertained of his entire restoration;
and he spoke confidently of being able to reënter his
pulpit on Easter Sunday.

The society of his favorite pupil seemed to render
him completely happy, and his countenance shone in
the blessed light that gladdened his heart. After a
long, dark, stormy day, the sun of his life was preparing to set in cloudless peace and glory.

Into all of Edna's literary schemes he entered eagerly. She read to him the MS. of her new book as far
as it was written, and was gratified by his perfect satisfaction with the style, plot, and aim.

Mrs. Murray came every day to the parsonage, but
Edna had not visited Le Bocage; and though Mr.
Murray spent two mornings of each week with Mr.
Hammond, he called at stated hours, and she had not
yet met him. Twice she had heard his voice in earnest conversation, and several times she had seen his
tall figure coming up the walk, but of his features she
caught not even a glimpse. St. Elmo's name had
never been mentioned in her presence by either his
mother or the pastor, but Huldah talked ceaselessly of
his kindness to her. Knowing the days on which he
came to the parsonage, Edna always absented herself
from the invalid's room until the visit was over.

One afternoon she went to the church to play on the
organ; and after an hour of mournful enjoyment in
the gallery so fraught with precious reminiscences,
she left the church and found Tamerlane tied to the
iron gate, but his master was not visible. She knew
that he was somewhere in the building or yard, and
denied herself the pleasure of going there a second
time.

Neither glance nor word had been exchanged since
they parted at the railroad station, eighteen months
before. She longed to know his opinion of her book,
for many passages had been written with special reference to his perusal; but she would not ask; and it

was a sore trial to sit in one room, hearing the low, in-distinct murmer of his voice in the next, and yet never to see him.

Few women could have withstood the temptation; but the orphan dreaded his singular power over her heart, and dared not trust herself in his pres-ence.

This evening, as she sat with the firelight shining on her face, thinking of the past, she could not realize that only two years had elapsed since she came daily to this quiet room to recite her lessons; for during that time she had suffered so keenly in mind and body that it seemed as if weary ages had gone over her young head. Involuntarily she sighed, and passed her hand across her forehead. A low tap at the door di-verted her thoughts, and a servant entered and gave her a package of letters from New York.

Every mail brought one from Felix; and now open-ing his first, a tender smile parted her lips as she read his passionate, importunate appeal for her speedy return, and saw that the closing lines were blotted with tears. The remaining eight letters were from persons unknown to her, and contained requests for auto-graphs and photographs, for short sketches for papers in different sections of the country, and also various inquiries concerning the time when her new book would probably be ready for press. All were kind, friendly, gratifying, and one was eloquent with thanks for the good effect produced by a magazine article on a dissipated, irreligious husband and father, who, after its perusal, had resolved to reform, and wished her to know the beneficial influence which she exerted. At the foot of the page was a line penned by the rejoicing wife, invoking heaven's choicest blessings on the author's head.

" Is not the laborer worthy of his hire ?" Edna felt that her wages were munificent indeed; that her cof-fers were filling, and though the " Thank God !" was not audible, the great joy in her uplifted eyes attracted the attention of the pastor, who had been silently watching her, and he laid his hand on hers.

"What is it, my dear?"

"The reward God has given me!"

She read aloud the contents of the letter, and there was a brief silence, broken at last by Mr. Hammond.

"Edna, my child, are you really happy?"

"So happy that I believe the wealth of California could not buy this sheet of paper, which assures me that I have been instrumental in bringing sunshine to a darkened household; in calling the head of a family from haunts of vice and midnight orgies back to his wife and children; back to the shrine of prayer at his own hearthstone! I have not lived in vain, for through my work a human soul has been brought to Jesus, and I thank God that I am accounted worthy to labor in my Lord's vineyard! Oh! I will wear that happy wife's blessing in my inmost heart, and like those old bells in Cambridgeshire, inscribed, '*Pestem fungo! Sabbata pango!*' it shall ring a silvery chime, exorcising all gloom, and loneliness, and sorrow."

The old man's eyes filled as he noted the radiance of the woman's lovely face.

"You have indeed cause for gratitude and great joy, as you realize all the good you are destined to accomplish, and I know the rapture of saving souls, for, through God's grace, I believe I have snatched some from the brink of ruin. But, Edna, can the triumph of your genius, the applause of the world, the approval of conscience, even the assurance that you are laboring successfully for the cause of Christ—can all these things satisfy your womanly heart—your loving, tender heart? My child, there is a dreary look sometimes in your eyes, that reveals loneliness, almost weariness of life. I have studied your countenance closely when it was in repose; I read it I think without errors; and as often as I hear your writings praised, I recall those lines, written by one of the noblest of your own sex:

' To have our books
Appraised by love, associated with love,
While *we* sit loveless ! is it hard, you think ?
At least, 'tis mournful.'

Edna, are you perfectly contented with your lot ?"

A shadow drifted slowly over the marble face, and
though it settled on no feature, the whole countenance
was changed.

"I can not say that I am perfectly content, and
yet I would not exchange places with any woman I
know."

"Do you never regret a step which you took one
evening, yonder in my church ?"

"No, sir, I do not regret it. I often thank God that
I was able to obey my conscience and take that step."

"Suppose that in struggling up the steep path of
duty one soul needs the encouragement, the cheering
companionship which only one other human being can
give ? Will the latter be guiltless if the aid is obstinately withheld ?"

"Suppose the latter feels that in joining hands both
would stumble ?"

"You would not, oh, Edna ! you would lift each
other to noble heights ! Each life would be perfect,
complete. My child, will you let me tell you some
things that ought to——"

She threw up her hand, with that old, childish
gesture which he remembered so well, and shook her
head.

"No, sir ; no, sir ! Please tell me nothing that will
rouse a sorrow I am striving to drug. Spare me, for
as St. Chrysostom once said of Olympias the deaconess,
I 'live in perpetual fellowship with pain.' "

"My dear little Edna, as I look at you and think of
your future, I am troubled about you. I wish I could
confidently say to you, what that same St. Chrysostom
wrote to Pentadia : 'For I know your great and lofty
soul, which can sail as with a fair wind through many
tempests, *and in the midst of the waves enjoy a white
calm*' "

She turned and took the minister's hand in hers, while an indescribable peace settled on her countenance, and stilled the trembling of her low, sweet voice :

" Across the gray stormy billows of life, that 'white calm' of eternity is rimming the water-line, coming to meet me. Already the black pilot-boat heaves in sight ; I hear the signal, and Death will soon take the helm and steer my little bark safely into the shining rest, into God's 'white calm.'"

She went to the piano and sang, as a solo, "Night's Shade no Longer," from Moses in Egypt.

While the pastor listened, he murmured to himself :

> "Sublime is the faith of a lonely soul,
> In pain and trouble cherished ;
> Sublime the spirit of hope that lives
> When earthly hope has perished."

She turned over the sheets of music, hunting for a German hymn of which Mr. Hammond was very fond, but he called her back to the fireplace.

" My dear, do you recollect that beautiful passage in Faber's 'Sights and Thoughts in Foreign Churches'? 'There is seldom a line of glory written upon the earth's face but a line of suffering runs parallel with it ; and they that read the lustrous syllables of the one, and stoop not to decipher the spotted and worn inscription of the other, get the least half of the lesson earth has to give.'"

"No, sir ; I never read the book. Something in that passage brings to my mind those words of Martin Luther's, which explain so many of the 'spotted inscriptions' of this earth : 'Our Lord God doth like a printer, who setteth the letters backward. We see and feel well His setting, but we shall read the print yonder, in the life to come !' Mr. Hammond, it is said that, in the Alexandrian MS., in the British Museum, there is a word which has been subjected to microscopic examination, to determine whether it is οϲ, who, or θϹ—which is the abbreviation of θεος, God.

Sometimes I think that so ought we to turn the lens of faith on many dim, perplexing inscriptions traced in human history, and perhaps we might oftener find God."

"Yes, I have frequently thought that the MS. of every human life was like a Peruvian Quippo, a mass of many colored cords or threads, tied and knotted by unseen, and, possibly, angel hands. Here, my dear, put these violets in water; they are withering. By the way, Edna, I am glad to find that in your writings you attach so much importance to the ministry of flowers, and that you call the attention of your readers to the beautiful arguments which they furnish in favor of the Christian philosophy of a divine design in nature. Truly,

> 'Your voiceless lips, O flowers! are living preachers,
>   Each cup a pulpit, and each leaf a book;
>   Supplying to my fancy numerous teachers
>   From lowliest nook.'"

At this moment the door-bell rang, and soon after the servant brought in a telegraphic dispatch, addressed to Mr. Hammond.

It was from Gordon Leigh, announcing his arrival in New York, and stating that he and Gertrude would reach the parsonage some time during the ensuring week.

Edna went into the kitchen to superintend the preparation of the minister's supper; and when she returned and placed the waiter on the table near his chair, she told him that she must go back to New York immediately after the arrival of Gordon and Gertrude, as her services would no longer be required at the parsonage and her pupils needed her.

Two days passed without any further allusion to a subject which was evidently uppermost in Mr. Hammond's mind.

On the morning of the third, Mrs. Murray said, as she rose to conclude her visit: "You are so much

better, sir, that I must claim Edna for a day at least.
She has not yet been to Le Bocage ; and as she goes
away so soon, I want to take her home with me this
morning. Clara Inge promised me that she would
stay with you until evening. Edna, get your bonnet.
I shall be entirely alone to-day, for St. Elmo has carried Huldah to the plantation, and they will not get
home until late. So, my dear, we shall have the
house all to ourselves."

The orphan could not deny herself the happiness
offered ; she knew that she ought not to go, but for
once her strength failed her, she yielded to the temptation.

During the drive Mrs. Murray talked cheerfully of
various things, and for the first time laid aside entirely
the haughty constraint which had distinguished her
manner since they travelled south from New York.

They entered the avenue, and Edna gave herself
up to the rushing recollections which were so mournfully sweet. As they went into the house, and the
servants hurried forward to welcome her, she could
not repress her tears. She felt that this was her home,
her heart's home ; and as numerous familiar objects
met her eyes, Mrs. Murray saw that she was almost
overpowered by her emotions.

" I wonder if there is any other place on earth half
so beautiful !" murmured the governess several hours
later, as they sat looking out over the lawn, where the
deer and sheep were browsing.

" Certainly not to our partial eyes. And yet without you, my child, it does not seem like home. It is
the only home where you will ever be happy."

"Yes, I know it ; but it cannot be mine. Mrs.
Murray, I want to see my own little room."

"Certainly ; you know the way. I will join you
there presently. Nobody has occupied it since you
left, for I feel toward your room as I once felt toward
the empty cradle of my dead child."

Edna went up-stairs alone and closed the door of the
apartment she had so long called hers, and looked with

childish pleasure and affection at the rosewood furniture.

Turning to the desk where she had written much that the world now praised and loved, she saw a vase containing a superb bouquet, with a card attached by a strip of ribbon. The hothouse flowers were arranged with exquisite taste, and the orphan's cheeks glowed suddenly as she recognized Mr. Murray's handwriting on the card: "For Edna Earl." When she took up the bouquet a small envelope similarly addressed, dropped out.

For some minutes she stood irresolute, fearing to trust herself with the contents; then she drew a chair to the desk, sat down, and broke the seal:

"My DARLING: Will you not permit me to see you before you leave the parsonage? Knowing the peculiar circumstances that brought you back, I cannot take advantage of them and thrust myself into your presence without your consent. I have left home today, because I felt assured that, much as you might desire to see 'Le Bocage,' you would never come here while there was a possibility of meeting me. You, who know something of my wayward, sinful, impatient temper, can perhaps imagine what I suffer, when I am told that your health is wrecked, that you are in the next room, and yet, that I must not, shall not see you —my own Edna! Do you wonder that I almost grow desperate at the thought that only a wall—a door— separates me from you, whom I love better than my life? Oh, my darling! Allow me one more interview! Do not make my punishment heavier than I can bear. It is hard—it is bitter enough to know that you can not, or will not trust me ; at least let me see your dear face again. Grant me one hour—it may be the last we shall ever spend together in this world.

"Your own,   ST. ELMO."

"Ah, my God! pity me! Why—oh! why is it that I am tantalized with glimpses of a great joy never to be mine in this life ! Why, in struggling to do my duty, am I brought continually to the very gate of the only Eden I am ever to find in this world, and yet can never surprise the watching Angel of Wrath, and have to stand shivering outside, and see my Eden only by the flashing of the sword that bars my entrance ?"

Looking at the handwriting so different from any other which she had ever examined, her thoughts were irresistibly carried back to that morning wnen, at the shop, she saw this handwriting for the first time on the blank leaf of the Dante ; and she recalled the shuddering aversion with which her grandfather had glanced at it, and advised her to commit it to the flames of the forge.

How many such notes as this had been penned to Annie and Gertrude, and to that wretched woman shut up in an Italian convent, and to others of whose names she was ignorant ?

Mrs. Murray opened the door, looked in, and said :
" Come, I want to show you something really beautiful."

Edna put the note in her pocket, took the bouquet, and followed her friend down-stairs, through the rotunda, to the door of Mr. Murray's sitting-room.

" My son locked this door and carried the key with him ; but after some search, I have found another that will open it. Come in, Edna. Now look at that large painting hanging over the sarcophagus. It is a copy of Titian's 'Christ Crowned with Thorns,' the original of which is in a Milan church, I believe. While St. Elmo was last abroad, he was in Genoa one afternoon when a boat was capsized. Being a fine swimmer, he sprang into the water where several persons were struggling, and saved the lives of two little children of an English gentleman, who had his hands quite full in rescuing his wife. Two of the party were drowned, but the father was so grateful to my son that he has written him several letters, and last year he sent him this picture, which, though of course much smaller than the original, is considered a very fine

ST. ELMO.

copy. I begged to have it hung in the parlor, but fearing, I suppose, that its history might possibly be discovered (you know how he despises anything like a parade of good deeds), St. Elmo insisted on bringing it here to this Egyptian Museum, where, unfortunately, people can not see it."

For some time they stood admiring it, and then Edna's eyes wandered away to the Taj Mahal, to the cabinets and book-cases. Her lip began to quiver as every article of furniture babbled of the By-Gone—of the happy evenings spent here—of that hour when the idea of authorship first seized her mind and deter-mined her future.

Mrs. Murray walked up to the arch, over which the curtains fell touching the floor, and laying her hand on the folds of silk, said hesitatingly :

"I am going to show you something that my son would not easily forgive me for betraying; for it is a secret he guards most jealously——"

"No, I would rather not see it. I wish to learn nothing which Mr. Murray is not willing that I should know."

"You will scarcely betray me to my son when you see what it is ; and beside, I am determined you shall have no room to doubt the truth of some things he has told you. There is no reason why you should not look at it. Do you recognize that face yonder, over the mantelpiece ?"

She held the curtains back, and despite her reluc-tance to glancing into the inner room, Edna raised her eyes timidly, and saw, in a richly-carved oval frame, hanging on the opposite wall, a life-size portrait of herself.

"We learned from the newspapers that some fine photographs had been taken in New York, and I sent on and bought two. St. Elmo took one of them to an artist in Charleston, and superintended the painting of that portrait. When he returned, just before I went North, he brought the picture with him, and with his own hands hung it yonder. I have noticed that since that day he always keeps the curtains down over the arch, and never leaves the house without locking his rooms."

Edna had dropped her crimsoned face in her hands, but Mrs. Murray raised it forcibly and kisse ˙ her.

" I want you to know how well he loves you—how necessary you are to his happiness. Now I must leave you, for I see Mrs. Mo tgomery's carriage at the door. You have a note to answer ; there are writing materials on the table yonder."

She went ou , closing the door softly, and Edna was alone with surroundings that pleaded piteously for the absent master. Oxalis and heliotrope peeped at her over the top of the lotos vases ; one of a pair of gauntlets had fallen on the carpet near the cameo cabinet ; two or three newspa˛ ers and a meerschaum lay upon a chair ; several theological works were scattered on the sofa, and the air was heavy with lingering cigar-smoke.

Just in front of the Taj Mahal was a handsome copy of Edna's novel, and a beautiful morocco-bound volume containing a collection of all her magazine sketches.

She sat down in the crimson-cushioned armchair that was drawn close to the circular table, where pen and paper told that the owner had recently been writing, and near the inkstand was a handkerchief with German initials. 𝕾. 𝕰. 𝕸.

Upon a mass of loose papers stood a quaint bronze paperweight, representing Cartaphilds, the Wandering Jew ; and on the base was inscribed Mr. Murray's favorite Arabian maxim : " *Ed dunya djifetun ve talibeha kilab* " : " *The world is an abomination, and those who toil about it are dogs.*"

There, too, was her own little Bible ; and as she took it up it opened at the fourteenth chapter of St. John, where she found, as a book-mark, the photograph of herself from which the portrait had been painted. An unwithered geranium sprig lying among the leaves whispered that the pages had been read that morning.

Out on the lawn birds swung in the elm-twigs, sing-

ing cheerily, lambs bleated and ran races, and the little
silver bell on Huldah's pet fawn, "Edna," tinkled
ceaselessly.

"Help me, O my God! in this the last hour of my
trial."

The prayer went up moaningly, and Edna took a
pen and turned to write. Her arm struck a portfolio
lying on the edge of the table, and in falling loose
sheets of paper fluttered out on the carpet. One
caught her eye; she picked it up, and found a sketch
of the ivied ruins of Phyle. Underneath the drawing,
and dated fifteen years before, were traced, in St.
Elmo's writing, those lines which Henry Soame is said
to have penned on the blank leaf of a copy of the
"Pleasures of Memory":

> "Memory makes her influence known
> By sighs, and tears, and grief alone.
> I greet her as the fiend, to whom belong
> The vulture's ravening beak, the raven's funeral song!
> She tells of time misspent, of comfort lost,
> Of fair occasions gone forever by;
> Of hopes too fondly nursed, too rudely crossed,
> Of many a cause to wish, yet fear to die;
> For what, except the instinctive fear
> Lest she survive, detains me here,
> When all the 'Life of Life' is fled?"

The lonely woman looked upward, appealingly, and
there upon the wall she met—not as formerly, the
gleaming, augurous, inexorable eyes of the Cimbrian
Prophetess—but the pitying God's gaze of Titian's
Jesus.

When Mrs. Murray returned to the room, Edna sat
as still as one of the mummies in the sarcophagus, with
her head thrown back, and the long, black eyelashes
sweeping her colorless cheeks.

One hand was pressed over her heart, the other
held a note directed to St. Elmo Murray; and the
cold, fixed features were so like those of an Angel of
Death sometimes sculptured on cenotaphs, that Mrs.
Murray uttered a cry of alarm.

As she bent over her, Edna opened her arms and said in a feeble, spent tone :

"Take me back to the parsonage. I ought not to have come here; I might have known I was not strong enough."

"You have had one of those attacks. Why did you not call me? I will bring you some wine."

"No; only let me go away as soon as possible. Oh! I am ashamed of my weakness."

She rose, and her pale lips writhed as her sad eyes wandered in a farewell glance around the room.

She put the unsealed note in Mrs. Murray's hand, and turned toward the door.

"Edna! My daughter! you have not refused St. Elmo's request?"

"My mother! Pity me! I could not grant it."

CHAPTER XXXIII.

" THEY have come. I hear Gertrude's birdish voice."

The words had scarcely passed Mr. Hammond's lips ere his niece bounded into the room, followed by her husband.

Edna was sitting on the chintz-covered lounge, mending a basketful of the old man's clothes that needed numerous stitches and buttons, and, throwing aside her sewing materials, she rose to meet the travellers.

At sight of her Gordon Leigh stopped suddenly, and his face grew instantly as bloodless as her own.

" Edna! Oh! how changed!   What a wreck!"

He grasped her outstretched hand, folded it in his, which trembled violently, and a look of anguish mastered his features, as his eyes searched her calm countenance.

" I did not think it would come so soon. Passing away in the early morning of your life! Oh, my pure, broken lily!"

He did not seem to heed his wife's presence, until she threw her arms around Edna, exclaiming:

" Get away, Gordon! I want her all to myself. Why, you pale darling! What a starved ghost you are! Not half as substantial as my shadow, is she, Gordon?   Oh, Edna! how I have longed to see you, to tell you how I enjoyed your dear, delightful, grand, noble book! To tell you what a great woman I think you are; and how proud of you I am. A gentleman who came over in the steamer with us, asked me how much you paid me *per annum* to puff you. He was a

miserable old cynic of a bachelor, ridiculed all women
unmercifully, and at last I told him I would bet both
my ears that the reason he was so bearish and hateful,
was because some pretty girl had flirted with him outrageously. He turned up his ugly nose especially at
'blue stockings'; said all literary women were 'hopeless pedants and slatterns,' and quoted that abominable
Horace Walpole's account of Lady Mary Wortley
Montagu's 'dirt and vivacity.'   I really thought
Gordon would throw him overboard.   I wonder what
he would say if he could see you darning Uncle
Allan's socks. Oh, Edna, dearie! I am sorry to find
you looking so pale."

All this was uttered interjectionally between vigorous hugs and warm, tender kisses, and as Gertrude
threw her bonnet and wrappings on the lounge, she
continued:

"I wished for you just exactly ten thousand times
while I was abroad, there were so many things that you
could have described so beautifully. Gordon, don't
Edna's eyes remind you very much of that divine picture of the Madonna at Dresden?"

She looked round for an answer, but her husband
had left the room, and, recollecting a parcel that had
been stowed away in the pocket of the carriage, she
ran out to get it.

Presently she reappeared at the door, with a goblet
in her hand.

"Uncle Allan, who carries the keys now?"

"Edna.   What will you have, my dear?"

"I want some brandy.   Gordon looks very pale, and
complains of not feeling well, so I intend to make him
a mint-julep. Ah, Edna! These husbands are such
troublesome creatures."

She left the room jingling the bunch of keys, and a
few moments after they heard her humming an air
from "Rigoletto," as she bent over the mint-bed,
under the study window.

Mr. Hammond, who had observed all that passed,

and saw the earnest distress clouding the orphan's brow, said gravely :

"She has not changed an iota; she never will be anything more than a beautiful, merry child, and is a mere pretty pet, not a companion in the true sense of the word. She is not quick-witted, or she would discern a melancholy truth that might overshadow all her life. Unless Gordon learns more self-control, he will ere long betray himself. I expostulated with him before his marriage, but for once he threw my warning to the winds. I am an old man, and have seen many phases of human nature, and watched the development of many characters ; and I have found that these pique marriages are always mournful—always disastrous. In such instances I would with more pleasure officiate at the grave than at the altar. Once Estelle and Agnes persuaded me that St. Elmo was about to wreck himself on this rock of ruin, and even his mother's manner led me to believe that he would marry his cousin ; but, thank God ! he was wiser than I feared."

" Mr. Hammond, are you sure that Gertrude loves Mr. Leigh ?"

" Oh ! yes, my dear ! Of that fact there can be no doubt. Why do you question it ?"

" She told me once that Mr. Murray had won her heart."

It was the first time Edna had mentioned his name since her return, and it brought a faint flush to her cheeks.

" That was a childish whim which she has utterly forgotten. A woman of her temperament never remains attached to a man from whom she is long separated. I do not suppose that she remembered St. Elmo a month after she ceased to meet him. I feel assured that she loves Gordon as well as she can love any one. She is a remarkably sweet-tempered, unselfish, gladsome woman, but is not capable of very deep, lasting feeling."

" I will go away at once. This is Saturday, and I

will start to New York early Monday morning. Mr. Leigh is weaker than I ever imagined he could be."

The outline of her mouth hardened, and into her eyes crept an expression of scorn, that very rarely found a harbor there.

"Yes, my dear; although it grieves me to part with you, I know it is best that you should not be here, at least for the present. Agnes is visiting friends at the North and when she returns, Gordon and Gertrude will remove to their new house. Then, Edna, if I feel that I need you, if I write for you, will you not come back to me? Dear child, I want your face to be the last I look upon in this world."

She drew the pastor's shrunken hand to her lips, and shook her head.

" Do not ask me to do that which my strength will not permit. There are many reasons why I ought not to come here again; and, moreover, my work calls me hence, to a distant field. My physical strength seems to be ebbing fast, and my vines are not all purple with mellow fruit. Some clusters, thank God! are fragrant, ripe, and ready for the wine-press, when the Angel of the Vintage comes to gather them in ; but my work is only half done. Not until my fingers clasp white flowers under a pall, shall it be said of me, ' Yet a little sleep, a little slumber, a little folding of the hands to sleep.' *In coelo quies !* The German idea of death is to me peculiarly comforting and touching, ' Heimgang'—*going home.* Ah, sir ! humanity ought to be homesick ; and in thinking of that mansion beyond the star-paved pathway of the sky, whither Jesus has gone to prepare our places, we children of earth should, like the Swiss, never lose our home-sickness. Our bodies are of the dust—dusty, and bend dustward ; but our souls floated down from the sardonyx walls of the Everlasting City, and brought with them a yearning *maladie du pays*, which should help them to struggle back. Sometimes I am tempted to believe that the joys of this world are the true lotos, devouring which, mankind glory in exile, and forget the

Heimgang.   Oh! indeed, 'here we have no continuing
city, but seek one to come.'   Heimgang!   Thank
God! going home for ever!"

The splendor of the large eyes seemed almost unearthly as she looked out over the fields, where in
summers past the shout of the merry reapers rose like
the songs of Greek harvesters to Demeter!   Nay, nay,
as a hymn of gratitude and praise to Him who 'feedeth
the fowls of the air,' and maketh the universe a vast
Sarepta, in which the cruse never faileth the prophets
of God.   Edna sat silent for some time, with her
slender hands folded on her lap, and the pastor heard
her softly repeating, as if to her own soul, those lines
on "Life":

> " A cry between the silences,
>   A shadow-birth of clouds at strife
>   With sunshine on the hills of life;
>   Between the cradle and the shroud,
>   A meteor's flight from cloud to cloud!"

Several hours later, when Mr. Leigh returned to the
study, he found Edna singing some of the minister's
favorite Scotch ballads; while Gertrude rested on the
lounge, half propped on her elbow, and leaning forward to dangle the cord and tassel of her *robe de cham-
bre* within reach of an energetic little blue-eyed kitten,
which, with its paws in the air, rolled on the carpet,
catching at the silken toy.   The governess left the
piano, and resumed her mending of the contents of the
clothes-basket.

In answer to some inquiries of Mr. Hammond, Mr.
Leigh gave a brief account of his travels in Southern
Europe; but his manner was constrained, his thoughts
evidently preoccupied.   Once his eyes wandered to
the round, rosy, dimpling face of his beautiful child-
wife, and he frowned, bit his lip, and sighed; while his
gaze, earnest and mournfully anxious, returned and
dwelt upon the weary but serene countenance of the
orphan.

In the conversation, which had turned accidentally upon philology and the MSS. of the Vatican, Gertrude took no part; now and then glancing up at the speakers, she continued her romp with the kitten. At length, tired of her frolicsome pet, she rose with a half-suppressed yawn, and sauntered up to her husband's chair. Softly and lovingly her pretty little pink palms were passed over her husband's darkened brow, and her fingers drew his hair now on one side, now on the other, while she peeped over his shoulder to watch the effect of the arrangement.

The caresses were inopportune, her touch annoyed him. He shook it off, and, stretching out his arm, put her gently but firmly away, saying, coldly :

"There is a chair, Gertrude."

Edna's eyes looked steadily into his, with an expression of grave, sorrowful reproof—of expostulation ; and the flush deepened on his face as his eyes fell before her rebuking gaze.

Perhaps the young wife had become accustomed to such rebuffs; at all events she evinced neither mortification nor surprise, but twirled her silk tassel vigorously around her finger, and exclaimed :

"Oh, Gordon! have you not forgotten to give Edna that letter, written by the gentleman we met at Palermo? Edna, he paid your book some splendid compliments. I fairly clapped my hands at his praises —didn't I, Gordon?"

Mr. Leigh drew a letter from the inside pocket of his coat, and, as he gave it to the orphan, said with a touch of bitterness in his tone :

"Pardon my negligence ; probably you will find little news in it, as he is one of your old victims, and you can guess its contents."

The letter was from Sir Roger ; and while he expressed great grief at hearing, through Mr. Manning's notes, that her health was seriously impaired, he renewed the offer of his hand, and asked permission to come and plead his suit in person.

As Edna hurriedly glanced over the pages, and put

them in her pocket, Gertrude said gayly, "Shame on
you, Gordon! Do you mean to say, or, rather to
insinuate, that all who read Edna's book are victimized ?"

He looked at her from under thickening eyebrows,
and replied with undisguised impatience :

"No ; your common sense ought to teach you that
such was not my meaning or intention. Edna places
no such interpretation on my words."

"Common sense! Oh, Gordon, dearie! how unreasonable you are ! Why, you have told me a thousand
times that I had not a particle of common sense,
except on the subject of juleps ; and how, then, in the
name of wonder, can you expect me to show any ? I
never pretended to be a great shining genius like Edna,
whose writings all the world is talking about. I only
want to be wise enough to understand you, dearie, and
make you happy. Gordon, don't you feel any better ?
What makes your face so red ?"

She went back to his chair, and leaned her lovely
head close to his, while an anxious expression filled
her large blue eyes.

Gordon Leigh realized that his marriage was a terrible mistake, which only death could rectify ; but even
in his wretchedness he was just, blaming only himself
—exonerating his wife. Had he not wooed the love
of which, already, he was weary ? Having deceived
her at the altar, was there justification for his dropping
the mask at the hearthstone ? Nay, the skeleton must
be no rattling of skull and crossbones to freeze the
blood in the sweet laughing face of the trusting bird.

Now her clinging tenderness, her affectionate humility, upbraided him as no harsh words could possibly
have done. With a smothered sigh he passed his arm
around her, and drew her closer to his side.

"At least my little wife is wise enough to teach her
husband to be ashamed of his petulance."

"And quite wise enough, dear Gertrude, to make
him very proud and happy ; for you ought to be able
to say with the sweetest singer in all merry England :

> ' But I look up, and he looks down,
>   And thus our married eyes can meet ;
> Unclouded his, and clear of frown,
>   And gravely sweet.' "

As Edna glanced at the young wife and uttered
these words, a mist gathered in her own eyes, and col-
lecting her sewing utensils she went to her room to
pack her trunk.

During her stay at the parsonage she had not attended service in the church, because Mr. Hammond
was lonely, and her Sabbaths were spent in reading to
him. But her old associates in the choir insisted that,
before she returned to New York, she should sing with
them once more.

Thus far she had declined all invitations ; but on the
morning of the last day of her visit, the organist called
to say that a distinguished divine, from a distant State,
would fill Mr. Hammond's pulpit ; and as the best and
leading soprano in the choir was disabled by severe
cold, and could not be present, he begged that Edna
would take her place, and sing a certain solo in the
music which he had selected for an opening piece.
Mr. Hammond, who was pardonably proud of his
choir, was anxious that the stranger should be greeted
and inspired by fine music, and urged Edna's compliance with the request.

Reluctantly she consented, and for the first time
Duty and Love seemed to signal a truce, to shake
hands over the preliminaries of a treaty for peace.

As she passed through the churchyard and walked
up the steps, where a group of Sabbath-school children sat talking, her eyes involuntarily sought the dull
brown spot on the marble.

Over it little Herbert Inge had spread his white
handkerchief, and piled thereon his Testament and
catechism, laying on the last one of those gilt-bordered
and handsome pictorial cards, containing a verse from
the Scriptures, which are frequently distributed by
Sabbath-school teachers.

Edna stooped and looked at the picture covering
the blood-stain. It represented our Saviour on the
Mount, delivering the sermon, and in golden letters
were printed his words :

" Judge not, that ye be not judged. For with what
judgment ye judge, ye shall be judged ; and with what
measure ye mete, it shall be measured to you again."

The eyes of the Divine Preacher seemed to look
into hers, and the outstretched hand to point directly
at her.

She trembled, and hastily kissing the sweet red lips
which little Herbert held up to her, she went in, and
up to the gallery.

The congregation assembled slowly, and as almost
all the faces were familiar to Edna, each arrival
revived something of the past. Here the flashing silk
flounces of a young *belle* brushed the straight black
folds of widow's weeds ; on the back of one seat was
stretched the rough brown hand of a poor laboring
man ; on the next lay the dainty fingers of a matron
of wealth and fashion, who had entirely forgotten to
draw a glove over her sparkling diamonds.

In all the splendor of velvet, feathers, and sea-green
moire, Mrs. Montgomery sailed proudly into her pew,
convoying her daughter Maud, who was smiling and
whispering to her escort ; and just behind them came
a plainly-clad but happy young mechanic, a carpenter,
clasping to his warm, honest heart the arm of his
sweet-faced, gentle wife, and holding the hand of his
rosy-cheeked, bright-eyed, three-year-old boy, who tod-
dled along, staring at the brilliant pictures on the
windows.

When Mr. Leigh and Gertrude entered there was a
general stir, a lifting of heads and twisting of necks, in
order to ascertain what new styles of bonnet, lace, and
mantle prevailed in Paris.

A moment after, Mrs. Murray walked slowly down
the aisle, and Edna's heart seemed to stand still as she
saw Mr. Murray's powerful form. He stepped forward, and while he opened the door of the pew, and

waited for his mother to seat herself, his face was visible ; then he sat down, closing the door.

The minister entered, and, as he ascended the pulpit, the organ began to breathe its solemn welcome. When the choir rose and commenced their chorus, Edna stood silent, with her book in her hand, and her eyes fixed on the Murrays' pew.

The strains of triumph ceased, the organ only sobbed its sympathy to the thorn-crowned Christ, struggling along the *Via Dolorosa*, and the orphan's quivering lips parted, and she sang her solo.

As her magnificent voice rose and rolled to the arched roof, people forgot propriety, and turned to look at the singer. She saw Mrs. Murray start and glance eagerly up at her, and for an instant the grand, pure voice faltered slightly, as Edna noticed that the mother whispered something to the son. But he did not turn his proud head, he only leaned his elbow on the side of the pew next to the aisle, and rested his temple on his hand.

When the preliminary services ended, and the minister stood up in the shining pulpit and commenced his discourse, Edna felt that St. Elmo had at last enlisted angels in his behalf ; for the text was contained in the warning, whose gilded letters hid the blood-spot, " Judge not, that ye be not judged."

As far as two among his auditory were concerned, the preacher might as well have addressed his sermon to the mossy slabs, visible through the windows. Both listened to the text, and neither heard any more. Edna sat looking down at Mr. Murray's massive, finely-poised head, and she could see the profile contour of features, regular and dark, as if carved and bronzed.

During the next half-hour her vivid imagination sketched and painted a vision of enchantment—of what might have been, if that motionless man below, there in the crimson-cushioned pew, had only kept his soul from grievous sins. A vision of a happy, proud, young wife reigning at Le Bocage, shedding the warm,

rosy light of her love over the lonely life of its master;
adding to his strong, clear, intellect and ripe experience, the silver flame of her genius; borrowing from
him broader and more profound views of her race, on
which to base her ideal æsthetic structures; softening,
refining his nature, strengthening her own; helping
him to help humanity; loving all good, being good,
doing good; serving and worshipping God together;
walking hand and hand with her husband through
earth's wide valley of Baca, with peaceful faces full of
faith, looking heavenward.

> "God pity them both! and pity us all,
> Who vainly the dreams of youth recall.
> For of all sad words of tongue or pen
> The saddest are these, 'It might have been!'"

At last, with a faint moan, which reached no ear but
that of Him who never slumbers, Edna withdrew her
eyes from the spot where Mr. Murray sat, and raised
them toward the pale Christ, whose wan lips seemed to
murmur:

"Be of good cheer! He that overcometh shall in-
herit all things. What I do, thou knowest not now,
but thou shalt know hereafter."

The minister, standing beneath the picture of the
Master whom he served, closed the Bible and ended
his discourse by hurling his text as a thunderbolt at
those whose upturned faces watched him:

"Finally, brethren, remember under all circumstances
the awful admonition of Jesus, 'Judge not, that ye be
not judged!'"

The organ peals and the doxology were concluded;
the benediction fell like God's dew, alike on sinner and
on saint, and amid the solemn moaning of the gilded
pipes, the congregation turned to quit the church.

With both hands pressed over her heart, Edna
leaned heavily against the railing.

"To-morrow I go away for ever. I shall never see
his face again in this world. Oh! I want to look at it
once more."

As he stepped into the aisle, Mr. Murray threw his head back slightly, and his eyes swept up to the gallery and met hers. It was a long, eager, heart-searching gaze. She saw a countenance more fascinating than of old ; for the sardonic glare had gone, the bitterness, " the dare-man, dare-brute, dare-devil " expression had given place to a stern mournfulness, and the softening shadow of deep contrition and manly sorrow hovered over features where scoffing cynicism had so long scowled.

The magnetism of St. Elmo's eyes was never more marvellous than when they rested on the beautiful white face of the woman he loved so well, whose calm, holy eyes shone like those of an angel, as they looked sadly down at his. In the mystic violet light with which the rich stained glass flooded the church, that pallid, suffering face, sublime in its meekness and resignation, hung above him like one of Perugino's saints over kneeling mediæval worshippers. As the moving congregation bore him nearer to the door, she leaned farther over the mahogany balustrade, and a snowy crocus which she wore at her throat, snapped its brittle stem and floated down till it touched his shoulder. He laid one hand over it, holding it there, and while a prayer burned in his splendid eyes, hers smiled a melancholy farewell. The crowd swept the tall form forward, under the arches, beyond the fluted columns of the gallery, and the long gaze ended.

> " Ah ! well for us all some sweet hope lies
> Deeply buried from human eyes ;
> And in the hereafter, angels may
> Roll the stone from its grave away."

CHAPTER XXXIV.

"I AM truly thankful that you have returned! I
am quite worn out trying to humor Felix's whims, and
take your place. He has actually lost ten pounds;
and if you had staid away a month longer I think it
would have finished my poor boy, who has set you up
as an idol in his heart. He almost had a spasm last
week, when his father told him he had better reconcile
himself to your absence, as he believed that you would
never come back to the drudgery of the schoolroom.
I am very anxious about him ; his health is more feeble
than it has been since he was five years old. My dear,
you have no idea how you have been missed! Your
admirers call by scores to ascertain when you may be
expected home ; and I do not exaggerate in the least
when I say that there is a champagne basketful of
periodicals and letters upstairs, that have arrived
recently. You will find them piled on the table and
desk in your room."

"Where are the children?" asked Edna, glancing
around the sitting-room into which Mrs. Andrews had
drawn her.

"Hattie is spending the day with Lila Manning,
who is just recovering from a severe attack of scarlet
fever, and Felix is in the library trying to sleep. He
has one of his nervous headaches to-day. Poor fellow!
he tries so hard to overcome his irritable temper and
to grow patient, that I am growing fonder of him
every day. How travel-spent and ghastly you are!
Sit down, and I will order some refreshments. Take
this wine, my dear, and presently you shall have a cup
of chocolate."

"Thank you, not any wine. I only want to see Felix."

She went to the library, cautiously opened the door, and crept softly across the floor to the end of the sofa.

The boy lay looking through the window, and up beyond the walls and chimneys, at the sapphire pavement, where rolled the sun. Casual observers thought the cripple's face ugly and disagreeable; but the tender, loving smile that lighted the countenance of the governess as she leaned forward, told that some charm lingered in the sharpened features overcast with sickly sallowness. In his large, deep-set eyes, over which the heavy brows arched like a roof, she saw now a strange expression that frightened her. Was it the awful shadow of the Three Singing Spinners, whom Catullus painted at the wedding of Peleus? As the child looked into the blue sky, did he catch a glimpse of their trailing white robes, purple-edged—of their floating rose-colored veils? Above all, did he hear the unearthly chorus which they chanted as they spun?

" *Currite ducentes, subtemina currite fusi!* "

The governess was seized by a vague apprehension as she watched her pupil, and bending down, she said, fondly:

" Felix, my darling, I have come back! Never again while I live will I leave you."

The almost bewildering joy that flashed into his countenance mutely but eloquently welcomed her, as kneeling beside the sofa she wound her arms around him, and drew his head to her shoulder.

" Edna, is Mr. Hammond dead?"

" No, he is almost well again, and needs me no more."

" I need you more than anybody else ever did. Oh, Edna! I thought sometimes you would stay at the South that you love so well, and I should see you no more; and then all the light seemed to die out of the world, and the flowers were not sweet, and the stars were not bright, and oh! I was glad I had not long to live."

" Hush ! you must not talk so. How do you know that you may not live as long as Ahasuerus, the 'Ever-lasting Jew'? My dear little boy, in all this wide earth, you are the only one whom I have to love and cling to, and we will be happy together. Darling, your head aches to-day ?"

She pressed her lips twice to his hot forehead.

" Yes ; but the heartache was much the hardest to bear until you came. Mamma has been very good and kind, and staid at home and read to me ; but I wanted you, Edna. I do not believe I have been wicked since you left ; for I prayed all the while that God would bring you back to me. I have tried hard to be patient."

With her cheek nestled against his, Edna told him many things that had occurred during their separa-tion, and noticed that his eyes brightened suddenly and strangely.

" Edna, I have a secret to tell you ; something that even mamma is not to know just now. You must not laugh at me. While you were gone I wrote a little MS., and it is dedicated to you ! and some day I hope it will be printed. Are you glad, Edna ? My beauti-ful, pale Edna !"

" Felix, I am very glad you love me sufficiently to dedicate your little MS. to me ; but, my dear boy, I must see it before I can say I am glad you wrote it."

" If you had been here, it would not have been writ-ten, because then I should merely have talked out all the ideas to you ; but you were far away, and so I talked to my paper. After all, it was only a dream. One night I was feverish, and mamma read aloud those passages that you marked in that great book, Maury's Physical Geography of the Sea, that you admire and quote so often ; and of which I remember you said once, in talking to Mr. Manning, that ' it rolled its warm, beautiful, sparkling waves of thought across the cold, gray sea of science, just like the Gulf Stream it treated of.' Two of the descriptions which mamma read were so splendid that they rang in my ears like the music of the Swiss Bell-Ringers. One was the account of the atmosphere, by Dr. Buist of Bombay, and the other was the description of the Indian Ocean, which was quoted from Schleiden's Lecture. My fever was high, and when at last I went to sleep, I had a queer dream about madrepores and medusæ, and I wrote it down as well as I could, and called it 'Algæ Adventures, in a Voyage Round the World.' Edna, I have stolen something from you, and as you will be sure to find it out when you read my little story, where there is a long, hard word missing in the MS., I will tell you about it now. Do you recollect talking to me one evening, when we were walking on the beach at The Willows, about some shell-clad animalcula, which you said were so very small that Professor Schultze, of Bonn, found no less than a million and a half of their minute shells in an ounce of pulverized quartz, from the shore of Mola di Gaeta? Well, I put all you told me in my little MS.; but, for my life, I could not think of the name of the class to which they belong. Do you recollect it?"

"Let me think a moment. Was it not Foraminifera?"

"That's the identical word—'Foraminifera!' No wonder I could not think of it! Six syllables tied up in a scientific knot. Phew! it makes my head ache worse to try to recollect it. How stoop-shouldered your memory must be from carrying such heavy loads! It is a regular camel."

"Yes; it is a meek, faithful beast of burden, and will very willingly bear the weight of that scientific name until you want to use it; so do not tax your mind now. You said you stole it from me, but my dear, ambitious authorling, my little round-jacket scribbler, I wish you to understand distinctly that I do not consider that I have been robbed. The fact was discovered by Professor Schultze, and bequeathed by him to the world. From that instant it became universal, common property, which any man, woman, or child may use at pleasure, provided a tribute of gratitude is paid to the donor. Every individual is in some sort an intellectual bank, issuing bills of ideas (very often specious, but not always convertible into gold or silver); and now, my precious little boy, recollect that just as long as I have any capital left, you can borrow; and some day I will turn Shylock, and make you pay me with usury."

"Edna, I should like above all things to write a book of stories for poor, sick children; little tales that would make them forget their suffering and deformity. If I could even reconcile one lame boy to being shut up indoors, while others are shouting and skating in the sunshine, I should not feel as if I were so altogether useless in the world. Edna, do you think that I shall ever be able to do so?"

"Perhaps so, dear Felix; certainly, if God wills it. When you are stronger we will study and write together, but to-day you must compose yourself and be silent. Your fever is rising."

"The doctor left some medicine yonder in that goblet, but mamma has forgotten to give it to me. I will take a spoonful now, if you please."

His face was much flushed; and as she kissed him and turned away, he exclaimed:

"Oh! where are you going?"

"To my room, to take off my hat."

"Do not be gone long. I am so happy now that you are here again. But I don't want you to get out of my sight. Come back soon, and bathe my head."

On the following day, when Mr. Manning called to welcome her home, he displayed an earnestness and depth of feeling which surprised the governess. Putting his hand on her arm, he said in a tone that had lost its metallic ring:

"How fearfully changed since I saw you last! I knew you were not strong enough to endure the trial; and if I had had a right to interfere, you should never have gone."

"Mr. Manning, I do not quite understand your meaning."

"Edna, to see you dying by inches is bitter indeed!

I believed that you would marry Murray—at least I knew any other woman would—and I felt that to refuse his affection would be a terrible trial, through which you could not pass with impunity. Why you rejected him I have no right to inquire, but I have a right to ask you to let me save your life. I am well aware that you do not love me, but at least you can esteem and entirely trust me; and once more I hold out my hand to you and say, give me the wreck of your life! oh! give me the ruins of your heart! I will guard you tenderly; we will go to Europe—to the East; and rest of mind, and easy travelling, and change of scene will restore you. I never realized, never dreamed how much my happiness depended upon you, until you left the city. I have always relied so entirely upon myself, feeling the need of no other human being; but now, separated from you I am restless, am conscious of a vague discontent. If you spend the next year as you have spent the last, you will not survive it. I have conferred with your physician. He reluctantly told me your alarming condition, and I have come to plead with you for the last time not to continue your suicidal course, not to destroy the life which, if worthless to you, is inexpressibly precious to a man who prays to be allowed to take care of it. A man who realizes that it is necessary to the usefulness and peace of his own lonely life; who wishes no other reward on earth but the privilege of looking into your approving eyes, when his daily work is ended, and he sits down at his fireside. Edna, I do not ask for your love, but I beg for your hand, your confidence, your society—for the right to save you from toil. Will you go to the Old World with me?"

Looking suddenly up at him, she was astonished to find tears in his searching and usually cold eyes.

Scandinavian tradition reports that seven parishes were once overwhelmed, and still lie buried under snow and ice, and yet occasionally those church-bells are heard ringing clearly under the glaciers of the Folge Fond.

So, in the frozen, crystal depths of this man's nature, his long silent, smothered affections began to chime.

A proud smile trembled over Edna's face, as she saw how entirely she possessed the heart of one, whom above all other men she most admired.

"Mr. Manning, the assertion that you regard your life as imperfect, incomplete, without the feeble complement of mine—that you find your greatest happiness in my society, is the most flattering, the most gratifying tribute which ever has been, or ever can be paid to my intellect. It is a triumph indeed ; and, because unsought, surely it is a pardonable pride that makes my heart throb. This assurance of your high regard is the brightest earthly crown I shall ever wear. But, sir, you err egregiously in supposing that you would be happy wedded to a woman who did not love you. You think now that if we were only married, my constant presence in your home, my implicit confidence in your character, would fully content you ; but here you fail to understand your own heart, and I know that the consciousness that my affection was not yours would make you wretched. No, no ! my dear, noble friend ! God never intended us for each other. I can not go to the Old World with you. I know how peculiarly precarious is my tenure of life, and how apparently limited is my time for work in this world, but I am content. I try to labor faithfully, listening for the summons of Him who notices even the death of sparrows. God will not call me hence, so long as He has any work for me to do on earth ; and when I become useless, and can no longer serve Him here, I do not wish to live. Through Christ I am told, 'Let not your heart be troubled, neither let it be afraid.' Mr. Manning, I am not ignorant of, nor indifferent to, my physical condition ; but, thank God ! I can say truly, I am not troubled, neither am I afraid, and my faith is—

'All as God wills, who wisely heeds,
    To give or to withhold,
And knoweth more of all my needs
    Than all my prayers have told.' "

The editor took off his glasses and wiped them, but the dimness was in his eyes; and after a minute, during which he recovered his old calmness, and hushed the holy chime, muffling the Folge Fond bells, he said gravely and quietly:

"Edna, one favor, at least, you will grant me. The death of a relative in Louisiana has placed me in possession of an ample fortune, and I wish you to take my little Lila and travel for several years. You are the only woman I ever knew to whom I would entrust her and her education, and it would gratify me beyond expression to feel that I had afforded you the pleasure which can not fail to result from such a tour. Do not be too proud to accept a little happiness from my hands."

"Thank you, my generous, noble friend! I gratefully accept a great deal of happiness at this instant, but your kind offer I must decline. I can not leave Felix."

He sighed, took his hat, and his eyes ran over the face and figure of the governess.

"Edna Earl, your stubborn will makes you nearly akin to those gigantic fuci which are said to grow and flourish as submarine forests in the stormy channel of Terra del Fuego, where they shake their heads defiantly, always trembling, always triumphing, in the fierce lashing of waves that wear away rocks. You belong to a very rare order of human algæ, rocked and reared in the midst of tempests that would either bow down, or snap asunder, or beat out most natures. As you will not grant my petition, try to forget it; we will bury the subject. Good-by! I shall call to-morrow afternoon to take you to drive."

With renewed zest Edna devoted every moment stolen from Felix, to the completion of her new book. Her first had been a "bounteous promise"—at least so said criticdom—and she felt that the second would determine her literary position, would either place her reputation as an author beyond all cavil, or utterly crush her ambition.

Sometimes as she bent over her MS., and paused to reread some passage just penned, which she had laboriously composed, and thought particularly good as an illustration of the idea she was striving to embody perspicuously, a smile would flit across her countenance while she asked herself:

"Will my readers see it as I see it? Will they thank me for my high opinion of their culture, in assuming that it will be quite as plain to them as to me? If there should accidentally be an allusion to classical or scientific literature, which they do not understand at the first hasty, careless, novel-reading glance, will they inform themselves, and then appreciate my reason for employing it, and thank me for the hint ; or will they attempt to ridicule my pedantry? When will they begin to suspect that what they may imagine sounds 'learned' in my writings, merely appears so to them because they have not climbed high enough to see how vast, how infinite is the sphere of human learning? No, no, dear reader, shivering with learning-phobia, I am not learned. You are only a little, a very little more ignorant. Doubtless you know many things which I should be glad to learn ; come, let us barter. Let us all study the life of Giovanni Pico Mirandola, and then we shall begin to understand the meaning of the word 'learned.'"

Edna unintentionally and continually judged her readers according to her own standard, and so eager, so unquenchable was her thirst for knowledge, that she could not understand how the utterance of some new fact, or the redresssing and presentation of some forgotten idea, could possibly be regarded as an insult by the person thus benefited. Her first book taught her that what was termed her "surplus paraded erudition," had wounded the *amour propre* of the public ; but she was conscientiously experimenting on public taste, and though some of her indolent, luxurious readers, who wished even their thinking done by proxy, shuddered at the "spring-water pumped upon their nerves," she good-naturedly overlooked their grimaces

and groans, and continued the hydropathic treatment
even in her second book, hoping some good effects
from the shock. Of one intensely gratifying fact she
could not fail to be thoroughly informed, by the ava-
lanche of letters which almost daily covered her desk ;
she had at least ensconced herself securely in a citadel,
whence she could smilingly defy all assaults—in the
warm hearts of her noble countrywomen. Safely sheltered in their sincere and devoted love, she cared little
for the shafts that rattled and broke against the rocky
ramparts, and, recoiling, dropped out of sight in the
moat below.

So with many misgivings, and much hope, and great
patience, she worked on assiduously, and early in summer her book was finished and placed in the publisher's hands.

In the midst of her anxiety concerning its reception,
a new and terrible apprehension took possession of
her, for it became painfully evident that Felix, whose
health had never been good, was slowly but steadily
declining.

Mrs. Andrews and Edna took him to Sharon, to
Saratoga, and to various other favorite resorts for in-
valids, but with no visible results that were at all encouraging, and at last they came home almost dis-
heartened. Dr. Howell finally prescribed a sea-voyage,
and a sojourn of some weeks at Eaux Bonne in the
Pyrenees, as those waters had effected some remarkable cures.

As the doctor quitted the parlor, where he held a
conference with Mr. and Mrs. Andrews, the latter
turned to her husband, saying :

" It is useless to start anywhere with Felix unless
Miss Earl can go with us ; for he would fret himself to
death in a week. Really, Louis, it is astonishing to
see how devoted they are to each other. Feeble as
that woman is, she will always sit up whenever there is
any medicine to be given during the night ; and while
he was so ill at Sharon, she did not close her eyes for
a week. I can't help feeling jealous of his affection

for her, and I spoke to her about it. He was asleep at the time, with his hand grasping one of hers; and when I told her how trying it was for a mother to see her child's whole heart given to a stranger, to hear morning, noon, and night, 'Edna,' always 'Edna,' never once 'mamma,' I wish you could have seen the strange, suffering expression that came into her pale face. Her lips trembled so that she could scarcely speak, but she said meekly, 'Oh! forgive me if I have won your child's heart; but I love him. You have your husband and daughter, your brother and sister; but I—oh! I have only Felix! I have nothing else to cling to in all this world!' Then she kissed his poor little fingers, and wept as if her heart would break, and wrung her hands, and begged me again and again to forgive her if he loved her best. She is the strangest woman I ever knew; sometimes, when she is sitting by me in church, I watch her calm, cold, white face, and she makes me think of a snow statue; but if Felix says anything to arouse her feelings and call out her affection, she is a volcano. It is very rarely that one finds a beautiful woman, distinguished by her genius, admired and courted by the reading public, devoting herself as she does to our dear little crippled darling. While I confess I am jealous of her, her kindness to my child makes me love her more than I can express. Louis, she must go with us. Poor thing! she seems to be failing almost as fast as Felix; and I verily believe if he should die, it would kill her. Did you notice how she paced the floor while the doctors were consulting in Felix's room? She loves nothing but my precious lame boy."

"Certainly, Kate, she must go with you. I quite agree with you, my dear, that Felix is dependent upon her, and would not derive half the benefit from the trip if she remained at home. I confess she has cured me to a great extent of my horror of literary characters. She is the only one I ever saw who was really lovable, and not a walking parody on her own writings. You would be surprised at the questions constantly

asked me about her habits and temper. People seem
so curious to learn all the routine of her daily life.
Last week a member of our club quoted something
from her writings, and said that she was one of the few
authors of the day whose books, without having first
examined, he would put into the hands of his daughters. He remarked : ' I can trust my girls' characters
to her training, for she is a true woman ; and if she
errs at all in any direction, it is the right one, only a
little too rigidly followed.' I am frequently asked how
she is related to me, for people can not believe that
she is merely the governess of our children. Kate,
will you tell her that it is my desire that she should
accompany you ? Speak to her at once, that I may
know how many staterooms I shall engage on the
steamer."

"Come with me, Louis, and speak to her yourself."

They went up-stairs together, and paused on the
threshold of Felix's room to observe what was passing
within.

The boy was propped by pillows into an upright
position on the sofa, and was looking curiously into a
small basket which Edna held on her lap.

She was reading to him a touching little letter just
received from an invalid child, who had never walked,
who was confined always to the house, and wrote to
thank her, in sweet, childish style, for a story which
she had read in the Magazine, and which made her
very happy.

The invalid stated that her chief amusement consisted in tending a few flowers that grew in pots in her
windows ; and in token of her gratitude, she had made
a nosegay of mignonnette, pansies, and geranium leaves,
which she sent with her scrawling letter.

In conclusion, the child asked that the woman whom,
without having seen, she yet loved, would be so kind
as to give her a list of such books as a little girl ought
to study, and to write her " just a few lines " that she
could keep under her pillow, to look at now and then.

As Edna finished reading the note, Felix took it, to examine the small, indistinct characters, and said :

"Dear little thing ! Don't you wish we knew her ?
'Louie Lawrence.' Of course, you will answer it,
Edna ?"

"Yes, immediately, and tell her how grateful I am
for her generosity in sparing me a portion of her pet
flowers. Each word in her sweet little letter is as
precious as a pearl, for it came from the very depths of
her pure heart."

"Oh ! what a blessed thing it is to feel that you are
doing some good in the world ! That little Louie says
she prays for you every night before she goes to sleep !
What a comfort such letters must be to you ! Edna,
how happy you look ! But there are tears shining
in your eyes, they always come when you are glad.
What books will you tell her to study?"

"I will think about the subject, and let you read my
answer. Give me the 'notelet'; I want to put it
away securely among my treasures. How deliciously
fragrant the flowers are ! Only smell them, Felix !
Here, my darling, I will give them to you, and write
to the little Louie how happy she made two people."

She lifted the delicate bouquet so daintily fashioned
by fairy child-fingers, inhaled the perfume, and, as she
put it in the thin fingers of the cripple, she bent forward and kissed his fever-parched lips. At this instant
Felix saw his parents standing at the door, and held up
the flowers triumphantly.

"Oh, mamma ! come smell this mignonnette. Why
can't we grow some in boxes in our windows ?"

Mr. Andrews leaned over his son's pillows, softly put
his hand on the boy's forehead, and said :

"My son, Miss Earl professes to love you very much,
but I doubt whether she really means all she says ; and
I am determined to satisfy myself fully. Just now I
can not leave my business, but mamma intends to take
you to Europe next week, and I want to know
whether Miss Earl will leave all her admirers here, and

go with you and help mamma to nurse you. Do you think she will?"

Mrs. Andrews stood with her hand resting on the shoulder of the governess, watching the varying expression of her child's countenance.

" I think, papa—I hope she will; I believe she——"

He paused, and, struggling up from his pillows, he stretched out his poor little arms, and exclaimed:

"Oh, Edna! you will go with me? You promised you would never forsake me! Tell papa you will go."

His head was on her shoulder, his arms were clasped tightly around her neck. She hid her face on his, and was silent.

Mr. Andrews placed his hand on the orphan's bowed head.

"Miss Earl, you must let me tell you that I look upon you as a member of my family; that my wife and I love you almost as well as if you were one of our children; and I hope you will not refuse to accompany Kate on the tour she contemplates. Let me take your own father's place; and I shall regard it as a great favor to me and mine if you will consent to go, and allow me to treat you always as I do my Hattie. I have no doubt you will derive as much benefit from travelling, as I certainly hope for Felix."

"Thank you, Mr. Andrews, I appreciate your generosity, and I prize the affection and confidence which you and your wife have shown me. I came, an utter stranger, into your house, and you kindly made me one of the family circle. I am alone in the world, and have become strongly attached to your children. Felix is not merely my dear pupil, he is my brother, my companion, my little darling! I can not be separated from him. Next to his mother he belongs to me. Oh! I will travel with him anywhere that you and Mrs. Andrews think it best he should go. I will never, never leave him."

She disengaged the boy's arms, laid him back on his pillows, and went to her own room.

In the midst of prompt preparations for departure

Edna's new novel appeared. She had christened it
"SHINING THRONES ON THE HEARTH," and dedicated it "To my countrywomen, the Queens who
reign thereon."

The aim of the book was to discover the only true
and allowable and womanly sphere of feminine work,
and, though the theme was threadbare, she fearlessly
picked up the frayed woof and rewove it.

The tendency of the age was to equality and com-
munism, and this, she contended, was undermining the
golden thrones shining in the blessed and hallowed
light of the hearth, whence every true woman ruled
the realm of her own family. Regarding every *pseudo*
"reform" which struck down the social and political
distinction of the sexes, as a blow that crushed one of
the pillars of woman's throne, she earnestly warned
the Crowned Heads of the danger to be apprehended
from the unfortunate and deluded female malcontents,
who, dethroned in their own realm, and despised by
their quondam subjects, roamed as pitiable, royal
exiles, threatening to usurp man's kingdom; and to
proud, happy mothers, guarded by Prætorian bands of
children, she reiterated the assurance that

"Those who rock the cradle rule the world."

Most carefully she sifted the records of history,
tracing in every epoch the sovereigns of the hearth-
throne who had reigned wisely and contentedly,
ennobling and refining humanity; and she proved by
illustrious examples that the borders of the feminine
realm could not be enlarged, without rendering the
throne unsteady, and subverting God's law of order.
Woman reigned by divine right only at home. If
married, in the hearts of husband and children, and
not in the gilded, bedizened palace of fashion, where
thinly veiled vice and frivolity hold carnival, and
social upas and social asps wave and trail. If single,
in the affections of brothers and sisters and friends, as
the golden sceptre in the hands of parents. If or-

phaned, she should find sympathy and gratitude and usefulness among the poor and the afflicted.

Consulting the statistics of single women, and familiarizing herself with the arguments advanced by the advocates of that "progress," which would indiscriminately throw open all professions to women, she entreated the poor of her own sex, if ambitious, to become sculptors, painters, writers, teachers in schools or families ; or else to remain mantua-makers, milliners, spinners, dairymaids ; but on the peril of all womanhood not to meddle with scalpel or red tape, and to shun rostra of all descriptions, remembering St. Paul's injunction, that "*It is not permitted unto women to speak ;*" and even that "*It is a shame for women to speak in the church.*"

To married women who thirsted for a draught of the turbid waters of politics, she said : "If you really desire to serve the government under which you live, recollect that it was neither the speeches thundered from the forum, nor the prayers of priests and augurs, nor the iron tramp of glittering legions, but the ever triumphant, maternal influence, the potent, the pleading 'My son !' of Volumnia, the mother of Coriolanus, that saved Rome."

To discontented spinsters, who travelled like Pandora over the land, haranguing audiences that secretly laughed at and despised them, to these unfortunate women, clamoring for power and influence in the national councils, she pointed out that quiet, happy home at "Barley Wood," whence immortal Hannah More sent forth those writings which did more to tranquilize England, and bar the hearts of its yeomanry against the temptations of red republicanism than all the eloquence of Burke, and the cautious measures of Parliament.

Some errors of style, which had been pointed out by critics as marring her earlier writings, Edna had endeavored to avoid in this book, which she humbly offered to her countrywomen as the best of which she was capable.

From the day of its appearance it was a success; and
she had the gratification of hearing that some of the
seed she had sown broadcast in the land fell upon good
ground, and promised an abundant harvest.

Many who called to bid her good-by on the day
before the steamer sailed, found it impossible to disguise their apprehension that she would never return;
and some who looked tearfully into her face and whispered "God-speed!" thought they saw the dread signet
of death set on her white brow.

To Edna it was inexpressibly painful to cross the
Atlantic while Mr. Hammond's health was so feeble;
and over the long farewell letter which she sent him,
with a copy of her new book, the old man wept. Mrs.
Murray had seemed entirely estranged since that last
day spent at Le Bocage, and had not written a line
since the orphan's return to New York. But when she
received the new novel, and the affectionate, mournful,
meek note that accompanied it, Mrs. Murray laid her
head on her son's bosom and sobbed aloud.

Dr. Howell and Mr. Manning went with Edna
aboard the steamer, and both laughed heartily at her
efforts to disengage herself from a pertinacious young
book-vender, who, with his arms full of copies of her
own book, stopped her on deck, and volubly extolled
its merits, insisting that she should buy one to while
away the tedium of the voyage.

Dr. Howell gave final directions concerning the
treatment of Felix, and then came to speak to the
governess.

"Even now, sadly as you have abused your constitution, I shall have some hope of seeing gray hairs about
your temples, if you will give yourself unreservedly to
relaxation of mind. You have already accomplished
so much that you can certainly afford to rest for some
months at least. Read nothing, write nothing (except
long letters to me), study nothing but the aspects of
nature in European scenery, and you will come back
improved to the country that is so justly proud of you.
Disobey my injunctions, and I shall soon be called to

mourn over the announcement that you have found an
early grave, far from your native land, and among
total strangers. God bless you, dear child! and bring
you safely back to us."

As he turned away, Mr. Manning took her hand and
said:

"I hope to meet you in Rome early in February;
but something might occur to veto my programme. If
I should never see you again in this world, is there
anything that you wish to say to me now?"

"Yes, Mr. Manning. If I should die in Europe,
have my body brought back to America and carried to
the South—my own dear South, that I love so well—
and bury me close to Grandpa, where I can sleep
quietly in the cool shadow of old Lookout; and be
sure, please be sure, to have my name carved just below Grandpa's, on his monument. I want that one
marble to stand for us both."

"I will. Is there nothing else?"

"Thank you, my dear, good, kind friend! Nothing
else."

"Edna, promise me that you will take care of your
precious life."

"I will try, Mr. Manning."

He looked down into her worn, weary face and
sighed, then for the first time he took both her hands,
kissed them and left her.

Swiftly the steamer took its way seaward; through
the Narrows, past the lighthouse; and the wind sang
through the rigging, and the purple hills of Jersey
faded from view, proving Neversink a misnomer.

One by one the passengers went below and Edna
and Felix were left on deck, with stars burning above,
and blue waves bounding beneath them.

As the cripple sat looking over the solemn, moaning
ocean, awed by its brooding gloom, did he catch in
the silvery starlight a second glimpse of the rose-
colored veils, and snowy vittæ, and purple-edged robes
of the Parcæ, spinning and singing as they followed

the ship across the sobbing sea ? He shivered, and
clasping tightly the hand of his governess, said :

"Edna, we shall never see the Neversink again."

"God only knows, dear Felix. His will be done."

> *"How silvery the echoes run—*
> **Thy will be done—Thy will be done."**

CHAPTER XXXV.

"WORTHY? No, no! Unworthy! most unworthy! But was Thomas worthy to tend the wandering sheep of Him, whom face to face he doubted? Was Peter worthy to preach the Gospel of Him, whom he had thrice indignantly denied? Was Paul worthy to become the Apostle of the Gentiles, teaching the doctrine of Him whose disciples he had persecuted and slaughtered? If the repentance of Peter and Paul availed to purify their hands and hearts, and sanctify them to the service of Christ, ah! God knows my contrition has been bitter and lasting enough to fit me for future usefulness. Eight months ago, when the desire to become a minister seized me so tenaciously, I wrestled with it, tried to crush it; arguing that the knowledge of my past life of sinfulness would prevent the world from trusting my professions. But those who even slightly understand my character, must know that I have always been too utterly indifferent to, too unfortunately contemptuous of public opinion, to stoop to any deception in order to conciliate it. Moreover, the world will realize that in a mere worlaly point of view, I can possibly hope to gain nothing by this step. If I were poor, I might be accused of wanting the loaves and fishes of the profession; if unknown and ambitious, of seeking eminence and popularity. But when a man of my wealth and social position, after spending half of his life in luxurious ease and sinful indulgence, voluntarily subjects himself to the rigid abstemiousness and self-sacrificing requirements of a ministerial career, he can not be suspected of hypocrisy. After all, sir, I

care not for the discussion, the nine days' gossip and
wonder, the gibes and comments my course may occasion.   I am hearkening to the counsel of my conscience ; I am obeying the dictates of my heart.   Feeling that my God accepts me, it matters little that men
may reject me.   My remorse, my repentance, has been
inexpressibly bitter ; but the darkness has passed away,
and to-day, thank God ! I can pray with all the fervor
and faith of my boyhood, when I knew that I was at
peace with my Maker.   Oblivion of the past I do not
expect, and perhaps should not desire.   I shall always
wear my melancholy memories of sin, as Mussulmen
wear their turban or pall—as a continual memento of
death.   Because I have proved so fully the inadequacy
of earthly enjoyments to satisfy the demands of a soul ;
because I tried the alluring pleasures of sin, and was
satiated, ah! utterly sickened, I turned with panting
eagerness to the cool, quiet peace which reigns over the
life of a true Christian pastor.   I want neither fame
nor popularity, but peace ! peace I must have ! I
have hunted the world over and over; I have sought it
everywhere else, and now, thank God ! I feel that it is
descending slowly, slowly, but surely, upon my lonely,
long-tortured heart.   Thank God ! I have found peace
after much strife and great weariness——"

Mr. Murray could no longer control his voice ; and
as he stood leaning against the mantelpiece at the
parsonage, he dropped his head on his hand.

"St. Elmo, the purity of your motives will never be
questioned, for none who knows you could believe you
capable of dissembling in this matter; and my heart
can scarcely contain its joy when I look forward to
your future, so bright with promise, so full of usefulness.   The marked change in your manner during the
past two years has prepared this community for the
important step you are to take to-day, and your influence with young men will be incalculable.   Once your
stern bitterness rendered you an object of dread ; now
I find that you are respected, and people here watch
your conduct with interest, and even with anxiety.

Ah, St. Elmo! I never imagined earth held as much pure happiness as is my portion to-day. To see you one of God's anointed! To see you ministering in the temple! Oh! to know that when I am gone to rest you will take my place, guard my flock, do your own work and poor Murray's, and finish mine! This, this is indeed the crowning blessing of my old age."

For some minutes, Mr. Hammond sobbed; and, lifting his face, Mr. Murray answered:

"As I think of the coming years consecrated to Christ, passed peacefully in endeavoring to atone for the injury and suffering I have inflicted on my fellow-creatures; oh! as the picture of a calm, useful, holy future rises before me, I feel indeed that I am unworthy, most unworthy of my peace; but, thank God!

'Oh! I see the crescent promise of my spirit hath not set;
Ancient founts of inspiration well through all my fancy yet.'"

It was a beautiful Sabbath morning, just one year after Edna's departure, and the church was crowded to its utmost capacity, for people had come for many miles around to witness a ceremony, the announcement of which had given rise to universal comment. As the hour approached for the ordination of St. Elmo Murray to the ministry of Jesus Christ, even the doors were filled with curious spectators; and when Mr. Hammond and St. Elmo walked down the aisle, and the old man seated himself in a chair within the altar, there was a general stir in the congregation.

The officiating minister had come from a distant city to perform a ceremony of more than usual interest; and when he stood up in the pulpit, and the organ thundered through the arches, St. Elmo bowed his head on his hand, and sat thus during the hour that ensued.

The ordination sermon was solemn and eloquent, and preached from the text in Romans:

"For when ye were the servants of sin, ye were free from righteousness. But now being made free from

sin, and become servants to God, ye have your fruit
unto holiness, and the end everlasting life."

Then the minister, having finished his discourse,
came down before the altar and commenced the services ; but Mr. Murray sat motionless, with his countenance concealed by his hand. Mr. Hammond approached and touched him, and, as he rose, led him to
the altar, and presented him as a candidate for ordination.

There, before the shining marble pulpit which he had
planned and built in the early years of his life, for the
idol of his youth, stood St. Elmo ; and the congregation, especially those of his native village, looked with
involuntary admiration and pride at the erect, powerful form, clad in its suit of black—at the nobly-pro-
portioned head, where gray locks were visible.

"But if there be any of you who knoweth any im-
pediment or crime, for the which he ought not to be
received into this holy ministry, let him come forth, in
the name of God, and show what the crime or im-
pediment is."

The preacher paused, the echo of his words died
away, and perfect silence reigned. Suddenly St.
Elmo raised his eyes from the railing of the altar, and,
turning his face slightly, looked through the eastern
window at the ivy-draped vault where slept Murray
and Annie. The world was silent, but conscience and
the dead accused him. An expression of intolerable
pain crossed his handsome features, then his hands
folded themselves tightly together on the top of the
marble balustrade, and he looked appealingly up to
the pale Jesus staggering under his cross.

At that instant a spotless white pigeon from the
belfry found its way into the church through the
open doors, circled once around the building, fluttered
against the window, hiding momentarily the crown of
thorns, and, frightened and confused, fell upon the
fluted pillar of the pulpit.

An electric thrill ran through the congregation;
and as the minister resumed the services, he saw on

St. Elmo's face a light, a great joy, such as human countenances rarely wear this side the grave.

When Mr. Murray knelt and the ordaining hands were laid upon his head, a sob was heard from the pew where his mother sat, and the voice of the preacher faltered as he delivered the Bible to the kneeling man, saying :

" Take thou authority to preach the word of God, and to administer the holy sacraments in the congregation."

There were no dry eyes in the entire assembly, save two that looked out, coldly blue, from the pew where Mrs. Powell sat like a statue, between her daughter and Gordon Leigh.

Mr. Hammond tottered across the altar, and knelt down close to Mr. Murray ; and many who knew the history of the pastor's family, wept as the gray head fell on the broad shoulder of St. Elmo, whose arm was thrown around the old man's form, and the ordaining minister, with tears rolling over his face, extended his hands in benediction above them.

" The peace of God, which passeth all understanding, keep your hearts and minds in the knowledge and love of God, and of his Son Jesus Christ our Lord ; and the blessing of God Almighty, the Father, the Son, and the Holy Ghost, be among you, and remain with you alway."

And all hearts and lips present whispered " Amen !" and the organ and the choir broke forth in a grand " Gloria in excelsis."

Standing there at the chancel, purified, consecrated henceforth unreservedly to Christ, Mr. Murray looked so happy, so noble, so worthy of his high calling, that his proud, fond mother thought his face was fit for an archangel's wings.

Many persons who had known him in his boyhood, came up with tears in their eyes, and wrung his hand silently. At last Huldah pointed to the white pigeon, that was now beating its wings against the gilded pipes of the organ, and said, in that singularly sweet,

solemn, hesitating tone, with which children approach
sacred things :

"Oh, Mr. Murray! when it fell on the pulpit, it
nearly took my breath away, for I almost thought it
was the Holy Ghost."

Tears, which till then he had bravely kept back,
dripped over his face, as he stooped and whispered to
the little orphan :

"Huldah, the Holy Spirit, the Comforter, came
indeed ; but it was not visible, it is here in my heart."

The congregation dispersed. Mrs. Murray and the
preacher and Huldah went to the carriage ; and, leaning on Mr. Murray's arm, Mr. Hammond turned to
follow, but observing that the church was empty, the
former said :

"After a little, I will come."

The old man walked on, and Mr. Murray went back
and knelt, resting his head against the beautiful glittering balustrade, within which he hoped to officiate
through the remaining years of his earthly career.

Once the sexton, who was waiting to lock up the
church, looked in, saw the man praying alone there at
the altar, and softly stole away.

When St. Elmo came out, the churchyard seemed
deserted ; but as he crossed it, going homeward, a
woman rose from one of the tombstones and stood
before him—the yellow-haired Jezebel, with sapphire
eyes and soft, treacherous red lips, who had goaded
him to madness and blasted the best years of his life.

At sight of her he recoiled, as if a cobra had started
up in his path.

"St. Elmo, my beloved ! in the name of other days
stop and hear me. By the memory of our early love,
I entreat you !"

She came close to him, and the alabaster face was
marvelously beautiful in its expression of penitential
sweetness.

"St. Elmo, can you never forgive me for the suffering I caused you in my giddy girlhood?"

She took his hand and attempted to raise it to her

lips; but shaking off her touch, he stepped back, and steadily they looked in each other's eyes.

" Agnes, I forgive you. May God pardon your sins, as He has pardoned mine!"

He turned away, but she seized his coat-sleeve and threw herself before him, standing with both hands clasping his arm.

"If you mean what you say, there is happiness yet in store for us. Oh, St. Elmo! how often have I longed to come and lay my head down on your bosom, and tell you all. But you were so stern and harsh I was afraid. To-day when I saw you melted, when the look of your boyhood came dancing back to your dear eyes, I was encouraged to hope that your heart had softened also toward one, who so long possessed it. Is there hope for your poor Agnes? Hope that the blind, silly girl, who, ignorant of the value of the treasure, slighted and spurned it, may indeed be pardoned, when, as a woman realizing her folly, and sensible at last of the nobility of a nature she once failed to appreciate, she comes and says—what it is so hard for a woman to say—'Take me back to your heart, gather me up in your arms, as in the olden days, because— because I love you now; because only your love can make me happy.' St. Elmo, we are no longer young; but believe me when I tell you that at last—at last— your own Agnes loves you as she never loved any one, even in her girlhood. Once I preferred my cousin Murray to you; but think how giddy I must have been, when I could marry before a year had settled the sod on his grave? I did not love my husband, but I married him for the same reason that I would have married you then. And yet for that there is some palliation. It was to save my father from disgrace that I sacrificed myself; for money entrusted to his keeping—money belonging to his orphan ward—had been used by him in a ruinous speculation, and only prompt repayment could prevent exposure. Remember I was so young, so vain, so thoughtless then! St. Elmo, pity me! love me! take me back to your heart!

God is my witness that I do love you entirely now! Dearest, say, 'Agnes, I will forgive all, and trust you and love you as in the days long past.'"

She tried to put her arms up around his neck and to rest her head on his shoulder; but he resisted and put her at arm's length from him.

Holding her there, he looked at her with a cold scorn in his eyes, and a heavy shadow darkening the brow that five minutes before had been so calm, so bright.

"Agnes, how dare you attempt to deceive me after all that has passed between us? Oh, woman! In the name of all true womanhood I could blush for you!"

She struggled to free herself, to get closer to him, but his stern grasp was relentless; and as tears poured down her cheeks, she clasped her hands and sobbed out:

"You do not believe that I really love you! Oh! do not look at me so harshly! I am not deceiving you; as I hope for pardon and rest for my soul— as I hope to see my father's face in heaven—I am not deceiving you! I do—I do love you! When I spoke to you about Gertrude, it cost me a dreadful pang; but I thought you loved her because she resembled me; and for my child's sake I crushed my own hopes —I wanted, if possible, to save her from suffering. But you only upbraided and heaped savage sarcasms upon me. Oh, St. Elmo! if you could indeed see my poor heart, you would not look so cruelly cold. You ought to know that I am terribly in earnest when I can stoop to beg for the ruins of a heart, which in its freshness I once threw away, and trampled on."

He had seen her weep before, when it suited her purpose, and he only smiled and answered:

"Yes, Agnes, you ruined it and trampled it in the mire of sin; but I have rebuilt it, and, by the mercy of God, I hope I have purified it. Look you, woman! when you overturned the temple, you crumbled your own image that was set up there; and I long, long ago swept out and gave to the hungry winds the despised dust of the broken idol, and over my heart you can reign no more! The only queen it has known since that awful night, twenty-three years ago, when my faith, hope, charity were all strangled in an instant by the velvet hand I had kissed in my doting fondness —the only queen my heart has acknowledged since then, is one who, in her purity soars like an angel above you and me, and her dear name is—Edna Earl."

" Edna Earl!—a puritanical fanatic! Nay, a Pharisee! A cold prude, a heartless blue! A woman with some brain and no feeling, who loves nothing but her own fame, and has no sympathy with your nature. St. Elmo, are you insane! Did you not see that letter from Estelle to your mother, stating that she, Edna, would certainly be married in February to the celebrated Mr. Manning, who was then on his way to Rome to meet her? Did you see that letter?"

" I did."

" And discredit it? Blindness, madness, equal to my own in the days gone by! Edna Earl exists no longer ; she was married a month ago. Here, read for yourself, or you will believe that I fabricate the whole."

She held a newspaper before his eyes and he saw a paragraph, marked with a circle of ink, " Marriage in Literary Circles:"

" The very reliable correspondent of the New York —— writes from Rome that the Americans now in that city are on the *qui vive* concerning a marriage announced to take place on Thursday next at the residence of the American Minister. The very distinguished parties are Miss Edna Earl, the gifted and exceedingly popular young authoress, whose works have given her an enviable reputation, even on this side of the Atlantic, and Mr, Douglass G. Manning, the well-known and able editor of the —— Magazine. The happy pair will start, immediately after the ceremony, on a tour through Greece and the Holy Land."

Mr. Murray opened the paper, glanced at the date, and his swarthy face paled as he put his hands over his eyes.

Mrs. Powell came nearer, and once more touched his hand; but, with a gesture of disgust, he pushed her aside.

"Away! Not a word—not one word more! You are not worthy to take my darling's name upon your lips! She may be Manning's wife—God forbid it!—or she may be in her grave. I have lost her, I know, but if I never see her dear angel face again in this world, it will be in consequence of my sins, and of yours; and with God's help I mean to live out the remainder of my days, so that at last I shall meet her in eternity! Leave me, Agnes! Do not make me forget the vows I have to-day taken upon myself, in the presence of the world and of my Maker. In future, keep out of my path, which will never cross yours; do not rouse the old hate toward you, which I am faithfully striving to overcome. The first time I went to the communion-table, after the lapse of all those dreary years of sin and desperation, I asked myself, ' Have I a right to the sacrament of the Lord's Supper?—can I face God and say I forgive Agnes Powell?' Finally, after a hard struggle, I said, from the depths of my heart, ' Even as I need and hope for forgiveness myself, I do fully forgive her.' Mark you, it was my injuries that I pardoned, your treachery that I forgave. But recollect there is a mournful truth in those words —*There is no pardon for desecrated ideals!* Once, in the flush of my youth, I selected you as the *beau ideal* of beautiful, perfect womanhood; but you fell from that lofty pedestal where my ardent, boyish love set you for worship, and you dragged me down, down, almost beyond the pale of God's mercy! I forgive all my wrongs, but ' take you back, love you?' Ah! I can never love anyone, I never, even in my boyhood, loved you, as I love my pure darling, my own Edna! Her memory is all I have to cheer and strengthen me in my lonely work. I do not believe that she is married; no, no, but she is in her grave. For many days past I have been oppressed by a horrible presentiment that she has gone to her rest in Christ—that the next steamer will bring me the tidings of her death. Do not touch me, Agnes! If there be any truth in what you have to-day asserted so solemnly (though I can not believe it, for if you ridiculed and disliked me in my noble youth, how can you love the same man in the melancholy wreck of his hopes?), if there be a shadow of truth in your words, you are indeed to be pitied. Ah! you and I have learned at a terrible price the deceitfulness of riches, the hollowness of this world's pleasures ; and both have writhed under the poisonous fangs that always dart from the dregs of the cup of sin, which you and I have drained. Experience must have taught you, also, what I was so long in learning—the utter hopelessness of peace for heart and soul save only through that religion, which so far subdues even my sinful, vindictive, satanic nature, that I can say to you—you who blasted all my earthly happiness—I forgive you my sufferings, and hope that God will give you that pardon and comfort which after awful conflicts I have found at last. Several times you have thrust yourself into my presence ; but if there remains any womanly delicacy in your nature you will avoid me henceforth when I tell you that I loathe the sight of one whose unwomanliness stabbed my trust in womanhood, and sunk me so low that I lost Edna Earl. Agnes, go yonder— where I have spent so many hours of agony—yonder to the grave of your victims as well as mine. Go down on your knees yonder, and pray for yourself, and may God help you !"

He pointed to the gray vault and the slab that covered Annie and Murray Hammond ; and disengaging her fingers, which still clutched his sleeve, he turned quickly and walked away.

Her mournful eyes, strained wide and full of tears, followed him till his form was no longer visible; and sinking down on the monument—whence she had risen at his approach—she shrouded her fair, delicate features, and rocked herself to and fro.

CHAPTER XXXVI.

"How lovely! Oh! I did not think there was any place half so beautiful this side of heaven!"

With his head on his mother's bosom, Felix lay near the window of an upper room, looking out over the Gulf of Genoa.

The crescent curve of the olive-mantled Apennines girdled the city in a rocky clasp, and mellowed by distance and the magic enamelling of evening light, each particular peak rose against the chrysoprase sky like a pyramid of lapis lazuli, around whose mighty base rolled soft waves of golden haze.

Over the glassy bosom of the Gulf, where glided boats filled with gay, pleasure-seeking Italians, floated the merry strains of a barcarole, with the silvery echo of " Fidulin " keeping time with the silvery gleam of the dipping oars.

> "And the sun went into the west, and down
> Upon the water stooped an orange cloud,
> And the pale milky reaches flushed, as glad
> To wear its colors ; and the sultry air
> Went out to sea, and puffed the sails of ships
> With thymy wafts, the breath of trodden grass."

"Lift me up, mamma! higher, higher yet. I want to see the sun. There! it has gone—gone down into the sea. I can't bear to see it set to-day. It seemed to say good-by to me just then. Oh, mamma, mamma! I don't want to die. The world is so beautiful, and life is so sweet up here in the sunshine and the starlight, and it is so cold and dark down there in the grave. Oh!

where is Edna? Tell her to come quick and sing
something to me."

The cripple shuddered and shut his eyes. He had
wasted away, until he looked a mere shadow of humanity, and his governess stooped and took him from
his mother's arms as if he were a baby.

"Edna, talk to me! Oh! don't let me get afraid to
die. I——"

She laid her lips on his, and the touch calmed their
shivering; and, after a moment, she began to repeat
the apocalyptic vision of heaven:

"And there shall be no night there; and they need
no candle, neither light of the sun; for the Lord God
giveth them light; and they shall reign for ever and
ever."

"But, Edna, the light does not shine down there in
the grave. If you could go with me——"

"A better and kinder Friend will go with you, dear
Felix."

She sang with strange pathos "Motet," that beautiful
arrangement of "The Lord is my Shepherd."

As she reached that part where the words, "Yea,
though I walk through the valley of the shadow of
death," are repeated, the weak, quavering voice of
the sick boy joined hers; and, when she ceased, the
emaciated face was placid, the great dread had
passed away for ever.

Anxious to divert his thoughts, she put into his hand
a bunch of orange flowers and violets, which had been
sent to her that day by Mr. Manning; and taking a
book from the bed, she resumed the reading of "The
Shepherd of Salisbury Plain," to which the invalid had
never wearied of listening.

But she soon saw that for once he was indifferent;
and, understanding the expression of the eyes that
gazed out on the purple shadows shrouding the Apennines, she closed the volume, and laid the sufferer back
on his pillow.

While she was standing before a table, preparing

some nourishment to be given to him during the night, Mrs. Andrews came close to her, and whispered :

" Do you see much change ? Is he really worse, or do my fears magnify every bad symptom ?"

" He is much exhausted, but I trust the stimulants will revive him. You must go to bed early, and get a good sound sleep, for you look worn out. I will wake you if I see any decided change in him."

Mrs. Andrews hung for some time over her child's pillow, caressing him, saying tender, soothing, motherly things ; and, after a while, she and Hattie kissed him, and went into the adjoining room, leaving him to the care of one whom he loved better than all the world beside.

It was late at night before the sound of laughter, song and chatter died away in the streets of Genoa the magnificent. While the human tide ebbed and flowed under the windows, Felix was restless, and his companion tried to interest him by telling him the history of the Dorias, and of the siege during which Massena won such glory. Her conversation drifted away, even to Ancona, and that sad, but touching incident, which Sismondi records, of the noble, patriotic young mother, who gave to a starving soldier the milk that her half-famished babe required, and sent him, thus refreshed and strengthened, to defend the walls of her beleaguered city.

The boy's fondness for history showed itself even then, and he listened attentively to her words.

At length silence reigned through the marble palaces, and Edna rose to place the small lamp in an alabaster vase.

As she did so, something flew into her face, and fluttered to the edge of the vase, and as she attempted to brush it off, she started back, smothering a cry of horror. It was the *Sphinx Atropos*, the Death's Head Moth ; and there, upon its breast, appallingly distinct, grinned the ghastly, gray human skull. Twice it circled rapidly round the vase, uttering strange, stridulous sounds, then floated up to the canopy overarching

Felix's bed, and poised itself on the carved frame, waiting and flapping its wings, vulture-like. Shuddering from head to foot, notwithstanding the protest which reason offered against superstition, the governess sat down to watch the boy's slumber.

His eyes were closed, and she hoped that he slept; but presently he feebly put out his skeleton hand and took hers.

" Edna, Mamma can not hear me, can she?"

"She is asleep, but I will wake her if you wish it."

" No, she would only begin to cry, and that would worry me. Edna, I want you to promise me one thing——" He paused a few seconds and sighed wearily.

" When you all go back home, don't leave me here; take me with you, and lay my poor little deformed body in the ground at 'The Willows,' where the sea will sing over me. We were so happy there! I always thought I should like my grave to be under the tallest willow, where our canary's cage used to hang. Edna, I don't think you will live long—I almost hope you won't—and I want you to promise me, too, that you will tell them to bury us close together; so that the very moment I rise out of my grave, on the day of judgment, I will see your face! Sometimes, when I think of the millions and millions that will be pressing up for their trial before God's throne, on that great, awful day, I am afraid I might lose or miss you in the crowd, and never find you again; but, you know, if our coffins touch, you can stretch out your hand to me as you rise, and we can go together. Oh! I want your face to be the last I see here, and the first— yonder."

He raised his fingers slowly, and they fell back wearily on the coverlet.

"Don't talk so, Felix. Oh, my darling! God will not take you away from me. Try to sleep, shut your eyes; you need rest to compose you."

She knelt down, kissed him repeatedly, and laid her

face close to his on the pillow; and he tried to turn
and put his emaciated arm around her neck.

"Edna, I have been a trouble to you for a long
time, but you will miss me when I am gone, and you
will have nothing to love. If you live long, marry
Mr. Manning, and let him take care of you. Don't
work so hard, dear Edna; only rest, and let him make
you happy. Before I knew you I was always wishing
to die; but now I hate to leave you all alone, my own
dear, pale Edna."

"Oh, Felix, darling! hush! Go to sleep. You
wring my heart!"

Her sobs distressed him, and, feebly patting her
cheek, he said:

"Perhaps if you will sing me something low, I may
go to sleep, and I want to hear your voice once more.
Sing me that song about the child and the rose-bush,
that Hattie likes so much."

"Not that! anything but that! It is too sad, my
precious little darling."

"But I want to hear it; please, Edna."

It was a painful task that he imposed, but his
wishes ruled her; and she tried to steady her voice as
she sang, in a very low, faltering tone, the beautiful,
but melancholy ballad. Tears rolled over her face as
she chanted the verses; and when she concluded, he
repeated very faintly:

> "Sweetly it rests, and on dream-wings flies,
>   To play with the angels in paradise!"

He nestled his lips to hers, and, after a little while,
murmured:

"Good-night, Edna!"

"Good-night, my darling!"

She gave him a stimulating potion, and arranged his
head comfortably. Ere long his heavy breathing told
her that he slept, and, stealing from his side, she sat
down in a large chair near the head of his bed, and
watched him.

For many months he had been failing, and they had travelled from place to place, hoping against hope that each change would certainly be beneficial.

Day and night Edna had nursed him, had devoted every thought, almost every prayer to him; and now her heart seemed centred in him. Scenery, music, painting, rare MSS., all were ignored; she lived only for that poor dependent boy, and knew not a moment of peace when separated from him. She had ceased to study aught but his comfort and happiness, had written nothing save letters to friends; and notwithstanding her anxiety concerning the cripple, the frequent change of air had surprisingly improved her own health. For six months she had escaped the attacks so much dreaded, and began to believe her restoration complete, though the long banished color obstinately refused to return to her face, which seemed unable to recover its rounded outline. Still, she was very grateful for the immunity from suffering, especially as it permitted more unremitting attendance upon Felix.

She knew that his life was flickering out gently but surely; and now, as she watched the pale, pinched features, her own quivered, and she clasped her hands and wept, and stifled a groan.

She had prayed so passionately and continually that he might be spared to her; but it seemed that whenever her heart-strings wrapped themselves around an idol, a jealous God tore them loose, and snatched away the dear object, and left the heart to bleed. If that boy died, how utterly desolate and lonely she would be; nothing left to care for and to cling to, nothing to claim as her own, and anoint with the tender love of her warm heart.

She had been so intensely interested in the expansion of his mind, had striven so tirelessly to stimulate his brain, and soften and purify his heart; she had been so proud of his rapid progress, and so ambitious for his future, and now the mildew of death was falling on her fond hopes. Ah! she had borne patiently many trials, but this appeared unendurable. She had set all her earthly happiness on a little thing—the life of a helpless cripple ; and as she gazed through her tears at that shrunken, sallow face, so dear to her, it seemed hard ! hard ! that God denied her this one blessing. What was the praise and admiration of all the world in comparison with the loving light in that child's eyes, and the tender pressure of his lips?

The woman's ambition had long been fully satisfied, and even exacting conscience, jealously guading its shrine, saw daily sacrifices laid thereon, and smiled approvingly upon her ; but the woman's hungry heart cried out, and fought fiercely, famine-goaded, for its last vanishing morsel of human love and sympathy. Verily, these bread-riots of the heart are fearful things, and crucified consciences too often mark their track.

The little figure on the bed was so motionless that Edna crept nearer and leaned down to listen to the breathing ; and her tears fell on his thick, curling hair, and upon the orange-blossoms and violets.

Standing there she threw up her clenched hands and prayed sobbingly :

"My Father ! spare the boy to me ! I will dedicate anew my life and his to thy work ! I will make him a minister of thy word, and he shall save precious souls. Oh ! do not take him away ! If not for a lifetime, at least spare him a few years ! Even one more year, O my God !"

She walked to the window, rested her forehead against the stone facing, and looked out ; and the wonderful witchery of the solemn night wove its spell around her. Great, golden stars clustered in the clear heavens, and were reflected in the calm, blue pavement of the Mediterranean, where not a ripple shivered their shining images. A waning crescent moon swung high over the eastern crest of the Apennines, and threw a weird light along the Doria's marble palace, and down on the silver gray olives, on the glistening orange-groves, snow-powdered with fragrant bloom , and in that wan, mysterious, and most melancholy light—

" The old, miraculous mountains heaved in sight,
    One straining past another along the shore
    The way of grand, dull Odyssean ghosts,
    Athirst to drink the cool, blue wine of seas,
    And stare on voyagers."

From some lofty campanile, in a distant section of
the silent city, sounded the angelus bell ; and from the
deep shadow of olive, vine, and myrtle that clothed the
amphitheatre of hills, the convent bells caught and
reëchoed it.

              " Nature comes sometimes,
    And says, ' I am ambassador for God;' "

and the splendor of the Italian night spoke to Edna's
soul, as the glory of the sunset had done some years
before, when she sat in the dust in the pine glades at
Le Bocage ; and she grew calm once more, while out
of the blue depths of the starlit sea came a sacred
voice, that said to her aching heart :
    " Peace I leave with you, my peace I give unto you ;
not as the world giveth, give I unto you. Let not
your heart be troubled, neither let it be afraid."
    The cup was not passing away ; but courage to drain
it was given by Him who never calls his faithful children into the gloom of Gethsemane without having
first stationed close at hand some strengthening angel.
The governess went back to the bed, and there, on the
pillow, rested the moth, which at her approach flew
away with a humming sound, and disappeared.
    After another hour she saw that a change was steal-
ing over the boy's countenance, and his pulse fluttered
more feebly against her cold fingers.   She sprang into
the next room, shook his mother, and hastened back,
trying to rouse the dying child, and give him some
stimulants.   But though the large, black eyes opened
when she raised his head, there was no recognition in
their fixed gaze ; for the soul was preparing for its
final flight, and was too busy to look out of its
windows.

In vain they resorted to the most powerful restoratives ; he remained in the heavy stupor, with no sign
of animation, save the low irregular breath, and the
weak flutter of the thread-like pulse.

Mrs. Andrews wept aloud and wrung her hands, and
Hattie cried passionately, as she stood in her long
white nightgown at the side of her brother's bed ; but
there were no tears on Edna's cold, gray face. She had
spent them all at the foot of God's throne ; and now
that He had seen fit to deny her petition, she silently
looked with dry eyes at the heavy rod that smote her.

The night waned, the life with it ; now and then the
breathing seemed to cease, but after a few seconds a
faint gasp told that the clay would not yet forego its
hold on the soul that struggled to be free.

The poor mother seemed almost beside herself, as
she called on her child to speak to her once more.

"Sing something, Edna; oh! perhaps he will hear!
It might rouse him!"

The orphan shook her head, and dropped her face
on his.

"He would not hear me ; no, no! He is listening
to the song of those, whose golder harps ring in the
New Jerusalem."

Out of the whitening east rose the new day, radiant
in bridal garments, wearing a star on its pearly brow ;
and the sky flushed, and the sea glowed, while silvery
mists rolled up from the purple mountain gorges, and
rested awhile on the summits of the Apennines, and
sunshine streamed over the world once more.

The first rays flashed into the room, kissing the
withered flowers on the bosom of the cripple, and falling warm and bright on the cold eyelids and the pulseless temples. Edna's hand was pressed to his heart,
and she knew that it had given its last weary throb ;
knew that Felix Andrews had crossed the sea of glass,
and in the dawn of the Eternal day wore the promised
morning-star, and stood in peace before the Sun of
Righteousness.

*   *   *   *   *

During the two days that succeeded the death of Felix, Edna did not leave her room; and without her knowledge Mrs. Andrews administered opiates that stupefied her. Late on the morning of the third she awoke, and lay for some time trying to collect her thoughts.

Her mind was clouded, but gradually it cleared, and she strained her ears to distinguish the low words spoken in the apartment next to her own. She remembered, as in a feverish dream, all that passed on the night that Felix died; and pressing her hand over her aching forehead, she rose and sat on the edge of her bed.

The monotonous sounds in the neighboring room swelled louder for a few seconds, and now she heard very distinctly the words:

" And I heard a voice from heaven, saying unto me, Write, Blessed are the dead which die in the Lord from henceforth."

She shivered, and wrapped around her shoulders a bright blue shawl that had been thrown over the foot of the bed

Walking across the floor, she opened the door, and looked in.

The boy's body had been embalmed, and placed in a coffin which rested in the centre of the room; and an English clergyman, a friend of Mr. Manning's, stood at the head of the corpse, and read the burial service.

Mrs. Andrews and Hattie were weeping in one corner and Mr. Manning leaned against the window, with his hand on Lila's curls. As the door swung open and Edna entered, he looked up.

Her dressing gown of gray merino trailed on the marble floor, and her bare feet gleamed like ivory, as one hand caught up the soft merino folds sufficiently to enable her to walk. Over the blue shawl streamed her beautiful hair, making the wan face look even more ghastly by contrast with its glossy jet masses.

She stood irresolute, with her calm, mournful eyes

riveted on the coffin, and Mr. Manning saw her pale
lips move as she staggered toward it. He sprang to
meet and intercept her, and she stretched her hands in
the direction of the corpse, and smiled strangely, murmuring like one in a troubled dream :

"You need not be afraid, little darling, 'there is no
night there.'"

She reeled and put her hand to her heart, and
would have fallen, but Mr. Manning caught and carried her back to her room.

For two weeks she hovered on the borders of eternity; and often the anxious friends who watched her,
felt that they would rather see her die than endure
the suffering through which she was called to pass.

She bore it silently, meekly, and when the danger
seemed over, and she was able to sleep without the
aid of narcotics, Mrs. Andrews could not bear to look
at the patient white face, so hopelessly calm.

No allusion was made to Felix, even after she was
able to sit up and drive; but once, when Mr. Manning
brought her some flowers, she looked sorrowfully at
the snowy orange-blossoms, whose strong perfume
made her turn paler, and said faintly :

"I shall never love them or violets again. Take
them away, Hattie, out of my sight; put them on
your brother's grave. They smell of death."

From that day she made a vigorous effort to rouse
herself, and the boy's name never passed her lips ;
though she spent many hours over a small manuscript
which she found among his books, directed to her for
revision. "Tales for Little Cripples," was the title he
had given it, and she was surprised at the beauty
and pathos of many of the sentences. She carefully
revised and rewrote it, adding a brief sketch of the
young writer, and gave it to his mother.

About a month after Felix's death the governess
seemed to have recovered her physical strength, and
Mrs. Andrews announced her intention of going to
Germany. Mr. Manning had engagements that called
him to France, and, on the last day of their stay at

Genoa, he came as usual to spend the evening with Edna.

A large budget of letters and papers had arrived from America; and when he gave her the package containing her share, she glanced over the directions, threw them unopened into a heap on the table, and continued the conversation in which she was engaged, concerning the architecture of the churches in Genoa.

Mrs. Andrews had gone to the vault where the body of her son had been temporarily placed, and Edna was alone with the editor.

"You ought to look into your papers; they contain very gratifying intelligence for you. Your last book has gone through ten editions, and your praises are chanted all over your native land. Surely, if ever a woman had adulation enough to render her perfectly happy and pardonably proud, you are the fortunate individual. Already your numerous readers are in-quiring when you will give them another book."

She leaned her head back against her chair, and the little hands caressed each other as they rested on her knee, while her countenance was eloquent with hum-ble gratitude for the success that God had permitted to crown her efforts; but she was silent.

"Do you intend to write a book of travels, embrac-ing the incidents that have marked your tour? I see the public expect it."

"No, sir. It seems now a mere matter of course that all scribblers who come to Europe, should afflict the reading world with an account of what they saw or failed to see. So many noble books have been already published, thoroughly describing this continent, that I have not the temerity, the presumption to attempt to retouch the grand old word-pictures. At present, I expect to write nothing. I want to study some sub-jects that greatly interest me, and I shall try to inform and improve myself, and keep silent until I see some phase of truth neglected, or some new aspect of error threatening mischief in society. Indeed, I have great cause for gratitude in my literary career. At the beginning I felt apprehensive that I was destined to sit always under the left hand of fortune, whom Michael Angelo designed as a lovely woman seated on a revolving wheel, throwing crowns and laurel wreaths from her right hand, while only thorns dropped in a sharp, stinging shower from the other; but, after a time, the wheel turned, and now I feel only the soft pattering of the laurel leaves. God knows I do most earnestly appreciate His abundant blessing upon what I have thus far striven to effect; but, until I see my way clearly to some subject of importance which a woman's hand may touch, I shall not take up my pen. Books seem such holy things to me, destined to plead either for or against their creators in the final tribunal, that I dare not lightly or hastily attempt to write them; and I can not help thinking that the author who is less earnestly and solemnly impressed with the gravity, and, I may almost say, the sanctity of his or her work, is unworthy of it, and of public confidence. I dare not, even if I could, dash off articles and books as the rower shakes water-drops from his oars; and I humbly acknowledge that what success I may have achieved is owing to hard, faithful work. I have received so many kind letters from children, that some time, if I live to be wise enough, I want to write a book especially for them. I am afraid to attempt it just now; for it requires more mature judgment and experience, and greater versatility of talent to write successfully for children than for grown persons. In the latter, one is privileged to assume native intelligence and cultivation; but the tender, untutored minds of the former permit no such margin; and this fact necessitates clearness and simplicity of style, and power of illustration that seem to me very rare. As yet I am conscious of my incapacity for the mission of preparing juvenile books; but perhaps, if I study closely the characteristics of young people, I shall learn to understand them more thoroughly. So much depends on the proper training of our American youth, especially in view of the great political questions that now agitate the country, that I confess I feel some anxiety on the subject."

"But, Edna, you will not adhere to your resolution of keeping silent. The public is a merciless task-master; your own ambition will scourge you on; and having once put your hand to the literary plough, you will not be allowed to look back. Rigorously the world exacts the full quota of the author's *arura*."

"Yes, sir; but 'he that plougheth should plough in hope'; and when I can see clearly across the wide field, and drive the gleaming share of truth straight and steady to the end, then, and not till then, shall I render my summer-day's *arura*. Meantime, I am re-solved to plough no crooked, shallow furrows on the hearts of our people."

At length when Mr. Manning rose to say good-night, he looked gravely at the governess, and asked:

"Edna, can not Lila take the vacant place in your sad heart?"

"It is not vacant, sir. Dear memories walk to and fro therein, weaving garlands of *immortelles*—sing-ing sweet tunes of days and years—that can never die. Hereafter I shall endeavor to entertain the precious guests I have already, and admit no more. The past is the realm of my heart; the present and future the kingdom where my mind must dwell, and my hands labor."

With a sigh he went away, and she took up the let-ters and began to read them. Many were from strangers, and they greatly cheered and encouraged her; but finally she opened one, whose superscription had until this instant escaped her cursory glance. It was from Mr. Hammond, and contained an account of Mr. Murray's ordination. She read and reread it, with a half-bewildered expression in her countenance, for the joy seemed far too great for credence. She looked again at the date and signature, and passing her hand over her brow, wondered if there could be any mistake. The paper fell into her lap, and a cry of delight rang through the room.

" Saved—purified—consecrated henceforth to God's
holy work? A minister of Christ? O most merciful
God! I thank Thee! My prayers are answered
with a blessing I never dared to hope for, or even to
dream of! Can I ever, ever be grateful enough? A
pastor, holding up pure hands! Thank God! my
sorrows are all ended now; there is no more grief for
me. Ah! what a glory breaks upon the future!
What though I never see his face in this world? I
can be patient indeed; for now I know, oh! I know
that I shall surely see it yonder!"

She sank on her knees at the open window, and
wept for the first time since Felix died. Happy,
happy tears mingled with broken words of rejoicing,
that seemed a foretaste of heaven.

Her heart was so full of gratitude and exultation
that she could not sleep, and she sat down and looked
over the sea, while her face was radiant and tremulous.
The transition from patient hopelessness and silent
struggling—this most unexpected and glorious fruition
of the prayers of many years—was so sudden and in-
toxicating, that it completely unnerved her.

She could not bear this great happiness as she had
borne her sorrows, and now and then she smiled to
find tears gushing afresh from her beaming eyes.

Once, in an hour of sinful madness, Mr. Murray had
taken a human life, and ultimately caused the loss of
another; but the waves that were running high beyond the mole told her in thunder-tones that he had
saved, had snatched two lives from their devouring
rage. And the shining stars overhead grouped themselves into characters that said to her, "Judge not,
that ye be not judged"; and the ancient mountains
whispered, "Stand still, and see the salvation of God?"
and the grateful soul of the lonely woman answered:

> "That all the jarring notes of life
> Seem blending in a psalm,
> And all the angles of its strife
> Slow rounding into calm."

CHAPTER XXXVII.

IMMEDIATELY after her return to New York, Edna resumed her studies with renewed energy, and found her physical strength recruited and her mind invigorated by repose. Her fondness for Hattie induced her to remain with Mrs. Andrews in the capacity of governess, though her position in the family had long ceased to resemble in any respect that of a hireling. Three hours of each day were devoted to the education of the little girl, who, though vastly inferior in mental endowments to her brother, was an engaging and exceedingly affectionate child, fully worthy of the love which her gifted governess lavished upon her. The remainder of her time Edna divided between study, music, and an extensive correspondence, which daily increased.

She visited little, having no leisure and less inclination to fritter away her mornings in gossip and chitchat ; but she set apart one evening in each week for the reception of her numerous kind friends, and of all strangers who desired to call upon her. These reunions were brilliant and delightful, and it was considered a privilege to be present at gatherings where eminent men and graceful, refined, cultivated Christian women assembled to discuss ethical and æsthetic topics, which all educated Americans are deemed capable of comprehending.

Edna's abhorrence of *double entendre* and of the fashionable *sans souci* style of conversation, which was tolerated by many who really disliked but had not nerve enough to frown it down, was not a secret to

any one who read her writings or attended her recep-
tions. Without obtruding her rigid views of true
womanly delicacy and decorum upon any one, her de-
portment under all circumstances silently published
her opinion of certain latitudinarian expressions prev-
alent in society.

She saw that the growing tendency to free and easy
manners and colloquial license was rapidly destroying
all reverence for womanhood ; was levelling the distinction between ladies' parlors and gentlemen's club-
rooms ; was placing the sexes on a platform of equality
which was dangerous to feminine delicacy, that God-
built bulwark of feminine purity and of national morality.

That time-honored maxim, "*Honi soit qui mal y
pense,*" she found had been distorted from its original
and noble significance, and was now a mere convenient
India-rubber cloak, stretched at will to cover and excuse allusions which no really modest woman could
tolerate. Consequently, when she heard it flippantly
pronounced in palliation of some gross offense against
delicacy, she looked more searchingly into the characters of the indiscreet talkers, and quietly intimated to
them that their presence was not desired at her recep-
tions. Believing that modesty and purity were twin
sisters, and that vulgarity and vice were rarely if ever
divorced, Edna sternly refused to associate with those
whose laxity of manners indexed, in her estimation, a
corresponding laxity of morals. Married belles and
married beaux she shunned and detested, regarding
them as a disgrace to their families, as a blot upon all
noble womanhood and manhood, and as the most dangerous foes to the morality of the community, in which
they unblushingly violated hearthstone statutes and
the venerable maxims of social decorum.

The ostracized banded in wrath, and ridiculed her
antiquated prudery ; but knowing that the pure and
noble mothers, wives, and daughters, honored and
trusted her, Edna gave no heed to raillery and envious

malice, but resolutely obeyed the promptings of her womanly intuitions.

Painful experience had taught her the imprudence, the short-sighted policy of working until very late at night ; and in order to take due care of her health, she wisely resorted to a different system of study, which gave her more sleep, and allowed her some hours of daylight for her literary labors.

In the industrial pursuits of her own sex she was intensely interested, and spared no trouble in acquainting herself with the statistics of those branches of employment already open to them ; consequently she was never so happy as when the recipient of letters from the poor women of the land, who thanked her for the words of hope, advice, and encouragement which she constantly addressed to them.

While the world honored her, she had the precious assurance that her Christian countrywomen loved and trusted her. She felt the painful need of Mr. Manning's society, and even his frequent letters did not fully satisfy her ; but as he had resolved to remain in Europe, at least for some years, she bore the irreparable loss of his counsel and sympathy, as she bore all other privations, bravely and quietly.

Now and then alarming symptoms of the old suffering warned her of the uncertainty of her life ; and after much deliberation, feeling that her time was limited, she commenced another book.

Mr. Hammond wrote begging her to come to him, as he was now hopelessly infirm and confined to his room ; but she shrank from a return to the village so intimately associated with events which she wished if possible to forget ; and, though she declined the invitation, she proved her affection for her venerable teacher, by sending him every day a long, cheerful letter.

Since her departure from the parsonage, Mrs. Murray had never written to her ; but through Mr. Hammond's and Huldah's letters, Edna learned that Mr. Murray was the officiating minister in the church

which he had built in his boyhood ; and now and then
the old pastor painted pictures of life at Le Bocage,
that brought happy tears to the orphan's eyes. She
heard from time to time of the good the new minister
was accomplishing among the poor ; of the beneficial
influence he exerted, especially over the young men of
the community; of the charitable institutions to which
he was devoting a large portion of his fortune; of the
love and respect, the golden opinions he was winning
from those whom he had formerly estranged by his
sarcastic bitterness.

While Edna fervently thanked God for this most
wonderful change, she sometimes repeated exultingly :

> " Man-like is it to fall into sin,
>   Fiend-like is it to dwell therein,
>   Christ-like is it for sin to grieve,
>   God-like is it all sin to leave !"

One darling rose-hued dream of her life was to
establish a free-school and circulating library in the
village of Chattanooga ; and keeping this hope ever in
view, she had denied herself all superfluous luxuries,
and jealously hoarded her savings.

She felt now that, should she become an invalid, and
incapable of writing or teaching, the money made by
her books, which Mr. Andrews had invested very
judiciously, would at least supply her with the neces-
sities of life.

One evening she held her weekly reception as usual,
though she had complained of not feeling quite well
that day.

A number of carriages stood before Mrs. Andrews's
door and many friends who laughed and talked to the
governess little dreamed that it was the last time they
would spend an evening together in her society. The
pleasant hours passed swiftly ; Edna had never conversed more brilliantly, and the auditors thought her
voice was richer and sweeter than ever, as she sang the
last song and rose from the piano.

The guests took their departure—the carriages rolled away.

Mrs. Andrews ran up to her room, and Edna paused in the brilliantly lighted parlors to read a note, which had been handed to her during the evening.

Standing under the blazing chandelier, the face and figure of this woman could not fail to excite interest in all who gazed upon her.

She was dressed in plain black silk, which exactly fitted her form, and in her hair glowed clusters of scarlet geranium flowers. A spray of red fuchsia was fastened by the beautiful stone cameo that confined her lace collar; and, save the handsome gold bands on her wrists, she wore no other ornaments.

Felix had given her these bracelets as a Christmas present, and after his death she never took them off; for inside he had his name and hers engraved, and between them the word " Mizpah."

To-night the governess was very weary, and the fair sweet face wore its old childish expression of mingled hopelessness, and perfect patience, and indescribable repose. As she read, the tired look passed away, and over her pallid features, so daintily scultured, stole a faint glow, such as an ivory Niobe might borrow from the fluttering crimson folds of silken shroudings. The peaceful lips stirred also and the low tone was full of pathos as she said :

" How very grateful I ought to be. How much I have to make me happy, to encourage me to work diligently and faithfully. How comforting it is to feel that parents have sufficient confidence in me to be willing to commit their children to my care. What more can I wish? My cup is brimmed with blessings. Ah ! why am I not entirely happy ?"

The note contained the signatures of six wealthy gentlemen, who requested her acceptance of a tasteful and handsome house, on condition that she would consent to undertake the education of their daughters, and permit them to pay her a liberal salary.

It was a flattering tribute to the clearness of her intellect, the soundness of her judgment, the extent of her acquirements, and the purity of her heart.

While she could not accede to the proposition, she appreciated most gratefully the generosity and good opinion of those who made it.

Twisting the note between her fingers, her eyes fell on the carpet, and she thought of all her past ; of the sorrows, struggles, and heart-aches, the sleepless nights and weary, joyless days—first of adverse, then of favorable criticism ; of toiling, hoping, dreading, praying ; and now, in the peaceful zenith of her triumph, popularity, and usefulness, she realized

> " That care and trial seem at last,
> Through Memory's sunset air,
> Like mountain ranges overpast,
> In purple distance fair."

The note fluttered to the floor, the hands folded themselves together, and she raised her eyes to utter an humble, fervent "Thank God !" But the words froze on her lips ; for as she looked up, she saw Mr. Murray standing a few feet from her.

"God has pardoned all my sins, and accepted me as a laborer worthy to enter His vineyard. Is Edna Earl more righteous than the Lord she worships ?"

His face was almost as pale as hers, and his voice trembled as he extended his arms toward her.

She stood motionless, looking up at him with eyes that brightened until their joyful radiance seemed indeed unearthly ; and the faint, delicate blush on her cheeks deepened and burned, as with a quivering cry of gladness that told volumes, she hid her face in her hands.

He came nearer, and the sound of his low, mellow voice thrilled her heart as no other music had ever done.

"Edna, have you a right to refuse me forgiveness, when the blood of Christ has purified me from the guilt of other years ?"

She trembled and said brokenly:

" Mr. Murray—you never wronged me—and I have nothing to forgive."

" Do you still believe me an unprincipled hypocrite ?"

" Oh ! no, no, no !"

" Do you believe that my repentance has been sincere, and acceptable to my insulted God ? Do you believe that I am now as faithfully endeavoring to serve Him, as a remorseful man possibly can ?"

" I hope so, Mr. Murray."

" Edna, can you trust me now ?"

Some seconds elapsed before she answered, and then the words were scarcely audible.

" I trust you."

" Thank God !"

There was a brief pause, and she heard a heavily-drawn sigh escape him.

" Edna, it is useless to tell you how devotedly I love you, for you have known that for years ; and yet you have shown my love no mercy. But perhaps if you could realize how much I need your help in my holy work, how much more good I could accomplish in the world if you were with me, you might listen, without steeling yourself against me, as you have so long done. Can you, will you trust me fully ? Can you be a minister's wife, and aid him as only you can ? Oh, my darling, my darling ! I never expect to be worthy of you ! But you can make me less unworthy ! My own darling, come to me."

He stood within two feet of her, but he was—too humble ? Nay, nay, too proud to touch her without permission.

Her hands fell from her crimson cheeks, and she looked up at the countenance of her king.

In her fond eyes he seemed noble and sanctified, and worthy of all confidence ; and as he opened his arms once more, she glided into them and laid her head on his shoulder, whispering :

" Oh ! I trust you ! I trust you fully !"

Standing in the close. tender clasp of his strong

arms, she listened to a narration of his grief and loneliness, his hopes and fears, his desolation and struggles
and prayers during their long separation. Then for
the first time she learned that he had come more than
once to New York, solely to see her, having exacted a
promise from Mr. Manning that he would not betray
his presence in the city. He had followed her at a
distance as she wandered with the children through
the Park; and, once in the ramble, stood so close to
her, that he put out his hand and touched her dress.
Mr. Manning had acquainted him with all that had
ever passed between them on the subject of his unsuccessful suit; and during her sojourn in Europe, had
kept him regularly advised of the state of her health.

At last, when Mr. Murray bent his head to press his
lips again to hers, he exclaimed in the old, pleading
tone that had haunted her memory for years:

"Edna, with all your meekness you are wilfully
proud. You tell me you trust me, and you nestle your
dear head here on my shoulder—why won't you say
what you know so well I am longing, hungering to
hear? Why won't you say, 'St. Elmo, I love you'?"

The glowing face was only pressed closer.

" My little darling!"

"Oh, Mr. Murray! could I be here."

" Well, my stately Miss Earl! I am waiting most
respectfully to allow you an opportunity of expressing
yourself."

No answer.

He laughed as she had heard him once before, when
he took her in his arms and dared her to look into
his eyes.

" When I heard your books extolled; when I heard
your praises from men, women, and children; when I
could scarcely pick up a paper without finding some
mention of your name; when I came here to-night,
and paced the pavement, waiting for your admirers to
leave the house; whenever and wherever I have heard
your dear name uttered, I have been exultingly
proud! For I knew that the heart of the people's pet

was mine! I gloried in the consciousness, which alone strengthened and comforted me, that, despite all that the public could offer you, despite the adulation of other men, and despite my utter unworthiness, my own darling was true to me! that you never loved any one but St. Elmo Murray! And as God reigns above us, His happy world holds no man so grateful, so happy, so proud as I am! No man so resolved to prove himself worthy of his treasure! Edna, looking back across the dark years that have gone so heavily over my head, and comparing you, my pure, precious darling, with that woman, whom in my boyhood I selected for my life-companion, I know not whether I am most humble, or grateful, or proud!

> ' Ah! who am I, that God hath saved
>   Me from the doom I did desire,
>   And crossed the lot myself had craved
>   To set me higher?
>   What have I done that he should bow
>   From heaven to choose a wife for me?
>   And what deserved, he should endow
>   My home with THEE?' "

* * * * * *

As Mr. Hammond was not able to take the fatiguing journey north, and Edna would not permit any one else to perform her marriage ceremony, she sent Mr. Murray home without her, promising to come to the parsonage as early as possible.

Mr. and Mrs. Andrews were deeply pained by the intelligence of her approaching departure, and finally consented to accompany her on her journey.

The last day of the orphan's sojourn in New York was spent at the quiet spot where Felix slept his last sleep; and it caused her keen grief to bid good-bye to his resting-place, which was almost as dear to her as the grave of her grandfather. Their affection had been so warm, so sacred, that she clung fondly to his memory; and it was not until she reached the old village depot, where carriages were waiting for the party,

that the shadow of that day entirely left her counte.
nance.

In accordance with her own request, Edna did not
see Mr. Murray again until the hour appointed for
their marriage.

It was a bright, beautiful afternoon, warm with sunshine, when she permitted Mrs. Murray to lead her
into the study where the party had assembled. Mr.
and Mrs. Andrews, Hattie, Huldah, and the white-
haired pastor, were all there, and when Edna entered,
Mr. Murray advanced to meet her, and received her
hand from his mother.

The orphan's eyes were bent to the floor, and never
once lifted, even when the trembling voice of her beloved pastor pronounced her St. Elmo Murray's wife.
The intense pallor of her face frightened Mrs. Andrews,
who watched her with suspended breath, and once
moved eagerly toward her.   Mr. Murray felt her lean
more heavily against him during the ceremony; and,
now turning to take her in his arms, he saw that her
eyelashes had fallen on her cheeks—she had lost all
consciousness of what was passing.

Two hours elapsed before she recovered fully from
the attack; and when the blood showed itself again in
lips that were kissed so repeatedly, Mr. Murray lifted
her from the sofa in the study, and passing his arm
around her, said:

"To-day I snap the fetters of your literary bondage.
There shall be no more books written! No more
study, no more toil, no more anxiety, no more heart-
aches! And that dear public you love so well, must
even help itself, and whistle for a new pet. You belong solely to me now, and I shall take care of the life
you have nearly destroyed in your inordinate ambition.
Come, the fresh air will revive you."

They stood a moment under the honeysuckle arch
over the parsonage gate, where the carriage was waiting to take them to Le Bocage, and Mr. Murray
asked :

"Are you strong enough to go to the church?"

"Yes, sir; the pain has all passed away. I am perfectly well again."

They crossed the street, and he took her in his arms and carried her up the steps, and into the grand, solemn church, where the soft, holy, violet light from the richly-tinted glass streamed over gilded organ-pipes and sculptured columns.

Neither Edna nor St. Elmo spoke as they walked down the aisle ; and in perfect silence both knelt before the shining altar, and only God heard their prayers of gratitude.

After some moments Mr. Murray put out his hand, took Edna's, and holding it in his on the balustrade, he prayed aloud, asking God's blessing on their marriage, and fervently dedicating all their future to His work.

The hectic flush of the dying day was reflected on the window high above the altar, and, burning through the red mantle of the Christ, fell down upon the marble shrine like sacred, sacrificial fire.

Edna felt as if her heart could not hold all its measureless joy. It seemed a delightful dream to see Mr. Murray kneeling at her side; to hear his voice earnestly consecrating their lives to the service of Jesus Christ.

She knew from the tremor in his tone, and the tears in his eyes, that his dedication was complete ; and now to be his companion through all the remaining years of their earthly pilgrimage, to be allowed to help him and love him, to walk heavenward with her hand in his ; this—this was the crowning glory and richest blessing of her life.

When his prayer ended, she laid her head down on the altar-railing, and sobbed like a child.

In the orange glow of a wintry sunset they came out and sat down on the steps, while a pair of spotless white pigeons perched on the blood-stain ; and Mr. Murray put his arm around Edna, and drew her face to his bosom.

"Darling, do you remember that once, in the dark

days of my reckless sinfulness, I asked you one night, in the library at Le Bocage, if you had no faith in me? And you repeated so vehemently, 'None, Mr. Murray!'"

"Oh, sir! do not think of it. Why recur to what is so painful and so long past? Forgive those words and forget them! Never was more implicit faith, more devoted affection, given to any human being than I give now to you, Mr. Murray; you, who are my first and my last and my only love."

She felt his arm tighten around her waist, as he bowed his face to hers.

"Forgive? Ah, my darling! do you recollect also that I told you then that the time would come when your dear lips would ask pardon for what they uttered that night, and that when that hour arrived I would take my revenge? My wife! my pure, noble, beautiful wife! give me my revenge, for I cry with the long-banished Roman:

'Oh! a kiss—long as my exile,
Sweet as my revenge!'"

He put his hand under her chin, drew the lips to his, and kissed them repeatedly.

Down among the graves, in the brown grass and withered leaves, behind a tall shaft, around which coiled a carved marble serpent with hooded head—there, amid the dead, crouched a woman's figure, with a stony face and blue *chatoyant* eyes, that glared with murderous hate at the sweet countenance of the happy bride. When St. Elmo tenderly kissed the pure lips of his wife, Agnes Powell smothered a savage cry, and Nemesis was satisfied as the wretched woman fell forward on the grass, sweeping her yellow hair over her eyes, to shut out the vision that maddened her.

Then and there, for the first time, as she sat enfolded by her husband's arm, Edna felt that she could thank him for the monument erected over her grandfather's grave.

The light faded slowly in the west, the pigeons ceased their fluttering about the belfry, and as he turned to quit the church, so dear to both, Mr. Murray stretched his hand toward the ivy-clad vault, and said solemnly:

"I throw all mournful years behind me; and, by the grace of God, our new lives, commencing this hallowed day, shall make noble amends for the wasted past. Loving each other, aiding each other, serving Christ, through whose atonement alone I have been saved from eternal ruin. To Thy merciful guidance, O Father! we commit our future."

Edna looked reverently up at his beaming countenance, whence the shadows of hate and scorn had long since passed; and, as his splendid eyes came back to hers, reading in her beautiful, pure face all her love and confidence and happy hope, he drew her closer to his bosom, and laid his dark cheek on hers, saying fondly and proudly:

> "My wife, my life.   Oh! we will walk this world,
>   Yoked in all exercise of noble end,
>   And so through those dark gates across the wild
>   That no man knows.   My hopes and thine are one
>   Accomplish thou my manhood, and thyself,
>   Lay thy sweet hands in mine and trust to me."

THE END.

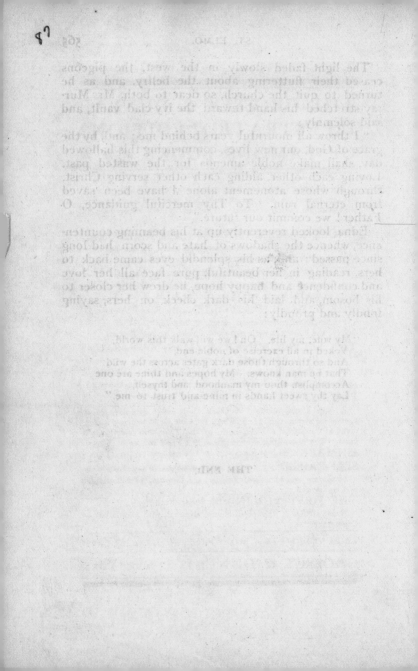